GERMINAL

ÉMILE ZOLA was born in Paris in 1840, the son of a Venetian engineer and his French wife. He grew up in Aix-en-Provence where he made friends with Paul Cézanne. After an undistinguished school career and a brief period of dire poverty in Paris, Zola joined the newly founded publishing firm of Hachette which he left in 1866 to live by his pen. He had already published a novel and his first collection of short stories. Other novels and stories followed until in 1871 Zola published the first volume of his Rougon-Macquart series with the sub-title *Histoire naturelle et sociale d'une famille sous le Second Empire*, in which he sets out to illustrate the influence of heredity and environment on a wide range of characters and milieux. However, it was not until 1877 that his novel *L'Assommoir*, a study of alcoholism in the working classes, brought him wealth and fame. The last of the Rougon-Macquart series appeared in 1893 and his subsequent writing was far less successful, although he achieved fame of a different sort in his vigorous and influential intervention in the Dreyfus case. His marriage in 1870 had remained childless but his extremely happy liaison in later life with Jeanne Rozerot, initially one of his domestic servants, gave him a son and a daughter. He died in 1902.

PETER COLLIER is Emeritus Fellow in French at Sidney Sussex College, Cambridge, and University Lecturer in French.

ROBERT LETHBRIDGE is Master of Fitzwilliam College, Cambridge and Emeritus Professor of French Language and Literature at the University of London. For Oxford World's Classics he has edited Zola's *L'Assommoir* (1995) and *La Débâcle* (2000) and Maupassant's *Bel-Ami* (2001) and *Pierre et Jean* (2001).

OXFORD WORLD'S CLASSICS

*For over 100 years Oxford World's Classics have brought
readers closer to the world's great literature. Now with over 700
titles—from the 4,000-year-old myths of Mesopotamia to the
twentieth century's greatest novels—the series makes available
lesser-known as well as celebrated writing.*

*The pocket-sized hardbacks of the early years contained
introductions by Virginia Woolf, T. S. Eliot, Graham Greene,
and other literary figures which enriched the experience of reading.
Today the series is recognized for its fine scholarship and
reliability in texts that span world literature, drama and poetry,
religion, philosophy and politics. Each edition includes perceptive
commentary and essential background information to meet the
changing needs of readers.*

OXFORD WORLD'S CLASSICS

ÉMILE ZOLA

Germinal

Translated by
PETER COLLIER

With an Introduction by
ROBERT LETHBRIDGE

OXFORD
UNIVERSITY PRESS

OXFORD
UNIVERSITY PRESS

Great Clarendon Street, Oxford OX2 6DP

Oxford University Press is a department of the University of Oxford.
It furthers the University's objective of excellence in research, scholarship,
and education by publishing worldwide in

Oxford New York

Auckland Bangkok Buenos Aires Cape Town Chennai
Dar es Salaam Delhi Hong Kong Istanbul Karachi Kolkata
Kuala Lumpur Madrid Melbourne Mexico City Mumbai Nairobi
São Paulo Shanghai Taipei Tokyo Toronto

Oxford is a registered trade mark of Oxford University Press
in the UK and in certain other countries

Published in the United States
by Oxford University Press Inc., New York

Translation and Notes © Peter Collier 1993
Introduction © Robert Lethbridge 1993
Chronology © Roger Pearson 1993

British Library Cataloguing in Publication Data

Data available

Library of Congress Cataloging in Publication Data
Zola, Émile, 1840–1902.
[Germinal. English]
Germinal / Émile Zola ; translated by Peter Collier ; with an
introduction by Robert Lethbridge.
1. Labor disputes—France—Fiction. I. Title. II. Series.
PQ2504.A33 1993 843'.8—dc20 93-12854

ISBN 978-0-19-953689-4

17

Printed in Great Britain by
Clays Ltd, Elcograf S.p.A.

CONTENTS

CONTENTS

INTRODUCTION

Germinal is a resonant title, in every sense. Fifty thousand people followed behind Émile Zola's funeral procession on 5 October 1902, and among them a delegation of miners from the Denain coalfield rhythmically chanted, 'Germinal! Germinal!' through the streets of Paris. Even today, the novel has a special place in the folklore of the mining communities of France. It also enjoys a critical reputation as Zola's masterpiece. When it was first published, in 1885, it caused a sensation. A nineteenth-century public needed no reminding that 'Germinal' was the name given to the month of April in the immediate aftermath of the French Revolution, when those convinced that 1789 marked a new beginning had recast the calendar, starting with year I. More precisely, it was on '12 Germinal, year III' that starving Parisians staged a famous uprising against the government of the Convention.

Such revolutionary echoes did not make of *Germinal* an urgent recall to the barricades. Zola himself claimed that he was looking forward rather than back. In his work-notes for the novel, he deliberately termed it 'prophetic'; it posed, as he said, 'the twentieth century's most important question', namely the conflict between the forces of modern Capitalism and the interests of the human beings necessary to its advance. The Industrial Revolution had come later to France than to England. Zola had already devoted a novel (*L'Assommoir* in 1877) to one of its consequences, the urban slum. The growth of the heavy industries, linked to the development of the railways and the means to make and power them, provided the writer with a subject of greater dramatic potential. A series of miners' strikes, from the late 1860s onwards, brought to national attention the fact that the working class was becoming unionized as the only effective way of protesting against inhuman exploitation. For the leaders of these early proletarian movements, party politics as such were irrelevant. There were more fundamental issues at stake when children of 11 were working a fourteen-hour day, pitiful wages were habitually further reduced to starvation level in response to what we now call 'market forces', and troops were sent at the first sign of trouble.

Before *Germinal*, Zola had never visited a coalfield, let alone gone down a mine or witnessed a strike at first hand. Industrial unrest in the Valenciennes area, in February 1884, gave him the opportunity to do so. When he went there, in order to familiarize himself with his subject, he was struck not by the violence which had been reported in the press, but by a chilling resignation and despair. What Zola found in the region close to the Belgian border was human suffering in contemporary form. Although he conceived *Germinal* as a political novel, it has an epic sweep which transcends a particular time and place. And Zola's stance is ultimately to be located between compassion and an awareness of fatalities which combine to render almost insignificant the vicissitudes of individual lives (on both sides of the class struggle). There has been more than a century of debate about whether *Germinal* is a revolutionary or reactionary work. It can be argued that it leaves unexamined the ideological implications of the social issues foregrounded by the text. Modern commentators have stressed that even its mythical dimension is problematic. For if Zola's title self-consciously warns of revolutionary forces at work, it literally refers to the germinating spring with which the novel ends. Revolution, in the other sense, speaks of coming full circle. Economics and politics are thus reinscribed in the eternal cycle of the seasons. But what is certain is that those same timeless qualities have been responsible for *Germinal*'s effect on generations of readers. It is widely recognized as one of the finest novels ever written in French.

Germinal was the thirteenth novel in Zola's twenty-volume Rougon-Macquart series. The latter's subtitle is 'A Natural and Social History of a Family under the Second Empire', thereby making explicit the seminal influence of Hippolyte Taine, most notoriously formulated in the Positivist philosopher's isolation of three principal determinants on human behaviour: heredity, environment, and the historical moment. By tracing the destiny of a single family and its descendants,

Zola felt he could give due weight to biological imperatives
lent added intellectual credibility in France by the 1865 translation of Darwin's *On the Origin of Species*. That is to suggest
neither that Zola uncritically subscribed to theories of heredity
being popularized at the time, nor that these are systematically
illustrated in his Rougon-Macquart novels. Preliminary notes
for the series as a whole, drawn up in 1868–9, make it clear
that he considered heredity a conveniently scientific substitute
for the outmoded concept of Fate. Above all, it was intended
that the twin focus on the Rougon and Macquart branches of
the family would endow Zola's fictional world with an internal
coherence. This would be afforded not only by blood ties and
comparative experiences, but also by reappearing characters.
Étienne, the hero of *Germinal*, is the son of Gervaise Macquart,
whose alcohol-ravaged decline is chronicled in *L'Assommoir*.
Just over half-way through this earlier novel, and while still a
boy, he is sent away from Paris to find work in Lille. It is
accordingly from here that he comes into *Germinal*.

Cross-references (see pp. 46, 384) serve, or seek, to enhance
the illusion of overlapping books and lives. It was not one Zola
himself necessarily respected. In the initial planning stage of
Germinal, Étienne Lantier, with his 'tainted blood', appears as
a homicidal maniac rather than with a personality more compatible with that of a leader of striking miners. And the
arbitrary status of Zola's exploitation of hereditary principles is
confirmed by the novelist subsequently, and belatedly, having
to invent another Lantier brother with the requisite psychotic
disorder to sustain the murderous plots of *La Bête humaine*
(1890). Although his protagonists have nominal relationships
across different texts, they remain as autonomous as the separate frames which constitute the Rougon-Macquart, and their
construction is subordinate to Zola's shaping of the novel in
hand.

A less suspect unity of design is to be found in the historical
ambitions advertised by the subtitle of Zola's series. Each of
the Rougon-Macquart novels explores a specific milieu so that,
together, they form a panorama of Second Empire society.
Notwithstanding differences of authorial approach which Zola
was at pains to point out, he aimed to provide for the reign of

Napoleon III what Balzac had done for the Restoration and
the July Monarchy. This is what distinguishes the novel-cycle
from Zola's earlier work. A text like *Thérèse Raquin* (1867),
for example, is equally informed by a physiological explanation
of private dramas; but its characters are not positioned in
relation to external events. Zola's rereading of *La Comédie
humaine* in 1869, coinciding as it did with his assimilation of
Positivist thought, left him in no doubt that the determining
social context of his own age was a ready-made subject for
the young writer working in Balzac's gigantic footsteps. That
does not prevent us from resisting the claim that the Rougon-
Macquart are exclusively anchored in the years 1852–70. When
Zola was preparing the opening novel of the series, *La Fortune
des Rougon*, in 1869, its satirical evocation of Louis-Napoleon's
coup d'état of 2 December 1851 was of the utmost topicality at
a moment when the illegitimacy of the regime was the polemical concern of those opposed to it. By the time Zola completed
his encyclopedic project in 1893, it was inevitable that events
subsequent to the Second Empire's demise in 1870 should be
superimposed on a period increasingly consigned to an archival
past.

    In this respect, *Germinal* is an exemplary case. Although
precise allusions and chronological co-ordinates are few and far
between, the novel supposedly takes place in the closing years
of the Second Empire. It could be said to be loosely based on
two major coal-strikes which occurred in 1869, the first at La
Ricamarie (near Saint-Étienne) and the second at Aubin (in
the Aveyron), both of them marked by bloody confrontations
between soldiers and miners. But Zola was perfectly aware that
such incidents merely offered him an *ex post facto* justification
consistent with his series' self-imposed historical constraints.
Not only is the real model the Anzin strike he went to observe
in 1884; without it, the novel might have borne only a superficial resemblance to *Germinal* in its definitive form. The subject
had not been included in Zola's original (ten-volume) outline
for the series. It is clear that the Commune was decisive in
persuading him that, at some stage, a novel needed to be
devoted to revolutionary action in a contemporary setting. In
retrospect, at least, the savagery of 1871 could be interpreted

as the culmination of strains and tensions which imperial dictatorship had tried to suppress.

During the preparation of *L'Assommoir*, Zola promised himself that he would complement it with another study of the working class, but this time with politics at its centre. Only towards the end of 1883, however, does he seem to have made up his mind to proceed with such a novel; and it would therefore bring together his reflections on two decades of a militant socialism neither checked by, nor limited to, a failed revolution. *Germinal*'s impact derives, at least in part, from this sequence of temporal displacements. Rather than being circumscribed by its origins in specific events of 1869 or 1884, the novel accommodates the conflicts of the century extended, by a process of repetition, from 1789 onwards. If its title announces the paradigm, nowhere are the implied analogies more forcefully aligned than in the 'vision' of revolution articulated in Part V, Chapter V. The collective demand for bread reminds the reader of a famous vanguard of women, with the same battle-cry, advancing on Versailles during the Terror. And a supplementary conflation of time-frames is effected by points of contact between, on the one hand, miners rampaging across the landscape and, on the other, the mindlessly destructive hordes roaming across the plains of France described by historians of 1789—themselves writing in the equally terrifying shadow of the Commune.

This widening of perspectives is one of the most remarkable features of *Germinal* as a whole. Because it is grounded in identifiable realities, its compelling story is also a plausible one. The novel's richness lies in its associative texture and symbolic patterning. Replying to expressions of admiration for such an interplay of the factual and the poetic in *Germinal*, Zola defined this dynamic as 'a leap to the stars on the springboard of the exactly observed'. The latter is assured by the process of documentation which is perhaps the best known of his habits of composition. For *Germinal* this involved substantial research. Zola read numerous books on the economics of the mining industry, the topography of the Valenciennes coal-basin, and the history of working-class politics; and, in order to minimize the possibility of anachronisms, he consulted

Second Empire accounts of the day-to-day life of miners and
their families as well as those detailing the technical workings
of the pits. This note-taking operation occupied him during the
early months of 1884, from late January until the beginning of
April. By far the most important phase of it was the week or so
(23 February–2 March) spent in Valenciennes itself. From
there he visited Denain, Bruay-sur-Escaut, and, especially,
Anzin, where 12,000 miners had gone on strike a few days
before. To a colleague in Paris Zola wrote that he had found a
'superb landscape in which to set my book'. He drew sketches
and maps; he questioned union officials and mining engineers;
he talked to colliers, sat in their cafés, and was invited into
their homes. He was taken deep underground, in the tunnels
of the Renard pit at Denain, which was still working. In the
evenings, in his hotel, Zola transcribed his pencil jottings. And
he returned to the capital with a sheaf of papers under the
generic heading 'My Notes on Anzin' which form a unique
document in their own right, as an extraordinary record of
things seen and heard. *Germinal* is indelibly marked by these
personal impressions, overlaid on the other sources of information which guarantee its 'exactitude'.

The function of such documentation is often misunderstood.
In *Le Roman expérimental* (1880) Zola claimed that the docu-
ments assembled by Naturalist novelists like himself were
entirely responsible for the structure and content of their
works: they both preceded the elaboration of character and plot
and were transposed so directly that the creative imagination
was virtually redundant. Even Zola's metaphor of the 'springboard', applied to his procedures in *Germinal*, repeats this
prioritization of the verifiable over the inventive. Scholars with
access to the preparatory notes for his novels have since shown
the more dogmatic statements to be highly misleading, and
intelligible only in a critical climate in which Zola was violently
attacked for his depiction of unaesthetic physical appetites and
social conditions; in other words, as his opponents insisted that
obscenity and bias resulted from a perverse and politically
motivated representation of reality, Zola found himself denying
that any such distortion had taken place; quasi-scientific evidence, he argued, was at the heart of his objective realism.

Yet to acknowledge that polemical pressures vitiated Zola's accounts of his own achievement does not mean that we can invert the proposition and relegate his documentation to a secondary position. Its relative significance, in the composition of *Germinal*, is to be gauged by the fact that, before he went to Valenciennes, work on the novel's properly fictional outline was already in progress. Zola began this *ébauche* (a pictorial term for such an outline) on 10 February 1884, and completed over a third of it prior to his visit to the coalfields. These first thirty manuscript pages, in the form of an interior monologue, are crucial in determining the directions which subsequent planning would take. They speak of Zola's intention to end the novel with the defeat of the miners, while simultaneously suggesting the provisional nature of such a conclusion to the informing conflict of capital and labour; and they contain, in embryo, many of *Germinal*'s scenes and characters, as well as the matrix of its images and thematic structures. Nor are 'My Notes on Anzin' those of a social scientist; they too are interspersed by novelistic reflections and play with potential scenarios and descriptive effects. On the other hand, this documentation radically modified some of Zola's original ideas; it prompted as many new ones; it acted as a restraint on melodramatic intensity. Its role is thus creative as well as authenticating. The preparation of *Germinal* bears witness to such a fertile interpenetration of narrative requirements and the historically true, artistic licence and factual detail.

Less visible within this dialectic, but none the less present, are the more indirect sources of the novel. Zola's long career as a journalist, for example, had put him in close touch with issues and attitudes of the day over the preceding twenty years. There are other aspects of *Germinal* which seem to have no basis in reality at all, and which may have more to do with the writer's subconscious than it is possible to confirm. In any case, however scrupulously he planned its scenes, chapters, and fictional portraits, there remains an irrecuperable distance between even the fullest of his notes and the corresponding finished page. What we do know is that this enormous novel took Zola hardly ten months to write; he penned its opening lines on 2 April 1884, and finished it on 23 January 1885.

Serial publication in *Le Gil Blas* had begun on 26 November 1884 and lasted until 25 February 1885. The next month *Germinal* appeared in volume form.

Those first lines of *Germinal* are a marvellously conceived way of bringing the reader into the novel. Far from starting to fill in a recognizable background, they plunge us into a world which, at every level, is difficult to negotiate. We are thus put precisely in the position of the man, as yet unnamed, who emerges into a disturbingly alien location, relying on his sense impressions to try to situate himself in relation to a profoundly unfamiliar context. All we register initially is the blackness and the numbing cold, a brutally physical environment properly incapacitating to the extent that it is beyond the control of the rational intelligence. As the man gradually makes out fearful sights and sounds, the reader is confronted with a fantastic vision, alerted to a monstrous presence barely seen but (and with lasting consequences) already personified. Hallucinatory silhouettes are synonymous with material shapes; and metaphors are immediately substituted for points of reference. Even before Étienne simultaneously introduces himself to the reader and to the stranger he comes across in the midst of a tangible desolation, the mood of *Germinal* is set. But so too is the creative tension between the novel's realistic effects and its symbolic meanings.

The latter have been subjected to such a wealth of critical scrutiny that *Germinal*'s realism is sometimes taken as read rather than underlined. Readers of the novel are, of course, virtually saturated with prosaic information: about mine-shafts, tunnelling techniques, working conditions, the price of coal, wage-levels, underground accidents, respiratory diseases, the lexical, sexual, and eating habits of miners; it ranges from the anecdotal details of their growing vegetables to the organization of working-class associations, and from wash-tubs to syndicalist theory. To learn all this is to be forcibly reminded, not only of Zola's documentation, but also of the pedagogic aspirations of much nineteenth-century French fiction. In an era of educational enthusiasm, reflected in publishing ventures like dictionaries and encyclopedias, novels in the realist tradition teach their readers about realities behind appearances or beyond horizons. That is not to conclude that *Germinal* is a compendium of facts re-presented with artistic skill, or that these form a residual body of knowledge ensuring that we suspend our disbelief. It is certainly one of the reasons why we take the novel seriously. Though it is told in the past historic of narrative convention, we are absorbed into the present tense of a world which patently exists.

These effects are also integral to the means whereby the novel, as opposed to a treatise, a history, or a newspaper report, assumes its more general significance. Not the least important is the representative status of Zola's scenes and characters. If the very topography of *Germinal*'s setting, for example, is typical of the somewhat featureless countryside of much of northern France, so too its mining community could be any such community of the period. But this broadening of perspectives is not merely spatial or temporal. The archetypal is engendered from the same descriptive fabric which highlights the typical. A specific industrial landscape is transformed into the barren stage on which we see enacted the basic human struggle for existence. There are certain repeated sequences— the descent into the pit, the miners, pickaxe in hand, at the coal-face—which become recurrent motifs of the text rather than simply indications of a routine: men are momentarily seized in the statuesque incarnation of their lives; their ritual tasks are those of allegorical figures of toil and suffering. And the multiple connotations of the mine itself reinforce such suggestions. While it is through Étienne's bewildered eyes that we are first alerted to the voracious appetite of the appropriately named Le Voreux, what was introduced as an unreliable image is, for the rest of the novel up until its destruction, a substantive: the monstrous presence is an ever-present monster. Its labyrinthine corridors evoke the buried cities of legend; in it the miners are entombed, as the living dead vainly searching for an escape from claustrophobic oppression. It is also a primeval world where bestiality breaks out in murder and sex; and it is a place of torture and eternal damnation, irresistibly associated with Hades or hell. For these are the comparisons to which Zola has explicit recourse in explaining the intolerable temperature or the choking dust. In the process of detailing utterly factual determinants, his descriptive language generates associations which are the shared references of the cultural imagination.

A similar mythological enrichment of the text can be seen in Zola's handling of his characters. Their movements and conversations have a crucial documentary function; but *Germinal*'s central figures are also organized into a narrative pattern as old as literature itself. In both respects, Étienne plays a structuring role. His progress through the novel delineates its shape, with his departure at the end symmetrically balancing his arrival at the beginning. In between, it is his struggles, his loves and friendships, his moments of triumph and defeat which carry the reader forward. From the opening sentence, which picks out the solitary hero on the road, what is set in motion is, both literally and figuratively, a quest. His meeting with Bonnemort takes the analogy with the prologue to a classical fable one stage further. For the old man is more than simply a retired collier of 1866 fortuitously found, but strategically positioned, to answer Étienne's (and the reader's) questions; he is the spokesman for the suffering of over half a century; and he is the voice of wisdom. He initiates the young hero into the nature of his future battle with the malevolent beast swallowing its daily ration of human flesh. Complementary to this encounter is the initiating journey into the mine with Maheu. Whereas Bonnemort, however, is a guide only to an external décor and prepares action by speech, Maheu is a kind of king of the underworld who dispenses knowledge, work, and food; he also brings Étienne to his daughter. And the narrative model is completed by the meeting with Chaval, thereby plotting a rivalry in both work and love which must, of dramatic necessity, be violently resolved.

We can accept the intentionally symbolic naming of people and places, and still ask whether it was consciously or not that this plot was drawn from the legacy of story-tellers down the ages. Such curiosity is ultimately less rewarding than an awareness of the far-reaching implications of the allegories encoded in *Germinal*'s exposition. In particular, the synthesis of the archetypal and the documentary creates a logic which owes as much to narrative imperatives as to the dictates of reality. The series of intersecting affective triangles relating the protagonist to Maheu, Catherine, and Chaval ensures that Étienne is given a freedom of movement enjoyed by no other character. As he appears at every moment of drama, so his visits to each of the novel's locations, whether domestic or public, allow him to become the roving focus of Zola's textual vehicle of information. But these comings and goings are inseparable from a narrative dynamic perhaps less easily reconciled with *Germinal*'s realism.

The successive elimination, for example, of all four figures so significantly met by Étienne in the opening chapters is explicable in terms other than the statistics of mortality in nineteenth-century coalfields. It is directly linked to the phasing of Étienne's quest, discreetly aligning his desire for Catherine and his desire for social justice. In the preparatory notes for *Germinal*, it is exactly at the point that personal and collective destinies are synchronized that the strike-leader becomes, in Zola's mind, 'a hero': 'and the counterpoint of his attraction to Catherine, his conflict with Chaval the traitor.' This antithesis is developed on opposing sides of Maheu's authority. Chaval is the outsider: he quits the leader's team, violates the family sanctuary, ravishes the daughter, and removes her from the paternal hearth. Étienne, by contrast, is the prodigal son, taken in under Maheu's roof, reintegrated into the communities of work and leisure. In such a scheme, it is inevitable that the ensuing duel should see him heroically prevail over Chaval as villain.

Yet Maheu's death is also necessary. While Étienne sleeps alongside fraternal bodies in Catherine's room, his sexual longing is kept in check by a taboo akin to incest. Only once the father-figure is removed can he become her lover. Nor can she live on, however, after the failure of the strike. As the filial bond with Maheu is broken and Étienne's quest for justice is abandoned, he returns to solitude. With Bonnemort terminally paralysed, there is a sense that Étienne takes his place: when he emerges from the mining disaster, having survived as miraculously as Bonnemort had earned his nickname, it is now Étienne who is described as the 'old man' (p. 512); and he takes with him into an untold future his own version of a bitter experience once recounted to him. Here, in other words, is a saga working itself out in pre-ordained fashion, a story which can have no other conclusion.

Nor is Zola's arrangement of his characters limited to putting in place these 'eternal triangles' as a source of dramatic tension and narrative development. There are also parallels and inverted symmetries as obliquely related to verisimilitude but no less signifying. The trio of Jeanlin, Bébert, and Lydie, for example, deliberately echoes the Étienne–Chaval–Catherine triangle. And this suggestion of reduplicated scenarios across the generations is heightened by the rigorous correlation of parents and children. Between the corresponding members of the Grégoire and Maheu families there is an opposition which speaks of a class struggle with its origins in an ancestral past and which will be inherited by the future. Many such juxtapositions merely serve to bring out essential contrasts: between Hennebeau's tortured sexuality and the miners' uncomplicated promiscuity; between a Catherine inaccessible to Étienne and La Mouquette's availability. Other patterns are less straightforward, such as Ma Brûlé's butchering of Maigrat, and the murders of the sentry, Chaval, and Cécile, by (respectively) Jeanlin, Étienne, and Bonnemort.

The degree to which characters are subject to *Germinal*'s thematic structures, as much as representative of the social and political realities it depicts, is illustrated by the antithesis between Étienne and Souvarine. The latter's documentary function is to articulate, within the collectivist debate which opposes Étienne and Rasseneur, the anarchist objection to Marxist evolutionary theory; and although he is not based on a specific individual, his Russian origins are testimony to Zola's reading about Kropotkin and Bakunin. Étienne, on the other hand, is the repository of ideas which make him into a composite portrait of union officials the novelist met during his fact-finding tour of the coalfields. But beyond the dialogues which serve to affirm their alternative conceptions of working-class history, Étienne and Souvarine have fictional destinies which dramatize the cosmic themes of life and death, and of destruction and rebirth. They evolve in opposite directions. In sabotaging the mine, Souvarine renounces humanity in the name of his intellectual nihilism. That same cataclysm is instrumental in awakening in Étienne a regenerative hope. For as he emerges from the flooded mine into Négrel's embrace, he can be seen to reject Souvarine's despair; and his sun-drenched departure at the end of the novel is contrasted with Souvarine's silent exit into the night.

We should nevertheless refrain from reading into the final pages of *Germinal* the triumph of positive forces. Zola leaves us with the impression that Souvarine and Étienne both go on. As that quite extraordinary episode in the depths of the mine makes clear, it is Souvarine's act of destruction which creates the very conditions in which Étienne can kill Chaval and then make love to the dying Catherine. In an elemental space realistically mapped but resonant with mythological associations, Eros and Thanatos intertwine as precisely as consummation and corpse. Within perspectives constrained by neither politics nor credibility, Étienne and Souvarine play out the same dialectical relationship which orders the seasons into cycle rather than sequence.

Zola's characters are seldom admired for their innate psychological complexity or the subtlety with which nuances of mood and feeling are conveyed to us. Consistent with physiological explanations, his technique is to work from the outside, to isolate expression and gesture. Thus the contradictions in Souvarine, for example, are exemplified by his habit of watching the smoke from his cigarette drift upwards in a mysterious reverie while, at the same time, caressing the soft coat of the rabbit which points to his lingering human instincts. The instinctual, indeed, is privileged at the expense of the inner life. What impels Étienne forward as *Germinal* begins is, first and foremost, the need to warm his hands. When he retreats to the enclosing warmth of the disused mine-shaft of Réquillart he is like a hibernating animal. Above all, the characters are driven by their appetites; and amongst these basic physical needs, food and sex take pride of place, nowhere more graphically imbricated than in Maigrat's exchange of one for the other and the revenge wrought on him by the women who stuff earth into his mouth while holding his mutilated genitals aloft.

To measure Zola's characterization against that of a Henry James would be just about as perverse! His achievement in *Germinal* is to have constructed a set of interlocking and inexorable causalities: historical, social, and physical; but also textual and cosmic. And if we are moved by the novel it is surely because we are pressed up close to the suffering of its characters, and simultaneously made aware that the universal drama in which they play their given parts is plotted beyond their control.

Together with his role in the Dreyfus Affair, it is *Germinal* which has been largely responsible for Zola's reputation as a writer of the Left. Few novels, of any period or in any language, so forcefully dramatize the cruel exploitation of men, women, and children in the interests of unseen shareholders; and perhaps none shows with such clarity the emergence of a new historical force in the shape of the working-class struggle for dignity and justice. Within the text, a key moment in this respect occurs in Part IV, Chapter II: for there, and in a language which cuts across political theorizing, Maheu gives expression, at first haltingly but then increasingly fluently, not to union demands but to a human protest; Hennebeau, the miners' delegation, Étienne, the narrator too, are all reduced to silence, thus allowing Maheu to speak directly to *Germinal*'s readers. And many of the latter would subscribe to Irving Howe's view that the novel itself tells one of the great stories of the modern era, 'the story of how the dumb acquire speech';[1] or, to put it another way, of how the passive objects of manipulation at the bottom of the system begin, at least, to transform themselves into active subjects determined to create their own history.

What seems less certain is the outcome of the crisis and impending conflict which *Germinal* predicts. That future is articulated most explicitly in the novel's final paragraph. Although its images of fecundity are anticipated, in passing, earlier in the text (see pp. 166–7, 288), only at the moment we put the book down does our reading of *Germinal* in terms of

---

[1] 'Zola: The Genius of *Germinal*', *Encounter*, 34 (1970), 53–61.

the thematic signposting of its title appear to be confirmed. It is interesting to note, therefore, that what readers of 1885 found most confusing was that, within the novel, there was no evidence whatsoever to justify its lyrical conclusion. Huysmans summed up their reaction to a catalogue of unrelenting misery when he spoke of being overwhelmed by *Germinal*'s 'terrible sadness'.[2] Even socialist commentators pointed not to the radiant future it announced, but to what it revealed in the present about the appalling conditions in which the proletariat lived and worked. The most famous contemporary response is that of the eminent critic Jules Lemaître: for him, the final page of the novel was so 'enigmatic' that it was virtually meaningless; he described *Germinal* as a 'pessimistic epic of human animality';[3] and when Zola replied to this, it is significant that it was only to the 'animality' that he objected.[4]

This pessimism is due, in part, to the failure of revolutionary action. Its leaders, like Rasseneur and Pluchart, are portrayed by Zola with a distrust which reflects his lack of sympathy for the demagogues of the Commune. Even Étienne is not invulnerable to such charges, as Zola traces a self-aggrandizement in which the character sees himself as an 'apostle' of truth (p. 281), ultimately despising the ignorance of those who reject his leadership. The experience of the Commune also informs Zola's nightmarish vision of the unleashed mob. He had intended that 'the bourgeois reader should feel a *frisson* of terror' at the spectacle. To this end, he plays on fears of evil spirits and hobgoblins emerging from the dark in order to conjure up the uprising of the disinherited from the bowels of the earth; a localized industrial incident thereby becomes a vision of the apocalypse. But in the evocation of demonic wolfmen and collective dementia there is more than a hint of Zola's own revulsion. Unforgettable his crowd-scenes may justly be; here revolution and anarchy are perilously synonymous.

[2] J.-K. Huysmans, in *Lettres inédites à Émile Zola*, ed. Pierre Lambert (Geneva: Droz, 1953), 113–15.

[3] J. Lemaître, review of *Germinal* in *Revue politique et littéraire*, 14 Mar. 1885.

[4] Zola's reply, dated the same day, in his *Correspondance*, ed. B. H. Bakker (Montreal: Presses Universitaires de Montréal, 1978), v. 244–5.

There is, at best, a precarious balance between the despairing prediction of social catastrophe and regenerative optimism. If Zola's politico-economic analysis is subordinate to the myth of Eternal Return, it is sustained by a conception of society as an organic unity forever evolving towards a utopian order of justice and harmony situated somewhere down the endless corridors of time. The class struggle is thus relativized within the same antithetical pattern which opposes fertility and sterility, mortality and rebirth, winter and spring. *Germinal* is organized in these binary terms, starting with its topography.

We get the impression that the miners' houses are so cut off from the rest of the world that the occasional visits to the Grégoire mansion are like expeditions to a foreign planet. We tend to overlook the fact that Montsou is an industrial city with a sugar-refinery, workshops, and a number of other factories; and that while the miners live in one of its outlying suburbs, the bourgeois family of the novel live two kilometres to the east of Montsou, on the other side. We do so because, as a consequence of the conflict which structures every aspect of *Germinal*'s fictional reality, the territory between these poles is only intermittently in focus. That polarization is sometimes so schematic as to be heavy-handed: on the one hand there is the rich Cécile Grégoire of pale complexion, staying in her cosy bed until all hours of the morning and then getting up to her hot chocolate and deliciously fresh brioche; on the other there are the poor, miserable, sallow-skinned Maheu children rising at 4 a.m. desperate for their thin gruel and dry crust. So too when the miners trudge into Hennebeau's sumptuous drawing-room, there is a dramatic contrast between rich and poor. What is not filled in is the causal mechanism by which bourgeois affluence is in precisely inverse proportion to working-class starvation. Responsibility for the latter is delegated instead to an impersonal god of Capitalism crouching in a tabernacle.

Nor is this antithetical structuring limited to Zola's elaboration of a conflict between social classes. The same principle opposes night and day, darkness and light, under the ground and above it, the haves and the have-nots; and these work across the class divide, so that Hennebeau, for example, shares the suffering of deprivation at the very moment he watches a sexual satisfaction which compensates for the miners' lack of food. But it is also the correlation between natural and social oppositions which suggests their permanence. This is undoubtedly the implication of Zola's choice of metaphors in his description of revolution. The crowd streams across the landscape like a river overflowing its banks; its thundering is compared to a stampeding herd. Human action is transposed, in effect, into natural schemes of catastrophe like floods, fires, and earthquakes. And the assimilation of men and the animal kingdom is underpinned by common physiological determinants. The effect of such equations, it can be argued, is to reinscribe the specificities of politics or history into the unchanging, and unchangeable, natural order of things. Time and again, in *Germinal*, human beings are described as insects, insignificant dots powerless to modify a cosmic process.

The directions of that process are far from being entirely elucidated by the novel's closing lines. To be sure, the bursting fertility of Réquillart is a prophetic symbol of what Le Voreux will one day be. But the renewal of the natural world operates within a cycle less infinitely prolonged than liberal-positivist promises of human happiness. The cycle of individual lives, in *Germinal*, is one of monotony and repetition. The symbolic parallel between the horses and the miners is double-edged. If only the latter have a capacity for rebellion, Bataille and Trompette share both their misery and their dreams: of light and air, of breaking out of their imprisonment, of wide horizons; and these are indistinguishable from the utopian future imagined by the assembled miners in the forest clearing—which is, ironically, the high-point of their illusions.

Less illusory, of course, is the violence which punctuates the second half of *Germinal*. But though the deaths of the sentry, Maigrat, and Cécile may all be motivated by social revenge, in reality they have the status of ritual sacrifices; they achieve nothing. Nor does the destruction of the mine. For if the future is simply a continuation of the past and present, the novel ushers in the possibility that it will be a continuing degradation: when the miners are forced back to work at the end, conditions are even worse than before; and La Maheude herself has to return to the pit where she had slaved like her daughter, this time simply to keep the rest of her broken family alive. More disturbing still is that virtually the last survivor in this Darwinian scheme is the animalized Jeanlin. Throughout the text he is closely identified with Étienne: structurally, within the infantile version of the hero's rivalry; emotionally, in the murder so obsessively witnessed; thematically, at Réquillart. Such a chain of substitutions may well make us wonder whether he is also the leader's obscene successor. To set such undertones against *Germinal*'s rousing finale is not to deny the latter's impact or the feeling that it somehow 'fits' nevertheless. It is to stress that, resulting from the meeting of the lucid observer and the lyrical optimist, there are ambiguities in Zola's novel which can be more easily reconciled in terms of poetic coherence than in those of political discourse.

Readers will judge for themselves whether *Germinal* remains a novel about revolution rather than a revolutionary novel. A related question is the extent to which the text itself reveals an awareness, on Zola's part, of its limits as an effective instrument of political change. The question is prompted by the recognition that between Étienne and his creator there are a number of telling analogies. At the simplest level Zola seems to have projected on to the fictional character aspects of his own career and personality. More sophisticated analysis of the rhetorical strategies employed by both the novelist and his more articulate protagonists has allowed Naomi Schor to conclude that 'Zola's leaders are all variants on the writer'.[5] It is also worth remembering that, within the Rougon-Macquart series, *Germinal* is situated between two of Zola's most introspective novels, namely *La Joie de vivre* (1884) and *L'Œuvre* (1886). In Claude Lantier, the artist-hero of the latter, Zola provides a partial self-portrait. And it has been shown that Claude's failed ambitions precisely echo those of Étienne in *Germinal*.

As far as the potentially autobiographical dimension of Étienne is concerned (always allowing for differences of con-

---

[5] *Zola's Crowds* (Baltimore: Johns Hopkins University Press, 1978), 77.

text), there are coincidences it is difficult to ignore. As in *L'Assommoir*, Zola refers to Étienne sending back money to his impoverished mother, as he himself had done when he had first left his home in the Midi. In *Germinal* a whole career is evoked: the thrill of earning fees from his early writing, the beginnings of popularity, the hopes of playing a major role in the shaping of the future, becoming head of a militant group, gradually listened to and increasingly admired. As in *L'Œuvre*, this mirroring process by no means precludes self-irony, whether at the expense of inflated vanity or messianic pretensions; and a bitterness, about the progressive disaffection of disciples, inseparable from the fact that in 1884–5 Zola's own (literary) grouping was starting to disintegrate. Étienne and the novelist certainly have more in common than just their southern accents. The character shares, for example, Zola's long-held fear (dating from a childhood trauma) of being buried alive, as well as a repressed sexuality.

It is possible that this kind of unconscious projection was catalysed by the actual preparation of *Germinal*. In his notes, Zola identifies so closely with Étienne that he often substitutes a first-person pronoun in his vivid imagining of the character's actions or feelings. Above all, if it is Étienne's responsibility to distribute Zola's information within the text, the novel also ascribes to him the very process of documentation which had been the writer's own. Thus when Étienne first goes down the mine, his intense anguish is exactly that felt by Zola himself during the exploratory descent recorded in 'My Notes on Anzin'. His evening conversations with Souvarine are those Zola had with Turgenev about anarchist movements in Russia. And Étienne has to work through much of Zola's bibliography, including 'treatises on political economy [. . .] full of arid and incomprehensible technical detail' (p. 164). Both of them undertake an education in socialist theory, leading to the repudiation of the naïve idealism with which they had set off.

To approach the novel in this way is also to register moments when Zola appears to prefigure its reception. We know that *Germinal* was planned with one eye on its reading. The writer's notes testify to his concern to alternate between action and description, narrative development and panoramic views of the landscape. And he is continually alive to what should be withheld from the reader at certain junctures in order to heighten the suspense. When the miners are trapped underground, for example, there is a highly deliberate deferral of the climax through interweaving the narrative of their plight with scenes simultaneously taking place elsewhere. Powerful linguistic effects are self-evidently integral to our response to *Germinal*, whether this is one of fear, pity, or excitement. The novel's own reflections on language are thus of considerable interest. Sometimes these are merely wry: for instance immediately after his own evocative rendering of a vision of revolution designed to scare bourgeois readers out of their wits, Zola refers to handwritten texts 'threatening to rip open the bellies of the bourgeois; and although nobody had read one, there were still those who could quote from them word for word' (p. 351); and the terrifying accounts of the strike which appear in the Parisian press provoke 'a violent polemic' (p. 380) but are of no practical consequence—with the added irony, as Zola well knew, that the subscribers to *Le Gil Blas* were thoroughly enjoying his own.

More significant is that Étienne's role as surrogate novelist is at its most explicit when his facility with words is mocked. Zola continually uses the term 'histoire' to liken his eloquence to that of a story-teller. For as he expands his metaphors of hope into a dazzling version of the future, his listeners are entranced, as carried away as he is himself by the beauty of his construction. Even La Maheude's pragmatism ('Can't you see he's telling us fairy-tales?' (p. 169)) yields to Étienne's rhetorical talents. The most damning critique of them is Souvarine's, 'the only one who had a lively enough intelligence to analyse the situation' (p. 174). He calmly warns Étienne that verbal skills will serve no purpose whatsoever, and that revolution involves action rather than 'phrases lifted from literature' (p. 242). As Zola imaginatively elaborates *Germinal*, his notes are full of reminders to himself to 'analyse' this or that problem, alcoholism, diet, child labour; and to ensure that all aspects of the plot are 'logically' worked out. One of Souvarine's functions is thus to act as a counterpoint to a textual fabric so poetically

charged that there is a risk of the novel leaving behind its
original intention to 'study' the social conflicts of the day.

These unresolved tensions are perfectly illustrated by
Étienne's great speech at Le Plan-des-Dames which is, in
every sense, the culmination of Part IV of the novel (pp. 279–
91). It is prepared by the character with the same care Zola
had devoted to this long-foreseen chapter. All the half-formed
ideas assimilated by Étienne were to be welded together into a
coherent political programme; and, indeed, all those Zola had
drawn from his own reading; for, prior to writing the speech,
he went right back through his notes, often adding the cross-
reference '(in the forest)'. Here, as he put it, was to be a
reasoned exposition of the necessity of a future radically different from the social injustices of the present. But Zola the
novelist also wanted it to be a chapter of tremendous 'momen-
tum' which would dramatize, for the reader, the apogee of
Étienne's popularity with, and power over, the crowd. The
result is that we are offered both a summary of *Germinal*'s
ideas and a microcosm of our response to the book as a whole.
The shifts in narrative focus may distance us from the quasi-
religious fervour of Étienne's listeners; but, like the clouds
passing over the moonlit scene, these interruptions do not so
much break the spell as create a lull which paradoxically
intensifies its rhythm. Similarly the gap between the suffering
Étienne recalls and the brave new world he evokes justifies the
dream rather than deflates it. It is as difficult for the reader as
for the crowd not to be swept away by the sheer force of
Étienne's language. To reread the final paragraph of *Germinal*
in the light of his speech is to realize how precise an echo it
contains of Étienne's earlier image of a germinating army of
men breaking upwards through the ground and into the sun.

If *Germinal* poses such questions about the relationship
between imaginative language and reality, it also asks them of
us. At one extreme we may ponder Bonnemort's blunt remark
that Étienne's fictions will do nothing to improve the soup (p.
170); at the other, there is the admiration of Lucie and Jeanne
exulting over the aesthetic qualities of the horror (pp. 348–9,
486). Where do we ourselves stand in relation to the inhuman
violence viewed through the barn-door by the bourgeois

characters? Are we dispassionate observers, or fearfully transfixed by the novel's spectacle of human distress? The problems raised by _Germinal_ have to be addressed from within the admission that, alongside the novel's terrible sadness, there is also a terrible beauty.

ROBERT LETHBRIDGE

NOTE ON THE TRANSLATION

THE text on which the translation is based is the revised edition of *Germinal* by Colette Becker published in the 'Classiques Garnier' series (Paris, 1989), although a number of other editions were extensively consulted.

This translation is the result of a sustained effort to reconcile an accurate rendering of nineteenth-century French dialogue, description, and technical terminology with the twentieth-century English language, while trying to preserve the force of Zola's poetic realism. When I wanted to test what I had written on a potential audience, I was exceptionally lucky in finding a series of willing and talented readers, Catherine Collier, Anne Dunan, Elinor Dorday, Kate Tunstall, and Meryl Tyers who between them read aloud, listened to, pondered over, and criticized every word of Zola's original, and every word of my draft. Their linguistic flair has helped me in my ambition to write as far as possible as Zola might have written, had he been writing in modern English. If there are moments when my readers are able to forget that they are reading a translation, I hope that they will join me in thanking Cathy, Anne, Ellie, Kate, and Meryl.

PETER COLLIER

SELECT BIBLIOGRAPHY

Germinal was first published in book form by the Librairie Charpentier in Paris in 1885 (it had been serialized in *Le Gil Blas* between 26 November 1884 and 25 February 1885). Modern scholarly editions are *Germinal*, 'Classiques Garnier', revised edition by Colette Becker (Paris, 1989), or volume iii of *Les Rougon-Macquart* in the 'Bibliothèque de la Pléiade' (Paris: Gallimard, 1964), edited by Henri Mitterand. Paperback editions exist in the following popular collections: 'Garnier-Flammarion' (ed. Henri Guillemin, Paris, 1968); 'Folio' (ed. Henri Mitterand, Paris, 1978); and 'Livre de Poche' (ed. Auguste Dezalay, Paris, 1983).

The standard account of Zola's life is the 'biographie romancée' by Armand Lanoux, *Bonjour, Monsieur Zola* (Paris: Hachette ('Livre de Poche'), 1972). Studies of the whole cycle of the Rougon-Macquart include Philippe Hamon, *Le Personnel du roman: Le Système des personnages dans 'les Rougon-Macquart' d'Émile Zola* (Geneva: Droz, 1983), and Auguste Dezalay, *L'Opéra des 'Rougon-Macquart'* (Paris, Klincksieck, 1983).

Comprehensive studies of Zola written in English are: Elliot M. Grant, *Émile Zola* (New York: Twayne ('World Authors'), 1966); F. W. J. Hemmings, *Emile Zola* (2nd edn., Oxford: Oxford Paperbacks, 1970); Philip Walker, *Zola* (London: Routledge & Kegan Paul, 1985); R. Lethbridge and T. Keefe (eds.), *Zola and the Craft of Fiction* (Leicester: Leicester University Press, 1990); Naomi Schor, *Zola's Crowds* (Baltimore: Johns Hopkins University Press, 1978).

Monographs on *Germinal* have been written by Colette Becker, *Germinal* (Paris, PUF ('Études littéraires'), 1984), E. M. Grant, *Zola's 'Germinal': A Critical and Historical Study* (Leicester: Leicester University Press, 1962), C. Smethurst, *Émile Zola: 'Germinal'* (London: Arnold, 1974), and Philip Walker, *'Germinal' and Zola's Philosophical and Religious Thought* (Amsterdam: John Benjamins, 1984). Those in search of a single, stimulating essay may consult one or other of the chapters on *Germinal* in Henri Mitterand, *Le Discours du roman* (Paris: PUF, 1980), while two of the best essays in English are Irving Howe, 'Zola: The Genius of *Germinal*', *Encounter*, 34 (1970), 53–61, and David Baguley, 'The Function of Zola's Souvarine', *Modern Language Review*, 66 (1971), 186–97.

Those interested in more specialized enquiries into the documentary sources and social background of the novel should refer to Richard H.

Zakarian, *Zola's 'Germinal': A Critical Study of its Primary Sources*
(Geneva: Droz, 1972), Colette Becker, *La Fabrique de 'Germinal'*
(Paris: SEDES, 1986) (which presents Zola's preparatory dossier),
Henri Marel, *'Germinal': Une documentation intégrale* (Glasgow: University of Glasgow French and German publications, 1989) (which
includes a specialized bibliography), or two special issues of *Les
Cahiers naturalistes* (Paris: Fasquelle): no. 50 (1976), entitled *'Germinal' et le mouvement ouvrier en France*, and the centenary number, 59
(1985).

   As for the wider context of Zola's writing, David Baguley has
recently completed an authoritative study of Naturalism, *Naturalist
Fiction: The Entropic Vision* (Cambridge: Cambridge University Press,
1990). Finally, the fascinating history of the Second Empire in France
can be followed up either concisely in Roger Magraw's contribution
to the 'Fontana History of Modern France', *France 1815–1914: The
Bourgeois Century* (London: Fontana, 1987), or at leisure in Theodore
Zeldin's *France* (2 vols., Oxford: Oxford University Press, 1973).

CHRONOLOGY

1840	(2 April) Born in Paris, the only child of Francesco Zola (b. 1795), an Italian engineer, and Émilie, née Aubert (b. 1819), the daughter of a glazier. The Naturalist novelist was later proud that 'zolla' in Italian means 'clod of earth'
1843	Family moves to Aix-en-Provence
1847	(27 March) Death of father from pneumonia following a chill caught while supervising work on his scheme to supply Aix-en-Provence with drinking water
1852–	Becomes a boarder at the Collège Bourbon at Aix. Friendship with Baptistin Baille and Paul Cézanne. Zola, not Cézanne, wins the school prize for drawing
1858	(February) Leaves Aix to settle in Paris with his mother (who had preceded him in December). Offered a place and bursary at the Lycée Saint-Louis. (November) Falls ill with 'brain fever' (typhoid) and convalescence is slow
1859	Fails his *baccalauréat* twice
1860	(Spring) Is found employment as a copy-clerk but abandons it after two months, preferring to eke out an existence as an impecunious writer in the Latin Quarter of Paris
1861	Cézanne follows Zola to Paris, where he meets Camille Pissarro, fails the entrance examination to the École des Beaux-Arts, and returns to Aix in September
1862	(February) Taken on by Hachette, the well-known publishing house, at first in the dispatch office and subsequently as head of the publicity department. (31 October) Naturalized as a French citizen. Cézanne returns to Paris and stays with Zola
1863	(31 January) First literary article published. (1 May) Manet's *Déjeuner sur l'herbe* exhibited at the Salon des Refusés, which Zola visits with Cézanne
1864	(October) *Tales for Ninon*
1865	*Claude's Confession*. A *succès de scandale* thanks to its bedroom scenes. Meets future wife Alexandrine-Gabrielle Meley (b. 1839), the illegitimate daughter of teenage parents who soon separated, and whose mother died in September 1849

1866 Forced to resign his position at Hachette (salary: 200 francs a month) and becomes a literary critic on the recently launched daily *L'Événement* (salary: 500 francs a month). Self-styled 'humble disciple' of Hippolyte Taine. Writes a series of provocative articles condemning the official Salon Selection Committee, expressing reservations about Courbet, and praising Manet and Monet. Begins to frequent the Café Guerbois in the Batignolles quarter of Paris, the meeting-place of the future Impressionists. Antoine Guillemet takes Zola to meet Manet. Summer months spent with Cézanne at Bennecourt on the Seine. (15 November) *L'Événement* suppressed by the authorities

1867 (November) *Thérèse Raquin*

1868 (April) Preface to second edition of *Thérèse Raquin*. (May) Manet's portrait of Zola exhibited at the Salon. (December) *Madeleine Férat*. Begins to plan for the Rougon-Macquart series of novels

1868–70 Working as journalist for a number of different newspapers

1870 (31 May) Marries Alexandrine in a registry office. (September) Moves temporarily to Marseilles because of the Franco-Prussian War

1871 Political reporter for *La Cloche* (in Paris) and *Le Sémaphore de Marseille*. (March) Returns to Paris. (October) Publishes *The Fortune of the Rougons*, the first of the twenty novels making up the Rougon-Macquart series

1872 *The Kill*

1873 (April) *The Belly of Paris*

1874 (May) *The Conquest of Plassans*. First independent Impressionist exhibition. (November) *Further Tales for Ninon*

1875 Begins to contribute articles to the Russian newspaper *Vestnik Evropy* (*European Herald*). (April) *The Sin of the Abbé Mouret*

1876 (February) *His Excellency Eugène Rougon*. Second Impressionist exhibition

1877 (February) *L'Assommoir*

1878 Buys a house at Médan on the Seine, forty kilometres west of Paris. (June) *A Page of Love*

1880   (March) *Nana*. (May) *Les Soirées de Médan* (an anthology
        of short stories by Zola and some of his Naturalist 'disci-
        ples', including Maupassant). (8 May) Death of Flaubert.
        (September) First of a series of articles for *Le Figaro*. (17
        October) Death of his mother. (December) *The Experimen-
        tal Novel*

1882   (April) *Pot-Bouille*. (3 September) Death of Turgenev

1883   (13 February) Death of Wagner. (March) *Au Bonheur des
        dames*. (30 April) Death of Manet

1884   (March) *La Joie de vivre*. Preface to catalogue of Manet exhi-
        bition

1885   (March) *Germinal*. (12 May) Begins writing *The Master-
        piece* (*L'Œuvre*). (22 May) Death of Victor Hugo. (23
        December) First instalment of *The Masterpiece* appears in
        Le Gil Blas

1886   (27 March) Final instalment of *The Masterpiece*, which is
        published in book form in April

1887   (18 August) Denounced as an onanistic pornographer in
        the *Manifesto of the Five* in *Le Figaro*. (November) *Earth*

1888   (October) *The Dream*. Jeanne Rozerot becomes his mis-
        tress

1889   (20 September) Birth of Denise, daughter of Zola and
        Jeanne

1890   (March) *The Beast in Man*

1891   (March) *Money*. (April) Elected President of the Société
        des Gens de Lettres. (25 September) Birth of Jacques, son
        of Zola and Jeanne

1892   (June) *The Débâcle*

1893   (July) *Doctor Pascal*, the last of the Rougon-Macquart
        novels. Fêted on a visit to London

1894   (August) *Lourdes*, the first novel of the trilogy *Three Cities*.
        (22 December) Dreyfus found guilty by a court martial

1896   (May) *Rome*

1898   (13 January) 'J'accuse', his article in defence of Dreyfus,
        published in *L'Aurore*. (21 February) Found guilty of
        libelling the Minister of War and given the maximum
        sentence of one year's imprisonment and a fine of 3,000
        francs. Appeal for retrial granted on a technicality. (March)

Paris. (23 May) Retrial delayed. (18 July) Leaves for England instead of attending court

1899   (4 June) Returns to France. (October) *Fecundity*, the first of his *Four Gospels*

1901   (May) *Toil*, the second 'Gospel'

1902   (29 September) Dies of fumes from his bedroom fire, the chimney having been capped either by accident or anti-Dreyfusard design. Wife survives. (5 October) Public funeral

1903   (March) *Truth*, the third 'Gospel', published posthumously. *Justice* was to be the fourth

1908   (4 June) Remains transferred to the Panthéon

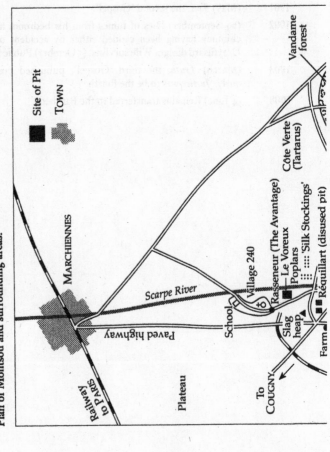

Plan of Montsou and surrounding areas.

■ Site of Pit
▨ TOWN

MARCHIENNES

Railway to PARIS

Plateau

Paved highway

Scarpe River

School

Village 240

Rasseneur (The Avantage)
Le Voreux
Poplars

Slag heap

'Silk Stockings'

Réquillart (disused pit)

Farm

To COUGNY

Côte Verte (Tartarus)

Vandame forest

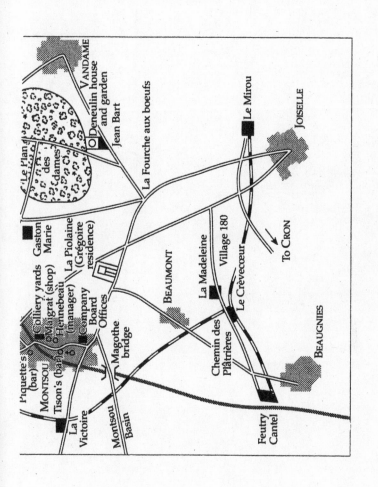

Germinal*

PART I

CHAPTER I

CROSSING the open plain, wading through the thick, dark ink of a starless night, a solitary figure followed the highway from Marchiennes to Montsou,* which cut its paved pathway straight through ten kilometres of beet fields. The man could not even see the black earth beneath his feet, and his only sense of the vast, flat horizons came from the gusting March wind, blowing in wide swathes as if sweeping across the sea, but icy cold from its passage over leagues of marshland and barren earth. Not a tree marked the sky with its shadow, and the paved road jutted forward like a pier straight out into the murky waves of this world of shadows.

He had left Marchiennes around two o'clock. He was walking with long strides, shivering in his thin, worn, cotton jacket and corduroy trousers. He was rather hampered by a small bundle, tied up in a check handkerchief, which he wedged against his ribs, first under one arm, then under the other, so that he could keep both hands plunged deep in his pockets, since they were already numb and chapped from the whiplash of the east wind. He was unemployed and homeless, and had only one thought in his head; the hope that the cold would be less keen after daybreak. He had been struggling onward like this for an hour, and was still a good way from Montsou, when he noticed the red glow of three braziers, burning apparently suspended in mid-air. At first he hesitated, apprehensively; then he could no longer resist the painful need to warm his hands, if only for a moment.

There was a dip in the road, and the vision vanished. On his right a fence appeared, a rough wooden barricade blocking off a railway track; while over to the left rose a grass mound, covered with a jumbled arrangement of gables, giving the impression of a village with a low, regular line of rooftops. About 200 paces further on, a sudden bend in the road brought the fires back into sight, nearer this time, yet he could not guess how they could be burning so high up in the lifeless sky, looking like smouldering moons. But then he was suddenly brought to a halt by the sight at ground level of a great shapeless heap of low buildings topped by the outline of a factory chimney rising from its midst; here and there a lonely light flickered through a filthy window, five or six miserable lanterns were hung up outside on brackets whose blackened timber projected mysterious silhouettes like giant scaffolds, and, from the midst of this fantastic apparition, swimming in smoke and darkness, there rose a lone voice, the prolonged, loud wheezing of a steam engine exhaust valve, hidden somewhere out of sight.

Then he recognized it as a pit-head. A feeling of defeat came over him again. What was the use? There wouldn't be any work for him. Instead of walking towards the buildings, he decided at last to climb up the slag-heap where the three coal fires were burning in cast-iron braziers, lighting and heating the working area. The stonemen, digging the tunnels, must have been working late, they were still sending out the rubble. Now he could hear the sorters pushing the coal-tubs over the trestles, and was able to distinguish moving shadows emptying the tubs near each of the fires.

'Morning,' he said, going nearer to one of the braziers.

The driver was standing upright with his back to the brazier. He was an old man, clad in a mauve woollen jersey and a rabbit-skin cap; while his big, sand-coloured horse stood still as a statue, waiting for the six tubs which he had hauled up there to be emptied. The workman operating the tippler,* a gangling, red-haired fellow, took his time, pulling the lever with a sleepy hand. And over their heads the wind howled fiercer than ever, an icy winter wind cutting like a scythe in strong, rhythmical blasts.

'Morning,' the old man replied.

They fell silent. The young man felt that he was under suspicion, so he said who he was straight away.

'My name is Étienne Lantier.* I'm a mechanic . . . I suppose there isn't any work going here?'

The flames lit him up. He had a very dark complexion, and seemed about twenty-one years old. He was handsome and looked strong, although his limbs were rather spare.

The driver looked reassured and shook his head.

'No, there's no work for a mechanic, nothing ... There were two more of you asking only yesterday. There's nothing at all.'

A blast of wind carried their words away. Then Étienne pointed at the dark heap of buildings at the foot of the slag-heap, and asked:

'It is a pit, isn't it?'

But this time the old man couldn't answer. He was choked by a violent fit of coughing. Finally he managed to cough up a great gobbet of phlegm which made a black stain on the flame-tinted ground.

'Yes, it's a pit, it's Le Voreux* ... Look, the mining village is just next door.'

Then it was his turn to reach out and point into the night towards the village whose roofs the young man had dimly glimpsed. But the six tubs were empty, and he followed them back with his stiff rheumatic gait, without so much as a flick of the whip, while the big sandy horse went off without needing to be prompted, straining laboriously along the tracks in the teeth of a fresh squall of wind which made his hackles rise.

Now Le Voreux started to emerge from its shadowy dream world. Étienne was engrossed in the process of warming his poor chapped hands at the brazier, and, as he watched, each part of the pit took shape before his eyes: the pitch-roofed screening shed, the headgear* standing over the shaft, the great winding-engine house, the square tower of the drainage pump. The pit, with its squat brick buildings crammed into the bottom of the valley, raised its chimney like a threatening horn, and seemed to take on the sinister air of a voracious beast, crouching ready to pounce and gobble you up. As Étienne looked it up and down, he thought of himself and his nomadic existence seeking work for the last week; he pictured himself in his railway workshop, hitting his boss, thrown out of Lille, thrown out of everywhere; on Saturday he had got to Marchiennes, where he had heard there was work at the Les Forges* metalworks; but no luck, not at Les Forges's, and not at Sonneville's either, he'd had to spend Sunday holed up in a woodpile in a cartwrights' timber yard, where he had just been kicked out by the watchman at two o'clock in the morning. No luck, not a penny, not even a crust of bread: how long could he hold out like this, wandering aimlessly over the countryside, without the slightest shelter from the winter wind? Yes, of course, now he recognized the pit, as the scattered lanterns lit the paved yard, and a door suddenly flew open, giving him a glimpse of the generator furnaces, blazing with light. He worked out what everything was, and could even locate the pump letting off steam, with its long, raucous, repetitive wheezing, like the hoarse snorting of some monster.

The tippler operator was doubled up over his work and had not bothered even to look up at Étienne, who was just about to pick his small bundle up from where he had dropped it, when a fit of coughing announced the return of the driver. He gradually emerged from the shadows followed by his sandy horse, pulling six more loaded tubs.

'Are there any factories in Montsou?' the young man asked.

The old man coughed up some black phlegm* and then spoke up loudly against the wind:

'Oh, there are plenty of factories, all right. You should've seen 'em three or four years ago, thundering away, they couldn't find enough workmen, never was so much money about . . . but now we've got to tighten our belts again. It's a crying shame round here, people laid off, workshops closing down,* one after the other . . . Maybe it's not the Emperor's* own fault; but why does he need to go off to fight in America?* Not to mention the cattle that's dying of cholera,* like everyone else.'

Thus the pair of them swapped complaints, in short, wind-swept phrases. Étienne listed the futile approaches he had made over the last week; so should he give up and die of hunger? Soon the roads would be chock-full of beggars. Yes, said the old man, things couldn't go on like that, after all, for Christ's sake, you couldn't just keep on throwing all God's creatures out on the streets like that.

'You don't get to eat meat every day, either.'

'It wouldn't be so bad if there was enough bread to go round.'

'That's true, if only there was enough bread!'

Their voices were pummelled and funnelled into a melancholy wailing by the blustering gale.

'Look!' the driver continued at the top of his voice, turning towards the south, 'there's Montsou . . .'

And stretching his arm out again he pointed at places invisible in the darkness, and he named them. Over there, at Montsou, the Fauvelle sugar-refinery was still working, but the Hoton refinery had just cut back its work-force, there was really only the Dutilleul flour-mill and the Bleuze works, which made mine cables, which weren't going under. Then with a sweep of his arms he marked out an area covering half of the northern horizon: the Sonneville building works had had less than two-thirds of their normal orders; only two of the three blast-furnaces at Les Forges, in Marchiennes, were burning; and, last but not least, a strike was in the offing at the Gagebois glassworks, because they were talking of cutting the men's wages.

'I know, don't tell me,' the young man repeated after every assertion, 'that's where I've just been.'

'Over here we're all right so far,' the driver added. 'But the pits have cut back their production. And look, over the other side there, at La Victoire, they've only lit two of their batteries of coke ovens.'

He spat, then followed on after his sleepy horse, after hitching it up to the empty tubs.

Now Étienne was able to survey the whole countryside. The shadows were still deep, but the old man's hand had somehow fleshed them out with a breadth of suffering that the young man could now intuitively feel living in the limitless space that surrounded him, as if the March wind were wringing a cry of famine from the bare countryside. The squalls of wind shrieked crazily, as if they were murdering work, bringing a famine which would cause untold slaughter. And his eyes darted back and forth as he tried to penetrate the darkness, racked with an anguished urge to see and understand.

Everything was swallowed up in the unknowable darkness of night; all he could see, far off, were the blast-furnaces and the coke ovens. The latter, with their batteries of 100 chimneys each set at a slant, traced out their parallel slopes of scarlet flames; while further over to the left the two tall stacks blasted their blue light high into the heavens, like giant torches. It was a tragic vision, like a town gutted by a disastrous blaze. There were no stars rising over the lowering horizon other than these northern lights hanging over the land of coal and iron.

'Would you be from Belgium?' The driver spoke again, he had come up behind Étienne on his way back up.

This time he had brought along only three tubs. They might as well tip those out to be going on with: there had been a breakdown in the cage, due to a broken nut, which would halt work for at least a quarter of an hour. Around the base of the slag-heap things had gone quiet; the labourers could no longer be heard shaking the trestles with their continuous rumbling and rattling. All you could hear was the distant sound of a hammer beating on an iron plate down in the pit shaft.

'No, I'm from the south,' the young man replied.

The tippler operator emptied the trucks, then sat down on the ground, pleased at the interruption; he remained locked in his awkward silence, merely looking up at the driver with wide, lifeless eyes, as if all this talking bothered him. Indeed, the old man was not usually so talkative. He must have taken a fancy to the newcomer's face and been bitten with one of those sudden urges to confide which sometimes make old people talk to themselves out loud.

'I'm from Montsou, myself,' he said, 'my name is Bonnemort.'*

'That's never your real name!' said Étienne in astonishment.

The old man chuckled delightedly, and pointed at Le Voreux:

'No, of course not . . . I've been dragged out of there three times in little pieces, once with my hair singed to the roots, once with my guts bunged up with mud, the third time with my belly blown up with water like a frog . . . So when they saw I wasn't going to kick the bucket they called me Bonnemort for a laugh.'

He laughed with renewed vigour, like the creaking of a rusty pulley, but his mirth tailed off into a terrible fit of coughing. The light from the brazier now shone directly on his head. He had a large, flat face, sparse white hair, and a livid complexion covered in slate-coloured blotches. He was a short man, with a massive neck and bandy legs. He had long arms, and his square hands reached down to his knees. Moreover, like his horse, which was standing there motionless, apparently untroubled by the wind, he resembled a stone statue, seeming not to notice the cold, nor the wind buffeting and whistling around his ears. When he had finished coughing up, raking his throat with a great rasping noise, he spat out on the ground beneath the brazier, staining it black.

Étienne looked at him, then looked at the soil which he had just discoloured.

'Have you been working at the mine for long?' he asked.

Bonnemort flung his arms open wide.

'For long? Oh, yes! ... I was still only seven when I first went down, just here as it happens, down Le Voreux, and now here we are and I'm fifty-eight. Work it out for yourself ... I've done the lot in there, pit boy to start with, then trammer* pushing coal-tubs when I was strong enough to push, then hewer for eighteen years. Then with my gammy legs they made me a stoneman, on digging tunnels, then seam-filler, then repair man, until they had to drag me back up to the daylight in the end because the doctor said otherwise I'd never come out alive. So now that's five years ago and they made me a driver ... Hey, that's quite something, isn't it, fifty years at the pit, and forty-five of those underground!'

While he was speaking, the pieces of burning coal which dropped from the brazier from time to time lit up his pale face, giving it a bloodshot appearance.

'They keep telling me to take a rest,' he continued, 'but I won't buy that one, I'm not that daft ... I'm going to see out the next two years till I'm sixty, to get my hundred-and-eighty-franc pension. If I said my goodbyes today they'd jump at the chance of paying me off with the hundred-and-fifty-franc one, the crafty buggers ... Anyway I'm fighting fit, apart from the legs. It's only the water that got under my skin,* you see, what with being rained on at the coal-face. Some days I can't put one foot in front of the other without crying out loud.'

He was interrupted by another fit of coughing.

'And it's given you that cough, too, hasn't it?' said Étienne.

But Bonnemort shook his head in violent dissent. And as soon as he could speak, he said:

'No, it's not that, I caught a cold a month or so ago. I never had a cough before, now I can't get rid of it . . . and the funny thing is that now I just keep on coughing all the time, coughing and coughing.'

A rasping sound came up from the back of his throat, and he spat out more black phlegm.

'Is that blood?' Étienne asked, finally plucking up the courage to put the question.

Bonnemort wiped his mouth with the back of his hand, slowly.

'No, it's coal . . . I've got enough of it stored in my bones to keep me warm till my dying day. And I haven't put a foot underground for the last five years. So I must have been stocking it up in my cellars in advance without realizing it. Oh well, keeps you young.'

They fell silent. The sound of the hammer rang out rhythmically from far down in the pit, the wind wailed past them like a cry of hunger and fatigue torn from the bowels of the night. The flames danced frantically as the old man picked up his story, chewing over his memories in a quieter voice now. Oh yes, of course, he was no newcomer to cutting the coal, him and his family. They'd been working for the Montsou Mining Company since it was founded; and that was long enough ago, a hundred and six years now. One of his grandfathers, Guillaume Maheu, a fifteen-year-old kid at the time, had discovered the soft-coal measures at Réquillart, the Company's first pit, an old pit, disused now, over there by the Fauvelle sugar-refinery. The whole neighbourhood knew it was true, on account of the seam he discovered was called the Guillaume seam after his grandfather's Christian name. He never knew him himself, a big man so people said, died of old age at sixty years old. Then his father, Nicolas Maheu, they called him The Red, only just forty when he breathed his last, down under in Le Voreux which was just being sunk at the time: tunnel collapsed, squashed him flat as your hand, blood, bones, and everything swallowed up by the rocks. Two of his uncles and three brothers later on had met their maker down below. He himself, Vincent Maheu, had come out more or less in one piece, with just his legs out of kilter; he was the smart one, if you asked what folks thought. But what could you do about it, anyway? You had to work. It was handed down from father to son like any other job. His own son, Toussaint Maheu, was wearing himself out at the same game, and his grandsons, and the whole family, who lived just opposite, in the mining village. A hundred and six years of hard labour, first the old men then the kids, all for the same boss: hey, there weren't many of your upper-class blokes who could give you such a good long family history!*

'And even then, it's all right as long as you have enough to eat!' Étienne murmured again.

'That's what I always say, as long as you've got enough bread to eat, you can keep alive.'

Bonnemort fell silent, and turned his gaze towards the mining village, where the lights were coming on one by one.

The bells of Montsou rang out four o'clock. The cold turned sharper.

Étienne was the next to speak: 'Is your Company rich?'

The old man raised his shoulders, then let them fall limp again, as if he had suddenly been buried by a landslide of gold coins.

'Oh yes, you can say that again . . . Maybe not as rich as the d'Anzin* Company, next door. But worth millions and millions all the same. You couldn't count it all up . . . Nineteen pits, thirteen producing, Le Voreux, La Victoire, Crèvecœur, Mirou, Saint-Thomas, Madeleine, Feutry-Cantel, and still more, and six for drainage or ventilation, like Réquillart . . . Ten thousand workers, concessions covering sixty-seven parishes, producing 5,000 tons a day, railway links to every pit, and workshops, and factories . . . Oh yes, you can say that again, there's money there all right!'

The sound of tubs rumbling over the trestles made the big sandy horse prick up its ears. Down below the cage must have been repaired, for the sorters had returned to their labours. While he harnessed the horse to go back down again, the driver added quietly, addressing the animal confidentially:

'Mustn't get used to nattering, lazy old boy! . . . What

would Monsieur Hennebeau think if he knew how you wasted your time?'

Étienne looked out into the night, meditatively. He asked:

'So the mine belongs to Monsieur Hennebeau, then, does it?'

'No,' the old man explained, 'Monsieur Hennebeau is only the manager. He draws his wages like the rest of us.'

The young man pointed towards the vast domain that lay hidden in the darkness.

'So who does it all belong to, then?'

But Bonnemort was momentarily choked by another attack, so violent that he had to fight for breath. When he had finally spat out, and wiped the black foam off his lips, he spoke against the wind, which was gusting more fiercely than ever:

'What? Who does it all belong to? . . . Who knows? Other people.'

And with his hand he indicated an imaginary point in the shadows, some distant, unknown place, inhabited by those other people, for whom the Maheu family had been hacking their hearts out for over a century.

His voice had taken on a kind of religious awe; it was as if he had spoken of some untouchable tabernacle which concealed the crouching, greedy god to whom they all offered up their flesh, but whom they had never seen.

'If only we had enough bread to eat,' Étienne repeated for the third time, with no apparent connection.

'Lord, yes, if we had all the bread we could eat, that would be too good to be true!'

The horse had started off, then the driver disappeared after him with his cripple's limp. By the tippler, the operator hadn't moved an inch; he was still sitting hunched up with his chin between his knees, staring at nothing with his wide, vacant eyes.

Étienne picked up his bundle, but he didn't move off again straight away. He felt the icy blasts of wind biting into his back, while his chest was roasting in front of the blazing fire. Perhaps, all the same, he could do worse than ask at the pit: the old man might not be well informed: and then, he was resigned to the fact that he would have to accept whatever was on offer. Where could he go; and what future was there for him anywhere in this country starving from unemployment? Why leave his carcass behind a wall somewhere like a dead dog? Yet one thing still made him hesitate, a feeling of fear as he looked at Le Voreux, in the middle of that bare plain, drowned so deep in such black night. With every new squall the wind seemed to gather strength, as if the horizons it blew from kept opening wider. There was no sign of dawn to relight the dead sky, only the blast-furnaces burning alongside the coke ovens, bloodying the shadows without illuminating their hidden depths. And Le Voreux lay lower and squatter, deep in its den, crouching like a vicious beast of prey, snorting louder and longer, as if choking on its painful digestion of human flesh.

CHAPTER II

AMID the fields of wheat and sugar-beet, mining village number Two Hundred and Forty* slumbered in the depths of night. You could just detect the bulk of the four massive blocks of small back-to-back houses, running geometrically in parallel lines like a barracks or a hospital, and divided by three wide avenues, laid out with regular gardens. And, over the deserted plain, the only sound to be heard was the wailing of the wind, tearing the trellises away from the fences.

In the Maheus' house, which was number 16 of the second block, nothing moved. The single first-floor bedroom was cloaked in thick shadows, as if their very weight was driving sleep into the creatures whose presence could almost be felt, as they lay there in a heap, with their mouths open, drugged with fatigue. Despite the sharp cold outside, the fetid air gave out a living warmth, the suffocating warmth of even the most comfortable sleeping quarters, with their smell of human cattle.

The cuckoo clock on the ground floor struck four o'clock, but nothing stirred; there was the whistle of faint breathing, accompanied by two deeper snores. But suddenly Catherine started. Despite her fatigue she had intuitively recognized the

Germinal

four chimes of the clock echoing up through the floorboards,
without having the energy to wake up altogether. Then she
swung her legs out of bed, groped for a match, and lit the
candle. But she stayed sitting down, her head so heavy that it
sagged back behind her shoulders, drawn irresistibly by the
urge to collapse on to the bolster.

Now the candle lit up the square room, its two windows,
and the three beds which were crammed into it. There was a
wardrobe, and a table and two chairs, all made of old walnut
wood, whose smoky hues clashed starkly with the bright
yellow paint on the walls. There was no other furniture, only
some clothes hung up on nails, and a jug on the floor,
alongside a red cooking pot which served as a basin. In the
left-hand bed, Zacharie, the oldest child, a lad of twenty-one,
lay alongside his brother Jeanlin, who was nearly eleven years
old; in the right-hand bed there were two kids, Lénore and
Henri, one six and the other four, asleep in each other's arms;
while Catherine shared the third bed with her sister Alzire,
who was so skinny for her nine years that she wouldn't even
have felt her presence at her side, if the poor little cripple's
hump hadn't dug into her ribs. The glass-panelled door was
open, and you could see the landing, where in a kind of recess
the father and mother slept in a fourth bed, beside which they
had managed to lodge the cradle of their youngest, Estelle,
who was only just three months old.

Catherine forced herself to make a supreme effort. She
stretched out her arms, and tugged at the red hair which
cascaded over her neck and forehead. She was slim for a fifteen-
year-old, and all that could be seen of her limbs, tightly
wrapped in her nightshirt, were her feet, seemingly tattooed
with bluish coal-stains, and her delicate arms, whose milky
whiteness glowed in contrast to her sallow complexion, which
was already worn by repeated scrubbing with black soap. A
final yawn revealed a generous mouth, and gleaming teeth set in
anaemic gums; while from her grey-green eyes, brimming with
the wreckage of sleep, seeped a broken and suffering expression
which radiated out from her naked body in waves of fatigue.

But a voice croaked out from the landing, as Maheu stammered through the mists of sleep:

'God damn! It's time . . . Did you put the light on, Catherine?'

'Yes, Father . . . The clock's just chimed, downstairs.'

'Well hurry up then, lazybones! If you hadn't spent all Sunday night dancing, you could have woken us earlier this morning . . . What a life of idle luxury!'

And he carried on scolding her, but he lapsed into sleep again, and his complaints became confused and died away in a new fit of snoring.

The girl crossed the bedroom in her nightshirt, walking barefoot on the tiled floor. As she went past Henri and Lénore, she tucked in the blanket, which had slipped off their bed; they didn't awake, but stayed drowned in their deep, childish sleep. Alzire opened her eyes, and turned over to take the warm place left by her big sister, without saying a word.

'Hey, Zacharie! Hey, there, Jeanlin, come on!' Catherine said, twice over, standing over her two brothers, as they remained oblivious, with their heads buried in the bolster.

She had to grab her elder brother by the shoulders and shake him; then, while he was mumbling insults at her, she decided to strip off the sheet. She thought the two boys looked funny as they thrashed out their bare legs in protest, and she laughed out loud.

'Let go, stupid!' grumbled Zacharie sulkily, as he sat up. 'I don't like your games . . . My God, just think! We've got to get up!'

He was a thin, gangling young man, whose long face was darkened at the chin, shadowed by a few scraps of nascent beard. He had the same straw-coloured hair and anaemic complexion as the rest of the family. His nightshirt had ridden up around his belly, and he tugged it down again, not from modesty, but to keep himself warm.

'It's struck four downstairs,' Catherine repeated. 'Come on, move it, Father's getting mad.'

Jeanlin, who had curled back up into a ball, closed his eyes again, and said:

'Piss off, I'm tired!'

She gave another good-natured laugh. He was so small, with his thin limbs, and his oversized joints swollen with scabs, that she swept him up bodily in her arms. But he wriggled furiously, and his livid monkey-like features were lit up by his fierce green eyes. His tight, curly hair and his big ears emphasized the pallor of his sullen, angry features, and, humiliated by his impotence, he said nothing, but bit her right breast.

'Rotten bastard!' she swore quietly, choking back a cry and putting him down on the ground.

Alzire remained silent, the sheet drawn up to her chin, but she had not gone back to sleep. Her pensive, sickly eyes followed the movements of her sister and her two brothers as they started to get dressed. Another quarrel broke out around the basin, with the boys elbowing the girl aside because she was taking too long to get washed. Then they threw off their nightshirts and relieved themselves, still half-asleep, naturally and unembarrassedly, like a litter of puppies raised together. In fact, Catherine was the first to be ready. She slipped on her miner's breeches, put on her cotton jacket, tied her hair into a bun and tucked it into her blue cap. In her clean Monday-morning clothes she looked like a little man, with nothing betraying her gender but a slight swaying of the hips.

'When the old man comes in,' said Zacharie spitefully, 'he'll be really pleased to see the bed in a mess . . . and you can bet I'll tell him it's your fault.'

The old man was their grandfather, Bonnemort, who worked at night and slept in the daytime: so the bed never cooled off, there was always someone snoring away in it.

Catherine said nothing, but started to straighten out the blanket and tuck it in. But a few moments earlier she had heard noises behind the wall, coming from the neighbours' house. These brick partitions, one of the Company's more frugal investments, were so thin that the slightest whisper was audible on the other side. The occupants lived back to back; nothing private stayed secret, even in front of the children. A heavy footstep had shaken the staircase; then there was a sort of soft thump, followed by a sigh of relief.

'Well!' said Catherine, 'Levaque's gone downstairs, so now it's Bouteloup's turn to go up and keep La Levaque warm.'

Jeanlin sniggered, and even Alzire's eyes lit up. Every morning they joked over the *ménage à trois* next door, made up of a hewer, his lodger, who was a stoneman,* and the hewer's wife, who was thus provided with two men, one working nights, and the other on the day shift.

'Philomène's coughing,' said Catherine, after listening quietly for a moment.

This was the eldest Levaque child, a tall nineteen-year-old girl, who was Zacharie's mistress, and had already had two children by him, although she had such a weak chest that she had always worked as a sorter at the pit, because she had never been able to work below ground.

'Oh yes, like hell!' Zacharie replied. 'Philomène doesn't give a damn, she's fast asleep ... What a slut, to think she can sleep until six o'clock!'

He put his breeches on, then opened a window, struck by a sudden thought. Outside, in the darkness, the village awoke, as the lights came twinkling one by one through the slats of the blinds. And that caused another quarrel: he leant forward, peering out, hoping to see the overman* emerge from the Pierrons' house over the way, since he was reputed to be sleeping with La Pierronne; while his sister shouted out that the husband had gone over to a day shift at the loading bay since yesterday, so that, obviously, Dansaert couldn't have shacked up there last night. The wind burst through in icy gusts, as Zacharie and Catherine shouted at each other, both equally convinced of the accuracy of their information, until they were interrupted by a fit of screaming and crying, coming from Estelle's cot. She had been disturbed by the cold.

This woke Maheu up. What the hell had got into his bones, to make him doze off again like a layabout? And he swore so loud that the children in the next room fell silent. Zacharie and Jeanlin were finishing washing, with a slowness that betrayed their fatigue. Alzire had opened her eyes wide and was looking around her. The two youngsters, Lénore and Henri, were still asleep in each other's arms, breathing quietly and rhythmically in time together, despite the row.

'Catherine, give me the candle!' shouted Maheu.

She finished buttoning up her jacket, then took the candle into the recess on the landing, leaving her brothers to look for their clothes in the faint light that filtered through the doorway. Her father jumped out of bed. But she didn't stop, she felt her way down the stairs in her thick woollen stockings and lit another candle at the bottom, so that she could see to get the coffee ready. The family all kept their clogs under the dresser.

'Will you shut up, you little rat!' Maheu shouted, exasperated by Estelle, who was still crying.

He was short, like old Bonnemort, and in fact he was like a plumper version of him, with a large head, a flat, pallid face, and straw-coloured hair cut very short. The child screamed louder, frightened by the big muscular arms waving around over her head.

'Leave her alone, you know she won't shut up,' said La Maheude, lying back in the middle of the bed.

She too had just woken up, and she complained how rotten it was never to be able to get a proper night's sleep. Couldn't they just go out quietly? All that emerged from under the blanket tucked snugly round her was her long face, with its striking features, whose ripe beauty had already been undermined at the age of only thirty-nine by a life of poverty and the seven children she had borne. She stared up at the ceiling and spoke slowly, while her old man got dressed. Neither of them noticed the baby, who was gradually running out of breath to scream with.

'Look, you realize I'm clean out of cash, and it's only Monday: another six days to go before we get our fortnight's pay* . . . it can't go on like this. All the lot of you earn is nine francs. How can you expect me to make ends meet? There are ten of us to feed.'

'Oh! Nine francs!' protested Maheu. 'Me and Zacharie are both on three, that makes six . . . Catherine and Father on two, that makes four; four and six is ten . . . and Jeanlin gets one, which makes eleven.'

'All right, eleven, but don't forget there's Sundays and days off work . . . so you never get more than nine, do you?'

He was too busy looking on the floor for his leather belt to reply. Then he straightened up, and said:

'You shouldn't complain, I'm good and strong. There are plenty of fellows who are reduced to repair work by the time they're forty-two.'

'Maybe, my friend, but that doesn't bring home the bacon ... What the hell am I supposed to do, then? Haven't you got a penny on you?'

'I've got two sous.'*

'Keep them for the pub ... My God! What the hell am I going to do? Six days to go, it's endless. We owe sixty francs to Maigrat, who shut the door on me the day before yesterday. That won't stop me going back to see him. But if he keeps on turning me down ...'

And La Maheude droned on, without moving her head, closing her eyes from time to time to shut out the sad light of the candle. She said the cupboard was bare, the little ones kept asking for bread and butter, there wasn't even any coffee left, the water gave you the runs, and day after day you kept your mind off the hunger by chewing boiled cabbage leaves. She must have been gradually raising her voice, to make herself heard over the screams of the baby. This screaming was now too much to bear. Maheu suddenly seemed to hear it, he couldn't stand it, he snatched the kid out of her cot and dumped her on her mother's bed, stammering with rage:

'Here! take her, before I do her an injury ... God almighty, what a child! She has everything she wants, she gulps it down, and she moans worse than the others!'

And sure enough Estelle had started sucking. She was already buried under the blankets, enveloped in the soothing warmth of the bed, and the only sign of life she gave was a greedy little slurping of the lips.

'Didn't the bourgeois* at La Piolaine tell you to go and see them?' the father resumed, after a moment of silence.

The mother pursed her lips, with an air of doubt and discouragement.

'Yes, I met them. They give out clothes for poor children ... All right, I'll take Lénore and Henri to see them this morning. If they'd just give me a hundred sous,* even.'

Silence fell again. Maheu was ready. He stayed motionless for a moment, then he concluded, with his gruff voice:

'What do you expect, that's the way things are, it's your job to rake up the food ... Sitting here talking won't do any good, I'd do better to get off to work.'

'Of course,' replied La Maheude. 'Blow the candle out, I don't need to see what my thoughts look like.'

He blew the candle out. Zacharie and Jeanlin were already on their way downstairs; as he followed them down, the wooden stairs creaked under the heavy tread of their woollen-stockinged feet. Behind them, the recess and the bedroom had relapsed into darkness. The children were asleep, and even Alzire had closed her eyes. But now their mother was staring wide-eyed into the darkness, while Estelle, pumping away at the exhausted woman's empty breast, purred like a kitten.

Downstairs, Catherine had started by lighting the fire. The cast-iron hearth, which had a griddle in the centre and a stove on each side, was permanently lit with a coal fire. Once a month the Company handed out to each family eight hectolitres of slack, the hard coal flakes which accumulated beside the tracks. It was difficult to get it to light, so the girl merely damped down the fire every night and then stoked it up in the morning, adding little pieces of carefully chosen soft coal. Then, when she had put a kettle on the griddle, she squatted down in front of the dresser.

It was a fairly large room, which took up the whole of the ground floor. It was painted apple green, and gleamed with Nordic cleanliness, since its flagstones were sluiced down with water and then sprinkled with white sand. In addition to the dresser, of varnished pine, the furniture consisted of a table and chairs of the same wood. The walls were covered with garish prints, including portraits of the Emperor and Empress,* donated by the Company, as well as copiously gilded soldiers and saints, contrasting blatantly with the stark austerity of the room; and the only ornaments to be seen were a pink cardboard box on the sideboard, and the multicoloured cuckoo clock, whose loud tick-tock seemed to echo right up through the air to the ceiling. Next to the door at the foot of the stairs was another door, leading down to the cellar.

Despite the cleanliness, the warm air was tainted with a smell of fried onion which had lingered captive overnight and now hung rankly in the warm air, permanently thick and heavy with the acrid tang of burning coal.

In front of the open sideboard, Catherine reflected. There

was only one piece of bread left, there was enough cottage cheese, but only a single pat of butter; and she was supposed to prepare slices for four of them. But then she made up her mind, cut the bread into slices, spreading cheese on one piece and smearing butter on another, then sticking them together: making a 'slab',* the sandwich which they took to the pit each morning. Soon she had lined up the four slabs on the table, having calculated their size with the most rigorous justice, from the father's man-size bite down to Jeanlin's little nibble.

Catherine, who seemed quite absorbed by her housework, was no doubt dreaming of the stories that Zacharie had been telling about the overman and La Pierronne, for she pushed the door half-open and glanced ouside. The wind was still strong, but the light playing on the low walls of the village buildings was brighter now, and the air was filled with the muffled sounds of people waking up. Already doors were opening and closing, as dark lines of workmen moved off into the night. What a fool she was to get cold, because you could bet that the cage-loader was still asleep; he was in no hurry to go off to his shift, which didn't start until six o'clock! But she stayed there looking at the house at the bottom of the garden. The door opened, and her curiosity was whetted. But it must only have been the Pierrons' daughter Lydie, going off to the pit.

A hiss of steam made her turn round. She shut the door and hurried back to the stove: the water was boiling and spilling over, putting the fire out. There was no coffee left, she had to make do with pouring the boiling water over yesterday's grounds; then she put some raw sugar in the coffee-pot. Just then her father and two brothers came down.

'Ye gods!' proclaimed Zacharie, raising his bowl to his lips, 'I reckon there's no danger to life and limb in this brew.'

Maheu shrugged his shoulders philosophically.

'Well, it's hot, so it's better than nothing.'

Jeanlin collected all the crumbs from the sandwiches to dunk in his bowl. Catherine finished drinking, and then poured what was left of the coffee out of the pot into their tin flasks. All four of them remained standing, as they drank up quickly, by the dim light of the smoking candle.

'That's it, and about time, too!' said their father. 'Anyone would think we had a private income!'

But they heard a voice from upstairs, through the door, which they had left open. It was their mother, La Maheude, who shouted out:

'Take all the bread, I've got a bit of vermicelli for the children.'

'Yes, all right,' answered Catherine.

She had damped down the fire, but put a drop of soup to simmer on a hot part of the griddle for the grandfather to find when he got home at six o'clock. They all took their clogs out from under the dresser, slung the straps of their flasks over their shoulders, and wedged their slabs down between their shirts and their jackets. Then they went out with the men leading and the girl bringing up the rear, after she had blown out the candle and locked the door. The house went dark again.

'Hello there! We're all off together,' said a man who was closing the door of the neighbouring house.

It was Levaque, with his son Bébert, a twelve-year-old kid who was a great friend of Jeanlin. Catherine was amazed, and had to smother her laughter, as she whispered to Zacharie: 'How about that? Now Bouteloup doesn't even wait till her husband has left!'

Back in the village the lights started to go out again. The last door banged shut, and sleep descended, as the women and children dozed off again, in their cosier beds. And all the way from the silent village to the roaring pit of Le Voreux, a slow procession of shadows wended its way through the gusts of wind, as the colliers set off for work, shoulders swaying and arms crossed on their chests to keep them out of the way, with their lunchtime slab giving them a hump in the small of the back. In their thin cotton clothes they shivered with cold, but never quickened their pace, as they tramped along the road like a wandering herd of animals.

CHAPTER III

WHEN Étienne finally came down from the slag-heap, he went into the pit-head at Le Voreux; and the men he approached to ask if there was any work shook their heads, but they all told him to wait until the overman arrived. They left him to his own devices amid the twilit buildings, with their pools of darkness, and their confusing maze of rooms and floors. He mounted a dark and ramshackle staircase, and found himself on a shaky gangway, leading across the screening shed, which was still so plunged in darkness that he groped his way forwards with his arms outstretched to avoid bumping into things. Suddenly two large yellow eyes cut through the darkness. He was right underneath the headgear, in the coal receipt hall at the top landing-stage, at the very mouth of the pit.

A deputy,* old Richomme, a fat man with a face like a benevolent policeman, and a wide grey moustache, was walking at that very moment towards the office of the receiving clerk, the checkweighman.

'Could you use a workman here, for any kind of job at all?' Étienne asked again.

Richomme was about to say no; but he thought twice and replied as the others had, as he walked away:

'Wait for Monsieur Dansaert, the overman.'

Four lanterns had been set up there, with reflectors, to cast their light right down into the pit, illuminating the iron railings, the signal levers and the cage keeps, and the timber beams of the guides which the two cages ran along. The rest of the vast hall seemed like the nave of a church, or a shipwrecked vessel, haunted by great, floundering shadowy souls. The only bright patch came from the lamp depot blazing at the end, while, in the coal receipt office, a weak lamp guttered like a waning star. Production had just started up again; a constant rumbling sound came from the cast-iron plates of the flooring as the coal trucks rolled endlessly by, and the labourers were running back and forth, their long curved spines occasionally visible above the dark, turbulent, noisy chaos.

For a moment Étienne stood motionless, deafened and

blinded. He felt frozen; there were draughts coming at him
from all sides. So he walked forward a few steps, drawn
towards the winding engine, watching its steel and copper
parts fitfully gleaming. It was set back from the shaft, twenty-
five metres higher up, in a separate room, and so solidly fixed
on its own brick foundations that despite its steam engine
running at top speed with its full 400 horsepower, its enormous
crank rod surged and dived with well-oiled smoothness, trans-
mitting not the slightest vibration to the surrounding walls.
The mechanic stood beside the operating lever, listening out
for the signal bells and watching the planning board with its
plan of the shaft, showing its various levels marked off against
a vertical groove, where lead weights hung on strings ran up
and down, representing the cages. And with each departure, as
the engine started up, the drums, two immense wheels ten
metres wide, around whose hubs the two steel cables were
constantly wound and then unwound in the opposite direction,
spun at such speed that they seemed like a grey cloud of dust.

'Watch out, there!' shouted three labourers, who were lug-
ging a gigantic ladder.

Étienne had nearly been crushed. As his eyes became accustomed to the darkness, he watched the cables whistling through
the air, their ribbons of steel cord flying over thirty metres high
up into the headgear, running over the pulleys, then hurtling
vertically down into the shaft where they latched on to the
production cages. The pulleys were supported by an iron
framework, like the tall framework of a bell-tower. The cable,
which constantly dipped and soared, flying smoothly and
silently as a bird despite its enormous weight, was capable of
lifting 1,200 kilograms at a speed of ten metres per second.

'Watch out there, for Christ's sake!' the labourers shouted
again, shifting the ladder over to the other side, to reach the
left-hand winding-drum.

Étienne walked slowly back to the receipt hall. The gigantic,
whirling flight over his head made him feel dizzy. And he
shivered in the cold draughts, as he watched the movement of
the cages, and felt his ears deafened by the tubs as they
thundered past. Near the shaft the signal rang out; it was a
heavy, swivelling hammer, which fell against a metal block

when pulled by a rope from below. One stroke to stop, two to
go down, three to come up: like great cudgel blows beating
down a riot, accompanied by the sharp ringing of a bell; while
the labourer directing the operation added to the din by
shouting orders to the mechanic through a loud hailer. The
cages surfaced suddenly amid this flurry of movement and
immediately dived down again; they emptied and were refilled,
without Étienne gaining any idea how these complex manœuvres were achieved.

There was only one fact that he really took in: the shaft was
swallowing men down in mouthfuls of twenty or thirty at a
time, with a swift gulping motion, showing hardly a ripple.
From four o'clock in the morning the workmen started their
descent. They came barefoot out of the shed, holding their
lamps in their hands, gathering in small groups until there
were enough of them. Soundlessly pouncing like a nocturnal
beast of prey, the iron cage rose out of the night, to lock into
its keeps, with its four decks each holding two tubs full of coal.
Labourers removed the tubs from each deck and replaced
them with others, either empty, or already loaded with props.
And the miners then squeezed into the empty tubs, in groups
of five, up to forty at a time, if all the tubs were filled. An
order was barked out through the loud hailer, a confused,
muffled braying, while the operator tugged the cord to ring
the signal four times down below, calling 'dinner's ready',
warning them that their next load of human cattle was on its
way down. Then the cage shuddered slightly, and plunged
silently downwards, falling like a stone, leaving no trace of its
passage but the swooping, throbbing cable.

'Is it deep?' Étienne asked a miner who was waiting alongside
him looking sleepy.

'Five hundred and fifty-four metres,' he replied. 'But there
are four stops on the way down, the first one's at three
hundred and twenty.'

They both fell silent, their eyes on the cable as it rose.
Étienne spoke again:

'And if it breaks?'

'Oh, if it breaks! . . .'

The miner finished his sentence with a gesture. His turn

had come, the cage had reappeared, with its slick, effortless movement. He squatted down inside one of the tubs with his workmates, it plunged down again, then, barely four minutes later, it surged back up again, ready to swallow down another load of men. For half an hour the pit gulped down these meals, in more or less greedy mouthfuls, depending on the depth of the level they were bound for, but without ever stopping, always hungry, its giant bowels capable of digesting a nation. It filled, and filled again, and the dark depths remained silent as the cage rose up from the void, silently opening its gaping jaws.

In the end Étienne felt the disquiet he had experienced earlier on the slag-heap returning. Why keep trying? This overman would turn him away as the others had. A strange feeling of fear made him take a sudden decision: he turned and walked away, and when he got outside he did not stop until he reached the building which housed the generators. Through the wide open doors he could see seven boilers with two furnaces each. Amid a white haze and the hiss of escaping steam a stoker was busy loading one of the furnaces, whose blazing fire could be felt from the entrance; and the young man, who was glad to feel some warmth, moved closer, when he met the next group of colliers arriving at the pit. It was the Maheu and Levaque families. When he saw Catherine at their head, her gentle, boyish demeanour inspired him with the sudden, irrational urge to make one last appeal.

'Listen, friend, isn't there room for another workman here, for any kind of job at all?'

She looked at him in surprise, a little frightened by this abrupt voice coming out of the shadows. But, behind her, Maheu had heard him, and he stopped to talk for a moment in reply. No, they didn't need anybody. But he was struck by this poor wretch of a workman wandering around the countryside. As he left he said to the others:

'You know, we could end up like that! ... Mustn't complain, it's not everyone who's dying of overwork.'

The group went straight into the changing shed, a great hall roughly plastered and whitewashed, its walls lined all round with padlocked lockers. In the centre there was an iron stove, a sort of open furnace, glowing brightly, and it was crammed so full of white-hot coal that pieces kept splitting open and shooting out over the earthen floor. The room was lit only by this brazier, which sent blood-red reflections dancing along the filthy woodwork and up on to the ceiling, which was stained with black dust.

As the Maheus arrived, they heard a gust of laughter billowing out from the direction of the blaze. About thirty workmen were standing with their backs to the flames, toasting themselves voluptuously. Before going down below, they all came to stoke up with a good skinful of heat to ward off the damp of the pit. But that morning there was an extra pleasure, they were teasing La Mouquette, an eighteen-year-old tram girl, a good-natured sort, whose ample breasts and buttocks threatened to burst out of her jacket and breeches. She lived at Réquillart with her father, old Mouque, a stable-man, and her brother Mouquet, a labourer; only, since their timetables weren't the same, she went to the pit on her own; and so, laid flat on her arse in a cornfield in summertime, or propped up against a wall in wintertime, she took her pleasure with whoever happened to be that week's lover boy. The miners had all had their turn, passing her on from mate to mate, without thinking twice about it. But on the day that she found herself accused of going with a nailsmith from Marchiennes she flew into a rage, shouting that she had more self-respect, that she'd rather lose an arm and a leg than let anyone boast he'd seen her with anyone but a collier.

'Is it all over with big tall Chaval, then?' asked one of the miners, mockingly. 'Have you snatched that little whippersnapper? I bet he'd need a ladder to get up there! . . . I saw the two of you behind Réquillart. And the proof is he had to climb up on a milestone.'

'So what?' said La Mouquette spiritedly. 'What the hell does it matter to you? Nobody asked you to come and give him a leg up.'

Her good-hearted coarseness made the men laugh even louder, as they shook their shoulders, half-toasted by the stove; while, roaring with laughter herself, she walked among them flaunting her indecent attire, with her grotesque but

provocative protrusions of flesh bursting through her clothes
like some obscene disease.

But the humour subsided when La Mouquette told Maheu
that Fleurahce, tall Fleurance, wouldn't be coming any more:
they had found her the night before stretched out stiff on her
bed; some said her heart had missed a beat, others blamed it
on a litre of gin she had downed too quickly. Maheu felt a
wave of despair: another bit of bad luck, there went another of
his tram girls, and no chance of finding an instant substitute!
He had to work on a subcontracting basis; there were four of
them as hewers in his seam, himself, Zacharie, Levaque, and
Chaval. If there was only Catherine left to push the tubs, their
output would suffer. Suddenly, he shouted out:

'Hey! How about that man who was looking for work?'

Just at that moment Dansaert was walking past the changing
shed. Maheu told his story, and asked permission to take the
new man on; and he reminded him that the Company wanted
to take on boys instead of girls as trammers, like at d'Anzin's.
At first the overman smiled, because the plan to remove the
women from underground usually offended the miners, who
were much more worried about finding work for their daughters than about any question of health or morality. But after
some hesitation he agreed, although he said he would have to
have his decision ratified by Monsieur Négrel, the engineer in
charge of the mine.

'Oh, that's great!' declared Zacharie. 'Our man must be
miles away by now if he hasn't dropped dead in the mean-
time.'

'No,' said Catherine, 'I saw him stop at the boiler-house.'

'Get a move on then, lazybones!' shouted Maheu.

The girl ran off, while a flood of miners headed for the
shaft, making room for others to warm themselves at the fire.
Without waiting for his father, Jeanlin went to get his lamp
too, with Bébert, a fat, innocent boy, and Lydie, a sickly ten-
year-old girl. La Mouquette, who had gone on ahead, shouted
out in the dark stairway that she'd slap the filthy little brats if
they pinched her.

And in fact Étienne was still in the boiler-house talking to
the stoker, who was loading the furnaces with coal. He felt a

deep chill come over him at the thought of going back out into the night. Yet he had to make up his mind and start to leave. Then he felt a hand on his shoulder.

'Come on,' said Catherine. 'We've got something for you.'

At first he didn't understand what she meant. Then he felt a rush of delight, and shook the girl's hands enthusiastically.

'Thank you, friend . . . You're a real mate, you are!'

She burst out laughing, and looked him up and down in the red light of the furnace which lit them. She enjoyed the fun of being taken for a boy, because of her slim figure and her long hair rolled into a bun and hidden under her cap. He laughed too, feeling safe at last; and they stood face to face for a moment laughing together, their cheeks glowing red in the firelight.

Maheu was squatting beside his locker in the changing shed, pulling off his clogs and his woollen stockings. When Étienne arrived, they settled their business in a couple of sentences: thirty sous a day, a tiring job, but he'd soon learn. The hewer advised him to keep on the shoes he was wearing, and he lent him an old skullcap, a leather headpiece designed to protect the cranium, a precaution spurned by the father and children themselves. They got their tools out of their toolbox, and there was Fleurance's shovel ready waiting for him. Then, when Maheu had shut their clogs and stockings inside, as well as Étienne's bundle, he suddenly got impatient.

'What's that damned oaf Chaval doing? Screwing another bit of skirt at the roadside! . . . We're half an hour late today.'

Zacharie and Levaque were quietly toasting their shoulders. After a while the former said:

'If it's Chaval you're waiting for . . . He got here before us, and he went straight down.'

'What? You knew that and you didn't tell me! . . . Come on! Come on! Hurry up!'

Catherine, who was warming her hands, went off after the group. Étienne let her past, then went up behind her. Again he found himself lost in a maze of dark stairways and corridors, where their bare feet made a soft slapping noise like old slippers. But then they came to the bright patch of the lamp depot, a glass-panelled room filled to the ceiling with racks,

where row after row of Davy lamps* were lined up, after
having been inspected and cleaned the previous night. They
sparkled like candles arrayed in a memorial chapel. As he
reached the counter, each workman took his own lamp, with
his number stamped on it; then he examined it, and sealed it
himself; while the clerk at the table recorded the time of
descent in his register.

Maheu had to ask for a lamp for his new trammer. And then
there was another check, when the workmen filed past an
inspector, who made sure that all the lamps were properly
sealed.

'Damn it! It's not very warm in here,' muttered Catherine,
shivering.

Étienne merely nodded his head. He found himself facing
the pit shaft, in the middle of the great entrance hall, swept by
draughts. He liked to think he was tough, and yet he felt an
unpleasant sensation grip him by the throat, amid all these
rumbling tubs, the dull thudding of the signal rapper, the
stifled bellowing of the loud hailers, and the unceasing flight
of the cables nearby, as they were wound and unwound at full
speed by the drums driven by the engine. The cages slid up to
the surface and then fell smoothly back down again like some
nocturnal beast, swallowing more and more men, drinking
them down the dark abyss of its throat. Now it was his turn,
and he felt very cold, he became tense and silent, and this
made Zacharie and Levaque laugh at him; for both of them
disapproved of the employment of this stranger, especially
Levaque, who had not been consulted. So Catherine was
pleased to hear her father explain things to the newcomer.

'Look, on top of the cage, there's a "parachute", an iron
anchor, with spikes that dig into the guides, if the cable
breaks. It's effective enough, unless it breaks down ... Yes,
that's right, the shaft is divided into three compartments,
separated by boards all the way down: in the middle there's
the cages, on the left there's the well for the ladders ...'

But he broke off to complain, although he kept his voice
cautiously low:

'What the hell are we hanging about here for, for Christ's
sake! It shouldn't be allowed, making us freeze like this!'

The deputy, Richomme, who was also waiting to go down, with his open lamp fixed on a stud set in his leather skullcap, heard him complaining.

'Take care, walls have ears!' he murmured paternally, with the reflexes of an ex-miner who still cared for his workmates. 'They've got to carry out the proper procedure . . . There! here we go, get your crew inside.'

And indeed the cage, which was strengthened with steel bands and covered in a fine wire mesh, was waiting for them, locked into its keeps. Maheu, Zacharie, Levaque, and Catherine slipped into a tub at the back; and, as they had to get five people into it, Étienne got inside too; but as the best places were taken, he had to huddle up close to the girl, and her elbow dug into his stomach. He did not know what to do with his lamp. Someone advised him to fix it to one of the button-holes of his jacket, but he didn't hear, and held it awkwardly in his hand. Above and below him people continued to fill up the tub, piling in wholesale like cattle. Why couldn't they start, what was happening? He seemed to have been waiting impatiently for several long minutes. At last he felt shaken by a sudden tremor, and everything keeled over, everything that had been at hand flew away; at the same time he felt pangs of anxiety and waves of vertigo tugging at his bowels, as if he were falling. This lasted as long as he could see daylight, while he was going down past the two floors of the landing-stage, plunging down through the middle of the soaring framework. Then, as they fell into the black depths of the shaft, he felt dazed, and was unable to perceive his sensations clearly.

'We're off,' Maheu said calmly.

Everyone was relaxed. From time to time Étienne wondered whether he was rising or falling. There seemed to be pauses, when the lift shot straight down without touching the guides; and then sudden tremors, when he felt himself swinging between the timbers, and he feared disaster was nigh. What was more, he was unable to make out the walls of the shaft even with his face pressed up against the wire. The lamps failed to shed much light on the huddle of bodies at his feet. Only the deputy's open lamp in the tub next to his shone like a beacon.

'This shaft is four metres in diameter,' continued Maheu, finishing his pupil's education. 'The wooden lining really needs replacing, because there's water seeping through all the way round ... Look! we've reached the water-table, can you hear it?'

In fact Étienne had just been wondering what this sound of rainfall could be. At first a few large drops had rung out on the roof of the cage, like the start of a downpour; and now the rain increased, streaming down as it turned into a veritable deluge. The roof of the cage must have been leaking, for a trickle of water ran down his shoulder and soaked through to his skin. The cold became icy as they plunged into the damp darkness; then they rushed through a sudden bright patch, glimpsing a momentary vision of men bustling around in a cave, lit by a flash of light. But they had already gone past and were falling into the void again.

Maheu said:

'That's the first level. We're three hundred and twenty metres down ... Look how fast we're going.'

He raised his lamp and shone it on one of the beams holding the guides, which shot past like a rail beneath a train going at full speed; and, beyond it, there was still nothing to be seen. Three other levels passed, each one a brief blur of light. The deafening rain battered away at the darkness.

'Isn't it deep!' murmured Étienne.

They must have been falling for hours. He suffered from the awkward position he had adopted, not daring to move, tortured most of all by Catherine's elbow. She didn't say a word, but he felt her against him, keeping him warm. When the cage at last touched bottom, at 554 metres, he was amazed to learn that the descent had only lasted a minute. But the sound of the keeps locking on to the cage, and the sensation of solid ground beneath his feet, suddenly cheered him up, and he turned to Catherine, teasing her humorously.

'How does a small chap like you manage to work up such a body heat, mate? ... You know your elbow's burning a hole in my guts, I suppose?'

She laughed in her turn. What a fool to keep thinking she was a boy! Had he got bandages over his eyes?

'Sounds more like you've got my elbow stuck in your eye,' she replied, to the accompaniment of gales of laughter on all sides, which the startled young man was unable to interpret.

The cage emptied, and the workmen crossed the loading bay, a room carved out of the rock face, its roof arched with brickwork, lit by three open lamps. The onsetters,* who loaded the full tubs, were pushing them roughly across the cast-iron floor. A cavernous smell of cold saltpetre seeped out of the walls, mingling with gusts of fetid air from the neighbouring stables. The entrances to four haulage roads gaped open in front of them.

'This way,' said Maheu to Étienne. 'You're not there yet. We've got a good two kilometres to go.'

The workmen split up into small groups and dispersed down into these black holes. One lot of about fifteen of them had just entered the left-hand opening; and Étienne brought up the rear, behind Maheu, who followed Catherine, Zacharie, and Levaque. It was a fine haulage road, cutting across the line of the solid rock, so that it only needed a little masonry support in places. They went forward in single file, and they kept walking onward without exchanging a word, each accompanied by the little flame of a lamp. The young man stumbled at every step, catching his feet in the rails. For a few moments now he had been disturbed by a low rumbling noise, sounding like a storm far away, which seemed to grow ever fiercer as it thundered towards them from out of the very bowels of the earth. Was it the thunder of a rock fall, about to fling down on their heads the solid mass of earth that separated them from the sky? A flash of light stabbed through the darkness, he felt the rock tremble; and as he flattened himself against the side of the tunnel like his workmates, he saw a big white horse pass by, harnessed to a train of tubs. Sitting on the first tub, and holding the reins, was Bébert; while Jeanlin ran barefoot behind the last one, holding on to the rim with both hands.

They started walking again. Further on they came to a crossing, where two new roads opened up, and the group split up again, and thus the workmen gradually spread out to man all the workings in the mine. Now the haulage road was lined with timber; there were oak stays supporting the roof, and a

timber framework lining the crumbling rock. Behind the woodwork they could glimpse the flakes of shale, sparkling with
mica, and the heavy mass of the sandstone, dull and rough.

Trains of full or empty tubs continually passed in both
directions, arriving with a thunderous roar and then swept
along into the darkness by shadowy beasts with their ghostly
tread. On the parallel tracks of the sidings the long black
serpent of a stationary train lay sleeping; as its horse snorted in
the pitch darkness, the vague forms of its hindquarters seemed
like a mass of rock that had broken away from the roof. The
trapdoors used for ventilation swung open, then slowly closed
again. And the further along the road they proceeded, the
narrower and lower it became, with its uneven roof forcing
them to keep bending their backs.

Étienne received a sharp crack on the head. Without his
leather skullcap, he would have split his skull open. Yet he had
been aping every movement that Maheu made, following the
dark silhouette sketched in front of him by the lamplight.
None of the other workmen bumped their heads; they must
have known by heart every pothole, every knot in the wood,
every outcrop of rock. The young man was also hindered by
the slippery terrain, which became more and more sodden. At
times he found himself walking through deep puddles, which
he realized only when his feet sank into a choppy sea of mud.
But what surprised him most were the sudden changes in
temperature. Down at the pit bottom it was very cold, and in
the haulage road, where all the air ventilating the mine was
channelled, there was an icy wind, which started blowing at
gale force as the tunnel walls got narrower and narrower.
Afterwards, as they plunged deeper into the byways, which
received only a meagre ration of ventilation, the wind dropped,
and the heat rose, a suffocating, leaden heat.

Maheu hadn't opened his mouth again. He turned down a
new tunnel which loomed up on the right, saying simply to
Étienne without turning round:

'The Guillaume seam.'

This was the seam where their coal-face was situated. No
sooner had he taken a few steps than Étienne bruised his head
and his elbows. The sloping roof was so low that for whole

stretches of twenty or thirty metres he had to walk bent double. The water came up to his ankles. They progressed in this fashion for 200 metres; then, all at once, he saw Levaque, Zacharie, and Catherine disappear, as if they had been swallowed up in a narrow crevice which had suddenly opened up in front of his eyes.

'We've got to climb up,' said Maheu. 'Hook your lamp on to one of your buttonholes, and hold on to the wooden beams.'

Then he too disappeared. Étienne had to follow him. This chimney, cut into the seam, was used by the miners for access to all the side passages. It was exactly the width of the coal-seam, hardly sixty centimetres across. Luckily the young man was slim, for he was still clumsy from inexperience and wasted a lot of muscular effort in hauling himself upwards, flattening his shoulders and hips, using his wrists to force himself forward, clutching frantically at the timber supports. Fifteen metres higher up they came across the first side passage, but they had to continue, for the face where Maheu and company were cutting was on the sixth passage, in what they called 'hell', and after every fifteen metres of climbing they came across another passage; there seemed no end to their ascent, struggling up this crack which tore the skin off his back and his chest. Étienne groaned as if the weight of the rocks had crushed his limbs, his wrists felt dislocated and his legs battered, and above all he was gasping for air till he felt the blood bursting out of his veins. Down one passage he thought he saw two animals on all fours, a small one and a large one, pushing tubs: it was Lydie and La Mouquette, hard at work already. And he still had to climb past another two coal-faces! He was blinded with sweat, and was afraid he would never catch up with the others, as he heard their limbs brush smoothly and confidently past the surface of the rocks.

'Cheer up, we're there!' said Catherine's voice.

But just as he did get there, another voice called out from the depths of the coal-face:

'Hey, what the hell have you lot been doing? What do you take me for? I've got a two-mile walk from Montsou, and I still got here first!'

It was Chaval, a tall, thin, bony man of twenty-five, with

strong features, who was protesting at having had to wait.
When he saw Étienne, he asked, with as much contempt as curiosity:

'What have we got here?'

And when Maheu had explained things, he added through
clenched teeth:

'So now the boys are stealing the girls' bread* out of their
mouths!'

The two men exchanged glances, charged with a flash of
instinctive hatred. Étienne felt himself insulted, without yet
understanding how or why. Silence fell as they all set to work.
Finally nearly all the seams were in production and every coal-
face busy, on every level, down each and every passage. The
gluttonous pit had swallowed its daily ration of men, with
nearly 700 workmen now sweating away in this giant ant-hill,
burrowing into the earth on all sides, riddling it with holes like
worms eating into wood. And despite the silence that hung
heavy beneath the pressure of the countless layers of rock, if
one had put an ear to the seam, one might have heard the
vibrations of these human insects on the march, from the
whirring of the cable as it raised and lowered the production
cage, to the chomping of the tools as they chipped away at the
coal, down in the depths of these sites of destruction.

As Étienne turned round he found himself pressing up
against Catherine again. But this time he felt the soft swelling
of her young breasts, and immediately recognized the source of
the warmth that he had felt suffuse him.

'So you're a girl, then?' he murmured in astonishment.

She replied in her usual cheerful way, quite unembarrassed:

'Right at last! . . . Took you long enough, didn't it!'

CHAPTER IV

THE four hewers had just spread themselves out, each lying at
a different height, so as to cover the whole expanse of the coal-
face. They were separated by boards, hung on hooks, which
caught the coal as they hewed it away; they each worked over

about four metres of the seam at a time; and the seam was so thin, hardly more than half a metre thick at that point, that they were more or less flattened between the roof and the wall, dragging themselves around on their knees and elbows, unable to turn round without bruising their shoulders. In order to get at the coal, they had to stay stretched out on one side, with their necks twisted, so that they could swing their arms far enough back to wield their short-handled picks at an angle.

First of all there was Zacharie, at the bottom; Levaque and Chaval were on the next two shelves up; and then right at the top came Maheu. Each one hewed away at the shale bedrock, hollowing it out with his pick; then he made two vertical cuts in the seam, and levered the block out by forcing an iron wedge into the top. The coal was soft, so the blocks broke up into little pieces which rolled down their stomachs and thighs. As these pieces were caught by the boards and piled up beneath the hewers, the latter gradually disappeared from view, and became walled into their narrow crevices.

It was Maheu who suffered most from this. At the top the temperature reached thirty-five degrees, and there was no air, so in time you could die of suffocation. In order to see what he was doing, he had had to fix his lamp on to a nail over his head, which in the end made his blood run hot. But his torment was aggravated by the wetness. The rock above him was only a few centimetres away from his face and large drops of water streamed from it rapidly and relentlessly, falling with an apparently obstinate rhythm, always hitting the same spot. However much he twisted and turned his neck backwards and sideways, the drops kept splashing his face, spattering and slapping him remorselessly. After a quarter of an hour, he was soaked, covered in his own sweat as well, giving off a stream of dirty, warm vapour. That morning a persistent dripping in one of his eyes made him swear. He didn't want to stop cutting, and hacked away so furiously that he shook with the vibrations, wedged between his two levels of rock, like a greenfly caught between the pages of a book which threatened to slam suddenly shut.

Not a word was exchanged. They were all hacking away, their irregular blows setting up a dull, distant-sounding, but

pervasive barrage of noise. The sound had a harsh timbre in
the thick air, which stifled any echo at birth. And the darkness
seemed to be coloured an unnatural black, with swirling waves
of coal-dust, and vapours which hung heavy on the eyelids.
The wicks of the lamps, beneath their gauze chimneys, failed
to penetrate the gloom with their small red glow. Hardly
anything could be seen at the coal-face, whose wide mouth led
diagonally upwards like a wide but shallow chimney, where the
soot had been gathering for a decade of winters to form an
impenetrable blackness. Ghostly figures could be seen gesticulating, as a stray gleam revealed at random an arched hip, a
muscular arm, or a grim face, camouflaged as if for some
crime. Sometimes, as a block of coal was dislodged, its surface
or corners would suddenly sparkle like crystal. Then everything
would be plunged into darkness again, the picks battering
away with their heavy, dull blows, and nothing was audible
but chesty breathing, and tired or painful grunts and groans,
muffled by the heavy air and the sound of running water.

Zacharie, whose arms felt limp after a hard night of fun,
soon gave up his work, on the pretext of needing to timber the
passage, which allowed him to relax enough to start whistling
quietly and let his eyes roam dreamily among the shadows.
Behind them, the hewers had left nearly three metres of the
seam hollowed out, without yet taking the trouble to shore up
the rock. They were in too much of a hurry to bother about
the danger.

'Hey, you there, your lordship!' the young man shouted at
Étienne. 'Pass me some wood.'

Étienne had to leave off learning from Catherine how to use
his shovel, and take the wood up to the coal-face. There were a
few pieces left over from the day before. Every day they were
supposed to bring down a fresh supply, cut to fit the size of
the seam.

'Move it, you bloody slowcoach!' added Zacharie, as he
watched the new trammer clambering awkwardly up into the
coal, his arms entangled with four lengths of oak.

With his pick he cut out one set of notches in the roof and
another set along the wall, and he jammed the ends of the
pieces of wood into these notches so that they propped up the

rock. In the afternoon the stonemen cleared away the rubble left at the end of the gallery by the hewers, and filled in the used trenches, props and all, leaving only the upper and lower tunnels free, in order to roll the tubs along.

Maheu stopped groaning. He had finally cut his block out. He wiped his streaming face on his sleeve, and started wondering what Zacharie had come up behind him to do.

'Leave that be,' he said. 'We'll worry about that after lunch ... We need to stick at the cutting if we want to have our tally of tubs.'

'Yes, but it's coming down,' his son replied. 'Look, there's a fault. I'm afraid it's going to cave in.'

But his father shrugged his shoulders. All right, so it might cave in! It wouldn't be the first time, after all, and they'd get away with it all the same. He grew impatient, and sent his son back to hewing at the coal-face.

But the others were getting restless, too. Levaque lay on his back, swearing away, studying his left thumb, whose skin had been cut by a falling rock. Chaval was angrily ripping off his shirt, to bare his chest and feel cooler. They were all blackened with coal already, swathed in a fine dust dissolved in sweat, running in rivulets and collecting in pools. And Maheu was the first to take up his pick again, striking lower down, with his head touching the floor of the rock. Now the drops of water rained on his forehead so persistently that he felt as if they were boring a hole in his skull.

'Don't take any notice,' Catherine explained to Étienne. 'They're always moaning about something.'

And she dutifully resumed her instruction from where she had left off.

Each loaded tub sent up from the coal-face arrived at the surface in exactly the same state as when it left, marked with a special token for the clerk to record it as part of the tally of the team that sent it. So they had to take great care to fill it right up, and to put in only clean coal: otherwise it would be rejected by the recording clerk.

Étienne, whose eyes were getting used to the darkness, looked at Catherine, whose young skin was still white, but anaemic, and he could hardly guess her age; he would have put it at twelve, she looked so frail. Yet he could sense that she was older, from her open, boyish manner and her naïve lack of shame, which he found rather embarrassing: he wasn't attracted to her; with her pale face under her tight cap she looked like a childish Pierrot. Yet he was amazed by the strength and speed of the child, which was based more on skill than on muscle. She filled her tub quicker than he could, with short, quick, regular thrusts of her shovel; then she pushed it up to the incline, with one long, slow, smooth movement, slipping effortlessly under the overhanging rocks. Whereas he kept banging and scraping himself, crashing his tub, and grinding to a halt.

To tell the truth, it certainly wasn't an easy trip. The distance from the coal-face to the incline was fifty or sixty metres; and the passage, which the stonemen had not yet widened, was hardly more than a gully, whose very uneven roof bulged and buckled all over the place: in some places, there was only just enough room to get the loaded tub through; the trammers had to crouch and push on hands and knees to avoid splitting their heads open. Besides, the props had already started to bend and split. You could see long, pale cracks running right up the middle of them, making them look like broken crutches. You had to watch out not to rip your skin on these splinters; and under the relentless pressure, which was slowly crushing these oak posts even though they were as thick as a man's thigh, you had to slip along on your belly, with the secret fear of suddenly hearing your back snap in two.

'Not again!' said Catherine, laughing.

Étienne's tub had derailed once more, at the most difficult part of the passage. He couldn't manage to push it straight along the rails, since they constantly failed to run true, in their passage over the muddy ground; and he lost his temper and swore, wrestling furiously with the wheels, but despite his titanic efforts he was unable to get them back on the track.

'Hold on,' she said, 'if you get mad you'll never manage.'

Already she had deftly slipped her backside underneath the tub; and taking its weight on the small of her back, she raised it off the ground and swivelled it back into place. It weighed 700 kilograms. He was surprised and ashamed, and stammered his apologies.

She had to show him how to walk with his legs apart, bracing his feet against the timbers on either side of the tunnel in order to get some solid leverage. His body should be bent forward, and his arms stretched out straight in front of him so as to use all his muscles, including those of his shoulders and hips. He spent one whole trip following her, watching her run, with her behind up in the air and her hands placed so low down that she seemed to be trotting on all fours, like some small circus animal. She sweated and panted, and her joints were creaking, but she didn't complain, displaying the dull acceptance acquired by habit, as if it were mankind's common lot to live in this wretched, prostrate condition. But he was unable to follow her example, for his shoes hurt, and his body ached, from walking in that position with his head bent down. After a few minutes the position became sheer torture, an intolerable anguish so painful that he had to stop and kneel down for a moment so as to straighten his back and breathe freely.

Then when he got to the ramp there was a new trial. She showed him how to load his tub quickly. There was a pit boy at the top and another at the bottom of this incline, which served all the coal-faces between two levels, a brake operator above and a collector below. These were urchins aged from twelve to fifteen who communicated in a series of vile oaths; thus in order to catch their attention you had to shout even louder. So, as soon as there was an empty tub to take up, the collector gave the signal, the tram girl loaded her full tub, and its weight sent the empty one upwards, when the operator released his brake. Down at the bottom, in the lower passage, the tubs were made up into trains for the horses to draw off to the shaft.

'Hey there, you bastards!' Catherine shouted at the incline, and her voice echoed along the whole hundred-metre length of the timber-lined structure, which acted like a gigantic loud hailer.

The pit boys must have been resting, since neither of them replied. The tubs stopped rolling on every level. Finally they heard a shrill, girlish voice call out:

'One of them's at work on La Mouquette, you might have guessed!'

There was an outbreak of laughter on all sides, and all the tram girls working on the seam split their sides.

'Who said that?' Étienne asked Catherine.

She told him that it was young Lydie, a saucy kid who knew a thing or two and could push a tub as fast as a grown woman despite her arms, which looked as if they belonged to a doll. And as for La Mouquette, she was as likely to be busy with both the pit boys at once as with just one of them.

But the collector's voice floated up, calling on them to load their tub. Doubtless there was a deputy in the offing down below. On each of the nine levels the trucks started moving again, and nothing could be heard but the regular calls of the pit boys and the coughing and spluttering of the girls as they brought their tubs up to the incline, sweating like overladen mares; and the atmosphere that reigned in the pit was bestial enough, with sudden violent outbursts of animal desire when a miner came across one of these girls bending over with her bottom up in the air and her round hips straining at the seams of her little boy's breeches.

And on every trip Étienne found himself faced once again with the suffocating heat of the coal-face, the irregular rhythm of the muffled pick strokes, the loud, painful groans of the hewers, straining at their task. All four had stripped to the waist, and had grown indistinguishable from the coal as they became covered all over in black mud right up to their caps. Once they had to pull Maheu out when he started groaning in agony, trapped under a pile of coal, which they had to spill out over the tracks by dislodging his boards for him. Zacharie and Levaque raged at the seam, which they said was getting too hard and would ruin the return on their contract. Chaval turned round, and rested on his back for a moment, insulting Étienne, whose presence it was obvious he couldn't abide.

'What a worm! Weaker than a girl! . . . Too tired to fill our tub, are we? Mustn't wear out our poor little arms, must we . . . God almighty! I'll fine you ten sous for every sou you make us lose!'

The young man refrained from answering, since he was still satisfied with having found this forced labour, and accepted the crude hierarchy subordinating the unskilled labourer to the trained team-leader. But he had simply stopped moving, his feet bleeding, his limbs racked with agonizing cramp, his chest and back clamped in an iron vice of pain. Fortunately it was ten o'clock, and the team decided to have lunch.

Maheu had a watch with him but he didn't even look at it. In the depths of this starless night, he was never more than five minutes out. They all put their shirts and jackets back on. Then they climbed down from the coal-face and squatted down on their heels, with their elbows against their thighs, a posture which miners get so used to that they adopt it even when they are not down the mine, feeling no need for a rock or a beam to sit on. And each man took out his slab and got down to the serious business of biting into the thick slices of bread, exchanging only the odd word about the morning's work. Catherine had remained standing, but after a moment or two she went to join Étienne, who had found a more or less dry place to lie down on, some distance away, where he could lean up against a pit-prop and stretch his legs out over the track.

'Aren't you hungry?' she asked, with her mouth full, holding her sandwich in her hand.

Then she remembered that the young man had been wandering around all night with no money, and perhaps even with nothing to eat.

'Do you want to share mine?'

And when he refused, swearing that he wasn't hungry, although his voice was trembling from the cramp in his stomach, she chattered on brightly:

'Oh, is it because I've had it in my mouth? ... Look, I've only chewed on this side, so you can have the other half.'

And she had already broken her slab into two pieces. Étienne took his half, and had to restrain himself to avoid wolfing it down in a single mouthful; and he rested his arms against his thighs so that she wouldn't see them shivering. With her calm, friendly air she came and lay down alongside him on her stomach, with her chin propped up in one hand, using the other to eat with, slowly. They were lit by each other's lamps.

Catherine watched him silently for a moment. She must have found him handsome, with his fine features and his dark moustache. She smiled with an ill-defined pleasure.

'So you're a mechanic, and you got sent off the railway . . . Why?'

'Because I hit my boss.'

She was dumbfounded, shocked to the depths of her hereditary notions of submission and passive obedience.

'I have to admit that I'd had too much to drink,' he went on, 'and when I drink, I lose control, I could kill myself or kill someone else . . . Yes, I can't drink more than a glass or two without feeling the need to kill someone . . . Then it makes me sick as a dog for a day or two.'

'You shouldn't drink,' she said solemnly.

'Oh, don't worry, I know my limits.'

And he shook his head. He had a hatred of spirits, the sort of hatred inspired in the last child of a long line of alcoholics,* who suffered in his very flesh from all this heredity soaked and warped by alcohol, to such an extent that the slightest drop had become poison to him.

'It's because of my mum that I'm sad I was thrown out,' he said, after swallowing a mouthful. 'Mum is unhappy, and I send her a hundred sous from time to time.'

'Where does your mother live, then?'

'In Paris . . . she's a laundress, in the rue de la Goutte d'Or.'*

He fell silent. When he thought of those things, his black eyes swam and went pale, for he was stricken with sudden anxiety at the thought of the hereditary flaw which festered unpredictably somewhere in the depths of his youthful vigour. For a moment he lay motionless with his eyes lost dreamily in the darkness of the mine; and, deep underground, feeling oppressed and suffocated by the earth itself, he conjured up his childhood, his mother still resourceful and good-looking when she was abandoned by his father, then taken back again by him after she had married someone else, living between these two men who devoured her, rolling with them into the gutter, swimming in cheap wine and wallowing in filth. He was transported back to Paris; he remembered the street, and other details came to mind: the dirty linen in the middle of the laundry, the smell of drunkenness stinking out the house, and the jaw-breaking blows.

He started talking again, slowly: 'Now my thirty sous I'll get here won't leave anything over to send her presents with . . . She's going to die of hunger, for sure.'

He shrugged his shoulders in misery, and took another bite of his sandwich.

'Do you want a drink?' asked Catherine, taking the cap off her bottle. 'Oh, it's only coffee, it won't do you any harm . . . It makes you choke swallowing all that dry bread.'

But he refused: it was bad enough to have taken half her bread. Yet she offered the coffee again with a sincere expression, and finally said:

'Oh well, if you're going to be such a gentleman, I agree to go first, but don't you be rude and turn it down now.'

And she held out the flask. She had got up on to her knees, and he saw her close up, lit by their two lamps. Why had he thought her ugly? Now that she was black, with a fine film of coal-dust all over her face, he found a strange charm in her. Her face was eaten by the shadows, and her mouth was too wide, but it showed off her sparkling white teeth; her eyes were wide open, flickering with a greenish light, like the eyes of a cat. A lock of red hair which had escaped from her cap was tickling her ear, and made her laugh. She didn't look as young as he had thought, she might even be about fourteen.

'Just for you,' he said, taking a drink and giving the flask back to her.

She took another swig, then forced him to take another, too, to share and share alike, she said; and they started to laugh as they kept passing the narrow neck of the flask back and forth between their two mouths. He suddenly wondered whether he wasn't going to grab her in his arms and kiss her on the lips. She had thick, pale pink lips, glittering with coal-dust, and he felt a painful surge of desire tug him towards them. But he didn't dare, feeling intimidated, because he'd only ever gone with the lowest kind of whores in Lille, and he didn't know how to go about it with a respectable working girl who was still living at home.

'So you'd be about fourteen, then?' he asked, after another bite of his bread.

She was surprised, annoyed even.

'What do you mean, fourteen! I'm fifteen, I'll have you know! It's true I'm not very plump, but girls don't grow up very quickly round here.'

He asked her more questions, and she answered everything openly, without a trace of embarrassment or provocation. Yet it was clear that she knew everything there was to know about men and women, although he sensed that she was physically a virgin, and not yet out of puberty, her sexual maturity stunted by the exhausting and airless environment she lived in. He got back on to the subject of La Mouquette, hoping to embarrass her, but she told him the most awful stories, with a calm, cheerful voice: 'Oh, she's done a thing or two!' And since he wanted to know whether she'd ever been in love herself, she replied jokingly that she didn't want to upset her mother, but it was bound to happen one day. She hunched her shoulders, shivering a little in her sweat-soaked clothes, and her expression was gently submissive, as if she were getting ready to submit to the ways of the world and its menfolk.

'Because it's easy enough to find a sweetheart, when you're all living together, isn't it?'

'Of course.'

'And then, it doesn't do anyone any harm . . . No need to tell the vicar.'

'Oh, I don't care a stuff about the vicar! . . . But there's the Black Man.'

'What Black Man?'

'The old miner's ghost that haunts the pit and strangles naughty girls.'

He looked at her, for he was afraid that she was making fun of him.

'You don't believe that nonsense, do you? Hasn't anyone taught you anything sensible?'

'Yes they have, I can read and write, I can . . . It's useful at home, because in Mum and Dad's time they never learnt.'

She was really very nice. As soon as she'd finished her sandwich he'd take her in his arms and kiss her thick, pink lips. His shy, young man's voice shook with the decision that he had imposed on himself, his thoughts pressing violently upon him. The boyish jacket and breeches that clung to the girlish body both excited and inhibited him. He had finished his last mouthful. He took a drink from the flask, and handed it to her to let her drain the last drops. Now the moment for action had arrived, and he glanced worriedly towards the miners at the other end of the tunnel, when a shadow fell over the passageway.

Chaval had been standing watching them for a moment. He came closer, made sure that Maheu couldn't see them; and, while Catherine was still sitting down on the ground, he grabbed her by the shoulders, pulled her head back and crushed her mouth with a brutal kiss, quite coldly, pretending not to notice Étienne. There was, in the kiss, a sort of claim to ownership, a kind of jealous bid for power.

However, the girl rebelled.

'Will you let go!'

He kept hold of her head, and looked deep into her eyes. His red moustache and pointed beard made his black face look as if it was on fire behind his large, aquiline nose. And then, at last, he let go, and went off, without saying a word.

Étienne felt a cold shudder go through him. What a fool to have waited. Obviously, he wasn't going to kiss her now, because she might think he was just copying the other man. In his wounded vanity he felt genuine despair.

'Why did you lie to me?' he asked, quietly. 'He's your sweetheart.'

'No he isn't, I swear he isn't!' she shouted. 'There's nothing like that between us. He just likes to fool around a bit sometimes ... He's not even local, you know, he only came here from the Pas-de-Calais six months ago.'

They had both stood up, it was time to go back to work. When she saw how cold he had turned, she seemed upset. She thought he was really rather better looking than the other man, and maybe she might have preferred him, if she'd had a chance. The thought of making it up to him with a friendly word or deed nagged away at her; and when Étienne saw in astonishment that the flame of his lamp had turned blue* and acquired a large, pale halo, she thought she might at least try to distract him.

'Come and look at something,' she murmured, in a good-natured, friendly tone.

When she had led him to the end of the coal-face, she pointed at a fissure in the seam. He heard a slight bubbling, and a faint noise, like a little bird singing.

'Hold out your hand, and you'll feel the breeze ... It's firedamp.'*

He was surprised. Was that all it was, that awful thing that blew things sky high? She laughed, and said that there was a lot of it about that morning, to turn the flames of the lamps so blue.

'When you've quite finished chattering, you idle buggers!' shouted Maheu, roughly.

Catherine and Étienne hurried to fill their tubs and push them up to the ramp, with stiff backs, crawling along the passage under the bumpy roof. By their second trip they were drenched in sweat and their bones were creaking again.

At the coal-face the hewers had started work once more. Often they cut short their lunch break to avoid catching cold; and their slabs, which they had wolfed down silently in the damp, dark air, lay like lead on their stomachs. Stretched out on their sides, they hacked away harder than ever, obsessed with the idea of filling as many tubs as possible. Everything else was swallowed up by this furious urge to hack out their hard-earned profit. They didn't even feel the dripping water which soaked into their limbs, making them swell, they were oblivious to the cramp brought on by their awkward postures, and they took no notice of the stifling darkness where they turned pale, like plants growing in a cellar. And yet, as the day drew on, the air got gradually fouler and warmer from the fumes of the lamps, their fetid breath, and the suffocating firedamp; the fug drifted irritatingly into their eyes like cobwebs, and only a night of ventilation would clear the air. For the men themselves, lying at the bottom of their molehill with the earth pressing down on top of them, had no breath of air of their own left in their burning lungs. And still they kept hacking away.

CHAPTER V

WITHOUT looking at his watch, which he had left in his jacket, Maheu stopped, and said:

'Nearly one o'clock . . . Zacharie, have you finished?'

His son had been putting up props for a while. But he had stopped in the middle of the job and, lying flat out on his back, was staring blindly into the distance, daydreaming over the game of 'cross' he had been playing the day before. He woke up, and answered:

'Yes, that'll do, for today at least.'

And he went back to man his post at the cutting face. Levaque and Chaval, too, put their picks down. They rested a moment. They all wiped their faces on their bare arms, looking at the surface of the roof, where the blocks of shale were cracking up. They rarely spoke of anything but work.

'We're in luck again!' muttered Chaval, 'we've hit another patch of soft rock . . . They don't add that to our expenses.'

'They're bloody crooks!' complained Levaque. 'They hope we'll get buried alive.'

Zacharie started to laugh. He didn't give a damn about the work, or about anything else, but he liked to hear them knock the Company. With his calm air Maheu explained that the state of the terrain changed every twenty metres. You had to be fair, you couldn't guess in advance. Then, as the other two kept on slagging off the bosses, he started to look anxiously over his shoulder.

'Shh! That's enough.'

'You're right,' said Levaque, and he too lowered his voice. 'It's not healthy.'

He was obsessed with the idea that he was being spied on, even at that depth, as if the very coal-seam could listen, and tell the shareholders.

'All the same,' said Chaval, loudly and defiantly, 'if that swine Dansaert talks to me like he did the other day, he'll be asking for a brick in the guts from me . . . I don't stop him screwing all his lily-skinned blondes, do I?'

This time it was Zacharie who burst out laughing. The

overman's affair with Pierron's wife was a standing joke in the pit. Even Catherine leant on her spade, shaking with laughter, and passed the word on to Étienne; meanwhile Maheu got angry, prey to a fear he didn't try to disguise.

'Will you shut up, you fool? . . . Wait till we've gone if you want to get into trouble.'

While he was still talking they heard the sound of approaching footsteps coming from the tunnel overhead. Almost immediately the pit engineer, young Négrel, as the workmen called him among themselves, appeared at the top of the cutting face, accompanied by Dansaert, the overman.

'Talk of the devil!' murmured Maheu. 'They pop up all over the place.'

Paul Négrel, Monsieur Hennebeau's nephew, was a twenty-six-year-old lad, slim and handsome, with curly hair and a brown moustache. His sharp nose and bright eyes made him look like a friendly ferret. He was intelligent and suspicious, and easily became authoritarian and intolerant when dealing with the workmen. He dressed as they did, and was smeared with coal just like them; and in order to gain their respect, he showed a daredevil bravery, going into the most difficult places, and was always first on the scene after a rock fall or a firedamp explosion.

'This is it, isn't it, Dansaert?' he asked.

The overman, a fat-faced Belgian with a wide, sensual nose, replied with exaggerated politeness:

'Yes, Monsieur Négrel . . . There's the man we took on this morning.'

They both slid down to the middle of the coal-face, and asked for Étienne to be sent up. The engineer raised his lamp and looked at him, without asking him anything.

'All right this once,' he said after a while. 'I'm not keen on picking people up off the streets . . . Better not do it again.'

And he paid no attention to the explanations he was offered, the requirements of the job, the desire to replace the women on the tubs with men. He had started to study the roof, while the hewers took up their picks again. Suddenly, he shouted out:

'Hey there, Maheu, what do you take me for? . . . You're going to do yourselves in, you stupid buggers.'

'Oh, it's safe enough,' the workman replied calmly.

'What do you mean, safe? ... The rock's started to shift, and you're leaving it for two metres at a stretch before you bother to stick a prop in! Oh, you're all the same, you'd rather have your heads squashed flat than leave off hewing and get timbering like you're meant to! ... Be so kind as to timber that lot, and look smart about it. Twice as many props, do you hear!'

And, faced with the resistance of the miners, who started arguing, saying that they were the best judges of their own safety, he got mad.

'Look here! When you've had your heads bashed in, are you going to pay for the damage? Not on your life! It'll be the Company who'll have to cough up to pay your pensions or support your wives ... Listen to me, we know what you're up to: you'd cut off your arms to fill up a couple of extra tubs a day.'

Despite the anger that was gradually rising within him, Maheu replied calmly enough:

'If we were properly paid we'd put up more props.'

The engineer shrugged his shoulders, and made no reply while he was making his way down the coal-face, and only when he had reached the bottom did he conclude:

'You've got an hour left, get back to work, the lot of you; and I'm telling you now, this team's being fined three francs.'

These words were greeted by muttered grumblings. They were only restrained by the force of hierarchical authority, that military command structure which ran from the lads at the incline right up to the overman, keeping everyone subservient to the person above him. Chaval and Levaque, however, shook their fists in fury, while Maheu frowned at them to keep them under control and Zacharie shrugged his shoulders obstreperously. But Étienne was perhaps the most upset. From the moment he had reached the bottom of this hell-hole, rebellion had been slowly simmering within him. He looked at Catherine, who had lowered her head submissively. How could they possibly drive themselves to death at such hard labour, in this mortal darkness, earning a pittance too small even to afford to buy their daily bread?

But by now Négrel was moving off with Dansaert, who had

merely stood by all the time nodding his head in approval. And then they raised their voices again: they had just come to a halt again, and were examining the timbering in the tunnel which the hewers were supposed to look after over a distance of ten metres back from the cutting face.

'Didn't I tell you they were a load of layabouts!' shouted the engineer. 'And what about you, damn it, don't you check up on them?'

'Of course I do,' stammered the overman. 'But you get fed up with telling them the same thing time after time.'

Négrel shouted out violently:

'Maheu! Maheu!'

They all came down. He continued:

'Look at that. You think that'll stay up? ... It looks like a pig's breakfast. The joints come away in your hand, they're so shoddily made ... Heavens! Now I know why we spend so much on repairs. Am I right? As long as you can get away with it, you think it's none of our business! And then the whole lot falls down, and the Company has to take on an army of repair men ... Look over there, what a bloody mess.'

Chaval wanted to say something, but Négrel shut him up.

'No point, I know what you're going to say. We need to pay you more, don't we? Well, let me tell you something. You're forcing the management to take steps, aren't you? So, all right, we'll pay you separately for the timbering, and we'll take the difference off the price of a tub-load of coal. We'll soon see who wins at that game ... Meanwhile, get moving and put that timber straight right away. I'll be back tomorrow.'

And while the miners remained dumbfounded by this outburst, he moved off. Dansaert, who had been so meek in his presence, stayed behind a few moments, to say bluntly to the workmen:

'You've got me into trouble, you have ... There'll be more than a three-franc fine to pay as far as I'm concerned, mark my word!'

Then, when he too had gone, it was Maheu's turn to explode.

'God almighty! That's not fair and anyone can see it's not fair. You know I like to keep my cool, because it's the only way to get any sense out of them; but in the end they drive you mad . . . Did you hear what he said? Pay us less for a tub-load, and count the timbering separately! Just another way of paying us less! . . . Good God almighty!'

He needed someone to shout at, and he noticed Catherine and Étienne standing idly by.

'Will you get a move on and pass me the timber! Who wants your opinion? . . . You'll get my boot up your . . .'

Étienne went off to load up, with no bitterness at this outburst, for he was so enraged with the bosses that he found the miners too meek.

Moreover, Levaque and Chaval had let off steam with a volley of oaths. All of them, even Zacharie, set to work furiously at the timbering. For nearly half an hour, nothing could be heard but the creaking of the posts as they were wedged into place with sledgehammer blows. No one opened his mouth. Gasping for air, they fought so desperately to force back the rock face, that they would have shifted it out of the way with their bare backs if they could.

'Enough is enough!' said Maheu at last, drained with anger and fatigue. 'Half-past one . . . Oh! What a right old day, we won't have made fifty sous! . . . I'm off, I'm sick of it.'

Although there was still half an hour of working time left, he put his jacket back on. The others followed suit. Just to look at the coal-face made them wild with anger. As the tram girl had started pushing again they called her back, and scolded her: if God had wanted coal to move so fast, he would have given it legs. Then all six of them put their kit under their arms and set off, with two kilometres to cover to get back to the shaft by the route they had travelled that morning.

In the chimney, Catherine and Étienne hung back, while the hewers slid down. They had met up with young Lydie, who had stopped in the middle of one of the roads to let them past, and who told them that La Mouquette had disappeared, she'd had such a nosebleed that she'd gone off an hour ago to bathe her face, but nobody knew where. Then, when they left the little girl, she went back to pushing her tub, covered in mud and racked with pain, straining with all the force of her matchstick arms and legs, like a skinny little black ant

struggling with too large a burden. Étienne and Catherine slid
down on their backs, pressing their heads and shoulders backwards, to avoid scraping the skin off their foreheads; and they
slid so swiftly down the slippery rock, which had been polished
by the behinds of all the miners from all the coal-faces, that
from time to time they had to catch hold of the props to slow
themselves down so that they didn't burn holes in their bums,
as they said, with a laugh.

When they got to the bottom, they found that they were
alone. They saw some red sparks disappearing round a bend in
the tunnel in the distance. Their high spirits subsided, and
they started to walk on with their legs heavy with fatigue,
Catherine in front and Étienne following her. Their lamps
were smoking, and he could hardly see her, for she was
surrounded by a sort of sooty halo; and the idea that she was
a girl disturbed him, because he felt he was a fool not to try to
kiss her, but the memory of the other man held him back.
Clearly she had lied to him: the other man was her lover, they
made love on every slag-heap, for she already swung her hips
like a little tramp. He sulked, irrationally, as if she had been
cheating on him. And yet she was constantly turning round,
warning him about some obstacle, and seemed to be encouraging him to be friendly. They were so lost, they could have had
a bit of harmless fun together! At last they emerged into the
haulage road, and this relieved him of his agony of indecision;
but the girl shot him one last, sad glance, mourning the
happiness they would not find again.

Now the hubbub of underground life was rumbling all
around them, with deputies continually walking past, and
trains hauled back and forth by trotting horses. The darkness
twinkled everywhere with the gleam of dancing lamps. They
had to flatten themselves back against the rock to let the
shadowy men and horses go past, and even felt their breath
against their faces. Jeanlin, running barefoot behind his train,
shouted out some insult which they couldn't hear because of
the rumbling of the wheels. They kept moving forward, but
she had fallen silent now, and he didn't recognize the pathways
or the turnings which they had taken that morning, imagining
that she was plunging him deeper and deeper underground;

and what he suffered from most was the cold, a growing cold which had gripped him as they left the coal-face, and was making him shiver more and more as they approached the shaft. Between the narrow walls, a rushing wind whistled stormily past. He had given up all hope of ever arriving, when suddenly, they found themselves in the loading bay at the pit bottom.

Chaval looked askance at them, grimacing in suspicion. The others were there, sweating in the icy draught, equally silent, choking back their angry mutterings. They had arrived too early, they weren't allowed to go up for another half-hour, especially as there was a complicated operation in progress to let a horse down. The onsetters were still packing the tubs in, with a deafening rattle of clattering ironmongery, and the cages flew up out of sight into the driving rain which was showering down the black hole. Down below, a drainage sump ten metres deep, which they called the 'bog', collected this streaming liquid, and gave off a peculiar dank, murky stench. There were men milling around the shaft all the time, pulling on signal ropes, and pushing levers down, amid this spray of water which soaked their clothes. The reddish light of the three open lamps marked out great moving shadows, and gave this underground room the appearance of a bandits' cave, or some clandestine forge by a mountain stream.

Maheu made one last attempt. He went up to Pierron, who had started his shift at six o'clock.

'Look, you could easily let us go up.'

But the onsetter, a handsome lad with strong limbs and a friendly look, refused with a frightened gesture.

'Out of the question, ask the deputy . . . I'd get fined.'

They muttered furiously under their breath again. Catherine leant over and whispered into Étienne's ear:

'Come and have a look at the stable. That's where it's warmest!'

They had to slip off without being seen, because it was forbidden to go there. It was on the left, at the other end of a short tunnel. The chamber, which had been cut out of the rock, was twenty-five metres long and four metres high. It had a brick-lined roof, and it could take twenty horses. And it

really was warm in there, with the radiant heat given off by the
animals, and the fine smell of fresh, regularly changed hay. A
single lamp burnt with a peaceful glow like a nightlight. The
resting horses turned their staring, childish eyes towards them,
then got back to slowly chewing their oats. They were well-
fed, healthy beasts, the workers that everyone liked.

But as Catherine read out their names from the zinc name-
plates above their mangers, she let out a little cry, as a body
suddenly rose up in front of her. It was La Mouquette,
jumping up in a fright from a bale of straw where she had
been sleeping. On Mondays, when she was too tired from
Sunday's carousing, she gave herself a violent punch on the
nose, and left the coal-face on the pretext of going to get some
water, and she went to hide there, with the animals, in their
warm bedding.

Her father, who was very indulgent towards her, let her get
away with it, although it could have got him into trouble.

And at that very moment old Mouque himself came in. He
was a short, bald, careworn man, but still stout, which was
rare in a fifty-year-old ex-miner. Since he had been put in
charge of the horses, he had taken to chewing so much tobacco
that his gums bled and his mouth was all black. When he saw
the other couple with his daughter he got angry:

'What do you think you're doing, you silly bitches? Come
on, piss off, fancy bringing a man in here! . . . . What a filthy
trick to come and arse around on my nice clean straw.'

La Mouquette thought that was funny, and shook with
laughter, but Étienne was embarrassed, and moved off, while
Catherine smiled at him. As the three of them arrived back at
the loading bay, Bébert and Jeanlin turned up with a trainload
of tubs. During the pause while the cages were being prepared,
the girl went up to their horse and stroked him, and told her
companion all about him. He was Bataille, the oldest horse in
the mine, a white horse who had spent ten years underground.
For ten years he had lived in this hole, staying in the same
corner of the stable, doing the same job, trotting up and down
the dark haulage roads without ever going back up to see
daylight. He was very fat, with a sleek coat and a benevolent
air, and seemed to pass his time living the good life, protected

from the misfortunes of the world above. Moreover, he had grown accustomed to the dark, and extremely clever. The passage he plied had finally become so familiar that he knew how to push open the ventilation doors with his head, and he remembered to stoop down to avoid bumping his head where the roof was too low. And he must have been able to count, for when he had done the regulation number of trips, he refused to start another, and insisted on being taken back to his manger. Now, with old age, his cat's eyes would sometimes cloud over with melancholy. Perhaps he had a vague vision, in the dim light of his dreams, of the mill where he was born, near Marchiennes, a mill set on the banks of the Scarpe, surrounded by broad meadows and swept by a constant breeze. There was something bright and burning in the air, a sort of huge lamp, but the creature could not recall it exactly. And he lowered his head, trembling on his aged legs in his futile attempts to remember what the sun was like.

Meanwhile, however, operations were proceeding in the shaft, the rapper had sounded four times, the horse was being lowered. It was always a worrying moment, for it sometimes happened that the animal was so seized with terror that it was dead by the time it arrived. At the top, trussed in a net, it struggled desperately; then, as soon as it felt the earth disappearing beneath it, it remained petrified, and as it vanished out of sight, with its great eyes staring, it didn't move a muscle. Today, the horse was too large to fit between the guides, and, once they had strung him below the cage, they had had to bend his head round and tie it back against his flanks.

It took nearly three minutes to winch the horse down, for they were careful to run the engine at low speed. So, down below, people started to get worried. What was up? Were they going to leave it half-way down, hanging up there in the darkness? At last it came into sight, rigid as a statue, with its staring, terrified eyes. It was a bay, only three years old, called Trompette.*

'Watch out!' shouted old Mouque, whose job it was to collect the horse. 'Bring it over here, but don't untie it yet.'

Soon Trompette was laid out on the iron slabs, a motionless mass, lost in the nightmare of the dark and bottomless pit, and the long, deafening hall. They were starting to untie him, when Bataille, who had been unharnessed a little earlier, came up and stretched out his neck to sniff at the new companion who had fallen from earth to meet him. The workmen formed a wide circle round them, and laughed. What was it that smelled so good? But Bataille was deaf to their mockery. He was excited by the good smell of fresh air, the forgotten scent of sunshine in the meadows. And he suddenly let out a resounding whinny, whose happy music seemed muted with a sorrowful sigh. It was a welcoming shout, and a cry of pleasure at the arrival of a sudden whiff of the past, but also a sigh of pity for the latest prisoner, who would never be sent back alive.

'Oh, Bataille, you old wag!' shouted the workmen, amused by their old comrade's antics. 'He's saying hello to his new friend.'

Trompette was untied, but still didn't move. He lay on his side as if he could still feel the netting tied around him, strangled with fear. At last, with a crack of the whip, they got him to stand up. He was still numb, and his legs were shaken by violent tremors. The two animals made friends with each other, as old Mouque led them away.

'Right, are we ready now, then?' asked Maheu.

They had to prepare the cages, and anyway, there were still ten minutes left until the official time for the return trip. Gradually the coal-faces were emptying and the workmen returning from all the tunnels. There were about fifty men there, wet and shivering, with chesty coughs flying around. Pierron, despite his good-natured expression, slapped his daughter Lydie, because she had left the face before time was up. Zacharie gave La Mouquette an underhand pinch, to warm himself up a bit. But they were all getting more and more annoyed. Chaval and Levaque spread the news of the engineer's threat to lower the price of the tub-load and pay for the timbering separately; and this prospect was greeted with exclamations of protest, as the seeds of rebellion started to grow in this narrow hole, nearly 600 metres below ground. Soon they forgot to restrain their voices, and these men, filthy with coal and frozen with waiting, accused the Company of killing off half the workmen down the mine and letting the other half die of hunger. Étienne listened, trembling with rage.

'Hurry along there, hurry along!' Richomme, the deputy repeated to the onsetters.

He hurried through the procedure for the ascent, and, not wanting to have to use his authority, pretended not to hear them. But the grumbling became so loud that he was obliged to intervene. Behind him someone shouted that it couldn't go on for ever and one fine day they'd blow the roof off.

'You're a sensible chap,' he said to Maheu; 'tell them to shut up. Better safe than sorry.'

But Maheu, who had calmed down, and was starting to get worried, didn't need to intervene. Suddenly their voices tailed off. Négrel and Dansaert had returned from their tour of inspection, and emerged from one of the tunnels, sweating as much as the workmen. Their ingrained obedience made the men move aside, while the engineer made his way through the group without a word. He got into one of the tubs, and the overman got into another; they pulled five times on the signal rope, main course coming up, as they said for the bosses; and the cage flew up into the air amid a melancholy silence.

CHAPTER VI

As the cage brought Étienne back up, squashed in with four other people, he resolved to continue his hungry search along the roads. He'd as soon drop dead on the spot as go back down again into that hell-hole, where you didn't even earn enough to live on. Catherine, who had been stacked higher up, was no longer there beside him, to soothe him with her warm body. Anyway it was better not to think in such stupid terms; he ought to get away from there; for, with his superior education, he didn't feel the same resignation as the rest of the herd, so he'd only end up strangling one of the bosses.

Suddenly, he was blinded. The ascent had been so swift that he felt stunned by the broad daylight, his eyelids trembling at the brightness, to which he had already grown unaccustomed.

None the less, he was relieved when he felt the cage lock back into the keep. A labourer opened the door and the flood of miners jumped out of the tubs.

'Hey, Mouquet,' Zacharie whispered in the workman's ear, 'fancy slipping off to the Volcan* tonight?'

The Volcan was a pub in Montsou. Mouquet winked slyly, and a silent laugh spread over his face. He was short and stout like his father, with the hard-nosed air of a lad greedy for life and careless of what the morrow might bring. And, as La Mouquette got out, he dealt her a mighty slap on the behind, as a sign of brotherly affection.

Étienne hardly recognized the high vault of the entrance hall, which, in the eerie, flickering light of the lanterns, had seemed unnerving to him. Now it was merely bare and dirty. A grimy light filtered through the dusty windows. The only source of brightness was the copper body of the engine, gleaming in the distance; the greasy steel cables flew past like inky ribbons; while the pulleys up above, with their enormous supporting framework, and the cages and the tubs, formed one vast, metallic mass, overshadowing the room like a great, grey heap of scrap iron. The ceaseless rumbling of the wheels made the cast-iron flooring shudder; while a fine dust rose from the coal being moved through the room, and threw a black veil all over the floor, the walls, and even the beams of the headgear.

But Chaval, who had taken a look at the number of tokens recorded on the board in the recording clerk's little glass-fronted office, had come back in a temper. He had noticed that two of their tubs had been rejected, one because it didn't contain the regulation amount, the other because it included some dirty coal.

'The perfect end to a perfect day,' he shouted. 'Another twenty sous down the drain . . . Serves us right for taking on layabouts with arms no more use than a pig's tail!'

And he looked sideways at Étienne to underline his point. Étienne was tempted to reply with a punch on the nose. But then he thought there was no point, if he was leaving. Now his mind was really made up.

'You can't learn it all in just one day,' said Maheu to keep the peace. 'He'll do better tomorrow.'

But they all felt just as bitter, and were spoiling for a quarrel. As they went past the lamp depot to hand in their lamps, Levaque had a run-in with the storekeeper, accusing him of not cleaning his lamp. They only started to unwind when they got to the shed, where the fire was still burning. They had even stoked it up too much, for the stove was red-hot, and the great windowless room seemed ablaze, with reflections from the brazier appearing to run molten down the walls. Then they let themselves go with voluptuous grunts, toasting their backs as near the fire as they dared until they were steaming like soup. When their backs started to burn, they turned round to cook their stomachs. La Mouquette had quite shamelessly rolled down her breeches to let her shirt dry. One or two lads essayed their wit; then the laugh was on them, as she suddenly flashed her backside at them, which, in her eyes, was the ultimate insult.

'I'm off,' said Chaval, who had already put his tools back in his locker.

Nobody moved except La Mouquette, who hurried off after him, on the pretext that they were both going the same way back to Montsou. But the banter continued, because everyone knew he had had enough of her.

Meanwhile Catherine had been speaking quietly to her father in worried tones. At first he seemed surprised, but then he nodded in approval, and calling Étienne to come over and collect his bundle, he mumbled:

'Look here, if you're out of cash, you're not going to last out till the end of next week when we get paid ... Do you want me to try and find someone to allow you some credit?'

The young man remained silent with embarrassment for a moment. In fact he had been about to claim his thirty sous and go, but he felt ashamed in front of the girl. She was staring at him, and might even be thinking he was work-shy.

'You know, I can't promise it'll work,' Maheu went on, 'but the worst they can do is refuse.'

So Étienne didn't say no. They would surely refuse. And anyway, it was not a commitment, he could always move on, after he had had something to eat. A moment later he was annoyed with himself for not having said no, when he saw how happy Catherine looked, as she laughed prettily with the pleasure of having been able to help him. What was the point of getting involved?

When they had retrieved their clogs and closed their lockers, the Maheu family left the changing shed, following their workmates as they left one by one when they had warmed themselves up. Étienne went with them, and Levaque and his lad tagged along. But then, just as they were walking through the screening shed, they were brought to a halt by a violent incident.

It was a huge shed, whose beams were blackened by the flying coal-dust, and whose open shutters let through a constant draught of air. The coal-tubs came straight in from receipt at the entrance hall, and then the tipplers emptied them out on to the screens, which were long chutes made of sheet-metal. Standing on steps on either side of the chutes were the sorting girls, who were armed with shovels and rakes to pick out the stones and push back the clean coal, which continued on its way down towards the railway wagons which were waiting at the sidings.

Philomène Levaque was there. She was a pale, thin girl, whose consumptive pallor gave her a sheep-like face. Her head was protected by a flimsy scrap of blue woollen material, and her hands and arms had gone black right up to the elbows. There she stood sorting, just below an old witch, La Pierronne's mother, old Ma Brûlé, as they called her, a fearsome creature with eyes like a screech-owl and lips clenched tighter than a miser's purse. They had come to blows as the younger accused the elder of filching her stones, which meant it took her more than ten minutes to get a basketful. They were paid by the basket, which led to endless quarrels, with much tearing of hair and sooty fingermarks on red faces.

'Give her a good poke!' Zacharie shouted down to his mistress.

All the sorting girls howled with laughter. But old Ma Brûlé flew bitterly at the young man.

'You can talk, you pig! You'd do better to own up to the two brats you stuffed her with! ... What a liberty, with an eighteen-year-old kid who's weak on her pins!'

Maheu had to prevent his son from going down to sort out the old bag of bones in person, as he put it. But then the supervisor hove into view, and the rakes started rattling through the coal again. All that could be seen all along the sides of the hoppers were the rounded backs of the women fiercely fighting each other for the stones.

Outside the wind had suddenly fallen and a cold, damp air fell from the grey sky. As they left in ones and twos, the colliers hunched their shoulders and hugged their chests tightly to keep warm, swaying lopsidedly as they walked, which made the shape of their bony hips show through the thin cotton of their garments. Out in the daylight they looked like a troupe of muddy negroes. Some of them hadn't finished their sandwiches; and the spare hunks of bread lodged between their shirts and their jackets made them look like hunchbacks.

'Look! There's Bouteloup,' said Zacharie, mockingly.

Without stopping, Levaque swapped a few words with his lodger, a stout dark man of thirty-five, who wore a placid, honest expression.

'Is the soup ready, Louis?'

'I think so.'

'Is the wife in a good mood today?'

'Yes, I think she's all right.'

More miners arrived, fresh groups of stonemen, and one by one they were swallowed up by the pit. It was the three o'clock shift, another meal for the mine, as the teams went down to take over the concessions that the hewers had been working on, at the far end of the tunnels. The mine never slept; night and day these human insects burrowed into the rock, 600 metres below the beetfields.

Meanwhile the boys led the way back home. Jeanlin was explaining to Bébert his secret and complicated plan of campaign to get four sous' worth of tobacco on tick; while Lydie hung around at a respectful distance. Catherine followed, accompanied by Zacharie and Étienne. Nobody spoke. And it was only when they got to the Avantage* bar that Maheu and Levaque caught up with them.

'Here we are,' said Maheu to Étienne. 'Do you want to come in?'

Germinal

They split up. Catherine had stopped for a moment, taking a last look at Étienne with her large, grey-green, crystal-clear eyes, which sparkled brighter than ever against her black skin. She smiled at him, then disappeared with the others, walking up along the steep path towards the miners' village.

The bar was located half-way between the village and the mine, at the crossroads. It was a two-storey brick building, whitewashed all over, with a sky-blue border painted gaily round the outline of the windows. On a square sign nailed up over the doorway was the following legend in yellow lettering: 'The Avantage, Premises licensed to Monsieur Rasseneur.'* Behind the building was a skittle alley, bordered by a privet hedge. And the Company, which had done its best to buy up this plot of land, was annoyed by the survival of this bar, planted in the fields in the middle of its vast estates and strategically placed at the very gates of Le Voreux.

'Come on in,' Maheu invited Étienne again.

The room was small and bare, but its white walls made it light; it was furnished with three tables, a dozen chairs, and a pine bar as big as a kitchen dresser. There were no more than a dozen mugs, three bottles of spirits, a carafe, a small zinc beer barrel with a tin tap; and nothing else, not a picture, not a shelf, not a game. In the glossily painted cast-iron stove a lump of coal burned softly. On the flagstones a fine layer of white sand soaked up the constant damp of this rainy country.

Maheu ordered 'a pint' from a plump blonde girl, a neighbour's daughter who sometimes minded the bar, and asked, 'Is Rasseneur around?'

The girl turned the tap on, and answered that the boss would be back soon. The miner drank half of his glassful with one long slow draught, sluicing away the dust which was blocking his throat. He didn't offer his workmate anything to drink. There was only one other client, another damp, messy miner, sitting at a table, drinking his beer in silence, with a profoundly meditative air. A third entered, was served on the nod, drank up, paid, and left without a word.

But then a big, clean-shaven man of thirty-eight arrived, with a round face and a sociable smile. It was Rasseneur, a former hewer who had been sacked by the Company three years previously, after a strike. He had been a very good worker, and, because he expressed himself well, he had taken the lead in every protest, and finished up as the ringleader of the malcontents. His wife already ran a bar, as did quite a few miners' wives; so, when he was thrown out, he set up as publican himself, raising enough money to establish his bar at the very gates of Le Voreux, as a challenge to the Company. Now business was flourishing, and he had become a centre of attraction, cashing in on the discontent which he had gradually nurtured in the hearts of his former workmates.

'This is the lad I took on this morning,' Maheu explained straight away. 'Is one of your two rooms free, and can you give him credit for a fortnight?'

Rasseneur's broad face suddenly took on an intensely suspicious look. He looked Étienne over and replied without even making the effort to show any regret:

'Both of my rooms are taken. Nothing doing.'

The young man had been expecting this rejection; and yet he was upset by it, and he was surprised by the surge of disappointment he felt at the prospect of going away. Never mind, he'd go as soon as he'd got his thirty sous. The miner who had been drinking at the table had gone. Others had come in one by one to wash out their throats, then set off again with the same lopsided gait. They just rinsed their gullets, feeling no pleasure or emotion, silently satisfying a simple need.

'So, nothing's happened, then?' Rasseneur asked with a meaningful tone, as Maheu was sipping at the last of his beer.

Maheu turned round, and saw that only Étienne was left.

'Only that we had another row . . . You know, about the timbering.'

He explained what had happened. The blood rose to the publican's face, and his eyes and skin glowed with hot fury. Then he blurted out:

'Well! Right then! If they start to lower the price, they're buggered!'

He felt uneasy in the presence of Étienne, and although he continued, he kept darting sidelong glances at him all the while, and what he said was veiled in hints and allusions. He discussed the manager, Monsieur Hennebeau, and his wife and nephew, the young Négrel, without mentioning them by name, repeating that it couldn't go on like this, that things would come to a head one of these fine days. The poverty was too awful, he told of factories closing down, and workers leaving. Over the last month he had distributed more than six pounds of bread a day. The day before someone had told him that Monsieur Deneulin, the owner of a local pit, was unable to make ends meet. And besides, he had received a letter from Lille which was full of worrying details.

'You know,' he muttered, 'it's to do with the person you saw here the other night.'

But he was interrupted by the entrance of his wife, a tall, thin, passionate woman, with a long nose and ruddy cheeks. She held much more radical political opinions than her husband.

'Pluchart's letter,' she said. 'Oh, he's your man; if he was in charge, then things would improve fast enough!'

Étienne had been listening for only a moment, but it was long enough for him to feel deeply moved by the impact of this suffering and the idea of revenge.

And the sudden mention of this name made him jump. He said aloud, as if in spite of himself:

'I know Pluchart, I do.'

As they turned and looked at him he had to add:

'Yes, I'm a mechanic, and he was my foreman, in Lille . . . He's a capable man, I've often talked to him.'

Rasseneur looked him over again; and his expression rapidly changed, reflecting a new-found sympathy. After a moment he said to his wife:

'Maheu's brought us this young gentleman, he's one of his trammers, in case there's a room for him upstairs, and we could give him a fortnight's credit.'

So the deal was done in the twinkling of an eye. There was a room free, for the lodger had left that morning. And the landlord got carried away and explained himself more fully, although he kept repeating that he only wanted the bosses to be reasonable, unlike so many other people, he didn't want to demand the impossible. His wife shrugged her shoulders, she wanted to hold out for her rights, and settle for nothing less.

'Time to say good-night,' Maheu called out, interrupting them. 'None of that will stop the miners going down the pit, and as long as anyone has to go down the pit, some of them will die of it . . . Look how you've been thriving over the last three years, since you came back up.'

'Yes, I've quite got my health back,' said Rasseneur contentedly.

Étienne walked over to the door, to thank the departing miner; but Maheu merely nodded his head, and said nothing, leaving Étienne to watch him tramp slowly up the path to the mining village. Madame Rasseneur, who was serving some customers, had just asked him if he would mind waiting a moment until she was free to take him up to his room so he could clean himself up. Ought he to stay? He felt pangs of indecision again, a feeling of uneasiness and a wave of nostalgia for the freedom of the open road, where hunger was tempered with the pleasure of being his own master, living in the sunshine. He felt as if he had been living there for years already, since his arrival at the slag-heap in the middle of the storm, and the hours he had spent crawling along the black tunnel floors on his belly. And he felt sick at heart at the idea of starting again; it was too unfair, too hard, his human pride rebelled at the idea of becoming a blinded and crippled beast of burden.

While Étienne thought through his dilemma, he let his eyes roam over the vast plain until they grew accustomed to its features. He was surprised, for he hadn't imagined that the landscape looked like that, when old Bonnemort had pointed at what lay out there in the depths of the night. He recognized Le Voreux easily enough, lying right in front of him in a dip in the ground, with its mixture of wooden and brick buildings, its pitch-roofed screening shed and slate-covered headgear, its engine-room with its tall, pale red chimney, all squatting down there in the hollow, looking menacing. But around the buildings there was a wider expanse of paved yard than he had thought, transformed into a lake of ink by the rising waves of stockpiled coal, bobbing with the tall pylons carrying the overhead railway, swamped at one end by a deluge of wood, the result of felling a whole forest of trees. Over to the right,

the slag-heap blotted out the horizon, like a colossal barricade
built by giants, already overgrown with grass on its earlier
slopes, and burning at the other end with an inner fire which
had been smouldering for a year, giving off a dense cloud of
smoke and staining the ghastly grey surface of shale and
sandstone with long streaks of blood-red rust. Then the fields
unwound, endless fields of wheat and sugar-beet, still bare at
this time of the year, and then marshes covered in rough
scrubland, punctuated by a few stunted willows, then, far off,
the meadows, divided by thin lines of poplars. Way off in the
distance some tiny, white patches showed up the position of
the towns, Marchiennes to the north and Montsou to the
south; while over to the east the forest of Vandame framed the
horizon with a dim violet line of bare-branched trees. And
beneath the livid sky and fading light of this winter afternoon,
it seemed as if all the blackness of Le Voreux, all the swirling
dust, had swept down over the plain, powdering the trees,
sanding the roads, impregnating the soil.

As Étienne kept looking, what surprised him the most was
the sight of a canal, or rather the river Scarpe* turned into a
canal, which he had not seen during the night. The canal ran
in a straight line all the way from Le Voreux to Marchiennes,
unwinding its dull silver ribbon for over two leagues, an
avenue bordered with tall trees, raised higher than the low-
lying land, drawing the gaze along its green banks, and its pale
waters parted by the vermilion keels of barges, until they
disappeared into infinity. Near to the pit was a landing-stage,
where the boats lay moored, waiting to be filled directly from
the tubs coming down the overhead railway. Then there was
a bend in the canal, as it cut diagonally across the marshes;
and the whole soul of this flat plain seemed to be subsumed
into this geometrical stretch of water which cut across it like a
great road, bearing its coal and iron away.

Étienne raised his eyes from the canal to the mining village,
which was built on the plateau. He could just make out the red
tiles of the roofs. Then he looked back towards Le Voreux,
and his gaze lingered on two enormous stacks of bricks lying at
the bottom of the clay slope. They must have been made and
baked on the premises. A branch of the Company's railway

line passed behind a fence on its way into the pit. The last stonemen must be going down. There was no sound except for the sharp screech of a wagon being pushed by a group of men. The scene had lost its nocturnal mystery, which had been charged with implausible thunder and the flaring of unfamiliar stars. In the distance the blast-furnaces and coke ovens had grown pale in the light of dawn. All that was left was the incessant exhaust of the pump, breathing out continually with the same long, heavy panting, like some insatiable ogre, whose grey fumes he could now see rising through the air.

Then, suddenly, Étienne made up his mind. Perhaps he had imagined seeing Catherine's bright eyes again, up there at the entrance to the mining village. Or perhaps it was a wind of rebellion blowing from Le Voreux. He wasn't sure which it was, but he wanted to go back down into the mine to suffer and struggle, he felt furious at the thought of those people mentioned by Bonnemort, of this greedy, squatting god, who fed off the flesh of 10,000 hungry people who didn't even know him.

PART II

PART II

CHAPTER I

THE Grégoires' property, La Piolaine, was situated two kilometres to the east of Montsou, on the Joiselle road. It was a large square house of no particular style, built at the beginning of the eighteenth century. Of the vast lands which had originally depended on it, there were little more than thirty hectares left, enclosed by a wall and easy to maintain. People spoke admiringly of their orchard and their vegetable garden, which produced the finest fruit and vegetables in the neighbourhood. In fact there was no formal park, only a small wood. The avenue of ancient lime trees, which formed an arcade of greenery 300 metres long, running from the boundary of the estate to the main steps, was one of the sights to see on this bald plain, where there were very few large trees anywhere between Marchiennes and Beaugnies.

That morning, the Grégoires had risen at eight o'clock. Usually they did not stir until an hour later, sleeping on soundly, with total conviction; but that night's storm had upset them. And while her husband had gone out forthwith to see whether the wind had done any damage, Madame Grégoire had just come down to the kitchen in her slippers and her flannel dressing-gown. She was a short, stout woman, but although she was already fifty-eight, her face was still plump beneath her glossy white hair, and bore a wide-eyed, innocent, doll-like expression.

'Mélanie,' she said to the cook, 'why don't you make the brioche* this morning, since the dough is ready? Miss Cécile won't be getting up for another half-hour yet, and she could have some with her chocolate ... wouldn't that be a lovely surprise?'

The cook, a thin, old woman who had been in service there for thirty years, started to laugh.

'That's true, it would be a marvellous surprise ... I've lit the stove and the oven must be hot by now; and anyway Honorine will lend a hand.'

Honorine was a girl of about twenty, who had been taken in

by the household when she was a little child and brought up almost as one of the family, and now worked as a chambermaid. Apart from these two women there were no other servants, except for the coachman, Francis, who also acted as handyman and labourer. A gardener and his wife looked after the fruit and vegetables, the flowers, and the little farmyard. And as this was a patriarchal regime, a cosy family affair, the small community lived in harmony.

Madame Grégoire, who had dreamed up the surprise of the brioche while she was lying in bed, stayed in the kitchen to watch the dough being put in the oven. The kitchen was huge, and one could see that it was the most important room in the house from its extreme cleanliness, and from its copious arsenal of pots and pans, and utensils. There was the good smell of fine food. The cupboards and shelves were overflowing with provisions.

'And you'll make sure it's nice and golden, won't you?' added Madame Grégoire as she went off into the dining-room.

Although the whole house was centrally heated by the main boiler, there was a coal fire to cheer up this room. Not that there was any luxury: just the large table, the chairs, and a mahogany sideboard; only two deep armchairs betrayed a love of comfort, and prolonged post-prandial relaxation. They never used the drawing-room; the family stayed in the dining-room together.

Just then Monsieur Grégoire came in, dressed in a heavy fustian jacket, and, despite his sixty years, he too had a pink complexion, with kind, honest, open features, crowned by a mass of curly white hair. He had seen the coachman and the gardener: there was no major damage, only a fallen chimney-pot. Every morning he liked to take a look round La Piolaine, which was not big enough to create significant problems, but gave him all the pleasures of property ownership.

'Where's Cécile?' he asked. 'Isn't she going to get out of bed at all, today?'

'I'm as surprised as you are,' his wife replied. 'I thought I heard her stir.'

The places were laid, with their three bowls on the white table-cloth. They sent Honorine to see what Miss Cécile was up to. But she came straight back down again, suppressing her laughter, lowering her voice as if she were still talking in the bedroom upstairs.

'Oh, if Sir and Madam could only see Miss Cécile! . . . She's as fast asleep as an angel in heaven . . . You can't imagine it, it's a pleasure to see.'

Father and Mother exchanged a tender look. He smiled and said:

'Shall we go and look?'

'Poor little dear!' she murmured. 'I'm coming.'

And up they went together. Her bedroom was the only luxuriously furnished room in the house. The walls were covered in blue silk, there was white lacquered furniture with blue borders, a childish fancy that her parents had gratified. Softly framed by the white bed-linen, in the half-light which slipped between the slightly parted curtains, their daughter lay sleeping with her cheek resting on her bare arm. She was too healthy, robust, and well developed for her eighteen years to be called pretty; but she had a fine firm body with milk-white skin, chestnut hair, and a stubborn little nose rather lost amid her round cheeks. The covers had slipped down, but she breathed so lightly that her full young bosom hardly moved.

'That wretched wind must have kept the poor creature awake,' her mother said quietly.

Father made a sign to his wife to stop talking. They both bent in pious adoration over the unadorned, virginal body of the daughter they had awaited so long, who had arrived so late in their lives, after they had lost all hope. In their eyes she was perfection itself, not too plump, never well-fed enough. She slept on, unaware of their presence beside her, of their faces next to hers. But then a slight tremor ruffled her limpid features. Afraid that they might wake her, they crept away on tiptoe.

'Shh!' said Monsieur Grégoire when they reached the door. 'If she hasn't slept, we must leave her to sleep on.'

'As long as she likes, the poor darling,' added Madame Grégoire. 'We can wait.'

They went downstairs and settled into the armchairs in the dining-room; while the two maids, laughing at Miss Cécile's long lie-in, good-humouredly kept the chocolate warming on the stove. Father had picked up a newspaper; Mother had started knitting a thick woollen counterpane. The house was snug and warm, and not a sound came to disturb the silence.

The Grégoires' fortune, around 40,000 francs a year in investment income, was derived entirely from their shares in the Montsou mines. They enjoyed telling how this had come to pass, way back at the time of the birth of the Company.

Towards the start of the eighteenth century, a feverish coal-rush had broken out all the way from Lille to Valenciennes. The success of those who had bought concessions, and who would later come together to form the d'Anzin Company, had gone to people's heads. In every village, people bored into the ground; companies were founded, and concessions were traded overnight. But, among the more stubborn entrepreneurs of the time, it was the Baron Desrumaux who had earned a reputation for the most heroic foresight. For forty years he had struggled relentlessly: failing in his first searches, working for long months to dig out new trenches only to be forced to abandon them in the end, his shafts blocked by rock falls and his workmen drowned by sudden flooding, thousands of francs dug in and buried; then the harassment by bureaucrats, the panic of the shareholders, the struggle with the hereditary landowners who were determined not to recognize the concessions leased by the Crown if they were not first consulted and cut in. He finally founded a company, called Desrumaux, Fauquenois, and Co., to work the Montsou concession, and the pits were just starting to show a slim profit when two neighbouring concessions, one at Cougny, which belonged to Count Cougny, and one at Joiselle, which belonged to the Cornille and Jenard Company, had almost driven him under with their ferocious competition. Fortunately, on 25 August 1760, a pact was signed between the three concessions which merged them into one. The Montsou Mining Company was created, in the form still existing today. As part of the agreement, the whole property had been divided up into twenty-four parts of one sou each, aligned on the gold standard of the period, each of which was subdivided into twelve deniers, making 288 deniers in all; and, since a denier was equivalent to

10,000 francs, the capital was worth a sum of nearly three million francs. Desrumaux had triumphed on his death-bed, for he had received six sous and three deniers in the share-out.

In those days, the Baron was the owner of La Piolaine, which brought with it 300 hectares of land, and he took into service an estates manager named Honoré Grégoire, a young man from Picardy, the great-grandfather of Léon Grégoire, Cécile's father. When the Montsou pact was signed, Honoré, who had nearly 50,000 francs of savings hidden under his mattress, succumbed faint-heartedly to his master's unshakeable faith. He took out 10,000 pounds in shining crowns,* and bought a denier's share, terrified that he might be stealing his children's inheritance. And it is true that his son Eugène received very slim dividends; and as he had espoused the bourgeois life, but had foolishly squandered the remaining 40,000 francs of the parental inheritance in a catastrophic business venture, he lived in rather straitened circumstances. But the returns from his denier gradually accumulated. It first started to add up to a fortune for Félicien, who was able to act out the dream which his grandfather, the former estates manager, had instilled in him from the cradle: the purchase of what was left of La Piolaine, for a mere pittance, after it had been confiscated by the State under the revolutionary regime.* Yet the next few years were unpromising, with the various disasters that beset the Revolution, and then the violent overthrow of Napoleon.* So that it was only Léon Grégoire who benefited from the staggering growth in the profits generated by the cautious and half-hearted investment of his great-grandfather. His 10,000 hard-won francs had increased and multiplied with the prosperity of the Company. By 1820 they had achieved a 100 per cent return, 10,000 francs. By 1844, this had increased to 20,000; by 1850, 40,000. And finally, two years ago, the dividend had attained the staggering sum of 50,000 francs: the value of a denier share, quoted at a million francs on the Lyons stock exchange, had multiplied a hundredfold during the course of the century.

Monsieur Grégoire, who had been advised to sell when the million had been reached, had refused, with his smiling, paternal air. Six months later there was a sudden industrial

slump, and the denier fell to 600,000 francs. But he kept
smiling, and felt no remorse, for the Grégoires had always had
a stubborn faith in their mine. Their shares would rise again,
as indestructible as God himself. Mingled in with this religious
faith was a profound gratitude for a valuable investment which
had kept the family in comfort and idleness for a century. It
was like a household god, the object of a self-indulgent cult,
the patron saint of their hearth and home, cradling them in
their big, soft beds and fattening them at their sumptuous
table. From father to son it had lasted: why risk offending
destiny by showing loss of faith? And at the heart of their
worship was a superstitious terror that the million of their
denier might suddenly dissolve if they withdrew it and placed
it in a drawer. They felt it was safer to keep it buried
underground, where a whole population of miners, starving
generation after starving generation, could dig up a little for
them every day, according to their needs.

Moreover, the house was blessed with happiness. While he
was still very young, Monsieur Grégoire had married the
daughter of the pharmacist at Marchiennes, a plain and penniless young woman whom he adored, and who had amply
repaid him in domestic bliss. She had thrown herself into her
household tasks and marital devotion, imagining no wishes but
her husband's; they were never separated by contradictory
tastes, and shared an identical goal of perfect contentment; and
thus they had lived for forty years, exchanging the daily tokens
of mutual concern and affection. Their existence was smoothly
self-regulating, for their 40,000-franc income as well as their
savings were all effortlessly consumed in the interests of Cécile,
whose belated birth had momentarily upset their budget. Even
today they satisfied her every whim: a second horse, two new
carriages, the latest Parisian fashions. But this only gave them
a further source of enjoyment, since nothing could be too fine
for their daughter, while they themselves found any personal
display so distasteful that they still dressed in the styles of
their youth. For themselves, they found any unprofitable
expenditure ridiculous.

Suddenly, the door opened, and a loud voice shouted:

'I say, whatever next, you've started breakfast without me!'

It was Cécile, who had just climbed out of bed, her eyes still bleary with sleep. She had merely pinned up her hair and slipped into a white woollen dressing-gown.

'Of course not,' her mother said, 'you can see that we were waiting for you ... can't you? The wind must have kept you awake, my poor darling!'

Her daughter looked at her in astonishment.

'Was it windy? ... How should I know, I've been fast asleep all night.'

This seemed a great joke to everyone, and all three started to laugh; and the maids who were bringing in their breakfast burst out laughing too, the whole household happily amused at the realization that Miss Cécile had slept for twelve hours at a stretch. The arrival of the brioche made their pleasure visibly complete.

'Good heavens, has it just come out of the oven?' asked Cécile. 'What a trick to play on me! ... How super to have warm brioche to dip in our hot chocolate!'

Then at last they sat down to table, with the chocolate steaming in their bowls, and their conversation lingered on the topic of the brioche. Mélanie and Honorine stayed on to supply details of the cooking, watching them tuck in with sticky lips, saying what a pleasure it was to bake a cake when their master and his family looked so happy to eat it.

But then the dogs started barking noisily, as if to welcome the arrival of the piano teacher, who came from Marchiennes on Mondays and Thursdays. There was also a literature teacher. The girl's whole education had thus taken place at La Piolaine, in a state of happy ignorance, for she threw her book out of the window as soon as she found a problem too tedious.

'It's Monsieur Deneulin,' said Honorine when she returned.

Deneulin, a cousin of Monsieur Grégoire, walked in casually behind her, talking loudly and gesticulating briskly, rather like some retired cavalry officer. Although he was over fifty, his close-cropped hair and thick moustache were jet black.

'Yes, it's me, hallo ... Please don't get up!'

He sat down immediately amid the volley of familiar greetings, and then waited for them to get back to their chocolate.

'Has something happened?' asked Monsieur Grégoire.

'No, nothing at all,' replied Deneulin, perhaps a shade too quickly. 'I just set out for a ride to stretch my legs, and as I was passing by your door I thought I'd look in to pass the time of day.'

Cécile asked after his daughters Jeanne and Lucie. He replied that they were fine, the former busy with her painting and the latter, the elder, practising singing at the piano morning and night. Yet there was a slight quaver to his voice, a hidden disturbance beneath the outbursts of cheerfulness.

Monsieur Grégoire asked again:

'And is everything all right at the pit?'

'God! I'm having trouble with this rotten slump, like all my friends . . . Ah! We're paying for the years of prosperity! We built too many factories and railway lines, tied up too much capital in planning a massive increase in production. And now the money is frozen, we don't have enough liquid cash to run the whole damn thing . . . Luckily things haven't gone too far, though, I'll get out of it somehow.'

Like his cousin he had inherited a denier share in Montsou. But as an engineer and a businessman, he was driven by the urge to make a fast fortune, and he had hastened to sell·as soon as the denier had reached the million level. For some months he had been hatching a plan. His wife had received from one of her uncles the small concession of Vandame, where there were only two active pits, Jean-Bart and Gaston-Marie, and these were in such a state of neglect, and their equipment so defective, that their production hardly covered their running costs. Now his dream was to refurbish Jean-Bart, replace the old machinery and widen the shaft in order to go deeper, saving Gaston-Marie entirely for pumping and ventilation. That way, he argued, they would strike gold by the shovelful. His project was shrewd enough. The only problem was that he had sunk his million in it and the damned industrial crisis had broken out just when the big profits were lining up to prove him right. In addition to which he was not a good administrator; he was erratically generous with his workmen, and had let everyone cheat him since his wife had died. He had also given his daughters free rein, with the elder talking of taking to the stage and the younger already rejected by the Salon* for three of her landscapes, although both girls were equally merry in the face of disaster, which stimulated their housekeeperly qualities.

'You see, Léon,' he continued, with a catch in his voice, 'you were wrong not to sell up at the same time as me. Now everything's falling apart, and you can't do a thing . . . and yet if you had let me use your money, you can't imagine what we would have done to our own little mine, at Vandame!'

Monsieur Grégoire was draining his chocolate in leisurely fashion. He replied calmly:

'Not on your life! . . . You know that I refuse to speculate. I live in perfect peace, and I would be crazy to plague myself with business worries. And as for Montsou, it could go even lower, and we'd still have enough to live on. You shouldn't be so greedy, for heaven's sake! And mark my words, you're the one who's going to be biting his nails one day, when Montsou comes back up again, and Cécile's children's children will still be living in clover off the proceeds.'

Deneulin listened to him with an embarrassed smile.

'So,' he murmured, 'if I asked you to put a hundred thousand francs into my business, you would refuse?'

But, when he saw the worried expressions on the Grégoires' faces, he regretted having said so much so soon, and he put off his thought of a loan until later, keeping it as a last resort.

'Oh, it hasn't come to that yet! I was only joking . . . Heavens! You may be right: the money which other people earn for you is the money which pays you best.'

They changed the subject of the conversation. Cécile got back to her cousins, whose tastes she found shocking but fascinating. Madame Grégoire promised to take her to see the two darlings, as soon as the fine weather arrived. Yet Monsieur Grégoire seemed absent, and didn't keep up with the conversation. He added aloud:

'If I was in your shoes I wouldn't hold out any longer, I'd make a deal with Montsou . . . They're keen enough, and you would get your money back.'

He was referring to the long-standing feud between the Montsou and Vandame concessions. Despite the relative insignificance of the latter, its powerful neighbour was furious at having to endure the presence of this alien patch, which was only a square league in area, ensconced in the midst of its sixty-seven-village territory; and having vainly attempted to stifle it, Montsou plotted to buy it up on the cheap when it was on its death-bed. There was no let-up in the war; each Company drove its tunnels to within 200 metres of the other's, in a duel to the death, although the directors and the engineers maintained diplomatic relations with their counterparts.

Deneulin's eyes blazed.

'Not on your life!' he cried in his turn. 'As long as there's breath in my body, Montsou shan't have Vandame . . . I had dinner with Hennebeau last Thursday, and I could see what he was angling for. Even last autumn when the top brass came down to see the Board, they were making all sorts of come-hither signals . . . Oh yes, I know all those dukes and marquesses and generals and ministers! They're no more than bandits hiding out in the woods getting ready to rob you of your shirt!'

He was unstoppable now. Besides, even Monsieur Grégoire didn't defend the Montsou Board, whose six trustees had been established by the 1760 pact. They ruled the Company like tyrants, and when any one of their number died, the five survivors selected the new member from among the richest and most powerful shareholders. The opinion of the owner of La Piolaine, a man of moderation, was that these gentlemen sometimes lacked discretion in their unbridled lust for money.

Mélanie had come back to clear the table. Outside, the dogs had started to bark again, and Honorine was on her way to the door when Cécile, who was stifling with heat and full of food, left the table.

'No, don't bother, that must be for my lesson.'

Deneulin too had got up. He watched the girl leave, and then he asked with a smile:

'Well then, how about this marriage with young Négrel?'

'Nothing's been decided,' said Madame Grégoire. 'It's just a thought . . . We need to sleep on it.'

'Of course,' he continued, with a suggestive laugh, 'I'm sure that the nephew and the aunt . . . What amazes me is that Madame Hennebeau should welcome Cécile with open arms.'

But Monsieur Grégoire became indignant. Such a distinguished lady, and fourteen years older than the young man! It was appalling, he didn't think one should joke about things like that. Deneulin, still laughing, shook hands and said goodbye.

'It still wasn't her,' said Cécile, as she came back. 'It's that woman with the two children, you know Mummy, the miner's wife that we met . . . Should we let them in?'

They hesitated. Were they very dirty? No, not really, and they could leave their clogs on the doorstep. Father and Mother had already stretched out in their deep armchairs to relax. Their reluctance to move decided them.

'Let them in, Honorine.'

And in came La Maheude and her children. They were frozen and famished, and were stricken with panic to find themselves standing in such a room, which was so warm, with its lovely smell of brioche.

CHAPTER II

IN the bedroom, some grey slivers of daylight had gradually started to filter through the slats of the closed shutters, and fanned out over the ceiling; the close air became muggier, as they all continued their night's sleep: Lénore and Henri lying in each other's arms, Alzire with her head thrown back on her hump; while old Bonnemort, taking up the whole of Zacharie's and Jeanlin's bed, was snoring with his mouth open. Not a whisper came from the recess on the landing, where La Maheude had fallen asleep again while suckling Estelle, with her breast hanging out on one side, and her little girl sprawling over her stomach, sated with milk and as drowsy as her mother, almost buried in the soft flesh of her breasts.

Downstairs the cuckoo clock struck six o'clock. The sound of doors slamming echoed down the streets of the village, followed by the clattering of clogs on the cobbled pavement: the sorting girls were off to the pit. Then silence fell again, until seven o'clock, when the shutters sprang open, and yawns and coughs started echoing through the walls. A coffee-grinder squeaked away for some time without anyone in the bedroom waking.

But suddenly an outbreak of slaps and screams in the distance made Alzire jump up with a start. She realized what the time was, and ran in her bare feet to shake her mother.

'Mum! Mum! it's late. Remember you've got to go out . . . Look out! you'll squash Estelle.'

And she retrieved the baby, who was almost suffocating under the great mass of her mother's breasts.

'For heaven's sake!' stammered La Maheude, rubbing her eyes, 'you get so whacked you could sleep all day . . . You dress Lénore and Henri and I'll take them with me; so you look after Estelle, I don't want to drag her along in case she catches cold in this lousy weather.'

She washed hurriedly, putting on her cleanest skirt, an old blue one, and a grey woollen jacket, which she had mended with two patches the night before.

'And then there's the soup, for heaven's sake!' she muttered again.

While her mother went crashing downstairs, Alzire went back to her room with Estelle, who had started to scream again. But she was used to the baby's tantrums, and although she was only eight she called on the tender wiles of a woman to soothe and distract her. She laid her gently down in her bed, which was still warm, and lulled her back to sleep by giving her a finger to suck. And only just in time, for another storm broke; which meant that she had to get straight out of bed again to go and make peace between Lénore and Henri, who had just woken up. The only time that these two children were ever in agreement, and put their arms lovingly round each other's necks, was when they were asleep. As soon as she awoke, the girl, who was six, fell upon the boy, who was two years younger, and pummelled him with blows that he was unable to return. They both had the same oversized, balloon-like head, with tangled, yellowish hair. Alzire had to grab her sister by the legs, and threaten to tan the skin off her backside. Then they kept squabbling while she was trying to get them washed, and she had to fight to get each garment on them. They kept the shutters closed, so as not to disturb old Bonnemort's sleep. He kept snoring away, despite the dreadful hullabaloo created by the children.

'It's ready! Have you finished up there?' shouted La Maheude.

She had opened the shutters, stoked the fire, and put on more coal. She had hoped that the old man wouldn't have wolfed down all the soup, but she found the pan cleaned out, so she cooked a handful of vermicelli, which she had been keeping in reserve for the last three days. They would have to eat it on its own, without any butter; there wouldn't be any of yesterday's pat left; yet she was surprised to see that Catherine, who had prepared the sandwiches, had miraculously managed to save them a lump as large as a walnut. Only this time the cupboard really was bare: nothing, not a crust, no left-overs, not a bone to gnaw. What was to become of them, if Maigrat was determined to cut off their credit, and if the bourgeois at La Piolaine wouldn't give her a hundred sous? When the men and the girl came back from the pit, they'd have to eat again; for nobody had yet discovered how to live without eating, unfortunately.

'Come on down, you lot!' she shouted, losing her temper. 'I ought to be gone by now.'

When Alzire and the children had come down, she shared the vermicelli out on to three small plates. She wasn't hungry herself, she said. Although Catherine had already boiled up yesterday's coffee-grounds, she added more water and downed two large mugs of coffee so weak it looked like dishwater. It would keep her going all the same.

'Listen,' she said to Alzire again, 'you must let grandfather sleep, and make really sure that Estelle doesn't hurt herself, and if she wakes up and screams too much, look, here's a sugar lump, you melt it and then give her spoonfuls to drink . . . I know you'll be a good girl and not eat it yourself.'

'But what about school, Mum?'

'School can wait . . . There's too much to do today.'

'And what about the soup, do you want me to make it, if you're going to be late?'

'What soup? Oh yes, the soup . . . No, better wait till I get back.'

Alzire had the quick intelligence of an invalid child, and knew perfectly well how to make the soup. But she must have guessed the problem, for she didn't insist. Now the whole village had woken up; groups of children were marching off to school, dragging their feet in their noisy galoshes. Eight o'clock struck, and the hum of chatter from the Levaques' house on the left grew louder. The women's day had started, as they manned the coffee-pots, with their hands on their hips and their tongues wagging tirelessly, thrashing like water-wheels. A withered face, with thick lips and a flattened nose, pressed up against one of the window panes, and called out to them:

'Have you heard the latest?'

'No, later!' replied La Maheude. 'I've got to go out.'

And fearing that she might succumb to the offer of a glass of hot coffee, she bundled Lénore and Henri quickly out of the house and walked away with them. Upstairs, old Bonnemort was still snoring, with a steady rhythm that gently rocked the whole household.

Outside La Maheude was surprised to find that the wind had died down. There had been a sudden thaw; the sky looked the same colour as the earth, the walls were oozing with greenish moisture, and the roads clogged with mud, a mud that only the coal country knew, as black as liquid soot, thick and sticky enough to suck your clogs under. The next moment she had to smack Lénore, because the little girl was playing at picking up the mud on the end of her galoshes as if they were shovels. She left the village, walked past the slag-heap, and set off in the direction of the canal, taking short cuts down rough pathways leading over the waste land, in between rows of mouldy fences. Then she went past a series of sheds, then some long factory buildings, with their tall chimneys spewing out soot, polluting the ravaged countryside of this industrial suburb. Behind a clump of poplars, the old Réquillart pit displayed its dilapidated headgear, with only its great, hollow frame still standing. And then La Maheude turned to the right, and found herself on the main road.

'Stop it, you dirty little pig!' she shouted. 'I'll teach you to make mud pies.'

Now it was Henri who had picked up a handful of mud and

was kneading it. Both children were smacked even-handedly, and they fell into line, squinting down at the tracks that they carved through the middle of the heaps of mud. They were soon exhausted by the effort of unsticking their soles after every step that they took, and they just skidded forward.

Over towards Marchiennes the road ran straight ahead like a ribbon dipped in tar, unreeling its two leagues of cobbles between the reddish fields. But in the other direction it wound its way down through Montsou, which was built on the side of one of the gentle slopes of the plateau. These roads were springing up all over the Nord* Department, shooting out like arrows from one manufacturing town to another, with only the slightest of curves and the smoothest of gradients, and they were turning the whole county into one single, industrial city. The small brick houses, which were brightly painted to make up for the dismal climate, some yellow, some blue, others black (the latter doubtless aspiring to reach their predestined state of blackness without undue delay), lined both sides of the road, following its curves right down to the bottom of the hill. One or two large detached two-storey houses, where the factory managers lived, interrupted the serried ranks of these mean terraces. There was even a church built of brick, looking like some new kind of blast-furnace, with its square belfry already discoloured by the flying coal-dust. And yet, amid all the sugar-refineries, cable-works, and flour-mills, what stood out most were the dance halls, pubs, and beershops, which were so thick on the ground that they accounted for more than 500 out of every 1,000 buildings.

As she approached the Company's yards, a vast series of warehouses and workshops, La Maheude decided to hold Henri's and Lénore's hands, to keep one child on either side of her. Beyond the yards, she saw the villa where the manager, Monsieur Hennebeau, lived, a kind of vast chalet set back from the road behind iron gates and a garden, planted with some rather neglected and spindly trees. And at that very moment a carriage had stopped at the door, delivering a gentleman with decorations and a lady in a fur coat, who must be Parisian visitors who had just turned up at the Marchiennes railway station; for Madame Hennebeau, who could just be

seen in the half-light of the hallway, let out a little cry of
surprise and delight.

'Walk properly, you lazy kids!' scolded La Maheude, dragging her two children away from their games in the mud.

She had reached Maigrat's, which made her feel very nervous. Maigrat lived right next door to the manager, in a little
house separated from the villa by only a wall; and here he kept
his general stores, in a long building which opened directly on
to the street, but had no shop window. He stocked everything
you could need, groceries, cooked meat, fruit, bread, beer, pots
and pans. Maigrat was a former supervisor from Le Voreux,
who had started by setting up a little snack bar; then, thanks to
his former bosses' protection, his business had grown steadily
until it had wiped out all the small shopkeepers in Montsou.
He was able to make bulk purchases and offer a variety of
goods in one place, for the considerable clientele of the mining
villages allowed him to sell cheaper and allow more credit.
Moreover, he remained in the lap of the Company, since it had
built his little house and his shop for him.

'It's me again, Monsieur Maigrat,' said La Maheude
humbly, when she saw him standing in front of his door.

He looked at her without answering. He was a fat, cold,
formal man, who prided himself on never changing his mind.

'Look, please don't send me away like you did yesterday.
We can't wait till Saturday for something to eat ... I know we
still owe you sixty francs from two years ago.'

She continued her plea in short, painful sentences. It was an
old debt, contracted during the last strike. Time and again
they had promised to settle the debt, but they really hadn't
been able to, they hadn't managed to spare even two francs a
fortnight to give him. And to make matters worse, she'd had a
stroke of bad luck just two days ago, when she'd had to pay
twenty francs to the cobbler, who was threatening to send in
the bailiffs. And that was why they were completely broke.
Otherwise they could have held out till Saturday, like their
workmates.

But Maigrat stood there with his arms firmly crossed over
his imposing stomach, shaking his head in rejection of every
plea.

'Only two loaves of bread, Monsieur Maigrat. It's not much. I'm not asking for coffee ... Just two three-pound loaves a day.'

'No!' he shouted at last, at the top of his voice.

His wife had come out, a sickly creature who spent all her days doing the books, without even daring to look up. She scuttled back again, frightened at the sight of this wretched woman turning her urgently pleading gaze on her. People said she vacated the marital bed when the tram girls came shopping, for it was a well-known fact that when a miner wanted his credit extended, he had only to send round his wife or his daughter, no matter whether they were pretty or plain, as long as they were compliant.

As La Maheude kept looking beseechingly at Maigrat, she felt embarrassed to see by the gleam in his pale, narrow eyes that he was mentally stripping her naked. That infuriated her, though she wouldn't have thought it so bad when she was young, before she had had seven children. So she left, dragging Lénore and Henri roughly away from the gutter, where they were picking up nutshells.

'It'll bring you bad luck, Monsieur Maigrat, don't you forget it!'

Now her last resort was the bourgeois at La Piolaine. If they didn't cough up a hundred sous, she might as well lie down and die and her whole family with her. She took the left fork towards Joiselle. The Board was over there, at the corner of the road, a genuine red brick palace, where the bigwigs from Paris, and the princes and generals and government figures, came every autumn to hold their grand dinners. And while she walked she was already thinking how to spend her hundred sous: first some bread, then a bit of coffee, plus a quarter of a pound of butter, and a bushel of potatoes for soup in the morning and *ratatouille* in the evening; finally perhaps a bit of brawn, to make sure Father had his ration of meat.

The vicar of Montsou, Father Joire, went by, holding up the hem of his cassock, mincing along like a well-fed cat afraid of getting his coat dirty. He was a mild man, who made a show of never getting involved in anything, in order to offend neither workers nor bosses.

'Good morning, vicar.'

He walked right past her, smiling at the children, leaving her standing in the middle of the road. She had no religious feelings, but she had suddenly imagined that this priest might do something for her.

And she started off on her trek again, through the black, sticky mud. There were still two kilometres to go, and the children were no longer enjoying themselves. They started dragging behind, showing signs of distress. On both sides of the road they passed the same patches of waste land bounded by mouldy fences, the same factory buildings, stained with soot and bristling with tall chimneys. Beyond them, the country-side unfurled its vast open fields, like an ocean of brown clods, without a single tree for a mast, over as far as the hazy violet line of the forest of Vandame.

'Carry me, Mum.'

She carried them, each in turn. There were puddles all over the road, and she tucked up her skirts, to avoid arriving too dirty. Three times she nearly fell over, the damned cobbles were so slippery. And, when they finally arrived at the steps to the house, two enormous dogs rushed at them, barking so loud that the children screamed with fright. The coachman had to take his whip to them.

'Take your clogs off, and come in,' Honorine repeated.

In the dining-room, the mother and her children stood motionless, dazed by the sudden heat and very embarrassed by the looks they got from the old gentleman and the old lady, reclining in their armchairs.

'My dear,' said the lady, 'you know what's expected.'

The Grégoires entrusted Cécile with their good works. It was part of their notion of a proper education. You had to be charitable, and they themselves said that their house was God's refuge for the needy. However, they prided themselves on the fact that they were thinking Samaritans, constantly worried that they might make a mistake and encourage some immoral tendency. So they never gave money, never ever! neither ten sous nor even two sous, for you know what the poor are like, as soon as they have two sous to rub together, they squander them on drink. Their alms, therefore, were always donations in kind, especially in warm clothes, which they gave out to needy children in winter-time.

'Oh, the poor little darlings!' cried Cécile. 'Aren't they pale from the nasty cold weather? ... Honorine, go and get the parcel from the wardrobe.'

The maids, too, looked at these wretches with the pity and the pang of concern of girls who never had to wonder where their next meal was coming from. While the chambermaid went upstairs, the cook forgot her duties, and put the remains of the brioche down on the table, and stood there with her arms dangling.

'It just happens that I've still got two woollen dresses and some scarves . . . You'll see, they'll be nice and warm, the poor little darlings.'

At that La Maheude found her tongue again, and stammered:

'Thank you, Miss . . . You are all very kind . . .'

Her eyes had filled with tears, she thought the hundred sous were within arm's reach, and she was only worried about the best way of asking for them if they didn't make the first move. There was no sign of the chambermaid, and there was a moment of embarrassed silence. Clinging to their mother's skirts, the children gazed at the brioche in wide-eyed wonder.

'Have you just those two children?' asked Madame Grégoire, to break the silence.

'Oh, no, Ma'am, I've got seven.'

Monsieur Grégoire, who had gone back to reading the paper, gave a start of indignation.

'Seven children, but whatever for, for heaven's sake?'

'It's hardly wise,' murmured the old lady.

La Maheude made a vague gesture of apology. What did you expect? You didn't think twice, they just came along, that was life. And then when they grew up they brought in a bit of money and that helped with the housekeeping. So, you see, they would have had enough to live on, if only the grandfather's bones hadn't seized up, and if only there were more than two of her boys and her eldest daughter old enough to go down the pit. You still had to feed the kids who did nothing all day.

'So,' Madame Grégoire replied, 'have you all been working at the mine for long?'

La Maheude's wan face lit up with silent laughter.

'Oh, dear, oh Lord, yes! ... I went down until I was twenty. The doctor said it would be the death of me when I had my second, because, so he said, it was doing my bones a mischief. Anyway that was when I got married and I had enough to do at home ... But on my husband's side, you see, they've been going down for ever. Ever since his grandfather's grandfather, well, nobody knows, right at the beginning, when they first started digging down there, at Réquillart.'

Monsieur Grégoire looked dreamily at this pitiful woman and her children, with their waxen flesh, discoloured hair, rickety bones, anaemic thinness, and sad, ugly, hungry expressions. A new silence had come over them, nothing could be heard but the crackling of the gas escaping from the burning coal. The room exuded the moist, heavy, comfortable atmosphere that cradles the bourgeois family in their contented slumbers.

'Whatever can she be doing?' cried Cécile impatiently. 'Mélanie, go up and tell her that the parcel is in the bottom of the wardrobe, on the left.'

Meanwhile, Monsieur Grégoire concluded aloud the results of his meditation on the sight of these starving creatures.

'This world is a difficult place, it is true; but, my good woman, I have to say that the workers are hardly wise ... You see, instead of putting money to one side like the peasants, the miners drink, run up debts, and in the end they can't feed their families.'

'You are right, Sir,' replied La Maheude, soberly. 'We don't always follow the straight and narrow. That's what I tell the layabouts, when they complain ... But I've been lucky, my husband doesn't drink. All the same, sometimes on a Sunday night out he takes a drop too much; but he never goes too far. It's all the nicer of him because he was a real swine of a drinker before we got married, excusing my language ... And you see it doesn't get us anywhere now he behaves himself. There are some days, like today, when you could turn out every drawer in the house and not find a brass farthing.'*

She was trying to turn their thoughts towards her hundred-sou piece, and she continued, in confidential tones, explaining the fatal debt, which at first was small and safe, but soon started snowballing at a frightening rate. You paid up regularly every fortnight ... But one day you got behind with it and it was all over, you could never catch up again. The hole in your pocket got deeper, the men got fed up with work, because it wouldn't even pay off their debts. Damn it all, you were in it up to there until the day of your death. And besides, you had to understand: a collier needed a mugful to wash down the dust. That's how it started and then as soon as you had any problems you couldn't tear them away from the bar. Maybe even, although it was nobody's fault, the workers didn't get paid enough.

'But', said Madame Grégoire, 'I thought that the Company paid for your rent and your heating.'

La Maheude cast a sidelong gaze at the coal crackling in the grate.

'Oh yes, we do get some coal, pretty rotten stuff, but at least it burns ... As for the rent it's only six francs a month: it doesn't sound much, but it's often dead hard to pay ... For instance, today, you could cut me up into little pieces, but you couldn't get ten sous out of me. You can't get something out of nothing.'

The master and his wife said nothing, relaxing in comfort, gradually finding it tedious and embarrassing to have this poverty spread before them. She was afraid that she had offended them, and she added, thoughtfully, as a fair and sensible woman:

'Oh, it's not that I want to complain, you have to accept things as they are; especially since we could try as hard as we liked, we'd never change them an inch ... The best thing, Sir, Ma'am, is to try to get on with life honestly, isn't it, in the place God gave you.'

Monsieur Grégoire approved of her sentiments entirely.

'With such feelings, my good woman, one rises above misfortune.'

At last Honorine and Mélanie came down with the parcel. Cécile undid it herself and took out the two dresses. She added some scarves, and even stockings and mittens. It would all be a marvellous fit, and she hastened to get the maids to wrap up the clothes she had chosen; for her piano teacher had just arrived, so she pushed the mother and her children towards the door.

'We really are short of money,' stammered La Maheude. 'If we could just lay hands on a single hundred-sou piece . . .'

She could hardly get the words out, for the Maheus were proud and were determined not to beg. Cécile looked anxiously at her father; but he refused point-blank, with a dutiful air.

'No, we don't agree with that sort of thing. We cannot.'

Then their daughter, upset by the tragic expression on the mother's face, wanted to shower the children with generosity. They were still staring at the brioche, so she cut off two slices to give to them.

'Here, this is for you.'

But then she took them back again, and asked the maids for some old newspaper.

'Wait, you must share it with your brothers and sisters.'

And under the tender gaze of her parents, she finally steered them out of the house. La Maheude's poor kids, who didn't have even a slice of bread to eat themselves, went away holding the brioche* respectfully in their cold, numb little hands.

She dragged them back over the cobbles, looking neither at the empty fields, nor the black mud, nor the great, livid sky hanging over her head. As she was going back through Montsou, she marched determinedly into Maigrat's and pleaded so fiercely that she finally made off with two loaves of bread, coffee, butter, and even her hundred-sou piece, for Maigrat also lent small sums of money. It wasn't her he fancied, it was Catherine, as she realized when he advised her to send her daughter to collect the groceries. They would deal with that when the time came, if they had to. Catherine would belt him one if he crept up too close for comfort.

CHAPTER III

THE clock on the little church of mining village Two Hundred and Forty was striking eleven. It was a brick chapel, where Father Joire came to say mass on Sundays. Beside it was another brick building, the school, where you could hear the repetitive chanting of the children, although the windows were closed because of the cold outside. Between the four large blocks of identical houses, the broad space that was divided up into little back-to-back gardens remained deserted; and these gardens, ravaged by winter, made a sorry sight, with their bare, clay soil sporadically defiled by a few late, stunted vegetables. People were preparing their soup, and the chimneys were smoking. Here and there a woman came into view somewhere along the terrace, opened a door, then disappeared inside. All along the street, the drainpipes dripped into the water-butts standing on the cobbled pavement, not because it was raining, but because of the heavy humidity in the grey air. And this village, built all of a piece in the middle of a vast plain, surrounded by its black roads as if by a mourning ribbon, had nothing more cheerful to show than the regular stripes of its red tiles, washed clean by the constant showers.

On the way home La Maheude stopped off to buy some potatoes from the wife of a supervisor, who still had some of her own crop left over. Behind a curtain of rickety poplars, the only trees visible on this open ground, was an isolated group of buildings, comprising individual blocks of four houses, set in their own gardens. As the Company had reserved this new development for their deputies, the workers had dubbed this end of the village 'Silk Stockings'; in the same vein they had called their own neighbourhood 'Bailiffs' Delight', with a good-natured irony which made light of their poverty.

'Phew! here we are,' said La Maheude, bundling her mud-spattered, worn-out children through the door before her and dumping her bulky packages.

Estelle was screaming by the fireside, cradled in Alzire's arms. When Alzire had run out of sugar, the only way she could think of to try to silence her was to pretend to suckle her. This pretence was often quite effective. But this time, although she had gone to the trouble of opening her dress and applying the baby's mouth to her skinny, sickly eight-year-old breast, the child was furious at chewing on empty skin and getting nothing from it.

'Give her here,' cried her mother, as soon as she had put everything down. 'We won't be able to hear ourselves think.'

And when she had pulled from her bodice a breast as full as a wineskin, and the screaming brat had plugged herself in and suddenly fallen silent, they were at last able to talk. Otherwise everything was all right, the little housekeeper had kept the fire going, swept the floor, and tidied the room. And in the sudden silence, the grandfather could be heard snoring upstairs, with the same regular rhythm that he had kept up all morning.

'What a lot of stuff!' murmured Alzire, smiling at the provisions. 'I'll make the soup, if you like, Mum.'

The table was piled high: there was a parcel of clothes, two loaves of bread, potatoes, butter, coffee, chicory, and half a pound of brawn.

'Oh, the soup!' said La Maheude wearily. 'I'd have to go and pick the sorrel and pull up the leeks ... No, I'll make some for the men afterwards ... Put the potatoes on to boil, we'll eat them with a bit of butter ... And the coffee, hey, don't forget the coffee!'

But suddenly she remembered the brioche. She looked at Lénore and Henri, who were already rested and refreshed enough to have started fighting on the floor, and she saw that their hands were empty. Would you believe it, the greedy monkeys had already quietly finished off the brioche on the way home! She smacked them both, but Alzire, who was putting the cooking pot on the fire, tried to pacify her.

'Leave them alone, Mum. If it's for my sake, you know I don't like brioche very much. They must have been hungry from such a long walk.'

The clock struck twelve, and then they heard the galoshes of the children as they came home from school. The potatoes were cooked, the coffee, which was mixed with at least its own volume of chicory to make it go further, was bubbling tunefully through the filter. They had cleared one end of the table; but only the mother was using it, the three children were happy to eat off their knees; and all the while the little boy was eyeing the brawn with silent greed, excited by the sticky paper.

La Maheude was drinking her coffee sip by sip, cupping the glass in her hands to warm them up, when old Bonnemort came down. Usually he got up later, and his lunch would be ready for him on the stove. But today he started grumbling, because there wasn't any soup. Then, when his daughter-in-law replied that you didn't always get what you wanted in life, he ate his potatoes in silence. From time to time he got up and went to spit politely into the cinders; then he sat huddled up in his chair with his head sunk on his chest, and concentrated on chewing his food slowly, moving it from one side of his mouth to the other, and staring into space.

'Oh, Mum, I forgot,' said Alzire, 'the next-door neighbour came round.'

Her mother broke in.

'She gets on my nerves!'

She bore La Levaque a lingering grudge, for she had cried poverty the day before so as not to lend her anything, and yet she knew full well that she was loaded at the time, because her lodger Bouteloup had just paid his fortnight's rent. The village households didn't go in for lending each other money.

'Oh, that reminds me,' continued La Maheude, 'wrap up a bit of coffee . . . I'll take it round to La Pierronne, I owe it her from the day before yesterday.'

And when her daughter had prepared the packet, she added that she would come straight back to put the men's soup on to heat up. Then she went out with Estelle in her arms, leaving old Bonnemort slowly chewing his potatoes, while Lénore and Henri fought for the skins that had fallen on the floor.

Instead of walking round by the road, La Maheude went straight across the gardens, to avoid being hailed by La Levaque; for her garden happened to back on to the Pierrons', and there was a gap in the dilapidated fence between that allowed them to get through. The communal well for the four households was there. To one side, behind a clump of spindly lilacs, was what they called the hutch, which was a low shed, full of old tools, where they always kept a rabbit, to have one to eat on holidays. The clock struck one, which meant coffee-time, and not a soul could be seen at the doors or windows. There was only one man out digging his vegetable patch, doubtless a stoneman killing time waiting for his shift, and he didn't even look up. But, as La Maheude reached the block of houses opposite, she was surprised to see a gentleman and two ladies walking past the church. She stopped for a second, and recognized them: it was Madame Hennebeau, who was taking her guests, the decorated gentleman and the fur-coated lady, on a tour of the village.

'Oh, why ever did you bother?' exclaimed La Pierronne, when La Maheude had given her the coffee. 'There was no hurry.'

She was twenty-eight years old, and was generally considered to be the village beauty. She was a brunette with a low forehead, big eyes, and fine lips: and she was smartly dressed to boot, as clean as the cat's whiskers. She had a shapely bosom, since she hadn't had any children. Her mother, old Ma Brûlé, the widow of a hewer who had died down the mine, had sent her daughter to work in a factory, swearing that she would never let her marry a coal-mining man, and now she lived in a permanent state of bad temper, after her daughter got married rather late on to Pierron, a widower if you please, who already had a little girl of eight. And yet the couple were perfectly happy, despite the tissue of tales woven around the husband's complaisance and his wife's lovers: they had no debts, they ate meat twice a week, and their house was so spick and span that you could use their saucepans for mirrors. And to add to their luck, because they knew the right people, the Company had authorized her to sell sweets and biscuits, which she displayed in jars on two shelves in her window. That meant a profit of six or seven sous a day, sometimes twelve on Sundays. And the only blots on all this happiness were the fact that old Ma Brûlé continued to scream fire and brimstone, spewing out her tireless revolutionary fury, fuelled by the urge to wreak vengeance on the bosses for the death of her man, and that little Lydie tended to collect more than her fair share of slaps in the course of their turbulent family life.

'Oh, aren't we a big girl now!' said La Pierronne, smiling and cooing at Estelle.

'Oh, you can't believe the trouble they cause!' said La Maheude. 'You're lucky you haven't got any. At least you can keep your house clean.'

Although her own home was perfectly tidy, and she did the washing every Saturday, she cast jealous housewifely eyes on this beautifully light room, where there were even some pretty ornaments, like the gilt vases on the sideboard, the mirror, and the three framed prints.

Meanwhile La Pierronne was drinking her coffee on her own, since her whole small family was at the pit.

'Do have a glass of coffee with me,' she said.

'No, thanks, I've only just drunk my own.'

'That doesn't matter, does it?'

And indeed it didn't matter. And they both sat down and started slowly drinking. Their gaze slipped past the jars of biscuits and sweets, and lighted on the houses opposite, with their row of little curtained windows, whose greater or lesser whiteness betrayed their owners' degree of housewifely virtue. The Levaques' were very dirty, veritable dishcloths, which looked as if they had been used to wash up with.

'How can anyone live in such filth!' murmured La Pierronne.

Then La Maheude launched into an unstoppable tirade. Oh, if only she had a lodger like that Bouteloup, wouldn't she have made the most of it for the housekeeping! When you knew how to manage them, lodgers were really good business, as long as you didn't get into bed with them. And then the husband drank, beat his wife, and chased after the girls who sang in the pubs at Montsou.

La Pierronne affected a profoundly disgusted look. Those singers gave you every disease in the book. One of them, at Joiselle, had infected a whole pitful of men.

'What surprises me is that you let your son go out with their daughter.'

'Well, how do you think I could stop him? . . . Their garden is next to ours. All summer Zacharie spent the whole time with Philomène under the lilacs, and they were at it all over the hutch—you couldn't draw water from the well without tripping over them.'

It was the usual story of promiscuity in the mining village, the boys and girls getting each other into trouble, going flat on their arses, as the saying went, on the low, sloping roof of the hutch, as soon as night fell. All the tram girls caught their first kids that way, except for those who took the trouble to walk all the way to Réquillart or to find somewhere to lie down in the wheatfields. It didn't really matter, they got married afterwards, only the mothers got angry when their boys started too soon, for a boy who got married stopped bringing his pay packet home to his parents.

'If I was you I'd try to have it over and done with,' continued La Pierronne. 'Your Zacharie's given her a bun in the oven twice already, and they'll go off and settle down somewhere else ... Anyway, you've already lost your money on that one.'

La Maheude was furious, and clenched her fists.

'You listen to me: I'll curse them if they get hitched ... Doesn't Zacharie owe us any respect? Haven't we spent money on him? Well, it's his turn to pay us back, before he gets weighed down with a woman on his hands ... what would become of us, for heaven's sake, if all our children went straight off to work for somebody else? We might as well drop dead straight away!'

But then she calmed down.

'I mean in general, of course, we'll just have to see what happens ... Your coffee's good and strong, isn't it, you don't do things by halves.'

And after another half-hour of gossiping, she slipped away, pleading that she hadn't got the men's soup ready yet. Outside the children were returning to school, a few women could be seen in their doorways, watching Madame Hennebeau, who was walking past one row of houses, pointing out the features of the village to her guests. Their visit was starting to create some excitement amongst the inhabitants. The tunnel worker stopped digging for a moment, and two disturbed hens cackled anxiously in their gardens.

As La Maheude was going home she bumped into La Levaque, who had gone out to catch Dr Vanderhaghen on his way past. He was one of the Company's doctors, a small, harassed man, who gave his consultations on the run.

'Doctor,' she said, 'I can't sleep a wink, I ache all over ... we must have a talk about it, really.'

He was equally familiar with all his clients, and replied without stopping.

'Get along with you, my dear, you drink too much coffee, that's all.'

'But what about my husband?' said La Maheude in her turn. 'You said you would call in and see ... he's still got those pains in his legs.'

'Only because you're wearing him out, get along with you!'

The women remained stock still, watching the retreating back of the doctor.

'Why don't you come in,' said La Levaque, when she and her neighbour had both shrugged their shoulders in exasperation. 'You haven't heard the news ... And you must have a drop of coffee, won't you, I've only just made it.'

La Maheude put up token resistance but easily succumbed. Go on, just a drop, so as not to offend her. And she went inside.

The room was black with grime, the floor and the walls were spattered with grease, the sideboard and the table thick with muck; and a rank whiff of sluttishness caught in your throat. Sitting by the fireside, with both elbows on the table and his nose plunged in his dish, she saw Bouteloup, a heavily built but easy-going fellow, who looked younger than his thirty-five years. He was finishing off the remains of his broth. Little Achille, Philomène's elder child, who was already over three years old, was standing beside him, watching him with the dumb pathos of a hungry animal. The lodger, who was a tender man at heart, behind his wild black beard, popped a piece of his meat right into the child's mouth from time to time.

'Wait for the sugar,' said La Levaque, putting the brown sugar straight into the coffee-pot.

She was six years older than him, hideous and worn out, with her breasts hanging down to her belly and her belly hanging down to her thighs. Her sagging face sprouted grey whiskers, and her hair was never combed. He had had her absent-mindedly, scrutinizing her no more than he did his soup, which often had hairs in it, or his bed, whose sheets did three months' service at a stretch. She was part of the deal, and, as her husband would say, good friends mean good business.

'So, as I was saying,' she went on, 'they saw La Pierronne nosing round Silk Stockings last night. You can guess which gent was waiting for her behind Rasseneur's, and they went off together along the canal ... eh, how about that, then, for a married woman!'

'Heavens,' said La Maheude. 'Before he married her, Pierron used to give the deputy his rabbits, now he finds it cheaper to lend him his wife.'

Bouteloup burst out with a loud guffaw of laughter, dunked a bit of bread in the stew, and launched it into Achille's mouth. The two women finished venting their feelings about La Pierronne, a flirt, no prettier than the others, but always examining her spots, washing herself, and putting on face cream. Anyway, she was her husband's problem, if he liked his bread buttered that way. Some men were so ambitious they would wipe the boss's bum, just to hear him say thank you. And they would have gone on all night if they hadn't been interrupted by the arrival of a neighbour who brought in a nine-month-old kid, Désirée, Philomène's youngest. The mother herself had her lunch at the screening shed, and arranged to have the little one brought over to her, so that she could give her the breast while she sat down on the coal for a moment.

'You know I can't leave mine alone for a second, she starts screaming straight away,' said La Maheude, looking at Estelle, who had fallen asleep in her arms.

But she didn't manage to avoid the show-down she had seen looming up for some time now in the whites of La Levaque's eyes.

'Look here, isn't it time we tried to get this thing settled?'

At first both mothers had been in agreement about not allowing the marriage, without even needing to discuss it. If Zacharie's mother wanted to keep on pocketing her son's fortnightly pay packet, Philomène's mother was equally obsessed by the idea of not losing her daughter's. There was no hurry, La Levaque had even preferred to stay at home and look after the baby as long as there was only one of them; but now he had started to grow up and share their food, and another baby had turned up, she found she was losing out on the deal; and, since she had no intention of subsidizing them, she had become a fervent advocate of marriage.

'Zacharie has made his choice, there's nothing stopping them . . . When do you fancy?'

'Let's leave it for the fine weather,' replied La Maheude, embarrassed. 'These things are a nuisance! As if they couldn't have waited to be married before they got together! . . . I give you my word, I'd strangle Catherine, if I found she'd been fooling around.'

La Levaque shrugged her shoulders.

'Don't worry, she'll do it same as everyone else!'

Bouteloup, with the relaxed air of a man thoroughly at home, searched the dresser looking for bread. Some half-peeled vegetables for Levaque's soup, potatoes and leeks, were strewn over the end of the table, where they had been started and abandoned again ten times over during La Levaque's endless gossiping. She had just got back to work once more, however, when she dropped everything yet again in order to take up her station by the window.

'What have we here . . . Hey! It's Madame Hennebeau with some people. And they're going in to see La Pierronne.'

With that, the two of them fell to criticizing La Pierronne again. Oh! you could count on it, as soon as the Company brought any people to visit a miners' village, they took them straight round to her house, because it was clean. And you could bet they didn't let on about the business with the overman. It's easy enough to keep clean and tidy when you have lovers who earn three thousand francs and have their heating and rent paid for them, not to mention the sweeteners. But even if it did look clean on top it wasn't so clean if you looked underneath. And all the time the visitors were in the house opposite, they held forth.

'They're coming out now,' said La Levaque at last. 'They're doing the rounds . . . Look out, dear, I think they're coming to see you.'

La Maheude was terror-stricken. Who could tell whether Alzire had remembered to wipe the table? Not to mention her soup, which wasn't ready either! She stammered out her goodbye and fled, running straight home without looking to left or to right.

But everything was spick and span. Seeing that her mother had failed to return, Alzire had decided to make the soup. She had donned a tea towel for an apron, pulled up the last leeks from the garden, picked some sorrel, and she was at that moment in the process of cleaning the vegetables, while a large cauldron of bath water was heating on the fire, for the men when they got home. Henri and Lénore were behaving themselves, for once, putting all their energy into tearing up an old calendar. Old Bonnemort was smoking his pipe in silence.

Just as La Maheude was catching her breath, Madame Hennebeau knocked.

'You don't mind, do you, my good woman?'

She was a tall, blonde woman in her forties, slightly heavy but splendidly blooming. She made a good attempt at an affable smile, and managed rather well to conceal her fear of dirtying the bronze silk outfit that she was wearing under her black velvet cape.

'Come in, come on in,' she repeated to her guests. 'Nobody minds ... Look, isn't this one clean, too? And the good woman has seven children! ... All our households are like this ... As I said, the Company lets them the house for six francs a month. There's a large room downstairs, two bedrooms upstairs, a cellar and a garden.'

The decorated gent and the fur-coated lady, fresh off the train from Paris that morning, stared vacantly round the room, showing by their expressions that they were out of their depth in this stark and unfamiliar world.

'And a garden,' repeated the lady. 'But it's divine, one could really live here!'

'We give them more coal than they can burn,' Madame Hennebeau went on. 'A doctor visits them twice a week; and, when they are old, they get pensions, although nothing is deducted from their wages.'

'It's Eldorado! The promised land!' murmured the gentleman, enchanted.

La Maheude had hastened to offer them chairs, but the ladies declined. Madame Hennebeau was already bored, although she had been amused for a moment to forget her weary exile and act the role of safari guide; but she was soon repelled by the stale odour of poverty, despite the carefully selected cleanliness of the houses where she ventured. Besides, she only ever repeated snatches of things she had heard people say, never bothering to understand this race of workers, who toiled and suffered so close by her side.

'What lovely children,' murmured the lady, who thought they were dreadful, with their oversized heads and their matted, straw-coloured hair.

Then La Maheude had to tell them their ages, and they asked her about Estelle, to be polite. As a mark of respect old Bonnemort had taken his pipe out of his mouth; but they still found him disturbing enough, he was so ravaged by his forty years down the pit, with his stiff legs and his broken frame and his ashen face. Just then, he was seized by a violent fit of coughing, so he thought he had better go outside and spit, in case the black phlegm upset the visitors.

Alzire was the main attraction. What a pretty little house-wife, with her tea towel! They complimented the mother on having a little girl who was so sensible so young. And no one mentioned her hump, although they did keep sneaking looks of embarrassed compassion at the poor little cripple.

'Well then,' Madame Hennebeau concluded, 'if they ask you about our mining villages when you get back to Paris, you know what to say. Never a voice raised in anger, traditional family morality, everyone healthy and happy as you can see, a place where you could go for a holiday, just for the fresh air and the peace and quiet.'

'It's marvellous, too marvellous!' cried the gentleman, with a final burst of enthusiasm.

They left with an air of enchantment, as if they had just seen a fairground side-show, and La Maheude saw them to the door, then waited there while they walked slowly away, talking at the top of their voices. The streets had filled with people, and they had to walk through groups of women, who had been attracted by the news of their visit, which they broadcast from house to house.

La Levaque, for instance, had intercepted La Pierronne at her front door, when she rushed up out of curiosity. Both claimed to be disagreeably surprised. Well, whatever next, were they going to spend the night there, at the Maheus'? There wasn't that much to see there, surely.

'Always broke, despite what they earn! Heavens, when you can't control yourself!'

'I've just heard that she went this morning to see the bourgeois at La Piolaine, and Maigrat who refused to give them any bread has given her some now ... you know what Maigrat wants to be paid with.'

'Nothing she's got to offer, I reckon, you'd have to be pretty desperate ... It's Catherine he wants it from.'

'Oh, just think, you wouldn't believe the cheek, she told me just now that she'd strangle Catherine if she caught her at it! ... As if that great oaf Chaval hadn't had her flat on her arse on the hutch ages ago!'

'Shh! ... Here they come.'

La Levaque and La Pierronne, affecting the courteous air of the discreetly incurious, contented themselves with watching the visitors leave out of the corner of their eyes. Then they made urgent signs to La Maheude, who was still carrying Estelle in her arms. And all three watched motionless while the well-dressed backs of Madame Hennebeau and her guests receded into the distance. As soon as they were about thirty paces away, the gossiping started up again more furiously than ever.

'They've got a gold mine on their backs, worth more than they are, I reckon!'

'You bet ... I don't know the stranger, but I wouldn't give tuppence for the one from round here, despite all the fine flesh on her. I've heard plenty of stories ...'

'Eh? What stories?'

'They say she has men, you know! ... First there's the engineer ...'

'That weedy little runt! ... Oh, he's too skinny, she'd lose him in the bedclothes.'

'Why should you care, as long as it keeps her happy? ... I have my doubts, you know, when I see a lady who looks so snooty that she's never satisfied wherever she is ... Look at her sticking out her backside as if she despised the lot of us. Is that decent?'

The tourists were moving away at the same slow pace, still talking, when a carriage, a barouche in fact, came down the road and drew up in front of the church. A gentleman of about forty-eight, wearing a tightly buttoned black frock coat, got out. His complexion was very dark, and he had a severe, formal expression.

'The husband!' murmured La Levaque, lowering her voice as if he could hear her, gripped by the hierarchical fear that the manager inspired in his 10,000 workmen. 'But it's true, you can see from his face he's a cuckold, can't you!'

By now the whole village had come outside. As the curiosity of the women increased, the groups came closer together and merged into a crowd; while bands of snotty-nosed kids hung about the roadside gawping. At one moment even the school-teacher's pale face popped up over the school hedge. In the middle of the gardens, the man who had been digging stood still with his foot on his spade, staring wide-eyed. And the murmur of their gossiping gradually grew into a rustling noise, like the wind blowing through dry leaves.

It was mainly in front of La Levaque's door that the meeting had congregated. Two women had come round, then ten, then twenty. La Pierronne fell cautiously silent, now that there were too many ears listening. La Maheude, who was one of the most sensible, was also content just to watch; and in order to pacify Estelle, who had woken up and started scream-ing, she had calmly taken out her maternal breast, which hung there in broad daylight like a cow's udder, distended by its bountiful flow of milk. When Monsieur Hennebeau had seated his ladies in the back of his carriage, and whisked them off towards Marchiennes, there was a last explosion of chattering voices. The women gesticulated, and talked too volubly to listen, creating a commotion reminiscent of an ant-hill in an emergency.

But the clock struck three. The stonemen, Bouteloup and the others, had gone. Suddenly, the first colliers hove into view around the church corner on their way back from the pit, with their black faces and soaking clothes, hunching their shoulders and hugging their chests. Their arrival sent a flurry of panic through the crowd, and all these housewives ran off home, upset at having been caught in the act of over-indulging in coffee and gossip. And on all sides there arose the same anxious lament, as they knew the trouble they had let themselves in for:

'Oh, my God, my soup! My soup isn't even ready yet!'

CHAPTER IV

WHEN Maheu got home, after leaving Étienne at Rasseneur's, he found Catherine, Zacharie, and Jeanlin already seated round the table finishing their soup. When they got back from the pit they were so hungry that they ate in their damp clothes before even cleaning themselves up, and nobody waited, the table was laid from morning to night, there was always someone there swallowing his rations, depending on the time of his shift.

As soon as he came through the door, Maheu noticed the provisions. He said nothing, but his worried face lit up. All morning he had been plagued by the thought of the empty cupboard, the house with no coffee or butter, it had racked him with sudden pangs while he was hacking at the seam in the suffocating heat of the coal-face. How would his wife have got on? And what was to become of them if she returned empty-handed? And now, he saw that they had everything they needed. She would explain later. He laughed with relief.

Catherine and Jeanlin had already left the table and were drinking their coffee standing up; while Zacharie, who still felt empty after the soup, cut himself a large slice of bread and covered it in butter. Of course he had seen the brawn on the plate; but he didn't touch it; if there was only one portion of meat, then it was for Father. They had all chased their soup down with a great gulp of cold water, the fine clear drink that marked the end of the fortnight.

'I haven't got any beer,' said La Maheude when Father had taken his turn to sit at the table. 'I wanted to keep a bit of money over . . . But if you want some, the little one can run and get you a pint.'

He looked at her and beamed. She even had some money left over as well!

'No, no need,' he said. 'I've had a glass already, thanks.'

And slowly but surely Maheu started to swallow the mixture of bread, potatoes, leeks, and sorrel, eating it straight out of the brimming bowl which he used as a dish. La Maheude, still holding Estelle in her arms, helped Alzire make sure that he had everything he wanted, pushed the butter and the pork within his reach, and put his coffee back on the stove to keep it nice and warm.

Meanwhile, beside the fire, the ablutions commenced, in a half-barrel converted into a bath-tub. Catherine, who went first, had filled it with lukewarm water; and she took her clothes off with no embarrassment, first her cap, then her jacket, her breeches, and finally her shirt, as she had ever since she was eight years old, a habit she had grown up with without seeing anything wrong in it. She did turn her body towards the fire, however, then she rubbed herself vigorously with a piece of black soap. Nobody watched her; even Lénore and Henri were no longer curious to see what she looked like. When she was clean, she went upstairs stark naked, leaving her soaking shift and her other clothes in a heap on the floor. But then a quarrel broke out between the two brothers. Jeanlin had quickly leapt into the tub, arguing that Zacharie was still eating; and the latter pushed him aside and claimed that it was his turn first, shouting that he might be kind enough to let Catherine take her dip first, but he didn't want to swim in that urchin's dishwater, especially as, by the time he had finished with the water, you might as well fill the school ink-wells with it. In the end they got washed together, both facing the fire too, and they even lent each other a hand to scrub their backs. Then, like their sister before them, they went upstairs stark naked.

'What a mess they make!' muttered La Maheude, picking their clothes up off the floor and hanging them up to dry. 'Alzire, mop up a bit, will you?'

But the sound of an uproar on the other side of the wall cut short her complaint. There was a man swearing and a woman crying, then the whole din of battle, including some dull thuds which sounded like someone kicking a sack of potatoes.

'La Levaque's facing the music,' stated Maheu calmly, as he

scraped the bottom of his bowl with his spoon. 'It's odd, Bouteloup claimed the soup was ready.'

'Like hell it was,' said La Maheude. 'I saw the vegetables on the table, she hadn't even peeled them.'

The shouts and cries got louder, something lurched violently against the wall, making it shake, then a long silence fell. Then the miner, swallowing his last spoonful, concluded with an air of impartial justice:

'It's fair enough, if the soup wasn't ready.'

And when he had drunk a full glass of water, he started on the brawn. He cut it into square pieces, spearing them on his knife and eating them on his bread without a fork. Nobody spoke while Father was eating. He himself fell silent while he was busy satisfying his hunger; although he didn't recognize Maigrat's usual cold meat, and thought it must have come from somewhere else; he didn't ask his wife any questions. He just asked whether the old man was still asleep up there. No, Grandfather had already gone out for his usual walk. And silence reigned again.

But the smell of meat had alerted Lénore and Henri, who looked up from their game of making rivers with the spilled bathwater. They both came and stood beside their father, the little boy in front. Their eyes followed the fate of every morsel, watching hopefully as it left the dish, and observing tragically its demise in their father's mouth. After a while, he noticed that they were pale with greed and were licking their lips.

'Have they had some?' he asked.

And when he saw his wife hesitate, he said:

'You know I don't like to be unfair. It spoils my appetite to see them hanging around me begging.'

'Yes, they damn well have,' she shouted angrily. 'Of course, if you listen to them you'd give them your share and everyone else's, and they'd stuff their faces till they burst ... It's true, isn't it, Alzire, we've all had some brawn?'

'Of course we have, Mum,' replied the little hunchback, who on great occasions like this could lie with all the sang-froid of a grown-up.

Lénore and Henri were dumbstruck with emotion, disgusted by such spectacular mendacity, when they would have been whipped if ever they didn't tell the truth. Their little hearts beat furiously, and they were sorely tempted to protest, to say that they weren't there, personally, when the others had had theirs.

'Be off with you then!' continued their mother, who shooed them away to the other end of the room. 'You should be ashamed to be nosing around your father's plate like that. And even if he was the only one to have some, why shouldn't he, he does all the work, doesn't he, while you little layabouts do nothing all day but spend our money, piles of it, more than your weight in gold!'

Maheu called them back to his side. He sat Lénore down on his left knee and Henri on his right; then he turned the rest of his lunch into a picnic, cutting the brawn into little pieces, one for you, one for me. The children were delighted and wolfed it all down.

When he had finished he said to his wife:

'No, don't serve the coffee yet. I'm going to get washed first . . . And lend me a hand to get rid of the dirty water.'

They grabbed hold of the handles of the tub, and were emptying it into the gutter outside the door, when Jeanlin came downstairs, wearing dry clothes, a faded woollen jacket and breeches which were too big for him, having already done their share of service for his brother. Seeing him trying to slip through the open door on the sly, his mother stopped him.

'Where are you going?'

'Out.'

'Out where? . . . Listen, you can go and gather some dandelion leaves for the salad this evening. Hey, are you listening, if you don't bring the dandelion leaves back, I'll give you what for.'

'Oh, all right.'

Jeanlin went off with his hands in his pockets, dragging his feet, swaying his skinny, rickety ten-year-old hips as if he were a mature miner. Then Zacharie came down, more neatly dressed, sporting a tight black woollen sweater with blue stripes. His father shouted out to him not to be late home, and he nodded his head as he left, but without removing his pipe from between his teeth.

Once again the tub was filled with warm water. Maheu was already slowly peeling his jacket off. Alzire caught her mother's eye and took Lénore and Henri to play outside. Father didn't like getting washed in the tub surrounded by the rest of the family, although lots of the other men in the village didn't mind. Not that he had anything against it, he just said that it was all right by him if the children wanted to splash around together.

'What are you doing up there?' La Maheude shouted upstairs.

'I'm mending my dress, I tore it yesterday,' Catherine answered.

'That's all right . . . Don't come down, your father's getting washed.'

So Maheu and his wife were alone. She had decided to put Estelle down on a chair, and by some miracle the baby was pleased to be by the fireside, and didn't scream, but merely turned her mindless little infant eyes towards her parents. Maheu squatted quite naked in front of the tub, dipping his head in first, when he had finished scrubbing it with the black soap whose constant use from generation to generation turns the hair of a whole race of miners into a discoloured, yellow thatch. Then he got into the water, smeared soap over his chest and stomach, arms and thighs, and scrubbed away energetically with both hands. His wife stood watching him.

'You know,' she started, 'I saw the look on your face when you came in . . . You were worried, weren't you? You weren't half relieved when you saw the groceries . . . Can you believe it, the bourgeois at La Piolaine wouldn't cough up a single sou. Oh, they were kind enough, they've given us clothes for the little ones, and I felt too ashamed to ask for money, the words just stick in my throat.'

She broke off for a moment, to wedge Estelle more securely in the chair, in case she fell off. Father continued to rub away at his skin, not wanting to spoil the story by asking any questions, despite his curiosity, patiently waiting to be enlightened.

'And you know Maigrat had already turned me down, point blank, just like I was a dog he was kicking out . . . Guess how cheerful I felt! Woollen clothes keep you warm, but you can't eat them, can you?'

He looked up, and still said nothing. Nothing from La Piolaine, nothing from Maigrat, so how come? But as usual she merely rolled up her sleeves, and started washing his back and the other bits that were hard to reach. Besides, he enjoyed it when she covered him in soap, and then rubbed him all over till her wrists were aching. She picked up the soap and pummelled his shoulders, while he tensed his muscles to resist the pressure.

'So, back I went to Maigrat, I told him what I thought, I really told him . . . I said he must be made of stone, and he'd come to a sticky end, if there was any justice in this world . . . He didn't like that much, he looked the other way, he would have liked to escape . . .'

She moved down the back to the buttocks; then swept onwards into the nooks and crannies, leaving not an inch of his body unscrubbed, making him shine like her three saucepans when she did her Saturday spring cleaning. But she got terribly hot and sweaty from lathering away with her arms, all shaken and breathless, so that her words came out in fits and starts.

'Anyway, he called me an old leech . . . We've got enough bread to last till Saturday, and best of all, he lent me a hundred sous . . . I got the butter and the coffee and the chicory from him, and I was even going to get the cold meat and the potatoes, but I saw he was getting annoyed . . . Seven sous for the brawn, and eighteen for the potatoes, so I've got three francs seventy-five left over for a stew and some boiled beef . . . Well, I didn't waste my day, did I?'

Then she wiped him dry, patting away with a towel at the places which stayed obstinately wet. He was enjoying this, and, without stopping to worry about the extra debt they were laying up for the morrow, burst out laughing and grabbed her in his arms.

'Let me go, you big silly! You're soaking, you're getting me wet . . . The only thing is, I hope Maigrat hasn't got the wrong idea . . .'

She was going to mention Catherine, but she stopped. Why bother Father with it? She'd never hear the end of it.

'What idea?' he asked.

'Like taking us for a ride, of course! We must get Catherine to check the bill twice over.'

He grabbed hold of her again, and this time refused to let go. The bath always finished this way, she excited him with her brisk rubbing, then by patting him all over with towels, which tickled the hairs on his arms and his chest. In fact this was the time when his workmates in the village usually started fooling around, only to find themselves fathering more children than they intended. At night you had the whole family under your feet. He pushed her towards the table, teasing her, he'd been waiting all day for a nice bit of pudding, as he called it, and a free helping at that. And she pretended to struggle, all part of the game, with her stomach and her breasts softly heaving.

'For heaven's sake, what a silly! With Estelle watching us! Wait till I turn her head the other way.'

'Oh, heavens, do you think they know what's going on at three months old?'

When they had finished, Maheu simply put on some dry breeches. His little treat, when he was nice and clean and had had his bit of fun with his wife, was to leave his chest bare for a while. His pale skin, as white as that of an anaemic girl, was covered in tattoo marks scraped and scored by the coal, 'cuttings', as the miners call them; and he displayed them proudly, flexing his strong arms and broad chest, which gleamed like blue-veined marble. In summer, all the miners sat out on their doorsteps like this. Despite the day's wet weather, he even went outside for a moment, to exchange ribald remarks with another bare-chested neighbour, on the other side of the gardens. Other men came out too. And the children, who had been playing on the pavements, looked up, and laughed with pleasure at the sight of all this tired flesh released from work and at last allowed to breathe in some fresh air.

While he was drinking his coffee, and still had no shirt on, Maheu told his wife how the engineer had got mad about the timbering. He was calm and relaxed, and he nodded his head in approval of La Maheude's wise counsel, for she was always full of good advice on these occasions. She always maintained that there was no point in butting your head up against the Company. Then she told him about Madame Hennebeau's visit. Although neither of them said so, they both felt proud of it.

'Can we come down?' asked Catherine from the top of the stairs.

'Yes, it's all right, your father's getting dried.'

Their daughter was wearing her Sunday dress, an old one made of bright blue poplin, already faded and worn at the pleats. She had put on a very plain black tulle bonnet.

'Well, you're all dressed up . . . Where are you going, then?'

'I'm going to Montsou to buy a ribbon for my bonnet . . . I've taken the old one off, it was too dirty.'

'So you've got some money, then?'

'No, but Mouquette has promised to lend me ten sous.'

Her mother let her go. But when she reached the door she called her back.

'Listen, don't go and buy your ribbon from Maigrat . . . he'll only rip you off and he'll think we're rolling in money.'

Her father, who was squatting in front of the fire to dry his neck and armpits quicker, merely added:

'And try not to be out on the streets after dark.'

That afternoon Maheu was busy in the garden. He had already sown his potatoes, beans, and peas, and the previous day he had heeled in his cabbages and lettuce plants, which he was now ready to prick out. This patch of garden kept them in vegetables, except for potatoes, which they never had enough of. In fact he was very good at growing things, and even managed to grow artichokes, which the neighbours thought he did just to show off. While Maheu was preparing his trench, Levaque came to smoke a pipe in his own patch, admiring the cos lettuce that Bouteloup had planted that morning; for without the lodger's energetic spade work, there would have been nothing growing there but nettles. And they started to chat over the fence. Levaque, refreshed and reinvigorated after beating his wife, tried in vain to persuade him to come round to Rasseneur's. Look, he wasn't afraid of a pint of beer, was he? They'd play a round of skittles, they'd stop and say hallo to their mates, then they'd come back home for dinner. That's what life was all about, after a day down the pit. Maheu wasn't saying that there was anything wrong with it, but he stuck to his guns, because if he didn't prick out his lettuces, they would be dead by the morning. But his real motive for refusing was thrift—he didn't want to have to ask his wife for as much as a farthing out of the change from the hundred sous.

The clock was striking five when La Pierronne came to see if it was Jeanlin that her Lydie had gone off with. Levaque replied that something like that must have happened, for Bébert had disappeared too, and the two ruffians were always up to their tricks together. When Maheu had calmed them down, explaining about the dandelion salad, he and his mate started to taunt the young woman, with good-humoured coarseness. She protested, but didn't depart, for she was secretly excited by their rude language, although it had her gasping for breath and screaming for mercy. She soon received succour in the shape of a thin woman, stammering with fury like a clucking hen. Other women, further down the street, came to their doors and shouted out protests in sympathy. Now school was over, and all the brats were wandering around, there was a swarm of little creatures tumbling about, whining and fighting; while the fathers who hadn't gone to the pub formed little groups of three or four, found a wall to shelter behind, squatted down on their heels as if they were at the bottom of the mine, and stayed there smoking their pipes, exchanging only the occasional word. La Pierronne departed in a fury, after Levaque had tried to pinch her thighs to see if the flesh was firm; and he decided to go off to Rasseneur's on his own, since Maheu was still planting away.

The day suddenly drew in, and La Maheude lit the lamp, annoyed that neither her daughter nor her boys had returned. She might have bet on it: you could never get them together for the one meal where she could have had everyone round the same table. And then she was waiting for the dandelion leaves, too. How could he be picking anything at this time of night, it was black as pitch, the stupid little brat! The salad would have gone so well with the *ratatouille* that she had put to simmer on the stove, made of potatoes, leeks, and sorrel chopped up with fried onion! The whole house wallowed in the rich smell of fried onion, which soon turns rancid, impregnating the bricks of the village with noxious vapours so strong that your nostrils are assailed by the violent odour of this poor man's cuisine from miles away across the country.

Maheu left the garden as night was falling. He slumped down into a chair straight away, resting his head against the wall. As soon as he sat down in the evening he fell asleep. The cuckoo clock struck seven, Henri and Lénore had just broken a plate through insisting on helping Alzire lay the table, when old Bonnemort arrived back first, in a hurry to have his dinner and return to the pit. So La Maheude woke Maheu.

'Oh well, let's eat, what the hell . . . They're old enough to find their way back home. But it's a shame about the salad.'

CHAPTER V

AT Rasseneur's, Étienne had eaten his soup and gone upstairs to the narrow attic bedroom, overlooking Le Voreux, which was going to be his home. He had fallen on to his bed fully clothed, numb with fatigue. He had not slept more than four hours in the past two days. When he awoke, night was falling, and for a moment he lay dazed, not recognizing where he was; he felt so dizzy, and his head seemed so heavy, that he had to force himself to struggle to his feet, feeling he ought to go out and get some fresh air before having dinner and retiring for the night.

Outside the weather had become milder and milder, the sooty sky was turning a copper colour, and lowering with the threat of one of those endless falls of rain that the Nord is known for, and whose imminent arrival you could sense in the warm, damp air. The darkness swept down, drowning the furthest points of the plain in great misty swathes. Over this huge sea of reddish earth, the low sky seemed to be dissolving into black dust, with not a breath of air left to enliven the darkness. The whole scene was as sad, wan, and lifeless as the grave.

Étienne set off walking nowhere in particular, with no thought in mind other than shaking off his feverish headache. When he reached Le Voreux, already difficult to distinguish in its murky lair, especially since none of the lanterns had yet been lit, he stopped for a moment, to watch the workers from the day shift emerge. It must have just struck six o'clock, for whole groups of labourers, onsetters, and stablemen were leaving, mingling with the blurred figures of the sorting girls, who could be heard laughing in the shadows.

First came old Ma Brûlé and her son-in-law Pierron. She was scolding him because he had not supported her in a dispute with one of the supervisors over her tally of stones.

'Oh, you weak-kneed weed! How can you call yourself a man if you bow and scrape to one of those bastards who bleed us to death!'

Pierron followed her quietly without answering. Finally he said:

'So I suppose I was meant to jump at the boss and hit him. Thanks a lot, for all the good that would do us!'

'Well, bend over and offer him your arse then!' she shouted. 'God! If my daughter had only listened to me ... It's not enough for them to have killed her father, perhaps you expect me to thank them as well. No, you listen to me, I'll have their guts in the end!'

Their voices faded away, and Étienne watched her disappear, with her aquiline nose and straggling white hair, and her long, thin arms flailing wildly. But he pricked up his ears at the conversation of two young lads behind him. He had recognized the voice of Zacharie, who had been waiting there, and had just been hailed by his friend Mouquet.

'Are you coming?' asked Mouquet. 'We're going to get a slice of bread, then we're off to the Volcan.'

'Not yet, I'm busy.'

'Doing what?'

The labourer turned round and saw Philomène coming out of the screening shed. He thought he understood.

'Oh, I see ... Okay, I'll go on ahead.'

'Yes, I'll catch you up.'

As Mouquet went off, he met his father, old Mouque, who

was also leaving Le Voreux; the two men simply said good-night to each other, and the son took the high road while his father went down by the canal.

Zacharie had already dragged Philomène down the same, lonely path, despite her reluctance. She was in a hurry, next time maybe; and they argued together like an old married couple. It wasn't much fun only ever seeing each other out-doors, especially in the winter, when the ground is wet and there isn't even any wheat in the fields to bed down in.

'No, it's not for that,' he muttered impatiently. 'There's something I want to tell you.'

He put an arm round her waist, and led her gently along with him. Then, when they were in the shadow of the slag-heap, he asked her if she had any money.

'What for?' she asked.

Then he launched into a confused story about a debt of two francs which would be the ruin of his family.

'Get lost! . . . I saw Mouquet, you're off to the Volcan again, where they have those dirty chorus girls.'

He denied the charge, crossing his heart and giving his word of honour. But then, when she shrugged her shoulders, he suddenly said:

'You can come with us, if you like . . . you can see I've got nothing to hide. What would I want a chorus girl for? . . . D'you want to come?'

'What about the baby?' she replied. 'How can I go anywhere with a baby crying all the time . . . Let me go back, I bet they're rowing at home.'

But he caught hold of her, and pleaded with her. Come on, it was so as not to look silly in front of Mouquet, he had promised him. A man couldn't go to bed early every night like a rooster. She gave in, and turned up one of the flaps of her jacket, snapped the thread with her nail and pulled out several ten-sou pieces from under the hem. She was afraid of being robbed by her mother, so she hid there what she earned from overtime at the pit.

'Look, I've got five,' she said. 'I can give you three, if you like . . . But you must promise me you'll persuade your mother to let us get married. I've had enough of this life of hanging around waiting! And even then my Mum counts the cost of every mouthful of food that I swallow ... Swear you will, then you can have it.'

She was a sickly, gangling, apathetic girl, who spoke in lifeless tones. She was fed up with the life she was leading. He swore blind that it was a promise, honest to God; then, when he had the three coins safely in his hand, he kissed her and tickled her, making her laugh, and he would have gone all the way there and then, up against the side of the slag-heap that had become a familiar winter bedroom for the jaded couple, if she hadn't kept saying no, for it wouldn't give her the slightest pleasure. She went back to the village on her own, while he cut across the fields, to catch up with his mate.

Étienne had been following them absent-mindedly at a distance without understanding, thinking that it was an ordinary date. The pit girls were precocious; and he remembered the working girls at Lille that he used to meet behind the factories, those gangs of immoral fourteen-year-olds, whom poverty had already corrupted. But he was more surprised by the next encounter he made. He stopped dead.

There, at the bottom of the slag-heap, in a hollow between some large fallen rocks, was Jeanlin, roughly berating Lydie and Bébert, who were seated on either side of him.

'Hey? What did you say? ... You'll both get a smack in the eye if you argue ... Whose idea was it, anyway?'

And Jeanlin had indeed had an idea. After spending an hour wandering along the canal and wading into the meadows gathering dandelion leaves with the two others, he had just realized, when sizing up the mass of greenery, that they'd never get through all that salad at home; so, instead of going back to the village, he had gone to Montsou, taking Bébert to keep watch, and sending Lydie in to ring on the doors of the posh houses, to sell them the dandelion leaves. Armed with experience beyond his years, he argued that girls could sell whatever they wanted. They had got so carried away by the excitement of the trade that they had sold the whole lot, but the girl had made eleven sous. And now that they had disposed of the goods, the three of them were splitting the proceeds.

'It's not fair!' said Bébert. 'You should divide it by three ... If you keep seven sous, we'll only get two each.'

'Why's that unfair?' Jeanlin replied angrily. 'I picked more
than you did, for a start.'

Usually Bébert submitted, from fear and admiration, with
the credulity of the born victim. Although he was older, and
stronger, he would even let Jeanlin punch him. But this time,
the thought of all that money inspired him to resist.

'It's true, isn't it, Lydie, he's robbing us ... if he doesn't
share it out, we'll tell his mother.'

At that Jeanlin brandished his fist under his nose.

'Just you dare. I'll go and say that you were the one who
sold our mum's salad ... And besides, you bloody fool, how
the hell can I divide eleven sous by three? Why don't you try
it yourself, mastermind ... There's your two sous each. Hurry
up and take them before I put them back in my pocket.'

Bébert admitted defeat and accepted his two sous. Lydie
was trembling and hadn't said anything, for in the presence of
Jeanlin she felt the fear and affection of a beaten child bride.
As he held out the two sous to her, she put out her hand with
a submissive smile. But he suddenly changed his mind.

'Hey? what the hell would you do with all that money
anyway? ... Your mother's bound to pinch it, if you've got
nowhere to hide it ... I'd better keep it for you. When you
need some money, just come and ask me for it.'

And the nine sous disappeared again. To stifle her protests
he jumped on her, laughing and rolling over with her on the
slag-heap. She was his little wife, and they got together in dark
corners to try out the love that they heard going on at home
behind walls, or saw happening through keyholes. They knew
all about it, but they were too young to manage, so they would
spend hours fumbling and tumbling, playing like a pair of
naughty puppies. He called it 'playing mums and dads'; and
where he led, she eagerly followed, letting him grab her with a
deliciously instinctive thrill. She often got angry with him but
she always gave way, hoping for something exciting which
never happened.

As Bébert wasn't allowed in on these games, and got
thumped black and blue any time he tried to have a turn with
Lydie, he would stand awkwardly by, torn between anger and
embarrassment, while the two others amused themselves, which

they often did quite openly in his presence. So his only hope was to frighten and interrupt them by shouting out that someone was watching.

'The game's up, there's a bloke watching!'

This time he was not making it up, there was someone coming, as Étienne had decided to walk on further. The children leapt up out of his way and ran out of sight as he walked past the slag-heap, following the canal, amused at giving the rascals such a fright. Well, obviously they were too young; but what of it? They saw such goings-on and heard such rude stories that you would have had to clap them in irons if you wanted to stop them trying. But deep down inside, Étienne felt a twinge of sadness.

A hundred paces further down the road, he came across some more couples. He had arrived at Réquillart, which was where all the girls from Montsou came with their lovers to haunt the ruins of the disused pit. This distant and deserted spot was the common meeting-place, where the tram girls came to contract their first babies, when they were afraid of being seen at the local hutch. Anyone could get through the broken fences into the old yard, which had become a waste-land, littered with the debris of the two sheds which had collapsed, and with the skeletons of some of the pylons from the overhead railway that were still standing. There were broken tubs scattered around, and old timbers lay rotting in stacks; while nature was vigorously reclaiming its rights to colonize this plot of land, covering it with thick grass and riddling it with sturdy, thrusting young trees. So every girl could make herself a little nest here, for there was a hideaway suitable for every one of them: their sweethearts could lay them flat on their arses on piles of beams, or behind stacks of timber, or inside the tubs. They all settled down side by side without worrying about the couple in the slot next door, even though they were near enough to touch. And the result was that all round this lifeless machinery, in the shadow of the pit which had grown weary of spewing forth coal, creation was exacting its revenge, in the form of a free love spurred on by wild instinct, which sowed babies in the bellies of these girls who were still hardly women.

Yet there was a watchman on the premises, old Mouque, who had been given two rooms by the Company, situated almost directly beneath the dilapidated headgear, whose last remaining beams threatened to fall on his head from one moment to the next. He had even had to prop up part of the ceiling; and yet he lived there very comfortably with his family; himself and Mouquet in one room, La Mouquette in the other. As there wasn't a single pane of glass left in the windows, he had taken a hammer and nails and boarded them up solid: you couldn't see your hand in front of your face, but it did keep the place warm. Meanwhile, despite being called a watchman he didn't watch a thing, because he went off to Le Voreux to look after his horses, and took no interest in the ruins of Réquillart, whose only going concern was the shaft, which they used as a chimney for a single furnace which drove the ventilation pump for the neighbouring pit.

And thus it came to pass that old Mouque spent his old age surrounded by lovers. Ever since she had turned ten, La Mouquette had been hoisting her skirts in every corner of the ruins, not with nervous and immature insolence like Lydie, but from a precociously voluptuous disposition, able to satisfy lads whose beards had already started growing. Her father had no cause to object, for she showed due respect, and never brought her sweethearts home. And then again, he knew all about life's little incidents. Whenever he went off to Le Voreux, and whenever he returned, every time that he ventured out of his den, he could hardly take a step without stumbling upon some couple lying in the grass; and it was even worse if he went to gather firewood to heat his soup, or to look for burdock for his rabbit at the other end of the mine: then he espied all the young girls of Montsou taking it in turns to raise their lips hungrily towards the heavens, and he had to be careful not to trip over their legs, stretched right out over the pathway. Besides, after a while these encounters had finally ceased disturbing any of the parties concerned, neither old Mouque, whose main concern was to avoid tripping over, nor the girls, whom he left to bring their business to a peaceful conclusion, as he continued gently on his way like a nature-lover anxious not to disturb the wild-life. The only thing was that just as they had now got used to his comings and goings, so he had come to recognize them, just as you get to know the shameless magpies whose frolics play havoc with the pear trees at the bottom of your garden. How greedy were the young, oh, how they clutched and sucked at life! Sometimes he shook his head, his chin trembling in silent regret, turning away from the noisy hussies who were panting too loudly in the darkness. Only one thing upset him: two lovers had developed the bad habit of embracing right up against his bedroom wall. Not that it kept him awake at nights, of course, but they went at it so hard that in the long run they were damaging the wall.

Every evening old Mouque entertained his friend old Bonne-mort, who regularly took the same walk before dinner. The two cronies hardly exchanged more than a dozen words during the half-hour that they spent together. But it cheered them up to be together chewing over old times without needing to talk. At Réquillart they sat down on a beam side by side, let slip a word from time to time, then went off into their daydreaming, staring at the ground. No doubt they were reliving their youth. All around them there were lovers bedding their loved ones, in a flurry of whispered laughs and kisses, and a warm scent of girls' flesh rose from the depths of the cool, crushed grass. It was forty-three years now, since Bonnemort had gone behind the pit to take his wife, a tram girl so small and frail that he had to lift her up on to a tub to kiss her in comfort. Ah, those were the days! And the two old men, nodding their heads, finally left for the night, often without even saying good-night.

But that evening, just as Étienne was approaching, old Bonnemort happened to be getting up off his beam to go back to the village, and saying to Mouque:

'Good-night, me old mate! . . . Hey, look, did you ever get to know a girl called La Roussie?'

Mouque stayed silent for a moment, shrugging his shoulders, then replied, as he went back indoors:

'Good-night, good-night, mate!'

Étienne came and sat down on the beam that they had just left. He felt even more miserable than before, without under-standing why. Watching the old man's back disappear had reminded him of his arrival that morning, the flood of words that the tormenting wind had wrung from that taciturn fellow. All that suffering! and all those girls, dropping with tiredness, who were still stupid enough to go off in the evening and produce babies, more flesh fit only for toil and suffering! There would never be an end to it all, if they kept on filling themselves up with an endless supply of newborn starvelings. Wouldn't they do better to plug up their bellies and keep their legs tightly crossed, battening down the hatches in the face of disaster? Or perhaps he was only mulling over these melancholy thoughts because he was upset at his loneliness, while everyone else at this hour was pairing off in search of pleasure. The muggy weather made him feel rather stifled, and a few scattered drops of rain started to fall on his hot, sweaty hands. Yes, all the girls succumbed, it was a force stronger than reason.

And in fact, while Étienne was sitting motionless in the shadows, a couple who had come down from Montsou brushed past him without noticing him, and walked on to the waste ground at Réquillart. The girl, who was obviously a virgin, was struggling, and resisted with a quiet, pleading voice; but the young man took no notice and silently pushed her over to a dark corner of one of the sheds that was still standing, where there was a pile of mouldy old rope. It was Catherine and big tall Chaval. But Étienne had not recognized them as they went past, and he watched the story unfold, gripped by a sensual excitement which coloured his thoughts. Why should he intervene? When girls say no, it's only because they fancy a fight before they agree to say yes.

On leaving village Two Hundred and Forty, Catherine had taken the main road towards Montsou. Ever since she had turned ten and started earning her living at the pit, she had walked all round the country by herself, left in total freedom as everyone in a miner's family was; and if she had reached the age of fifteen without a man laying hands on her, it was because of her retarded puberty, which showed no signs of coming. When she got to the Company's yards, she crossed the road and went into a laundry where she was sure she would find La Mouquette; for she spent half her life there, with women who took it in turns to stand each other rounds of coffee from morning to night. But Catherine was disappointed, for it so happened that La Mouquette had just paid for a round herself, so she couldn't lend her the ten sous she had promised. To console her, they offered her a glass of hot coffee. She wouldn't even let her friend borrow the money off one of the other women. She had a sudden urge to economize, a sort of superstitious fear, making her feel sure that, if she insisted on buying the ribbon now, it would bring her bad luck.

She hurried to take the road back to the village, and had reached the last houses of Montsou when a man called out to her from the doorway of Piquette's*.

'Hey, Catherine, where are you off to so fast?'

It was big tall Chaval. She was annoyed, not because she didn't like him, but because she didn't feel in the mood for a laugh.

'Come in and have something to drink . . . A little glass of sweet wine, if you like.'

She refused, courteously: night was falling, and they were expecting her at home. But he came out of the tavern, and pleaded with her under his breath in the middle of the road. He had been laying plans for some time now to persuade her to come and see the room he lived in on the first floor of Piquette's; it was a lovely room with a nice wide bed, just right for two. Was she afraid of him, then, was that why she kept on rejecting him? She laughed good-naturedly, and said she'd go upstairs with him the week that children stopped growing. Then one thing led to another, and without quite knowing how, she got round to mentioning the blue ribbon which she hadn't been able to buy.

'But why don't I buy you one?' he cried.

She blushed, for she felt that she really ought to keep on refusing, but she was racked by a secret urge to possess that ribbon. The idea of a loan came to her mind again, and she finally accepted his offer, on condition that she paid him back whatever he spent on her. That led to another exchange of pleasantries: and they agreed that if she didn't sleep with him, she would give him his money back. But there was another problem, when he spoke of going to Maigrat's.

'No, not Maigrat's, Mum told me I mustn't.'

'Don't worry, there's no need to say where we went! . . . He's got the nicest ribbons in Montsou!'

When Maigrat saw Catherine and big tall Chaval enter his shop like a loving couple choosing their wedding present, he went bright red, and showed his pieces of blue ribbon with the fury of a man who feels he is being made a laughing stock. Then, when he had served the young couple, he went out and stood rooted to the doorstep of his shop, watching them move off into the twilight; and, when his wife came to ask a timid question, he fell upon her, and swore at her, crying that he'd make the bastards sorry one day for showing no gratitude when they should be grovelling at his feet and licking his boots.

Walking along the road big tall Chaval kept Catherine company. He walked alongside her, swinging his arms; but he nudged her hips and casually guided her in the direction he intended. Suddenly she realized that he had led her off the cobbled road and that they were walking down the narrow path to Réquillart together. But she didn't have time to get angry: he already had his arm round her waist and he dazed her with a continuous patter of soothing words. Wasn't she silly to be afraid! Would anyone want to harm a sweet little thing like her, as soft as silk, tender enough to eat? And he breathed on her neck behind her ear, which made a thrill pass over her skin all down her body. She was choking with emotion and found nothing to say. It was true that he seemed to love her. Saturday evening, after she had put the candle out, she had asked herself precisely this question, what would happen if he took her like that; then as she fell asleep, she had dreamed that she stopped saying no, as her courage was overwhelmed by her pleasure. Why then did she feel repelled or even saddened by the same idea today? While he was tickling her neck with his moustache, so gently that she closed her eyes, the silhouette of another man, the lad she had seen that morning, went past her closed eyes in the darkness.

Suddenly Catherine looked around and realized that Chaval had led her into the ruins of Réquillart, and she started back with a shiver from the shadows of the dilapidated shed.

'Oh, no! Oh, no!' she murmured, 'please leave me alone.'

She panicked, with that instinctive fear of the male that stiffens a girl's muscles in self-defence even when she is willing, as she feels the man's triumphal approach. Her virginity was not based on ignorance, but she was still as terrified as if she had been threatened with a beating, faced with the wound whose unknown pain she dreaded.

'No, no, I don't want to! You know I'm too young ... It's true! Wait till later on, at least till I'm grown up.'

He growled under his breath:

'Silly! that means there's no danger ... Why should you worry?'

Then he stopped talking. He grabbed hold of her firmly, and thrust her into the shed. And she fell backwards on to the pile of old rope, stopped resisting, and, although her body wasn't ready, she let the male have his way with her, with the hereditary submissiveness that sent all the girls of her race rolling flat on their backs while they were little more than children. Her terrified stammerings died away, and nothing could be heard except the man's fierce breathing.

Meanwhile Étienne had been listening motionless. Another one taking the plunge! And now that he had finished watching the show, he got up, filled with an awkward feeling of mounting anger and a kind of jealous excitement. He stopped trying to be tactful, and walked right across the beams, for the pair were far too busy by now to take any notice of him. So he was surprised when he had walked about a hundred paces down the road to look round and see that they were already on their feet again, and that they seemed to be following the same path as him back down to the village. The man had taken hold of the girl's waist again, squeezing her with a grateful air, and talking with his face nuzzling her neck; and she was the one who seemed impatient to get back home quickly, looking as if she were more worried about being late than about anything else.

Then Étienne was tormented by a desire to see their faces. It was a stupid whim, and he quickened his stride so as not to give in to it. But his feet slowed down all by themselves, and as soon as he reached the first street lamp, he stopped and hid in the shadows. He was rooted to the spot with stupefaction when he recognized Catherine and big tall Chaval as they walked past. At first he could hardly believe his eyes, could it really be her, that young lady wearing a bonnet and a bright blue dress? Was that the urchin he had seen in breeches, with a cotton cap pulled down over her ears? That explained how she had managed to brush past him without him guessing who she was. But he could doubt it no longer, as soon as he recognized the limpid green tint of her eyes, as clear and deep as water from a spring. What a whore! and he felt an irrational contempt for her, together with a furious desire to get his revenge. Besides, it didn't suit her to be got up as a girl: she looked awful.

Slowly, Catherine and Chaval went past, with no idea that they were being spied on, and he held her back to kiss her behind the ear, while she started to slow down as he caressed her, for it made her laugh. Since he had hung back, Étienne was now obliged to follow them, but he was annoyed to realize that they were blocking his path, and forcing him to see things that tried his patience. So it was true, what she had sworn to him that morning: she had never been anyone's mistress; and to think he hadn't believed her, that he had even resisted her so as not to act like the other fellow! And that he had let her be snatched away from him right under his nose, that of all the damn fool things to do he had enjoyed getting into a lecherous mood over watching them! That made him feel mad, and he clenched his fists, he would have torn the man to shreds if he'd got into one of his blind, murderous rages.

The promenade lasted for another half an hour. As Chaval and Catherine approached Le Voreux, they walked even slower; stopping twice on the banks of the canal and three times on the side of the slag-heap, for they had become very gay, and were amusing themselves with tender little games. Étienne had to stop each time too and await their pleasure, for fear of being seen. He tried to feel only a crude disappointment: this would teach him to respect girls and act politely! Then, when they had left Le Voreux, and he was at last free to go and dine at Rasseneur's, he continued to follow in their footsteps as far as the village, and stayed standing in the shadows there for a quarter of an hour waiting for Chaval to let Catherine go home. Then, when he was sure that they were no longer together, he set off again, and walked a long way out over the road to Marchiennes, tramping along mindlessly, too choked with sadness to go and shut himself up in his room.

Not until an hour later, towards nine o'clock, did Étienne come back through the village, realizing that he must eat and go to bed, if he wanted to be up again at four in the morning. The village was already asleep, and plunged in darkness. There was not a single ray of light to be seen through the closed shutters, and the long terraces stretched away in front of him, as heavy with sleep as a barracks full of snoring soldiers. A solitary cat emerged, and fled across the empty gardens. It was the end of the day, and the workers fell heavily from table to bed, crushed with fatigue and full of food.

Back at Rasseneur's there was still a light on in the bar, where a mechanic and two day-shift workers were drinking pints. But before he went in, Étienne stopped, and cast a last look into the gathering night. He discovered the same fathomless darkness as that morning, when he had arrived in the middle of a gale. In front of him lay Le Voreux, crouching like some evil beast, its shape unclear, except where it was picked out here and there by the gleam of a lantern. The three braziers at the slag-heap were burning in mid-air, like bleeding moons, episodically projecting the gigantic shadows of old Bonnemort and his straw-coloured pony. And further away the shadows had engulfed everything all over the flat plain—Montsou, Marchiennes, the forest of Vandame, the great ocean of wheat and sugar-beet, where the only lights, gleaming like beams from distant lighthouses, were blue flames from the blast-furnaces and red flames from the coke ovens. Gradually everything became drowned in darkness, as the rain started falling, slowly and persistently, swamping the empty space with its monotonous drizzle; while only one voice could still be heard, the heavy, slow wheezing of the drainage pump, panting away day after day and night after night.

PART III

PART III

CHAPTER I

THE next day, and the following days, Étienne went back to his work at the pit. He got used to it, and his life became attuned to the rhythms of the new tasks and habits which he had found so hard at first. Only one incident interrupted the monotony of the first fortnight, a passing attack of fever which kept him in bed for forty-eight hours, with his limbs aching and his head burning, daydreaming in a state of near delirium that he was pushing his tub down a passage too narrow for his body to pass. But it was merely beginner's cramp, an excess of fatigue which he soon shook off.

And one day started to feel like the next, and weeks, and then months, went by. Now, like his mates, he rose at three in the morning, drank his coffee, and picked up the sandwich that Madame Rasseneur had prepared for him the night before. On his way to the pit he regularly met old Bonnemort on his way home to bed, and when he came back out again in the afternoon, he passed Bouteloup going the other way to clock on for his shift. Dressed in his cap, his breeches, and his cotton jacket, he was shivering when he arrived at the shed, and went to warm his back at the great open fire. Then he had to wait barefoot in the entrance hall, with all its icy draughts. But the engine, whose great steel limbs in their copper casing gleamed high above him in the shadows, had lost its fascination for him, as had the cables, swooping silently past like the black wings of some nocturnal bird of prey, and the cages rising and falling amid the chaos of signals ringing, orders shouted, and tubs shaking the iron flooring. His lamp was not burning properly, the damn lamp keeper must have forgotten to clean it; and he only started to unwind when Mouquet piled them all in, dealing great theatrical smacks to the girls' behinds. The cage was released, and it fell like a stone down a well, without Étienne even bothering to turn his head to watch the daylight disappear. He never dreamed of the likelihood of an accident, and the deeper he plunged down into the darkness and the driving spray the more he felt at home. At the pit bottom, at the loading bay, when Pierron had let them out with his hypocritically submissive air, they would mill around like a herd of animals, as each team shuffled slowly off to its own coal-face. Now Étienne, too, knew the passages of the mine better than the streets of Montsou, knew that you had to turn here, duck down later on, avoid a puddle somewhere else. He had got so used to his two-kilometre walk underground that he could have done it in the dark with his hands in his pockets. And each time there were the same encounters, a deputy turning his lamp on the workmen's faces as they went by, old Mouque bringing up a horse, Bébert driving Bataille snorting onwards, Jeanlin running along behind the train to close the ventilation doors, and fat Mouquette and skinny Lydie pushing their tubs.

In the end, Étienne also found the dampness and the suffocating lack of air at the coal-face much less oppressive. The chimney seemed easy to climb, as if he had shrunk, and could pass through crannies where he wouldn't have dared venture an arm earlier on. He breathed in the coal-dust without feeling sick, saw clearly in the dark, and sweated freely, now that he had got used to the feeling of having his body draped in soaking garments from morning to night. Besides, he no longer clumsily wasted his energy, now that he had acquired the necessary skills with a flair that astonished the whole team. After three weeks, he was mentioned as one of the pit's really good trammers: no one rolled his tub up to the incline more quickly, nor loaded it afterwards more carefully. His slim build enabled him to get past any obstacle, and although his arms were as thin and white as a woman's, they seemed to be made of iron beneath their delicate skin, so hardened were they to their task. He never complained even when dropping with fatigue, doubtless because he was too proud. The only fault they reproached him with was being unable to take a joke, and quick to lose his temper if someone tried to pick on him. All in all, he was accepted and considered as a real miner, as he yielded to the crushing force of habit which reduced him a little more each day to the status of a machine.

It was Maheu in particular who felt drawn to Étienne, for

he respected a job well done. And also, just like the others, he sensed that the lad was better educated than he himself was: he saw him reading and writing, or sketching little plans, and heard him discussing things which he didn't even know existed. He was not surprised at this, colliers are simple folk with bonier skulls than mechanics; but he was impressed by the guts of this little chap, with his plucky decision to have a bash at the coal rather than let himself die of hunger. Étienne was the first casual worker he had seen settle in so quickly. So when Maheu was behind with production and didn't want to interrupt any of the hewers, he entrusted the young man with the timbering, certain that his work would be carefully and reliably accomplished. The bosses were still pestering him over the question of the props, and he was afraid at every moment that Négrel, the engineer, would appear, with Dansaert in tow, shouting, arguing, and ordering them to start all over again; and he had noticed that his new trammer's timbering seemed to satisfy these gentlemen better, although they were careful never to show their approval, and kept repeating that one of these days the Company was going to do something drastic about it. Things dragged on like this, breeding sullen resentment throughout the mine, to such an extent that even Maheu, despite his easygoing nature, felt that he was ready for a fight.

At first there had been rivalry between Zacharie and Étienne. One evening they had threatened to come to blows. But Zacharie, who was an uncomplicated fellow, loath to cause himself unnecessary displeasure, was rapidly soothed by the friendly offer of a drink, and soon bowed to the newcomer's superiority. Levaque had decided to make the best of things now, and he got to talking politics with the trammer, who knew his own mind, he said. And of all the men in his team, the only one that Étienne felt still harboured some secret resentment was big tall Chaval; not that they openly snubbed each other, on the contrary, they had become mates; but all the same, even when they were joking together, they couldn't help exchanging hostile glances. Caught between the two of them, Catherine had relapsed into her routine, bending down to push her tub in a posture of tired and resigned female compliance, although she was always considerate towards her new workmate, who helped her in his turn; but she was submissive to the will of her lover, and openly welcomed his caresses. It was an accepted situation, an official couple to which even her family turned a blind eye, so much so that every evening Chaval took the tram girl off to the slag-heap, then brought her back to her parents' door, where he kissed her good-night in front of the whole village.

Étienne, who thought he had come to terms with this, often teased her about these walks, joking in the same crude language that all the lads and girls use down the mine; and she would reply in the same vein, telling him brazenly what her lover had got up to with her; she faltered and turned pale, however, when her eyes met those of her young companion. Then they would both avert their gaze, and sometimes went for an hour without talking to each other, as if they hated each other for reasons confused and untold.

Spring came. One day as he left the pit Étienne felt a sudden gust of April warmth, the wholesome scent of new growth, green shoots, and draughts of fresh air; and now each time he left the pit spring felt warmer and smelled sweeter, after his ten hours' work in the eternal winter of the pit bottom, surrounded by clouds of darkness that no summer ever dispersed. The days grew steadily longer, and by May when he went down in the morning the sun was starting to rise, as the ruby-red sky bathed Le Voreux in its dusty, dawn light, which made all the white steam rising from the pumping machines turn pink. He no longer shivered, now that warm breezes wafted in from the far reaches of the plain, and high over his head skylarks sang. Then at three o'clock he was dazzled by the blazing sunshine, which set the horizon alight and turned the bricks flaming red beneath their thick layer of soot. By June the wheat was already high, its blue-green tones contrasting with the blacker green of the beet. It was an uncharted sea, which rippled with every breeze, and seemed to rise and spread more each day; sometimes he found to his surprise that it had apparently grown fuller and greener be-tween the morning and the evening of a single day. The poplars along the canal grew plumes of leaves. Weeds invaded the slag-heap, flowers carpeted the meadows, in short, life was on the move, sprouting out of the same earth that weighed him down with fatigue and suffering as he toiled beneath it.

When Étienne went out for his evening stroll now, he no longer disturbed any lovers behind the slag-heap. He followed their tracks through the wheatfields, and guessed where the love-birds had made their nests from the movements of the tall red poppies and the ears of wheat, which were starting to turn yellow. Zacharie and Philomène went there as part of their long-familiar marital routine; old Ma Brûlé was always on the war-path after Lydie, and was constantly starting her out of the hides where she was so deeply ensconced with Jeanlin that it was only if you tripped over them that they were forced to take flight; and as for La Mouquette, she made her bed left, right, and centre, you couldn't cross a single field without seeing her take a header, as she threw herself down on the ground and lifted her legs up in the air. But they all had every right to do as they pleased, and Étienne only took offence on the evenings that he met Catherine and Chaval.

Twice he saw them founder suddenly out of sight in the middle of a field as he approached, and the sea of stalks close over them, silent as the grave. Another time, as he was going down a narrow path, he saw Catherine's crystal-clear eyes rise a moment above the level of the wheat, and quickly sink out of sight again. In the end the vast plain seemed too small for him, and he preferred to spend the evening with Rasseneur at the Avantage.

'Madame Rasseneur, give me a pint . . . no, I won't go out tonight, my legs are like jelly.'

And he turned to talk to one of his mates, who was sitting in his usual place at a table at the back of the room, leaning his head against the wall.

'Souvarine,* won't you have a pint?'

'No thanks, nothing at all.'

Étienne had got to know Souvarine from living alongside him. He was a mechanic from Le Voreux, who lived on the top floor in the furnished room next to his. He looked about thirty; he was slim and fair-skinned, with fine features framed by long hair and a slight beard. His sharp, white teeth, delicate nose and mouth, and pink complexion gave him a girlish air, an appearance of unshakeable gentleness, although this could on occasion be turned fierce by a sudden flash from his steely grey eyes. In his poor working man's room, he had no possessions except a box full of books and papers. He was Russian, but never spoke of himself, although he let people spread rumours about him. The colliers, who were very suspicious of foreigners, and guessed from his small, delicate hands that he was from a different class, had at first suspected some scandal, perhaps that he was a murderer on the run from justice. But when they saw how brotherly and warm and humble he was towards them, and how he turned out his pockets and gave all his change to the kids in the village, they came to accept him, and were further reassured by the rumour that he was a political refugee, a vague term that seemed to provide an excuse, even for committing a crime, and implied a fellowship of suffering.

During the first few weeks Étienne had found him implacably reserved. Thus he only discovered his story later. Souvarine was the youngest son of a noble family from the province of Tula. At St Petersburg, where he went to study medicine, the passion for socialism that fired his whole generation had inspired him to learn a trade, that of mechanic, in order to be able to mix with the people, to be able to get to know them and help them like a brother. And now he was earning his living from this skill, having fled after an abortive attempt on the life of the Tsar:* for a month he had lived in a greengrocer's cellar, digging a tunnel under the street, and priming his bombs, despite the constant risk of going up in smoke along with the whole building. Since being disinherited by his family, he had become penniless, and he had also been banned from joining any French workshops, because he was suspected of being a spy. In fact he was nearly dying of hunger when the Montsou Company had finally taken him on in a moment of labour shortage. For a year now he had been working there quietly and soberly, giving entire satisfaction, doing the day shift one week and the night shift the next, and he was so conscientious that the bosses held him up as an example.

'Don't you ever get thirsty?' Étienne asked him, laughing.

And he answered in his soft voice, with hardly any trace of an accent:

'I get thirsty when I eat.'

His friend teased him about girls, swearing that he had seen him with a tram girl in the wheatfields near Silk Stockings. But he shrugged his shoulders, indifferent and unruffled. Why should he want to do that to a tram girl? As long as she had the fraternal spirit and courage of a man, a woman was, for him, no different from a man, merely a comrade. And if not, what was the point of burdening your heart with potential betrayal? He wanted no ties, neither with women nor with friends—he felt free to do what he liked with his own life, and he wanted no new family commitments.

Every evening towards nine o'clock, when the bar started emptying, Étienne stayed on to talk to Souvarine like this. He sipped slowly at his beer, while the mechanic smoked cigarette after cigarette, staining his fine fingers the colour of tobacco. He mused on the spirals of smoke with his dreamy, mystical eyes, while he waved his left hand around nervously and incoherently, just for something to do; and in general he ended up sitting a pet rabbit on his knee, a fat mother rabbit who was always pregnant, and who had the run of the house. This rabbit, whom he had taken to calling 'Poland',* had started to love him, and she would come and sniff at his trousers, then stand up and beg, and scratch at him with her paws, until he picked her up like a child. Then she would nestle down in his lap, flatten her ears, and close her eyes; while absent-mindedly but tirelessly he stroked her silky grey fur, as if the soft warmth of this living creature brought him solace.

'You know,' said Étienne one evening, 'I had a letter from Pluchart.'*

Rasseneur was the only other person left. The last customer had gone back to the village, where everyone was going to bed.

'Oh, really?' the landlord exclaimed, walking up to his two lodgers. 'What's he up to these days?'

For two months Étienne had been corresponding regularly with the mechanic from Lille, wanting to tell him all about his job at Montsou; but Pluchart was using the correspondence to indoctrinate him, now that he saw a chance of spreading his propaganda among the mining community.

'He's doing everything he can to make sure that his

association is a great success. He's recruiting people on all fronts, so it seems.'

'And what do you think of their society?' Rasseneur asked Souvarine.

The latter, who was gently stroking Poland's head, blew out a stream of smoke, and murmured dispassionately:

'Another load of rubbish!'

But Étienne waxed lyrical. His whole rebellious temperament tempted him to embrace the struggle of labour against capital, in the first flush of his ignorant enthusiasm. It was the Workers' International Association,* the famous 'International', that had just been founded in London. Wasn't it a superb achievement, to have launched this campaign through which justice would at last triumph? With no more frontiers, the workers of the whole world would rise up and unite, to make sure that the worker kept the fruits of his labour. And what a simple but powerful organization: at the base was the section, which served the local community; then came the federation, linking the sections from within the same province; then the nation; and above it all, finally, was humanity itself, incarnated in a General Council, where each nation was represented by a corresponding secretary. In another six months they would have conquered the earth, and they would impose new laws on the bosses, if they tried to turn nasty.

'Rubbish!' Souvarine repeated. 'Your Karl Marx still believes in letting natural forces take their course. No politics, no conspiracies, am I right? Everything out in the open, and nothing to fight for but wage rises ... To hell with you and your gradual evolution! Set fire to every town and city, cut the populace to shreds, raze everything to the ground, and when there's nothing left of this whole, vile world, maybe a better one will grow up in its place.'

Étienne started laughing. He didn't always listen to his workmate's arguments, he took this theory of destruction to be a pose. Rasseneur, who was even more down to earth than Étienne, and had that fund of good sense which comes with experience, didn't even bother to take offence. He just wanted Étienne to spell out the details.

'Well, then? Are you going to try to set up a section in Montsou?'

That was what Pluchart wanted, since he was secretary of the federation of the Nord Department. He was careful to point out the services which the Association could render the miners if they were to go on strike one day. And it just so happened that Étienne thought that a strike was imminent: the argument over timbering would turn sour, and it would only need one more demand from the Company to drive all the pits to revolt.

'The real nuisance is the subscriptions,' Rasseneur declared judiciously. 'Fifty centimes a year for the general fund, two francs for the section— it may not sound much, but I bet that a lot of people will refuse to pay up.'

'Especially', said Étienne, 'since we ought first of all to set up a provident fund here, which could become a fighting fund if necessary . . . Be that as it may, it's time we started thinking about these things. I'm ready, if the others are.'

There was a silence. The oil lamp was smoking on the counter. Through the wide open doorway, you could distinctly hear the sound of a boilerman's shovel at Le Voreux loading one of the engine's furnaces.

'Everything is so expensive!' Madame Rasseneur chimed in. She had come in and had been listening disapprovingly, looming imposingly over them in her eternal black dress. 'When you think that I've just had to pay twenty-two sous for the eggs. Something's got to give.'

This time all three men were of one opinion. One by one they spoke, each adding his tale of misery to the ever-growing list of complaints. The workman could no longer survive, the Revolution had only added to his misery, it was the bourgeoisie who had grown fat since 1789, and they had become so greedy that they didn't even leave anything on their plates for the workers to lick clean. Could anyone claim that the workers had had a fair share of the extraordinary growth of wealth and comfort that had taken place over the last hundred years? In declaring them free, the bourgeoisie had clearly taken them for a ride: yes, they were free to die of hunger, and they made liberal use of this right. But it brought home no bacon to vote for lads who then proceeded to live the life of Riley without giving any more thought to the poor than they would to their old boots. No, one way or another, it had to stop, either peacefully, with an amicable arrangement to change the law, or violently, by burning everything to the ground and everyone destroying his neighbour. Their children would certainly live to see it happen, if their parents didn't, for the century couldn't finish without another revolution, and this time it was the workers' turn, and they would upset the apple cart and turn society upside down, and rebuild it more decently and more justly.

'It's got to be blown away,' Madame Rasseneur repeated, vigorously.

And all three of them cried together, 'Yes, blow it all away!'

Souvarine was stroking Poland's ears now, and the rabbit's nose wrinkled with pleasure. His eyes took on a glazed look, and he spoke under his breath, as if he were talking to himself:

'As for raising wages, how can they? It is graven in tablets of bronze* that wages should be fixed at the absolute minimum, just the barest sum necessary for the workers to eat a crust of bread and have children ... If wages fall too low, the workers die, and the demand for new workmen makes them rise again. If they rise too high, the surplus offer makes them drop again ... It's the balanced budget of empty bellies, a life sentence condemning the workers to the prison camp of poverty.'

When he let himself go in this way, debating topics as an intellectual socialist, Étienne and Rasseneur felt uneasy; they were disturbed by his depressing allegations, but had no answer to them.

'Make no mistake!' he went on, in the same peaceful tone of voice, as he looked at them, 'we must destroy everything, or hunger will spring up again. Yes! Anarchy,* an end to everything, the earth bathed in blood and purified by fire ... Then we'll have another think.'

'Monsieur Souvarine is quite right,' declared Madame Rasseneur, who was always most polite even when seized by revolutionary fervour.

Étienne, in despair at his ignorance, refused to prolong the discussion. He rose, saying:

'Let's go to bed. All this doesn't stop me having to get up at three o'clock.'

Souvarine, who had already stubbed out the cigarette end that had been stuck to the corner of his lips, placed a hand gently under the fat rabbit's stomach and lifted her on to the floor. Rasseneur locked up. They went to bed without exchanging a word, their ears humming and their heads reeling with the grave questions that they had been debating.

And every evening there were similar conversations, in the bare room, around the single pint mug that Étienne took an hour to empty. A crowd of confused ideas which had been lying dormant within him started to wake, and gradually took on substance. He was devoured above all by the need to learn, but he had long hesitated to borrow books from his neighbour, who unfortunately owned hardly anything that wasn't written in German or Russian. Finally he got him to lend him a French book on co-operative societies,* another load of rubbish, according to Souvarine; and he also regularly read a journal that Souvarine subscribed to, *Le Combat*, an anarchist paper published in Geneva. Besides, despite their daily meetings, he found Souvarine still just as difficult to draw out, with his semblance of just passing through life, with no interests or emotions or possessions of any kind.

It was towards the beginning of July that Étienne's situation improved. The monotonous life of the mine, eternally recommencing each morning, had been interrupted by an accident: the teams working on the Guillaume seam had just encountered an obstacle, a major disturbance in the stratum, which doubtless announced the proximity of a fault; and sure enough they soon ran into the fault, which the engineers, despite their detailed knowledge of the terrain, had been unaware of. This upset the life of the pit, and the miners talked of nothing but the missing seam, which must have fallen and continued at a lower level on the other side of the fault. The old miners were already sniffing it out with nostrils flaring, chasing after the scent of coal like well-trained hounds. But meanwhile the teams couldn't down tools and sit back and do nothing, and notices appeared announcing that the Company would put some new concessions up for auction.

One day after work Maheu followed Étienne on his way home from the mine and offered him a place as a hewer in his concession instead of Levaque, who had gone over to a different team. The deal had already been approved by the overman and the engineer, who both said they were very pleased with the young man. So it was easy for Étienne to accept this rapid promotion, and he was pleased with the increasing esteem that Maheu had shown him.

That very evening, they returned together to the pit to see what the notices said. The sections put up for auction were situated at the end of the Filonnière seam, in the northern section of Le Voreux. They didn't sound very promising, and the miner shook his head when the young man read the conditions out to him. And in fact the next day, when they had gone down so that Maheu could show him the seam, he pointed out how far it was from the loading bay, how unstable the rock was, and how thin and hard the coal was. And yet if they wanted to eat, they had to work. So the next Sunday they went to the auction, which was held in the changing shed and was presided over by the pit engineer, assisted by the overman, in the absence of the divisional engineer. Five or six hundred coal workers were there, facing the small platform which had been set up in the corner of the room; and the lots were adjudicated at such a speed that you could hear nothing but a confused babble of voices, as figures were shouted out only to be immediately drowned by more figures.

For a moment, Maheu was afraid that he would not be able to obtain any of the forty concessions offered by the Company. All his competitors lowered their offers, worried by rumours of a slump, and terrified by the prospect of unemployment. Négrel, the engineer, was in no hurry to stem this savage competition, for he wanted the bids to drop as low as possible, while Dansaert, who was hoping to speed things up, lied about the qualities of the bargains offered. In order to win a patch of coal fifty metres nearer the shaft, Maheu had to struggle against a comrade who was just as determined; they took it in turns to drive down the price of a tub-load of coal, centime by centime; and even though he emerged victorious from the contest, it was only by lowering their income so much that Richomme, the deputy, who was standing behind him, muttered between his teeth and nudged him with his elbow, growling angrily that he would never make a go of it at that price.

When they emerged, Étienne was swearing. And he lost his temper when he saw Chaval wandering casually back from the wheatfields accompanied by Catherine, while his father-in-law had been doing all the urgent business.

'In heaven's name!' he cried, 'it's a massacre! ... Now they're setting the workers at each other's throats!'

Chaval was furious; he would never have lowered his price, himself! And Zacharie, who had only turned up out of sheer curiosity, declared that it was disgusting. But Étienne silenced them with an expression of contained violence.

'It's got to stop. We'll be the masters, one day!'

Maheu, who had remained silent since the end of the auction, seemed to come to life again. He repeated:

'The masters! God almighty, and about bloody time, too!'

CHAPTER II

IT was the last Sunday in July, the day of the Montsou fair, the Ducasse.* By Saturday evening, the good village housewives had sluiced their living-rooms down with floods of water, throwing whole bucketfuls over the flags and down the walls; and their floors weren't yet dry, although they had been strewn with fine white sand, which was an extravagant expense for a pauper's budget. Meanwhile, it looked as if it was going to be a sweltering day, with the sort of stormy summer sky that seems to stifle the flat, bare, endless expanses of the Nord countryside.

Sundays always upset the Maheu family's morning routine. While Father was bored to tears with staying in bed by five o'clock, and impatiently rose and dressed, the children lay in until nine o'clock. Today Maheu went to smoke a pipe in the garden, and then eventually came in to eat some bread and butter on his own, to kill time. Thus he whiled away the morning, doing nothing in particular: he repaired a leak in the basin, then he pinned up under the cuckoo clock a portrait of the Imperial Prince,* which had been given to the children. Meanwhile, the others came downstairs one by one; old Bonnemort took a chair out to sit in the sunshine, Mother and Alzire had settled down in the kitchen straight away. Catherine appeared, with Lénore and Henri in tow, when she had finished dressing them: and it was striking eleven o'clock, and the smell of stewed rabbit and boiled potatoes was already pervading the house, when Zacharie and Jeanlin came down last, still yawning, their eyes puffy with sleep.

The whole village was all agog, excited by the festivities, impatient for dinner, which had been brought forward so that they could go off in groups to Montsou. Hordes of children hopped and skipped along, while the men slouched around in their shirt sleeves, dragging their feet lazily as they always did on holidays. The windows and doors were wide open because of the fine weather, showing off a whole row of sitting-rooms, all full to overflowing with the assembled families, gesticulating and shouting. And all the way down the terraces, there was a rich, rabbity smell of cooking, which for once overcame the persistent smell of fried onion.

The Maheus dined at twelve noon exactly. They didn't make very much noise compared to the door-to-door gossip and promiscuous congregation of the village women, with their continual toing and froing of questions, answers, and borrowings, of brats shooed away or called back with a smack. Besides, they had been on cool terms for three weeks with their neighbours, the Levaques, over the issue of Zacharie and Philomène's marriage. The men were still talking to each other, but the women acted as if they were strangers. This feud had strengthened their ties with La Pierronne. The only problem was that La Pierronne, leaving Pierron and Lydie with her mother, had gone out half-way through the morning to spend the day with a cousin, at Marchiennes; and they were much amused, because they knew the identity of the lady in question, who had a moustache, for she was in fact none other than the overman of Le Voreux. La Maheude said that it was hardly decent to leave your family on a holiday Sunday.

Apart from the potatoes, and the rabbit that they had been fattening up in the hutch for the past month, the Maheus had a rich soup and some beef, for their fortnight's pay had arrived the day before. They couldn't remember when they had last had such a feast. Even last St Barbe's day, on the miners' three-day holiday, the rabbit had not been so fat and tender. So from little Estelle, whose teeth were only just starting to come through, right up to old Bonnemort, who was losing all of his, ten pairs of jaws were working flat out, crunching up even the bones. It was lovely to have meat, of course, but it was not easy to digest, since they had it so rarely. Everything disappeared, there was only a bit of boiled beef left over for the evening. They would finish it up with some bread and butter, if they were still hungry.

Jeanlin was the first to slip off. Bébert was waiting for him behind the school. And they had to hang around for some time before they managed to enlist Lydie, who was trapped in the house with old Ma Brûlé, who didn't want to go out herself. When she realized that the child had done a bunk, she screamed and waved her skinny arms around, while Pierron, who found that the din got on his nerves, wandered off for a relaxing walk, basking in the role of a husband unashamedly enjoying himself knowing that his wife too is taking her pleasure.

Old Bonnemort was the next to go, then Maheu decided to stretch his legs, after asking La Maheude if she wanted to join him out there. No, how could she, it was a real drag with the kids; or perhaps she might after all, she'd think about it, they'd meet up somewhere or other. Once he was outside he hesitated, then he went next door, to see if Levaque was ready. But he bumped into Zacharie, who was waiting for Philomène; and La Levaque had just launched into her pet topic, their marriage, shouting that nobody took her seriously, that she would have it all out with La Maheude once and for all. What sort of a life was it to look after her daughter's fatherless kids while the daughter herself was screwing around with her lover? When Philomène had quietly finished adjusting her bonnet, Zacharie went off with her, repeating that he had no objection as long as his mother agreed. Meanwhile Levaque had made his getaway, and Maheu advised his lady neighbour to consult his wife, and hurried off. Bouteloup, who was sitting with his elbows firmly planted on the table, polishing off his piece of cheese, doggedly resisted his invitation to come out for a pint. He was staying at home, just like a good husband.

Gradually, however, the village became empty, as all the men went off one after the other, while the girls, who had been keeping watch in the doorways, went off in the opposite direction, on the arms of their sweethearts. As her father disappeared behind the church, Catherine caught sight of Chaval and hastened to join up with him, and walk down the road to Montsou with him. And Mother was left on her own, surrounded by the children, who had been left to their own devices, and she felt she hadn't the energy to leave her chair, so she poured herself another glass of piping hot coffee, which she sipped slowly. Only the women were still left in the village, inviting each other round to drain the dregs of the coffee-pots, and sitting at their tables, which were still warm and sticky from dinner.

Maheu guessed that Levaque would be at the Avantage, and he stopped off at Rasseneur's, without bothering to hurry. And sure enough, Levaque was having a game of skittles with some friends in the narrow garden behind the bar, under the shadow of the hedge. Old Bonnemort and old Mouque were standing beside them, but not playing, both of them so absorbed in the game that they even forgot to nudge each other. The hot sun beat straight down on them, there was only a single shaft of shadow down the middle of the tavern; Étienne was there, sitting over a pint, disappointed that Souvarine had left him and gone upstairs to his room. Nearly every Sunday, the mechanic shut himself in his room to read or write.

'Are you playing?' Levaque asked Maheu.

But the latter refused. It was too hot, he was already dying of thirst.

'Rasseneur!' Étienne called, 'Bring him a pint.'

And, turning to Maheu, he said:

'This is my round, you know.'

By now, Étienne was on familiar terms with all of them. Rasseneur was in no hurry, and they had to call out three times running; until finally it was Madame Rasseneur who brought them their lukewarm beer. The young man had lowered his voice to complain about the house: they were good people all right, with all the right ideas; but the beer was hopeless and the soup disgusting! He would have changed lodgings ten times already, if it hadn't meant such a long walk from Montsou. Sooner or later he'd go and find himself a family in the village.

'Of course,' repeated Maheu with his slow voice, 'of course you'd be better off in a family.'

But there was an outburst of shouting, Levaque had knocked over all the skittles at one go. Mouque and Bonnemort were staring at the ground, marking their dignified and silent approval amid all the tumult. And the men's pleasure at this lucky strike overflowed into a series of jokes, especially when the players saw La Mouquette's cheerful face peeping over the top of the hedge. She had been prowling around for an hour, and had plucked up courage to approach them when she heard the laughter.

'Whatever are you doing all alone?' cried Levaque. 'What have you done with all your lovers?'

'My lovers? I've pensioned them all off,' she replied with cheerful impudence, 'and I'm looking for a new one.'

They all offered their services, and excited her with ribald suggestions. She shook her head, but laughed even louder, good-naturedly sharing the fun. Her father also took in the performance without taking his eyes off the scattered skittles.

'Get along with you!' Levaque went on, casting a glance at Étienne. 'We can guess who you fancy, my girl! . . . But you'll have to use force on him.'

This made Étienne laugh. And he was indeed the tram girl's target. Although he was amused, he declined the invitation, for he had not the slightest desire for the girl.

She hung around behind the hedge a few minutes longer, standing and gazing at him with her big eyes; then she went away slowly, her face abruptly grown serious, as if suddenly oppressed by the hot sun.

Lowering his voice, Étienne had once again started rehearsing for Maheu's benefit his long explanations of the necessity for the Montsou miners to set up a provident fund.*

'Since the Company claims that we are free,' he repeated,

'what have we got to fear? We only have their pensions, and
they give them out however they see fit, because they don't
dock our wages for contributions. Well then, it makes sense to
set up a mutual assistance society, to add to their grace and
favour, so that we at least have something to fall back on in an
emergency.'

And he went on to give details, discussing the organization,
promising to do all the work himself.

'I'm willing,' said Maheu at last, convinced by Étienne's
arguments. 'But what about the others . . . Try and persuade
the others.'

Levaque had won, and they abandoned the skittles in favour
of draining their glasses. But Maheu refused to drink a second
pint: there was plenty of time, the day was still young. He had
just remembered Pierron. Wherever could he be? Probably at
the Lenfant bar. And he persuaded Étienne and Levaque to go
off with him to Montsou, just as a new gang of skittlers came
into the Avantage.

On their way down the cobbled street they were obliged to
go into Casimir's bar, and then the Progrès Inn. Some of their
mates hailed them through the open doorway: so there was no
way they could refuse. Each time that meant another pint, or
two, if they were kind enough to reciprocate. They stayed for
ten minutes, and exchanged a few words, and then moved off
again for a drink next door, quite abstemiously, for they knew
their beer, and could fill their boots with it quite harmlessly,
apart from the nuisance of having to keep on pissing out jets of
clear water, to lower the level. At the Lenfant they bumped
right into Pierron, who was emptying his second pint, and who
then downed a third, so as not to refuse to drink their health.
And they of course followed suit. Now there were four of them,
as they set out with the idea of trying to see whether Zacharie
might be at the Tison.* The room was empty, so they called
for a pint to help them wait for a moment. Then they thought
of trying the Saint-Éloi, accepted a round from Richomme, the
deputy, when they got there, and from then on wandered from
bar to bar without any excuse other than going for a walk.

'We must go to the Volcan!' said Levaque, who had suddenly
woken up and shown an interest.

The others laughed rather hesitantly at first, but then followed their comrade, along with the growing crowd on their way to the fair. In the long narrow room at the Volcan, five chorus girls paraded about on a trestle stage erected at the back of the hall, the dregs of the low life of Lille, gesticulating grotesquely and flaunting their cleavages; it cost the punters ten sous if they wanted to have one of them behind the trestle stage. There were mostly trammers and labourers, and even fourteen-year-old pit boys, all the young men from the pits, drinking more gin than beer. One or two old miners slipped in too, the randy husbands from the villages, those whose marriages were going down the drain.

As soon as their group had sat down at a little table, Étienne latched on to Levaque, to explain his idea of a provident fund. He was driven by the missionary zeal of the new believer, seeking an audience to convert.

'Every member', he said, 'could pay in, say, four francs a month. As these four francs accumulate, in four or five years you'd have quite a pile; and when you've got money behind you, you're strong, aren't you? Ready for anything . . . Hey, what do you think?'

'I've got nothing against it myself,' answered Levaque absent-mindedly. 'We must talk about it some time.'

He was excited by the sight of an enormous blonde; and even when Maheu and Pierron had finished their pint, and wanted to leave without waiting for the next performance, he was determined to stay.

No sooner had Étienne followed them outside than he found himself face to face with La Mouquette again, as if she had been following them. She was still there, looking at him with her great, staring eyes, laughing cheerfully and innocently, as if to say: 'Don't you want me?' The young man made a joke and shrugged his shoulders. Then she flung off angrily and disappeared into the crowd.

'Where the hell has Chaval got to?' asked Pierron.

'That's a point,' said Maheu. 'He's bound to be at Piquette's . . . let's go to Piquette's.'

But as the three of them arrived at Piquette's, they were brought up short by the sound of a fight in the doorway.

Zacharie was brandishing his fist at a stocky and phlegmatic Walloon* nailsmith; while Chaval stood looking on with his hands in his pockets.

'Look, there's Chaval,' Maheu went on calmly. 'He's with Catherine.'

For a good five hours the tram girl and her sweetheart had been walking around the fair. All the way from Montsou there was a stream of people, pouring down the wide street with its brightly painted houses, filing out into the sunshine and down the winding road, forming one long crocodile, like a colony of ants that had lost its way crossing the flat, bare plain. The inevitable black mud had dried, giving off a black dust, floating around like a storm cloud. On both pavements the pubs were bursting at the seams, and had set out their tables right up to the edge of the road, where the stallholders were two deep with their open-air displays, with scarves and mirrors for the girls and knives and caps for the lads, not to mention the sweetmeats like biscuits and sugared almonds. In front of the church there was an archery contest, and a bowls match opposite the Company yards. At the corner of the road to Joiselle, opposite the Board, people were rushing up to see a cock-fight in a wooden ring, where two big red cocks, armed with steel spurs, were hacking blood out of each other's throats. Further on, at Maigrat's, you could win an apron or a pair of breeches at billiards. And there were long silences while the mob drank and stuffed itself soundlessly, stoking up an indigestible mixture of beer and chips in their stomachs, festering in the great heat which was aggravated by the frying pans blazing away in the open air.

Chaval bought a nineteen-sou mirror and a three-franc scarf for Catherine. At every turn in the road they met old Mouque and Bonnemort who had come to the fair, and who were determined to see everything there was to see, in a spirit of systematic reflection, despite their shaky legs. But their next encounter made them feel indignant, for they chanced on Jeanlin in the process of inciting Bébert and Lydie to steal bottles of gin from a makeshift stall set up on a piece of waste land. Catherine only had time to smack her brother, for the little girl had already taken to her heels with a bottle. Those damned children would finish up in gaol.

Then, when they arrived at the Tête-Coupée* bar, Chaval wanted to take his beloved in to see the finch contest* that had been advertised on a notice on the door for the last week. Fifteen nailsmiths from the Marchiennes nailworks answered the call, each bringing a dozen cages; and the tiny, dark cages, where the finches remained, sightless and motionless, had already been hung up on a fence in the courtyard of the pub. You had to count which bird sang its song the most times during the course of an hour. Every nailsmith took a slate and stood behind the cages, marking his own score and noting his neighbours', who kept an eye on him too. Then the finches started, both the 'warblers' with their throaty song and the 'chirrupers' with their shriller tones, timid at first, chancing a few random notes, then egging each other on, accelerating their rhythm, and finally carried away by such a spirit of emulation that some of them even fell off their perches, dead from exhaustion. The nailsmiths spurred them on fiercely with their voices, calling out to them in Walloon to keep singing, again, come on, just one more time, while a good hundred spectators looked on silently, fascinated by this infernal music of 180 finches all reproducing the same refrain in dispersed order. It was one of the 'chirrupers' that won the first prize, which was a wrought-iron coffee-pot.

Catherine and Chaval were there when Zacharie and Philomène entered. They shook hands and stayed together. But suddenly Zacharie became angry, when he caught a nailsmith, who had come over with his comrades out of curiosity, pinching his sister's thighs; and she went very red, but told him to keep quiet, fearing a massacre, if Chaval was determined to stop her from being pinched and all the nailsmiths were to throw themselves at him. She had felt what the man was doing, but preferred to play safe and pretend not to notice, and indeed, her sweetheart's only reaction was to sneer at the man, so the four of them left, the affair seemingly settled. But hardly had they gone into the Piquette to have a drink, when the nailsmith showed up again to make fun of them, laughing in their faces with an air of defiance. Zacharie, whose family feelings were outraged, rushed at the man.

'That's my sister, you bastard! . . . Just you wait, God damn you, and I'll learn you some respect!'

People rushed to keep the two men apart, while Chaval, remaining quite calm, repeated:

'Leave off, it's my business . . . and I tell you he's not worth the trouble!'

Maheu and his group arrived, and he consoled Catherine and Philomène, who were already in tears. Soon the whole group of them were laughing, and the nailsmith had disappeared. To drown the whole problem in alcohol, Chaval, who felt quite at home in Piquette's, offered to buy a round. Étienne had to clink glasses with Catherine, as they all drank together, the father, the daughter and her sweetheart, the son and his mistress, politely wishing each other: 'Health and happiness!' Pierron then insisted on paying for another round. And harmony reigned, until Zacharie was suddenly goaded into a new fit of rage on the arrival of his friend Mouquet. He called him over to go and settle the nailsmith's hash, as he put it.

'I've got to do him in! . . . look, Chaval, hang on to Philomène and Catherine. I'll be back.'

Then it was Maheu's turn to pay for the pints. After all, if the lad wanted to avenge his sister, it wasn't such a bad example to set. But as soon as she had seen Mouquet arrive, Philomène had stopped worrying, and shaken her head: you could bet that the two bastards had run off to the Volcan.

In the evening the whole fair always finished up in the dance hall at the Bon-Joyeux.* Widow Désir ran the ball. She was a stout matron in her fifties, round as a barrel, but so sprightly that she still had six lovers, one for each day of the week, she said, and all six together on Sundays. She called all the colliers her children, and waxed sentimental over the oceans of beer that she had poured down their throats over the last three decades; and she prided herself too on the fact that not a single tram girl had become pregnant without first having learnt how to two-step at the back of her dance hall. There were two rooms at the Bon-Joyeux; the bar, with the counter and some tables; then immediately adjoining through a wide archway was the dance hall, a vast room with a wooden floor laid only in the middle, with a brick surround. It had been decorated for the event with two streamers of paper flowers which ran from the corners of the hall and were tied up in the middle in a garland made of the same flowers, while all round the walls were gilded crests, bearing saints' names: St Éloi, the patron saint of iron workers, St Crispin, the patron saint of cobblers, St Barbe, the patron saint of the miners, the whole calendar of the guilds. The ceiling was so low that when the three musicians mounted the stage, which was as high off the floor as a preacher's lectern, they bumped their heads. To light up the room at night there were four oil lamps, one hung in each corner of the room.

That Sunday they started dancing at five o'clock, while the sunlight was still streaming through the windows. But it was nearly seven o'clock before the hall really got crowded. Outside a stormy wind had risen, blowing up great clouds of black dust, which got in your eyes and made the frying pans spit. Maheu, Étienne, and Pierron, who had come in to find a seat, had just met Chaval at the Bon-Joyeux, where he was dancing with Catherine, while Philomène stood on her own watching them. Neither Levaque nor Zacharie had reappeared. As there were no benches round the hall, Catherine went to sit down at her father's table after each dance. They called Philomène over, but she preferred to stand. Night was falling, the three musicians were in full swing, and the whole hall was seething with hips and bosoms swaying amid a turmoil of limbs. The sudden lighting of the lamps was greeted with a loud clamour, as all at once everything was illuminated, the red faces, the dishevelled hairstyles straggling down the girls' faces, the flying skirts fanning the air with the heavy scent of sweating couples. Maheu pointed out La Mouquette to Étienne: she looked as round and firm as a suet dumpling, as she spun wildly around on the arm of a tall, thin labourer: she had obviously lost hope of seducing Étienne and was consoling herself with another man.

It was eight o'clock by the time La Maheude finally appeared, carrying Estelle at her breast and followed by her ramshackle army—Alzire, Henri, and Lénore. She had come straight over to find her man, certain she would find him there. They'd have supper later, nobody was hungry yet, their stomachs were lined with coffee and bloated with beer. Other women arrived, and La Levaque created a stir of whispers as she came in after La Maheude, accompanied by Bouteloup, who was holding Philomène's children, Achille and Désirée, by the hand. The two mothers seemed to be in good humour, turning and chatting to each other. They had talked the whole thing over on the way, and La Maheude had resigned herself to Zacharie's marriage, disappointed at losing her eldest son's earnings, but forced to agree that she couldn't hold him back any longer without being unfair. So she did her best to put a brave face on it, although, like any careful housewife, her heart sank as she wondered how she would manage to make ends meet, now that the main contributor to the housekeeping was leaving.

'Sit yourself there, neighbour,' she said, pointing out a table close to the one where Maheu was drinking with Étienne and Pierron.

'Isn't my husband with you?' asked La Levaque.

His comrades told her that he would be back soon. Everyone moved up to make room for the women, as well as for Bouteloup and the kids, although they were so tightly pressed in the crush of drinkers that the two parties merged into one. They ordered some beer. When she saw her mother and the children, Philomène decided to come over and join them. She accepted a seat, and seemed pleased at the news that her marriage had at last been agreed; then, when they asked after Zacharie, she replied in her toneless voice:

'I'm expecting him any moment, he's not far away.'

Maheu exchanged glances with his wife. So she had given her consent? He became serious, and smoked in silence. He too was seized with doubts about the future, faced with the ingratitude of these children who were getting married one after the other, leaving their parents in poverty.

The dancing progressed. As the quadrille came to an end, drowning the hall in clouds of red dust, the walls shook, and a cornet shrieked its whistle-shrill blasts, like a train sounding the alarm. When the dancers finally stopped, they were steaming like horses.

'Do you remember,' said La Levaque, bending over to talk into La Maheude's ear, 'that you said you'd strangle Catherine, if she did anything silly?'

Chaval brought Catherine round to the family table, and both of them stood behind her father and finished their beer.

'Well!' murmured La Maheude resignedly, 'you say these things . . . But what relieves me is that she can't have a baby yet, and I'm certain of that! . . . Just imagine if she went and had a baby, too, and I was forced to marry her off! What would we live on then?'

Now the cornet was piping out a polka; and as the room was filled with noise again, Maheu slipped a word under his breath to his wife. Why didn't they take a lodger, Étienne for instance, who was looking for digs? They would have room, since Zacharie was leaving them, and that way they would get back some of the money he was making them lose. La Maheude's face lit up: of course, what a good idea, they must see to it. She seemed saved from starvation once again, and her good humour revived so vigorously that she ordered another round of beer.

Meanwhile Étienne was trying to indoctrinate Pierron, explaining his idea of a provident fund to him. He had got him to promise to join, when he unwisely revealed his true aim.

'And if we come out on strike, you can see how useful the fund will be. We won't have to give a damn what the Company thinks, we'll have our own funds to call on once we start to resist . . . Well, what do you say to that?'

Pierron had lowered his eyes and gone pale. He stammered:

'I'll have to think about it . . . The best insurance policy is really just to behave ourselves properly.'

Then Maheu took Étienne to one side and offered right away, man to man, to take him in as a lodger. Étienne accepted outright, since he was very keen to live in the village, so that he could spend more time with his workmates. The affair was settled in a couple of moments, although La Maheude said they would have to wait for the children's marriage first.

And just then Zacharie returned, with Mouquet and Levaque. All three of them smelled of the Volcan, breathing out gin and a musky scent of loose women. They were extremely drunk, and looked very pleased with themselves, nudging each other and sniggering. When he heard that he was at last to be married, Zacharie laughed so loud that he nearly choked.

Unperturbed, Philomène declared that she'd rather see him laugh than cry. As there were no chairs left, Bouteloup moved over to leave half of his to Levaque. And the latter, who was suddenly overcome with emotion at seeing them all together as one happy family, asked for yet another round of beer.

'God almighty! We don't often have so much fun, do we?' he bellowed.

They stayed there until ten o'clock. Women kept arriving, to meet up with their menfolk and take them home; hordes of children trailed after them; and their mothers felt no shame in heaving out their breasts as if they were long, pale sacks of oats, and pumping up the chubby cheeks of their nurselings with a dose or two of milk, while the kids that were already toddling were full of beer, and crawled around under the tables pissing happily whenever the spirit moved them. The evening swam past on a rising tide of beer, with all Widow Désir's barrels being sucked dry, their contents pouring into people's bellies and then streaming out again, through their noses, eyes, and elsewhere. They swelled visibly, until everyone was sticking his shoulder or knee into his neighbour, and they all wallowed warmly and cheerfully in the closeness of the contact. A continuous laugh went the rounds, with mouths perpetually split from ear to ear. It was so hot that they felt they were roasting in an oven, and they let themselves go, not minding if their flesh spilled out of their clothes, glowing with a golden tint in the smoky light of the men's pipes; and the only problem was the nuisance of having to get up and pee; every now and then a girl got up, went down to the back of the hall near the pump, lifted her skirts, and then returned. Under the fancy paper streamers, the dancers could hardly see each other any more for sweat; and this encouraged the pit boys to send the tram girls flying flat on their arses, when they were able to catch a nice pair of hips off balance. But when a lass fell back with a man on top of her, the cornet covered their fall with its furious piping, and the trampling feet flowed over and round them, as if the ball were a landslide burying them alive.

Someone came up to Pierron and told him that his daughter Lydie was lying outside the door on the pavement, where she had fallen asleep. She had imbibed her share of the stolen bottle and got drunk, so he had to hoist her on to his shoulders, while Jeanlin and Bébert, who had held their drink better, followed at a distance, finding it all very funny. This gave the cue for the families to leave the Bon-Joyeux, and the Maheus and the Levaques decided to go back to the village. At that moment old Bonnemort and old Mouque were also leaving Montsou, with the same sleepwalking gait, lost in the stubborn silence of their memories. Thus they all went home together, walking back through the fair for the last time, as the fat congealed in the frying pans, and the inns poured their last pints out into the middle of the road. The storm was still brewing up, but they were surrounded by louder echoes of laughter, as they left the brightly lit buildings and struck out into the darkness of the countryside. Torrid gusts of passion wafted through the fields of ripened wheat, and many a child must have been conceived in the heat of that night. They straggled into the village. Neither the Levaques nor the Maheus had much appetite for supper, and the latter fell asleep in the process of finishing off what was left of the morning's boiled beef.

Étienne had invited Chaval to come round to Rasseneur's for another drink.

'Count me in!' said Chaval, when his comrade explained his idea about the mutual provident fund. 'Let's shake on it. I'm your man!'

Étienne's eyes were starting to glimmer with the first signs of drunkenness. He cried out:

'Yes, let's agree . . . You see, as far as I'm concerned you can keep it all, drink as well as women, as long as you can have justice. There's only one thing that warms my heart, and that's the thought of knocking the bourgeoisie flat on their backs.'

CHAPTER III

TOWARDS the middle of August, Étienne moved in with the Maheus, after Zacharie had married and was able to obtain an empty house in the village from the Company for Philomène and her two children; and, at first, the young man felt embarrassed in the presence of Catherine.

They were forced into intimate proximity at every moment, for he took the elder brother's place at every turn, sharing Jeanlin's bed beside his big sister's. When he got up in the morning and went to bed at night he had to get dressed and undressed alongside her, and watch her while she put on and took off her own clothes. When the underskirt came off she looked very pale, with the transparent, snowy whiteness typical of anaemic blondes; and he felt moved anew every time he saw this whiteness against the prematurely worn texture of her hands and face, as if she had been dipped in milk from her heels to her neck, whose strip of weathered skin stood out sharply like an amber necklace. He went through the motions of turning away; but he gradually got to know her: first her feet, which caught his lowered eyes; then a glimpse of a knee, when she slipped under the blanket; then her bosom, with her tiny, pointed breasts, when she bent over the wash-basin in the morning. And although she didn't look at him, she hurried as fast as she could, so that it took her only ten seconds to get undressed and slip into bed beside Alzire, with a swift, slippery motion like a grass snake, so that he had hardly got his shoes off before she had disappeared, turning her back and leaving nothing visible but her hair, tied up into a thick bun.

Besides, she never had cause for complaint. Although a kind of obsession drove him in spite of himself to watch out for the moment when she went to bed, he never tried to tease her and never allowed his hands to wander. The parents were close at hand, and besides, he looked on her with mixed feelings of tenderness and resentment, which prevented him from treating her as a girl to be desired, amid all the promiscuity of their new life in common, washing, eating, resting, and working together, with nothing between them ever remaining private, even their most intimate needs. The last remaining shreds of family modesty were preserved in the ritual of the daily bath, which the girl conducted alone in the upstairs room, while the men took it in turns to bathe downstairs.

And in fact by the end of the first month Étienne and Catherine already seemed not to notice each other any more at bedtime, and they went about the room in a state of undress before snuffing out the candle. She had given up trying to hurry, and had adopted her previous habit of sitting on the edge of her bed to tie up her hair, raising her arms, which lifted her shirt up over her thighs; and even if he had no trousers on, he would sometimes help her to look for a lost hairpin. Habit dulled the shame of being naked, and they found it natural, for they were doing nothing wrong and it was hardly their fault if there was only one bedroom for all of them. Yet suddenly they would feel disturbed, at moments when they were thinking of nothing indecent. Sometimes, when he had paid no attention to her pale body for several nights in a row, he would suddenly notice her nakedness, glowing with a whiteness that started him trembling, obliging him to turn away, for fear of yielding to the desire to take her. And there were other evenings when she herself, for no apparent reason, fell prey to an attack of nervous modesty, trying to avoid the young man, and slipping between the sheets as if she had felt his hands starting to grope her. Then, when the candle was out, each realized that the other couldn't sleep and that they couldn't stop thinking about each other despite their fatigue. This left them feeling disturbed and withdrawn all the next day, for they preferred the peaceful nights when they were able to relax and just be good friends.

Étienne had only one cause for complaint, which was that Jeanlin slept curled up like a gundog. Alzire breathed almost imperceptibly while she slept, and Lénore and Henri were to be found every morning lying in each other's arms just as they had been put to bed. Nothing could be heard throughout the darkened house apart from the snores of Maheu and his wife, rising and falling at regular intervals like the bellows of a forge. All in all, Étienne found himself better off than at Rasseneur's; the bed was quite good, and they changed the sheets once a month. The soup was better too; the only problem was that they didn't eat meat so often. But everyone was in the same boat, he could hardly expect to have rabbit at every meal for forty-five francs' rent. These forty-five francs helped the family, and they were able to make ends meet, although they were always dogged by the odd little debt; and

the Maheus showed their gratitude to their lodger, by washing
and darning his linen, sewing on his buttons, and keeping
things tidy for him; so that at last he felt himself surrounded
by the cleanliness and care that a woman brings to the home.

It was at this time that Étienne started to listen to the ideas
that were swarming around in his head. Until then he had felt
only an instinctive rebellion, amid the inarticulate discontent
of his comrades. He asked himself all sorts of confused questions: why should some people be so wretched and others so
rich? Why should the former be trampled underfoot by the
latter, with no hope of ever taking their places? And the first
progress he made was to understand how ignorant he was.
From then on he was devoured by a secret feeling of shame
and sorrow; since he knew nothing, he didn't dare talk of the
things which most moved him, that all men should be equal,
and that the principle of equity required fair shares for all in
the wealth of the world. So he found himself seized with the
uncritical taste for study that strikes the ignorant who are
hungry for knowledge. By now he was in regular correspondence with Pluchart, who was more learned than he, and deeply
committed to the socialist movement. He sent away for books,
and his imagination was inflamed by his hasty reading: especially a medical work, *Miners' Hygiene,** where a Belgian doctor
made a survey of the mortal ailments that afflicted the mining
community; not to mention the treatises on political economy
which were full of arid and incomprehensible technical detail,
the anarchist pamphlets which moved him to tears, copies of
old newspaper articles which he collected, hoping that they
would provide him with incontestable proof in some future
argument. In addition, Souvarine lent him books, and a work
on co-operative societies had made him dream for a whole
month of a society built on universal exchange, abolishing
money and basing the whole of social life on the value of
labour. His shame at his ignorance diminished, and he grew in
pride as he came to feel himself capable of thinking.

During these early months, Étienne enjoyed the ecstasy of
the convert, his heart overflowing with generous indignation
against the oppressor, yearning hopefully for the imminent
triumph of the oppressed. He hadn't yet got round to creating

a system out of his mass of reading. Rasseneur's practical claims were mixed up inside him with Souvarine's destructive violence; and every time he left the Avantage, where he joined them every day to relieve in public his feelings against the Company, he walked away in a kind of dream, where he imagined the populations of the earth being totally transformed without a single window being broken or a drop of blood being spilled. In fact, he was vague about how to achieve this, and preferred to think that things would proceed smoothly all by themselves, for he lost track of the argument as soon as he tried to form any specific plans for the rebuilding of society. He tended to preach moderation and fail to push his arguments to their logical conclusion, even repeating on occasions that politics should be banned from the social debate, which was a phrase that he had read and which sounded as if it would go down well with the phlegmatic colliers that he lived among.

Now every evening at the Maheus' they stayed downstairs for half an hour before they went upstairs to bed. Étienne kept returning to the same topic. Since he had become more sophisticated, he found himself more and more offended by the promiscuity of village life. Were they animals, to be herded together like cattle in the fields, and crammed in so tightly on top of one another that they couldn't change their shirts without showing their behinds to their neighbours! And it was hardly very good for anyone's health; and the boys and girls were so thrown together that they were bound to go to rack and ruin!

'Good Lord,' said Maheu, 'if we had more money, we'd be more comfortable ... All the same, it's true enough that it doesn't do anyone any good to live on top of each other. It always ends up with the men blind drunk and the girls in trouble.'

And this got the family going, everyone wanting to get his word in, while the oil lamp added its fumes to the stale air of the room, already reeking with fried onion. No, you had to agree life wasn't much fun. You already had to work like beasts of burden at a job which would have been a punishment for convicts in olden days, and more often than not you didn't get out alive, and you still didn't make enough out of it to have meat on the table for dinner. Of course, you got your daily bread, you did eat, but so little that it was only just enough to keep you alive so you could enjoy being half-starved, piling up debts and hounded remorselessly as if you had stolen every mouthful you ate. When Sunday came round you were so tired that you slept all day. Life's only pleasures were getting drunk or giving your wife a baby; and even then the booze gave you a beer belly and the baby would grow up and wouldn't give a damn for you. No, too true, life was not a bowl of cherries.

Then La Maheude had her say.

'The worst of it, I think, is when you realize that nothing can change . . . When you're young you think that you're going to be happy later on, there are things you look forward to; and then you keep finding you're as hard up as ever, you stay bogged down in poverty . . . I don't blame anyone for it, but there are times when I feel sick at the injustice of it all.'

There was a moment of silence, as they caught their breath for a moment, at the thought of this locked horizon. Only old Bonnemort, if he was there, would open his eyes wide in surprise, for in his day nobody bothered themselves with that kind of question: you were born in the coal, you hacked away at the seam, and you asked no questions; whereas nowadays, there was something in the air which gave the miners ideas.

'Beggars can't be choosers,' he would murmur. 'A pint in the hand is a pint indeed . . . The bosses are often a load of bastards; but there'll always be bosses, won't there? No point in getting het up over that.'

That set Étienne going. What did he mean? Couldn't a worker think for himself? In fact that was just why things would change one day soon, because nowadays the workers were starting to think. In the old man's time, the miners lived out their life down the mine like dumb brutes, as if they were just machines for excavating coal, always underground, with their ears and their eyes blocked to anything happening in the outside world. So the rich who ran the country found it easy enough to get together and buy and sell the workers and live off their very flesh; while the workers didn't even realize what was happening. But now the miners were waking from their slumbers in the depths of the earth and starting to germinate

like seeds sown in the soil; and one morning you would see how
they would spring up from the earth in the middle of the fields
in broad daylight: yes, they would grow up to be real men, an
army of men fighting to restore justice. Hadn't all citizens been
equal since the Revolution? Since they all voted in the same
elections, why should the worker stay the slave of the boss who
employed him? The big companies and their machines crushed
everything in their path and against them you couldn't even use
the safeguards you would have had in olden days, when people
in the same trade joined the same guild and were able to defend
themselves. For God's sake, that, and more besides, was why
everything would have to go up in smoke one day, it was
education that would do it. You didn't have to look further than
your own village: while the grandfathers couldn't have signed
their names, the fathers were able to write now, and as for the
sons, they could read and write like professors. Oh, things were
moving, sure enough, there was a right little harvest of men
growing up and ripening in the sunshine! As soon as each man
wasn't stuck in the same place all his life long, and you could
hanker after taking your neighbour's place, why ever shouldn't
you flex your muscles a bit and see if you couldn't be stronger?

Maheu was shaken, but he remained deeply suspicious.

'As soon as you make a move they hand you your booklet,'*
he said. 'The old man's right, it's always going to be the miner
who does the work, and he's never going to be paid for his
pains with a leg of roast lamb.'

La Maheude had been silent for a moment, but now she
awoke as if from a dream.

'And if only what the vicar said was true, if only the people
who are poor in this world were rich in the next!'

She was interrupted by hoots of laughter, and even the
children shrugged their shoulders, for none of them believed
these things out in the open air, and although they hid in their
hearts a secret fear of the ghosts that haunted the pit, they
laughed at the empty heavens.

'Oh my gawd, yes, the vicar!' cried Maheu. 'If they really
believed that, they'd eat less and work harder, to try at least to
keep a place warm for them up there later on . . . oh, no, once
you're dead, you're good and damn well dead.'

La Maheude sighed deeply.

'Oh dear God, oh dear God!'

Then letting her hands fall to her knees, she said with an air of profound weariness:

'Well then, there's no answer, we've had it, the lot of us.'

They all looked at each other. Old Bonnemort spat out into his handkerchief, while Maheu forgot to take his pipe out of his mouth although it had gone out. Alzire was listening, sitting between Lénore and Henri, who had fallen asleep at the table. But it was Catherine above all who sat there with her chin in her hands, and kept her crystal-clear eyes fixed on Étienne, whenever he cried out in protest, proclaimed his faith, and revealed his vision of the enchanted society of the future. All around them the village was putting out the lights, and nothing could be heard but the stray wails of the odd child or the ramblings of some drunkard late home. Inside the room the cuckoo clock ticked slowly away, and a cool and humid air arose from the sand-covered flagstones, despite the muggy atmosphere.

'What a crazy idea!' said the young man. 'Do you need a damn God and his paradise to make you happy? Can't you make your own happiness on earth all by yourselves?'

He talked on endlessly, in increasingly passionate tones. And suddenly, the bolts locking the horizon burst open to let a gleam of light break through and illuminate the grim lives of these poor people. The endless chain of poverty, the brutish labour, the doomed and bestial life they led, first shorn of their fleeces and then led to the slaughter, all this suffering disappeared, as if a great blaze of sunshine had swept it away; and in a dazzling, magical vision, justice descended from heaven. Since God himself was dead, it would be justice which would now ensure the happiness of men, by opening up a kingdom of equality and fraternity. Just like in fairy-tales, a new society would grow up overnight, a great city, shimmering like a mirage, where each citizen would fulfil his appointed duties and take his part in the community of joy. The rotten old world would crumble to dust, a new young breed of humanity purged of its crimes would form a single, united race of workers, who would have for their motto: to each according to his worth, and each one's worth to be judged according to his efforts. And the dream grew continually vaster and finer, all the more seductive for riding higher and higher into the realms of impossible fantasy.

At first La Maheude refused to listen, for she was seized with a vague feeling of panic. No, really, it was too fantastic, you shouldn't get carried away by such ideas, for they made life even more revolting afterwards, and then you would kill anyone who got in your way, just to be happy. When she noticed the anxious gleam in Maheu's eyes, she grew worried, seeing him so carried away, and cried out, interrupting Étienne:

'Don't you listen, my dear! Can't you see he's telling us fairy-tales? . . . D'you think the bourgeoisie will ever agree to work as hard as we do?'

But little by little the charm started to work on her too. She finally started to smile as her imagination was aroused, tempting her to enter this marvellous world of hope. It was so sweet to forget the pain of reality, if only for an hour! When you live like an animal, with your nose to the grindstone, you need at least a little pocket of lies, so that you can enjoy gloating over things you can never possess. And what really excited her, what made her agree with the young man, was the idea of justice.

'You're right there!' she cried. 'For me, once something's just, I'll go to hell for it . . . And it's true, it would be only justice for us to have fun for a change.'

Then Maheu felt able to let himself go.

'In the name of all that's holy! I'm not a rich man, but I'd certainly give a hundred sous not to die before I've seen all that . . . What an upset, eh? Will it happen soon, and how are we going to do it?'

Étienne started talking again. The old society was falling apart, for, he affirmed outright, it couldn't last more than a few months longer. As for the means of putting it into practice, he seemed to be less sure of himself, confusing his sources and, given the ignorance of his audience, feeling no scruples at launching into explanations where he himself was out of his depth. All the systems he knew of went into his maw, smoothed over by his certainty of an easy triumph, of a universal embrace which would put an end to the misunderstandings between the classes; apart from the ill will of one or two individual bosses or bourgeois who might perhaps have to be made to see reason. And the Maheus appeared to understand and approve, accepting his miraculous solutions with the blind faith of converts, like the early Christians at the beginnings of the Church who awaited the emergence of a perfect society out of the very compost of the ancient world. Little Alzire hung on every word, imagining happiness as a vision of a very warm house where the children would play all the time and eat as much as they wanted to. Catherine sat transfixed, still holding her chin in her hands, staring at Étienne, and when he fell silent, she shivered slightly, as if she suddenly felt cold.

But La Maheude looked at the cuckoo clock.

'Past nine o'clock, what are we thinking of! We'll never get up in the morning.'

And the Maheus left the table, feeling sick at heart, and near to despair. They had suddenly felt as if they were going to be rich, and now they fell back with a crash into the mire. Old Bonnemort, who was leaving for the pit, complained that that sort of story didn't make the soup taste any better; while the others went upstairs one by one, suddenly noticing the damp on the walls and the foul, fetid air. Upstairs, once Catherine, who was last into bed, had blown out the candle, Étienne heard her tossing and turning feverishly in the midst of the silent and slumbering village before she was able to sleep.

Often there were neighbours who wanted to sit in on their conversations; Levaque, who was enthusiastic about the idea of fair shares, and Pierron, who felt that prudence commended he should leave when they got round to attacking the Company. Every now and again Zacharie came in for a moment; but politics bored him to tears, he preferred to go out to the Avantage to down a pint. As for Chaval, he egged them on, calling for blood. Almost every evening he spent an hour at the Maheus'; although some of his assiduity might be attributed to secret jealousy, the fear that he might lose Catherine. He had already started to find her boring, but he felt all the more drawn to her, now that she was sleeping alongside another man who might be able to take her during the night.

Étienne's influence increased; he gradually revolutionized the village. It was not an official campaign, which made it all the more effective in helping him to grow in everyone's esteem. Despite the suspicion she felt, like any cautious housewife, La Maheude treated him considerately, since the young man paid his rent on the dot, neither drank nor gambled, and always had his nose in a book; when she talked of him to the neighbours she vaunted his reputation as an educated lad, and they took advantage of this by getting him to write their letters. He became a kind of business adviser, who looked after their correspondence and was consulted by households on delicate issues. In this way, by September he had set up his much-vaunted provident fund, which was very insecure at first, since the only members were the residents of his village; but he hoped soon to enrol colliers from all the pits, especially if the Company continued to remain passive, and didn't raise any particular objection. He had just been appointed secretary of the association, and even had a small income from the fees he charged for his writing. That almost made him seem rich. Although a married miner might have trouble making ends meet, a clean-living young man with no dependants might actually manage to put some savings aside.

From this moment on Étienne underwent a gradual transformation. An instinctive pride in his appearance and love of comfort, which had been buried beneath his poverty, were awakened, and he yielded to the temptation to buy himself some woollen clothes and a pair of soft leather boots, and this immediately marked him out as a leader, with the whole village ready to follow him. This fed his ego with the most delicious satisfaction, and the first thrill of popularity went to his head: finding himself leading a group of people and giving orders, despite being so young and until just recently only an unskilled labourer, filled him with pride, and fuelled his dream of an imminent revolution with a role for him in it. His very features changed, as he took on a reflective air and studied the sound of his own voice; while his nascent ambition inflamed his theories and whipped up his taste for confrontation.

However, autumn was drawing to a close and the October frosts had turned the little village gardens a rusty colour. Behind the straggling lilac trees, the pit boys had stopped laying the tram girls flat on their arses on the hutch; and all that was left were the winter vegetables, the cabbages iced with diamonds of frost, the leeks, and any greens they had managed to pickle. Once again the showers whipped across the red rooftops and crashed noisily down the gutters into the rain-butts. In every house the fires were kept piled high with coal burning day and night, poisoning the airless rooms with their fumes. Another season of wretched poverty had begun.

In October, during one of these freezing nights, Étienne, who was carried away from talking downstairs, found he couldn't get to sleep. He had watched Catherine slip under the covers and blow out the candle. She too seemed quite upset, tormented by one of the fits of modesty that still occasionally made her hurry her toilet awkwardly and actually show even more of her body. She lay still in the darkness like a dead creature; but he could tell that she was not asleep; and he could feel that she was thinking of him just as he was thinking of her: this silent exchange of their innermost feelings had never before filled them with such a disturbing sensation. The minutes passed, but neither of them moved, and only their breathing betrayed their emotion, despite their efforts to control it. Twice he was on the point of going over to take her. It was so stupid for both of them to be wanting each other so badly and depriving themselves of the satisfaction. Why should they keep fighting their natural desires? The children were asleep, and she wanted him urgently, he was sure she was waiting for him, choking with frustration, and that she would wrap her arms around him silently and keep her mouth tightly shut. Almost an hour passed, but he didn't go over to take her, and she didn't turn round, for fear of calling out to him. The longer they lived side by side, the more their friendship placed between them a kind of barrier of shame, reluctance, and tact, which they could hardly have explained themselves.

CHAPTER IV

'Look,' said La Maheude to her man, 'if you're going to Montsou for your pay, will you bring me back a pound of coffee and a kilo of sugar?'

He was stitching one of his shoes himself, to save on the repair.

'All right!' he muttered, without stopping work.

'Can you go to the butcher's too? ... Get a bit of veal, will you? It's so long since we saw any.'

This time he looked up at her.

'Sounds as if you think I'm going to be paid ten times over ... The fortnight's wages are slim pickings with their bloody mania for stopping work.'

They both fell silent. It was after lunch on a Saturday at the end of October. On the pretext that pay-day disrupted work, the Company had once again called a halt to production in all the pits for the day. Seized with panic at the galloping industrial slump, and reluctant to increase its oversized stockpile of coal, it seized on the slightest excuse to stop its 10,000 workers from working.

'You know that Étienne is waiting for you at Rasseneur's,' went on La Maheude. 'Take him with you. He'll be cleverer than you at working it out if they don't count all of your hours.'

Maheu nodded in approval.

'And talk to those gentlemen about your father's problem. The doctor's been paid to agree with the management ... That's right, isn't it, old man, the doctor's wrong, you can still work, can't you?'

For the last ten days old Bonnemort, whose pins were numb, as he put it, had been sitting rooted to his chair. She had to repeat the question, and he replied gruffly:

'Of course I can go back to work. You're not done for just because your legs hurt. The whole thing's a plot so they don't have to give me my hundred-and-eighty-franc pension.'

La Maheude thought of the old man's forty sous, which he might never bring home to her again, and she cried out in anguish.

'My God! We'll all be dead soon if this goes on much longer.'

'When you're dead,' said Maheu, 'you don't feel hungry any more.'

He finished mending his shoes by knocking in a few nails and then decided to leave. Village Two Hundred and Forty wasn't due to be paid until four o'clock. So the men hung about and took their time, leaving in ones and twos, pursued by their wives, who pleaded with them to come back home straight away afterwards. A lot of them gave them errands to run so that they wouldn't go off and get blind drunk in the pubs.

Étienne was at Rasseneur's catching up with the news. There were worrying rumours abroad, to the effect that the Company was getting more and more dissatisfied with the timbering. It kept piling on the fines, and a battle looked certain. Besides, this dispute was merely a superficial symptom, which hid a whole network of more secret and serious issues.

And just as Étienne arrived, one workmate who had stopped for a pint on his way back from Montsou told them that there was a notice posted up at the cashier's; but he wasn't sure what it said. Another man came in and then a third; and each of them had a different story to tell. It seemed certain, at all events, that the Company had decided to take action.

'What do you think, then?' Étienne asked Souvarine as he sat down at his table, where there was only a packet of tobacco to be seen, and nothing to drink.

The mechanic finished rolling his cigarette, as if they had all the time in the world.

'I think anyone could have seen it coming. They're going to push you to the brink!'

He was the only one who had a lively enough intelligence to analyse the situation. He explained it all with a tranquil air. The Company had been badly affected by the slump, and was obviously forced to cut its expenses to avoid going under; and naturally enough it was the workers who were supposed to tighten their belts, for the Company needed to save on their wages, using any pretext that came to hand. For two months now, the coal had been piling up at the pit heads, and nearly all the factories had ground to a halt.

As the Company wanted to avoid a total shut-down, because it was terrified at the prospect of the disastrous effect it would have on the plant, it was casting around for a compromise solution, perhaps a strike, from which its whole work-force of miners would emerge cowed, and settle for lower wages. And, finally, the new provident fund worried the Company, for it posed a threat for the future, whereas a strike would get rid of it by emptying it before it was fully funded.

Rasseneur had sat down beside Étienne, and they both listened in consternation. As there was nobody else there except Madame Rasseneur, sitting behind the counter, they were able to talk openly.

'What an idea!' muttered the landlord. 'Why take so much trouble? The Company has nothing to gain from a strike, any more than the workers. It'd be better to come to an agreement together.'

This was the sensible thing to do. He was always in favour of making sensible claims. And since his former lodger had become so popular, he waxed even more lyrical in defence of the politics of what was possible, declaring that if you tried to get everything all at once you would end up with nothing at all. But behind his plump, jovial, beery exterior he fostered a secret jealousy, aggravated by the scarcity of customers, for the workers from Le Voreux had started coming in less often to drink at the bar and listen to him; and he sometimes even ended up defending the Company, forgetting his grudge for having been sacked from his job at the mine.

'You mean you're against a strike?' cried Madame Rasseneur, without leaving the bar.

And when he vigorously replied that he was, she ordered him to be quiet.

'Well, you've got no heart, so let these other gents talk!'

Étienne was musing, his eyes riveted to the mug of beer she had served him. Finally he looked up.

'Everything our friend's been telling us is perfectly possible, and we'll just have to resign ourselves to the strike, if we're forced into it . . . It just so happens that Pluchart has written me something very good on that subject. He's against the strike too, for the workers suffer as much as the bosses, without getting any useful result. Except that he sees it as an excellent opportunity to persuade our men to join his great enterprise . . . Anyway, here's his letter.'

And in fact Pluchart, who was dismayed at the Montsou miners' reluctance to join the International, hoped to see them join up *en masse* if a struggle forced them to pit their strength against the Company. Despite his efforts, Étienne hadn't been able to recruit a single member, even if he had put most of his effort into the relief fund, which went down much better. But this fund was still so meagre that it would run out in no time, as Souvarine said, and then the strikers would surely rush to join the Workers' Association so that their brothers from countries all over the world would come to their assistance.

'How much have you got in the fund?' asked Rasseneur.

'Barely three thousand francs,' replied Étienne. 'And you know that the management called me to see them the day before yesterday. Oh, they were very polite, and they confirmed that they wouldn't prevent their workmen building up a reserve fund. But I understood perfectly well that they want to control it themselves . . . In any case, we'll have to fight for it.'

The publican had started to walk up and down, whistling contemptuously. Three thousand francs! What the hell did you expect to be able to do with that? You wouldn't get six days' bread out of it, and if you relied on foreigners, people living in England, you might as well take to your bed and give up the ghost straight away. Really, this strike was a damn silly idea!

Then, for the first time, bitter words were exchanged between these two men who normally ended up united by their mutual hatred of capitalism.

'Well, then, and how about you?' Étienne asked again, turning to Souvarine.

But the latter replied in his usual dismissive tones:

'Strikes? A load of rubbish!'

Then, amid the angry silence that had fallen, he added gently:

'Well, actually, I don't entirely object, if it makes you happy: it ruins some and kills off others, that's a start, at least . . . The only problem is that it would take a thousand years to renew the world at that rate. Why don't you start by blowing up the prison that you're all dying in!'

With his slim hand he gestured towards Le Voreux, whose buildings were visible through the open door. Then he was interrupted by an unexpected drama: Poland, the fat pet rabbit, who had ventured outside, came bounding inside fleeing a hail of stones thrown by a band of pit boys; and in her terror, her ears laid back and her tail raised in alarm, she came to seek shelter between Souvarine's legs, scratching at him piteously for him to pick her up. When he had placed her on his knees, he covered her with his hands, and as he stroked her soft warm fur he fell into a familiar state of drowsy reverie.

Almost immediately, Maheu entered. He didn't want anything to drink, despite the gracious insistence of Madame Rasseneur, who offered her beer for sale as if it were a gift. Étienne got to his feet and they both left for Montsou.

On pay days, Montsou seemed to flock to the Company yards, as if celebrating a public holiday on a fine Sunday at the fair. Crowds of miners came from all the villages in the neighbourhood. The cashier's office was very small, so they preferred to wait outside the door, and congregated in groups in the yard, blocking the way with an endlessly renewed queue of people. There were hawkers who cashed in on the situation, setting up their mobile stalls selling everything including crockery and cooked meats. But it was the pubs above all that made a killing, for the miners went for a drink for something to do while they were waiting to be paid, and then went back again to celebrate being paid as soon as they had the money in their pockets. And that was if they were on their best behaviour, and not going on to blow the rest of it at the Volcan.

As Maheu and Étienne moved forward through the groups of men that day, they felt a tide of exasperation rising among them. There wasn't the usual carefree attitude to the money they pocketed and then started to squander in the pubs. There were clenched fists, and angry words flying from mouth to mouth.

'Is it true, then?' Maheu asked Chaval, whom he met outside Piquette's. 'Have the bastards really done it?'

But Chaval's only answer was to spit furiously, looking sideways at Étienne. Since the last round of contracts, he had signed on again with a different team, but was increasingly

consumed with envy for this new workmate who set himself
up as a master, and whose boots the whole village was queueing
up to lick, so he said. It was further aggravated by a lovers'
quarrel, for every time he took Catherine off to Réquillart or
behind the slag-heap, he accused her in the vilest terms of
sleeping with her mother's lodger; then, seized with an upsurge
of brutal desire, he would crush her in his embrace.

Maheu put another question to him.

'Have they got to Le Voreux yet?'

And as Chaval just shook his head and turned his back on
him, the two men decided to go into the Company yards.

The cashier's office was a small rectangular room, divided
in two by a grille. Five or six miners were sitting waiting on
benches lined against the walls; while the cashier and his clerk
were paying another miner who was standing at the window
with his cap in his hand. Up above the left-hand bench
someone had posted a yellow notice, which stood out bright
and clear against the smoke-stained grey plaster walls; and
there it was that the men had been filing by all day since
morning. They came in two or three at a time, stood in front
of it, then went off without saying a word, with· just a
twitching of the shoulders, as if their backs had been broken.

There were two colliers looking at the notice as they went
in, a young man with a square, brutish head and a very thin
old man, his face dulled with age. Neither of them could read,
but the young one spelled out the letters, moving his lips,
while the old man merely looked on vacantly. Many of the
men came in and reacted in the same way, since they didn't
understand a word of it.

'Read it out for us, then,' said Maheu to his companion, for
he was no great reader either.

So Étienne set to reading out the notice. It was an address
by the Company to each and every miner in all its pits. It drew
their attention to the fact that, given the lack of care taken over
timbering, and tired of levying ineffectual fines, the Company
had resolved to introduce a new mode of payment for the
cutting of coal. Henceforth, it would pay for the timbering
separately, so much per cubic metre of wood taken below and
used, basing the price on the quantity needed to accomplish

the task satisfactorily. The price of a tub-load of coal would therefore be lowered to forty centimes in lieu of the fifty given previously, paying due regard, however, to the quality and accessibility of the coal-face of origin. And a fairly obscure calculation followed, attempting to prove that this reduction of ten centimes would be exactly compensated for by the payment for the timbering. The Company added finally that, in order to grant everyone time enough to appreciate the advantages of the new system, it would delay its application until Monday, 1 December.

'Couldn't you read more quietly, over there!' cried the cashier. 'We can't hear ourselves think.'

Étienne finished reading, taking no notice of this remark. But his voice was trembling, and when he had finished they all continued to stare at the notice. The old miner and his young companion seemed to be waiting for some further explanation; but then they left, with shoulders bowed.

'God in heaven!' murmured Maheu.

Both he and his friend had sat down. While the queue continued to file past the yellow notice, they sat with their heads in their hands, lost in their mental calculations. What did the Company take them for? They would never make up on the timbering the ten centimes they lost on the tub-load. At best they would make eight centimes, so the Company would be robbing them of two centimes, and even that was not allowing for the time that the work would take them if they did it properly. So that was how the Company was going to manage to lower their wages on the sly! It would be lining its pockets with money stolen from the miners.

'Good God almighty!' repeated Maheu, looking up again. 'We're a load of silly buggers if we fall for that one!'

But the window was free, and he went up to receive his pay. The team-leaders went up to the cash desk on their own, and then shared out the money between their men, in order to save time.

'Maheu and associates,' said the clerk, 'Filonnière seam, coal-face number seven.'

He looked down the lists which were compiled from the books in which the overmen at each site recorded each day's tally of tubs filled. Then he repeated:

'Maheu and associates, Filonnière seam, coal-face number seven . . . A hundred and thirty-five francs.'

The cashier handed over the money.

'Excuse me, Sir,' stammered the hewer in dismay, 'are you sure there isn't some mistake?'

He looked at the small pile of coins without picking them up, and he felt a cold shiver chill him to the heart. He had certainly expected the pay packet to be disappointing, but it couldn't have shrunk so low, unless he had made some mistake in his calculations. Once he had paid out their share to Zacharie, Étienne, and the other workmate who had taken over from Chaval, there would be no more than fifty francs left for him, his father, Catherine, and Jeanlin.

'No, no, there's no mistake,' the cashier replied. 'You've got to take off two Sundays and four days laid off: so that makes nine days' work.'

Maheu followed his calculation, working out the sum under his breath: nine days would make about thirty francs for him, eighteen for Catherine, nine for Jeanlin. As for old Bonnemort, he had earned only three days' pay. But even so, by the time you added ninety francs for Zacharie and his two workmates, it should surely come to more than that.

'You're forgetting the fines,' the clerk added. 'Twenty francs in fines on account of your shoddy timbering.'

The hewer made a gesture of despair. Twenty francs in fines and four days laid off! So the sum was correct. And to think that he had brought home as much as a hundred and fifty francs some fortnights, when old Bonnemort was working normally and Zacharie had not yet set up home!

'Are you going to take the money or not?' cried the cashier impatiently. 'You can see that there are people waiting . . . If you don't want it, say so.'

As Maheu made up his mind to pick up the money with his large shaking hand, the clerk asked him to wait.

'Wait a moment, I see your name's on my list. It's Toussaint Maheu, isn't it? . . . The General Secretary wants to have a word with you. You can go in, he's free.'

The surprised workman found himself in an office full of antique mahogany furniture, with walls draped in faded green fabric. He spent five minutes listening to the General Secretary, a tall, pale gentleman, who talked at him from behind a pile of papers on his desk, without getting up. But the buzzing in his ears prevented him from taking in what was being said. He understood vaguely that it was about his father, whose retirement at the rate of 150 francs was under consideration, given that he was fifty-eight years old and had clocked up fifty years of service. Then it seemed to him that the Secretary's voice hardened. It was a reprimand, he was accusing him of going in for politics, he was referring to the lodger and his provident fund; finally, he was advised not to compromise himself in such foolish undertakings, when he was one of the best workmen in the pit. He wanted to protest but could only come out with a jumble of disconnected words, twist his cap nervously in his fingers, and withdraw, stammering:

'Certainly, Mr Secretary, Sir . . . I promise you, Sir . . .'

Outside, when he had joined Étienne, who was waiting for him, he exploded.

'I'm a useless bugger, I should have answered him back! . . . We can hardly feed ourselves as it is, and now they're making it worse! You realize it's you they're getting at? He told me the village was poisoned . . . And what can we do, for God's sake! Bow down and say thank you? He's right, it's the safest thing to do.'

Maheu fell silent, racked with mixed feelings of anger and fear. Étienne looked sombre and thoughtful. They walked back through the crowds who were still blocking the road. The exasperation of these peaceful people was mounting. There were no violent gestures, but you could feel a dark, silent, storm cloud gathering ominously over this great mass of people. One or two quick thinkers had done their mental arithmetic, and the two centimes that the Company would claw back on the propping went the rounds, exciting even the cooler heads among them. But their rage centred chiefly on this disastrous fortnight's pay, their revolt was driven by hunger and by protest at the lay-offs and fines. Already they hadn't enough to eat, what was to become of them if their wages fell still lower? In the pubs their anger broke out openly, and their throats were so heated with fury that the

182

Germinal

little money they had received went straight into the publicans'
tills.

All the way back from Montsou to the village Maheu and
Étienne didn't exchange a single word. When Maheu got
home, his wife, who was alone with the children, noticed
immediately that he was empty-handed.

'Well, you're a great help!' she said. 'What about my coffee
and my sugar and my meat? A bit of veal wouldn't have ruined
you.'

He couldn't answer, choked with pent-up emotion. Then
his rough face, hardened by years of labour down the mine,
swelled up with despair, and great warm tear-drops poured
down his cheeks. He collapsed on a chair, weeping like a child,
and threw his fifty francs on the table.

'There you are!' he stammered. 'That's what I've brought
you . . . That's our wages, for the lot of us.'

La Maheude looked at Étienne and saw that he was silent
and crushed. So she cried too. How could you keep nine
people alive for a fortnight on fifty francs? Her eldest had left
them, the old man could no longer move a muscle: they would
soon be dead. Alzire threw her arms round her mother's neck,
upset at hearing her cry. Estelle screamed, Lénore and Henri
sobbed.

And similar cries of distress rang out from every corner of
the village. Now that the men had come home, every family
lamented their disastrously meagre pay packet. Doors flew
open, and women came out shouting aloud, as if their protests
would have burst through the ceilings and walls if they had
stayed indoors. A fine drizzle was falling, but they didn't even
notice it as they went out on to the pavement and called from
house to house, holding out their hands to show each other
how little money they had received.

'Look! That's all they've given him, who do they think
they're kidding?'

'Look at us! I haven't even got enough to pay for a fortnight's bread.'

'Well what about me! Just work it out, I'll have to sell my
shirts again.'

La Maheude had gone outside like everyone else. A group

formed around La Levaque, who was shouting the loudest; for her drunken husband hadn't even returned, she guessed that his pay packet, big or small, would be spirited away at the Volcan. Philomène was looking out for Maheu, to prevent Zacharie from making inroads into the money. And the only person who seemed relatively calm was La Pierronne, for that sly fox Pierron always managed to fix things, who knows how, in order to tot up more hours than his comrades in the deputy's books. But old Ma Brûlé thought her son-in-law's behaviour was cowardly, and she was at the heart of the angry crowd. Her skinny figure could be seen standing erect in the middle of the group, shaking her fist in the direction of Montsou.

'To think', she cried, without naming the Hennebeaus, 'that this morning I saw their maid go by in a carriage! . . . Yes, the cook swans off in a two-horse carriage, galloping away to Marchiennes to buy fish, you mark my words!'

A clamour arose, and the cries became more violent. That maid in her white apron who rode off in her masters' carriage to go to market in town provoked their wrath. When the workers were dying of hunger, did their masters really need to eat fish? They might not eat fish for ever though: the turn of the poor would come one day. And the ideas that Étienne had sown grew and multiplied in their cries of revolt. They were impatient to discover the promised land, and hungered to taste their share of happiness, beyond the horizon of their misery, which seemed to seal them inside a tomb. The injustice had become too great, and it was time they claimed their due, now that they were having the bread taken out of their mouths. The women, especially, were ready to mount the attack straight away, to storm this ideal city of progress, where poverty would be outlawed. It was almost dark, and the rain fell harder than ever, but they still filled the village with their tearful cries, surrounded by hordes of yelping children.

That evening at the Avantage they decided on the strike. Rasseneur resisted no longer, and Souvarine accepted it as a first step. Étienne summed up the situation in a word: if it was a strike that the Company wanted, then a strike they would get.

CHAPTER V

A WEEK went by, and the miners carried on working as usual, but they were sullen and suspicious, as they prepared for the coming struggle.

At the Maheus', the fortnight's pay looked likely to be even slimmer than before. And so La Maheude became bitter, despite her moderation and good sense. Hadn't her daughter Catherine taken it into her head to spend a whole night out on the tiles? The next morning she had returned so tired and sick from her adventure that she hadn't been able to go to the pit; and she cried, saying it wasn't her fault, because it was Chaval who had forced her to stay, threatening to beat her if she ran away. He was going mad with jealousy, and wanted to stop her returning to Étienne's bed, where he said he was sure that the family made her sleep. La Maheude was furious, and after she had forbidden her daughter ever to see that brute again, she said she would go to Montsou to thump him. But they had still lost a day's work, and now that the girl had a sweetheart she preferred not to look for another one.

Two days later there was another drama. On Monday and Tuesday Jeanlin, who was supposed to be at Le Voreux, quietly working, took off on a wild escapade across the marshes and the forest of Vandame with Bébert and Lydie. He had seduced them into God knows what precocious looting and tomfoolery together. He received stiff punishment, a thrashing administered by his mother outside in the street under the eyes of the terrified brats of the village. Would you believe it? Her own children, who had depended on her since the day they were born and who now ought to be bringing in some money of their own at last! And in her cry there was the memory of her own hard childhood, with inherited poverty making her family see each new baby as a future bread-winner.

That morning, when the men and the girl left for the pit, La Maheude got out of bed to say to Jeanlin:

'You know if you ever do that again, you wicked little scoundrel, I'll tan the skin right off your backside.'

At Maheu's new workings, it was hard going. This part of the Filonnière seam was so narrow that the hewers were wedged between the walls and the roof, and scraped the skin off their elbows as they cut the coal. In addition, it started to get very wet, and they were afraid that at any moment there might be a sudden flood from one of those torrents that can burst through the rocks and even carry a man away. The previous day, as Étienne was pulling back his pick after having driven it in particularly hard, he had received a spurt of water in his face, from some spring; but it had appeared to be a false alarm, and had just made the coal-face a bit wetter and nastier. Besides, he hardly gave a thought to the likelihood of an accident, he quite forgot about the danger himself while he was there with his comrades. They lived surrounded by fire-damp, without even noticing how it weighed on their eyelids and span a spidery web over their eyelashes. Sometimes, when the flames of their lamps grew paler and bluer than usual, they remembered it, and one of the miners would press his head against the seam and hear the thin hiss of the gas as if there were bubbles of air breaking the surface at every crack in the rock. But the most constant menace was of rock falls: for, apart from the inadequate timbering, which had always been cobbled up in too much of a hurry, the earth was made unstable by the water soaking through it.

Three times that day Maheu had had to get them to reinforce the timbering. It was half-past two, and the men were about to go back up. Étienne was lying on his side, and had just finished dislodging a block of coal, when a distant but thunderous roar shook the whole mine.

'Whatever's that?' he cried, dropping his pick to listen.

He thought that the gallery had started collapsing behind him.

But Maheu had already thrown himself down the sloping coal-face, saying:

'It's a rock fall . . . Come on, quick!'

They all tumbled downwards as fast as they could, carried onward by an upsurge of fraternal anxiety. Their lamps seemed to dance in their hands, as they ran in single file along the railway track, surrounded by an eerie silence, with their backs bent double as if they were galloping on all fours; and without slackening their pace, they exchanged a series of hurried questions and answers: where? maybe the coal-face? no, it sounded lower down! by the haulage, more like! When they reached the chimney, they flung themselves into it and were swept down on top of each other, not even caring if they got battered and bruised.

Jeanlin, whose skin was still raw from his hiding the day before, hadn't dared play truant again. He trotted barefoot behind his train, closing the ventilation doors one by one; and he occasionally jumped up for a ride on the last tub when he thought he was safely out of sight of the deputy, although this was forbidden, because of the danger of falling asleep. But his greatest entertainment, which occurred every time the train drew into a siding to let another one pass, was to go up to the front to catch Bébert, who was holding the reins. He would slip up stealthily behind his comrade, without his lamp, and give him a savage pinch, or spring some other practical joke on him. He looked like a wicked monkey, with his yellow hair, big ears, and sharp snout, and his tiny green eyes gleaming in the darkness. He was unhealthily precocious, and seemed to have the obscure intelligence and lively skill of some mutant creature, half human, half wild.

That afternoon it was Bataille's turn to work, and Mouque had brought him over to the pit boys; and as the horse caught its breath in a siding, Jeanlin, who had sneaked up behind Bébert, asked him:

'What's that bloody old nag stopped dead for? . . . He nearly broke my legs.'

Bébert was unable to reply; he had to hold Bataille back because he was getting excited at the approach of the other train. The horse had caught the scent of his comrade Trompette, still some way off; he had felt drawn to him since the day he had seen him delivered to the pit. He felt the tender sympathy of an old philosopher wanting to help a young friend by teaching him resignation and patience; for Trompette couldn't seem to settle in, and hauled his trains listlessly, keeping his head down, blinded by the darkness and still yearning for the sunshine. So every time Bataille met him, he stretched out his neck, snorted a greeting, and encouraged him with a great wet kiss.

'God almighty!' Bébert swore; 'there they go slobbering all over each other again!'

Then, when Trompette had passed, he answered the question about Bataille.

'Yes, he's a really crafty bugger, that old nag! ... when he stops like that it's because he's seen something in the way, like a stone or a hole; and he's taking care of himself, he doesn't want to do himself an injury ... There's something bugging him today, over there, behind that door. He pushes at it but then he won't go past ... Did you notice anything?'

'No,' said Jeanlin, 'apart from the water; it's up to my knees.'

The train set off again. And on the next trip, when he had pushed the ventilation door open with his head, Bataille once more refused to proceed, whinnying and trembling. At last he suddenly made up his mind, and lunged through the doorway.

Jeanlin had stayed behind to close the door. He bent down and looked at the muddy pool that he was wading through; then, raising his lamp, he noticed that the props had bent under the constant dripping from the spring. Just then a hewer named Berloque, but called 'Chicot',* because of his habit of chewing and spitting tobacco, came past on his way up from his coal-face, hurrying back to see his wife, who was in labour. He too stopped to look at the props. And all of a sudden, just as the kid was going to run back to catch up with his train, they heard a tremendous crash, and a rock fall covered both man and child.

There was a deep silence. The draught from the collapse sent a dense cloud of dust billowing along the tracks. And on all sides, even from the furthest workings, the miners descended, blinded and choking, with their lamps swinging as they ran, but shedding hardly any light on the galloping file of black figures scurrying along the bottom of this molehill. When the first arrivals bumped into the rock fall, they called out, to warn their comrades. A second group, arriving from the further coal-face, found themselves on the other side of the mass of earth, which had cut the tunnel in two. They quickly realized that the roof had only collapsed over a distance of about ten metres. The damage wasn't particularly serious. But their hearts missed a beat when they heard a strangled moan from beneath the rubble.

Bébert left his train and rushed up repeating:

'Jeanlin's underneath it! Jeanlin's underneath it!'

At that very moment Maheu tumbled down out of his chimney, accompanied by Zacharie and Étienne. He was seized with horror and despair, and could only keep swearing:

'God almighty! God almighty! God almighty!'

Catherine, Lydie, and La Mouquette, who had also rushed up, started sobbing and screaming with terror, at the sight of the terrifying chaos, made worse by the darkness. The men tried to shut them up, but they panicked and screamed louder at every moan they heard.

Richomme, the deputy, had run up, and he was upset by the news that neither Négrel, the engineer, nor Dansaert was at the pit. He pressed his ear to the pile of rocks to listen; and he finally declared that it didn't sound like a child, there must be a man under there. Maheu had already called Jeanlin's name a dozen times. But not a whisper could be heard in reply. The kid must have been crushed.

But still the monotonous moaning could be heard. They called to the dying man, asking who he was, but they heard only more groans in reply.

. 'Hurry up!' repeated Richomme, who had already started to organize the rescue. 'We'll talk later.'

The miners were digging into the rock fall from both ends with picks and shovels. Chaval worked away silently alongside Maheu and Étienne; while Zacharie saw to the removal of the rubble. It was time for the end of their shift, and nobody had eaten, but no one was going home for his soup while his comrades' lives were in danger. They did realize, however, that the whole village would be anxious if they didn't see anyone return, so they proposed to send the women back up. But neither Catherine nor La Mouquette, nor even Lydie, wanted to go, for they were rooted to the spot by the need to know what was happening, and they were helping to clear the debris. So Levaque took it upon himself to go up there to

announce the landslide, and describe it as a routine incident
that they were in the process of clearing up. It was nearly four
o'clock; in less than an hour the workmen had done the
equivalent of a day's work; and already half of the earth would
have been removed if there hadn't been a new fall of rocks
from the roof. Maheu flung himself into the task with such
fury that he dismissed a colleague with a savage gesture when
the man came up and offered to take over for a while.

'Go easy!' said Richomme at last. 'We're nearly there . . . we
mustn't finish them off.'

And the moaning was indeed getting louder and clearer.
The workers had been guided by this continual moaning
sound; and now they seemed to hear the man breathing at the
very tips of their picks. But suddenly he stopped.

They all looked at each other in silence, shivering as they
felt the cold wing of death brush past them in the darkness.
They dug away, bathed in sweat, their muscles stretched to
breaking-point. They uncovered a foot, and from then on they
pulled the earth away with their bare hands, freeing the limbs
one by one. The head hadn't been damaged. They shone the
lamps on him, and murmured his name, Chicot. He was still
warm, but his spine had been broken by a rock.

'Wrap him in a blanket, and put him on a tub,' the deputy
ordered. 'Now for the kid, and let's get a move on.'

Maheu struck a final blow with his pick and broke through
to the men who were clearing the rock fall from the other side.
They shouted out that they had just found Jeanlin unconscious,
with both legs broken, but still breathing. His father picked
him up in his arms, and all he could utter were repeated cries
of 'God almighty!' through his clenched teeth; while Catherine
and the other women had started screaming again.

They hurriedly formed a procession. Bébert had brought
Bataille back, and hitched him to two tubs: in the first lay the
corpse of Chicot, supported by Étienne; and in the second was
Maheu, squatting down holding the unconscious Jeanlin in his
lap, covered by a piece of woollen cloth torn from one of the
ventilation doors. And off they set, walking in step. On each
tub they had hung a lamp, shining like a red star. Then behind
came a line of miners, some fifty shadowy figures. By now

they were broken with fatigue, their feet caught and slipped in the mud, looking like a mournful herd of cattle decimated by an epidemic. It took them nearly half an hour to reach the loading bay. The subterranean convoy seemed never-ending, as it wound its way in thick darkness past the crossroads, round the bends, and down the tunnels.

At the loading bay, Richomme had already gone on ahead and given the order to reserve an empty cage. Pierron loaded the two tubs immediately. In one of them Maheu held his wounded child on his knees, while in the other Étienne had to guard Chicot's body, holding it in his arms to keep it still. When the workmen had piled into the other levels, the cage ascended. It took two minutes. An icy rain fell from the lining of the shaft, and the men kept looking impatiently upwards, eager to see daylight again.

Luckily a pit boy who had been sent to fetch Dr Vander-haghen had found him in and brought him along. Jeanlin and the dead man were carried into the deputies' room, where there was always a great fire blazing throughout the year. Someone put away the buckets of hot water which always stood ready for people to wash their feet in; and when they had spread out two mattresses on the flagstones they laid the man and the child down on them. Only Maheu and Étienne were allowed in. Outside there was a group of tram girls, miners, and youths who had come running up to see what was happening, and were talking in whispers.

As soon as the doctor had glanced at Chicot, he murmured:

'Done for! . . . You can wash him now.'

Two supervisors undressed him, then sponged down his body, which was still black with coal-dust and smeared with the sweat of his labour.

'His head's all right,' the doctor remarked, kneeling on Jeanlin's mattress. 'So's his chest . . . Ah! It's his legs that caught it.'

He undressed the child himself, loosening his cap and slipping off his jacket and breeches with the skill of a nurse-maid. And the poor little body appeared, as thin as a stick-insect, smeared with black dust and yellow mud, mottled with bloodstains. You couldn't tell what was what, so they had to wash him, too. As they passed the sponge over his body he appeared to become even thinner, for his flesh was so pale and transparent that you could see his bones. It was tragic to see this degenerate offshoot of a wretched breed, this insignificant, suffering creature, half-crushed by the collapse of the rocks. When he was clean, they discovered the bruises on the thighs, two red streaks on the white skin.

Jeanlin regained consciousness, and groaned. Maheu stood at the foot of the mattress watching him, with great tears rolling down his cheeks.

'Are you the father, then?' asked the doctor, raising his head. 'No need to cry, you can see he's not dead . . . Better come and help me.'

He noted that there were two simple fractures. But the right leg worried him: he'd probably have to lose it.

At that moment Négrel, the engineer, and Dansaert, who had at last been informed, arrived with Richomme. Négrel listened to the deputy's account with an air of exasperation. He exploded: still the same old story with those damn props! Hadn't he repeated a hundred times that someone would lose his life! And those brutes dared to threaten to strike if they were forced to put up better props! And the worst thing was that the Company would have to pay for the damage now. What was Monsieur Hennebeau going to think?

'Who is it?' he asked Dansaert, who was silently studying the body as they wrapped it in a sheet.

'It's Chicot, one of our good workmen,' the overman replied. 'He's got three children . . . poor bastard!'

Dr Vanderhaghen asked for Jeanlin to be transported immediately to his parents' house. Six o'clock struck and twilight was falling already, so they ought to move the corpse too; the engineer gave orders for horses to be harnessed to the hearse, and for a stretcher to be brought. The wounded child was put on the stretcher, while they loaded the dead man and his mattress on to the hearse.

The tram girls were still waiting outside the door, chatting with the miners who had lingered on to see what would happen. When the deputies' room opened again, silence descended on the group. A new procession formed, with the hearse in front and the stretcher behind, followed by the others, walking in line. They left the yard, and walked slowly up along the steep road to the village. The first November frosts had stripped the vast plain bare, and it seemed to be buried alive by the gathering darkness which fell like a shroud from the leaden sky.

Then Étienne advised Maheu quietly to send Catherine to warn La Maheude, to soften the blow. Her father, who was following the stretcher looking distracted, nodded his agreement; and the girl ran off quickly, for they were nearly there now. But already the familiar black outlines of the hearse had been sighted. Women rushed crazily out on to the pavement, and three or four of them started running wildly around, bareheaded. Soon there were thirty of them, then fifty, all choking with the same terror. Someone was dead then? Who was it? Levaque's story had reassured them all at first, but now it threw them into nightmarish fantasies: it wasn't one man, but ten who had perished, and the hearse would bring them back one by one.

Catherine had found her mother disturbed by a premonition: and as soon as she stammered out her first words, her mother cried out:

'Your father's dead!'

Her daughter protested in vain, and tried to tell her about Jeanlin, but La Maheude didn't stop to listen, she ran off straight away. And when she saw the hearse come past the front of the church she collapsed, looking deathly pale. Some of the women stayed rooted to their doorsteps, struck dumb with fear, turning their heads to follow the progress of the hearse, while others followed, trembling at the thought of discovering whose house the procession would stop at.

The hearse went past; and behind it La Maheude noticed Maheu walking alongside the stretcher. Then, when they put the stretcher down at her door, when she saw Jeanlin alive, with his legs broken, her reaction was so violent that she choked with anger, stammering with dry eyes:

'Now we've seen everything! Now they've started hacking our children to pieces! ... Both his legs, my God! What am I going to do with him?'

'Just you be quiet.' said Dr Vanderhaghen, who had come along to bandage up Jeanlin. 'Would you prefer to see him dead and buried down there?'

But La Maheude flew into an ever fiercer rage, surrounded by the tears of Alzire, Lénore, and Henri. While helping the wounded boy and passing the doctor whatever he needed, she cursed her fate, asking where they expected her to find the money to look after her invalids. Wasn't it enough to have the old man on her hands, without the kid losing his feet into the bargain? And she didn't let up, while other cries, heart-rending laments, emerged from a neighbouring house: it was the wife and children of Chicot who were weeping over the body.

It was pitch-dark now, and the exhausted miners were at last able to eat their soup, while the village was plunged in a gloomy silence, broken only by these piercing cries.

Three weeks passed. They had managed to save both Jeanlin's legs from amputation, but he would always walk with a limp. After an inquiry, the Company had reluctantly offered fifty francs in assistance. In addition, it had promised to find the young cripple a surface job as soon as he was fit. Their poverty would still be worse than before, however, for the father had been so shaken that he fell ill with a high fever.

But by the Thursday, Maheu had returned to the pit. Sunday came. And that evening Étienne discussed the looming deadline of the first of December, wondering anxiously whether the Company would carry out its threat. They stayed up until ten o'clock waiting for Catherine, who must have stayed out late with Chaval. But she didn't come home. La Maheude shut her door and bolted it furiously without saying a word. Étienne felt disturbed at the thought of the empty bed where Alzire took up so little room, and he found it very difficult to get to sleep.

The next day there was still no sign of her; and only in the afternoon on their return from the pit did the Maheus learn that Chaval was keeping Catherine to live with him. He kept creating such terrible scenes that she had decided to stay. To avoid recriminations, he had abruptly walked out of Le Voreux and signed on at Jean-Bart, Monsieur Deneulin's pit, where Catherine was joining him as a tram girl. But the young couple would continue to live in Montsou, at Piquette's.

At first Maheu said he would go and hit the man and bring his daughter back with a few good kicks up the backside. Then he raised his arms in resignation: what was the point? It was always happening, you couldn't prevent girls getting shacked up when they'd made up their minds. It would be better to sit quietly and wait for them to get married. But La Maheude didn't take things so well.

'Did I beat her, when she took up with this Chaval?' she shouted at Étienne, who sat listening, looking pale and very silent. 'Come on, I want you to tell me, you're a fair-minded man ... We left her free enough, didn't we? Because they all go the same way in the end, for heaven's sake. Look at me, I was expecting when her father married me. But that didn't make me run off and leave my parents; I'd never have played a dirty trick like taking my wage packet when I was that young and giving it away to a man who didn't need it ... Oh, it's disgusting, don't you think? It's enough to put you off having children!'

And as Étienne still made no reply apart from occasionally nodding his head, she persisted.

'A daughter who went out wherever she liked every evening! What's got into her! Why couldn't she wait and help us get through our bad patch and then let me get her married? It's natural enough, isn't it? You have a daughter so she can go out to work ... And there you are, we were too kind to her, we shouldn't have let her go out and have fun with a man. You give them an inch and they take a mile.'

Alzire nodded her head in agreement. Lénore and Henri, who had been upset by this storm, sobbed quietly, while their mother launched into a catalogue of their sorrows: first they had had to marry off Zacharie; then old Bonnemort just sat there on his chair with his twisted feet; then there was Jeanlin who would have to spend another ten days in bed, with his bones still not stuck back in place; and now the last straw, that bitch Catherine gone off with a man! The whole family was falling apart. Only Father was left now to go down the mine. How could they live on Father's three francs? There were seven of them, even if you didn't count Estelle. You might as well throw the whole bloody lot of yourselves in the canal.

'It's not going to get us anywhere if you sit around moping,' said Maheu in a low voice. 'Who knows, there may be worse to come.'

Étienne, who had been staring at the stone floor, with his eyes lost in a vision of the future, raised his head and murmured:

'Ah! The time has come, the time has come!'

PART IV

PART IV

CHAPTER I

THAT Monday, the Hennebeaus had invited the Grégoires and their daughter Cécile round to lunch. They had arranged a full day's entertainment: after lunch Paul Négrel was going to show the ladies round one of the mines, Saint-Thomas, which was being luxuriously refitted. But all this was little more than a friendly charade; Madame Hennebeau had organized the outing in order to precipitate the marriage between Cécile and Paul.

And suddenly that very Monday at four in the morning the strike had just broken out.* When the Company had applied its new wage structure on the first of December, the miners had stayed calm. At the end of the fortnight, on pay-day, no one had made the slightest protest. All the staff from the manager down to the humblest supervisor thought the rates had been accepted; so there was considerable surprise in the morning at this declaration of war whose tactics and organization seemed to suggest the presence of a strong leader.

At five o'clock Dansaert woke Monsieur Hennebeau to warn him that not a single man had gone down the pit at Le Voreux. He had come through village Two Hundred and Forty, and found it plunged in sleep, with all its doors and windows closed. And as soon as the manager had jumped out of bed, his eyes still swollen with sleep, he was swamped: every quarter of an hour another messenger arrived, and dispatches fell on to his desk as thick as hailstones. At first he hoped that the rebellion was limited to Le Voreux; but the news became worse by the minute: there was Mirou, there was Crèvecœur, and then there was Madeleine, where only the stablemen had turned up for work; there were La Victoire and Feutry-Cantel, the most loyal pits, where the work-force was down by a third; only Saint-Thomas was working at full strength and seemed unaffected by the action. Until nine o'clock he dictated dispatches, sending them by telegraph* in all directions, to the Prefect at Lille,* to the directors of the Company, warning the authorities and asking for instructions.

He had sent Négrel to tour the neighbouring pits, to get accurate information.

Suddenly Monsieur Hennebeau remembered the lunch; and he was just about to send the coachman to warn the Grégoires that the outing would have to be postponed when he hesitated, his nerve failed him, although he had had no trouble in preparing his plan of action in a few curt, military-style phrases. He went up to see Madame Hennebeau, whose chambermaid was in the last stages of arranging her hair in her boudoir.

'So they're on strike, are they?' she said casually, when he had explained his problem and asked her opinion. 'Well, then, what's that to us? . . . We're not going to stop eating, are we?'

And she persisted; it was no use his telling her that the lunch would be spoiled, that the visit to Saint-Thomas would have to be cancelled; she had an answer to everything: why should they waste a meal that was already in the oven? And as for visiting the pit, they could always decide to give up that idea later on if it looked as if it was going to be a problem.

'Besides,' she said, when the chambermaid had left, 'you know why I want to invite these good people. This marriage ought to mean more to you than the pranks your workmen get up to . . . Anyway, I've made up my mind, so don't contradict me.'

As he watched her, his hard, inscrutable features twitched slightly, despite his habitual self-control, betraying the secret pain of a bruised heart. She had left her shoulders uncovered, and, although she was already past her prime, she was radiant and still desirable, the goddess Ceres, with her ripe autumnal charms.

For a moment he was seized with a rough desire to take her, to plunge his face between her swelling breasts, in the warmth of this luxuriously intimate and sensually feminine room, which was spiced with the disturbing fragrance of musk; but he drew back, for they had slept apart for the last ten years.

'Fair enough,' he said as he left her. 'We won't change a thing.'

Monsieur Hennebeau had been born in the Ardennes. His beginnings in life had been difficult, for he had been a penniless orphan, raised on the streets of Paris. He had managed to struggle through the curriculum of the École des Mines, and at twenty-four he had left for La Grand-Combe to become the engineer at the Sainte-Barbe mine. Three years later he was appointed divisional engineer at the Marles collieries in the Pas-de-Calais; and it was there that he married the daughter of a rich cloth merchant from Arras, the sort of lucky prize that tended to fall into the laps of mining-school graduates. For fifteen years the couple had lived in the same small provincial town, without a single event interrupting the monotony of their existence, not even the birth of a child. Madame Hennebeau, who had been brought up to respect money, became increasingly irritated, and contemptuous of her husband, who worked hard to earn such a moderate salary, and who brought her none of the glamorous satisfaction she had dreamed of at boarding school. He was strictly honest, refused any financial speculation, and carried out his professional functions with an almost military devotion to duty. Their discord had grown, aggravated by one of those strange mismatches of the flesh which can freeze the warmest heart: he adored his wife, and she had all the sensuality of a voluptuous blonde, but already they slept apart, ill at ease with each other, quick to take offence. She soon took a lover, unbeknown to her husband. Finally he left the Pas-de-Calais to take up an office job in Paris, thinking that she would be grateful for this. But Paris finally separated them, for she had dreamed of Paris since she had dressed her first doll as a child, and they had hardly been there a week before she had shed all her provincial airs, become suddenly elegant, and thrown herself into all the luxurious follies of the period. The ten years she spent there were filled with a grand passion, which she flaunted in public, until her lover abandoned her, and she nearly died of grief. This time her husband had not been able to preserve his ignorance, and he resigned himself to the situation after a series of dreadful scenes, rendered powerless by this woman's tranquil impropriety, as she took her pleasure wherever she found it. It was after her abandonment, when he saw how ill with grief she had become, that he had accepted the management of the Montsou collieries, hoping that life in the sober black countryside might bring her to her senses.

Since they had moved to Montsou, the Hennebeaus had
relapsed into the irritable boredom of the early days of their
marriage. At first she appeared to be soothed by the unbroken
peace and quiet, finding solace in the monotonous flatness of the
surrounding plains; and she buried herself away like a woman
whose life was over, acting as if her heart were dead for ever, so
detached from the world that she didn't even care that she was
putting on weight. Then, behind this mask of indifference, a last
fever broke out, a sudden urge to live again, which she kept
under control by indulging her tastes in refitting and furnishing
their small official villa. She said it was hideous, and filled it
with tapestries and trinkets and all sorts of artistic luxuries,
which were talked about as far away as Lille. By now she was
exasperated with the whole area, its stupid fields stretching as
far as the eye could see, and its endless black roads, with never
a tree to be seen, was crawling with repulsive creatures who
disgusted and frightened her. She started to complain of living
in exile, and accused her husband of having sacrificed her
happiness for the sake of his 40,000-franc salary, which was a
pittance hardly even adequate for the household expenses.
Couldn't he have done like the others, demanded a partnership
and a share in the business, done something successful for once?
And she lost no opportunity to remind him of this, showing all
the cruelty of the heiress who has provided the fortune. He
remained polite, and took refuge in a duplicitous administrative
coolness, ravaged by his desire for the woman, one of those late
but violent desires which increase with age. He had never had
her as a lover, and he was haunted by an obsessive fantasy, to
have her fully to himself for once, as she was when she gave
herself to other men. Every morning he dreamed of winning her
affections in the evening; then, when he looked into her
cold eyes and felt that her whole being expressed her rejection of
him, he avoided even touching her hand. It was a sickness
whose suffering, although concealed beneath his rigid exterior,
was incurable, the suffering of a tender soul secretly tortured at
failing to find happiness in his marriage. After six months, when
the villa was finally furnished and Madame Hennebeau had lost
interest in it, she fell into a state of languor and boredom,
claiming to be dying of exile and happy to succumb.

And then Paul Négrel arrived in Montsou. His mother was the widow of a captain from Provence, living in Avignon on a small pension, and she had dined off bread and water in order to send her son to study to be a military engineer at the École Polytechnique. He had graduated with a mediocre diploma, and his uncle, Monsieur Hennebeau, had recently bought him out of the army and offered him a job as engineer at Le Voreux. From that moment on he was treated as one of the family, and even had his own room. Living and eating with the Hennebeaus enabled him to send his mother half his salary of 3,000 francs. In order to disguise his generosity, Monsieur Hennebeau spoke of the problems that a young man would face if he had to set up home from scratch in one of the little chalets reserved for the mining engineers. Madame Hennebeau had immediately assumed the role of the bountiful aunt, calling her nephew by his first name, and making sure he had everything he needed. During the first months especially, she overflowed with maternal advice on every conceivable topic. But she remained very feminine with him, and gradually let him into her confidence. This lad was so young and so practical, his intelligence was so uncluttered, he held such philosophical theories of love, and she was amused by the lively pessimism which often lit up his slim face, with its sharp little nose. Naturally enough she ended up one night in his arms; seeming to yield out of kindness, although she told him that her heart was burnt out and that she wanted him only as a friend. And in fact she wasn't jealous, she teased him about the tram girls, whom he found repulsive, and almost turned sulky when she discovered that he had no ribald youthful escapades to entertain her with. Then she became engrossed with the idea of marrying him off, and dreamed of sacrificing herself to the pursuit of some rich girl on his behalf. But their relationship continued to flourish, and she devoted all her emotional resources as a woman of leisure and experience into grooming and cosseting her little playmate.

Two years went by in this way. One night Monsieur Hennebeau had his suspicions when he heard a pair of naked feet brush past his bedroom door. But he was too shocked at the thought that she could have started a new affair in their own

home, under his own roof, between a mother and a son, to
believe it. And besides, the very next day his wife revealed that
she had chosen Cécile Grégoire for her nephew. She was so
enthusiastically wrapped up in her plans for this marriage that
he blushed at his own monstrous imagination. So he simply
felt grateful to the young man for making the household less
gloomy since his arrival.

As he came down from her boudoir into the hall, Monsieur
Hennebeau happened to meet Paul, who had just come in. He
seemed amused by the talk of the strike.

'Well, then?' asked his uncle.

'Well, then, I've been round the villages. They seem very
quiet in there ... I think that they are just going to send a
delegation.'

But at that moment Madame Hennebeau's voice called
down from the first floor.

'Is that you, Paul? ... Come up and tell me the news.
Aren't those people silly to misbehave, when they're so well
off!'

And the manager had to abandon all hope of obtaining any
further information, since his wife had kidnapped his messenger. He went back to sit at his desk, on which a new pile of
dispatches had collected.

At eleven o'clock, when the Grégoires arrived, they were
surprised to find Hippolyte, the manservant, standing guard,
and he bundled them into the house rather unceremoniously,
as soon as he had had time to cast an anxious glance up and
down the road. The drawing-room curtains were drawn, and
they were ushered straight into the study, where Monseiur
Hennebeau apologized for such a welcome; but the drawing-
room gave on to the road, and it was pointless to provoke
people deliberately.

'Good heavens! Do you mean that you haven't heard?' he
went on, when he saw their surprise.

When Monsieur Grégoire heard that the strike had finally
broken out, he shrugged his shoulders placidly. Bah! It would
come to nothing, they were honest workmen at heart. Nodding
her head, Madame Grégoire confirmed his belief in the traditional submissiveness of the coal-miners; while Cécile, who

was in a particularly cheerful mood, bursting with health and resplendent in a nasturtium-coloured outfit, was amused at the talk of a strike, which reminded her of her visits to the villages to distribute alms.

But Madame Hennebeau, with Négrel in tow, made her appearance, swathed in black silk.

'Oh, how tiresome!' she cried as she entered the doorway. 'As if those people couldn't have waited! . . . Just fancy, Paul refuses to take us round Saint-Thomas.'

'We'll have to stay here, then,' said Monsieur Grégoire, obligingly. 'But we shall enjoy ourselves just as much.'

So far Paul had merely welcomed Cécile and her mother with a formal bow. Annoyed with this lack of enthusiasm, his aunt propelled him towards the girl with a flash of her eyes; then, when she heard them laughing together, she enveloped them with her maternal gaze.

Meanwhile Monsieur Hennebeau finished reading his dispatches and drafted some replies. Around him the conversation continued, his wife explaining that she hadn't touched a thing in the study, letting him keep the faded red wallpaper, the clumsy old mahogany furniture, and the scruffy cardboard filing boxes. Three-quarters of an hour went by, and they were ready to go in to lunch, when the manservant announced the arrival of Monsieur Deneulin, who came in looking somewhat overwrought, but went straight to pay his respects to Madame Hennebeau.

'Oh, you're here, are you?' he said when he saw the Grégoires. And then he turned to the manager and addressed him urgently.

'So this is it then? I've just heard about it from my engineer . . . At my pit all the men went down this morning. But it could spread. I'm worried . . . Tell me, what's it like at your pit?'

He had just arrived on horseback, and his degree of concern could be judged from his loud voice and abrupt gestures, which made him seem like a retired cavalry officer.

Monsieur Hennebeau was starting to fill him in on the exact state of affairs, when Hippolyte opened the dining-room door. So he broke off to say:

'Stay and have lunch with us. I'll tell you the rest over dessert.'

'Yes, if you like,' replied Deneulin, so intent on his mission that he accepted outright, oblivious of etiquette.

He realized, however, that he had been impolite, and he turned to Madame Hennebeau to apologize. But she was all charm. When she had had a seventh place laid for him she settled her guests: Madame Grégoire and Cécile on either side of her husband, then Monsieur Grégoire on her right and Deneulin on her left; and then finally Paul, whom she placed between the young lady and her father. As they were tucking in to the *hors-d'œuvre* she smiled, and said:

'You'll have to excuse me, I wanted to give you oysters . . . You know there's a delivery of Ostends at Marchiennes on Mondays, and I intended to send the cook in the carriage . . . But she was afraid they might throw stones at her . . .'

They all broke out into a great roar of cheerful laughter. They found the story very funny.

'Shh!' said Monsieur Hennebeau, looking nervously towards the windows, from which they could see the road. 'There's no need for everybody to know we're having a party this morning.'

'Well, this is one slice of garlic sausage they won't get,' declared Monsieur Grégoire.

They broke out laughing again, but more discreetly. The guests all started to feel at ease in the room, which was decorated with Flemish tapestries and furnished with antique oak cabinets. The silverware gleamed through the glass panels of the dressers, and there was a great copper chandelier, whose shiny golden surface reflected the green foliage of a palm and an aspidistra, planted in majolica pots. Outside, the December day was made even icier by a bitter north-east wind. But not a draught could be felt in the house, which seemed as warm as a greenhouse, and was suffused with the scent of a pineapple, cut into slices and served in a crystal bowl.

'Perhaps we ought to draw the curtains?' suggested Négrel, who was amused by the idea of terrifying the Grégoires.

The chambermaid, who was helping the manservant, took this to be an order and went over to the window. This gave rise to an interminable series of jokes: nobody put their knife or their glass on the table without taking elaborate precautions; each successive dish was greeted as if it had been saved from the pillage of some plundered city; yet behind their strained hilarity there was a hidden fear, which was betrayed by involuntary glances in the direction of the road, as if a gang of starving beggars lay in wait outside, spying on the table.

After the scrambled eggs and truffles came the fresh trout.

The conversation had turned to the industrial slump, which had been getting worse for the last eighteen months.

'It was inevitable,' said Deneulin. 'The affluence of these last years was bound to end like this . . . Just think of the enormous amount of capital that has been tied up, in railways, and ports and canals, think of all the money wasted in absurd speculation. Even round here they set up enough sugar-refineries for three times the annual harvest of the Department . . . And, my word, the money's started to dry up now, and we've got to wait for people to get their interest back from the millions they've spent: that's why there's been fatal overproduction and a large-scale commercial slump.'

Monsieur Hennebeau challenged this theory, but he agreed that the years of prosperity had spoiled the workers.

'When I think', he cried, 'that these fellows used to be able to make as much as six francs a day in our collieries, twice what they're earning now! And they lived well, and they developed a taste for luxury . . . Today, of course, it seems hard to them to go back to being frugal like they were before.'

'Monsieur Grégoire,' Madame Hennebeau broke in, 'I beg of you, have a little more trout . . . They are delicious, aren't they?'

The manager continued:

'But are we really to blame? We have suffered grievously too . . . Since our factories have been closing one by one, we have had the devil's own job to unload our stock; and with the accelerating fall in demand, we have been forced to lower our production costs . . . That's what the workers refuse to understand.'

Silence reigned. The manservant brought in the roast partridge, while the chambermaid started to pour out the Château Chambertin for the guests.

'There's been a famine in India,' Deneulin went on in an undertone, as if he were talking to himself. 'And when America cancelled her orders for iron and cast iron, she dealt our furnaces a dreadful blow. It's all linked, one tremor is enough to shake the whole world . . . And our Empire was so proud of our rate of industrial growth!'

He tucked into his partridge wing. Then he raised his voice:

'The worst thing is, that to lower the production costs, logically, we ought to produce more: otherwise, we have to make the savings by reducing wages, and the workers are right to say that we are making them pay our bills.'

This admission, which he had been led into by his own honesty, gave rise to an argument. The ladies were not having much fun. Besides, they were all busy with the business of eating, their hunger still hardly abated. When the manservant came back in, he looked as if he wished to speak, then he hesitated.

'What is it?' asked Monsieur Hennebeau. 'If it's more dispatches, give them to me, I'm expecting some replies.'

'No, Sir, it's Monsieur Dansaert in the hall . . . But he's afraid of disturbing you.'

The manager begged his guests to excuse him, and asked the overman to come in. Dansaert remained standing, at a distance from the table; while everyone turned round to look at this big man, who was breathless with the news he had to tell. The villages were peaceful; but they had decided to send a delegation, which was due to arrive in a few minutes' time.

'That's fine, thank you,' said Monsieur Hennebeau. 'I want you to report morning and evening, is that understood?'

And, as soon as Dansaert had left, they started joking again. They wolfed down the Russian salad, declaring that there was not a moment to be lost if they wanted to finish it in peace. And their hilarity knew no bounds. When, after Négrel had asked the chambermaid for some bread, she had replied with a 'Yes, Sir' so quiet and terrified that it sounded as if she could feel an army of brigands breathing down her neck, ready for rape and murder, Madame Hennebeau said condescendingly:

'You can speak up. They haven't come yet.'

The manager, who had received another pile of letters and

dispatches, insisted on reading one of the letters out loud. It was a letter from Pierron, in which, in formal and respectful language, he advised that he felt bound to go on strike with his comrades in order to avoid maltreatment; and he added that he had not even been able to refuse to take part in the delegation, although he disapproved of the initiative.

'So much for the freedom of the worker!' cried Monsieur Hennebeau.

And so they got back to the subject of the strike, and asked for his opinion.

'Oh,' he replied, 'it won't be the first time ... They'll take a week's holiday, or at most a fortnight, like the last time. They'll go on a pub crawl; then when they start to get really hungry, they'll go back down under again.'

Deneulin shook his head.

'I'm not so sure ... This time they seem better organized. Haven't they got a provident fund?'

'Yes, but they've got hardly more than three thousand francs: what can they do with that? ... I suspect a certain Étienne Lantier of being their ringleader. He's a good workman, I'd be sorry to have to give him his booklet, like we had to do with the famous Rasseneur, who continues to poison Le Voreux with his ideas as well as his beer ... No matter, within a week half of the men will have returned to work, and in a fortnight all ten thousand will be back underground.'

He had no doubt about it. His only worry was the possibility of his own disgrace if headquarters were to put the blame for the strike on his shoulders. For some time now he had felt that he was out of favour. So, abandoning the spoonful of Russian salad which he had taken, he reread the latest dispatches from Paris, and tried to interpret all the overtones in their replies to his queries. The others let him leave the table, and they felt rather like soldiers eating their last rations on the battlefield before the shooting started.

Then the ladies started to offer their opinions. Madame Grégoire felt sorry for those poor people who were going to suffer from hunger; and Cécile had already started to plan the distribution of coupons for bread and meat.

But Madame Hennebeau was astonished at the idea that the

colliers of Montsou might be badly off. Weren't they extraordinarily lucky people, to be housed, heated, and cared for by the Company? In her indifference to the common herd, she knew only what she had been told, which was the lesson she always used to recite in order to impress visiting Parisians; and she had ended up believing it herself, so that she felt indignant at the ingratitude of the people.

Meanwhile Négrel continued to frighten Monsieur Grégoire. He found Cécile not unattractive, and he didn't mind marrying her to keep his aunt's favour; but he brought no amorous passion to the business, for he was an experienced young man who no longer lost his head, as he put it. He claimed to be a republican, which didn't prevent him from handling his workforce with the utmost severity, and making subtle fun of them, when there were ladies in the audience.

'I don't share my uncle's optimism,' he went on. 'I'm afraid there will be serious disturbances ... So, Monsieur Grégoire, I'd advise you to lock up La Piolaine. You might get looted.'

At that very moment, without abandoning the smile that illuminated his kindly face, Monsieur Grégoire was expressing paternal sentiments towards the miners even more fervently than his wife.

'Looted, me?' he cried out in stupefaction. 'Why ever would they want to loot me?'

'Aren't you a shareholder in Montsou? You do nothing, you live off the labour of others. In fact you are the original capitalist monster, with no mitigating features ... You can be sure that if the revolution ever triumphs, they will force you to hand over your fortune, as stolen goods.'

Monsieur Grégoire immediately lost his childish tranquillity, his habitual, uncritical serenity. He stammered:

'What, my fortune stolen goods! Didn't my great-grandfather work hard to make his small investment prosper? Haven't we shouldered all the risks of running the business? And have I ever used any of the income unwisely myself?'

Madame Hennebeau was alarmed to see that the mother and daughter too were white with fear, and she hastened to intervene, saying:

'Paul is only joking, my dear Monsieur Grégoire.'

But Monsieur Grégoire was beside himself. As the manserv-ant went by with a platter of crayfish, he took three, mechani-cally, and started absent-mindedly crunching at the claws.

'Oh! I don't say that there aren't shareholders who don't play the game. For instance, I've heard that some ministers received shares in Montsou as perks for services rendered to the Company. And then there's a distinguished person whose name I won't mention, a duke who's our biggest shareholder, whose whole life is the most ostentatious scandal, he throws millions down the drain chasing women, showing off, and buying unnecessary luxuries . . . But you know us, we never do anything wasteful, we wouldn't dream of such extravagance! We don't speculate, we try to live soberly on what we have, and even give some to the poor! . . . For heaven's sake! our workers would have to be the most arrant scoundrels to want to take so much as a pin that belonged to us!'

Négrel had to intervene personally in order to calm him down, although he was greatly amused by his anger. The crayfish were passed round again, and a restrained crunching of shells accompanied the conversation as it veered round to politics. Monsieur Grégoire argued, with a tremulous voice, that he was a Liberal, in spite of all this; and that he regretted the overthrow of Louis-Philippe.* As for Deneulin, he was in favour of strong government, and declared that the Emperor had gone too far down the road of dangerous concessions.*

'Remember 1789,'* he said. 'It was the nobles who made the Revolution possible through their complicity and their taste for new philosophical ideas . . . Well, there you are, the bourgeoisie today is playing the same idiotic game, encouraging liberalism, enjoying destruction, and flattering the people . . . Oh, yes, you are sharpening the monster's teeth so that it can devour us. And it will devour us, you can count on it!'

The ladies silenced him and tried to change the subject, asking for news of his daughters. Lucie was at Marchiennes, where she was singing with a friend; Jeanne was painting the portrait of an old beggarman. But he gave this information absent-mindedly, and he kept his eyes glued to the manager, who was absorbed in reading his dispatches, and had forgotten about his guests. Behind these flimsy pieces of paper he could feel the weight of Paris, where the orders of the Board would decide the outcome of the strike. So he couldn't resist harping back to his main concern.

'Well, what are you going to do?' he asked brusquely.

Monsieur Hennebeau jumped, then evaded the issue with the vaguest of phrases.

'We'll have to wait and see.'

'Of course you have quite a mattress to fall back on, you can hold out,' Deneulin said, thinking aloud again. 'But I'll go under straight away, if the strike reaches Vandame. It's all very well to have renovated Jean-Bart, I can only survive on a single pit if there's no break in production ... Oh, it's no laughing matter for me, I assure you!'

This involuntary confession seemed to impress Monsieur Hennebeau. As he listened a plan took shape in his mind: if the strike turned nasty, why shouldn't he make the most of it, and leave things to fester until his neighbour was ruined, then buy out his concession for a song? That would be the best way of buying himself back into favour with the Board, who had been dreaming for years of getting their hands on Vandame.

'If Jean-Bart is such a nuisance to you,' he said, laughing, 'why don't you get rid of it?'

But Deneulin already regretted having made his confession.

'Over my dead body!' he cried.

His vehemence caused some amusement, and they finally forgot about the strike when the dessert arrived. An apple charlotte with meringue attracted fulsome praise all round. Then the ladies started discussing the recipe for the pineapple, which was also judged to be exquisite. And then the fruit arrived, grapes and pears, putting the finishing touch to the feeling of mellow ease which accompanies the end of a copious meal. Everyone spoke at once, and the mood turned sentimental, as the manservant served them a hock, instead of champagne, which they felt would have been too predictable.

And the marriage of Paul and Cécile definitely took a step forward in the atmosphere of *bonhomie* encouraged by the dessert. The young man's aunt had cast him such urgent looks that he forced himself to be pleasant, using his charms and flattery to win back the Grégoires from their shock at the idea of being looted. For a moment Monsieur Hennebeau, seeing his wife and his nephew in such close harmony, felt his dreadful suspicions rise up within him again, as if he had caught them holding hands rather than exchanging glances. But he was soon reassured again by the thought of the marriage which was being planned before his very eyes.

Hippolyte was serving the coffee when the chambermaid ran up in a state of terror.

'Sir, Sir, they're here!'

It was the delegation. Doors slammed, and a wave of panic rippled through to the assembled company in the adjoining room.

'Show them into the drawing-room,' said Monsieur Hennebeau.

The guests, who were still sitting round the table, felt momentarily unnerved, and exchanged worried glances. But then they started joking again: they pretended to put the remains of the sugar in their pockets, and spoke of hiding the silver. But the manager refused to laugh, and the laughter died away, to be replaced by whispering, as the heavy footsteps of the delegates being shown into the drawing-room and trampling over the carpet reverberated close at hand.

Lowering her voice, Madame Hennebeau said to her husband:

'I hope that you are going to drink your coffee.'

'Of course,' he replied, 'they'll just have to wait.'

He was nervous, and pricked up his ears to listen to what was happening in the next room, although he looked entirely absorbed by his coffee.

Paul and Cécile had just got up, and he had persuaded her to have a dangerous peep through the keyhole. They were trying not to laugh, and were talking under their breath.

'Can you see them?'

'Yes ... I can see one fat one, with two other little men behind him.'

'Well, don't they look awful?'

'Not at all, they look very nice.'

Suddenly Monsieur Hennebeau leapt up from his chair, saying that the coffee was too hot and that he would drink it afterwards. As he went out he put his finger to his lips to counsel prudence. Everyone else remained seated, silently, not daring to move, listening intently and uncomfortably to the muffled sound of gruff male voices.

CHAPTER II

THE day before, during a meeting held at Rasseneur's, Étienne and some friends had chosen the delegates who were to meet the management the next day. That evening, when La Maheude found out that her man was to be one of them, she was upset, and asked him if he wanted to get them thrown out of their home. Maheu himself had not been keen to accept. When the moment for action arrived, they both relapsed into the traditional resignation of their kind, however unjust their wretched poverty, for they were fearful of what the morrow might bring, and preferred instead to bow to authority. Usually Maheu himself relied on his wife's judgement for the running of their lives, for her advice was always wise. This time however he finally showed his anger, all the more so because deep down he shared her doubts.

'Leave me alone, for Christ's sake,' he said as he went to bed, turning his back on her. 'That would be a fine thing to do, to let my comrades down! . . . I'm only doing my duty.'

She came to bed too. Neither of them spoke. Then, after a long silence, she answered him:

'You're right, you should go. But don't forget, dear, that we haven't got a chance.'

Noon was striking as they sat down to eat, for the appointment was for one o'clock, at the Avantage, where they had agreed to meet before setting out for Monsieur Hennebeau's. They had potatoes, but as there was only one small piece of butter left, nobody touched it. They would save it to spread on their bread in the evening.

'You know that we're counting on you to speak,' Étienne said suddenly to Maheu.

Maheu was transfixed, his voice shaking with emotion.

'Oh, no, that's the limit!' cried La Maheude. 'I don't mind him going, but I'm not going to have him play leader ... Anyway, why him rather than someone else?'

So Étienne explained, with all his ardour and eloquence. Maheu was the best workman in the pit, the most popular and the most respected, the one whose good sense was quoted as an example. Thus the miners' claims would take on real importance, if they were voiced by him. The first idea had been that he, Étienne, should speak, but he hadn't been at Montsou long enough. They would pay more attention to someone local. And besides, his mates were relying on their interests being defended by the most worthy man: he couldn't refuse, it would be cowardly.

La Maheude looked desperate.

'Go on then, my dear man, ruin yourself for the sake of the others. I don't care, why should I?'

'But I'll never be able to,' stammered Maheu. 'I'll say all the wrong things.'

Étienne, who was pleased to see that he accepted, clapped him on the shoulder.

'You only have to say what you feel, and everything will be fine.'

Old Bonnemort was sitting there waiting for his swollen legs to recover, but he had his mouth full, so he just listened, and nodded his head. They all fell silent ... When they had potatoes to eat the children always stuffed their mouths full and were very well behaved. When he had swallowed his mouthful, the old man murmured sagely:

'You can say what you like, and you might as well not have said anything at all ... Oh, I've seen a lot, I've seen 'em all! Forty years ago they threw us out of the manager's offices, and they drew their swords on us! Maybe they'll let you in today, but you won't get any more sense out of them than out of a brick wall ... Heavens! they're the ones who are sitting on the money, they don't give a damn!'

Silence fell again. Maheu and Étienne got up and left the family sitting gloomily over their empty plates. As they went out, they picked up Pierron and Levaque, then all four of them went round to Rasseneur's, where the delegates from the neighbouring villages were arriving in small groups. Then, when the twenty members of the delegation had all gathered there, they drew up the conditions that they thought should replace those imposed by the Company; and finally they left for Montsou.

The bitter north-east wind swept over the cobbles. It was striking two o'clock as they arrived.

At first the manservant told them to wait, closing the door in their faces; but then, when he returned, he let them into the drawing-room and drew back the curtains. Daylight filtered gently through the frills of the lace *guipure*. And the miners, left on their own, did not dare sit down, feeling embarrassed, although they were all perfectly clean, and had shaved that morning, combed their yellow hair and moustaches, and put their best woollen clothes on. They fingered their caps uneasily, and looked out of the corners of their eyes at the furniture, which was an amalgam of every style imaginable that the current taste for antiquity had made fashionable: Henri II armchairs, Louis XV chairs, an Italian cabinet from the seventeenth century and a Spanish *contador** from the fifteenth, an altar-front used as a mantelpiece, and gold braid taken from antique chasubles and sewn on to the *portières*.* All this old gold and tawny-hued silk, with its air of ecclesiastical luxury, filled them with respectful discomfort. The oriental carpets seemed to entangle their feet in their deep woollen pile. But what overcame them most powerfully was the heat from the stove, filling the room so evenly it took them by surprise, especially since their cheeks were frozen from the icy wind. Five minutes passed. Their embarrassment increased, in the comfort of this luxurious and secluded room.

At last Monsieur Hennebeau came in, his frock coat formally buttoned like an officer's, and the little rosette of his Légion d'honneur adorning his buttonhole in regulation fashion. He spoke first.

'Ah, there you are! ... I hear that you are planning a rebellion ...'

And he broke off, to add with studied politeness:

'Sit down, I'm perfectly happy to talk things over.'

The miners turned round, looking for something to sit on.

Some took the risk of sitting on the chairs; while the others, intimidated by the embroidered silk, preferred to remain standing.

There was a pause. Monsieur Hennebeau, who had pulled his armchair up to the fireside, looked them carefully up and down, trying to recall their faces. He had just recognized Pierron, hidden in the back row; and his gaze fell upon Étienne, sitting opposite him.

'Now then,' he asked, 'what have you got to say for yourselves?'

He expected to hear the young man speak up, and he was so surprised to see Maheu come forward, that he couldn't help adding:

'Whatever next! You've always been a sensible man and a good workman, you've grown up at Montsou and your family has worked down the mine since the first shaft was sunk! ... Oh, this is a bad business, it hurts me to see you at the head of these malcontents!'

Maheu listened, with his eyes lowered. Then he started, at first with a gruff, hesitant voice.

'Sir, it's because I'm a peaceful man with no complaints against my name that my comrades have chosen me. That should show you that it's not a rebellion by hotheads or rabble-rousers trying to make trouble for the sake of it. We only want justice, we are fed up with dying of hunger, and we thought it was time to sort things out, to make sure we at least had some bread to eat every day.'

His voice had got stronger. He raised his eyes, and continued, looking straight at the manager:

'You know very well that we can't accept your new system ... We've been accused of skimping on the timbering. It's true that we don't spend long enough on it. But if we did, our working day would be even shorter, and since we can't earn enough to feed ourselves as it is, it would be all over for us, we'd all be wiped out like a clean slate. Pay us more and we'll put better props up, we'll spend as long as we should on the timbering, instead of exhausting ourselves hacking away, which is the only thing we get paid for. There's no other way possible, the work's got to be paid for if we've got to do it ...

And what did you come up with instead? Something we'd never even dreamed of in our worst nightmares, for heaven's sake! You lower the price of a tub of coal, then you say you'll pay for the timbering separately to make up for the loss. If that was true, it'd still be daylight robbery, because the timbering would still take us longer. But what makes us furious is that it's not even true: the Company isn't paying us the difference at all, it's just pocketing two centimes for every tub-load, that's all!'

'Yes, he's right, it's the truth,' the other delegates muttered, when they saw that Monsieur Hennebeau was reacting violently, as if he were about to interrupt Maheu.

However, Maheu himself silenced the manager. Now that he had got going, the words came out unaided. At times he listened in surprise to the sound of his own voice, as if some stranger were speaking within him. Things which had been building up deep down inside him, things which he didn't even know he thought, came tumbling out as if his heart would burst. He spoke of the wretched poverty they all suffered, their exhausting labour, their animal existence, their wives and children at home reduced to tears from hunger. He mentioned the last few dreadful pay packets, the pathetic fortnightly pittance whittled away by fines and lay-offs, which reduced their families to tears when they brought it home. Did the Company want to destroy them for good?

'So there you are, Sir,' he eventually concluded, 'that is why we have come to tell you that if we're going to die because we can't make enough to live on, we'd rather die doing nothing. At least we won't wear ourselves out . . . Now that we've walked out of the pit, we are not going back down again unless the Company accepts our conditions. They want to lower the price of the tub, and pay separately for the timbering. What we want is to keep things as they were, and in addition we want an extra five centimes a tub . . . Now it's up to you to show that you're on the side of justice and labour.'

Several of the miners raised their voices.

'That's right . . . He's said what we all think . . . We only want what's right.'

Others, although they said nothing, nodded their heads in

approval. The luxurious room with its old gold and embroidery, and its mysterious accumulation of ancient bric-à-brac, had dissolved into thin air; and they no longer felt the carpet that they were trampling under their heavy feet.

'Give me a chance to reply,' Monsieur Hennebeau finally shouted, getting angry. 'First of all, it isn't true that the Company makes two centimes on every tub ... Let's have a look at the figures.'

A confused argument followed. The manager tried to divide the men against each other, asked Pierron to speak, but he declined, stammering, and it was Levaque who took the most aggressive stance, offering confused explanations, and alleging facts that he was unable to substantiate. The rising hubbub of voices became an indistinguishable mass, muffled by the tapestries and the heat.

'If you all talk at once,' Monsieur Hennebeau broke in, 'we'll never reach an agreement.'

He had calmed down again, and was showing no signs of resentment, the bluff politeness of the manager who is acting on instructions and intends to make sure that they are respected. Right from the beginning of the discussion he had been watching Étienne, and looking for an opportunity to get round to drawing the young man out of the silence into which he had withdrawn. So, dropping the question of the two centimes, he suddenly opened up the debate.

'No, let's get to the bottom of things, you are being worked on by vile agitators, there's a veritable plague abroad among the work-force now, and it's corrupting the best of you ... Oh! there's no need for anyone to confess, I can see that you've been changed, you were so peaceful before. It's true, isn't it? You've been promised milk and honey instead of bread and butter, they've told you it's your turn to be the masters ... And now they've enrolled you in the famous International, which is an army of brigands dreaming of destroying society ...'

Then Étienne interrupted him.

'There you are wrong, Sir. Not a single collier from Montsou has joined yet. But if they are provoked, every man in every pit will enrol. It all depends on the Company.'

From this moment on, combat was joined by Étienne and Monsieur Hennebeau, as if the other miners were not there.

'The Company is sheer providence for its employees, you are wrong to threaten it. This year it spent three hundred thousand francs on building mining villages, which bring in less than two per cent profit, not to mention the pensions it pays, nor the free coal and medical care. You're an intelligent man, in a few months you've become one of our best workmen, wouldn't you do better to broadcast the true facts rather than dissipate your energy on keeping bad company? Yes, I mean Rasseneur, you know that we had to let him go in order to protect our pits from his socialist filth ... You're always being seen in his company, and I'm sure he's the one who has forced you to set up your provident fund, which we would be pleased enough to allow if we thought it was just a savings scheme, but we can see that it's meant to be a weapon to use against us, a fighting fund to subsidize your battle. And while we're on that subject, I must inform you that the Company intends to keep a check on those funds.'

Étienne let him keep talking, looking into his eyes, but his lips were affected by a slight nervous twitch. On hearing the last statement he smiled, and simply replied:

'So now that's a new demand from the management, isn't it, Sir, for you haven't claimed the right to check it previously ... Unfortunately, what we want is less interference from the Company, and instead of it claiming to offer charity, we want it quite simply to be fair and to give us our due, our fair share in the profits we create for it. Is it fair that every time there's a slump the workers die of hunger in order to safeguard the shareholders' dividends? ... I don't see how you can deny, Sir, that the new system is a disguised cut in wages, and that's what we find intolerable, for if the Company does have to make savings, there's no reason why they should all be borne by the workers.'

'Ah! Here we are at last!' cried Monsieur Hennebeau. 'I was waiting for that, accusing us of starving the people and living off the sweat of their brows! How can you say such stupid things, when you must know what enormous risks capital investment is subject to in industry, in the mines for instance?

A properly equipped pit today costs between fifteen hundred thousand and two million francs; and it's long enough before you get your petty interest back from the mass of capital that you've sunk into it! Nearly half of the mining companies in France have gone bankrupt ... Besides, it's stupid to accuse the successful ones of cruelty. When their workers suffer, they suffer too. Do you think that the Company hasn't as much to lose as you have, in the current slump? It can't decide wages on its own, it has to obey the laws of competition or go bust. Argue with the state of the economy, not the Company. But you don't want to listen, you don't want to understand!'

'Oh yes we do,' said the young man, 'we understand very well that nothing can improve for us as long as things continue as they are, and that's exactly the reason why sooner or later the workers are going to make sure that something changes.'

Although these words were moderate enough in substance, they were pronounced with such quiet conviction and dangerous emotion that a sudden silence fell. A feeling of embarrassment and a shudder of fear ran through the suddenly thoughtful company. Although they didn't follow the details of the argument, the other delegates felt that their comrade had staked their claim to a share in the surrounding luxury; and they started to cast sidelong glances at the warm tapestries, the comfortable chairs, and the whole luxurious environment, where the tiniest trinket would have paid for a month's supply of soup.

At last Monsieur Hennebeau, who had remained pensive for a moment, got up to invite them to leave. Everyone rose when he did. Étienne gently nudged Maheu's elbow; and Maheu spoke up again, with a voice that had already become embarrassed and awkward again:

'Well, Sir, is that all you have to say to us? ... We'll have to tell the men that you've rejected our terms.'

'But, my good man,' the manager cried, 'I haven't rejected anything! I'm a wage-earner like yourself, I have no more say here than the youngest pit boy. I get my orders, and my only concern is to make sure that they are carried out properly. All I've said to you is what I feel it's my duty to tell you, but the last thing I can do is take a decision ... You express your demands, I pass them on to the Board, and I'll give you their answer as soon as I get it.'

He had adopted the impartial tone of the civil servant, avoiding emotional involvement in the dispute, speaking drily but courteously as if he were a neutral instrument of authority. But now the miners were unconvinced by him; they were suspicious of his motives, and wondered what lay behind this approach, why he found it in his interest to tell lies, and they imagined that he must be cheating them or stealing from the Company, by setting himself up between them and the real bosses, and they assumed that he must be on the fiddle, since he was paid like a worker, but lived like a lord!

Étienne took it upon himself to intervene again.

'In that case, Sir, it is most unfortunate that we can't put our case to the people in charge. We could explain a lot, we could clear up so many misunderstandings which you can't be expected to see from our point of view . . . If only we knew who to talk to!'

Monsieur Hennebeau showed no anger. He even smiled.

'Good heavens! We are getting confused. If you don't trust me any longer, you'll have to go higher up.'

The delegates followed the vague gesture he made with his arm in the direction of one of the windows. Where exactly was higher up? Paris, obviously. But they couldn't quite put their fingers on it, and it receded frighteningly into the distance, into a sacred and inaccessible land, ruled by an unknown god, lying in wait in the depths of his tabernacle. They would never meet him, they could only feel his power at a distance, weighing on the destinies of the 10,000 colliers of Montsou. And when the manager spoke, it was this hidden, oracular power that bore him up.

They felt enormously depressed. Even Étienne had to shrug his shoulders and tell them that they might as well go; while Monsieur Hennebeau took Maheu amicably by the arm and asked him for news of Jeanlin.

'That should certainly give you food for thought, when you feel like defending bad timbering! . . . If you stop to think, my friends, you will understand that a strike would be a disaster for everyone. You'll die of hunger before the week's out: how will you manage? . . . But I'm sure that I can count on your good sense and that you will go back down to work again by Monday at the latest.'

Then they all left, stumbling over each other like a herd of animals as they went out of the drawing-room, their shoulders bowed, refusing to say a word in reply to this plea for submission. The manager, who saw them out, was obliged to conclude the discussion: the Company on the one hand with its new tariff, and the workers on the other with their request for an increase of five centimes per tub. In order not to foster any illusions, he felt bound to warn them that their terms were sure to be rejected by the Board.

'Think it over before you do anything rash,' he repeated, worried by their silence.

In the hall, Pierron bowed with exaggerated politeness, but Levaque made a show of putting his cap back on. Maheu was trying to think of a parting word, when Étienne, once again, nudged his elbow. And they all left, with nothing dispelling the ominous silence but the loud banging of the door as it slammed shut behind them.

When Monsieur Hennebeau came back into the dining-room, he found that his guests had got to the liqueurs, but were silent and motionless. He explained the situation rapidly to Deneulin, whose face darkened and fell. Then, while he finished off his cold coffee, they tried to change the subject of conversation. But even the Grégoires came back to the strike, astonished that there were no laws to prevent the workmen from downing their tools. Paul reassured Cécile, and declared that they would call in the gendarmes.

After a while Madame Hennebeau called the manservant.

'Hippolyte, before we go into the drawing-room, open the windows to let some air in.'

CHAPTER III

Two weeks had gone by; and, on the Monday of the third week, the attendance records received by the management indicated a further decrease in the number of men reporting for work. That morning they had expected more people to go back to work; but the Board's obstinacy in refusing to yield exasperated the miners. Le Voreux, Crèvecœur, Mirou, and Madeleine were no longer the only pits lying idle; at La Victoire and at Feutry-Cantel there were now hardly more than a quarter of the men at work; and even Saint-Thomas was affected. Gradually the strike was becoming general.

At the Le Voreux pit-head a heavy silence reigned. The whole works seemed dead, the yards and buildings deserted and abandoned. Under the grey December sky, three or four tubs stranded up on the overhead track expressed a silent, inanimate sadness. Down below, between the legs of the trestles, the stock of coal was nearly used up, leaving the earth naked and black; while the stacks of timber props were rotting in the rain. At the quayside on the canal, a half-laden barge was moored, as if it had fallen asleep in the murky water; and on the deserted slag-heap, whose decomposing sulphur continued to smoulder in spite of the rain, a cart raised its melancholy arms. But it was above all the buildings which seemed lifeless, the screening shed with its shutters closed, the headgear which no longer vibrated with the rumblings from the landing-stage, the strangely cool generator room, and the giant chimney too wide for its few wisps of smoke. The winding engine was only fired in the mornings. The stablemen took fodder down for the horses, and the deputies went down below unaccompanied, like ordinary workmen now, keeping a look-out for the disasters which are liable to beset tunnels as soon as they cease to be maintained; then, after nine o'clock, the rest of the service was carried out using ladders. And above these moribund buildings, buried in their shroud of black dust, the only thing that could still be heard was the exhaust of the pump breathing out with its loud and protracted panting, the last sign of life at the pit, which would be swallowed up by flood water if that breathing were to cease.

Over on the plain beyond, village Two Hundred and Forty seemed lifeless, too. The Prefect had hurried down from Lille, and a company of gendarmes had come to guard the highway; but when they saw that the strikers were peaceful, the Prefect and the gendarmes had decided to go home. The mining village had never before set such a good example for its neighbours on the vast plain. In order to avoid going out to the pubs, the men spent the whole day at home in bed; the women, forced to ration their coffee, were less nervous, and less excited by gossip and quarrels; and even the gangs of children seemed to understand, behaving themselves so well that they ran about barefoot and were careful not to make a noise when they got into a fight. The slogan which was repeated and passed from mouth to mouth was: we've got to behave ourselves.

And yet the Maheus' house was filled with a continual coming and going of people. As secretary, Étienne had divided out the 3,000 francs from the provident fund among the most needy families; then a few hundred francs more had been raised by subscriptions and collections here and there. But already their combined resources were running out, the miners had no money left to support the strike, and starvation was looming. Maigrat, having at first promised a fortnight's credit, had suddenly changed his mind after the first week, cutting off their supplies of food. Usually he followed the directives of the Company; perhaps, then, the Company had decided to force a swift conclusion by starving the villages. In any case, Maigrat acted in an arbitrary and tyrannical way, offering or withholding his bread depending on the looks of the girl that the parents sent to do the shopping; and he closed his door most sharply on La Maheude, seething with resentment and wanting to punish her for making him lose Catherine. The last nail in their coffin was the weather, which turned absolutely freezing, so that the housewives saw their supplies of coal diminish, and were worried by the knowledge that it couldn't be replenished by production from the pits as long as the men refused to go back to work. As if it wasn't bad enough to die of hunger, they would die of cold as well.

The Maheu household was short of everything. The Levaques still had enough to eat, having borrowed a twenty-franc piece from Bouteloup. As for the Pierrons, they still had some money left; but, in order not to seem any less starving than the others, afraid that they would be approached for loans, they bought on credit from Maigrat, who would have given La

Pierronne the freedom of his shop if she had only offered to lift her skirt for him. By the Saturday many families had gone to bed with no supper. And yet, despite the prospect of days of terrible deprivation, not a single complaint could be heard, everyone observed the conventions, calmly and courageously. They showed absolute confidence, an almost religious faith, making an unconditional self-sacrifice like a persecuted confessional minority. Since they had been shown the promised land of justice, they were ready to suffer on the road to universal happiness. Hunger went to their heads, and, in their wretched, hallucinating eyes, the flat, dull horizon had never seemed to open up on to such a vast and infinite perspective. When their eyes became blurred with fatigue, they could see the ideal city of their dreams beyond the horizon, but now somehow close and real; there all men were brothers, in a golden age where meals and labour were shared between equals. Nothing could shake their conviction that they were already on the threshold. The fund was empty, the Company would never yield, every day could only make the situation worse, and yet they kept faith in their hope, showing a blithe contempt for reality. Even if the earth were to quake beneath their feet, a miracle would save them. This faith replaced their missing bread and warmed their stomachs. When the Maheus, like the others, had swallowed their watery soup all too quickly, they glided off into a state approaching vertigo, dreaming ecstatically of a better life, with the same conviction that drove the early Christians into the arena.

From now on Étienne became the undisputed leader. During their evening conversations, he made oracular statements, as he continued his studies and developed firm opinions on everything. He spent his nights reading, he received more and more letters; he had even subscribed to *The Avenger*, a socialist broadsheet from Belgium, and this review, the first of its kind which anyone in the village had seen, had brought him extraordinary prestige in the eyes of his comrades. His growing popularity made him daily more excited. Keeping up an extensive correspondence, discussing the fate of the workers in every corner of the province, holding consultations for the miners from Le Voreux, above all becoming a focus of attention and feeling the whole world revolving around him, constantly boosted his vanity, especially as he had scaled these heights after being a mere mechanic and hewer with greasy black hands. In fact, he had moved up a rung, he had entered the despised world of the bourgeoisie, enjoying intellectual and material satisfactions, although he couldn't admit this to himself. He still felt awkward about one thing, his lack of formal education, which made him embarrassed and shy as soon as he found himself face to face with a gentleman dressed in a frock coat. Although he continued to learn, devouring every book he could lay hands on, his lack of method made the process of assimilation very slow, and he became so confused that he came to know more things than he was able to understand. So it was that, in his more sensible moments, he lost confidence in his mission, and feared that he was not the right man for the situation. Perhaps they should have chosen a barrister or a scholar, someone who could speak and act without compromising his comrades? But he soon rebelled against these doubts. No, not a barrister! They were all scoundrels, exploiting their knowledge in order to grow fat on the backs of the people! Whatever the outcome of the crisis, the workers had to settle their own affairs. And he started to dream again of becoming a popular leader: once Montsou was at his feet, Paris would beckon from the misty distance, and, who knows, election to Parliament, speaking to a packed audience from the hallowed benches, and he saw himself slaying the bourgeoisie in the first speech ever made to Parliament by a working man.

For some days, Étienne had been puzzled. Pluchart kept writing letter after letter, offering to come to Montsou, in order to whip up the fervour of the strikers. The idea was to organize a private meeting, which the mechanic would preside over; and behind this project was the idea of using the strike to win over the miners, who until then had been suspicious, to the International. Étienne was worried that this might cause trouble, but he would still have let Pluchart come, if Rasseneur hadn't been highly critical of such an intervention. Despite his new power, Étienne had to take into consideration the opinions of the publican, who had given service for longer, and who had loyal supporters among his customers. So he continued to hesitate, and didn't know how to reply.

And then, on Monday towards four o'clock, a new letter arrived from Lille, while Étienne was on his own with La Maheude in the downstairs room. Maheu, bored with the enforced idleness, had gone fishing: if he managed to catch a decent fish, below the canal lock, they would sell it to buy bread with. Old Bonnemort and little Jeanlin had just slipped away to stretch their newly healthy legs; while the children had gone out with Alzire, who spent hours on the slag-heap scavenging for cinders. Sitting by the pathetic fire, which they dared no longer stoke up, La Maheude had unbuttoned her corsage, let one of her breasts hang down over her belly, and was feeding Estelle.

When the young man folded his letter up after reading it, she enquired:

'Is it good news? Are they going to send us any money?'

He shook his head, and she continued:

'I don't know how we're going to survive till the end of next week . . . Never mind, we'll survive somehow or other. When you've got justice on your side it keeps you going, doesn't it? We'll beat them in the end.'

She had now come to approve of the strike, within reason. It would have been better to gain satisfaction from the Company without stopping work. But since they had stopped, they shouldn't start again until they had obtained justice. She absolutely refused to budge from that principle. Rather die than seem to be in the wrong when they were in the right!

'Ah!' cried Étienne, 'what we could do with is a nice little outbreak of cholera to get rid of all those parasites from the Company!'

'Oh, no,' she replied, 'you shouldn't wish for anyone's death. It wouldn't get us anywhere, more of them would spring up to take their places . . . All I ask is for them to come to their senses, and I don't see why not, there are nice people in all walks of life . . . You know I don't agree with your politics at all.'

She did indeed frequently criticize him for the violence of his language, and for being too aggressive. You wanted your work to be paid for at the price it was worth, that was only right; but why get so involved in everything, including the bourgeoisie and the government? Why interfere in other people's business, when you could only get into trouble? But she still respected him, because he didn't get drunk, and he paid his forty-five francs' rent regularly. When a man was well behaved, you could excuse his other faults.

Then Étienne spoke of the Republic, which would provide bread for all. But La Maheude shook her head, for she remembered the 1848 Revolution,* a dreadful year which had left them stripped to the bone, her and her husband, at the beginning of their marriage. She let herself go in this reminiscence of their tribulations with an expressionless voice, her eyes unfocused, and her bosom uncovered, while her baby daughter Estelle had fallen asleep on her lap without relinquishing the breast. And Étienne, his thoughts elsewhere, stared at the massive breast, whose soft whiteness contrasted so starkly with the blotchy, yellow complexion of her face.

'Not a farthing,' she murmured, 'not a crumb to eat, and all the pits stopped work. And what did it all come to? The poor starving to death, like today!'

But at that moment the door opened and they were reduced to silence as Catherine walked in. Since eloping with Chaval, she had not shown her face in the village again. She was so unsure of herself that she did not close the door behind her, but just stood there trembling and speechless. She had hoped to find her mother on her own, and the sight of the young man spoiled the sentence she had been preparing in her mind on the way.

'What the hell have you come here for?' cried La Maheude, without even getting up from her chair. 'I don't want to see you again, be off with you.'

Then Catherine tried to pull herself together and say her piece.

'Mum, here's some coffee and sugar ... Yes, it's for the children ... I've done overtime, I did it for them ...'

She brought out of her pockets a pound of coffee and a pound of sugar, and plucked up the courage to place them on the table. She had been feeling upset by the fact that Le Voreux was on strike while she was working at Jean-Bart, and the only way she could think of of helping her parents a little like this was to use the pretext of the children. But this kindness failed to disarm her mother, who replied:

'Instead of bringing us treats you would have done better to stay at home and earn us more bread.'

She vented her feelings by attacking her daughter, throwing in her face everything that she had been saying about her for the last month. Going off with a man and getting tied down at sixteen, when you had a family in need! You'd have to be the most unnatural of daughters. You could forgive a silly mistake, but a mother could never forget such an act. And even then, you could understand it if they had kept her locked in! Far from it, she had been as free as the air as long as she came home to sleep at night.

'Whatever got into you, at your age?'

Catherine, who was standing motionless beside the table, listened, with lowered head. Her skinny, undeveloped body was shaking as she tried to reply, in short, breathless sentences.

'Oh, if it was only me, for all the fun I get! .... It's him. When he wants to I've got to want to too, haven't I? Because, you see, he's stronger than me ... You can't tell how things are going to turn out, can you? Anyway, what's done is done, and you can't undo it, it doesn't make any difference now, whether it's him or someone else. I'll have to get married.'

She defended herself, not on account of any sense of rebellion, but only with the passive resignation of all girls who come under the male thumb at an early age. Wasn't it the common fate? She had never dreamed of anything else, a rough and tumble behind the slag-heap, a child at sixteen, then poverty and unhappiness in marriage, if her lover would marry her. And she only blushed for shame, and trembled so, because she was shaken to be treated as a tramp in front of this lad, whose presence made her feel oppressed and desperate.

Meanwhile Étienne had got up and busied himself with stoking the dying embers of the fire, so as to keep out of the argument. But their eyes met. She looked pale and exhausted, but she was still pretty, with bright, clear eyes, and a browner face than he remembered; and he experienced a strange feeling as his resentment ebbed away; he would have simply liked her to be happy, with this man that she had chosen in preference to him. He felt the need to look after her, the urge to go to Montsou to force the fellow to respect her properly. But she saw nothing but pity in this constant show of tenderness, and thought he must despise her to keep staring at her like that. Then her heart felt so heavy that she choked and was unable to stammer any further words of apology.

'That's right, you might as well shut up,' broke in La Maheude, still unmoved. 'If you've come home to stay, come in; otherwise get out of here right away, and think yourself lucky that I'm busy, otherwise I'd have given you a good kick you know where.'

As if this threat had suddenly materialized, Catherine received a flying kick in the behind, with a violence that stunned her with shock and pain. It was Chaval, who had rushed in through the open doorway, and had lashed out at her like an enraged beast. He had been watching her from outside for a minute or two.

'Ah, you bitch!' he shouted, 'I've been following you, I was sure you'd come round here to get yourself fucked up to the eyeballs! And you're paying the bugger! I paid for the coffee that you're pouring down the bastard's throat!'

La Maheude and Étienne were so stunned that they remained rooted to the spot. Chaval pushed Catherine violently towards the door.

'Will you get out of here, for Christ's sake!'

And as she hid in a corner of the room, he lashed out at her mother.

'So that's what you're up to, then, you keep watch downstairs, while your whore of a daughter lies flat on her back upstairs with her legs apart.'

Finally he grabbed Catherine by the wrist, shook her, and dragged her outside. When he reached the door, he turned round again to face La Maheude, who sat glued to her chair. In the turmoil she had forgotten to put her breast away. Estelle had fallen asleep, face down, half-buried in her woollen skirt; and the massive breast swung naked and free like the udder of a milch cow.

'When the daughter's not on the job, it's the mother's turn

to get screwed,' shouted Chaval. 'Go on, flash your meat at him! Your dirty old lodger's got a strong stomach, hasn't he?'

At that, Étienne wanted to hit his workmate. Only his fear of alerting the whole village if he started a fight had prevented him from snatching Catherine away from Chaval. But now he too was carried away by his fury, and the two men found themselves face to face, with the blood rushing to their faces. Their deep-rooted hatred and long-suppressed jealousy burst out into the open. Now each wanted to finish off the other.

'Watch out!' Étienne muttered between his clenched teeth. 'I'll flay you alive.'

'Just you try!' replied Chaval.

They stood watching each other for a few seconds more, standing so close that each could feel the other's hot breath on his cheeks. And it was Catherine who pleaded with her lover and pulled him out of the house and the village, running straight ahead without looking back.

'What a brute!' muttered Étienne, slamming the door violently, shaken with such anger than he had to sit down again.

Opposite him La Maheude had still not moved. She raised her arms in despair, and then there was a long silence, heavy with the painful things they were unable to say. Despite his efforts to avoid it, Étienne's gaze kept returning to her breast, with its almost liquid expanse of white flesh, which he now found both voluptuous and embarrassing. Of course she was over forty and she had lost her figure from too many pregnancies, like any prolific mother; but many men still found her desirable, she was strong and well built, with a long, full face which retained traces of her former girlish beauty. Slowly and unhurriedly she had taken her breast in both hands and put it back in place. A rebellious pink extremity resisted, which she thrust back with her fingers, then she buttoned up her camisole, and slumped back in her chair, and became just a shapeless black body once more.

'He's a pig,' she said at last. 'Only a filthy pig could have such disgusting ideas ... Why should I care! He didn't deserve a reply.'

Then, still looking the young man in the face, she added, with her voice unwavering:

'I have my faults, of course, but not that one ... I've only ever been touched by two men, a trammer in the past, when I was fifteen, and then Maheu. If he'd left me like the first one did, God alone knows what would have happened, and if I've behaved myself ever since we've been married, that doesn't mean I'm a saint, because when we don't do anything wrong, it's often because we haven't had the chance ... But I'm telling the truth, and I know some of our neighbours who couldn't say as much, don't you?'

'That's perfectly true,' replied Étienne, standing up.

And he went out, while she tried to light the fire again, after placing Estelle, who was still asleep, on two chairs. If Father had caught a fish and sold it, they would still be able to make some soup.

Outside night was already falling, and Étienne walked away into the freezing darkness, plunged in gloom and despair. He no longer felt anger against the man and pity for the girl he was abusing. The violent scene receded and became blurred in his mind while he started thinking about the universal suffering and the abominable poverty of the people. He thought of the whole village without bread, its women and children who would go hungry that evening, the whole populace engaged in the struggle, despite their empty stomachs. And the doubts which disturbed him on occasion were now rekindled within him, in this dreadfully melancholy twilight, torturing him with misgivings which he had never felt so violently before. What a terrible responsibility he had taken upon himself! Should he still spur them on, now that there was neither money nor credit left? And how would things turn out, if no help arrived, if everyone's spirits were vanquished by hunger? Suddenly, he saw a vision of disaster: children dying, mothers sobbing, while the men, thin and haggard, marched back down into the pits. Étienne kept on walking, without noticing the stones he stumbled over, filled with intolerable anguish at the idea that the Company would win and that he would have led his comrades to disaster.

When he raised his head, he saw that he had arrived at Le Voreux. The dark bulk of the buildings loomed heavily in the growing darkness. Rising up from the deserted pit-head and its network of great, still shadows, they looked like part of an abandoned fortress. As soon as the winding engine stopped, the life went out of the walls. At this time of night, nothing stirred, not a lantern, not a voice; and even the exhaust from the pump itself was only a far-off death-rattle, rising from heaven knows where, as the whole pit slithered into oblivion.

As Étienne watched, the blood came coursing back into his heart. The workers might be suffering from hunger, but that meant that the Company would be breaking into its millions. Did it have to be the winner, in this war of labour against capital? Whatever happened, victory would cost it dear. Afterwards, each side would have to count its casualties. He was swept along once again by a militant frenzy, by a fierce need to put an end to poverty, even if the price to be paid was death. It would be better for the village to die there and then, rather than continue to die little by little every day from famine and injustice. A mixture of ill-digested ideas from books he had read passed through his mind, examples of inhabitants who had burnt their cities to stop the enemy, vague stories where mothers saved children from slavery by dashing their heads against stones, where men let themselves starve to death rather than eat the bread of tyrants. This carried him away, and a blaze of good cheer rose up from the ashes of his attack of darkest despair, banishing doubt and making him ashamed of his momentary cowardice. And, as his faith was rekindled, he felt borne upward by great gusts of pride, by the thrill of being a leader and seeing himself obeyed even if it meant a sacrifice, and by the burgeoning dream of the power he would assume on the night of his triumph. Already he pictured the simple grandeur of the scene, with his refusal to seize power, and his decision to return all authority to the people when he had become master.

But he awoke, and shivered at Maheu's voice telling him of his good luck in catching a superb trout and selling it for three francs. They would have their soup after all. So he let his comrade return to the village, saying that he would follow on later; and he went in to sit down at the Avantage, waiting for a customer to leave so that he could warn Rasseneur openly that he was going to write to Pluchart to come as soon as possible.

He had taken his decision: he wanted to organize a private meeting, for he felt that victory was assured, as long as the miners of Montsou joined the International *en masse*.

CHAPTER IV

IT was at the Bon-Joyeux, run by the Widow Désir, that the private meeting was arranged, for Thursday at two o'clock. The widow, who was outraged by the suffering imposed on the colliers, whom she considered her children, was in a state of constant fury, especially since her tavern was nearly empty. They had never had a less thirsty strike; even the heavy drinkers locked themselves in at home, for fear of disobeying the policy of sobriety. So Montsou, which was packed with people at the time of the Ducasse fair, now revealed its wide street in all its silence, dullness, and desolation. The beer had ceased flowing into and out of the miners' bellies; the gutters were dry. On the cobbles outside Casimir's bar and the Progrès Inn, the only signs of human life to be seen were the pale faces of the landladies looking hopefully down the street; then, at Montsou itself, the whole row of pubs was deserted, from the Lenfant to the Tison, including the Piquette and the Tête-Coupée; only the Saint-Éloi Inn, which was patronized by the deputies, was still serving up the odd pint; and the solitude was felt even at the Volcan, whose ladies were unemployed for lack of admirers, although they had lowered their price from ten sous to five in view of the hard times. The whole country seemed to be wallowing in a state of mourning.

'God almighty!' Widow Désir had yelled, slapping her thighs with her open palms, 'I blame the gendarmes! Let them clap me in gaol, but I'll have their guts for garters!'

For her all the authorities, all the bosses, were gendarmes, which was a term of general abuse which she used to characterize the enemies of the people. She had been thrilled by Étienne's request: her whole house belonged to the miners, she would lend her dance hall free, and she would send out the invitations herself, since the law required her to. Besides, if the law was annoyed, so much the better, they'd just have to lump it. The very next morning the young man brought her nearly fifty letters to sign, which he had had copied by some of his literate neighbours in the village; and they sent these letters off to the pits, to the delegates and a number of other reliable men. Ostensibly, their agenda was to discuss the continuation of the strike; but in fact they were expecting Pluchart to come and deliver a speech in order to urge mass membership of the International.

On the Thursday morning Étienne felt a sudden pang of anxiety, when he saw no sign of his former foreman, who had sent a dispatch promising to be there on Wednesday evening. Whatever could have happened? He was dismayed not to be able to talk things over with him before the meeting. At nine o'clock he went over to Montsou, hoping that the mechanic might have gone there direct without stopping at Le Voreux.

'No, I haven't seen your friend,' answered Widow Désir. 'But everything's ready, why not come and have a look?'

She led him into the dance hall. The decorations had not changed, there were the same streamers strung across the ceiling and meeting in a wreath of coloured paper flowers, and the arms of the saints, painted in gold on cardboard shields, lining the walls. The only difference was that they had replaced the musicians' stage with a table and three chairs in one corner; and the hall itself was set out with rows of benches, placed diagonally.

'That's perfect,' said Étienne.

'And, you know,' the widow continued, 'you must make yourself at home. You can shout the roof down ... If the gendarmes come, they'll have to march over my dead body.'

Despite his concern, he couldn't help smiling as he looked at her, because of her enormous size, with a pair of breasts either of which it would have taken all a man's energies to embrace; which led people to say that, even with six lovers a week, she needed two at a time every night, because of the size of the task.

But Étienne was astonished to see Rasseneur and Souvarine come in; and as the widow turned to leave the three of them in the great empty hall, he cried out:

'You're early, aren't you!'

Souvarine, who had been working the night shift at Le Voreux, because the mechanics weren't on strike, had come out of sheer curiosity. As for Rasseneur, he had been looking embarrassed for two days now, and his round face had lost its indulgent smile.

'Pluchart hasn't arrived, and I'm very worried,' Étienne added.

The publican looked away and replied between his teeth:

'I'm not surprised, I don't think he's coming.'

'What do you mean?'

Then Rasseneur pulled himself up and looked Étienne in the face and spoke out simply:

'The truth is, that I sent him a letter, too; and in my letter I begged him not to come ... That's right, I think that we ought to settle our own affairs, without involving outsiders.'

Étienne was beside himself and, trembling with anger, he stared his comrade in the face, and kept repeating:

'You didn't! You can't have!'

'Yes, that's just what I did do. And you know I believe in Pluchart! He's tough and he's clever, he's a good man to have by your side ... But the problem is, you see, that I don't give a damn for your ideas! I don't give a damn for government and politics and all that! What I want is better treatment for the miners. I worked below ground for twenty years, and I sweated so much with poverty and fatigue that I swore I would try to make things easier for the poor buggers I left down there; and I can feel it in my bones, you're not going to get anywhere with all this performance, you're going to make the condition of the workers even more wretched ... When they're forced by hunger to go back to work, the Company will lay it on even thicker, it'll reward them by beating them black and blue, sending them running back like dogs that have escaped from their kennels!'

He raised his voice, and stood his ground squarely, with his stout legs and imposing stomach. And all of his patience and good sense poured forth in an untroubled flow of effortlessly clear declarations. Wasn't it foolish to believe that you could change the world at a stroke, put the workers in charge of the bosses, and share out the money like an apple? You would need thousands and thousands of years even if it ever did come to pass. So you could stop pestering him with your miracles! The most sensible thing to do, if you didn't want to come a cropper, was to behave yourself, make realistic claims, in fact improve the workers' conditions at every possible opportunity. That's what he would do, if he was in charge, he'd make the Company improve conditions; instead of which, damn and blast it, they would all end up dead if they were so stubborn.

Étienne had let him talk on, his indignation preventing him from replying. Then he cried out:

'Great heavens! Haven't you a drop of blood in your veins?'

For a moment, he felt like hitting him; and to resist the temptation, he strode violently across the hall, venting his fury on the benches, which he kicked aside as he made his way forward.

'You might at least close the door,' Souvarine remarked. 'We don't want everyone to hear us.'

After he had gone to close the door himself, he sat down calmly on one of the chairs on the stage. He had rolled a cigarette, and he looked at the other two with his soft, critical air, and his lips curled in a knowing smile.

'When you get angry, we get nowhere,' Rasseneur replied judiciously. 'I thought at first that you were a man of good sense. It was fine to advise your comrades to keep quiet, to force them to stay at home, and to use your influence over them to make sure they behaved within the law. And now you want to throw them to the wolves!'

After each foray through the benches, Étienne kept coming back up to the publican, seizing him by the shoulders, and shaking him, shouting his replies into his face.

'But by all that's holy! I do want to keep the peace. Yes, I did impose discipline! And, yes, I am still advising them to stay at home! But in the end we mustn't allow people to make fools of us! You enjoy staying cool, don't you, but I don't, there are times when I feel that my head's going to burst.'

Now Étienne made his own confession. He mocked his novice's illusions, and his religious dreams of a compassionate society where justice would triumph and all men would be brothers. But if you were just going to fold your arms and sit back and wait, then you could stay there till the end of the world and man would still be eating man, like a pack of wolves. No! You had to do something about it, otherwise injustice would be eternal, the rich would go on sucking the blood of the poor for ever. So he couldn't excuse himself for the stupidity of having said previously that politics should be kept out of social problems. He was ignorant then, and since then he had read books, and studied. Now his ideas had matured, he was proud to say that he could think systematically. But he didn't explain it very well, for his arguments were full of the confused remnants of a number of theories* that he had successively worked through and abandoned. Looming largest was still Karl Marx's idea that capital had been acquired through theft, that it was the right and duty of labour to win back this stolen wealth. As for the practical means, he had at first followed Proudhon in believing in the mirage of mutual credit, of a vast bank of exchange, which would cut out all middle men; then, at a later stage, Lassalle's co-operative societies, funded by the State, gradually transforming the planet into one great industrial city, had fascinated him, until the day when he had felt disillusioned, realizing the difficulty of keeping control of such a creation; and latterly he had come to adopt collectivization, requiring all the instruments of production to be owned by the community. But it all remained vague, he had no idea how to put this new idea into practice, inhibited as he was by rational and emotional scruples, not daring to support the extreme claims of the most sectarian believers. He would go so far as to say that the workers should take charge of the government of the country, first of all. Then afterwards, they would have to see how things turned out.

'But what's got into you? Why are you defending the bourgeoisie?' he added violently, returning to stand right in front of the publican. 'You used to say it yourself, before: it just can't last, something's got to give!'

Rasseneur flushed slightly.

'Yes, I did say so. And if something does happen, you know that I won't be afraid to come forward . . . But what I do object to is increasing the chaos to better your personal position.'

Now it was Étienne's turn to flush. The two men had
stopped shouting; they had turned bitter and spiteful, feeling
cold and hostile as their rivalry was revealed. That was the
fundamental reason behind the exaggerated difference between
the systems they expounded, throwing one into revolutionary
excess and forcing the other into an affectation of prudence, so
that they both tended to get transported in spite of themselves
to extremes which did not represent their true convictions, as
they found themselves caught up in the fatal logic of the roles
which they had found thrust upon them. And as he listened to
them, Souvarine's pale, effeminate face betrayed a silent contempt, the crushing contempt of a man ready to pay with his
life, in total obscurity, without even the compensation of
recognition as a martyr.

'You wouldn't mean me, by any chance?' asked Étienne.
'Are you jealous?'

'Jealous of what?' asked Rasseneur. 'I don't claim to be a
great man, I'm not trying to found a branch of the International
at Montsou so that I can become its secretary.'

His opponent tried to interrupt him, but he continued:

'Why don't you admit it? You don't care a damn about the
International, you're just itching to take charge, so that you
can live like a lord corresponding away with the famous
Federal Council for the Nord Department!'

For a while silence reigned. Then Étienne replied, still
trembling:

'All right . . . I thought I was doing everything the proper
way. I always consulted you, because I knew that you had
been involved in the struggle here, long before me. But, since
you can't bear to work with someone else, I'll work on my own
from now on . . . And first of all I'm warning you that the
meeting will take place, even if Pluchart doesn't come, and
that our comrades will join whether you like it or not.'

'Oh, will they?' muttered the publican. 'It's not as easy
as all that . . . First you've got to get them to pay the
subscription.'

'That's not true. The International allows striking workers
to wait. We'll pay later, but they'll come to our assistance
straight away.'

That made Rasseneur see red.

'All right then, we'll see ... I'm coming to your meeting myself, and I shall speak. You can count on me, I'm not going to let you confuse my friends, I'll explain where their true interests lie. We'll see whether they prefer to follow me, whom they've known for thirty years, or you, who've turned everything upside down round here in less than one ... No, I've had enough! To hell with you! It's you or me now, a fight to the finish!'

And he went out, slamming the door behind him. The flowery streamers flapped against the ceiling, and the gilded coats of arms jumped away from the walls. Then the large hall relapsed into its previous state of peaceful torpor.

Souvarine was still sitting at the table, smoking peacefully. After walking up and down for a moment in silence, Étienne felt the need to relieve his pent-up feelings. Was it his fault if people forsook that great layabout and followed him instead? And he denied trying to become popular, he didn't even know how it had come about, how he had won the friendship of the villagers, the confidence of the miners, and the power that he now had over them. He was indignant at the accusation that he was trying to cause trouble in order to further his own ambitions, and thumped his chest, protesting his fraternal loyalty.

Suddenly, stopping in front of Souvarine, he cried out:

'You know, if I thought I would cause a friend to spill a single drop of his blood, I'd run away to America tomorrow!'

The mechanic shrugged his shoulders, and a faint smile flickered over his lips again.

'Oh, blood,' he muttered. 'What difference does that make? It's good for the soil.'

Étienne calmed down, took a chair, and sat down at the other side of the table, cupping his chin in his hands. This pale face, whose dreamy eyes were sometimes lit by a fierce and fiery gleam, worried him, and exercised a strange influence on his will-power. Without his comrade needing to speak, he was persuaded by his very silence, feeling himself gradually won over.

'Look,' he asked, 'what would you do in my place? Wasn't I

right to insist on positive action? . . . Isn't it best if we join this Association?'

Souvarine let a stream of smoke flow slowly from his lips; then he answered, using his favourite term:

'A load of rubbish! But meanwhile, it's better than nothing . . . Besides, their International will be successful sooner than you think. He's taking charge.'

'Who do you mean?'

'The man himself!'

He said this under his breath, with an air of religious fervour, looking toward the East. He was speaking of the master, of Bakunin* the exterminating angel.

'He's the only man who can deliver the sledgehammer blow we need to get things moving,' he continued, 'while all your intellectuals are cowards, waiting for things to evolve . . . In three years' time, under his command, the International should be able to overthrow the old world order.'

Étienne listened very attentively. He ached to know more, to understand this cult of destruction, on whose subject the mechanic dropped only the darkest hints, as if he were keeping its mysteries for himself.

'But I wish you'd explain . . . What is your aim?'

'To destroy everything . . . No more nations, no more governments, no more property, no more God, and no more religion.'

'Fair enough. But then what does that leave you with?'

'With the primal, unstructured community, with a new world, and a new beginning to everything.'

'And by what means? How are you going to set about it?'

'By fire and the sword, and poison if need be. The bandit is the real hero, the popular avenger, the active revolutionary who despises phrases lifted from literature. What we need is a series of shattering terrorist attacks which will terrify the authorities and awaken the people.'

While he spoke, Souvarine took on a terrible appearance. He drew himself up ecstatically in his chair, a mystical light burning in his pale eyes, his delicate hands clenching the edge of the table as if they would throttle it. Gripped with fear, Étienne looked at him, thinking of the garbled stories which had been passed on to him, of mines placed in the cellars of the Tsar's palace, of police chiefs hunted down and torn to shreds with knives like wild boars, of his mistress, the only woman he had ever loved, hanged one rainy morning in Moscow* while, watching from the crowd, he embraced her with his eyes for the last time.

'No, surely not!' murmured Étienne, sweeping these abominable visions away with a vigorous wave of his arm, 'we haven't reached those extremes in our country. Murder and arson we will never accept! It's monstrous, it's unjust, all our comrades would rise up to strangle the guilty party.'

Apart from which, he still failed to understand. It wasn't in his or his comrades' nature to be attracted by this dismal dream of a whole world exterminated, razed to the ground like a field of rye. And afterwards, what would they do, how would the nations rise again? He demanded an answer.

'Tell me what your programme is. The rest of us want to know where we're going.'

Then Souvarine concluded calmly, his gaze misty and unfocused:

'All arguments about the future are criminal, because they prevent sheer destruction, and obstruct the progress of the revolution.'

This made Étienne laugh, despite the cold shiver that the reply sent down his spine. In fact he admitted openly that there was some sense in these ideas, whose terrifying simplicity attracted him. However, it would make Rasseneur's task too easy, if they retailed them unadulterated to their comrades. They had to think of practicalities.

Widow Désir offered them lunch. They accepted and went into the bar, which was separated from the dance hall by a sliding partition during the week. When they had finished their omelettes and cheese, the mechanic wanted to leave, and, as Étienne tried to persuade him to stay, he said:

'What's the point? You'd only be repeating the same useless load of rubbish! ... I've heard enough of it already. Good-night.'

And he left, gentle and obstinate as ever, his cigarette still dangling from his lips.

Étienne's anxiety mounted. It was one o'clock, and it looked certain that Pluchart had not kept his word. Towards half-past one, the delegates started to arrive, and Étienne had to greet them, since he wanted to check who was coming in, for fear that the Company would be sending the usual spies. He examined each letter of invitation, scrutinized all the faces; many of them, however, could be allowed in without a letter of invitation; as long as he recognized them the door would be opened. As two o'clock struck, he saw Rasseneur arrive, and calmly proceed to finish his pipe at the bar, chatting away in leisurely fashion. This insolent lack of concern made him even more nervous, especially since some of the audience had come just for fun, like Zacharie, Mouquet, and a few others too: they didn't give a damn about the strike, they thought it was a great laugh to have nothing to do; and they had settled down at tables in the bar to spend their last few coins on a pint, cracking jokes and sneering at their more gullible comrades for their eagerness to receive a crashingly boring lecture.

Another quarter of an hour went by. The audience started to become impatient. Then Étienne in desperation came to a decision. But just as he was about to enter the hall, Widow Désir, who had been hanging out of the window, cried out:

'Look, there he is, your gentleman's arrived!'

And Pluchart it was. He arrived in a carriage drawn by a tired old nag. He jumped straight out on to the cobbles, a slim and rather sleek man, despite his somewhat large, square head, and wearing a fine black woollen frock coat over the Sunday best of a well-to-do working man. It was now five years since he had last wielded a spanner, and he had become very careful how he dressed, and especially how his hair was groomed. He was vainly proud of his success as a popular orator; but he still walked stiffly, and his nails, worn away by working with metal, had obstinately refused to grow again. He was an extremely active man, who tirelessly criss-crossed the countryside, trying to implant his ideas.

'Oh, I hope you're not angry!' he said, anticipating questions and reproaches. 'Yesterday morning a lecture at Preuilly, then a meeting at Valençay in the evening. Today lunch at Marchiennes with Sauvagnat ... Anyway, I did find a cab. I'm exhausted, you can tell by my voice. But it doesn't matter, I'll speak all the same.'

He was just about to enter the Bon-Joyeux when he remembered something.

'Heavens above! I nearly forgot the cards! We'd have made right fools of ourselves!'

He went back to the cab, which the driver was putting away in the yard, and he drew a little black wooden case out of the luggage compartment, and tucked it under his arm.

Étienne walked radiantly in his shadow, while Rasseneur, who was quite overcome, dared not hold out his hand, although Pluchart immediately grasped it and shook it, and mentioned his letter casually in passing: what a strange idea! Why shouldn't they hold this meeting? You should always hold meetings, if you got the chance. Widow Désir offered him a drink, but he refused. No need! He never drank when he had to speak. And besides he was in a hurry because that evening he was hoping to go on to Joiselle, where he wanted to discuss things with Legoujeux. Then they all went through into the dance hall in a group. Maheu and Levaque, who had turned up late, followed the gentlemen in. And then the door was locked, so that they wouldn't be disturbed, which remark led the hecklers to laugh even louder, and Zacharie shouted to Mouquet that anyone would think the whole damn village was bedding down for a right old orgy.

There were nearly a hundred miners waiting on the benches, in the musty air of the hall, where the odour of the last dance still lingered in the tepid air. Whispered comments spread all round the room, and heads turned, while the newcomers sat down in the empty seats reserved for them. Everyone looked at the gentleman from Lille, whose black frock coat surprised his audience and made them feel ill at ease.

But at Étienne's suggestion they immediately set up a committee. He called out the names, and the others approved with raised hands. Pluchart was appointed chairman, then Maheu and Étienne himself were nominated as deputies. There was a scraping of chairs, as the committee members took their seats; and for a moment the chairman seemed to have disappeared under the table, where he was depositing the case, which he had been firmly holding on to until then. When he resurfaced, he rapped lightly on the table with his knuckles to command attention; then he started speaking, with his hoarse voice:

'Citizens . . .'*

A side-door opened, which made him stop speaking. It was Widow Désir, who had gone round through the kitchen to get in, bringing six beer mugs on a tray.

'No need to move,' she murmured. 'Talking is thirsty work.'

Maheu took the tray and Pluchart was able to continue. He said how touched he was by the friendly welcome extended to him by the miners of Montsou, and he apologized for his late arrival, mentioning his tiredness and his sore throat. Then he granted citizen Rasseneur's request to speak.

Rasseneur had already taken up his position beside the table, near the mugs. He stood up on a chair which had been turned round to serve as a rostrum. He seemed very emotional, and coughed before he launched out in full voice:

'Comrades . . .'

The source of his influence over the pit workers was his eloquence, the casual ease with which he was able to talk to them for hours without ever getting tired. He never ventured the slightest gesture, but would stand motionless and smiling, deafening and drowning them with words, until they all cried out, 'Yes, of course, you're right!' And yet, today, as soon as he started to speak he sensed a covert resistance. So he proceeded cautiously. He dealt only with the continuation of the strike, waiting to attract their applause, before confronting the question of the International. Certainly, their honour required them to reject the demands of the Company; but what suffering this entailed! What a terrible future was in store for them if they had to hold out much longer. And, without actually proposing that they abandon the strike, he sapped their resolve, describing the villages dying of hunger, and wondering what unsuspected resources the partisans of resistance were counting on. Three or four friends started to applaud, but this only underlined the cold impassivity of the majority and their mounting irritation as he persisted in his argument. Then, when he felt it was hopeless trying to win them over, he gave way to his anger, and predicted all sorts of misfortune if they allowed themselves to be swept into provocative action at the instigation of outsiders.

Two-thirds of the audience had risen to their feet in anger, trying to stop him continuing, because they felt he was insulting them by treating them as if they were badly behaved children. But Rasseneur stood his ground, took regular swigs of his beer, and kept on talking regardless of the surrounding uproar, crying violently that no man alive, he was sure, would be able to stop him doing his duty!

Pluchart had stood up. As he had no bell, he banged on the table with his fist, repeating in his hoarse voice:

'Citizens . . . citizens . . .'

At last he obtained a measure of calm, and the meeting voted to terminate Rasseneur's address. The delegates who had represented the pits in the interview with the manager led on the others, who were equally goaded by hunger and eager for new ideas. The vote was a foregone conclusion.

'You don't give a damn, do you? You've got plenty to eat!' screamed Levaque, shaking his fist at Rasseneur.

Étienne had leaned over behind the president to pacify Maheu, who had gone very red, furious as he was at such a hypocritical speech.

'Citizens,' said Pluchart, 'I beg you to allow me to speak.'

There was a complete silence. Then he spoke. His voice emerged awkwardly and hoarsely, but he knew how to deal with it, he was constantly on the road, and his laryngitis was part of his agenda. After a while he started forcing his voice and exploiting it for its pathos. Opening his arms wide and letting his shoulders sway in time to his rhythmical prose, he preached a kind of rhetorical sermon, with an almost religious delivery, allowing his sentences to die away in a subdued echo which seemed to lend them all the more authority.

He focused his speech on the greatness and the benefits of the International, which had always been his introductory ploy when he had to speak in a new place. He explained its aim, the emancipation of the workers; then he explained its impressive structure, from the village at the base and the region higher

up, to the nation still higher, and the whole of humanity as its
summit. His arms rose progressively, building up the layers,
constructing the great cathedral of the world of the future.
Then there was its internal structure: he read out the statutes,
spoke of the congresses, explaining the growing importance of
their activities and the expansion of their programme, which at
first had merely argued for higher wages but had now moved
on to tackle the dissolution of society in order to put an end to
the whole class of hired labour. There would be no more
nationalities, and the workers of the whole world would be
united in the common cause of justice, sweeping away the
corrupt bourgeoisie and finally founding a free society where
anyone who didn't work would receive nothing! His voice
roared and vibrated, and the paper flowers up on the low
smoky ceiling danced nervously to the booming echoes of his
words.

The faces of his audience seemed to be swept by a tide of
emotion. Voices shouted:

'That's right! . . . Count us in!'

But he continued speaking. They would conquer the world
within three years. And he listed the nations that were already
being won over. People were queueing up on all sides asking to
join. No new religion had ever won such a following. Then
when they were the masters they would rewrite the laws and it
would be their old masters who would feel their hands at their
throats.

'Yes! Right! . . . It's their turn now, send them down!'

He motioned for silence. Now he came on to the question of
strikes. In principle he disapproved, they were too slow an
instrument, and they tended to make the suffering of the
workers even worse. But until they could find something
better, when they became inevitable, you had to make up your
mind to use them, for they did have the advantage of undermin-
ing the capitalist order. And this being the case, he explained
how the International was providential for the strikers, quoting
examples: in Paris, when the bronzeworkers had struck, their
bosses had caved in to all of their demands, terrified at the
news that the International was flying to their help; in London,
they had saved the miners at one colliery, by repatriating at

their expense a convoy of Belgian workers who had been drafted in by the owner of the mine. You only needed to become a member, to make the companies tremble, now that the workers were organizing themselves into a great army of labour, and determined to die for each other, rather than remain the slaves of capitalist society.

He was interrupted by a round of applause. He mopped his brow with his handkerchief, but refused the mug of beer that Maheu offered him. When he tried to start speaking again, he was interrupted by renewed applause.

'That's it!' he said quickly to Étienne. 'They're ready for it . . . Quick! the cards!'

He had dived under the table, and reappeared with his little black wooden case.

'Citizens,' he shouted, making himself heard above the din, 'here are the membership cards. Let the delegates through and I'll give them the cards to distribute . . . then we'll settle all the other details afterwards.'

Rasseneur leapt up and started protesting again. Étienne for his part was getting nervous, because he was supposed to make a speech. There was a state of considerable confusion. Levaque was waving his fists as if he were about to start a fight. Maheu was standing up and speaking, but it was impossible to make out a word of what he was saying. As the agitation increased, the dust rose up from the floorboards, the fine dust of former dances, turning the air sour with the powerful odour of the tram girls and the pit boys.

Suddenly the side-door opened, and Widow Désir planted her stomach and bosom in the doorway and bellowed thunderously:

'Shut up for Christ's sake! . . . The gendarmes are here!'

It was the local superintendent who had arrived, rather late in the day, to close down the meeting and make a report. He was accompanied by four gendarmes. For five minutes the widow had been keeping them busy at the door, telling them that she had a right to do what she liked on her own premises, that there was nothing wrong in entertaining a few friends. But then they brushed her aside, so she ran in to warn her 'children'.

'You must go out this way,' she continued. 'There's a bloody gendarme guarding the courtyard. Never mind, my little woodstore gives on to the alleyway ... Get a move on, there!'

The superintendent was already beating on the door with his fist; and as nobody opened up to let him in, he threatened to break it down. An informer must have been at work, for he shouted that the meeting was illegal, because there were a number of miners there without invitations.

In the hall the confusion mounted. They couldn't just run off like that, they hadn't even voted, either on joining the International or on continuing the strike. Everyone wanted to talk at once. Finally the chairman hit on the idea of a vote by popular acclaim. Arms were raised, and the delegates declared hastily that they requested membership on behalf of their absent comrades. And in this way the 10,000 colliers of Montsou became members of the International.

Meanwhile, however, the rout had commenced. Widow Désir was protecting their retreat by leaning her back against the door, which the gendarmes were battering away at with the butts of their rifles. The miners leapt over the benches, running out through the kitchen and the woodstore one after the other. Rasseneur was one of the first to escape, followed by Levaque, forgiving him his offence in the hope of being stood a drink to help him recover. Étienne went and salvaged the little case, and then waited with Pluchart and Maheu, who made it a point of honour to be last out. Just as they were on their way out, the lock burst, and the superintendent found himself faced with the last barricade, Widow Désir's bosom and stomach.

'Now what's the point in breaking my house down?' she asked. 'You can see there's nobody here.'

The superintendent, who was a stolid man, with no taste for drama, merely threatened to take her to prison. He took himself and his four gendarmes off to draw up his report, accompanied by guffaws from Zacharie and Mouquet, who were so delighted by the clever trick which their comrades had pulled off that they had lost all fear of the firepower of the law.

Outside in the alley Étienne, who was hampered by the

case, took to his heels, followed by the others. He suddenly thought of Pierron, and wondered why he hadn't seen him; and Maheu, still running, replied that he was ill: a diplomatic illness, for fear of compromising himself. They tried to get Pluchart to wait; but without stopping he declared that he had to leave immediately for Joiselle, where Legoujeux was waiting for instructions. So they shouted 'bon voyage' but kept on running, showing the gendarmes their heels as they all cantered through Montsou. They exchanged a few words whenever they could catch their breath. Étienne and Maheu were laughing with excitement, certain now of their triumph: once the International sent help, it would be the Company's turn to beg them to go back to work. And, as their galloping boots rang out along the cobbled road, another feeling mingled with the hope that surged up in their breasts, something bitter and fierce, a violence which the wind blew feverishly into the villages in every corner of the region.

CHAPTER V

ANOTHER fortnight went by. It was the beginning of January, with a cold mist blanketing the vast plain. The poverty and suffering had grown worse, the villages were getting hourly closer to their end, with the mounting famine. Four thousand francs sent from London by the International had given them no more than three days' bread. Then they had received nothing more. The death of this great hope dampened their spirits. Who could they count on, now that their own brothers had abandoned them? They felt lost amid the depths of winter, cut off from the world outside.

By Tuesday, village Two Hundred and Forty had no provisions left. Étienne and the delegates had left no stone unturned: they canvassed for new subscriptions in the neighbouring towns, and even as far away as Paris; they made collections, organized lectures. Most of these efforts came to nothing, for public opinion, which had at first been stirred, relapsed into indifference as the strike dragged on tediously, with no exciting dramatic incidents. The meagre charitable offerings which were donated were hardly enough to keep the poorest families alive. The others survived by pawning clothes, and selling off utensils and furnishings piece by piece to the flea market. Everything disappeared, the woollen stuffing from the mattresses, the pots and pans from the kitchen, even the furniture. For a brief period they thought they were saved: the small shopkeepers of Montsou, who had been put out of business by Maigrat, had offered credit to try to win back their customers from him; and, for a week, Verdonck the grocer, and the two bakers, Carouble and Smelten, did keep open shop; but their own financial reserves ran out, and all three had to stop. The bailiffs rubbed their hands gleefully, for the net result was a mountain of debts which would weigh long and heavy on the miners. There was no more credit to be had anywhere, not so much as one old saucepan left to sell, they might as well lie down and die in a corner like a pack of mangy dogs.

Étienne would have sold his own flesh. He had had to give up his income from fees; he had gone to Marchiennes to pawn his best trousers and his frock coat, happy to keep the Maheus' cooking pot simmering a little longer. The only thing he kept was his pair of boots, he kept them to make sure that he looked after his feet, he said. He despaired at the idea that the strike had started too soon, before they had had time to build up the provident fund. He saw this as the sole cause of the disaster, for the workers would surely triumph over the bosses one day, when they had saved enough money to put up an effective resistance. And he recalled Souvarine's words, accusing the Company of encouraging the strike in order to wipe out the first reserves accumulated by the fund.

When he looked around the village, where the poor people had no bread to eat and no fire to light, he was shaken. He preferred to go out, and tire himself by taking long walks. One evening when he was coming back home, walking past Réquillart, he noticed an old woman who had collapsed by the roadside. Doubtless she was dying of starvation; and after he had picked her up, he started to call out to a girl that he saw on the other side of the fence.

'Hey there, hallo!' he said, recognizing La Mouquette. 'Come here and help, we've got to get her to drink something.'

La Mouquette, moved to tears, went quickly inside, into the tumbledown shack that her father had set up amid the ruins of the old pit-head. She came straight back out with some bread and gin. The gin brought the old woman round and she started to eat the bread greedily without saying a word. She was a miner's mother from a village near Cougny, and she had fallen here on her way back from Joiselle, where she had tried in vain to borrow ten sous from one of her sisters. When she had eaten, she went off, still dazed.

Étienne had stayed outside waiting on the waste ground, where the ruined sheds of the old Réquillart mine could just be glimpsed through the brambles.

'Well then, aren't you going to come in for a little drink?' La Mouquette asked him, cheerfully.

And, as he hesitated, she added:

'So you're still scared of me, are you?'

He followed her, won over by her laughter. He was moved by her generous gesture in giving the old lady her bread. She didn't want to take him into her father's room, so she took him into her own instead, where she immediately poured out two little glasses of gin. Her room was very clean, and he complimented her on it. Moreover the family didn't seem to be in need of anything: the father was still working as a stableman at Le Voreux; and in order to keep herself busy she had taken a job as a laundress, which brought in thirty sous a day. Just because you enjoy fooling around with men, that doesn't mean you're bone idle.

'Look,' she murmured suddenly, coming up to him and putting her arm round him gently, 'why don't you want to love me?'

Now it was his turn to laugh, for she had come out with it so sweetly and innocently.

'But I do like you, a lot,' he replied.

'No, that's not what I mean ... You know I want to, ever so badly. Why not? It would be so nice for me!'

It was true that she had been after him for six months. He watched as she clung to him, wrapping her trembling arms round him, raising her face in such a plea for love that he was very moved. Her plump, round face had nothing beautiful about it, and her complexion was sallow and mottled with coal-dust; but such a flame burnt in her eyes that her whole body radiated charm and urgent desire, making her seem young and fresh and pink. And in the end, faced with this humble, ardent offering, he dared no longer refuse.

'Oh! you do like me,' she stammered, in ecstasy. 'Oh! you do like me!'

And she gave herself to him, awkwardly, swooningly, as if she were a virgin making love for the first time, with the first man she had ever known. Then, when he left her, it was she who rushed to express her gratitude: she said thank you, she kissed his hands.

Étienne felt a bit ashamed at this sudden windfall. You could hardly be proud of gaining La Mouquette's favours. As he left, he swore to himself that he wouldn't do it again. And yet, thinking back on it, he felt kindly towards her, she was a good girl.

And besides, when he got back to the village, the grave news which he heard made him forget his escapade. The rumour was abroad that the Company might perhaps agree to make concessions, if the delegates made a new approach to the manager. At any rate, the deputies had spread this rumour. The truth was that, as the bitter struggle dragged on, the mines were suffering even more than the miners. The stubbornness of both sides was leading them to ruin: while the workers were dying of hunger, the owners were watching their capital bleed away. Every day of lost production cost them hundreds of thousands of francs. An idle machine is a dead machine. The plant and fittings deteriorated, the starved bank balances started to crumble away like sand dunes in the wind. As soon as the meagre stock of coal at the pit-heads had been used up, their customers warned that they would have to seek provision from Belgium; and that boded ill for the future. But what frightened the Company most, although it took pains to hide it, was the increasing damage to the tunnels and the coal-faces. The deputies couldn't keep up with the repairs, the props were breaking up all over the place, there were rock falls almost by the hour. Soon the disaster seemed of such a scale that it would require long months of repair before any coal could be cut again. Already stories were getting around: at Crèvecœur 300 metres of tunnel had collapsed at once, blocking access to the Cinq-Paumes seam; at Madeleine, the Maugrétout seam had started splitting and filling up with water. The management refused to acknowledge these problems until two new accidents occurring one after the other suddenly forced them to admit what was happening. One morning, near La Piolaine, the ground started to split above the northern section of Mirou, where there had been a rock fall the day before; and the following day there was a collapse inside Le Voreux which rocked a whole street in the village so severely that two houses were nearly reduced to rubble.

Étienne and the delegates were reluctant to risk a new approach without knowing the intentions of the Board. Dansaert, when they asked his advice, was evasive: it was true that they sincerely regretted the misunderstanding, they would do everything in their power to come to an agreement; but he wouldn't give any details. In the end they decided that they should go round to see Monsieur Hennebeau, so that they wouldn't be in the wrong if anyone tried later on to accuse them of depriving the Company of its chance to admit its shortcomings. Nevertheless, they swore that they would make no concessions, that they would stick to their demands come what may, since theirs were the only just terms.

The meeting took place on the Tuesday morning, the day when the village had reached the depths of deprivation. It was less cordial than the earlier one. Maheu spoke again, explaining that his comrades had sent him to ask whether these gentlemen had anything new to say to them. At first Monsieur Hennebeau affected surprise: he had received no orders, nothing could change as long as the miners persisted with their scurrilous rebellion; and his stiff authoritarian stance produced the most regrettable effect, so much so that, if the delegates had come with conciliatory intentions, the manner of their reception would have been enough to stiffen their resistance. Then the manager said he was willing to find grounds for mutual concessions: so if the workers would agree to the timbering being paid for separately, the Company would add two centimes to the payment, to avoid the accusation of profiteering.

Moreover, he added that he was taking the initiative of this offer himself, that nothing had been decided, and that he thought he could safely say that he could extract this concession from headquarters in Paris. But the delegates refused and repeated their demands: maintaining the existing system, but with a rise of five centimes per tub. So he then admitted that if they accepted his offer he was empowered to ratify it immediately, and he urged them to accept, for the sake of their wives and children who were dying of hunger. They still looked at the ground, stubbornly refusing to budge, and they said no, repeatedly, shaking with emotion.

They parted brusquely. Monsieur Hennebeau slammed the doors behind them. Étienne, Maheu, and the others went away, their heavy boots striking the cobbles with the silent rage of victims who had reached the end of their tether.

Towards two o'clock, the women from the village mounted their own delegation, to see Maigrat. The only hope they had left was to soften this man, to wrench another week's credit from him. It was La Maheude's idea, with her incurable belief in people's good nature. She persuaded Ma Brûlé and La Levaque to go with her; as for La Pierronne, she excused herself on the grounds that she couldn't leave Pierron, whose illness still hadn't cleared up. Other women joined the group, until there were nearly twenty of them. When the bourgeois of Montsou saw their dark and wretched forms looming up, straggling right across the road, they shook their heads anxiously. Doors were smartly closed, and one lady hid her silver. This was the first time they had been known to make such a direct approach, and nothing could have been a worse omen: it usually meant that things were going to the dogs when the women took to the streets in groups like that. At Maigrat's there was a violent scene. At first he let them in with a malicious laugh, pretending to believe that they had come to pay off their debts: how nice of them to get together and bring him the money they owed all at once. Then as soon as La Maheude had started speaking, he pretended to lose his temper. What did they take him for? More credit? Did they want to force him out on the streets to beg? No, not one single potato, not the tiniest crumb of bread! And he advised them to go

back to Verdonck the grocer and Carouble and Smelten the
bakers, since that was where they did their shopping nowadays.
The women looked humble and intimidated as they listened to
him, making their apologies, while watching his eyes to see if
he would relent. He started cracking jokes, offering the whole
shop to old Ma Brûlé if she would take him for a sweetheart.
They were all so lacking in courage that they merely laughed;
and La Levaque even took him up on the offer, saying that she
herself was quite prepared to go along with his wishes. But he
immediately became coarse again, and thrust them out through
the doorway. As they were reluctant to leave, and kept pleading
their case, he manhandled one of them. The others, out on the
pavement, called him a scab, while La Maheude, raising her
arms in the air in a rush of vengeful indignation, cried a plague
on him, such a man didn't deserve to live.

They returned lugubriously to the village. When they saw
their wives return empty-handed, the men lowered their eyes.
It was over, the day would close without even a spoonful of
soup; and more days stretched out their icy shadows in front
of them, without the slightest glimmer of hope. But they had
gone into this willingly, and no one was prepared to give in.
This surfeit of misery made them even more stubborn and
silent, like hunted animals, resolved to die at the bottom of
their lair rather than emerge. Who would have dared be the
first to talk of surrender? Everyone had sworn with his comrades that they would all stand firm to the last, and stand firm
they would, just as they stood firm at the pit when someone
was buried under a rock fall. It was hardly surprising, for they
had been so well trained to resign themselves: it was easy
enough to tighten your belt for a week when you had been
swallowing fire and water since the age of twelve; and their
loyalty was thus augmented by a kind of soldierly dignity,
showing pride in their profession, having come to feel that
there was a sacrificial glory in their daily struggle with death.

At the Maheus' it was a dreadful evening. They all sat
silently around the dying fire where the last cake of scavenged
cinders was smoking away. After emptying the mattress handful by handful they had decided two days earlier to sell the
cuckoo clock for three francs; and the room seemed dead and

Germinal

empty now that it no longer echoed to the sound of its familiar ticking. The only luxury item left now was the pink cardboard box on the middle of the sideboard; an old present from Maheu which La Maheude treasured as if it were made of precious metal. Since the two good chairs had gone, old Bonnemort and the children huddled together on a mouldy old bench which they had brought in from the garden. And the livid twilight as it fell seemed to increase the cold.

'What can we do?' La Maheude kept repeating, as she huddled up close to the stove.

Étienne remained standing, looking at the portraits of the Emperor and the Empress, which were still pinned to the wall. He would have liked to tear them down long ago, if the family hadn't forbidden him, in order to keep some decoration. And so he muttered between his teeth:

'To think that we won't get two sous from those layabouts stuck up there watching us starve to death!'

'What if I took the box?' ventured La Maheude, after hesitating a moment, and turning pale.

Maheu, who had been sitting on the edge of the table with his head on his chest and his legs dangling, suddenly sat bolt upright.

'No, I won't hear of it!'

La Maheude got up painfully and walked round the room. How in God's name could they have been reduced to such wretchedness! Not a crumb in the cupboard, nothing left to sell, nobody had any idea how to get even a loaf of bread! And the fire was about to go out! She flew at Alzire, who had been sent that morning to the slag-heap and had come back empty-handed, saying that the Company had banned any scavenging. Did they care a damn about the Company? As if you were stealing something if you picked up the pieces of waste coal! The little girl sounded desperate as she told how a man had threatened to hit her; but she promised to go back the next day even if he did hit her.

'And that scoundrel Jeanlin?' cried his mother. 'Where's he got to now, I ask you? ... He was supposed to be fetching some leaves: we could at least have had something to chew on, like animals! You see, he won't come home tonight. He spent last night out. I don't know what he's up to but the ruffian always seems to have a full stomach.'

'Perhaps', said Étienne, 'he picks up some money by the roadside.'

At this she brandished her fists furiously in the air.

'The thought of it! . . . My children begging! I'd rather kill them and myself straight away after.'

Maheu had slumped down against the edge of the table again. Lénore and Henri, who were dismayed that nobody was starting to eat, began to whine; while old Bonnemort silently and philosophically rolled his tongue around the inside of his mouth to cheat his hunger. Nobody spoke, as they all felt numbed by this aggravation of their suffering, the grandfather coughing and spitting up black phlegm, and seized by fresh attacks of his rheumatism, which was turning to dropsy; the father asthmatic, his knees swollen with water, the mother and the children eaten away by hereditary scrofula and anaemia. No doubt it went with the job: they only complained about it when they started to die from lack of food; and already people were dropping like flies in the village. Yet they had to find something for supper. What could they do and where could they go, for heaven's sake?

Then, in the twilight whose dismal gloom made the room increasingly darker, Étienne, who had been hesitating for a moment, came to a heart-rending decision.

'Wait for me,' he said. 'I've got to go out for a moment.'

And he left. He had thought of La Mouquette. She was bound to have a loaf of bread, and would be pleased to give them it. He was annoyed at having to return to Réquillart: the girl would kiss his hands with her servile and amorous airs; but you couldn't let down friends in need, he'd be kind to her again, if he had to.

'I'll go out and ask around, too,' said La Maheude. 'It's too crazy.'

She opened the door which the young man had just closed, and she slammed it violently behind her, leaving the others dumb and motionless, in the wan light of a candle end which Alzire had just lit. Outside she stopped short, struck by a sudden thought. Then she went in to the Levaques'.

'Look, I lent you a loaf of bread the other day. How about giving me one back.'

But she stopped abruptly; what she saw was hardly encouraging, and the house reeked of poverty even more than hers.

La Levaque was staring blankly at their cold fireplace, while Levaque, who had been out drinking with some nailsmiths on an empty stomach, was slumped over the table asleep. Bouteloup was leaning back rubbing his shoulders mechanically against the wall, with the surprised look of the easygoing fellow whose savings have been pillaged and who is shocked at having to tighten his belt.

'A loaf of bread, oh, dear me,' La Levaque replied, 'I was just thinking of asking you for one myself.'

Then, as her husband groaned painfully in his sleep, she pushed his face down on to the table.

'Shut up, you pig! Serves you right if it rots your guts! . . . Instead of getting people to stand you drinks, couldn't you have asked one of your friends to give you twenty sous?'

She went on swearing to relieve her feelings, amid the filth of the house, already abandoned for so long that an unbearable smell wafted up from the floor. Everything could go hang, she didn't care a stuff! Her son, that little beggar Bébert, hadn't shown his face since the morning, and she shouted that she'd be well rid of him if he never came home again. Then she said she was going to bed. At least she'd be warm there. She gave Bouteloup a shake.

'Look alive! Let's go upstairs . . . the fire's out, there's no need to keep the candle alight just to look at the empty plates . . . Come on, move yourself, Louis, I said we're going to bed. We can keep each other warm, we'll feel better . . . And let that drunken bastard die of cold down here on his own!'

When she was outside again, La Maheude cut straight across the gardens to go to the Pierrons'. She could hear laughter. She knocked, and there was a sudden silence. It was a full minute before they opened the door for her.

'Oh, so it's you!' cried La Pierronne, affecting complete surprise. 'I thought it was the doctor.'

Without giving her time to reply, she continued, pointing at Pierron, who was sitting in front of a great coal fire.

'Oh, he's not well at all, he's still just as ill. His face looks well enough, but it's eating away at his stomach. So he has to have the warmth, we're burning everything we've got.'

Sure enough, Pierron did look sprightly, with his rosy complexion and his firm flesh. He tried ineffectually to wheeze as if he were ill. Besides, La Maheude had just caught a strong whiff of rabbit as she entered: it was obvious that they had hidden the dish. There were still some stray crumbs on the table; and right in the middle there was a bottle of wine they had forgotten to remove.

'Mum's gone to Montsou to try to get a loaf of bread,' La Pierronne continued. 'We're sitting here biting our nails waiting for her.'

But her voice died away into a croak as she followed her neighbour's gaze and discovered the bottle. She pulled herself together straight away, and gave the reason: yes, it was wine, the bourgeois from La Piolaine had brought the bottle for her man, because the doctor had prescribed a cure of claret. And she couldn't praise those fine people enough; especially the young lady, who wasn't too proud to call on the workers and distribute her alms herself!

'I know,' said La Maheude, 'I know them.'

Her heart missed a beat at the thought that it's always the least needy who attract help. You could count on it, those Piolaine people would have tried to top up the river with water from their well if they could. How had she missed them in the village? Perhaps she might still have got something out of them.

'The reason I came', she finally admitted, 'was to see if you had better luck than us ... Even if you just had a bit of vermicelli, we'd pay you back later.'

La Pierronne suddenly sounded desperate.

'Nothing at all, dear. Not the tiniest grain of semolina ... If Mum isn't back it must be because she's had no luck. We'll have to go to bed hungry.'

At that moment there was the sound of crying in the cellar and she went to bang on the door. It was that slut Lydie that she'd locked up, she said, to punish her for not getting home until five o'clock, after wandering around all day. They couldn't keep her under control, she kept disappearing.

However, La Maheude remained rooted to the spot, unable to make up her mind to leave. The great fire filled her with hurtful pangs of warmth, and the thought of the meal they were enjoying carved a hole in her stomach. It was plain that they had dispatched the old girl and locked up the kid so that they could wolf down their rabbit on the sly. Oh, you could say what you liked, when a woman misbehaved it didn't do her family any harm!

'Good-night,' she said suddenly.

Outside night had fallen, and from behind the clouds the moon shed a murky light on the ground. Instead of walking back across the gardens, La Maheude went the long way round, so miserable that she was unable to face going home. But as she walked past the dead terraces, starvation seeped from every door, and every knock rang hollow. What was the point in knocking? It would just pile on the agony. After weeks of not eating, even the smell of onion had disappeared, that strong smell which betrayed the presence of the village from far across the countryside; now there was only a smell like that of ancient tombs, or musty caves where nothing living survives. The muffled sounds of stifled tears and stray oaths died away; and in the gradually thickening silence you could hear the sleep of hunger coming and the collapse of bodies as they slumped on to their beds, racked by the nightmares invoked by their empty bellies.

As she passed by the church, she saw a shadow slip rapidly past. She hurried hopefully towards the vicar of Montsou, Father Joire, whom she had just recognized. He came on Sundays to say mass at the miners' chapel: he must have just left the vestry, where he had gone to settle some business. He hurried by, keeping his eyes on the ground, a plump and friendly looking man, wishing to live in peace with all mankind. If he went about his business by night, it must be to avoid compromising himself by mingling with the miners. Besides, people said that he had just been offered promotion, and even that he had been walking around with his successor, a skinny priest with blazing red eyes.

'Father, Father,' stammered La Maheude.

But he did not stop.

'Good-evening, my good woman, good-evening.'

She found herself in front of her own house again. Her legs would carry her no further, so she went inside.

Nobody had moved. Maheu was still slumped over the edge of the table. Old Bonnemort and the children were huddled together on the bench trying to keep each other warm. And nobody had spoken a word, only the candle had burnt down so low that soon they wouldn't even have any light. When they heard the door the children turned their heads, but on seeing that their mother had returned empty-handed, they started staring at the floor again, choking back their strong urge to cry, for fear of being scolded. La Maheude slumped back into her seat again, near the dying fire. Nobody asked her any questions, the silence continued. They had all understood, they thought there was no point in tiring themselves further by talking; and as they sat waiting, they felt crushed and depressed, waiting for their last chance, that Étienne might somehow come up with some help from somewhere. The minutes dragged by and became hours. In the end they gave up hope.

When Étienne reappeared, he was carrying a dozen cold potatoes wrapped up in a cloth.

'This is all I could find,' he said.

La Mouquette hadn't any bread either: and it was her own dinner that she had made into a bundle for him, kissing him passionately.

'No thanks,' he said to La Maheude when she offered him his share. 'I've already eaten.'

It wasn't true, and he looked bleakly at the children as they wolfed down their food. Their father and mother also held back, in order to leave them more, but it was the old man who greedily swallowed all that was left. They had to take a potato back off him to give to Alzire.

Then Étienne told them that he had had some news. The Company, angered by the obstinacy of the strikers, was talking of sacking the miners who were involved. That would surely mean war. And then there was an even more serious rumour: the Company boasted of persuading large numbers of men to go back to work: the next day, La Victoire and Feutry-Cantel should be back to full strength; and even at Madeleine and Mirou they counted on a third of them going back. The Maheus were exasperated.

'My God!' cried Maheu, 'if we find the traitors we must deal with them!'

And he stood up, carried away by his suffering, and cried:

'Tomorrow evening, in the forest! . . . Since they've already stopped us talking at the Bon-Joyeux, we'll be more at home in the forest.'

His shouting had awakened old Bonnemort, who had fallen asleep after his gluttonous meal. It was the old rallying cry, the meeting-place for miners in olden days when they went off to plot resistance to the king's men.

'Yes, let's go, off to Vandame! Count me in!'

La Maheude shook her fists.

'We'll all go. We'll put an end to this injustice and treachery!'

Étienne decided that they would spread the word around all the mining villages to meet the next evening. But the fire was dead, as it had been at the Levaques', and the candle suddenly went out. There was no coal left, and no oil, so they had to feel their way to bed in the dark and bitter cold which froze their bones. The children were crying.

CHAPTER VI

JEANLIN was better now, and able to walk again; but his bones were so badly set that he limped with both legs, and he was quite a sight to behold, waddling like a duck, but still scuttling around as fast as ever, and still as cunning as a wicked, thieving fox.

That evening, at twilight, Jeanlin was keeping watch on the road towards Réquillart, accompanied by his faithful followers, Bébert and Lydie. He had laid an ambush on a patch of waste ground, behind a fence, opposite a tumbledown grocer's which backed on to a fork in the road. An old woman who was almost blind was setting out three or four sacks of lentils and beans, black with soot; and there was an ancient piece of dry cod, hung up in the doorway, streaked with fly dirt, which he was watching through narrowed eyes. He had already twice dispatched Bébert to unhook it. But, each time, someone had appeared round the bend in the road. There's always someone who gets in the way just when you're ready to do business!

A man on horseback appeared, and the children threw themselves down flat on the ground at the bottom of the fence when they recognized Monsieur Hennebeau. Since the beginning of the strike, he was often to be seen riding out along the highways and byways, travelling alone through the rebellious mining villages, calmly but courageously faring abroad to check up on the lie of the land. Nobody had ever thrown the least stone at his face, his only encounters were with taciturn men who were reluctant to greet him, and he mostly discovered courting couples who cared nothing for politics, and were busy taking their fill of pleasure in any odd corner. Trotting along on his mare, he passed by with his head held high, to avoid embarrassing anyone, his heart bursting with unsatisfied desires as he rode through this display of amorous debauchery. He saw the brats perfectly clearly, the boys piled up on top of the girls. Even the kids were joining in the fun in order to rub their sad bodies together! His eyes watered, and he disappeared, sitting bolt upright in the saddle, with his frock coat buttoned tightly like a military uniform.

'Hell's bells!' said Jeanlin. 'Will it never end . . . Go, Bébert, go! Go for the tail!'

But this time two men came along, and the kid stifled an oath when he heard the voice of his brother Zacharie, who was in the process of telling Mouquet how he had found a forty-sou coin sewn into the hem of his wife's skirt. They were both laughing heartily and slapping each other on the back. Mouquet thought it would be a fine idea to have a good old game of cross* the next day: they'd set out at two o'clock from the Avantage, and go down towards Montoire, near Marchiennes. Zacharie accepted. Why should people pester them with the strike? Better to have a laugh since they couldn't do any work anyway! And they were just turning the corner when Étienne, who was coming up from the canal, stopped them, and struck up a conversation.

'Are they going to spend the night here?' asked Jeanlin, exasperated. 'It's getting dark, and the old girl's taking her sacks in.'

Another miner was walking down towards Réquillart. Étienne walked away with him; and, as they passed by the fence, the boy heard them talking about the forest: they'd had to put the meeting off until the next day for fear of not being able to alert all the mining villages in one day.

'Look,' Jeanlin murmured to his two comrades, 'the balloon goes up tomorrow. Got to be there. Right? We'll go in the afternoon.'

And now that the coast was clear at last, he dispatched Bébert on his mission.

'Go for it! Go for the tail! . . . And watch out, the old girl's got her broom.'

Luckily it was now quite dark. Bébert had leapt up to grab the cod, and his weight had broken the string. He ran off, waving it overhead like a kite, followed by the other two, and the three of them hared off. The grocer came out of her shop, astonished and bemused, unable to identify the gang as they vanished into the darkness.

These little scoundrels had turned into the scourge of the countryside, which they had gradually invaded like a tribe of barbarians. At first they had been satisfied with the pit-head yard at Le Voreux, tumbling around in the piles of coal, which left them as black as negroes, playing hide and seek in the wood stacks, where they got lost as if they were in the depths of some virgin forest. Then they had taken over the slag-heap, sliding down its bare patches on their bottoms, even though it was boiling hot from the internal combustion; they slipped in and out of the brambles which had grown over the older parts of the pit, and spent whole days out of sight playing quiet, mischievous games, like naughty little mice. Then their campaigns became bolder, and they went off to do battle among the brick heaps until they bled, ran wild in the fields eating all sorts of juicy grasses, without even any bread to help them down, scavenged the banks of the canal to catch small fry in the mud and swallow them raw, wandering ever further afield, travelling for miles to reach the thickets of Vandame, where they holed up to gorge themselves on strawberries in spring, and hazelnuts and bilberries in summer. Soon they roamed victorious over the whole vast plain.

But what spurred them on in the raids they mounted in every direction from Montsou to Marchiennes, their greedy young eyes ablaze, was a growing delight in sacking and looting. Jeanlin remained the captain of these expeditions, directing his troops in their pillage, ravaging onion fields, looting orchards, raiding shelves in shops. In the country people accused the striking miners, and they talked of a great organized band. One day Jeanlin had even forced Lydie to rob her mother, getting her to bring two dozen barley-sugar sticks that La Pierronne kept in a jar on one of the window ledges; and the little girl hadn't betrayed him, despite being beaten black and blue, so great was her fear of his authority. The worst of it was that he kept the largest share for himself. Bébert, too, had to hand over his booty, and was happy if his captain kept the lot, as long as he didn't beat him.

Over the last few days, Jeanlin had been taking things to extremes. He beat Lydie up as if she were his lawfully wedded wife, and he exploited Bébert's credulity to get him embroiled in awkward situations, delighted at the idea of making an ass of the clumsy lad, who was stronger than he was, and who could have felled him with a single blow of his fist if he had thought of it. He despised them both, and treated them as his slaves, telling them that he had a princess for a mistress, and that they would be unworthy of appearing in her presence. And indeed, over the last week he had taken to disappearing suddenly, at the end of a road, at a fork in the path, wherever he happened to find himself, having first pocketed the swag and ordered them with a threatening air to go back to the village.

And that was what happened this evening.

'Give it here,' he said, snatching the cod from his friend's hands, when all three of them had stopped at a bend in the road, near Réquillart.

Bébert protested.

'Look, I want some. I was the one who got it.'

'What d'you mean?' Jeanlin cried. 'You'll get some if I give

you some, and you can bet it won't be tonight: tomorrow, if
there's any left.'

He gave Lydie a few encouraging thumps, and pushed the
two of them into line together like soldiers shouldering arms.
Then he went behind them.

'Now you're going to stay there for five minutes without
turning round ... I swear by God that if you turn round
you'll be eaten alive by wild beasts ... And then you must go
straight home, and if Bébert tries to touch Lydie on the way,
I'll know about it, and I'll thump the pair of you.'

Then he disappeared into the shadows with such skill that
they didn't even hear the sound of his bare feet. The two
children stood stock still for five whole minutes, not daring to
look round behind them in case their invisible tormentor was
waiting to hit them. Gradually a great affection had grown up
between them in their common terror. He kept dreaming of
taking hold of her and squeezing her tightly in his arms the
way he had seen other people do it; and she would have liked
it to happen, because that would have been a nice change, to
be gently caressed. But neither of them would have dared to
disobey their orders. When they started back, although it was
pitch-dark, they didn't venture to embrace, but walked side by
side, plunged in love and despair, certain that if they were to
touch, the avenging captain would charge up from behind and
trounce them.

At the same moment Étienne had returned to Réquillart.
The previous night La Mouquette had begged him to return,
and he had come back, despite feeling ashamed, caught by a
desire which he refused to admit to himself for this girl who
worshipped him as if he were a saint. His reason for going
back, in any case, had been to break off the affair. He would
see her, he would explain to her that she must stop running
after him, because of his comrades. It was no time to be
enjoying themselves, it wasn't fair to be wallowing in such
pleasure when people were dying of hunger. And since he
hadn't found her at home, he had decided to wait, and was
watching every figure that passed in the shadows.

Beneath the ruined headgear, the old shaft gaped open, half-
obstructed. One beam sticking straight out with a bit of

roofing attached to it looked like a gallows raised over the black hole; two trees, a plane tree and a mountain ash, had grown up between the crumbling kerbstones, and seemed to spring up from the depths of the earth. It was a wild and abandoned place, the grassy, tangled entrance to an abyss, cluttered with old bits of wood, and invaded by sloe bushes and hawthorn hedges that teemed with warblers at nesting time. In order to save having to spend considerable sums on keeping it in good condition, the Company had been talking for the last ten years of filling in this disused pit; but they were waiting until they had installed a ventilation system* at Le Voreux, for the ventilation chamber for the two pits, which were interconnected, was sited at the bottom of Réquillart, whose former ventilation shaft served as its chimney. They had simply shored up the inner lining by wedging props in sideways to block the winding shaft tunnels, and they had abandoned the upper tunnels, maintaining only the bottom section, in which there blazed the enormous, hellish coal furnace whose powerful blast drew in tempestuous draughts of air right through the neighbouring pit. As a precaution, so that it was still possible to go into the pit and out again, they had given instructions to maintain the ladder well; only nobody actually did it, so the ladders were rotten with damp, and some platforms had already collapsed. At the surface, an overgrown bramble blocked the entrance to the well; and as the first ladder had lost a number of rungs, you had to swing down from the root of the mountain ash if you wanted to reach it, then let yourself drop by guesswork into the darkness.

Étienne was waiting patiently, hidden behind a bush, when he heard something slithering slowly through the branches. It sounded like a grass snake fleeing from danger. But he was suddenly taken aback to see a match being lit, and watched speechless as he recognized Jeanlin lighting a candle and disappearing down into the depths of the earth. His curiosity was so aroused that he went up to the edge of the hole: the boy had disappeared, but a dim light could be seen down on the second platform. He hesitated for a moment, then let himself slide down, keeping hold of the roots as he went, expecting to fall down the whole length of the 524-metre depth of the pit, but then he felt that he had touched a rung. From that point he climbed carefully down. Jeanlin must have heard nothing. Étienne could still see the light plunging lower beneath him, while the boy's shadow danced monstrously and menacingly, as he lurched downwards with his crippled gait. He swung down as nimbly as a monkey, using his hands and feet and even his chin to hold on with when there were no rungs. The seven-metre ladders stretched downwards one after the other, some of them still strong, others shaky and creaking, ready to break; the narrow platforms swept by, so green and rotten that it was like walking on moss; and as you went deeper down, the heat from the ventilation flue became stifling, a veritable furnace, although luckily it had not been working at full strength since the start of the strike, for at full blast, when the furnace devoured its 5,000 kilograms of coal a day, you couldn't have ventured near it without being roasted alive.

'Damn and blast the little rat!' Étienne swore as he felt himself suffocating. 'Where the hell is he going?'

Twice he had nearly fallen headlong, as his feet slipped on the damp wood. If only he had had a candle like the boy; but time and again he bumped into something, he could only guide himself by the faint glimmer that kept plunging down below him. He must have been on at least his twentieth ladder, and still he kept plunging downwards. So he started to count them: twenty-one, twenty-two, twenty-three, and still he went down, lower and lower. His head throbbed with the burning heat, it felt as if he was falling into an oven. At last he reached a loading bay, and he caught sight of the candle disappearing down the end of a tunnel. Thirty ladders, that made about two hundred and ten metres.

'How long is he going to make me run after him?' he wondered. 'I bet he's going to earth in the stables.'

But over to the left, the route to the stables was blocked by a rock fall. The chase recommenced, but it was even more difficult and dangerous. Frightened bats suddenly fluttered up into the air and clung to the ceiling of the loading bay. He had to make haste so as not to lose sight of the light, and flung himself into the tunnel he had seen it go down; only, where the child had been able to get through easily, slithering like a serpent, he couldn't squeeze through without bruising his limbs. This tunnel, like all the disused passages, had become narrower and was still getting narrower every day, with the ceaseless movements of the earth; and in some places it had shrunk to the width of a narrow gully, and would eventually disappear altogether. As he worked his way half-strangled through this passage, the torn and splintered pit-props became a menace, threatening to rip his flesh open or impale him as he passed with their jagged, sword-like spikes. He had to take great care as he edged his way forward, on all fours or flat on his belly, groping his way forward into the darkness ahead of him. Suddenly a family of rats scurried past, their feet pummelling him from head to toe in their panicky flight.

'God almighty! When are we going to get to the end of it all,' he groaned breathlessly, his back aching.

But that was it. After about a kilometre the gully opened up and they came out into a remarkably well preserved part of the passage. It was the end of the old haulage road, cut across the grain of the rock, opening out into something like a natural cave. He had to stop as he saw the child place the candle down on the ground between a couple of stones, settle down, and make himself comfortable, seeming relieved and relaxed as if he felt quite at home. There was a whole provision of comforts which made the end of the tunnel into a cosy dwelling. In one corner there was a pile of hay on the ground which made a soft bed; on some old props set up to form a table there was a whole larder of supplies, bread, apples, and half-drunk bottles of gin: a real robber's den, supplied with the fruits of weeks of pillage, even including useless booty, bits of soap and wax polish which were stolen for the sheer pleasure of stealing. And the child sat there alone surrounded by his loot, enjoying it with the selfish pleasure of a pirate king.

'Hey, you, who the hell do you think you are,' shouted Étienne, when he had had time to catch his breath, 'coming down here to stuff your face while the rest of us are dying of hunger up there?'

Jeanlin was dumbstruck, and trembled. But when he recognized the young man, he soon recovered.

'Will you have something to eat?' he finally said. 'How about a bit of grilled cod? . . . Try some.'

He had brought his cod safely home, and had started to clean off the fly dirt with a shiny new knife, one of those small sheath-knives with a motto engraved on its bone handle. This one was inscribed with the single world 'Love'.

'You've got a nice knife,' Étienne remarked.

'It was a present from Lydie,' Jeanlin replied, omitting to mention that Lydie had stolen it at his bidding from a hawker at Montsou, outside the Tête-Coupée bar.

Then, while he carried on scraping, he added proudly:

'I've made it really comfortable here, haven't I? . . . It's a damn sight warmer than up there, and it doesn't half smell better, too!'

Étienne had sat down, and was curious to hear what he had to say. He didn't feel angry any more, he felt interested in this delinquent child, who put so much honest effort into his misbehaviour. And in fact he did appreciate the comfort at the bottom of this hole: the heat was bearable, with an even temperature in all seasons, rather like a warm bath, while up above ground the sharp December cold was freezing his wretched comrades rigid. As they aged, the tunnels lost their noxious gases, all the firedamp had gone, and the only smell left was the scent of the old pit-props going musty, with their subtle whiff of ether, as if spiced with a hint of cloves. Besides, these props had become quite a sight, yellowish and pale like marble, fringed with whitish lace, while flaky excrescences seemed to drape them in an embroidery of silk and pearls. Others were covered with clouds of fungus. And there were swarms of white moths, snowy flies, and spiders, an albino population which would never know the sun.

'Aren't you afraid down here?' asked Étienne.

Jeanlin looked up at him in astonishment.

'What of? There's only me here.'

And now he had finished scraping the cod. He lit a small wood fire, spread out the hot ashes, and grilled it. Then he divided up a loaf of bread. It was a rough and salty feast, but tasted divine to their hardened stomachs.

Étienne had accepted his share.

'I'm not surprised that you're getting fatter while the rest of us are withering away. Don't you realize what a slob you are to stuff yourself like that? . . . What about the others, don't you ever think of them?'

'Why should I, if they're so damn stupid?'

'Though it's a good job you've got a hide-out; if your father found out you were thieving, he wouldn't half let you have it.'

'As if the bourgeois weren't robbing us themselves! You're always saying so yourself. When I filched some bread from Maigrat it was only what he owed us in the first place.'

Étienne fell silent, with his mouth full. That made him think. He looked at the boy, with his sharp features, green eyes, and big ears; his degenerate frame harboured a kind of occult intelligence and primitive cunning, as if he was slowly reverting to his animal origins. The mine had shaped him, but then it had broken his legs.

'And what about Lydie,' Étienne asked again, 'do you bring her down here sometimes?'

Jeanlin laughed contemptuously.

'That kid? You bet I don't! . . . Women can't keep their mouths shut.'

And he laughed again, full of boundless contempt for Lydie and Bébert. Did you ever see such dopey children? The thought of them swallowing all his schemes and going away empty-handed, while he sat there in comfort eating his cod, tickled his ribs with delight. Then he concluded philosophically, despite his youth:

'You're better off on your own, there's nobody to disagree with.'

Étienne had finished his bread. He took a swig at the gin. For a moment he had wondered whether he wouldn't repay Jeanlin's hospitality by dragging him out of his hide by the ear and ordering him to give up his outlaw career, threatening to tell his father all about it if he didn't. But, as he examined this underground retreat, an idea came to him: how did he know that he might not need it, for his comrades or for himself, in case things turned nasty up above? So he made the boy swear not to spend the whole night out, as he had taken to doing on occasion, when he fell asleep in the hay; and, taking up a candle end, he left first, leaving the lad to tidy up in his own good time.

La Mouquette, who was sitting out on an old beam waiting for him, despite the severe cold, was starting to lose hope that he would come. When she saw him she flung her arms around his neck; and when he told her that he had decided not to see her any more, she felt as if he had plunged a dagger in her heart. For God's sake, why ever not? Didn't she love him as much as ever? Since he himself was afraid of yielding to an urge to go inside with her, he drew her over towards the road, and explained to her, as gently as possible, that she would compromise him in the eyes of his comrades, that she was ruining his political credibility. She was astonished, whatever could it have to do with politics? Then the thought struck her that he was ashamed of being seen with her; but still she wasn't offended, it was natural enough; and she offered to let him slap her face in public, so that they would seem to be breaking up. But he'd come back to see her, just one more time, every now and then. Desperately she pleaded with him, she promised she'd stay hidden, she'd only take five minutes of his time. He was very touched, but he kept refusing. Then as he made to leave her he agreed at least to kiss her goodbye. Step by step they had arrived at the first houses of Montsou, and they had their arms right round each other, beneath the bright, full moon, when a woman who was passing by gave a sudden start, as if she had tripped against a stone.

'Who's that?' asked Étienne, worried.

'That was Catherine,' La Mouquette replied. 'She's on her way back from Jean-Bart.'

The young woman was moving away now, with her head lowered and her legs unsteady, looking very tired. And Étienne watched her, feeling despair at having been seen by her, his heart breaking with groundless remorse. Wasn't she going out with a man? Hadn't she made him suffer just as much over there on the road to Réquillart, when she had given herself to that man? But all the same, he felt sad to have paid her back in kind.

'Want to know what I think?' murmured La Mouquette tearfully as she left. 'If you don't want me, it's because you fancy someone else.'

The next day the weather was glorious, the air bright and

frosty, one of those fine winter days when the hard earth rings out like crystal under your feet. At one o'clock sharp Jeanlin had run off; but he had to wait for Bébert behind the church, and they nearly had to go without Lydie, who had been shut in the cellar by her mother again. She had just been let out and handed a basket, with instructions that, if she didn't bring it back full of dandelion leaves, she'd be locked in with the rats all night long. So because she was afraid she wanted to go off and gather her leaves straight away. Jeanlin put her off, saying they would get round to it later. For some time now he'd had a bee in his bonnet about Poland, the Rasseneurs' big fat rabbit, and he was just going past the Avantage, when at that very moment the rabbit emerged on to the road in front of him. He pounced on her and grabbed her by the ears, then stuffed her into the girl's basket; and all three of them cantered off. They would have a great time making her run like a dog all the way to the forest.

But they stopped to watch Zacharie and Mouquet, who, after they had drunk a pint with two other mates, were starting their great game of cross. The prizes were a new cap and a red silk scarf, deposited with Rasseneur. The four players, in two pairs, were bidding for the first leg, from Le Voreux to the Paillot farm, nearly three kilometres; and it was Zacharie who won, by bidding to do it in seven strokes, while Mouquet bid eight. The small, boxwood ball, shaped like an egg, was placed upright on the cobbles. Each man had a club, whose iron head was set crosswise at the end of a long wooden handle, which was bound tightly with twine. Two o'clock chimed as they set off. Zacharie went first, and took only three strokes to make a magnificent drive of over four hundred metres across the beetfields; for it was forbidden to play in the village or on the roads, because people had been killed in the past. Mouquet, who was also a tough player, returned the drive with such muscle power that his single shot knocked the ball a hundred and fifty metres back the other way. And so the game progressed, one team driving forward, the other team returning the ball, both constantly on the run, and bruising their feet on the frozen furrows of the ploughed earth.

At first, Jeanlin, Bébert, and Lydie had galloped along

behind the players, excited by their mighty swipes. Then they remembered Poland, who was being jolted around in their basket; and, breaking away from the game when it was out in the open countryside, they had let the rabbit go to see how fast she could run. She took off and they dived after her. They chased her for an hour, helter-skelter, twisting and turning, screaming to frighten her, their arms opening wide and then snapping shut on the empty air. If she hadn't been expecting yet again, they would never have caught her.

As they paused to catch their breath, the sound of swearing made them turn their heads. They had stumbled across the game of cross again, and Zacharie had only just missed splitting his brother's head open. The players were on the fourth leg: from the Paillot farm they had run out towards Quatre-Chemins, then from Quatre-Chemins to Montoire; and now they had bid to drive from Montoire to Le Pré-des-Vaches in six shots. That made two and a half leagues in an hour; not counting the time spent downing pints at Vincent's bar and the Trois Sages beershop. This time it was Mouquet who was on top. He had two more shots to loose off, and there was no doubt that he would win, when Zacharie gleefully took his turn and returned the ball so skilfully that it rolled down deep into a ditch. Mouquet's partner couldn't get it out, which was a disaster. All four players started shouting furiously, and everyone joined in the uproar, for the teams were neck and neck, and they were going to have to start all over again. But from Le Pré-des-Vaches it was not much more than two kilometres to the next stop, at Les Herbes-Rousses: five shots. Once there, they would slake their thirst at Lerenard's.

But then Jeanlin had an idea. He waited for the players to go, then got a piece of string out of his pocket and tied it on to one of Poland's hind paws, the left one. And that was terrific fun, the rabbit running along in front of the three tearaways, stretching its legs with such a pathetic limp that they laughed fit to bust. Then they tied the string round her neck, to let her gallop a bit; and when she was tired, they dragged her along like a toy carriage, first on her belly, and then on her back. They spent a whole hour at this pastime, and the rabbit was at her last gasp, but they had to stuff her quickly back into the basket when they reached the Cruchot woods and heard the players, whose game they had run into again.

Now Zacharie, Mouquet, and the other two were well into their stride, stopping only to down a pint in every bar that counted as a marker. From Les Herbes-Rousses they had run over to Buchy, then to La Croix-de-Pierre, then to Chamblay. The ground echoed to the clatter of their feet, as they galloped relentlessly after the ball, which bounced over the frozen soil: the conditions were favourable, you couldn't sink into the mud, the only danger was you might break a leg. The heavy shots rang out through the dry air as sharply as gunfire. Their muscular hands gripped the twine-bound handles, the movement rippled right through their bodies as if they were poleaxing oxen; and they kept at it for hours, from one end of the plain to the other, over ditches and hedges, road embankments and low farm walls. You had to have a pretty good pair of bellows in your chest and cast-iron hinges in your knees. The hewers seemed to use the game to blast the mine out of their systems. Some of the twenty-five-year-old fanatics would hack away over ten leagues of countryside. At forty you couldn't play any more, you couldn't work up the speed.

Five o'clock struck, and dusk was falling already. There was just one leg left, up to Vandame forest, to decide who would win the cap and silk scarf; and Zacharie joked about it with his vulgar indifference to politics: wouldn't it be fun to end up there with the lads? As for Jeanlin, since they had left the village he had been making for the forest, despite his pretence of running around aimlessly. He objected indignantly and threatened Lydie, when, assailed by fright and remorse, she asked him to let her go back to Le Voreux to pick dandelion leaves, and he asked her threateningly whether she intended to make them miss the meeting—he wanted to know what the old men had to say. He egged Bébert on, and offered to liven up the rest of the trip as far as the trees by letting Poland off the leash and throwing stones at her. He had an obscure desire to kill her, and an urge to carry her off and eat her down in his den at Réquillart. The rabbit raced off again, flaring her nostrils and flattening her ears; one stone grazed her back, another cut her tail; and, despite the gathering darkness, she would soon have breathed her last if the rascals hadn't spied Maheu and Étienne standing in the middle of a clearing. They pounced urgently on to the beast and got her back inside the basket. At almost the same moment Zacharie, Mouquet, and the others made their last drives, which sent the ball to a point only a few metres away from the clearing. The whole group fell right into the middle of the meeting.

From all over the countryside, as soon as dusk began falling, along every road and pathway that crossed the flat plain, there came a long procession of silently gliding shadowy forms, some slipping past on their own, others in groups, making their way towards the purple thickets of the forest. All the villages emptied, the women and even the children left as if they were just going out for a walk in the clear night air. Now the roads were cloaked in darkness and you could no longer see the crowds on the march as they glided towards the same goal; you could only dimly sense their presence as the rhythm of their hesitant footsteps seemed to shuffle to the beat of a single heart. All that could be heard between the hedges and among the bushes was a slight swishing sound and the faint whisper of nocturnal life.

Monsieur Hennebeau, who happened to be returning home at that moment, riding his mare, listened to these eerie sounds. He had passed a whole string of couples walking slowly along, enjoying the beautiful winter evening. An endless stream of courting couples whose lips already mingled as they went to take their pleasure somewhere behind a wall. Wasn't that what he usually came across, girls on their backside in every ditch, layabouts stoking up with the only genuinely free pleasure? And the fools complained that they had problems, when they could stuff their bellies full of the priceless happiness of making love! He would have been more than happy to die of hunger just like them, if he could start his life over again with a woman who would lie down on the ground and submit to him, open up her body and her soul to him. He felt a wave of inconsolable misery, of envy for these wretches. He rode home with lowered head, slowing his horse as the long-drawn-out murmurs emerging from the depths of the pitch-black countryside spoke to him of endless kisses.

CHAPTER VII

THEY met at Le Plan-des-Dames, in a great clearing* recently opened by some tree-fellers. It stretched away in a gentle slope, surrounded by a high thicket of lofty beeches, whose regular line of straight trunks made a white colonnade, speckled green with lichen; and some, like fallen statues, still lay stretched out full length in the grass, while to the left could be seen the neat cube of a pile of sawn logs. The cold sharpened as twilight fell, and the frozen moss crackled underfoot. It was pitch-black at ground level, but the topmost branches stood out clearly against the pale sky, where the full moon rising on the horizon had started to blot out the stars.

Nearly 3,000 colliers had come to the meeting, and a teeming crowd of men, women, and children gradually filled the clearing and spilled over into the edge of the wood; but still latecomers kept arriving, until the sea of faces, swimming in darkness, poured into the neighbouring copses. A murmuring sound arose like a stormy wind from the still, frozen forest.

Étienne stood at the top, overlooking the slope, with Rassenuer and Maheu. A quarrel had broken out, and you could hear the voices in sudden rough bursts. Close by, people were listening: Levaque shaking his fists, Pierron turning his back on them, very worried at not having been able to use his fever as an excuse any longer; and there was also old Bonnemort and old Mouque, side by side, on a log, looking lost in their thoughts. Then behind them were the jokers, Zacharie, Mouquet, and others, who had only come for a laugh; while a group of women on the other hand had gathered together as solemnly as if they were attending a church service. La Maheude nodded her silent agreement with the muttered oaths of La Levaque. Philomène was coughing with the bronchitis that caught up with her every winter. Only La Mouquette laughed out loud, amused by old Ma Brûlé's description of her daughter, the shameless hussy who banished her so that she could stuff herself with rabbit and sold her favours for food behind her spineless husband's back. And Jeanlin had taken up position on the pile of logs, dragging Lydie up with him and forcing Bébert to follow, so that all three of them rose up in the air over the heads of the crowd.

The quarrel had been started by Rasseneur, who wanted to set up a properly elected committee. He was still furious at having been defeated at the Bon-Joyeux; and he had sworn to himself that he would get his revenge, for he was convinced that he would recover his former authority when he came face to face, not with the delegates, but with the ordinary miners. Étienne was exasperated at the ridiculous idea of appointing this futile committee out in the middle of the forest. Since they were being hunted like wolves, they ought themselves to act with wild revolutionary violence.

When he realized that there was no end to the dispute in sight, he suddenly turned and tried to bring the crowd to order. He leapt up on to a tree trunk and shouted:

'Comrades, comrades!'

The confused babble of the crowd tailed off into a prolonged sigh, while Maheu tried to silence Rasseneur, who was still protesting. Étienne carried on speaking in ringing tones.

'Comrades, if they won't let us speak out, and now that they've sent the gendarmes out to get us as if we were bandits, we've got to discuss our problems out here! We're free out here, we're on our own ground, nobody can come to shut us up, we're as free as the birds and the beasts!'

He was answered by a thunderous round of cries and exclamations.

'Yes, it's ours, it's our forest, we've got a right to talk here . . . Go on!'

Then Étienne stood motionless for a moment on his tree trunk. The moon was still too low on the horizon to throw light on any but the topmost branches; and the crowd, who were gradually settling down and falling silent, remained plunged in darkness. Étienne also looked black, but his dark shadowy mass loomed over the crowd from the top of the slope like a statue.

Slowly he raised his arm, and started his speech; but instead of speaking roughly now, he had adopted the unemotional tones of a simple delegate of the people delivering a report. At last he was able to make the speech that the superintendent had

interrupted at the Bon-Joyeux; and he started with a brief
historical survey of the strike, presenting facts and nothing but
the facts in what he hoped was the language of pure science.
First he expressed his reluctance to strike: the miners hadn't
wanted to, they had been forced into it by the management
when they imposed their new tariff for timbering. Then he
reminded them of the first approach made by the delegates to
the manager, the hypocrisy of the Board, and, after the second
delegation, their belated concession, the ten centimes that they
had agreed to restore after attempting to steal them. Now that
was as far as they had got; he gave them the figures which
showed that the emergency fund was empty, listed the uses
made of the aid that they had received, and said a few words to
excuse the International, Pluchart, and the others for not being
able to do more for them, because of their concern to plan for
world-wide victory. Thus the situation was getting worse every
day, and the Company was returning people's booklets and
threatening to employ Belgian workers; in addition, they were
intimidating the weaker spirits and had persuaded a certain
number of miners to go back down to work again. He kept
insisting on the bad news, while continuing to speak in a
toneless voice. He spoke of the triumph of starvation, the
death of hope, and the last, feverish throes of their will to
resist. And then suddenly, without raising his voice, he
concluded:

'These are the circumstances, comrades, in which you have
to reach a decision tonight. Do you want the strike to continue?
And, if so, what do you propose to do in order to beat the
Company?'

A deep silence fell from the starry sky. The crowd was
invisible in the darkness, and struck dumb by this speech
which choked their spirits; and all that could be heard through
the trees was a sigh of despair.

But Étienne had already started up again in a different tone
of voice. Already he no longer spoke as the secretary of the
association, but as leader, or rather, as apostle entrusted with
revealing the truth. Were there any cowards among them who
would go back on their word? Really? Would they have
suffered for a month to no avail? They would go back down

the pit with their tails between their legs, and their endless suffering would start up all over again! Wouldn't it be better to die straight away and at least make the attempt to overthrow the tyranny of capital which was starving the workers to death? Wasn't it a fool's game, how could they bear it any longer, how could they allow themselves to be bullied by hunger, waiting until it finally drove even the mildest among them once more to rebel? And he portrayed the exploitation of the miners, explaining how they bore the whole brunt of every crisis, and every disaster, seeing themselves reduced to starvation as soon as the requirements of competition caused a reduction in revenue. No! The timbering tariff was not acceptable, it was only a crafty way of saving money by robbing each man of an hour's wages every day. This time they had gone too far, the time would come when the wretched of the earth would feel they had been pushed to their limit, and they would demand justice.

He stood still, his arms outstretched.

The crowd was shaken with a long tremor at the sound of the word 'justice', and they broke out in applause, which swept through the gathering with a sound like the wind rustling through autumn leaves. Voices cried out:

'Justice! . . . The time has come, justice!'

Étienne gradually warmed to his theme. He didn't have the smooth and easy fluency of Rasseneur. He was frequently lost for words, and he had to twist his sentences round, and wrench them out of himself with an effort that shook his shoulders. And yet each of these verbal struggles resulted in some lively, popular image which caught the imagination of the audience; while his gestures were those of a workman accomplishing some physical task, as he hunched up his shoulders and then stretched out his arms to thrust his fists forward, with his jaws following the rhythm, as if to bite. This also had an extraordinary effect on his comrades. Everyone agreed that, although he was small of stature, he imposed his presence.

'Wage-earning is a new form of slavery,' he continued in a more vibrant tone. 'The mine should belong to the miner, as the sea does to the fisherman, and as the land does to the farmer . . . Make no mistake! The mine is your property, it belongs to all of you, for you have paid for it for over a century with blood and starvation!'

He launched right into obscure legal considerations, including the intricate details of the special legislation on mines, and he became confused. The depths of the earth, like its surface, belonged to the nation: and yet a vile privilege allowed private companies to have the monopoly of it; all the more so because for Montsou the alleged legality of the concessions was complicated by the pacts signed formerly with the inheritors of the old feudal domains, according to the old custom of the Hainault region. The miners then had only to repossess what was theirs by right; and he held out his arms to embrace the whole countryside beyond the forest. At that moment the moon rose clear of the horizon, and its light, filtering through the topmost branches, shone on him. When the crowd, which was still plunged in darkness, saw him thus, his arms outstretched, bathed in white light, showering them with wealth, they cheered him again, with a long round of applause.

'Yes! True! He's right! Bravo!'

And then Étienne dived into his favourite topic, the assignment of the instruments of labour to the collective, as he rehearsed it in a single phrase, whose rebarbative ring gave him an almost physical satisfaction. Now his own transformation was complete. Starting with the brotherly love of the novice, hoping to improve the condition of the wage-earner, he had finished up with the intention of abolishing the system altogether. Since the meeting at the Bon-Joyeux, when his idea of the collective had still been humanitarian and untheorized, he had formulated a rigid and complicated programme, whose every article he could debate scientifically. He argued first that freedom could only be obtained through the destruction of the State.* Then, when the people had seized control of the government, the reforms could begin: the return to the primitive community, the substitution of a free and egalitarian family for the oppressive family of traditional morality, absolute civil, political, and economic equality, the guarantee of individual independence thanks to the integral possession of the instruments and the fruits of their labour, and finally a free vocational training at the expense of the collective. That would mean they would have to recast entirely the old corrupt society; he attacked marriage and the laws of inheritance, he would limit everyone's right to personal wealth, he would overthrow the dead weight of centuries of iniquity, and he made a well-rehearsed sweeping movement with his arm, the great swing of the reaper cutting down a field of ripe corn with his scythe; and he went on to rebuild with the other hand, reconstructing the humanity of the future, showing the house of truth and justice starting to rise up in the dawn of the twentieth century. At this peak of mental tension his rational arguments faltered and gave way to the obsession of the prophet. Scruples of sense and sensibility were swept aside, as nothing seemed easier than creating this new world: he had planned it all in detail, he spoke of it as if it were a machine that he could piece together in a couple of hours, and he would not flinch in the face of fire or the sword.

'Our time has come,' he shouted, in a final outburst. 'It's our turn now to be powerful and wealthy!'

The sound of applause echoed across to him in the clearing from the depths of the forest. By now the moon was shedding its white light on the whole clearing, giving sharper outline to what had been merely a shapeless ocean of heads, shining right into the murky depths of the forest between the great shadowy trunks. And beneath the chill air there rose a furious mass of faces, with gleaming eyes and open mouths, a tumult of people, men, women, and children, driven by starvation to demand restitution of the heritage which had been stolen from them. They forgot the cold as his burning words lit a fire in their hearts. A religious fervour lifted them towards the heavens, with the urgency that inspired the early Christians to hope that the reign of justice was about to materialize. Many of Étienne's more obscure phrases had escaped them, such technical and abstract arguments were over their heads; but their very obscurity and abstraction seemed to promise more, and to bear them aloft in a glowing cloud of expectation. What a dream, to be the masters, to see an end to their suffering, even to accede to the realm of pleasure!

'That's it, for heaven's sake, it's our turn! . . . Death to the oppressors!'

The women screamed in delirium, La Maheude lost her sang-froid, her head spinning from hunger, La Levaque was screaming, old Ma Brûlé was beside herself, waving her arms like a witch, and Philomène was shaken by a fit of coughing, while La Mouquette was so worked up that she shouted words of love at the speaker. Among the men, Maheu was won over and let out an angry war-cry, between a trembling Pierron and a garrulous Levaque; while the mockers, Zacharie and Mouquet, felt ill at ease but tried to keep joking, expressing astonishment that their comrade could make such a long speech without stopping for a drink. But up on his log-pile Jeanlin was creating even more fuss, egging on Bébert and Lydie, and brandishing the basket where Poland lay half-dead.

The uproar started anew. Étienne savoured the intoxicating taste of popularity. He felt his power take on material form in those 3,000 chests whose hearts he caused to beat in tune with his every word. If Souvarine had deigned to come, he would have applauded his ideas once he recognized them, and would have been pleased with the progress of his pupil in anarchy and approved of his programme, except for the chapter on education, a left-over of his childish naïvety, for it was the salutary force of holy ignorance that would bathe his own men with its baptismal waters. As for Rasseneur, he shrugged his shoulders in anger and contempt.

'Will you let me speak!' he shouted at Étienne.

The latter leapt down from his tree trunk.

'Go on, talk, and we'll see if they'll listen to you.'

Rasseneur had already taken his place and was motioning for silence. But the hubbub didn't die down, for his name ran through the crowd, from those in the front rows who had recognized him to those at the back lost among the beeches; yet nobody would listen to him, for he was a fallen idol, and just to look at him infuriated his former disciples. His smooth eloquence and his soothing, cheerful language had long kept them charmed, but now seemed to be like weak tea, designed to lull them into a cowardly sleep. He spoke in vain, his voice swallowed up in the noise, trying to piece together his usual arguments for reconciliation, the impossibility of changing the world by sudden decree, and the need to let social change evolve gradually: he was mocked and hissed, the defeat which he had suffered at the Bon-Joyeux was aggravated and confirmed. They finally started throwing bits of frozen moss at him, and one woman cried out:

'Down with the traitor!'

He explained that the mine couldn't become the property of the miner, as the loom belongs to the weaver, and he said that he would prefer the workers to share in the profits, because the worker with a stake in the business would be treated like one of the family.

'Down with the traitor!' came the cry, repeated now by a thousand voices, while stones started to fly through the air.

Then he went pale, and his eyes filled with tears of despair. His whole existence collapsed, twenty years of fraternal ambitions disintegrated under the ungrateful attacks of the mob. He got down from the tree trunk, struck to the heart, having lost the will to continue.

'Does that make you laugh?' he stammered, turning to the triumphant Étienne. 'All right, I just hope that it happens to you . . . And it will, you mark my words!'

And, as if to disclaim any responsibility for the misfortunes which he foresaw, he let his arms fall to his sides, and went off alone into the silent, white countryside.

People started booing, and, surprisingly, old Bonnemort showed up standing on the trunk, talking amid the uproar. Up until then he and Mouque had remained absorbed, with their usual air of being wrapped up in old stories. Doubtless he was succumbing to one of those sudden fits of verbosity which from time to time stirred up the past within him so violently that the memories welled up and spilled forth from his lips for hours on end. A deep silence fell as everyone listened to this old man, standing pale and ghostly in the moonlight; and since he was talking about things that had no immediate bearing on the argument, long stories that nobody could follow, the effect was even more arresting. It was his own youth he was talking about, he told of the death of his two uncles buried alive at Le Voreux, then he went on to the congestion of the lungs that had carried off his wife. Yet he stuck to his point: things had never worked properly, and never would. So they too had held a meeting right there in the forest, five hundred of them, because the king refused to reduce their working hours; but then he interrupted his own train of thought, and started telling them about a different strike: he had seen so many! They all ended up under the trees, sometimes like here, at Le Plan-des-Dames, sometimes over there at La Charbonnerie, or further away, near Le Saut-du-Loup. Sometimes it was freezing cold, sometimes it was burning hot. One evening it had rained so hard that they had gone back home again without being able to have a discussion at all. Then the king's soldiers arrived and it ended up in a shooting match.

'We raised our hands like that, we swore not to go back down . . . Oh, I swore, yes, I swore I wouldn't!'

The crowd was listening open-mouthed, seized with misgivings, when Étienne, who had been following the scene, jumped on to the fallen tree and stood up beside the old man. He had just recognized Chaval among his friends in the front row. The idea that Catherine must be there had rekindled his passion, with a desire to be applauded before her very eyes.

'Comrades, now you've heard what one of our elders has suffered, and what our children will suffer, if we don't put a stop to these thieves and assassins.'

He was implacable, never had he spoken so violently. He held on to Bonnemort with one arm, displaying him like an emblem of poverty and mourning, crying for vengeance. In a few rapid phrases he ran through the fate of the Maheu family from their beginnings, worn out by the mine, devoured by the Company, still starving after a hundred years of hard labour; and he contrasted this with the Board of Directors, sitting there with bloated bellies, positively dripping with money, and the whole crew of shareholders, kept in luxury for a hundred years like fancy women with no need to work, just pampering their bodies. Wasn't it horrifying: a whole race of men dying below ground from father to son, just to help out government ministers with their expense accounts and to enable generations of nobles and bourgeois to throw parties or grow fat staying at home by the fireside! He had studied the diseases of miners, and he listed them one by one, in all their horrifying detail:

anaemia, scrofula, the black phlegm of bronchitis, suffocation from asthma, paralysis from rheumatism. These wretched folk, thrown as fodder to the machines, herded like cattle into the mining villages, were gradually absorbed by the big companies who regulated their slavery, threatening to enlist all the workers of the nation, all their millions of arms, for the wealth of a few thousand layabouts. But the miner was no longer an ignorant brute, trodden down into the depths of the earth. Deep down in the mines an army was growing, a future crop of citizens, germinating like seeds that would burst through the earth's crust one day into the bright sunshine. And then they would see if, after forty years of service, they dared offer a hundred-and-fifty-franc pension to an old man of sixty, whose guts were full of coal and whose legs were pickled in the water that gushed from the coal-face. Oh yes, labour would call capital to account, challenging the anonymous god, who lay hidden in his mysterious tabernacle, somewhere out of sight of the workers, gorged on the blood of the sick and dying that he fed on! They would go to find him, they would see his face lit clearly at last in the blaze of his dwelling as it burnt to the ground, he would drown in his own blood like a filthy swine, that foul idol that fed on human flesh!

He fell silent, his arm still stretching into the darkness, challenging the enemy out there, wherever he might be, even at the other end of the earth. This time the clamour of the crowd was so loud that the good citizens of Montsou heard it, and looked out towards Vandame, quaking with fear at the thought of some awful rock fall. The birds of the night wheeled over the woods, silhouetted against the great white sky.

He decided to conclude immediately:

'Comrades, what is your decision? ... Do you vote to continue the strike?'

'Yes! We do!' the voices screamed.

'And what measures will you take? ... We are sure to lose, if any cowards go back down to work tomorrow.'

Voices were raised again, in a tempestuous blast:

'Death to all cowards!'

'So you decide to remind them of their duty, of their solemn oath . . . This is what we can do: go to the pits, persuade the traitors to join us, show the Company that we are united and that we will die rather than yield.'

'He's right, to the pits! To the pits!'

All the while he had been speaking, Étienne had been seeking out Catherine's face among the mass of pale, turbulent figures swaying before him. He was sure she wasn't there. But he could still see Chaval, who was sneering and shrugging his shoulders ostentatiously, consumed with jealousy, ready to sell his soul for a taste of such popularity.

'And if there are any spies among us, comrades,' Étienne continued, 'they had better watch out, we know who they are . . . Yes, I can see some colliers from Vandame who haven't left their pit yet . . .'

'Do you mean me?' asked Chaval, with an air of bravado.

'You or anyone like you . . . But since you've spoken, you should understand that people with enough to eat have nothing to tell those who go hungry. You're working at Jean-Bart . . .'

A raucous voice interrupted:

'Oh, you could say he's working . . . or you could say he's found a woman to go to work for him.'

Chaval's face flushed, and he swore.

'For God's sake! Is it a crime to work, then?'

'Yes!' cried Étienne. 'When your comrades are starving for the good of their neighbours it's a crime to be selfish and suck up to the bosses. If the strike had been general, we would have mastered them long ago . . . Should any man from Vandame have gone down to work when Montsou was out on strike? The best thing would have been for work to stop all over the region, at Monsieur Deneulin's as well as here. Do you hear? You're nothing but traitors at the coal-face at Jean-Bart, you are all traitors!'

Around Chaval the crowd became threatening, fists were raised, and cries of 'Kill them! Kill them!' started to ring out. He went pale. But in his furious urge to get the better of Étienne he was inspired by a new idea.

'Just listen to me, now! Come to Jean-Bart tomorrow and you'll see if I'm working! . . . We're on your side, they sent me to tell you. We must put out the furnaces, and the mechanics too must come out on strike. I don't care if that makes the pumps stop! The water will ruin the pits and that'll put an end to the whole bloody farce.'

He was applauded wildly in his turn, and from then on Étienne lost control of the meeting. Speaker after speaker stood on the tree trunk, gesticulated amid the uproar, making wild proposals. They were possessed with the divine folly of inspired believers, the impatience of a religious sect which, tired of waiting for the promised miracle to happen, decides to accomplish it unaided. They saw red, as their heads were light with hunger and spinning with visions of fire and slaughter, of a glorious apotheosis from which universal happiness would arise. The tranquil moonlight bathed this ocean swell, and the depths of the forest swathed their murderous cries in its silence. The only sound to be heard was the crunching of frozen moss beneath their feet; while the beeches, rising straight and strong, with the delicate tracery of their branches standing out darkly against the white sky, were deaf and blind to the miserable wretches surging at their feet.

As the crowd ebbed and flowed, La Maheude found herself next to Maheu, and both of them, taking leave of their senses, carried away by the gradually rising exasperation that had been racking them for months, applauded Levaque, who was asking for the heads of the engineers. Pierron had disappeared, and Bonnemort and Mouque were both talking at once, saying confused but violent things, which nobody followed. For a laugh, Zacharie called for the churches to be demolished, while Mouquet struck at the ground with his cross club, for the sheer pleasure of making even more noise. The women were like furies: La Levaque with her hands on her hips flew at Philomène, accusing her of laughing; La Mouquette said she would kick the gendarmes to pieces where it hurt most; old Ma Brûlé, who had just slapped Lydie for turning up with no salad and no basket, started thrashing the air around her, aiming punches at all the bosses that she would have liked to get hold of. For a moment Jeanlin had felt stunned, for a pit boy had told Bébert that Madame Rasseneur had seen them steal Poland; but having decided that he'd go back on the sly to let the creature go free near the door of the Avantage, he shouted even louder, drew out his new knife and made it spring open, brandishing its shining blade with pride.

'Comrades! comrades!' repeated Étienne, exhausted and hoarse from trying to obtain peace and quiet for a moment, to get them to agree to take a final decision.

At last they agreed to listen.

'Comrades! Tomorrow morning at Jean-Bart, is that agreed?'

'Yes, you bet, Jean-Bart here we come! Death to all traitors!'

The tempest of their 3,000 voices filled the heavens and gradually dissolved in the clear, bright moonlight.

PART V

CHAPTER I

By four o'clock, the moon had set and the night was pitch-black. Everyone was asleep at the Deneulins' old brick house, which stood dark and silent, with its doors and windows closed, at the end of a large, unkempt garden which separated it from the Jean-Bart pit. On the other side of the house you could see the deserted road to Vandame, a large country town about three kilometres away.

Deneulin, who was tired from spending part of the previous day down underground, was snoring, with his face pressed up against the wall, and dreaming that someone was calling him. He finally woke up, heard a real voice, and ran to open the window. It was one of his deputies, standing in the garden.

'What is it?' he asked.

'Sir, it's a rebellion;* half the men don't want to work any more and are stopping the others from going down.'

He didn't quite take it in, for his head was heavy and buzzing with sleep, and the freezing air shocked him like a cold shower.

'Make them go down, for Christ's sake!' he stammered.

'It's been going on for an hour now,' the deputy went on. 'So we thought we ought to fetch you. You're the only person who could get them to see sense.'

'All right, I'm coming.'

He got dressed quickly, with his mind clear now, but very worried. They could have looted the house, for neither the cook nor the manservant had moved. But on the other side of the landing there was a whispering of anxious voices; and as he emerged, he saw his daughters' door open, and they both appeared in their white dressing-gowns, which they had hastily put on.

'What's happening, Father?'

The elder sister, Lucie, was already twenty-two, and she was tall, dark, and distinguished-looking; while Jeanne, the younger, just nineteen, was small, with golden hair, and a gentle, gracious air. 'Nothing serious,' he replied, to reassure

them. 'It seems that there's some disturbance from trouble-
makers over there. I'm going to have a look.'

But they protested; they wouldn't let him leave without
having something warm to eat. Otherwise he'd come home ill,
with a chill on his stomach, as usual. He struggled to evade
them, and gave his word of honour that he was in too much of
a hurry.

'Listen,' said Jeanne finally, wrapping her arms round his
neck, 'at least drink a glass of rum and eat a couple of biscuits;
or I'll stay like this and you'll have to carry me along with you.'

He had to resign himself to it, swearing that the biscuits
would choke him. But they were already half-way downstairs,
each carrying her candle. Down in the dining-room they
hurried to serve him, one pouring out the rum, the other
running to the study to fetch a packet of biscuits. Having lost
their mother very young, they had been brought up on their
own rather laxly by their father, who spoiled them, the elder
haunted by her dream of singing on stage, the younger crazy
about painting, where she showed a singular boldness of taste.
But when they had to reduce their standard of living, after
some major business difficulties, these extravagant-looking girls
had suddenly turned into wise and shrewd housewives, whose
eyes could detect a single centime missing from the accounts.
And now, despite their boyish, artistic style, they held the
purse strings, counted the pennies, argued with tradesmen,
mended the same dresses several times over, and all in all
managed to survive with dignity the increasing pressures on
the household finances.

'Eat up, Daddy,' repeated Lucie.

Then, noticing that he was plunged in his thoughts again,
looking silent and sombre, she was seized by another attack of
anxiety.

'It must be serious, mustn't it, if you're making such a face?
... Look, we'll go with you, they can do without us for lunch.'

She was referring to a party planned for that morning.
Madame Hennebeau was to go in her carriage to fetch Cécile
at the Grégoires' first; then she would come and collect them,
and they were going to Marchiennes, to Les Forges, where the
manager's wife had invited them to lunch. It was an opportu-

nity to visit the workshops, the blast-furnaces, and the coke ovens.

'Of course we'll come,' declared Jeanne in turn.

But he became angry.

'What an idea! I've already told you it's nothing ... Be so kind as to snuggle back down under the bedclothes, and get dressed again for nine o'clock, as you were meant to.'

He kissed them goodbye, and hastened to leave. They could hear the noise of his boots fading away as he walked across the frozen soil of the garden.

Jeanne replaced the cork carefully in the rum bottle, while Lucie locked the biscuits up in the cupboard.

The room had the cold cleanliness of a household where every meal has to be carefully calculated. And they both took advantage of their early rising to see if anything had been left lying around from the previous evening. There was a napkin unfolded, the manservant would be scolded. Then at last they went back upstairs again.

While he walked briskly down a short cut along the narrow paths leading through his vegetable garden, Deneulin thought of the threat to his fortune, his share in Montsou, the million that he had made and had dreamed of multiplying tenfold, but which was so threatened today. He had had an uninterrupted run of bad luck, enormous and unforeseen repairs, ruinous rates of return, then the disaster of this industrial slump, just when they had started to make a profit. If the strike spread to his pit, he would be finished. He pushed open a little gate: amid the general darkness, he could just make out the buildings at the pit-head, from the darker shadows they cast, and the occasional flickering gleam of a lantern.

Jean-Bart was smaller than Le Voreux, but its modern plant made it an attractive pit, according to the engineers. They had not only enlarged the shaft by one and a half metres, and dug down to a depth of 708 metres, they had renewed all the equipment and fittings, installed a new winding engine and new cages, everything being chosen for its up-to-date scientific perfection; and there was even a hint of elegance in the buildings; the screening shed had a carved frieze, the head-gear was adorned with a clock, the landing-stage and the engine-house had the curved forms of a Renaissance chapel, adorned by a chimney whose black and red bricks were patterned with a spiral mosaic. The pump was situated at the other shaft owned by the concession, at the old Gaston-Marie pit, which was entirely reserved for drainage. Jean-Bart had only two wells, one on each side of the winding shaft, one for the steam-powered ventilator and one for the ladders.

Chaval had been the first to arrive, at three in the morning, demobilizing his comrades, persuading them to follow the Montsou example and ask for a rise of five centimes per tub. Soon the four hundred underground workers had spilled over from the changing shed into the entrance hall, amid a tumult of gestures and cries. Those who wanted to work stood barefoot, with a pick or a shovel under one arm; while the others, still wearing their clogs, with their coats over their shoulders because of the cold, were blocking the way to the shaft; and the deputies had shouted themselves hoarse trying to restore order, begging them to listen to reason, and not to get in the way of the men who had the sense and decency to go down to work.

But Chaval lost his temper when he saw Catherine in her breeches and jacket, and her blue cap pulled down over her ears. When he had left home he had told her roughly to stay in bed. But she was in despair over this lost work and had followed him regardless, for he never gave her any money, and she often had to pay for both of them; so, what was to become of her if she couldn't earn any more herself? She was haunted with the fear of ending up like many a starving and homeless tram girl, in the brothel* at Marchiennes.

'For God's sake!' shouted Chaval. 'What the hell are you doing here?'

She blurted out that she didn't have a private income and needed to work.

'So you'd stand in my way, would you, you bitch! . . . Go home straight away, or I'll kick you back there personally with my boot up your backside!'

She shrank back in fear, but she didn't leave, as she was determined to see how things would turn out.

Deneulin arrived, making his entrance through the stairway

of the screening shed. Despite the dim light of the lanterns, he took in the whole scene with one swift glance, the crowd drowned in the darkness, but whose every face he knew, the hewers, the loaders, the labourers, the tram girls, even the pit boys. In the great hall, which was still clean and new, work had stopped and was waiting: the engine was under pressure, and released little jets of steam; cages hung motionless from the cables, tubs lay abandoned on the tracks, blocking the way across the iron floor. Only eighty or so lamps had been taken out, the others were still burning in the lamp depot. But a word from him would surely be enough, and the whole process of labour would spring to life again.

'Well then, my children, whatever is happening?' he asked at the top of his voice. 'What are you angry about? Explain what the matter is, and we'll sort it all out.'

He commonly adopted a paternal tone with the men, although he demanded hard work. He was brusque and authoritarian, and tried at first to win them over with sudden blasts of brash *bonhomie*; he was often liked, and above all the workers respected his courage, for he would frequently go down to the coal-face with them, and he was the first to brave the danger when the pit was shaken by an accident. Twice he had had himself sent down on a rope looped under his arms after a firedamp explosion which had discouraged the boldest among them.

'Look,' he went on, 'you're not going to make me wish that I hadn't trusted you, are you? You know that I refused to let them send a garrison of gendarmes here ... Just take your time and tell me what's on your minds, I'm listening.'

Now they all fell into an embarrassed silence, and moved away from him; and it was Chaval who finally spoke up:

'You see, Monsieur Deneulin, we can't go on working like this, we need five centimes more for each tub.'

He looked surprised. 'Five centimes! Whatever gave you that idea? I have no quarrel with your timbering, I don't want to set a new tariff like the Board at Montsou.'

'That's as may be, but our comrades at Montsou have got the right idea. They've rejected the tariff, and they want a rise of five centimes, because there's no way we can work decently with these new rates ... We want five centimes more, don't we, all of us?'

Voices were raised in approval, the noise grew again and they started to brandish their fists. Gradually they had all closed in on him, forming a circle.

Deneulin's eyes blazed, and he clenched his fist, for he was a man with a taste for strong rule, and he was afraid of yielding to the temptation to seize one of them by the scruff of the neck. He knew it was better to win the argument rationally.

'You want five centimes, and I grant you that the job is worth it. But I just can't give you the money. If I did, I'd quite simply go bust ... You must realize that I've got to make a living in the first place, if I'm going to pay you a living wage. And I'm at the end of my tether, the slightest increase in costs will send me under ... Remember, two years ago, when we had the last strike, I gave in, and I could do the same again. But that pay rise was a ruin, all the same, that's why I've been struggling for the last two years ... Today I'd just as soon shut up shop straight away, rather than not know where to find the money to pay you with next month.'

Chaval laughed cynically at the sight of this master who talked so openly of his business. The others looked away, incredulous and unmoved, unable to get into their heads the idea that a boss didn't earn millions on the backs of his workers.

Then Deneulin really insisted. He explained how he had to struggle against Montsou, which was always on the look-out to do him down, if he was ever unlucky enough to come a cropper one day. The rivalry was fierce, and forced him to economize, especially since the great depth of Jean-Bart increased the cost of extraction, and this disadvantage was barely compensated by the thickness of the coal-seams. He would never have agreed to raise their wages after the last strike, if he hadn't been forced to imitate Montsou for fear of losing his work-force. And he threatened them with the consequences: what sort of a success would it be for them if they forced him to sell out and they had to come under the iron fist of the Board? He, Deneulin, wasn't an absentee landlord, a distant god; he wasn't one of those shareholders who pay managers to fleece the miners without ever going to see them; he was a real boss, he didn't just commit his money to the job, but his intelligence, his health, and his very life. A stoppage of work would mean death, no less, for he had no stocks behind him, and yet he had to fulfil his orders. And again, the capital he had sunk in his plant couldn't just be left to rot. How could he fulfil his commitments? Who would pay the interest on the loans that his friends had made him? He would go bankrupt.

'So there you are, my fine friends!' he concluded. 'I wish I could convince you ... You can't ask a man to sign his own death warrant, can you? And whether I give you your five centimes or let you go on strike, it'd still be like putting my head on the block.'

He fell silent. People started muttering among themselves. A group of the miners seemed to hesitate. One or two went back towards the shaft.

'At least,' said one of the deputies, 'let everyone decide freely ... Who wants to work?'

Catherine was one of the first to come forward. But Chaval was furious, and pushed her back, shouting:

'We're all agreed here, you'd have to be a real bastard to let your workmates down!'

From that moment on there was no hope of compromise. People started shouting again, there was a rush to chase people away from the entrance to the shaft, and some were nearly crushed against the walls. For a moment the manager tried desperately to struggle single-handed to hold back the crowd; but it was a pointless act of folly, he had to withdraw. And he remained for a few moments inside the clerk's office, sitting breathless on a chair, so dismayed at his inability to act that he couldn't muster a single idea. Finally he calmed down, he asked one of the supervisors to bring Chaval to see him; then, when the latter had agreed to talk to him, he waved the crowd away:

'Leave us alone.'

Deneulin's idea was to see what this strapping fellow was made of. As soon as he heard him start talking, he guessed that he was vain, and consumed with envious urges. So he tried to

flatter him, appearing to be surprised that a workman of his
class should take the risk of compromising his future prospects.
From the way he talked he made it sound as if he had marked
him out some time ago for rapid promotion; and he finished
off by openly offering to make him a deputy later on. And
Chaval listened, silently, with clenched fists, but then he
gradually relaxed. He ran through a whole scenario in his
mind: if he insisted on carrying on with the strike, he would
never escape playing second in command to Étienne, whereas
he now saw an alternative ambition beckoning, to become one
of the leaders. A flush of pride burnt his cheeks and made him
feel light-headed. Besides, the group of strikers that he had
been waiting for all morning wouldn't come now; some obstacle
must have prevented them, perhaps the gendarmes: it was time
to comply. But nevertheless he shook his head, acting the
incorruptible, beating his breast indignantly. And at last, without mentioning to his boss that he had invited the miners over
from Montsou, he promised to calm his comrades down and to
persuade them to go back down.

Deneulin kept out of the way, and the deputies themselves
stayed on the sidelines. For an hour they heard Chaval holding
forth, arguing, standing on a tub on the landing-stage. One
group of workers booed him, and 120 of them left in exasperation, obstinately sticking to the decision that he had made
them take previously. It was past seven o'clock, and day was
dawning brightly, radiant with sunlight and sharp frost. And
suddenly, the pit began to throb with the sounds of work as
things started moving again. First the crank rod of the engine
started plunging up and down, coiling and uncoiling the cables
on the winding-drums. Then, amid the din of signals, the men
went down; the cages filled up, plunged out of sight, and came
back up again; the shaft was swallowing up its ration of pit
boys, tram girls, and hewers; while the labourers pushed the
trucks over the iron floor with a thunderous rattle.

'For God's sake! What are you doing there?' Chaval shouted
to Catherine, who was waiting her turn. 'Get yourself down
there, and fast!'

At nine o'clock, when Madame Hennebeau arrived in her
carriage with Cécile, she found Lucie and Jeanne ready and

waiting, very elegant despite their much-mended dresses. But Deneulin was astonished to see Négrel riding on horseback alongside the carriage. Why were the men mixed up in the party? So Madame Hennebeau explained with her maternal air that she had taken fright from what people had told her about the roads being infested with dangerous characters, and that she preferred to take someone with her to defend her. Négrel laughed and reassured them: it was nothing to worry about, they were only the usual loud-mouthed windbags, who wouldn't dare throw a stone to break a window. Deneulin was still full of his success, and told them how he had crushed the rebellion at Jean-Bart. He felt that his problems were over now. And on the road to Vandame, while the young ladies got into their carriage, everyone rejoiced in the splendid day they had in view, without suspecting that far off in the countryside the first tremors of the people on the march could be heard, although had they pressed their ears to the ground, they would have heard them.

'Well, then, that's agreed,' repeated Madame Hennebeau. 'This evening you will come to collect your young ladies and have dinner with us . . . Madame Grégoire has also promised to come to collect Cécile.'

'You can count on me,' Deneulin replied.

The carriage went off in the direction of Vandame. Jeanne and Lucie leant out, laughing, to wave at their father, who was standing by the roadside; while Négrel trotted gallantly behind their speeding wheels.

They crossed the forest, and took the road from Vandame to Marchiennes. As they approached Tartarus, Jeanne asked Madame Hennebeau if she knew La Côte-Verte,* and the latter, despite having spent five years in the region already, had to admit that she had never been that far. So they made a detour. Tartarus, on the edge of the woods, was an uncultivated moor, whose sterile volcanic soil had lain for centuries over a burning coal-mine. Its history was lost in the mists of time, and the local miners told the tale of how a bolt from the heavens had fallen on this Sodom in the bowels of the earth, where the tram girls were guilty of the vilest abominations; it had happened so quickly that they had been unable to get back up to the surface, and still today they were roasting in their hell down below. The dark red, scorched rocks were covered in a leprous growth of alum. Sulphur grew like yellow flowers round the lips of the fissures in the rock. At night the foolhardy who risked their eyes to look through these cracks swore that they could see flames, and criminal souls crackling on the burning coals deep within. Wandering lights ran over the surface, and there was a constant stream of hot, poisonous vapours, rank with the faecal stench of this devil's kitchen. And like the miracle of eternal spring, in the middle of this moor of Tartarus, La Côte-Verte rose with its evergreen lawns, its beeches with leaves that grew as soon as they fell, and its fields which yielded three crops a year. It was a natural greenhouse, warmed by the fires from the lower regions. The snow never settled there. Right next door to the bare trees of the forest, this huge mantle of greenery was flowering lushly on that December day, without the frost having curled the slightest blade of grass.

Soon the carriage was speeding across the plain. Négrel made fun of the legend, explaining how the bottom of a pit often caught fire, because of the fermentation of coal-dust; and when you couldn't control it, it just went on burning; and he mentioned a pit in Belgium that they had had to flood, by diverting a river into the shaft. But he fell silent, as the carriage had started passing more and more groups of miners during the last few minutes. They went by noiselessly, casting shifty but insistent glances at the luxurious carriage that was forcing them off the road. Their numbers grew and grew, until the horses had to slow down to a walking pace over the little bridge of the Scarpe. Whatever could be happening, to bring the whole population out on to the roads? The young ladies took fright. Négrel became convinced that there must be trouble brewing somewhere out there in the seething country-side; and they were all relieved when they finally got to Marchiennes. In the sunlight which seemed to dull their flame, the batteries of coke ovens and the blast-furnace chimneys belched forth their smoke, raining their sempiternal soot over the face of the earth.

CHAPTER II

AT Jean-Bart Catherine had been pushing for at least an hour, taking the tubs to the relay point; and she was drenched in such a flood of sweat that she stopped for a moment to wipe her face.

Back at the coal-face, where he was cutting into the seam with his team-mates, Chaval was surprised not to hear the rumbling of the wheels any more. The lamps flickered weakly, with the coal-dust preventing them from seeing.

'What's up?' he cried.

When she replied that she was sure she was going to melt, and she could feel her heart starting to stop, he replied angrily:

'Why don't you take your shirt off like the rest of us, you fool!'

They were 708 metres under, at the northern end of the pit, in the first section of the Désirée seam, three kilometres away from the loading bay. When they spoke of this part of the pit, the local miners went pale and lowered their voices, as if they were speaking of hell, and often they did no more than shake their heads, as if they preferred not to talk about these burning depths. As the tunnels stretched further north, they came closer to Tartarus, and approached the underground furnace that scorched the rocks above. The coal-faces here averaged a temperature of forty-five degrees. It was a veritable hell, surrounded by the flames which people up on the plain only glimpsed through the faults in the rock, spewing forth sulphur and pestilential vapours.

Catherine, who had taken off her jacket, hesitated, then took off her breeches as well; and with naked arms and thighs, her shirt anchored round her hips by a piece of string like a tunic, she started hauling again.

'Surely that'll be better now,' she said out loud.

She had had a vague sensation of fear when she felt herself suffocating. Since they had started working there five days before, she had thought of the tales that she had heard all through her childhood, of those tram girls from the past who were still burning under Tartarus, punished for doing things nobody dared to repeat. Of course she was too old now to believe such foolish stories; and yet, what would she have done, if she had suddenly seen one of those girls pass through the wall, burning like a red-hot poker, with eyes blazing like coals? This thought made her break out in another sweat.

At the relay point, eighty metres away from the coal-face, another tram girl took the tub and pushed it eighty metres further, up to the foot of the incline, for the loader to dispatch it with those sent down from the upper tunnels.

'Damn it! You don't care, do you?' said this young woman, a skinny thirty-year-old widow, when she saw Catherine stripped down to her undershirt. 'I couldn't do that, the boys at the ramp would be after me with their filthy jokes.'

'Too bad!' the younger girl replied. 'I couldn't care less what the men think! I'm too uncomfortable.'

She went back, pushing an empty tub. The worst thing in this underground gallery was that there was another source of unbearable heat as well as the proximity to Tartarus. They were close to some old workings, an abandoned gallery of the Gaston-Marie pit, very deep down, where a firedamp explosion ten years before had set the coal-seam on fire, and it was still burning, behind the 'dyke', the clay wall built there and kept under constant repair, so as to limit the damage. Thus deprived of oxygen, the fire should have gone out; but it must have been nourished by unsuspected draughts, for it had kept going for ten years, warming the clay wall of the dyke like bricks in a kiln, so much so that you could feel the heat as you went past. And this was the rampart that they had to push the tubs past, for a distance of more than a hundred metres, in a temperature of sixty degrees.

After two trips, Catherine felt she was suffocating again. Luckily the tunnel was wide and comfortable in the Désirée seam, one of the thickest in the area. The seam was one metre ninety deep, so the miners could work standing up. But they would have preferred to work all bent double, if only the air had been cool.

'Hey there, have you gone to sleep?' Chaval shouted again, as soon as he couldn't hear Catherine moving any more. 'Where on earth did I find such a useless mule? Will you fill that tub and keep it moving!'

She was at the bottom of the coal-face, leaning on her shovel, and she felt a wave of nausea sweep through her, as she stood looking at them stupidly, and showed no signs of complying with the order. She couldn't see them clearly in the reddish glow of their lamps; they were stark naked like beasts, but so black and caked with soot and coal that she wasn't disturbed by their nudity. All you could see of their obscure labours was their spines twisting and turning like monkeys and an infernal vision of reddened limbs, toiling away amid the dull thuds and subdued groaning. But they must have been able to see her more clearly, for the picks stopped tapping, and they teased her for taking her breeches off.

'Hey, you'll catch cold up your bum, watch out!'

'Now that's what I call a real pair of legs! Come on, Chaval, share them with your friends.'

'Let's have a look! Lift it up. Higher, now, higher!'

Then Chaval, who didn't take offence at their laughter, flew at her again.

'That's right, for God's sake . . . She takes her time, doesn't she, when there's some dirty talk to listen to? She'll still be there in the morning at this rate.'

Catherine forced herself laboriously to fill the truck; then she started pushing again. The tunnel was too wide for her to use the props on either side for leverage, her bare feet kept catching in the rails as she tried to find a foothold, while she strained slowly forwards with her arms stretched stiffly out in front of her and her back painfully arched. And as soon as she passed by the dyke, she was tormented by the heat, sweat streamed all down her body in great drops like rain in a thunderstorm.

She had hardly covered a third of the distance to the relay point when she was soaked in sweat, spattered and blinded by black mud like the others. Her tight undershirt seemed as if it were soaked in ink; it stuck to her skin, and rode right up over her hips as she flexed her thighs; and it cut into her so painfully that she had to abandon the task again.

Whatever was wrong with her today? She'd never felt her legs so like jelly before. The air must be really bad. The ventilation didn't have any effect at the end of this distant gallery. You breathed in all sorts of gases that escaped from the coal with a little hissing and bubbling sound like a spring, and it was so concentrated sometimes that the lamps wouldn't burn; not to mention the firedamp, which nobody bothered about any more, since there was such a quantity of it pouring into the miners' nostrils from one week's end to another. She knew it well enough, this bad air, or dead air,* as the miners called it; lower down there were heavy, asphyxiating gases, while higher up there were lighter gases which could catch fire and blow up every coal-face in a shaft, hundreds of men at one go in a single thunderclap. From her childhood onwards she had swallowed so much of it that she was amazed that she was so affected by it, her ears ringing and her throat burning.

She felt so oppressed that she wanted to take her shirt off. The cloth was starting to torment her, as every fold cut into her and burnt her. She resisted the temptation, and tried to keep pushing, but she was forced to stop and stand up again. Then suddenly, telling herself that she'd cover up again when she got to the relay point, she took it all off, string and shirt together, feeling so feverish that she would have ripped her skin off if she had been able. And now, stark naked and reduced to the pitiful level of a scavenger scrabbling for a livelihood in the mud of the gutter, she struggled painfully along, her buttocks smeared with sweat and grime, wallowing belly-deep in the mire, pushing along on all fours, like a horse hitched to a cab.

But she was filled with despair, for she felt no relief even now that she was naked. What else could she remove? She was deafened by the ringing in her ears, she felt as if her temples were squeezed in the grip of a vice. She fell to her knees. The lamp, wedged in the coal on top of the tub, seemed to go out. The only thought that surfaced from her mental confusion was the idea of turning up the wick. Twice she tried to check it, and each time, as she placed it in front of her on the ground, she saw it grow dim, as if it too were running out of breath. Suddenly the lamp went out. Then everything slid away into the darkness, a millstone had started turning in her head, her heart weakened and stopped beating, numbed in its turn by the great fatigue that had overcome her limbs. She had fallen over flat on her back, and was suffocating from the lack of air at ground level.

'I do believe, for God's sake, that she's taking time off again!' growled Chaval.

He listened out from the top of the coal-face, but couldn't hear the rumble of wheels.

'Hey, Catherine, you lazy cow!'

His voice echoed down into the distance along the dark tunnel, and not a whisper came to answer it.

'Have I got to come and get you moving myself?'

Nothing stirred, there was still the same deathly silence. He climbed down in a fury and ran along with his lamp so hurriedly that he nearly tripped over the body of the tram girl, which was blocking the gallery. He looked down at her, open-mouthed. What had got into her? Was she trying it on, in order to take a quick nap? But the lamp, which he had lowered to get a look at her face, nearly went out. He lifted it and lowered it again and then he understood: there must be a pocket of bad air. His anger vanished, and his professional conscience awoke in the presence of a fellow miner in peril. He shouted immediately for someone to bring her shirt, and he seized the unconscious, naked girl in his arms, and lifted her as high up off the ground as he could. When they had thrown their garments over her shoulders, he raced off, holding his burden up with one arm, carrying the two lamps in the other hand. The deep tunnels sped by, as he raced along, turning right, turning left, rushing to find the life-giving air of the plains coming from the ventilator. At last he stopped when he heard the sound of a spring flowing through a crack in the rock. He had reached a crossroads on a haulage road which had previously served the Gaston-Marie pit. Here the ventilation blew like a hurricane, and it was so cold that, when he sat down on the ground and leaned against the props, he was shaken by a fit of shivering; he held on to his mistress, who lay unconscious, with her eyes closed.

'Come on, Catherine, for God's sake, stop mucking around . . . Hold on a moment while I dip this in the water.'

He was terrified to see how limp she was. But he managed to soak her shirt in the spring water, and he washed her face with it. She looked like a corpse, buried alive in the depths of the earth, with her slim, undeveloped body, where puberty had hardly yet sketched any female forms. Then a tremor ran through her childish breasts, and her pitiful, prematurely experienced stomach and thighs. She opened her eyes and stammered:

'I'm cold.'

'That's more like it, that's better!' cried Chaval, in relief.

He dressed her, slipping her easily into her shirt, but cursing at the difficulty of getting her breeches on, for she couldn't help much. She was still dazed, and unable to understand where she was, nor why she was naked. When she did remember, she was overcome with shame. How could she have dared to take all her clothes off! And she asked him whether anyone had seen her in that state, without even a kerchief round her waist to hide her. He laughed, and made up stories about it, alleging that he had just brought her there surrounded by workmates forming a guard of honour. What had got into her to take his advice literally and take her pants off! Then he gave her his word that his mates couldn't have guessed whether her behind was round or square, because of the speed it travelled at.

'Damn it, I'm dying of cold,' he said, getting dressed in his turn.

She had never seen him so kind. Usually every kind word he addressed to her was immediately followed by a couple of insults. And yet it would have been so nice to live in harmony! She was filled with tenderness, in the midst of her lassitude and fatigue. She smiled at him and murmured:

'Kiss me.'

He kissed her, and lay down alongside her, waiting until she was ready to get on her feet.

'You see,' she went on, 'you were wrong to shout at me down there, for I really couldn't go on, you know! You don't feel so hot at the coal-face; but you can't imagine how you get roasted alive further down the track!'

'Obviously,' he said, 'we'd be better off sitting under the trees in the shade . . . This pit is making you ill, I realize that, my poor girl.'

She was so touched to hear him agree that she put a brave face on it.

'Oh! I just had a bad turn. And today the air was really poisonous ... But you'll see, in a minute, that I'm not a lazy cow. When you have to work, you do work, don't you? I'd rather die than give up.'

Silence fell. With one arm round her waist, he held her against his chest, to keep her from harm. And although she felt strong enough to go back to work, she let herself go, enjoying her moment of pleasure.

'Except,' she went on very quietly, 'I do wish you'd be kinder to me ... You know it's so nice when we love each other a bit.'

And she started weeping softly.

'But I do love you,' he cried, 'after all, I've taken you to live with me.'

She could only nod her head in reply. It was common enough for a man to take a woman simply in order to have her, without worrying about her happiness. Her tears flowed hotly now; she felt suddenly miserable at the thought of the enjoyable life she might lead if she had happened upon a different young man, one whose arms she would always have round her waist. Another man? And she pictured the blurred outlines of this rival in the turmoil of her emotions. But it was already over, she felt no more than the wish to live out her days with the one she had got, if only he wouldn't be quite so rough with her.

'Well then,' she said, 'try to act like this every now and then.'

She broke off, sobbing, and he kissed her again.

'What a fool you are! ... Look, I swear I'll be kind. I'm no worse than the next man, you know!'

She looked at him, and started to smile again through her tears. Maybe he was right; you didn't often meet a happy woman. Then, although she only half-believed his promise, she let herself enjoy the happiness of having him act pleasantly. Oh God! If only it would last! They took hold of each other once again, and while they were locked in a prolonged embrace, they heard steps, and stood up. Three comrades, who had seen them pass, had come to see how they were getting on.

They went off again together. It was nearly ten o'clock, and they ate lunch in a cool spot before going back to the sweltering coal-face. But just as they were finishing off their sandwiches, and were about to take a swig of coffee from their flasks, a rumbling noise coming from the distant coal-faces disturbed them. What was it? Was it another accident? They got up and ran. Hewers, tram girls, and pit boys passed them running in every direction; but nobody knew what had happened, everyone was shouting, it must be something really bad. Gradually the whole mine was seized with terror, panicky silhouettes leapt out of the galleries, lanterns danced and ran through the shadows. Where was it? Why could nobody tell them?

Suddenly a deputy ran past, shouting:

'They're cutting the cables!* They're cutting the cables!'

Then there was a rush of panic. Everyone galloped madly down the dark galleries. They started to lose their heads. Why should anyone cut the cables? And whoever would cut them, with men down below? It seemed monstrous.

But the voice of another deputy rang out and then faded away.

'It's them from Montsou that are cutting the cables! Everybody out!'

As soon as he realized what was happening, Chaval stopped Catherine in her tracks. The thought of meeting the Montsou miners up there, if he got out, cut his legs from under him. So the Montsou group had given the gendarmes the slip and had come after all! For a moment he thought of turning back and going back up through the Gaston-Marie shaft; but it was no longer in working order. He hesitated, swearing in order to cover his fear, repeating how stupid it was to run so fast. They wouldn't leave them underground, surely to goodness!

The deputy's voice rang out again, getting nearer.

'Everybody out! Up the ladders, up those ladders!'

And Chaval was swept forwards along with his comrades. He jostled Catherine onwards, accusing her of running too slowly. Did she want to stay down the pit and die of hunger? For the thugs from Montsou were quite capable of smashing the ladders without waiting for everyone to get out. This ghastly suggestion finally made them lose their heads, and all along the tunnels there was one crazy stampede, a hysterical race to get there first, to climb out ahead of the others. People were shouting that the ladders were broken, that nobody could escape. And when the terrified groups started to reach the loading bay, there was a violent surge: they flooded into the shaft, and crushed each other in their rush to get through the narrow doorway leading to the ladder well; while an old stableman, who had just taken the precaution of leading his horses back into their stalls, watched them with supercilious unconcern, since he was used to spending his nights down the mine and was sure that he would get back up again some day or other.

'For God's sake! Will you get up in front of me!' said Chaval to Catherine. 'At least I'll catch you if you fall.'

Dazed and breathless from the three-kilometre dash that had covered her in sweat all over again, she had lapsed into a state of bewilderment, abandoning herself to the ebb and flow of the crowd. So he had to pull on her arm hard enough to break it; she shouted in pain, and tears welled up in her eyes; he had already forgotten his promise, she would never be happy.

'Go on, move!' he shouted.

But she was too afraid of him. If she went up ahead of him he would never stop bullying her. So she resisted, while the stream of desperate comrades swept them aside. The water that filtered through the shaft fell in great drops, and the floor of the pit bottom, shaken by the trampling herd, vibrated as they passed over what they called the 'bog', which was a muddy sump, ten metres deep. And in fact it had been here at Jean-Bart two years earlier that a terrible accident, caused by a broken cable, had sent the cage hurtling down to the bottom of the bog, where two men had drowned. And they were all thinking of it, they all feared they would go plunging down into it never to return, if the whole crowd kept piling on to the boards.

'Bloody blockhead!' cried Chaval. 'Drop dead if you like, I'll be better off!'

He went up, and she followed.

To reach daylight from the bottom of the well, you had to

climb up 102 ladders, each about seven metres high, and each
one perched on a narrow ledge that ran across the breadth of
the well, leaving a square hole only just wide enough to let
your shoulders through. It was like a flat chimney 700 metres
high between the outer wall of the winding shaft and its lining,
a damp, dark, endless tube, with its ladders following on
almost vertically in regular stages. It took a fit man twenty-five
minutes to climb this giant staircase. In fact the well was only
ever used in emergencies.

Catherine climbed quite briskly at first. Her bare feet were
hardened to the sharp coal chips of the gallery floor and felt
no discomfort on the square rungs, which were shod in iron to
prevent wear. Her hands, which were toughened from pushing
the tubs, grasped the uprights firmly, although they were too
wide for her grip. And this unforeseen climb even gave her
something to think about and made her forget her problems,
as she became one member of a slippery human serpent,
gliding upwards three at a time on each ladder, so that when
the head eventually reached daylight, the tail would still be
snaking over the top of the bog. But this hadn't happened yet,
the leaders must still be only a third of the way up the well.
Nobody spoke any more, there was only the dull slap of their
feet on the rungs; while their lamps became spaced further
apart the higher they rose, like an ever-lengthening stream of
shooting stars.

Behind her Catherine could hear a pit boy counting the
ladders. That gave her the idea of counting them too. They
had already gone up fifteen, and they had reached another
loading bay. But at that moment she stumbled into Chaval's
legs. He swore, shouting to her to watch out. As each man
stopped the next, the whole column ground to a halt. What
was up? What had happened? And their voices returned,
asking questions, expressing fears. Their anxiety had been
mounting since they had left the bottom of the shaft behind,
the fear of the unknown above their heads felt more and more
suffocating as they approached the daylight. Someone announced that they had to go back down again, for the ladders
were broken. That was what had haunted them all, the fear of
finding themselves lost in limbo. Another explanation was

passed down from mouth to mouth, a hewer had slipped and fallen down one of the ladders. Nobody was quite sure what was happening, with everyone shouting it was impossible to hear clearly, at this rate they'd be spending the night there. And at last, without them having any better idea of what had happened, the climb started up again, with the same tramping of feet and dancing of lamps. As for the broken ladders, they must be higher up, obviously.

By the thirty-second ladder, as they went past the third loading bay, Catherine felt her arms and legs growing stiff. At first she had felt a slight tingling of the skin. Now she had lost all feeling of the wood and the iron on her hands and feet. A vague but slightly burning ache spread through her muscles. And amid the numbness that invaded her, she remembered the stories told by grandfather Bonnemort, of the days when there used to be no ladder well and ten-year-old girls climbed up ladders placed against the side of the shaft, carrying the coal baskets on their shoulders; so that, if one of them slipped, or even if a piece of coal fell out of one of their baskets, three or four children would go tumbling down together, head first. The cramp in her muscles became unbearable, she'd never get to the top.

They had to stop again, and each time this happened she was able to catch her breath. But the terror which wafted down from above on these occasions finally made her head reel. Above and below her, people were breathing with increasing difficulty, the endless climb was causing a state of vertigo, and, like everyone else, she started to feel waves of nausea pass through her. She felt that she was suffocating, drowning in darkness, her head spinning with the pressure of the walls hemming her body in. And at the same time she was shivering from the dampness, for her body was soaked by heavy droplets of water as well as dripping in sweat. They were nearing the water-table, and the rain beat down so heavily that it threatened to extinguish the lamps.

Twice Chaval questioned Catherine without obtaining a reply. What was she up to down there, had she swallowed her tongue? She might at least tell him whether she was still all right. They had been climbing for half an hour; but so laboriously that they were only on the fifty-ninth ladder. Forty-three to go. Catherine finally stammered that she was still holding out. He would have called her a lazy cow if she'd admitted her exhaustion. The iron edges of the rungs must be eating into her feet, it felt as if someone was sawing into her very bones. After each pull up with her arms, she expected to see her hands fall away from the uprights, they were so skinned and stiff that she could no longer grip with her fingers; and she could feel herself on the point of falling backwards, with her shoulders and hips torn out of their sockets by their ceaseless straining. Above all it was the near-vertical slant of the ladders that exhausted her, since they were so steep she had to pull herself up by her wrists, with her stomach pressed up against the wood. The sound of people wheezing and gasping for breath was now louder than the rumbling of their footsteps, it sounded like one great, booming death-rattle, echoing tenfold off the sounding-board of the lining of the well, swelling up from the depths and dying away as it rose towards the daylight. There was a groan, rumours flew up and down the line, apparently a pit boy had split his head open against the rim of one of the landings.

Still Catherine kept on climbing upwards. They had got past the water-table. It stopped raining, and the underground air became heavy with the misty, poisonous vapours given off by the rusty iron and rotten wood. She forced herself to keep counting mechanically under her breath, eighty-one, eighty-two, eighty-three; nineteen to go. As she repeated the figures to herself their very rhythm kept her going. She had lost all consciousness of her movements. When she looked upwards, the lamps span round in a spiral. Her blood seemed to be ebbing out of her veins, she felt that she was dying, and that the slightest draught would blow her away. The worst was that the people below her were pressing upwards now, and the whole column was rushing, yielding to a growing rage, fuelled both by exhaustion and by the frenzied urge to get out into daylight. Some of their comrades, at the top of the column, had already emerged; so the ladders weren't broken; but the thought that someone might still have time to break them to stop the last people escaping, while the first in the queue were already breathing in the fresh air, finally drove them crazy. And when there was another bottleneck, they started swearing and kept on climbing, jostling each other and clambering over anyone who paused for a moment and got in their way, determined to get out at any cost.

Then Catherine fell. She had called out Chaval's name in a desperate appeal. But he didn't hear her, he was fighting with one of his comrades, kicking at his ribs with his heels to get past him. She was crushed and trampled. As she fainted she dreamed that she was one of the little tram girls of days gone by, and that a piece of coal that had fallen from a basket above her had just knocked her down to the bottom of the shaft, like a sparrow felled by a stone. There were only five ladders left to climb, after nearly an hour. She never knew how she got up to the surface, pushed upwards by the heaving mass of shoulders below her, held upright by the sheer narrowness of the well. Suddenly she found herself blinded by the sunlight, amid a crowd of people hissing and screaming at her.

CHAPTER III

IN the early morning, since before daylight, a tremor had been running through the villages, a tremor which had now become a rumbling which traversed the highways and the whole countryside. But they couldn't depart when they had planned, for they had heard the news that dragoons and gendarmes were scouring the plain. People said that they had arrived from Douai during the night, and Rasseneur was accused of betraying his comrades by warning Monsieur Hennebeau; there was even a tram girl who swore that she had seen the manservant go past taking the dispatch to the telegraphist. The miners clenched their fists, watching out for the soldiers from behind their shutters in the pale light of dawn.

Towards half-past seven, as the sun was rising, another rumour spread, which calmed their impatience: that it was a false alarm, a simple military manœuvre, like others which the general had organized from time to time since the start of the strike, at the instigation of the Prefect in Lille. The strikers abominated this official, whom they accused of deceiving them with the promise of arranging a compromise, but who did no more than parade his troops through Montsou once a week to show that they meant business. Thus, when the dragoons and gendarmes went off peacefully towards Marchiennes, satisfied with simply deafening the inhabitants of the villages with the trotting of their horses' hooves on the hard earth, the miners made fun of this foolish Prefect, with his soldiers who turned tail just when things were starting to hot up. Until nine o'clock they cheered each other up, standing peacefully in front of their houses, watching the unhurried backs of the last gendarmes marching away down the cobbled street. Deep in their comfortable beds, the good citizens of Montsou were still asleep, their heads sunk in their soft pillows. At the manager's house Madame Hennebeau had just been seen leaving by carriage, and must have taken Monsieur Hennebeau with her to drop him off at work, for their villa was closed, silent, and seemingly uninhabited. None of the pits had a military guard, which was a fatal act of imprudence in this hour of danger, showing people's usual stupidity when faced with disaster, and all the mistakes a government can make as soon as any insight is required. And nine o'clock was striking when the colliers finally took the road to Vandame, to keep the rendezvous they had fixed the night before in the forest.

Moreover Étienne understood straight away that there was no hope of finding at Jean-Bart the 3,000 comrades that he had been counting on. A lot of them thought that the demonstration had been postponed, but the worst of it was that two or three groups of men had already started out, and were bound to compromise their cause if he didn't go out and take charge of them, like it or not. Nearly a hundred men who had left home before daylight must have been sheltering under the beech trees in the forest to wait for the others. Souvarine, whom the young man went upstairs to consult, shrugged his shoulders: ten stout and resolute men could achieve more than a crowd; and he plunged immediately back into the book that was open in front of him, refusing to get involved with it. They were acting like a crowd of sloppy romantics, when all

they needed to do was burn Montsou to the ground, which
would be easy enough. As Étienne left the house by the front
path, he noticed Rasseneur sitting in front of the cast-iron
hearth, looking very pale, while his wife, wearing her changeless
black dress, seemed to have grown in stature as she insulted
him with elegance and precision.

Maheu's opinion was that they should keep their word.
Such a meeting was sacred. However, the night had cooled
everyone's ardour; now he was afraid of some tragedy, and he
explained that their duty was to go there, to make sure that
their comrades behaved themselves. La Maheude nodded her
approval. Étienne repeated reassuringly that, although they
had to act as revolutionaries, they must not threaten life and
limb. Before he left, he refused his share of a loaf of bread
which, along with a bottle of gin, he had been given the night
before; but he drank three small tots one after the other, just
to keep out the cold; and he even filled a flask to take along
with him. Alzire would look after the children. Old Bonnemort,
whose legs were weak from having walked too much the night
before, had stayed in bed.

They took the precaution of leaving separately. Jeanlin had
disappeared a long time before. Maheu and La Maheude went
off on their own, cutting across country to Montsou, while
Étienne made off towards the forest, where he hoped to join
his comrades. On the way he caught up with a band of women,
among whom he recognized old Ma Brûlé and La Levaque: as
they went along they were eating some chestnuts that La
Mouquette had given them, and even swallowed the skins to
have more in their stomachs. But he found nobody in the
forest; his comrades were already at Jean-Bart. So he ran off,
arriving at the pit just as Levaque and a hundred or so others
reached the pit-head. Miners were arriving from all sides, the
Maheus from the highway, the women from across the fields,
all in dribs and drabs, with no leaders, and no weapons,
flooding in like some natural stream that had overflowed its
banks and was pouring downhill. Étienne saw Jeanlin, who had
climbed up on to an overhead gangway and had settled down as
if to watch a show. Étienne ran faster so as to be among the
first to arrive. There were no more than 300 of them.

When Deneulin showed himself at the top of the staircase which led to the entrance hall, they faltered.

'What do you want?' he called out in a loud voice.

After he had watched the carriage depart out of sight, with his daughters still laughing inside, he had returned to the pit, seized by a vague anxiety. And yet everything was in good order, the men had gone down, the coal was coming up, and he felt reassured again. He was just talking to the overman when he was told of the approaching strikers. Swiftly he moved to a window in the screening shed; and seeing the surging flood of men filling the yard, he suddenly realized that he was powerless. How could he defend these buildings, which were open on all sides? He couldn't muster more than a score of men at his side. He was lost.

'What do you want?' he repeated, pale with suppressed anger, making an effort to put a brave face on disaster.

The men were surging back and forth and muttering among themselves. Étienne managed to break free and speak:

'Sir, we have not come to cause trouble. But work must cease in every pit.'

Deneulin treated him quite simply as an imbecile.

'Do you think you're going to cause me no harm if you stop people working for me? You might as well shoot me in the back at point-blank range . . . Yes, my men have gone down to work, and no, they won't come up again, unless you murder me first!'

This tough talk caused an uproar. Maheu had to restrain Levaque, who was rushing forward threateningly, while Étienne went on arguing, trying to convince Deneulin of the legitimate nature of their revolutionary action. But Deneulin answered that his men had the right to work.

And what's more he wasn't going to get involved in such stupid arguments, he was master of his works, and he was only sorry that he didn't have a handful of gendarmes with him to gun down the rabble.

'Fair enough, it's my own fault, it serves me right. With your kind of lout there's only force that counts. It's like the government, thinking they can buy you off by making concessions. You'll bring them down, sure enough, once they've given you the weapons.'

Étienne was shaking, but he continued to control himself. He lowered his voice.

'I beg of you, Sir, give your workers the order to come up. I can't answer for what my comrades might do. You can prevent a tragedy.'

'No, go to hell! Why should I have anything to do with you? I don't employ you, you've got nothing to discuss with me ... You're just a bunch of thugs roaming round the countryside looting people's houses.'

Angry protests covered his voice now, and the women especially hurled insults at him. But he continued to face up to them, and felt relieved at this open confrontation where he could give free rein to his authoritarian disposition. Since he was ruined, whatever happened, there was no point in resorting to cowardly platitudes. But the crowd kept growing, there were already over five hundred of them rushing towards the door, and he was about to get himself done in, when his overman pulled him roughly back.

'For heaven's sake, Sir! ... There'll be a massacre. There's no point in getting people killed for nothing.'

He struggled, protesting, and launched one last cry at the crowd.

'You bunch of thugs, just you wait till we get the upper hand again!'

They dragged him away, and a sudden surge of the crowd threw the people at the front up against the staircase, buckling the handrail. It was the women that pushed hardest, squealing with excitement and goading the men on. The door gave way immediately, for it had no lock, only a simple catch. But the staircase was too narrow, and the mob was all crushed up together and would have taken ages to get through, if the assailants at the back of the queue hadn't decided to go through the other entrances. And then they spilled over on all sides, overrunning the changing shed, the screening shed, and the boiler-house. In less than five minutes they were masters of the whole pit, they had the run of all three storeys, surrounded by a furious clamour of shouts and gestures, carried away by their intoxicating victory over a stubborn boss.

Maheu was horrified, and ran off with the first group, saying to Étienne:

'They mustn't kill him!'

Étienne had already started running too; then, when he realized that Deneulin had barricaded himself in the deputies' quarters, he replied:

'What if they did? Would it be our fault, with such a bloody-minded devil?'

Yet he felt deeply disturbed, and still too calm to give in to this wave of anger. His pride as leader was also offended, when he saw the crowd escape his authority, getting carried away and failing to execute the will of the people dispassionately as he had planned. He called in vain for calm, shouting that they mustn't give ammunition to their enemies by committing pointless acts of destruction.

'Get the boilers!' screamed old Ma Brûlé. 'Let's put out the fires!'

Levaque, who had found a file, was brandishing it like a dagger, and his awful cry could be heard above the din:

'Cut the cables! Cut the cables!'

Soon everyone had taken up his cry; only Étienne and Maheu continued to protest, but their voices were drowned out by the uproar, and they failed to make any impact. At last Étienne managed to make himself heard:

'But, comrades, there are men down below!'

The hubbub increased, shouts arose from all sides.

'Too bad, they shouldn't have gone down! ... Serve the traitors right ... Yes, and let them stay down there! ... Anyway, they've got the ladders!'

So when he saw that the thought of the ladders was inspiring them with renewed fury, Étienne realized that he'd have to give in. Fearing an even greater disaster, he rushed towards the engine, hoping at least to get the cages up first, to prevent the severed cables from falling down the whole depth of the shaft, and crushing the cages with their enormous weight. The mechanic in charge had disappeared, as had the handful of surface workers; and he grasped the control lever himself, pulling at it while Levaque and two others climbed up the iron framework which supported the pulleys. There was just time to lock the cages into their keeps before the harsh rasping of a file biting into the steel resounded. There was a deep silence, the sound seemed to fill the whole pit, everyone raised his head, looking and listening, feeling a wave of emotion. In the front row, Maheu felt himself possessed by a wild thrill of pleasure, as if every cut of the file was setting him free from the bonds of unhappiness, by hacking away at the cable leading to one of those hell-holes that they'd never have to go down into again.

But old Ma Brûlé had disappeared into the staircase at the back of the hall, still screaming:

'Empty the furnaces! Get the boilers! Go and get them!'

A group of women followed her. La Maheude hurried after, hoping to stop them from breaking everything up, just as her husband had wanted to make his workmates see reason. She was the most sensible among them, arguing that they could stand up for their rights without smashing things to pieces. By the time she reached the boiler-house, the women were already driving away the two boilermen, and old Ma Brûlé had armed herself with a large shovel, and was squatting down in front of one of the furnaces, emptying it violently, throwing the burning coal on to the brick floor, where it continued to burn, giving off a cloud of black smoke. There were ten furnaces fuelling the five generators. Soon all the women had set to work: La Levaque was wielding her shovel with both hands, La Mouquette tucking her skirt up over her thighs to avoid getting it burned, all of them blazing red in the reflection of the fire, sweating and dishevelled from this witches' sabbath. As they piled up the heaps of coal, the burning fumes scorched the ceiling of the great hall.

'That's enough!' cried La Maheude. 'The store room's on fire.'

'Who cares!' old Ma Brûlé replied. 'We'll have done our job ... Oh my God! I told them I'd make them pay for my man's death!'

At that moment they heard Jeanlin's shrill voice:

'Watch out! I'm going to put it out! Here goes!'

He had been one of the first on the scene, and was delighted at the prospect of a fight, looking out for any mischief he could contribute; and he had been struck by the idea of opening the safety valves, to let out the steam. The jets blew out as violently as gunshots, and the five boilers emptied with a tempestuous blast, whistling with such a thunderous roar that it made their ears bleed. Everything was drowned in steam, the coal seemed white, the women looked like ghosts, making dreamlike gestures. Only the boy showed up clearly, standing on the overhead platform where he had clambered, beyond the spirals of white vapour, looking delighted, with his mouth cracked open by the pleasure of having unleashed such destruction.

It lasted nearly a quarter of an hour. They had thrown a few buckets of water on the heaps of burning coal, to help extinguish them: there was no longer any danger of the building catching fire. But the anger of the crowd, instead of abating, was only whetted. Men came down wielding hammers, women armed themselves with iron bars; they talked of smashing the generators, breaking the engines, and demolishing the pit.

When Étienne realized what was happening, he ran up, accompanied by Maheu. Even he felt intoxicated, carried away by the hot breath of revenge. Nevertheless he struggled to urge them to stay calm, now that the broken cables, the doused flames, and the empty boilers rendered work impossible. But they still wouldn't listen to him, and his voice was about to be smothered again, when they heard a commotion outside, coming from a little low door, where the ladder well emerged.

'Down with the traitors! . . . Look at their filthy, cowardly faces! . . . Down with the lot of them!'

The underground workers had started to emerge. The first of them, blinded by the dazzling daylight, stopped still, blinking their eyelids. Then they filed off, trying to reach the road and escape.

'Down with cowards! Down with false friends!'

The whole band of strikers had run up. In less than three minutes, there was not a man left inside the buildings, and the 500 men from Montsou formed two lines, forcing the Vandame traitors, who had gone down the mine, to run the gauntlet. And as each new miner surfaced at the door of the well, covered in the muck of work and with his clothes in tatters, they renewed their insults and welcomed them with bitter sarcasm: 'Just look at him, Tom Thumb in person, with his arse scraping the ground, and how about that one, with his nose eaten off by the slags at the Volcan! And there's one with enough gunge in his eyes to make candlewax for a whole cathedral! And look at the one with no arse, he's taller than a Bible story!' An enormous tram girl who tumbled out, with breasts down to her belly and her belly billowing round into her behind, raised a gale of laughter. They wanted to have a feel, the jokes got cruder and crueller, and punches were soon going to fly; while the poor wretches continued to file past, suffering the insults shivering and in silence, keeping a wary eye on the strikers' fists, and much relieved when they were at last able to run free of the pit.

'Who'd believe it, how many of them are there down there?' asked Étienne.

He was astonished to see so many of them keep pouring out, and was upset at the idea that it wasn't just a handful of workers, driven by hunger or bullied by the deputies. So had they lied to him in the forest? Almost the whole of Jean-Bart had gone down to work. But he gasped out loud and dashed forward, as he saw Chaval loom up in the doorway.

'In God's name! Is this your idea of a strike?'

There was a volley of oaths, and a surge of people wanted to throw themselves at the traitor. Damn him, he had sworn to support them the night before, and now he had gone down the mine with the others! Who did he take them for?

'Get him! Off to the pit! Let's go!'

Chaval was white with fear, and tried to stammer out some excuse, but Étienne interrupted him furiously, carried away by the fury of the crowd.

'You wanted to join in, and so you bloody well shall, get walking, you bastard!'

Another cry drowned his words. It was Catherine's turn now to emerge, dazzled by the bright sunlight, terrified at finding herself surrounded by these savages. As she staggered forward, her legs giving way beneath her after the effort of climbing 102 ladders, her hands torn to shreds, and her breath failing, La Maheude saw her and rushed at her with her hand raised.

'Oh, you're here too, you bitch! ... While your mother's dying of starvation, you run off to work for your pimp!'

Maheu held her arm to stop her hitting her daughter. But he grabbed the girl and shook her, feeling as outraged as his wife over her behaviour; both of them quite lost control, and started screaming even louder than their comrades.

The sight of Catherine had finally made Étienne lose his temper:

'Let's go! Off to the other pits! And you're coming with us, you dirty bastard!'

Chaval just had time to retrieve his clogs from the shed, and to sling his woollen jersey over his freezing shoulders. The whole mob dragged him off, forcing him to gallop along in their midst. Filled with despair, Catherine also put on her clogs, buttoned up round her neck the shabby man's jacket that they had draped her in when she had caught cold; and she ran off behind her lover, afraid of leaving him, because she was sure they were going to do him in.

In another couple of minutes Jean-Bart was empty. Jeanlin, who had found a horn, blew a series of rough blasts on it, as if he were rounding up cattle. The women, including old Ma Brûlé, La Levaque, and La Mouquette, tucked up their skirts to run; while Levaque, with an axe in his hand, swung it round like a drum-major's baton. More and more comrades kept arriving, until there were nearly a thousand of them, spilling chaotically down the road like a swollen stream bursting its banks. The road out of the pit was too narrow, so they broke through the fences.

'To the pits! Down with traitors! Down with work!'

And Jean-Bart was suddenly reduced to absolute silence. Not a man could be seen, not a breath could be heard. Deneulin came out of the deputies' hut, and all by himself, forbidding anyone to follow him, he went to inspect the pit. He was very pale, but perfectly calm. First he stopped in front of the shaft, raised his eyes and looked at the severed cables: their steel strands hung limp and useless, the file had torn into their flesh, carving a raw wound which showed up like a livid open sore amid the greasy black mass. Then he went over to the engine, and studied the motionless crank rod, like the joint of a giant limb stricken with paralysis; and he touched the metal, which had already turned cold, so cold that he shivered as if he had touched a corpse. Then he went down to the boilers, walking slowly over to the extinguished furnaces, wide open and flooded, gave a kick at the generators, which rang with a hollow sound. Well then, that was it, he really was ruined! Even if he mended the cables and relit the furnaces, where would he find the men? Another two weeks of strike, and he would be bankrupt. And as he knew that disaster was inevitable, he felt no more hatred for the bandits from Montsou; for he felt that they were all in it together, he and they, all guilty accomplices from time immemorial. Doubtless they were brutes, but they were illiterate, starving brutes.

CHAPTER IV

AND in this fashion the group made off over the bare plain, white with frost beneath the pale winter sun, spilling over the sides of the road on to the beetfields.

By the time they had reached La Fourche-aux-Bœufs, Étienne had taken charge. Without anyone stopping, he called out orders and organized the march. Jeanlin galloped on ahead, blasting a barbarous music from his horn. Then, in the front ranks, the women advanced, some of them armed with sticks, La Maheude with wild eyes which seemed to burn with the vision of some distant city of instant justice; old Ma Brûlé, La Levaque, La Mouquette, all striding out in their rags, like soldiers marching off to war. If they met the enemy, they'd soon see if the gendarmes dared to strike women. And the men followed, in a straggling herd, fanning out in a widening tail, iron bars bristling everywhere, and Levaque's single axe waving overhead, its blade glinting in the sunlight. Étienne, in the centre, kept his eyes on Chaval, whom he forced to march in front of him; while Maheu, further behind, threw angry, sidelong glances at Catherine, the only woman in this group of men, determined to trot along behind her lover to prevent him coming to any harm. Their bare heads were dishevelled by the stiff breeze, the noise of clattering clogs, sounding like a herd of cattle on the loose, spurred on by Jeanlin's wild trumpeting.

But suddenly a new cry arose.

'Bread! Bread! We want bread!'*

It was noon, and the hunger born of six weeks of strike stirred in their empty bellies, whipped up by running across the open countryside. It was already a long time since they had shared their few pieces of bread in the morning and La Mouquette's few chestnuts; their stomachs were groaning, and this suffering added to their fury against the traitors.

'To the pits! No more work! We want bread!'

Étienne, who had refused to eat his share at the village, felt an unbearable tearing feeling in his chest. He didn't complain; but seized his flask from time to time with a mechanical motion and swallowed a mouthful of gin, for he was shivering so much that he thought he needed it to carry on. His cheeks were flushed, and his eyes blazed. Yet he kept a cool head; he still wanted to avoid any unnecessary damage.

As they arrived at the road to Joiselle, a hewer from Vandame, who had joined the band in order to avenge himself on his boss, urged his comrades over to the right, shouting out:

'Let's go to Gaston-Marie! Stop the pump! Let's flood Jean-Bart!'

The crowd had already started moving that way, carried away despite Étienne's protests, as he begged them to leave the drainage pumps alone. What was the point in ruining all the tunnels? That offended his deepest feelings as a workman, despite all his grievances. Maheu, too, found it was unfair to attack a machine. But the hewer kept shouting his cry for vengeance, so Étienne had to shout even louder:

'To Mirou! There are traitors down there! . . . To Mirou! To Mirou!'

With a wave of his arm he had swept the band round the corner on to the path leading to the left, while Jeanlin, taking the lead, blew harder and harder. They pushed and jostled as they ran off. For the moment, Gaston-Marie was saved.

And they covered the four kilometres to Mirou in half an hour, almost at running speed, over the limitless plain. The canal sliced through the surrounding landscape like a long ribbon of ice. Only the bare trees on its banks, transformed by the ice into giant candelabras, interrupted the endless, monotonous flatness of the plain, which fell away into the horizon, as if the sky were the sea. Montsou and Marchiennes were hidden behind a dip in the ground, and the immense terrain looked entirely bare.

As they reached the pit they saw a deputy go up on to one of the overhead tracks at the screening shed to meet them. They all knew old Quandieu well; he was the senior deputy at Montsou, an old man with white hair and skin who must have been seventy, a real miracle of health for a miner.

'What the hell are you doing here, you destructive louts?' he shouted.

The crowd stopped. He wasn't one of the bosses, he was one of their workmates; and they felt inhibited by their respect for an old workman.

'There are men at work down there,' said Étienne. 'Get them to come out.'

'Yes, there are some,' old Quandieu went on, 'There are six dozen or so, the others were afraid of you, you bastards! . . . But you can take it from me that not one of them is coming back up, over my dead body!'

Exclamations rang out, men pushed and shoved, the women moved nearer. The deputy got down off the gangway quickly now, and barred their way to the door.

Then Maheu tried to intervene.

'Look, old man, it's our right, how can we turn it into a general strike if we don't force our mates to come out on our side?'

The old man fell silent for a moment. Obviously his ignorance in questions of political alliances was as great as the hewers'. Finally, he replied:

'It's your right, I don't deny it. But as far as I'm concerned, rules are rules . . . I'm on my own here. The men are supposed to be below till three o'clock, and they're going to stay there till three o'clock.'

His last words were lost amid a tumult of booing and hissing. The men shook their fists at him, and the women shouted him down so deafeningly that he could feel their hot breath on his face. But he stood his ground, holding his head high, with his snow-white hair and little beard bristling; and his voice was so full of courage that it could be heard quite clearly despite the din.

'In God's name! I won't let you past! . . . As sure as the sun rises, I'd rather die than let anyone touch the cables . . . Stop pushing, or I'll throw myself down the bloody shaft before your very eyes!'

There was a general shudder, and the crowd drew back, shocked by what he had said. He continued:

'Is there any bloody fool who doesn't get the message? . . . I'm only a workman like the rest of you. I've been told to stand guard, so I'm standing guard.'

And that's about all there was to old Quandieu's intellectual capacities, as he dug his heels into his military duty, with his narrow forehead and his eyes dulled by half a century of dreary existence underground. His comrades looked at him, feeling moved, because somewhere deep within them they, too, felt an echo of what he was saying to them, with his soldierly obedience, fraternity, and resignation in the face of danger. He thought that they were still undecided, and he repeated:

'I'll throw myself down the bloody shaft before your very eyes!'

A shudder ran right through the group, and they all wheeled round away from him, and cantered off again down the open road which stretched away into infinity over the countryside. Once again their cries rang out:

'To Madeleine! To Crèvecœur! Down with work! We want bread, bread!'

But in their midst there was a disturbance in the rhythm of the march. Someone said that Chaval had tried to escape in the confusion. Étienne had just grabbed hold of one of his arms, threatening to break his back if he tried any tricks. And Chaval struggled, protesting furiously:

'What's all this about? Aren't I a free man? . . . I've been freezing for the last hour, I need a scrub. Let go of me!'

And he was indeed suffering from the coal-dust sticking sweatily to his skin, and his jersey was no protection.

'Keep moving, or we'll scrub you down ourselves,' replied Étienne. 'You shouldn't have gone on about asking for blood.'

As they galloped onwards Étienne finally turned round to look at Catherine, who was managing to keep up. He experienced a wave of despair at feeling her close to him, so wretched and shivering in her baggy man's jacket and her mud-stained breeches. She must have been fit to drop with fatigue, but she still kept on running.

'You can go, if you like,' he said at last.

Catherine didn't seem to hear. When her eyes met Étienne's they showed only the briefest glimmer of a reproach. And still she didn't stop. Why should she let her man down? Chaval was no gentleman, she knew, and he even beat her on occasions. But he was her man, the first man to have had her; and she felt furious when she saw the whole pack of them turn on him, more than a thousand of them against one man. Even if she had had no feeling for him, she would have defended him simply for honour's sake.

'Go away!' Maheu repeated, violently.

This order from her father slowed her down for a moment. She trembled, and her eyelids swelled with tears. Then, despite her fear, she kept running and took up her place again. So they left her alone.

The group crossed the road to Joiselle, followed the road to Cron for a while, and then went up towards Cougny. Over there the flat skyline was etched with factory chimneys; wooden sheds and brick workshops with wide dusty windows sped past them as they pounded over the cobbles. In quick succession they passed the low houses of two mining villages, one Hundred and Eighty and Seventy-Six; and from each, answering the call of the horn and the cries from every mouth, whole families emerged, men, women, and children, joining the stampede in the wake of their comrades. By the time they arrived at Madeleine, there must have been 1500 of them. The road sloped gently downwards, and the raging torrent of strikers then had to flow round the slag-heap before they could spread out over the flagstones at the entrance to the pit-head.

At that moment it was still only two o'clock. But the deputies, warned in advance, had hurried to get their men up early; and as the group arrived, the evacuation was almost complete; only a score of men had not yet left, and they were just emerging from the cage. They fled, under a hail of stones. Two of them were caught and beaten, another escaped, leaving the sleeve of his jacket behind. The man-hunt saved the plant, nobody touched the cables or the boilers. The sea of men was already surging on its way towards the next pit.

This pit, Crèvecœur, was only five hundred metres away from Madeleine. There, too, the group arrived just as the miners were on their way out. One of the tram girls was caught by the women, who tore her breeches apart and gave her a good whipping on her bare buttocks, while the men stood by and laughed. The pit boys were punched and slapped, and the hewers ran off with bloody noses and their ribs black and blue. And as the violence mounted, driven by a deep-rooted need for revenge, whose savage fury started sending everyone off their heads, they called in strangled cries for death to traitors, they screamed their hatred of underpaid work, and lamented their empty, starving bellies. They tried to cut the cables, but the file didn't make much impact, and it looked as if it would take too long, now that they felt driven feverishly onwards, ever onwards. In the boiler-room they broke a stopcock, and threw bucket after bucket of water inside the furnaces, making the cast-iron grids shatter.

Outside, they wanted to march on Saint-Thomas. This was the most obedient pit; the strike had not yet reached it, and nearly 700 men must have gone down to work; this infuriated the group, who decided to lie in wait for them with cudgels and do battle hand to hand, and then they'd see if any of them were left standing. But they heard a rumour that there were gendarmes at Saint-Thomas, the same gendarmes that they had seen and laughed at that very morning. How had someone found this out? Nobody could say. But the rumour was enough to strike fear into them and they decided to head for Feutry-Cantel instead. They were swept off their feet again, spinning dizzily back round on to the road, rushing along with their clogs clattering: Feutry-Cantel here we come, look out Feutry-Cantel! There were at least four hundred of the cowards down there, that would mean some fun! The pit was three

kilometres away, and hidden by a dip in the ground, near the
Scarpe. They had already reached the slope of Les Plâtrières,
after the road to Beaugnies, when a voice that they didn't
recognize threw out the notion that the dragoons might be
over at Feutry-Cantel. So all the way up and down the column
people repeated the news, that the dragoons were at Feutry-
Cantel. They faltered and slowed their pace, and panic started
to waft through their ranks. They must have been tramping
over the countryside for hours now, without shaking it out of
the torpor of its enforced idleness. Why had they not run up
against any soldiers? They were worried by their impunity,
and by the thought of the impending repression.

Without anyone knowing who had launched it, a new slogan
spurred them on towards another pit.

'La Victoire! Over to La Victoire!'

So were there no dragoons or gendarmes at La Victoire?
Nobody knew. That seemed to reassure them. And they
turned about and went down towards Beaumont, cutting across
the fields, to pick up the road to Joiselle. The railway line
blocked their path, but they knocked down the fences to cross
it. Now they were approaching Montsou, where the gently
undulating countryside flattened out and opened up on to a
sea of beetfields, stretching far, far away towards the black
houses of Marchiennes.

This time they were in for a run of at least five kilometres.
But they were driven on by such an urge that they didn't feel
their appalling fatigue or their bruised and aching feet. Their
column grew longer and longer, swelling with comrades picked
up along the way in the villages. When they had crossed the
canal at Magache bridge, and gathered in front of La Victoire,
there were 2,000 of them. But three o'clock had struck, the
men had come up, and there was not a soul left down below.
They vented their frustration in empty threats, and had to
console themselves with throwing brickbats at the stonemen
who turned up to start their shift, but now turned tail and
fled, leaving the group in control of the deserted pit. And as
they felt enraged at finding no traitors in front of them to
punch in the face, they turned to lash out at any object
they could find. Their rancour had swollen gradually but

poisonously within them, and now it burst like a boil. Year
after year of starvation spilled over into a feverish hunger for
murder and destruction.

Looking behind a shed, Étienne saw some men loading a
cart with coal.

'Get the hell out of here!' he cried. 'No one must move a
single piece of coal!'

A hundred or so strikers ran up to carry out his instructions;
and all the loaders had time to do was to run away. Some of
the men unharnessed the horses, and whipped their flanks,
making them take fright and run off; while others tipped the
carts over and broke their shafts.

Levaque had swung out wildly at the trestles with an axe to
cut down the overhead tracks. But as they withstood his blows,
he decided to tear out the rails to cut the track right across the
pit-head. Soon the whole gang had set to work to carry out
this task. Maheu dislodged the cast-iron clasps, using his
crowbar as a lever. Meanwhile old Ma Brûlé led the women on
and invaded the lamp depot, and they lashed out on all sides
with their sticks, strewing the ground with the wreckage of
shattered lamps. La Maheude was carried away and lashed out
as violently as La Levaque. They were all covered in oil, and
La Mouquette wiped her hands on her petticoat, laughing at
the filthy state she was in. Jeanlin had emptied a lamp down
her neck for a laugh.

But this orgy of vengeance didn't help fill their bellies,
whose claims became more vociferous. The great lament rose
again, drowning out other concerns:

'Bread! Bread! We want bread!'

As it happened, there was a former deputy from La Victoire
who ran a canteen there. He must have taken fright, because
his stall was abandoned. When the women returned and the
men had finally demolished the track, they stormed the canteen, whose shutters caved in at the first assault. They didn't
find any bread there, there were only a couple of pieces of raw
meat and a sack of potatoes. However, their pillage did bring
to light nearly fifty bottles of gin, which evaporated as quickly
as a drop of water in a sandpit.

Étienne emptied his flask, and was able to fill it up again.

Gradually his eyes became bloodshot with the unhealthy intoxication of a starving man, and his teeth seemed to stand out
like the fangs of a wolf between his ashen lips. Then suddenly
he noticed that Chaval had slipped away under cover of the
chaos. He swore loudly, and sent his men scurrying around
until they laid hands on the fugitive, who had been hiding
with Catherine behind the woodpile.

'You bastard, now you're afraid of getting involved!' Étienne
shouted. 'Out in the forest, you were the one who wanted to
call the mechanics out on strike, and shut down the pumps,
and now you're trying to leave us in the shit! All right, I swear
to God, we're going back to Gaston-Marie, and you're going
to smash the pump for us! Yes, I swear to God, you're going
to smash it!'

He was drunk, there he was launching his men to attack the
pump which he had saved just a few hours earlier.

'To Gaston-Marie! To Gaston-Marie!'

They all acclaimed his decision and rushed off; they grabbed
Chaval by the shoulders and dragged him off, while he asked
them again to let him wash himself.

'Go away!' shouted Maheu to Catherine, who had started
running with the rest of them.

This time she didn't even falter, but gave her father a fierce
look and kept on running.

The mob was now cutting across the flat plain again. They
retraced their route down the long straight roads, over the
widening fields. It was four o'clock, and the sun, as it sank on
the horizon, threw the long shadows of this rampaging horde
with their wild, threatening gestures across the frozen ground.

They went straight past Montsou, and picked up the road to
Joiselle further on; and to save having to make a detour round
La Fourche-aux-Bœufs, they passed beneath the walls of La
Piolaine. The Grégoires had just left, in order to call on their
notary, before dining with the Hennebeaus, where they planned
to meet up with Cécile. The estate seemed fast asleep, with its
deserted line of lime trees, and both the vegetable garden and
the orchard stood bare from winter. Nothing moved in the
house, whose closed windows were misty with the warm con-
densation inside; and this deep silence gave out an impression

of friendliness and well-being, a patriarchal feeling of comfortable beds and rich cooking, of well-tempered happiness, which surrounded the existence of the landlord and his family.

Without stopping, the mob looked menacingly through the iron bars of the gates and along the high perimeter walls bristling with broken bottles. The cry went up again:

'Bread, bread, we want bread!'

The only reply came from the dogs, a pair of tawny Great Danes, who barked fiercely and rose up on their hind legs, baring their fangs. And behind the closed blinds there were only the two maids, Mélanie, the cook, and Honorine, the chambermaid, attracted by the shouting but sweating with fear and deathly pale at the sight of this horde of savages dancing past. They fell down on their knees, believing that their doom was sealed, when they heard one of the windows in the next room shatter. But this single stone-throw was only one of Jeanlin's pranks: he had made himself a sling from a piece of string, and was merely sending a parting message to the Grégoires. He had already started blowing his horn again, and the mob disappeared into the distance, with their call dying away:

'Bread! Bread! We want bread!'

When they arrived at Gaston-Marie their ranks had further increased, until there were 2,500 of the desperadoes, smashing or sweeping aside everything in their path, with the unstoppable force of a raging torrent. Some gendarmes had been there an hour earlier, and had gone off towards Saint-Thomas, sent on a wild-goose chase by the local farm workers, leaving in such a hurry that they hadn't even taken the precaution of leaving a small picket of men to guard the pit. In less than a quarter of an hour the furnaces were emptied, the boilers drained, the buildings invaded and sacked. But it was the pump above all that they had it in for. It wasn't enough for it to give out a last dying gasp of steam, they threw themselves at it as if it were a living person that they wanted to throttle.

'You strike the first blow!' Étienne repeated, placing a hammer in Chaval's hands. 'Come on, you swore along with the others!'

Chaval trembled and stepped back a pace; and as the crowd

jostled him he dropped the hammer, while his workmates, without waiting, started hacking the pump to pieces, hitting it with bricks, crowbars, or anything else that came to hand. Some even tried to beat it with sticks, which split. The screws fractured, and the steel and copper plates broke loose, like dislocated limbs. A flying stroke with a pickaxe smashed the cast-iron lining, the water burst out, and the boiler emptied with a final gurgle, sounding like a death-rattle.

It was all over. The mob found themselves outside again in a state of hysteria, piling up behind Étienne, who refused to let Chaval go.

'Death to the traitor! Down the shaft with him!'

The wretch was livid and stammering, but still stubbornly obsessed with his compulsive need to clean himself up.

'Well, if that's bothering you,' said La Levaque, 'here's a basin for you, look!'

She had found a great puddle formed by the overspill of water from the pump seeping through the rock. It was white, and covered by a thick coat of ice; they pushed him towards it, broke the ice, and forced him to plunge his head into the icy water.

'Down you go!' repeated old Ma Brûlé. 'I swear to God, if you don't get your head under, we'll throw you in ... now have a drink, that's right, like an animal, get your snout in the trough!'

He had to get down on all fours and drink. They all laughed, enjoying the cruel fun. One woman pulled his ears, and another picked up a handful of fresh horse dung off the road to throw in his face. His old woollen jersey hung off him in shreds. He lurched about wildly, his back heaving with his desperate attempts to escape.

Maheu had pushed him, and La Maheude was one of the most ferocious of the women, for both of them were eager to take their long-overdue revenge; and even La Mouquette, who usually kept on good terms with her former lovers, had it in for him, calling him a good-for-nothing, and suggested taking his trousers down to see if he was still a man.

Étienne shut her up.

'That's enough! We don't all need to join in ... If you want, you and I will sort this out on our own.'

He clenched his fists, and his eyes lit up with homicidal fury, his intoxication brewing up within him an urge to kill.

'Are you ready? A fight to the death ... Give him a knife. I've got one already.'

Catherine looked at him, exhausted and terrified. She remembered what he had confided to her, how when he had been drinking he felt like tearing someone to pieces, poisoned with alcohol after only three glasses, because his tipsy parents had filled his body with so much of the muck already. Suddenly she threw herself at him, pummelled him with her small woman's fists, thrust her face up against his, and shouted at him, choking with indignation.

'You coward, you rotten coward! ... Wasn't all that filth enough for you? Do you want to murder the man now he's down on his knees?'

She turned to face her father and mother and then towards the others.

'You are all cowards! Rotten cowards ... Go on then, kill me along with him. I'll scratch your eyes out if you touch him again. Oh, you cowards!'

She had taken her stand in front of her man, defending him, forgetting his beatings and their poverty, borne on by the idea that she belonged to him, because he had taken her, and that it was shameful for her to let him be so degraded.

Étienne had turned pale under the blows that the girl had rained on him. His first reaction had been to strike her down. But then he drew his hand across his brow, with a gesture that showed him returning to his senses, and said to Chaval, amid a deep silence:

'She's right, that's enough ... bugger off!'

Chaval took to his heels immediately, and Catherine raced off after him. The crowd stood watching in stupefaction, until they disappeared round a bend in the road. Only La Maheude murmured:

'You're wrong, we should have held on to him. He's bound to pull some vile trick on us.'

But the mob had set off again already. It was nearly five o'clock, and low on the horizon the sun was as red as hot coals, scorching the whole vast plain. A passing pedlar told them that the dragoons were on their way, over by Crèvecœur. So they turned back, and the order flew among them:

'To Montsou! To the management! ... Bread! Bread! We want bread!'

CHAPTER V

MONSIEUR HENNEBEAU had stationed himself at the window of his study, in order to watch the departure of the carriage which was taking his wife off to lunch at Marchiennes. For a moment he had followed the progress of Négrel, trotting alongside the carriage door; then he had come back to sit down in peace and quiet at his desk. When it was not enlivened by the sounds of the existence of his wife or his nephew, the house seemed empty. And on this occasion, in fact, the coachman had gone to drive Madame; Rose, the new chambermaid, had her day off until five o'clock; and only Hippolyte, the manservant, was left, shuffling round the house in his slippers, apart of course from the cook, who had been up since dawn marshalling her whole battery of pots and pans in readiness for the dinner that her masters were giving that evening. So Monsieur Hennebeau was looking forward to a thorough day's work, amid the profound quietness of the deserted house.

At about nine o'clock, although he had orders not to let anyone in, Hippolyte thought he ought to show in Dansaert, who had brought news. It was only then that the manager learnt of the meeting in the forest the previous evening; and the report was so detailed that while he listened he had time to reflect on La Pierronne's amorous exploits, which were so notorious that two or three anonymous letters a week denounced the overman's indiscretions: obviously the husband must have been talking, the espionage reeked of the bedroom. He even took the opportunity to suggest that he was entirely in the know, and was content to recommend discretion, for fear of scandal. Horrified to hear such reproaches interrupt his report, Dansaert denied all, and stammered excuses, while the sudden reddening of his large nose admitted the crime. He didn't insist on his innocence too vigorously, however, pleased to be let off so lightly; for usually the manager showed an implacable puritan severity whenever one of his employees made himself a present of a pretty girl from the pit. They carried on discussing the strike: the forest meeting was nothing but bluff and bluster, with no serious consequences. In any case, the mining villages would surely stay calm for a few days, after the morning's military manœuvres had imbued them with a feeling of awe and respect.

When Monsieur Hennebeau was alone again, however, he felt like sending a dispatch to the Prefect. Only the fear of gratuitously admitting his anxiety restrained him. Already he couldn't forgive himself for having lacked intuition to the extent of telling everyone, and even writing to the Board, that the strike wouldn't last more than a fortnight. And now it had been dragging on for nearly two months, much to his surprise; and it was driving him to despair; every day he felt diminished and compromised, needing to achieve some signal victory if he wanted to return to favour in the eyes of the Board. And he had deliberately asked them for instructions in case of conflict. The reply was late in coming, he was expecting to find it in the afternoon's mail. And he said that then would be time enough to send out telegrams and have the military occupy the pits, if that was the wish of those gentlemen. He felt absolutely sure that there would be a pitched battle, with blood and bodies. He found such a responsibility disturbing, despite his usual vigour.

Until eleven o'clock he worked on quietly, hearing nothing in the abandoned house except the sound of Hippolyte, who was wax polishing one of the first-floor rooms at the far end of the house. Then he suddenly received two dispatches in quick succession, the first announcing the invasion of Jean-Bart by the gang from Montsou, the second giving details of the cut cables, the extinguished furnaces, and the rest of the destruction. He didn't understand. Why had the strikers gone off to Deneulin's mine instead of taking on one of their own Company's? Although they were welcome to sack Vandame, since it would further his plans for the take-over that he was contemplating. And at twelve o'clock he had lunch alone in the vast

room, served silently by the manservant, whose slippers he
didn't even hear. The solitude made him feel even more
gloomy and preoccupied, and he felt chilled to the heart when
an overman who had run all the way was ushered in, and told
him of the mob's march on Mirou. And almost immediately,
just as he was finishing his coffee, he learned from a telegram
that Madeleine and Crèvecœur were threatened in their turn.
So his dilemma was exacerbated. He expected more mail for
two o'clock: should he call for troops straight away? Or should
he wait patiently a while longer, to avoid acting before knowing
the orders of the Board? He went back to his study, he wanted
to read a note to the Prefect which he had asked Négrel to
draft the day before. But he couldn't discover where he had
put it; he wondered whether the young man might have left it
in his room, where he often wrote at night. And unable to
come to a decision, haunted by the thought of this note, he
walked rapidly upstairs to look for it in Négrel's bedroom.

As he entered the room, Monsieur Hennebeau was taken
aback: the room hadn't been tidied, no doubt through Hippolyte's negligence or laziness. There was a moist, warm atmosphere, the stale warmth of a bedroom which had been heated
all night by an open stove; and his nostrils were assailed by a
suffocating, penetrating scent, which he assumed was the smell
of the water the young man had washed in, for the basin was
full. The room was in a state of considerable disorder, clothes
scattered here and there, wet towels thrown over the backs of
chairs, the bed unmade, with an untucked sheet hanging down
over the side on to the carpet. However, at first he gave the
scene only a cursory glance, and walked straight over to a table
covered in papers, to start searching for the lost note. Twice
he went through all the papers one by one; it definitely wasn't
there. Where the hell had that scatter-brained Paul hidden it?

But as Monsieur Hennebeau moved back towards the middle
of the room, glancing at each piece of furniture, he noticed
something in the unmade bed which seemed to catch the light,
like a spark. He went over mechanically and stretched out his
hand. There, between two folds of the sheet, was a little
golden flask. He immediately recognized Madame Hennebeau's
flask of ether; she never went anywhere without it. But he

couldn't understand what this object was doing there: how could it have come to be in Paul's bed? And suddenly he went deathly pale. His wife had slept there.

'Excuse me, Sir,' Hippolyte murmured from the doorway, 'I saw Sir go upstairs . . .'

The manservant had come into the room, and was dismayed by the mess that the bedroom was in.

'Good heavens, the bedroom hasn't been tidied, that's for sure. So Rose went out and left me with all the housework to catch up on.'

Monsieur Hennebeau had hidden the flask in his hand, and was squeezing it hard enough to break it.

'What do you want?'

'Sir, there's another man . . . He's come from Crèvecœur, he's got a letter.'

'Well, leave me alone, tell him to wait!'

His wife had slept there! When he had bolted the door, he opened his hand up again, and looked at the flask, which had left a red mark on his flesh. Suddenly he could see and hear the obscenities which had been taking place in his own house for months. He recalled his previous suspicions, those rustling noises behind closed doors, sounds of bare feet creeping around the silent house at night. Yes, it was his wife coming upstairs to sleep in this bedroom!

He slumped into a chair, staring bemused at the bed in front of him, and spent several minutes in a kind of trance. He was awakened by the noise of someone knocking on the door; someone was trying to open it. He recognized the manservant's voice.

'Sir . . . Ah, Sir has locked himself in . . .'

'What now?'

'It seems to be urgent. The workmen are smashing everything to pieces. There are two other men downstairs. There are some telegrams too.'

'Leave me alone! I'll be down in a minute!'

The thought that Hippolyte would have discovered the flask himself, if he had cleaned the bedroom that morning, had just sent a chill through his bones. And besides, the servant must be in the know, a dozen times he must have found the bed warm from their adultery, Madame's hairs left on the pillow, disgusting stains defiling the bed-linen. And that was why he was deliberately pestering him, he was trying to rub salt in his wounds.

Perhaps he spent hours listening at the keyhole, excited by the debauchery of his masters.

So Monsieur Hennebeau remained motionless. He kept staring at the bed. The long litany of his past sufferings unfolded before his eyes, his marriage to this woman, their immediate misunderstanding of heart and body, the lovers she had had without him being aware of it, the one he had put up with for ten years as one humours a sick woman's cravings for some disgusting taste. Then came their arrival at Montsou, a crazy hope of curing her, months of languishing, of slumbering in exile, waiting for the approach of middle age which would finally yield her up to him. Then their nephew arrived, this Paul whose mother she became, to whom she spoke of her withered heart, buried for ever under ashes. And he suspected nothing, idiotic husband that he was; he adored the woman, who was his very own, yet she had belonged to others, and he alone could not possess her! He adored her with a shameful passion, and would have fallen on his knees in gratitude if she would only have thrown him the scraps from the favours she lavished on others! These scraps she was now throwing to a boy.

At that moment a distant ringing made Monsieur Hennebeau jump. He recognized it as the sound of the bell which had to be rung, on his orders, when the postman arrived. He got up, and spoke out loud, releasing a flood of coarse language which had been painfully strangling his throat despite his attempts to restrain it.

'Oh, damn and blast them, damn their bloody dispatches and letters!'

Now he was filled with rage, as if he wanted to open up the sewers to kick the filth back down them. That woman was a bitch, he sought the crudest words to sully her image. The sudden thought of the marriage between Cécile and Paul that she was organizing with such tranquil beatitude finally made him lose patience. Was there no passion, no jealousy, behind her sensual energy? Was there nothing left but playful perversity, the habit of male company, a recreation enjoyed like a favourite pudding? He accused her of the vilest crimes, and almost excused the youth, whom she had bitten into when her appetite revived, as if she were biting into the first unripe fruit stolen from over a garden wall. Whom would she gobble up, how low would she fall, when she had run out of indulgent nephews, sensible enough to share the family table, bed, and wife?

There was a nervous tap at the door, and Hippolyte's voice could be heard whispering through the keyhole:

'Sir, the mail ... And there's Monsieur Dansaert back again, he says that the bloodshed has started ...'

'I'm coming, for heaven's sake!'

What would he do to them? Throw them out as soon as they returned to Marchiennes, like rabid dogs he refused to shelter under his roof. He'd take a cudgel to them and would shout out loud at them to take their poisonous fornication elsewhere. It was their sighs and mingled breath that clotted the air in the room; the pervasive scent that had suffocated him was the odour of musk secreted by his wife's skin, another of her perverse tastes, her physical need for powerful scents; and he recognized the warmth and the smell of fornication, the living traces of adultery, in the jars left open in unemptied wash-basins, the tangled bed-linen and displaced furniture, in the whole room, which stank of immorality. In an impotent rage he flung himself on the bed and pounded it with his fists, messing it up entirely, thumping the places where he saw the imprint of their joined bodies, furious to find that the blankets he tore off and the sheets that he crumpled remained flabby and unresponsive under his blows, as if they themselves were worn out from a whole night of love-making.

But suddenly he heard Hippolyte coming back upstairs again, and he stopped, out of shame.

He stayed a few moments without moving, panting, wiping his brow, waiting for his racing heart to quieten down; standing in front of a mirror, he studied his face, which was so distraught that he hardly recognized himself. Then, when he had watched it gradually calm down, he made himself walk downstairs, through a supreme act of will.

Downstairs five messengers, as well as Dansaert, stood waiting. They all brought increasingly grave news about the march of the strikers from pit to pit; and the overman told him in full detail what had happened at Mirou, and how it had been saved by the fine stand taken by old Quandieu. He listened, nodding his head, but he wasn't taking it in, his mind was still up there in the bedroom. Finally he sent them away, saying that he would take the necessary steps. When he was left alone again, sitting at his desk, he seemed to nod off, with his head buried in his hands, and his eyes covered. His mail was there in front of him, and he decided to look out the long-awaited letter, the reply from the Board, but at first its lines span round in front of his eyes. However, he gradually made out that these gentlemen were in favour of some kind of battle: not that they were actually ordering him to make things worse; but they managed to suggest that the disturbances would precipitate the end of the strike by justifying vigorous reprisals. Thereupon he lost no further time in hesitation, he sent out dispatches in all directions, to the Prefect in Lille, to the army headquarters in Douai, to the gendarmerie at Marchiennes. He felt relieved, now all he had to do was stay in and wait, and he even let it be known that he was suffering from an attack of gout. And so he spent the whole afternoon shut away in the depths of his study, refusing to let anyone in, content to do nothing more than sit back and read the mounting flood of dispatches and letters. In this way he followed the progress of the mob from a distance, from Madeleine to Crèvecœur, from Crèvecœur to La Victoire, from La Victoire to Gaston-Marie. In addition, he received news of the confusion of the gendarmes and the dragoons, who had got lost along the way, and constantly found themselves marching away from whichever pit was being attacked. Let them murder and destroy, he had plunged his head into his hands again and, placing his fingers over his eyes, he let himself sink into the great silence of the empty house, where the only sound that emerged was the noise of the cook wielding saucepans, enthusiastically preparing that evening's dinner.

Twilight was already darkening the room when, at five o'clock, a sudden din made Monsieur Hennebeau jump, jolting him out of the state of stupefied inertia he was plunged in, still buried up to the elbows in his papers. He thought that the two wretched sinners must have returned home. But the tumult grew louder, and a terrible cry burst out just as he went over to the window.

'Bread, bread, we want bread!'

It was the strikers, who were now invading Montsou, while the gendarmes, thinking that Le Voreux was in danger of attack, were galloping away in the other direction to guard the wrong pit.

Meanwhile, two kilometres away from the first houses, just below the crossroads where the main highway met the road to Vandame, Madame Hennebeau and her young ladies had just watched the mob file past. They had spent a happy day at Marchiennes, including a friendly lunch with the manager of Les Forges, and then an interesting visit to his workshops and to a neighbouring glassworks, to fill up the afternoon, and as they were at last on their way home, in the limpid air of a fine winter evening, Cécile had suddenly had the urge to drink a mug of milk when she saw a little farm by the roadside. So they all got out of the carriage, Négrel having gallantly jumped off his horse to help them down; while the farmer's wife, aghast at this invasion by high society, rushed around trying to find a table-cloth before she would serve them. But Lucie and Jeanne wanted to see the cow being milked, and they all took their mugs right into the cowshed, to have a little country picnic, and laughed with delight as they sank into the straw.

Madame Hennebeau was still drinking her milk unenthusiastically, while radiating dutiful motherly approval, when a strange noise rumbling in the background outside disturbed her.

'Whatever can that be?'

The cowshed was situated by the roadside, and had a wide entrance gate, to let the haycart through, since the building also served as a barn. The girls had already poked their heads out and were astonished at what they could see over to the left, a great black crowd of people pouring like a flood down the road towards Vandame and yelling fiercely.

'My God!' murmured Négrel, who had also come to the

door. 'I wonder if our noisy brats are at last getting seriously angry?'

'Perhaps it's the colliers,' said the farmer's wife. 'That's the second time they've gone past. Seems things aren't going too well, they've taken over the countryside.'

She mouthed each word cautiously, watching for the effect it would have on her audience; and when she saw that they were all horrified, and realized how anxious this discovery had made them, she hastened to conclude:

'Oh, they're just beggars, that rabble!'

Négrel, seeing that it was too late to get back into the carriage and return to Montsou, gave the coachman the order to put the carriage away quickly inside the farmyard and hide the pair of horses behind a shed. He took his own horse, which a lad had been holding by the reins, and tethered it inside the same shed. When he came back, he found that his aunt and the girls were distraught, ready to follow the farmer's wife, who offered to shelter them in her home. But he felt that they would be safer where they were; surely nobody would think of looking for them in all that hay. But the double doors didn't shut at all well, and they were so full of cracks that they could see the road between the rotten planks.

'Come on, chin up!' he said. 'We'll make them pay dearly for our lives.'

This joke made them even more fearful. The noise increased, although there was nothing to be seen as yet, and it seemed as if a violent storm wind were blowing up along the empty road, like the sudden gusts which precede a great thunderstorm.

'No, I can't look, I won't look,' said Cécile, running to hide in the hay.

Madame Hennebeau had turned pale with anger, furious at these people for spoiling her pleasure, and she stood back, looking away with an expression of distaste, while Lucie and Jeanne, despite their shivers, had crept up to peep through a crack in the door, so as not to miss any of the action.

The thunderous noise came nearer, they felt the ground vibrate beneath their feet, and they saw Jeanlin at the head of the mob blowing his horn.

'Pass the smelling salts, please, here come the sweating

masses!' murmured Négrel, who, despite his republican convictions, liked to amuse the ladies by mocking the rabble.

But his witty remark was swept away in a hurricane of
shouting and gesticulating. The women had arrived, nearly a
thousand of them, their hair straggling untidily in the wind,
their rags showing patches of bare skin, the careless nudity of
women sick and tired of bearing more and more starving
young in an endless, animal cycle. Some of them had their
babes in their arms, and they raised them up in the air and
waved them about, like banners symbolizing mourning and
vengeance. Other, younger women, with firm and warlike
breasts, were brandishing sticks; while dreadful old crones
screamed so loud that their scraggy necks looked as if they
would stretch too far and snap. Then the men hove into view,
a raging mob 2,000 strong, pit boys, hewers, and wastemen, a
compact mass tumbling forwards like a single body, whose
discoloured breeches and ragged woollen jerseys merged into a
single mud-coloured mass. Only their burning eyes and the
dark holes of their gaping mouths could be seen as they sang
the 'Marseillaise',* and the verses tailed off into a vague
bellowing, echoing to the beat of their clogs clattering over the
hard ground. Over their heads, among the spikes of the iron
bars that stabbed at the air, they passed an axe, keeping it
upright; and this single axe, flaunted like the battle standard of
the band, took on the sharp profile of a guillotine blade against
the light evening sky.

'What dreadful faces!' stammered Madame Hennebeau.

Négrel said between his teeth:

'I'm damned if I recognize a single one of them! Where on
earth do these thugs come from?'

And in fact their anger, hunger, and the last two months of
suffering, as well as their crazy marathon from pit to pit, had
etched on to the placid faces of the Montsou colliers the savage
masks of wild animals. At that moment the sun was setting,
and its last, dark purple rays dyed the plain blood red. And
then the road seemed bathed in blood, as the men and women
continued to gallop onward, looking blood-stained, like butch-
ers in a slaughterhouse.

'Oh, how exquisite!' said Lucie and Jeanne under their

breath, moved in their artistic souls by the horrible beauty of the scene.

Yet they were afraid, and they huddled up to Madame Hennebeau, who was leaning against one of the troughs. The idea that a single glance between the gaping planks of the tumbledown doors would be enough to cause the massacre of the whole family made her blood run cold. Even Négrel, who was usually brave, felt himself turning pale too, as a wave of panic overwhelmed his will, a wave surging up out of the unknown. Down in the hay, Cécile didn't move a muscle. But the others, however strongly they would have liked to look away, found they couldn't stop themselves watching.

It was a scarlet vision of the revolution that would inevitably carry them all away, on some blood-soaked *fin de siècle* evening. That was it, one night the people would rise up, cast caution aside, and run riot like this far and wide all over the country-side; and there would be rivers of bourgeois blood, their heads would be waved on pikes, their strong-boxes hacked open, and their gold poured all over the ground. The women would scream, and the men would look gaunt as wolves, their fangs drooling and gnashing. Yes, these same rags and the same thunder of clogs, the same terrifying pack of animals with dirty skins and foul breath, would sweep away the old world, as their barbarian hordes overflowed and surged through the land. There would be blazing fires, not a stone of the towns would be left standing, and they would become savages again, living out in the woods, once the poor had enjoyed their great orgy and garnered their harvest, sucked the women dry and sacked the cellars of the rich. There would be nothing left, not a sou of inherited wealth, not a line of legal entitlement, until the day when, perhaps, a new order might at last spring up from the earth. And that was the future out there, tearing down the road like some natural disaster, and buffeting their faces with its great hurricane wind.

A great cry arose, drowning out the strains of the 'Marseillaise':

'Bread, bread, we want bread!'

Lucie and Jeanne huddled closer to Madame Hennebeau, who was on the point of fainting; while Négrel stood in front of them as if to shield them with his body. Was this then to be the night when traditional society went under? And what they saw next finally made them speechless. The mob had almost finished flowing past, there were only a few laggards bringing up the rear, when La Mouquette came into sight. She was taking her time, because she was on the look-out for any members of the bourgeoisie guarding their garden gates or peeping out of their windows; and when she discovered any, since she was too far away to spit in their faces, she showed them what was for her the utmost contempt. She must have spied one just then, for she suddenly lifted her skirts and thrust out her rear, displaying her enormous naked buttocks in the dying blaze of the setting sun. Her behind seemed savage rather than obscene, and there was nothing comic about it.

Then they had all disappeared, and the flood went off again towards Montsou, between the low houses daubed in bright colours. They had the carriage wheeled out of the yard, but the coachman didn't dare answer for Madame and her young ladies if the strikers had the run of the road. And the worst thing was that there was no other route.

'But we've got to get back, dinner will be ready,' said Madame Hennebeau, in a temper, her nerves frayed by fear. 'Those foul workmen deliberately chose the day when I had guests. What's the point of treating them decently?'

Lucie and Jeanne were busy extracting Cécile from the hay, while she fought them off, thinking that the savages were still on the war-path, and repeating that she didn't want to see them. At last they were all seated in the carriage. Négrel mounted his horse, and then thought it would be a good idea to return through the back streets of Réquillart.

'Drive slowly,' he said to the coachman, 'you know it's an awful road. Then if there are any gangs out there who stop you from getting back on to the road, you can stop behind the old pit, and we'll walk home through the side gate in the garden, and you'll just have to shelter the carriage and horses where you can, an inn-yard or somewhere.'

Off they went. In the distance the mob was pouring into Montsou. Since they had seen the gendarmes and the dragoons on two occasions, the inhabitants were agitated, and seized with panic. Abominable stories were going the rounds, telling of handwritten notices threatening to rip open the bellies of the bourgeois; and although nobody had read one, there were still those who could quote from them word for word. At the notary's, the panic was particularly hysterical, for he had just received an anonymous letter through the door, warning him that there was a barrel of gunpowder buried in his cellars, ready to blow him up if he didn't come out on the side of the people.

And the Grégoires, whose visit had been protracted by the arrival of this letter, were just in the process of discussing it and concluding that it was the work of a practical joker, when the invasion of the town by the mob sent the household into a state of terminal panic. The Grégoires, however, merely smiled. They drew a corner of the curtain aside to look out, and refused to admit that there was the slightest danger, saying that they were sure it would all come to an amicable conclusion. It had only just struck five o'clock, so they had plenty of time to wait for the road to clear before they went over the other side to dine with the Hennebeaus, where Cécile, who must have returned by now, would be waiting for them. But no one else in Montsou seemed to share their confidence: people were running around wildly, doors and windows were slammed fiercely shut. They noticed that Maigrat on the other side of the road was barricading his shop with every iron bar he could lay hands on, and his hands shook so much that his skinny little wife was obliged to tighten the nuts and bolts herself.

The mob had come to a halt in front of the manager's house, and their cry rang out:

'Bread, bread, we want bread!'

Monsieur Hennebeau was standing at the window when Hippolyte came in to close the shutters, afraid that the windows might be broken if they started to throw stones. He closed all the other ground-floor shutters too, then went up to the first floor, and the creaking of hasps and the clatter of shutters could be heard in quick succession. Unfortunately they couldn't close the main kitchen window, down in the basement, which left a dangerously exposed view of the saucepans and spit sizzling over the glowing fire.

Monsieur Hennebeau, who wanted to see what was happening, went mechanically up to the second floor, into Paul's room: it had the best position, over to the left of the house, overlooking the whole length of the road down as far as the Company's yards. And he stood behind the shutters, surveying the crowd. But he was struck anew by the state of the room: the dressing table had been wiped and tidied, and the bed looked cool, with its clean, neatly tucked sheets. His whole afternoon's fury, the inner struggle that had raged within the depths of his lonely silence, now fizzled out into a feeling of enormous fatigue. His inner being had already become like this room, cooled down, swept clean of the morning's filth, restored to its usual propriety. What was the point in creating a scandal? Had anything in the household changed? His wife had merely acquired another lover; it was hardly any worse because she had chosen one of the family; perhaps there might even be an advantage in it, for it would help to keep up appearances. He felt sorry for himself when he recalled the jealous fury he had felt. How ridiculous he had been to try to beat up the bed with his fists! Since he had already put up with another man, he could surely put up with this one. It would only mean that he would feel a little more contempt. His mouth seemed to be poisoned with the bitter taste of universal futility, the endless pain of existence, shame at himself for still adoring and desiring this woman in the filth that he allowed her to wallow in.

Beneath the window the shouting rang out louder and more violently than ever.

'Bread, bread, we want bread!'

'Fools!' said Monsieur Hennebeau between clenched teeth. He heard them insulting him because of his high salary, and calling him an idle, fat, dirty pig, making himself sick on fine food while the workers were dying of hunger.

The women had noticed the kitchen, and they hurled a barrage of insults at the pheasant that was roasting on the spit, and the sauces whose rich odour wrought havoc on their empty stomachs. Oh! How they would like to stuff the bourgeois so full of champagne and truffles that their guts would explode!

'Bread, bread, we want bread!'

'You fools!' Monsieur Hennebeau repeated. 'Do you suppose that I'm happy?'

He felt a wave of anger at these uncomprehending people. He would willingly have given them his high salary if he could have had their thick skins in exchange, allowing them to slip in and out of bed with no regrets. Why couldn't he invite them to dinner and let them stuff their faces with his pheasant while he went off to fornicate in the bushes, screwing the girls without giving a damn about whoever had screwed them before? He would have given everything, his education, his comfort, his luxury, his power as manager, if just for one day he could have been one of the lowliest of his employees, but crass and free enough in his body to beat his wife and take his pleasure with his neighbours' womenfolk. And he would like to be starving too, with nothing in his belly, and his stomach racked with cramps that made his head spin: perhaps that would dull his endless suffering. Oh, to live like a wild animal, to have no possessions, to tumble in the hay with the ugliest, dirtiest tram girl, and be able to be happy with that!

'Bread, bread, we want bread!'

Then his anger rose and he shouted furiously amid the din:

'Bread, is that all you want, you fools?'

He had enough to eat, and yet he still writhed in agony. His rickety marriage, his whole lifetime of suffering, rose up and caught in his throat to choke him, like a death-rattle. Life was not perfect just because you had bread to eat. What idiot would measure happiness in this world by the distribution of wealth? These unimaginative revolutionaries could go ahead and destroy one society and rebuild a different one, they wouldn't add a drop of happiness to humanity, they wouldn't cancel a single sorrow by cutting up the bread into equal slices. In fact they would spread even more misery over the face of the earth, until one day they would make even dogs howl in misery, if they forced them away from the simple satisfaction of their instincts and introduced them to the unquenchable suffering of frustrated passion. No, the best thing was not to be, and if you had to be, then let it be a tree or a stone, less even, a grain of sand, so as not to bleed when trampled underfoot.

And in this paroxysm of suffering, Monsieur Hennebeau's eyes swelled with tears, which poured in burning drops down his cheeks. The road was starting to disappear into the twilight when stones began to rake the front of the villa. Feeling no anger now against these starving creatures, but merely goaded by the raw wound in his heart, he kept on stammering through his tears:

'The fools, the fools!'

But the call from their empty bellies rang out louder, and the shouting re-echoed thunderously, sweeping all before it:

'Bread, bread, we want bread!'

CHAPTER VI

ÉTIENNE, who had sobered up after being slapped by Catherine, had stayed at the head of his comrades. But while he launched them into the attack on Montsou, shouting hoarsely, he heard another voice within him, the voice of reason, asking in astonishment what the purpose of all this could be. He hadn't wanted any of it to happen, so how could it have come about that he had left Jean-Bart with the intention of preventing a disaster and now here he was, at the end of a day of mounting violence, attacking the manager's residence?

And yet it was he who had just called a halt. Except that his first instinct had been merely to protect the Company's yards, when they had proposed going there to smash things up. And now that the first stones were already chipping away at the front of the villa, he cast around vainly in his mind for a legitimate target to launch the mob at, in order to avoid greater disasters. As he stood in the middle of the road feeling lonely and helpless, someone called him, it was a man standing in the doorway of the Tison bar, whose landlady had hurried to put up the shutters, just leaving the door clear.

'Yes, it's me . . . Listen to me.'

It was Rasseneur. A group of nearly thirty men and women, nearly all of them from village Two Hundred and Forty, who had stayed in during the morning and come out that evening when they heard the news, had invaded the bar when they heard the strikers coming. Zacharie was at one table with his wife Philomène. Further back, Pierron and La Pierronne, with their backs to the door, were hiding their faces. In fact nobody was actually drinking, they had all simply come in to take shelter.

Étienne recognized Rasseneur, and he started to walk away, when Rasseneur added:

'You're ashamed to see me here, aren't you? . . . You can't say I didn't warn you, your problems are only just starting. You can ask for all the bread you like now, but what you'll get is a bellyful of lead.'

So Étienne turned back towards him, and answered:

'What I'm more worried about is the cowards who are sitting down doing nothing but watch us while we risk our lives.'

'So you fancy going over the road for a bit of looting and pillage?' asked Rasseneur.

'I fancy staying with my comrades through thick and thin, even if we all have to die together.'

And Étienne, with heavy heart, returned to take his place among the crowd, ready to die. As they went down the road, three children started throwing stones, and he chased them to give them a good kick in the pants, and cried out, to stop his comrades from joining in, that they wouldn't get anywhere by breaking windows.

Bébert and Lydie, who had just come to join Jeanlin, were learning from him how to use the sling. They each slung a stone, betting who could cause the most damage. Lydie, with a clumsy throw, had cut open the head of a woman in the crowd; and the two boys split their sides laughing. Behind them, Bonnemort and Mouque sat on a bench watching them. Bonnemort's swollen legs were so weakened that he had had a terrible job getting that far, and yet nobody knew what he found so interesting, for he had that lifeless expression about him which meant that no one would get a word out of him.

By now, nobody obeyed Étienne any more. Despite his orders, the stones continued to fly, and he was astonished and dismayed to see these brutes that he had unleashed, so slow to

be roused, and yet so terrible afterwards, with their vicious
and implacable fury. All the old Flemish blood was there, in
these heavy, placid people; it took months for it to warm up,
but then they threw themselves into the most abominable
savagery, and were incapable of listening to reason, until the
beast had drunk its fill of atrocities. In the South of France,
where he came from, the crowds were more excitable, but they
were less destructive. He had to fight with Levaque to tear
away his axe, and he couldn't find a way to calm the Maheus,
who were throwing stones with both hands. And the women
were especially frightening, La Levaque and La Mouquette
and the others were shaking with murderous fury, baring their
teeth and nails, barking like bitches, goaded on by old Ma
Brûlé, whose tall, skinny figure stood out above them.

But they stopped abruptly, when a sudden surprise brought
the period of calm that Étienne's supplications had failed to
achieve. It was simply the Grégoires, who had decided to take
their leave of the notary, and cross over to go to the manager's
house; they seemed so peaceful, they looked so much as if they
thought that these kind miners whose passive compliance had
made their fortune for a century past were staging some kind
of practical joke, that the amazed miners themselves stopped
throwing stones, worried that they might hit this old lady and
gentleman who looked as if they had dropped in from heaven
on a visit. They allowed them to enter the manager's garden,
mount the steps, and ring at the barricaded door, which
nobody hurried to open. But at the same moment, Rose, the
chambermaid, returned from her day off, laughing in the
direction of the frenzied workers, for she knew all of them,
since she was from Montsou. And she it was who hammered at
the door until Hippolyte was forced to edge it open. The
Grégoires slipped through just in time, for the hail of stones
started up again. Once they had got over their astonishment
the crowd started clamouring even louder:

'Death to the bourgeoisie! Power to the people!'

Rose was still laughing as they came through the entrance
hall of the villa, as if she were enjoying the adventure, repeating
to the terrified manservant:

'They don't mean any harm, I know them well enough.'

Monsieur Grégoire hung up his hat carefully. Then, when he had helped Madame Grégoire remove her thick woollen cloak, he replied:

'I'm sure that they're not basically wicked. When they've had a good shout, they'll go home to supper with a better appetite.'

Meanwhile, Monsieur Hennebeau arrived downstairs from the second floor. He had seen what had happened, and he came to greet his guests with his usual cold, polite expression. Only the pallor of his face betrayed the fact that he had been shaken and weeping. The inner man was under control, there was no trace of anything other than the perfect executive, resolved to do his duty.

'Did you know', he said, 'that our ladies haven't returned yet?'

For the first time the Grégoires' feelings were upset by the worry that Cécile had not returned. How would she manage to get home if the miners continued their silly antics?

'I thought of sending for the gendarmes to clear them away from the house,' added Monsieur Hennebeau. 'But the problem is that I'm on my own here, and anyway I don't know where to send my servant to fetch them, otherwise four men and a corporal would easily get rid of the rabble for me.'

Rose, who had stayed to listen, felt bound to murmur again:

'Oh, Sir, they don't mean any harm.'

The manager nodded his head, while the din outside grew louder and they could hear the muffled impact of the stones against the front of the house.

'I have no grudge against them, in fact I excuse them; you have to be as stupid as they are to believe that we're wasting all our energy trying to make them miserable. But I have to guarantee peace and quiet ... To think that the gendarmes are running up and down the roads all over the countryside, everyone insists that it's true, and yet I haven't been able to find a single one of them all day!'

He broke off, and moved aside to let Madame Grégoire pass, saying:

'I beg of you, Madam, don't stay there, come into the sitting-room.'

But cook had come up from the basement, and she kept them talking in the hall for ten minutes more. She was at her wits' end and declared that she washed her hands of the dinner, since she was still waiting for the vol-au-vent cases that she had ordered from the *pâtisserie* at Marchiennes for four o'clock. Obviously the pastry-cook must have lost his way, for fear of meeting these bandits. Perhaps they had even pilfered his valuable wares. She saw her vol-au-vents waylaid and assaulted, ravished at gun-point and taken to swell the bellies of the 3,000 wretches who were calling for bread. Anyway, Sir should know the truth, that she'd rather throw the dinner into the grate and burn it than have it spoiled by a revolution.

'Be patient,' said Monsieur Hennebeau. 'All is not yet lost. There is still time for the pastry-cook to arrive.'

But, as he turned to let Madame Grégoire through the door to the sitting-room, he was extremely surprised to see that there was a man sitting on the bench in the hall, whom he hadn't noticed till then, because of the gathering dusk.

'Oh, it's you, is it, Maigrat? What's up then?'

Maigrat got to his feet and his plump face appeared in the light, his features pale and distorted with terror. He no longer cut his usual figure of a large, calm man, as he humbly explained that he had slipped in to see the manager, to ask for help and protection, Sir, in case the bandits attacked his shop.

'You can see that I'm threatened myself and that I've nobody to protect me,' replied Monsieur Hennebeau. 'You'd have done better to stay at home and look after your merchandise.'

'Oh, I've put up my iron bars, and I've left my wife in charge.'

The manager lost patience with him and didn't try to hide his contempt. What a fine guard she would make, that skinny creature, stunted by his bullying!

'Anyway, I can't do anything about it, try to look after yourself. And I advise you to go home immediately, because here they come again asking for bread . . . Listen.'

And indeed the tumult had broken out again, and Maigrat thought he heard his name among the words shouted. It was too late to go back home now, he would only be lynched. And besides, he was shattered by the idea of his ruin. He pressed his face up against the glass panel of the door, sweating, trembling, expecting a catastrophe; while the Grégoires decided to go through into the sitting-room.

Monsieur Hennebeau tried to proceed discreetly with the business of making his guests feel at home. But he asked them in vain to be seated. The room was shuttered and sealed, and lit by two lamps although night had not yet fallen, but it became filled with renewed terror each time a fresh clamour was heard outside. Muffled by the tapestries, the anger of the crowd was even more disturbing, its muttered threats vague and hideous. They couldn't help talking, however, and constantly returning to the subject of this unthinkable revolt. He was surprised that he had not foreseen anything like it, and he was so ill informed by his services that it was Rasseneur who was the main target of his anger, as he said that he could recognize his deplorable influence. However, the gendarmes would soon be coming, they couldn't possibly abandon him in this way. As for the Grégoires, they had thoughts for no one and nothing but their daughter: their poor darling who took fright so easily! Perhaps they had been warned of the danger and their carriage had returned to Marchiennes. Their wait lasted for another quarter of an hour, exacerbated by the uproar from the road outside, by the noise of stones striking the closed shutters from time to time, echoing like drumbeats. The situation was becoming intolerable, and Monsieur Hennebeau said he was going to go out and chase all those braggarts away single-handed and go to meet the carriage, when Hippolyte came in crying:

'Sir, Sir, here comes Madam, they're murdering Madam!'

The carriage had been unable to get further than the lane leading to Réquillart; surrounded by threatening groups, Négrel had put his plan into action, walking the hundred metres which separated them from the villa, then knocking at the little gate which gave on to the garden, near the outbuildings: the gardener would hear them, there was bound to be someone still there to open the gate for them. And at first everything had gone perfectly; Madame Hennebeau and the young ladies had arrived there safely and were already knocking at the door, when some women, who had got wind of it, rushed out into the lane. Things went from bad to worse. Nobody came to open the gate, and then Négrel failed in his attempts to force it open with his shoulders. The crowd of women grew, he was afraid of being swept away, so he decided in desperation to push his aunt and the girls in front of him, to break through the ranks of their assailants and reach the main steps at the front of the villa. But this manœuvre led to a scrum: they were unable to break away from a screaming group that followed them, while the mass of the crowd eddied around them on both sides, without understanding what was happening, but none the less astonished to see these ladies in their finery straying across the battlefield. At that moment the confusion reached such a peak that there occurred one of those extravagant events that are impossible to explain. Lucie and Jeanne had reached the steps and slipped through the door which the chambermaid held ajar; Madame Hennebeau had managed to follow them; Négrel finally came in behind them, and bolted the door, convinced that he had seen Cécile go in first. But she was not there, she had got lost along the way, swept away by such a fear that she had turned her back on the house and had plunged into the heart of the danger.

Immediately the cry went up:

'Up with the people! Death to the bourgeoisie! Kill them!'

Some of them, seeing her veiled face from a distance, thought it was Madame Hennebeau. Others guessed she must be a friend of the manager's wife, the young spouse of a local factory owner who was detested by his workmen. And in the end it made little difference, for it was her silk dress, her fur coat, and even the white feather in her hat, which drove them to a frenzy. She smelled of perfume, she wore a watch, her fine skin spoke of a life of idleness, never touching a piece of coal.

'Just you wait!' cried old Ma Brûlé. 'We'll stuff your lacy drawers right up your arse!'

'These bitches are robbing us to cover their bare bums in warm fur,' went on La Levaque, 'while we're dying of cold . . . Let's bloody well strip her naked, and teach her a thing or two about real life!'

Suddenly La Mouquette spat out:

'Yes, that's right, let's whip her, too.'

And the women exploded in a savage rivalry, holding up their rags, and each wanting to get her hands on a bit of this little rich girl. They bet her behind wasn't any finer than anyone else's. Lots of these creatures were worm-eaten enough under their fancy fur and feathers. This injustice had lasted long enough, it was time to force all those whores to dress like working women, and stop them spending fifty sous every time they had their petticoats laundered!

Amid this horde of furies Cécile was quaking with fear, her legs paralysed, stammering the same sentence over and over again:

'Ladies, please, ladies, please don't hurt me.'

But then she started screaming hoarsely: cold hands had come to seize her round the neck. It was old Bonnemort who had grabbed hold of her, when the crowd had pushed her close to him. He seemed drunk with hunger, drugged by his long-drawn-out suffering, but now suddenly shaken out of half a century of resignation, without anyone being able to tell which particular complaint had suddenly become unbearable. After having saved the lives of a dozen comrades during his career, risking his neck in firedamp and rock falls, he yielded to some force he couldn't explain, the irresistible fascination of the girl's white neck. And as he had lost his tongue that day, he tightened his fingers, taking on the look of an old, sick animal, chewing over his memories.

'No, no!', the women screamed. 'Get them off, let's have her arse!'

In the villa, as soon as they realized what was happening, Négrel and Monsieur Hennebeau had bravely reopened the door in order to fly to Cécile's rescue. But now the crowd was pressing up against the garden railings, and it was not easy to go out. A struggle started, as the Grégoires emerged on the steps in a state of terror.

'Leave her alone, Grandpa! It's the girl from La Piolaine!' cried La Maheude to her grandfather, recognizing Cécile, whose veil had been torn off by one of the women.

And Étienne for his part was shocked by this vengeful

attack on a child and tried to get the gang to let her go. He suddenly had an idea and brandished the axe which he had snatched from Levaque's hands.

'Let's go to Maigrat's, for God's sake! ... He's got bread there! Let's tear his shop to pieces!'

And he flew off immediately to strike the first blow at the door with his axe. A group of comrades, Levaque, Maheu, and a few others, followed him. But the women persisted. Cécile had fallen from Bonnemort's clutches into the hands of old Ma Brûlé. Lydie and Bébert, led by Jeanlin, had got down on their hands and knees and crawled under her skirts, to have a look at the lady's bottom. She was already being mauled, and her clothes were being torn off her, when a man on horseback arrived, spurring his mount forward and lashing out with his riding-crop at anyone who didn't get out of the way quick enough.

'You scum, you've started to whip little girls now, have you?'

It was Deneulin, who had turned up for his dinner appointment. He jumped down on to the road quickly, picked up Cécile by her waist, and with his other hand, manœuvring his horse with extraordinary skill and strength, used it as a living wedge, cutting through the crowd, which fell back beneath his charges. The battle was still in full swing by the railings. Yet he forced his way through, crushing one or two arms and legs on the way. This sudden help released Négrel and Monsieur Hennebeau from their ordeal of oaths, blows, and even worse perils. And while the young man at last made his way into the house with Cécile, who had fainted, Deneulin, who had reached the top of the steps, using his large frame as a shield to protect the manager, was struck so violently by a stone that it almost dislocated his shoulder.

'Go ahead,' he cried, 'break all my bones now you've broken my machines.'

He closed the door promptly behind him. A volley of stones pitted the woodwork.

'What maniacs!' he said. 'Another couple of seconds and they would have split my skull open like a ripe marrow ... There's no point in talking to them any more, that's obvious.

They're out of their minds, the only thing to do now is knock them down.'

In the sitting-room the Grégoires were weeping as they watched Cécile coming to her senses. She wasn't hurt, she hadn't even a scratch: all she had lost was her veil. But they became increasingly aghast when they recognized their cook Mélanie standing in the room, and she told them how the mob had destroyed La Piolaine. Crazed with fear, she had run to warn her masters. She too had got in by the half-open door in the thick of the struggle without anyone noticing her; and as her story grew longer and longer the single stone with which Jeanlin had broken just one window became a regular salvo, splitting the walls asunder. Now Monsieur Grégoire's ideas underwent a sea-change: his daughter was torn apart, his house was razed to the ground; did this really mean, then, that the miners had a grudge against him, just because he lived comfortably from providing them with work?

The chambermaid, who had brought a towel and some eau-de-Cologne, repeated:

'It's strange, all the same, they really don't mean any harm.'

Madame Hennebeau sat quite still and very pale, and could not get over the shock to her nerves; then suddenly she found a smile, when everyone congratulated Négrel.

Cécile's parents were most grateful to the young man; he could count on the marriage. Monsieur Hennebeau looked on in silence, casting his eyes now on the wife, now on the lover he had sworn to kill only that morning, now at the young lady who would doubtless soon take him away. He was in no hurry, for his main fear was that his wife might stoop even lower, and choose some manservant or suchlike.

'And how about you, my little dears?' Deneulin asked his daughters. 'Nothing broken, I hope?'

Lucie and Jeanne had been frightened enough, but they were pleased to have had the experience, and they had already started to laugh about it.

'Goodness gracious!' their father continued. 'What an exciting day! . . . If you want a dowry, it looks as if you're going to have to earn it yourselves; and even then you may well have to look after me as well.'

He was joking, but his voice quavered. His eyes were brimming with tears, and his daughters rushed into his arms.

Monsieur Hennebeau had listened to this confession of ruin. His face was lit by a luminous thought. For in fact Vandame would belong to Montsou; it was the compensation devoutly longed for, the stroke of luck which would bring him back into favour with the gentlemen of the Board. Each time in his life that he had been stricken by some disaster, he had taken refuge in the strict execution of orders received, and he drew from the military discipline with which he surrounded himself a limited form of solace.

But they recovered their nerves, and a tired peace fell on the room, beneath the soft light shed by the two lamps and the cosy warmth that had built up behind the *portières*. Whatever might be happening outside? They had stopped their hue and cry, and the stones no longer rained down on the front wall; and all that could be heard were some heavy, muffled thuds, like axe blows re-echoing in the depths of the forest. They wanted to find out, and they went back into the hallway to snatch a glimpse through the glass panel in the door. Even the good ladies and their daughters went upstairs to peep through the shutters on the first floor.

'Can you see that scoundrel Rasseneur, opposite us, in the doorway of that inn?' said Monsieur Hennebeau to Deneulin. 'I thought as much, you might have known he'd join in.'

And yet it wasn't Rasseneur, it was Étienne, staving in Maigrat's shop with his axe. And he kept calling out to his comrades: didn't the goods over there belong to the coal workers? Didn't they have the right to retrieve their own property from this thief who had been exploiting them for so long, and who was ready to starve them to death just because the Company told him to? Gradually, everyone left the manager's villa, and ran over to loot the neighbouring shop. The cry 'bread, bread, we want bread!' thundered out yet again. They would find some bread at last, behind this door. A hungry fury bore them on, as if they suddenly felt that if they waited any longer, they would just fall down in the road and die. They milled so violently around the door that Étienne was afraid of wounding someone with each swing of the axe.

Meanwhile Maigrat, who had left the entrance hall of the villa, had at first taken refuge in the kitchen; but he couldn't hear anything there, and he imagined all sorts of abominable outrages being perpetrated against his shop; so he had just come back to hide behind the pump outside, from where he quite distinctly heard the noise of the door splitting, and the sound of his own name mingled with the other cries of the looters. It wasn't just a bad dream, then: although he still couldn't see, at least he could hear, and he followed the progress of the assault, with his ears burning. Every splitting blow pierced his very heart. That must have been one of the hinges bursting; in another five minutes they would have stormed the shop. He saw it in clear, terrifying pictures inside his head, the brigands rushing in, then the drawers broken open, the sacks split down the middle, everything eaten up and drunk down, the house itself carried off, nothing left, not even a stick to pick up and go begging with from village to village. No, he wouldn't allow them to bring ruin down on his head, he'd rather risk his life to stop them. Standing there, he had noticed at one window of his house, situated in a wing which was set back from the front wall, the frail figure of his wife, pale and indistinct behind the pane: doubtless she was watching every blow, with her silent, hangdog expression. Below there was a shed, so situated that, from the garden of the villa, you could use a trellis on the adjoining wall to climb up on to it: then from there it was easy enough to climb on to the tiles, up to the level of the window. And the idea of getting back inside his house now obsessed him, for he bitterly regretted having gone out in the first place. Perhaps he might find time to barricade the shop up with furniture; and he even saw himself setting up further heroic defences, pouring boiling oil and burning paraffin down on the crowd. But his passion for his merchandise conflicted with his fear, and he groaned with tortured cowardice. Suddenly he made up his mind, when he heard another blow of the axe ring out louder than the previous ones. And it was avarice that won the day; he preferred to lay down his life, and his wife's, to protect his sacks of provisions with their very bodies, rather than relinquish a single loaf of bread.

Almost immediately the cries rang out.

'Look, look! . . . Look at the alley cat up there! Look at that tomcat! Catch the cat!'

The mob had caught sight of Maigrat on the roof of the shed. Carried away by his passion, he had scrambled swiftly up the trellis despite his bulk, paying no heed to the pieces of wood that split under his weight; and now he flattened himself against the tiles, trying to reach the window. But the slope of the roof was extremely steep, and he was encumbered by the size of his belly, and he tore his nails trying to cling on. Even so, he would have made it to the top if he hadn't started trembling with fear that they would throw stones at him, for although he couldn't see them, he could hear the crowd chanting away beneath him:

'Look at the tomcat! Bad cat! Kill the cat!'

And suddenly both his hands gave way at once; he tumbled downwards, bounced off a gutter, and fell on to the adjoining wall so awkwardly that he tumbled back over the other side into the road, and split his skull against the edge of a milestone. His brains spilled out. He was dead. His wife, above him, looked on, still pale and indistinct.

At first they were stupefied. Étienne came to a halt, and the axe slipped from his fingers. Maheu, Levaque, and the rest of them forgot the shop, and looked at the wall, down which a thin line of blood was gently running. Now the cries had ceased, and silence spread through the deepening gloom.

Suddenly the yelling recommenced. It was the women who rushed up to him, giddy with the scent of blood.

'Now I believe there's a God in heaven! It's all over now, you fat pig!'

They gathered round the warm corpse, and mocked it with insulting laughter, called the smashed skull an ugly mug, and screamed out the bitter litany of their endless starvation into the ears of the dead man.

'I owed you sixty francs, now I've paid you back, you thief!' said La Maheude, as furious as the rest of them. 'You won't refuse me credit any more . . . Wait a moment, just wait! I'm sure you've got room for more.'

And stretching out her fingers she dug deep into the soil,

tore up two full handfuls of earth and stuffed them violently right into his mouth.

'There you are! There's some food for you! . . . Eat it all up, like you ate us out of house and home!'

Then the insults exploded around the dead man, who lay there on his back looking up with staring eyes at the empty heavens which had become veiled by the gathering dusk. The earth crammed into his mouth was the bread that he had denied them. And he would never eat any other bread now. It hadn't brought him much luck to starve the poor.

But the women had other wrongs to avenge. They walked round him, nostrils flaring, vicious as vixens. They were on the look-out for some spectacular vengeance, some ferocious act which would release their pent-up passions.

Then the bitter voice of old Ma Brûlé made itself heard.

'Dirty tomcat! Cut it off!'

'Yes, get the dirty tomcat! . . . He's spent too long on the tiles, the dirty bastard!'

And already La Mouquette was hauling his trousers off, while La Levaque lifted his legs up in the air. And old Ma Brûlé, with her dry old hands, spread his bare thighs open, and grasped his lifeless virile organ. She seized the whole thing, tearing it all away with an effort that strained her skinny spine and stretched her bony arms. The soft flesh at first resisted, and she had to keep pulling, but it finally came away in her hands, a lump of hairy, bleeding flesh, and she waved it around, laughing in triumph:

'I've got it! I've got it!'

The ghastly trophy was greeted with a volley of shrill imprecations.

'You bastard, you won't stuff our daughters with that any more!'

'Right, we won't have to bend over and kiss that lump of mutton any more every time we can't afford to pay for a loaf of bread.'

'Hey, I owe you six francs, do you want a bit on account? I'm willing, if you still feel up to it!'

They rocked with terrible hilarity at this joke. They passed round the bleeding stump, as if they had finally exterminated a wild animal that had been preying on each and every one of them, and saw it there inert and in their power. They bared their teeth, and spat on it, repeating in a furious explosion of scorn:

'He can't get it up! He can't do a thing! ... Throw his bones to the crows, he's not even a man ... Rot in hell, you useless creature!'

Then old Ma Brûlé stuck the whole thing on the end of her stick; and she held it up in the air, bearing it aloft like a banner, and set out down the road followed by a screaming horde of women. The wretched lump of flesh dangled limply, dripping blood, like a strip of offal at the butcher's. Up above at her window, Madame Maigrat still didn't move; but the last rays of the setting sun refracted through the flaws in the glass distorted her pale face into the semblance of a smile. Since she had been beaten and deceived every hour of the day, and had spent her days bent double over the accounts, perhaps she was in fact laughing, as the mob of women galloped by with the wild, wicked beast crushed and impaled on the end of a stick.

This dreadful mutilation had been accompanied by a horrified silence. Neither Étienne nor Maheu, nor the others, had been able to intervene in time: they remained motionless in the face of these charging furies. At the door of the Tison bar faces could be seen, Rasseneur white-faced with revulsion, and Zacharie and Philomène stupefied at the sight. The two older men, Bonnemort and Mouque, shook their heads, impressed with the gravity of the affair. Only Jeanlin sniggered, nudged Bébert in the ribs, and forced Lydie to look up and watch. But the women were already on their way back, retracing their steps, passing beneath the windows of the manager's house. And behind the shutters, the ladies of the house peered out more intently. They hadn't been able to make out what had been happening, with the wall in the way, and they couldn't see anything distinctly in the gathering dark.

'Whatever have they got on the end of their stick?' asked Cécile, who had plucked up the courage to look out.

Lucie and Jeanne declared that it must be a rabbit skin.

'No, I don't think so,' murmured Madame Hennebeau,

'they must have raided the *charcuterie*, it looks more like a strip of pork.'

But then she suddenly gave a shudder and fell silent. Madame Grégoire had nudged her with her knee. They both remained transfixed. The young ladies had gone very pale, and asked no more questions, watching with staring eyes as the red vision swam away into the depths of the night.

Étienne had started wielding his axe again. But it was impossible to dispel the uneasy feeling, the corpse seemed to block the path to the shop and protect it. A lot of men had turned back. They all seemed suddenly appeased, as if their thirst had been quenched. Maheu was still downcast; then he heard a voice in his ear telling him to run for it. He turned round and recognized Catherine, still wearing the man's coat they had lent her, black with mud, and out of breath. He swept her aside with his hand. He refused to listen to her, and made as if to hit her. Then she gestured in despair, hesitated, and ran towards Étienne.

'Run for it, run for it, the gendarmes are coming!'

He too chased her away, swearing at her, feeling the blood rise to his cheeks with the memory of the slaps he had received. But she refused to be discouraged, she forced him to throw the axe away, and dragged him away by the arms, with irresistible strength.

'Listen to me, will you! . . . I'm telling you the gendarmes are coming! Chaval went to fetch them and he brought them here if you must know. I think it's disgusting, so I came back . . . Run for it, I don't want them to get you.'

And Catherine dragged him away, just as they heard the thunder of hooves beating over the cobbles in the distance. Suddenly the cry rang out: 'The gendarmes! The gendarmes!' There was such a hectic, chaotic scramble, with every man looking out for himself, that in only a couple of minutes the road was empty, swept absolutely clear as if by a hurricane. Maigrat's corpse made a solitary patch of shadow against the white ground. The only man still standing in front of the Tison bar was Rasseneur, whose relief could be seen in his radiant features, as he welcomed the swift success of the sword; while in the deserted town of Montsou, the bourgeois hid behind closed shutters with their lights extinguished, sweating with fear, their teeth chattering, not even daring to look out. The plain was drowned in the endless night; only the silhouettes of the blast-furnaces and the burnt-out coke ovens showed up tragically against the horizon. The thunder of hooves became louder, and the gendarmes surged into sight in one dark indistinguishable mass. And behind them, entrusted to their care, the pastry-cook's carriage arrived at last from Marchiennes; then out of this little vehicle the baker's boy sprang, and started cheerfully unpacking his vol-au-vent cases.

PART VI

CHAPTER I

The first fortnight of February went by, with the hard winter still gripping the miserable wretches pitilessly in its bitter cold. Again the authorities had swept through the region, sending the Prefect from Lille, a public prosecutor, and a general. And not content with sending in the gendarmes, the army had come* to occupy Montsou with a whole regiment, whose men were camped out from Beaugnies to Marchiennes. Armed pickets guarded the pits, and there were soldiers posted by every engine. The manager's villa, the Company yards, and even the houses of some of the bourgeoisie bristled with bayonets. There was no escaping the slow march of the squads patrolling up and down the cobbled streets. There was a sentry permanently standing guard on top of the slag-heap at Le Voreux, keeping watch over the featureless plain, facing the icy wind that blew up there; and every two hours the call of the changing of the watch rang out, as if on a hostile frontier.

'Halt! Who goes there? ... Advance, and give the password!'

Work had not started up again anywhere. On the contrary, the strike had hardened: Crèvecœur, Mirou, and Madeleine had stopped producing, like Le Voreux; Feutry-Cantel and La Victoire lost more workers each morning; at Saint-Thomas, which had previously been untouched, there were gaps in the ranks. Now that they were faced with the force of arms, the miners offered a quiet but obstinate resistance, for their pride had been wounded. The villages looked as if they had been left abandoned in the middle of the beetfields. Not a workman stirred, only the odd one might occasionally be seen, out on his own, looking away as he walked past the red-trousered troops. And amid this sullen peace, this passive resistance to the rifles that surrounded them, they showed the deceptive gentleness and the patient, forced obedience of wild beasts in cages, their eyes on the trainer, ready to snap his head off the moment he turns his back. The Company, ruined by the cessation of work, was talking of taking on miners from Le Borinage* on the Belgian frontier, but didn't dare do so; thus the battle lines remained static between the colliers, who stayed indoors, and the troops guarding the abandoned pits.

The very next morning after the terrible riot, this armed peace had arisen spontaneously, hiding a panic so deep that as little as possible was said about the damage and the atrocities. The official inquiry established that Maigrat had died from his fall, and the dreadful mutilation of his body was kept inexplicit, leaving it surrounded with an instant halo of legend. For its part, the Company declined to make public the damage it had suffered, just as the Grégoires preferred not to compromise the reputation of their daughter with the scandal of a trial, where she would have had to give evidence. However, there had been a few arrests, of bystanders as usual, all dazed, witless, and totally ignorant. By mistake they had taken Pierron in handcuffs to Marchiennes, which had his comrades laughing for days. Rasseneur, too, had almost been marched away by a pair of gendarmes. The management settled for drawing up lists of people to sack, sending whole batches of workmen their booklets: Maheu had received his, Levaque too, like thirty-four of their comrades in village Two Hundred and Forty alone. And the full rigour of the law was invoked against Étienne, who had disappeared on the night of the affray, but search as they might, they found no trace of him. Driven by personal hatred, Chaval had denounced him, but refused to name anyone else, yielding to Catherine's plea to him to spare her parents. As the days went by, there was a feeling of unfinished business; people were waiting for the end, their hearts sick with tension.

At Montsou from now on the bourgeoisie woke with a start in the middle of every night, their ears ringing with imaginary bells tolling and their nostrils reeking with the stench of gunpowder. But what finally drove them mad was a sermon by their new vicar, Father Ranvier, the skinny, red-eyed priest who had succeeded Father Joire. How different he was from that discreet, smiling, plump, and inoffensive man, whose only concern had been to avoid trouble and enjoy peace and quiet! Hadn't Father Ranvier dared take the defence of the disgraceful bandits who were the shame of the region? He found excuses for the strikers, and made a vicious attack on the bourgeoisie, whose fault it all was. It was the bourgeoisie who had stripped the Church of its ancient rights and was now misusing them, which had turned this world into a cursed place of injustice and suffering; it was the bourgeoisie that was encouraging the misunderstanding and was leading everyone to the brink of an appalling catastrophe, through its atheism, its refusal to return to the faith and the fraternal traditions of the early Christians. And he had dared to threaten the rich, he had warned them that, if they kept stubbornly refusing to hear the word of God, God would surely go over to the side of the poor: he would triumph over the faithless seekers after pleasure, and take back all their riches and redistribute them to the humble of the earth, in the pursuit of his glory. The devout church wives trembled at his words, the notary declared that it smacked of the worst brand of socialism, they all imagined the vicar brandishing his crucifix at the head of an armed mob, destroying with a few wild strokes the bourgeoisie that had been born in 1789.

When Monsieur Hennebeau was informed of what was happening, he merely shrugged his shoulders and said:

'If he becomes too much of a nuisance the Bishop will get rid of him for us.'

And while this wave of panic was sweeping back and forth right across the countryside, Étienne had gone to ground, in the depths of Réquillart, in Jeanlin's lair. Nobody imagined that he was hiding so close by, for his cool cheek in choosing to take refuge down the mine itself, in the abandoned gallery of an old pit, had thrown his pursuers off the scent. Up above, the mouth of the tunnel was blocked by sloe bushes and hawthorn shrubs which had sprouted up between the broken beams of the pulley frame; nobody dared enter; you had to know the routine, swing from the roots of the mountain ash, swallow your fear, let go, and drop down into the dark to reach the rungs that were still strong enough to take your weight; and there were other obstacles protecting Étienne, the suffocating heat of the well, the 120 metres of dangerous descent, then sliding painfully along on your belly for a quarter of a league, between the ever-narrowing walls of the tunnel, before you could discover the traitor's cave and its pirate's hoard.

Here he lived surrounded by lavish provisions; he had found some gin, the remains of the dried cod, and all sorts of other supplies. The great bed of hay was excellent, there wasn't a single draught in the room, which was bathed in a perfectly even warmth. The only problem was the imminent lack of light. Jeanlin, who had become his appointed purveyor, showing all the caution and cunning of the native delighted to dupe the occupying forces, brought him everything he wanted, including pomade, but was unable to lay his hands on a packet of candles.

By the fifth day, Étienne only lit a candle when he needed to eat. The food stuck in his throat if he tried to swallow it in the dark. This utter, endless night, with its invariable blackness, was a source of great suffering. Although he could sleep safely and eat his fill and was snug and warm, he had never in his life felt his head so invaded by darkness. It seemed to press down on him so that it crushed the life out of his own thoughts. Now he was living from robbery! Despite his communist theories, the old scruples inherited from his moral education made themselves felt, and he restricted himself to dry bread, eating as little of it as possible. But what was the point? He had to live on, his task was unfinished. He also felt burdened by another source of shame, remorse for his wild drinking session, when, in the bitter cold, the gin on an empty stomach had thrown him at Chaval with a knife in his hand. That stirred up within him a whole unknown area of terror, his hereditary ill, his long heritage of drunkenness, unable to stand a drop of alcohol without falling into a homicidal fury. Would he end up a murderer? When he had reached this haven, in the deep peace of the bowels of the earth, he had felt suddenly sated with violence, and slept for two whole days with the sleep of a gorged and stupefied beast; and his disgust persisted, he woke to find his muscles aching, his mouth bitter, his head swimming, as if he had been out on some terrible drinking spree. A week went by; but the Maheus, although they knew where he was, were unable to send him a candle: he had to accept his blindness, even when eating.

Now Étienne spent hours at a time stretched out on the hay. He was racked with vague ideas which he hadn't suspected to find in his head. He had a sensation of superiority that set him apart from his comrades, as the knowledge he was acquiring from his studies seemed to make his whole being expand. He had never reflected so much, and he wondered why he had felt so disgusted the day after his wild race from pit to pit; but he didn't dare answer his own question; there were memories that shocked him, the baseness of what people desired, the crudeness of their instincts, the smell of all that misery hanging in the air. Despite the torment he felt in the darkness, he found himself starting to dread the moment when he would have to return to the village. How revolting they were, these wretches piled one on top of the other, washing in each other's dirty water! Not a single one of them could hold a serious political conversation, they lived just like cattle, always surrounded by the same suffocating smell of onions! He would like to open up new horizons for them, to lead them towards the comfort and the good manners of the bourgeoisie, making them the masters; but how long it would take! And he felt he lacked the courage, plunged in the prison of hunger, to wait for victory to come. Gradually his vanity at being their leader and his constant concern to think on their behalf were detaching him from them, and creating within him the soul of one of those bourgeois that he so detested.

One evening Jeanlin brought him the remains of a candle that he had stolen from a carter's lantern; and Étienne was greatly relieved. When the darkness finally made him feel dazed, weighing so heavily on his head that he thought he would go mad, he lit it for a moment; then, as soon as he had dispelled his nightmares, he put the light out, as wary of wasting the life-giving light as he was of wasting bread itself. The silence throbbed in his ears, and he heard nothing but the scurrying of bands of rats, the creaking of old timber, and the tiny sounds made by a spider spinning its web. And as his eyes tried to penetrate the warm surrounding void, he kept returning to his obsession; that is, what his comrades were doing up above. Leaving them in the lurch would have seemed to him to be the most abject cowardice. If he was hiding out in this way, it was to remain free to be able to give them advice and act without constraint.

His long musings had clarified his ambitions: while awaiting something better, he would have liked to be Pluchart, give up work, and devote himself entirely to politics, but on his own, in a clean room, arguing that mental work absorbed all one's vital energies and required absolute peace and quiet.

At the start of the second week, when Jeanlin told him that the gendarmes thought he had crossed over into Belgium, Étienne thought it was safe to leave his hiding place at night-time. He wanted to check up on the situation, to see whether they should continue their struggle. He himself had thought the game was up even before the strike, and had doubted a successful outcome, but he had merely yielded to the pressure of events; and now, after feeling the intoxication of rebellion, he returned to these first doubts, since he despaired of making the Company give way. But he couldn't yet admit it to himself, he was still tortured by doubt when he thought of the misery of defeat, and of the heavy responsibility for the suffering which would weigh on his shoulders. Wouldn't the end of the strike mean the end of his role and the collapse of his ambitions, reducing his existence to the mindless routine of the mine and the repulsive life of the village? And sincerely, without mean or mendacious calculation, he tried to rekindle his faith in the strike, to persuade himself that resistance was still possible, that capitalism was bound to destroy itself in the wake of the heroic suicide of labour.

And indeed throughout the land there were long and ruinous consequences. At night, when he wandered round the country-side like a wolf venturing forth from the forest, he could almost hear the crash of bankruptcies re-echoing from end to end of the plain. Every road he walked down offered up its closed, dead factories, with their buildings rotting beneath the wan sky. The sugar-refineries had been especially hard hit; the Hoton and the Fauvelle refineries, after reducing the number of their workers, had been the latest to collapse. At Dutilleul's flour-mill the last grindstone had ceased to turn on the second Saturday of the month, and the Bleuze ropeworks, which made mine cables, was killed off for good by the local stoppages. Over at Marchiennes the situation worsened daily; all the furnaces at the Gagebois glassworks had been extinguished, there were constant redundancies at the Sonneville building works, only one of the blast-furnaces of Les Forges was lit, and not a single battery of coke ovens lit the horizon. The strike of the Montsou colliers, born of the industrial slump which had been worsening for the past two years, had aggravated it, and was now precipitating the débâcle. To the causes of the slump—the drying up of orders from America, and the log-jam of capital tied up in superfluous production—there now had to be added the sudden lack of coal for the few boilers which were still working; and that was the direst disaster of all, this lack of the very life-blood of the machines that the pits were no longer producing. Terrified by the scale of the slump, the Company had diminished its production and driven its miners to starvation, and so by the end of December had inevitably found itself without a single piece of coal at the pit-head. The long chain of disasters was all infernally logical, one collapse brought on another, the industries fell like dominoes, knocking each other down in such a rapid series of catastrophes that the repercussions were felt as far away as the heart of the neighbouring cities of Lille, Douai, and Valenciennes, where whole families were ruined by runaway bankers reneging on their obligations.

Often, as he rounded a bend in the road, Étienne would stop in the middle of the icy darkness to listen to the ruins crashing down around him. He drank in the night air, and was seized by a lust for destruction, a hope that when dawn broke it would reveal the extermination of the old order, leaving not a fortune standing, with equality cutting society down to ground level like a scythe. But what fascinated him most in this holocaust were the Company's pits. He started walking again, blinded by the darkness, visiting them one by one, delighted with each new depredation that he discovered. There were more and more rock falls, and the longer the tunnels lay neglected, the more serious they became. Above the northern sector of Mirou, the subsidence of the ground was so pronounced that the Joiselle road had collapsed over a distance of a hundred metres, as if hit by some earthquake; and the Company was so worried by the rumours surrounding these accidents that it had compensated the owners of the fields which had subsided, without haggling. Crèvecœur and Madeleine, where the rock was very unstable, were starting to become blocked up. There was talk of two deputies being buried alive at La Victoire; and a flood at Feutry-Cantel; they had had to line a kilometre of gallery at Saint-Thomas with bricks, where the timber was breaking up on all sides because it hadn't been properly maintained. Thus each hour that passed brought enormous expenses, ravaging the shareholders' dividends, rapidly destroying the pits, which threatened in the long term to swallow up the famous Montsou deniers, which had multiplied a hundredfold over the previous century.

So, in the face of this series of blows, Étienne's hopes were raised again; he finally came to believe that a third month of resistance would bring about the downfall of the monster, crouching sluggish and bloated out there in its lair, in the hidden depths of its tabernacle. He knew that the trouble at Montsou had shaken the Parisian press quite seriously, unleashing a violent polemic between establishment and opposition newspapers, over terrifying stories that were exploited above all in order to attack the International, which the Emperor and his government were scared of, after first encouraging it; and since the Board could hardly claim to be unconcerned by what was happening, two of their members had deigned to travel down to undertake an inquiry, but with an air of reluctance, and seemingly uninterested in the result, so much so, apparently, that they only stayed for three days, declaring as they left that everything was just perfect. And yet Étienne had been assured unofficially that those gentlemen had worked non-stop throughout their stay, had been rushing about feverishly, up to their elbows in negotiations that none of their entourage was allowed to mention. And Étienne accused them of whistling in the dark, and he came to see their precipitate departure as a panic-stricken flight; now he felt certain that he would triumph, since these much-feared men were dropping the reins.

Yet the very next night Étienne was in despair again. The Company was too well supported to be knocked sideways so easily: it could lose millions, and later it would get the money back from the workers, forcing them to eat less. That night, having struck out as far as Jean-Bart, he guessed the truth, when a supervisor told him that there was already talk of ceding Vandame to Montsou. They said that Deneulin's household was in the grips of the direst misery, the pauperization of the rich, with the father ill with frustration, prematurely aged by his financial worries, and his daughters struggling to satisfy their creditors and keep the shirts on their backs. The starving miners in the villages suffered less than this bourgeois family, living in a house where they had to hide for fear of people seeing that they were reduced to drinking water. Work had not started again at Jean-Bart, and they had had to replace the pump at Gaston-Marie; not to mention the fact that, despite all the speed with which this had been done, the pit had started to flood, which caused considerable expense. And finally Deneulin had taken the risk of asking the Grégoires for a loan of a hundred thousand francs, and their refusal, although expected, had finished him off: if they refused, it was out of kindness to him, in order to spare him an impossible struggle; and they advised him to sell. He repeated his refusal, vehemently. He was furious at the idea of paying for the strike, he'd rather burst a blood vessel, choke with apoplexy, and drop down dead. But what was the alternative? He had listened to their offers. They wanted to beat him down, to undervalue that superb prize, a pit that had been renovated and refurbished, and where only a lack of ready credit paralysed its exploitation. Now he would be lucky if he could get enough out of it to get his creditors off his back. He had spent two days arguing with the representatives of the Board who had invaded Montsou, furious at their casual exploitation of his difficulties, crying out in his booming voice that he would never surrender. And that had settled the affair; they had returned to Paris to wait patiently until he gave up the ghost. Étienne sensed the return of the pendulum that would compensate them for disaster, and felt discouraged again at the invincible power of the major capitalists, who were so battle-hardened that they were able to thrive on defeat, by eating the corpses of their lesser brethren who fell at their sides.

Fortunately Jeanlin brought him some good news the next day. At Le Voreux, the lining of the pit looked likely to burst, water was breaking through all of the joints, and they had had to put a team of carpenters to work to repair it in great haste.

Until then, Étienne had avoided Le Voreux, worried by the ever-present black silhouette of the sentry posted on top of the slag-heap, overlooking the plain. They couldn't avoid him, he stood up against the sky, towering aloft like the regimental standard. Towards three o'clock in the morning, the sky clouded over, and Étienne went over to the pit, where his comrades informed him of the precarious state of the shaft lining: they even thought that the whole thing needed urgently replacing, which would have prevented any production for three months. He spent a long time roaming around listening to the blows of the carpenters' mallets down in the shaft. He felt his heart leap at the thought of this wound that they were forced to bandage.

At daybreak, as he was returning home, he saw the sentry on the slag-heap again. This time he was sure to be spotted. He walked on, thinking how these soldiers were taken from the ranks of the people, and then armed against the people. How easy the revolution would have been if only the army could have come out and declared itself in its favour! It would be enough if the workman or the peasant in their barracks could remember what their own origins were. This was the supreme peril, the great terror that sent shivers down bourgeois spines, the thought of a possible defection by the troops. In a couple of hours they would be swept aside, exterminated, along with all the pleasures and abominations of their iniquitous lives. Already people were saying that whole regiments had been infected by socialism. Was it true? Would justice arrive, bursting forth from the cartridges provided by the bourgeoisie? And seizing on another hope, the young man dreamed that the regiment whose garrisons guarded the pits would join the strike, would gun down each and every member of the Company indiscriminately, and at last hand over the mines to the miners.

As he felt his head spinning with such notions, he suddenly realized that he was already climbing up the slag-heap. Why shouldn't he have a chat with the soldier? That would give him an idea of what they really thought. He continued to advance, looking unconcerned, pretending to scavenge for odd pieces of timber left in the rubble. The sentry still didn't move.

'Well, comrade, it's lousy weather, isn't it!' said Étienne at last. 'I think we're going to have some snow.'

The soldier was a short young man, with very fair hair, with a pale, gentle face, covered in freckles. He looked ill at ease in his cape, like a new recruit.

'Yes, I think so, you're right,' he murmured.

And he turned his blue eyes slowly up towards the livid sky, and studied the smoky dawn, whose soot weighed down over the distant plain like so much lead.

'Aren't they fools, to stick you up there leaving you frozen to the marrow!' Étienne continued. 'Anyone would think we were expecting the Cossacks* to attack! . . . And you know what a wind there always is up here, don't you.'

The little soldier was shivering uncomplainingly. There was a little drystone cabin where old Bonnemort used to take shelter on stormy nights; but the soldier had his orders not to leave the top of the slag-heap, so he didn't move an inch, although his hands were frozen so stiff that he could no longer feel his rifle. He was one of a garrison of sixty men guarding Le Voreux; and since the harsh sentry duty came round regularly, he had nearly breathed his last up there once already, when his feet had gone lifeless with the cold. But his duty demanded it, and his passive spirit of obedience made him even more numb and unresponsive, so that he answered Étienne's questions in the stammering tones of a half-sleeping child.

Étienne tried in vain for a quarter of an hour to get him to talk politics. He said yes or no without seeming to understand; some of his comrades reckoned that their captain was a republican; as for himself, he had no notion, he didn't mind either way. If they ordered him to shoot he would shoot, to avoid being punished.

The workman listened, swayed by the hatred that the people felt for the army, hatred of these brothers whose hearts were seduced away from them merely by dressing their behinds in a pair of red trousers.

'So, what's your name then?'

'Jules.'

'And where are you from?'

'From Plogoff, over there.'

He stretched out his arm, haphazardly. It was in Brittany, that was all he could say. His small, pale face lit up, he started to laugh, as he warmed to his theme.

'I live with my mother and my sister. They're waiting for me to come back, of course. My, but that won't be a day too soon . . . When I left they came with me as far as Pont-l'Abbé. We borrowed the Lepalmecs' horse, but he nearly broke his legs coming down from Audierne. Cousin Charles met us with some sausages, but the women were too upset, we couldn't swallow a thing . . . Oh, God! Oh, God! I'm so far from home!'

Tears came to his eyes, although he continued to laugh. The barren moors of Plogoff, that wild extremity of the Raz constantly swept by storms, appeared to him dazzling with sunshine, tinted with the pink of its heather in full bloom.

'Listen,' he asked, 'if I don't get any reprimands, do you think they'll let me have a month's leave in two years' time?'

Then Étienne spoke of Provence, which he had left when he was just a lad. Day was breaking, and snowflakes started to drift through the mud-coloured sky. And at last he started to get anxious, as he noticed Jeanlin roaming around in the brambles. The boy was astonished to see Étienne up there, and waved to warn him to leave. Étienne was wondering if there was any point to his dream of fraternizing with the soldiers. It would take years and years still, he felt upset at his futile attempt, as if he had expected to succeed. But he suddenly understood the meaning of Jeanlin's signal: they were coming to change the guard; and off he went, running home to go to earth at Réquillart, his heart breaking once again in the face of certain defeat; while the lad, trotting alongside him, accused that dirty slob of a trooper of calling out the garrison to shoot at them.

At the top of the slag-heap Jules remained motionless, his eyes peering sightlessly into the falling snow. The sergeant and his men arrived, and the regulation cries were exchanged.

'Halt! Who goes there? Advance, and give the password!'

And their heavy steps could then be heard returning, ringing out firmly as if in occupied territory. Despite the growing daylight, nothing stirred in the villages, where the colliers were lying low, fuming with rage at this military regime.

CHAPTER II

FOR two days it had been snowing; then that morning it had stopped, and the whole vast white carpet was frozen solid; thus this black country with its inky roads, whose walls and trees were covered in coal-dust, was white all over, absolutely white, stretching to infinity. Beneath the snow, village Two Hundred and Forty lay flattened, as if it had been obliterated. Not a curl of smoke rose from a rooftop. The houses had no fires, they were as cold as the paving stones on the roads, and they gave off no warmth to thaw the thick blanket covering the tiles. It looked like a massive quarry of white slabs, covering the white plain, like a dead village, wrapped in a shroud. Along the roads only the passing patrols had left the muddy traces of their march.

At the Maheus', the last shovelful of coal chips had been burnt the day before; and there was no question of scavenging any more on the slag-heap during such bitter weather, when even the sparrows couldn't find a blade of grass. Alzire was at death's door, from stubbornly persisting in searching through the snow with her poor weak little hands. La Maheude had to wrap her up in a scrap of blanket, and wait for Dr Vanderhaghen to call, after going round to his house twice without being able to find him in; however, the maid had just said that her master would go to the village before nightfall, so she stood guard in front of the window, while the sick child, who had insisted on getting out of bed, sat shivering on a chair, in the illusion that it was warmer there beside the cold stove. Old Bonnemort sat opposite, his legs poorly again, and seemed to have fallen asleep. Neither Lénore nor Henri was home yet; they were out on the road combing the countryside with Jeanlin, begging for coppers. Only Maheu moved, pacing heavily back and forth in the bare room, bumping clumsily into the wall at each turn, like a bewildered animal failing to notice the bars of its cage. The oil had been used up too; but the reflections from the snow outside were so white that they made the room glow slightly, despite the fact that night had fallen.

They heard the sound of clogs, and La Levaque threw the door open brusquely, in a temper, shouting as soon as she crossed the threshold:

'So you're the one that said I was forcing my lodger to give me twenty sous every time he slept with me!'

La Maheude shrugged her shoulders.

'Leave me alone, I never said a thing . . . And anyway, who told you that?'

'They told me you said it, never mind who told me . . . and you even said that you could hear us playing our dirty games through the wall, and that the dirt was piling up in our house because I spent all my time flat on my back . . . So tell me you didn't say so, then!'

Every day fresh quarrels broke out, as a result of the women's continual gossiping. Between neighbouring households with adjoining doors there were daily disputes and reconciliations. But never before had they been at each other's throats with such bitter ill will. Since the start of the strike, their rancour had been exacerbated by hunger, and they felt the need to lash out; an argument between two women tended to finish with a bloody show-down between their menfolk.

And just at that moment Levaque arrived, dragging Bouteloup along with him by force.

'Here's our friend, let him say whether he gave my wife twenty sous to sleep with her.'

The lodger, hiding his meekness and fear behind his thick beard, protested, stammering.

'Oh, never in my life, never ever!'

With this, Levaque became threatening, raising his fist in front of Maheu's face.

'You know, I don't like that one little bit. If you've got a wife like that, you should beat her up . . . If you don't, it means that you believe what she says, doesn't it?'

'For heaven's sake!' cried Maheu, furious at the interruption to his gloomy musings, 'What the hell is all this stupid gossip about? Haven't we got enough problems? Bugger off or I'll belt you one . . . And anyway, who said it was my wife who said it?'

'Who said so? . . . It was La Pierronne who said so.'

La Maheude shrieked with laughter; and turned round to face La Levaque:

'Oh, so it was La Pierronne ... Well, I might as well tell you what she told me. If you want to know, she said you slept with both of your men together, one on top and the other underneath!'

After that, any sort of agreement was out of the question. They all took offence, the Levaques riposting with the information that La Pierronne had had more home truths to tell about the Maheus, that they had sold Catherine, and that the whole family, including even the children, was rotting away with some filthy disease that Étienne had picked up at the Volcan.

'She said that, did she, she said that!' screamed Maheu. 'All right then! I'll go and see her myself, and if she says what they say she said I'll stuff my fist in her teeth.'

He was already outside, with the Levaques in his wake to bear witness, while Bouteloup, who detested arguments, went inside on the quiet. Excited by the idea of the show-down, La Maheude, too, was on her way out, when a cry from Alzire drew her up short. She folded the ends of the blanket over the shivering body, and went back to looking out of the window, with her eyes gazing into the distance. And still the doctor didn't come!

At the door of the Pierrons', Maheu and the Levaques met Lydie, who was tramping about in the snow. The house was closed, but a ray of light was visible through a crack in the shutters: and at first the child answered their questions with embarrassment: no, her dad wasn't there, he had gone to the laundry to see old Ma Brûlé, to fetch a bundle of washing. Then she became confused, and refused to say what her mum was doing. But in the end she let it all slip out, with a sullen, vindictive laugh: her mum had thrown her out, because Monsieur Dansaert was there, and she was stopping them from talking. Dansaert had been in the village since the morning, accompanied by two gendarmes, trying to rally the workmen, putting pressure on the weak ones, announcing on all sides that if they didn't go down to Le Voreux on Monday, the Company was determined to take on workmen from Belgium. And, as night was falling, he had sent away the gendarmes,

when he saw that La Pierronne was on her own; then he had
stayed with her to drink a glass of gin, in front of a roaring
fire.

'Shh! Be quiet, this we must see!' murmured Levaque, with
a bawdy laugh. 'We'll get back to our argument later . . . Clear
off, you little bitch!'

Lydie stepped back a few paces, while he put his eye to the
crack in the shutter. He spluttered under his breath, arching
his back, and a tremor ran down his spine. Then it was La
Levaque's turn to look; but she said it was disgusting, and
clasped her stomach as if she were having an attack of dia-
rrhoea. Maheu, who had pushed her out of the way, wanted to
look too, and then declared that at least you got your money's
worth. And they started again, each taking a peep in turn, as if
it were a show. The room was sparklingly clean, and was lit by
a great fire; there were cakes on the table, with a bottle and
glasses, a right old carnival. So much so that what they saw
finally made the men see red, whereas, in normal circumstances, they would have laughed about it for six months
afterwards.

It would have been funny enough if she had merely been
lying on her back with her skirt round her neck and having
herself stuffed up till it came out of her ears. But, God
almighty! Wasn't it filthy to have it away by a roaring fire,
with a provision of biscuits to keep up her strength, when her
comrades hadn't a crust of bread or a handful of coal-dust!

'Here's Dad!' cried Lydie, and made her escape.

Pierron was calmly returning from the laundry, with his
bundle of washing over his shoulder. Maheu addressed him
directly.

'Hey there, I hear your wife said we sold Catherine and that
we all had the clap at home . . . But how about you, then, does
the gent who scrubs your wife's fanny pay you to stay away
from home?'

Pierron was dumbfounded and didn't understand a word of
it, when La Pierronne, taking fright at the sound of the
hubbub of voices, lost her senses completely and half-opened
the door, to see what was happening. They saw that she was
flushed, that her bodice was undone, and her skirt still hitched

up into her belt, while, at the back of the room, Dansaert was desperately putting his trousers back on. Then he made a run for it, terrified that the manager might get to hear of his overman's scandalous behaviour. Then all hell broke loose, with laughter and hissing and insults.

'You're always saying that other women are dirty,' La Levaque shouted at La Pierronne, 'but it's no wonder you're so clean, if you get one of the bosses to scrub you night and day!'

'Oh, yes, she can talk!' Levaque chipped in. 'Just look at this bitch who said my wife was sleeping with me and the lodger, one on top and the other underneath! . . . Oh, yes, they told me you said so.'

But La Pierronne had recovered her composure, and stood up to the flood of insults with a contemptuous air, certain of her superior wealth and beauty.

'I said what I said, so leave me alone, then! . . . What business of yours is it what I do, you're all jealous because we put some money by in the savings bank! Get along with you, whatever you say, my husband knows perfectly well why Monsieur Dansaert was here.'

And indeed Pierron defended his wife vehemently. The quarrel changed direction, as they called him the Company's whore, snout, and lapdog, and accused him of hiding away to eat all sorts of titbits which the bosses gave him in exchange for his treachery. In reply he claimed that Maheu had put threatening letters under his door, with a dagger and crossbones drawn on the paper. And, inevitably, it all finished in an indiscriminate punch-up among the men, as all the women's quarrels did, since even the gentlest among them had become enraged with hunger. Maheu and Levaque rushed at Pierron with fists flying, and they had to be prised apart. When old Ma Brûlé arrived back from the laundry, blood was pouring from her son-in-law's nose. When she was informed of the state of play, she merely remarked:

'That slob's a disgrace to all of us.'

The street became deserted again, not a shadow stained the bare whiteness of the snow, and the whole village relapsed into its usual state of deathly stillness, with everyone dying of starvation and gripped by the bitter cold.

'And the doctor?' asked Maheu, closing the door behind him.

'Didn't come,' replied La Maheude, who hadn't moved from the window.

'Little ones back?'

'No, not yet.'

Maheu started pacing heavily back and forth again from wall to wall, looking like a stunned ox. Sitting stiffly on his chair, old Bonnemort hadn't even raised his head. Alzire too was silent, trying not to shiver, to avoid upsetting them; but despite her courage in the face of suffering, she did tremble so violently on occasion that they could hear the skinny body of the sick girl shivering beneath the blanket; while with her big staring eyes she watched the lunar glow that lit the ceiling with reflections from the stark white gardens outside.

Now the house, empty of all possessions and stripped to the bone, had entered into its death agony. The canvas mattress-covers had followed the woollen stuffing to the second-hand shop; then the sheets had gone, and all their linen, anything that could be sold. One evening they had sold one of Grand-father's handkerchiefs for two sous. The poor family shed tears for every object that they had to relinquish, and La Maheude still wept at having one day had to carry off hidden in her skirt the pink cardboard box which had been a gift from her man, as if she had been carrying a child that she wanted to abandon on someone's doorstep. They were stripped bare, they had nothing to sell but their skins, not that anyone would have given a fig for this soiled and wasted commodity. So they didn't even look for anything else, they knew there was nothing left, that it was the end of everything, that they had no hope of finding a candle end, nor a piece of coal, nor even a potato; and they sat waiting to die, which angered them only for the sake of the children, for they were revolted by the gratuitous cruelty that had made the poor little girl a cripple before choking her to death.

'At last, there he is!' said La Maheude.

A dark figure went past the window. The door opened. But it wasn't Dr Vanderhaghen; they recognized the new vicar, Father Ranvier, who showed no surprise at finding the house he entered dead, with no light, no fire, and no bread. He had already left three other houses nearby, going from family to family, trying to recruit men of goodwill, just like Dansaert with his gendarmes; and he came straight to the point, with his feverish, fanatical voice.

'Why didn't you come to mass on Sunday, my children? You do yourselves wrong, only the Church can save you ... Look now, promise me that you'll come next week.'

Maheu looked at him, but then started up his heavy pacing again, without speaking a word. It was La Maheude who replied.

'Go to mass, Father, whatever for? Isn't God making fools of us all? ... Look! What harm has my little girl ever done him, and she's trembling all over with fever! Don't you think we were wretched enough, without him making her ill, when I can't even get a cup of warm tea for her?'

Then the priest, still standing there, made a long speech. He used the strike, their dreadful suffering, and the furious resentment that hunger had filled them with, to teach a lesson exalting the glory of religion, displaying all the ardour of a missionary preaching to savages. He said that the Church was on the side of the poor, that one day it would make justice triumph, and would bring down the wrath of God on the iniquities of the rich. And that day would soon dawn, for the rich had usurped the place of God, and had started ruling without God, having impiously seized power. But if the workers wanted the fruits of the earth to be fairly distributed, they should place themselves immediately in the hands of their priests, as on the death of Jesus the humble and meek had followed the apostles. What strength the Pope would have, what an army the clergy would dispose of, once they were able to take command of the innumerable masses of the workers! In a single week the wicked would be banished from the world, unworthy masters would be deposed, and they would see the true kingdom of God, with everyone rewarded according to his deserts, and universal happiness deriving from the just regulation of labour.

Listening to him La Maheude heard echoes of Étienne's voice, when he had sat up late at night during the autumn,

announcing the imminent end of all their problems. But she
had never trusted a man in a cassock.

'That's all very well, the way you tell it, Father,' she said,
'but it's only because you don't get on with the bourgeois . . .
All our other vicars used to dine with the manager, and
threaten us with hell fire as soon as we asked for bread.'

He continued his argument, speaking of the deplorable
misunderstanding that had arisen between the Church and the
people. Now in veiled phrases he attacked the city priests,
bishops, and ecclesiastical dignitaries who were bloated with
pleasure and sated with power, supporting the liberal bourgeoisie in their imbecile blindness, not realizing that it was
that same bourgeoisie that deprived them of their influence in
the world. Deliverance would come from the country priests,
who would all rise up together to re-establish the kingdom
of Christ, with the aid of the poor; he seemed already to see
himself at their head, and, straightening his bony back as if he
were an outlaw chief, or an evangelical revolutionary, his eyes
filled with such light that they lit up the dark room around
him. He was carried away by his own ardent preaching in a
spate of mystical language, which the poor folk had long since
given up trying to grasp.

'We don't need all those words,' Maheu grumbled roughly.
'You'd have done better to start by bringing us some bread.'

'Come to Mass on Sunday,' cried the priest. 'God will see to
everything!'

And off he went, entering the Levaques' house to convert
them in their turn, floating so buoyantly on the tide of his
dream of the final triumph of the Church, showing such
disdain for the facts, that he did the rounds of the villages
thus, taking no alms, walking with empty hands through this
army of people dying from starvation, seeing himself as just
another poor devil, but thinking their suffering was a spur to
salvation.

Maheu still kept pacing up and down, and nothing could be
heard above his stubborn tramping, which shook the very
flagstones. There was a noise like a rusty pulley creaking, as
old Bonnemort spat into the cold fireplace. Then the rhythm
of Maheu's steps started up again. Alzire, dazed by her fever,

had started to ramble deliriously in a low voice, laughing, believing that it was hot, and that she was out playing in the sunshine.

'Damn and blast our luck!' muttered La Maheude, after touching her cheeks. 'Now she's burning . . . I don't think the bastard's going to come now, the thugs must have stopped him from coming.'

She meant the doctor, and the Company. And yet she uttered an exclamation of joy when she saw the door open again. But her arms fell back by her sides, and she remained motionless and grim-faced.

'Good-evening,' said Étienne quietly, when he had carefully closed the door again.

He often called in like this when it was fully dark. The Maheus had learned of his hide-out on the second day. But they had kept his secret, and nobody in the village was sure what had become of the young man. This gave him a legendary aura. They still had faith in him, and mysterious rumours abounded: he would return with an army, and with trunks full of gold; and they sat still waiting devotedly for their ideal to be miraculously realized, for him to lead them forthwith into the city of justice that he had promised. Some said they had seen him sitting in a carriage with three gentlemen on the road to Marchiennes; others affirmed that he had gone to England and wouldn't be back for another two days. In the end, however, their suspicions were roused; some jokers accused him of hiding out in a wine cellar with La Mouquette to keep him warm; for they knew of this affair and took a dim view of it. And his popularity started to be eaten away by a gradual disaffection, as the numbers of the disillusioned slowly grew.

'Bloody awful weather!' he added. 'And you? Nothing new? Still going from bad to worse? . . . They tell me young Négrel's gone to Belgium to recruit in Le Borinage. Heavens above, if it's true, we're done for!'

He had been racked by a sudden shudder as he entered this dark, icy room, where he had to wait for his eyes to grow accustomed to the gloom before he could see its wretched occupants, who only showed up as darker masses among the shadows. He felt the revulsion and unease of the working man who has risen out of his class, become refined through study, and harbours further ambitions. What misery, and what a smell, and all those bodies squeezed up against each other, and the terrible pity that seized him by the throat! The sight of this agony shook him so violently that he felt at a loss for words, as he tried to persuade them to give in.

But Maheu had suddenly come to a halt in front of Étienne.

'Belgians! They'll never dare, the useless buggers! ... Let them send their Belgians down, if they want us to smash up the pits!'

Looking embarrassed, Étienne explained that they couldn't lift a finger, that the soldiers who were guarding the pits would protect the Belgian workers who went down the mine. But Maheu clenched his fists, especially angry at the idea of having their bayonets stuck in his back, as he put it. So now the colliers were no longer masters in their own house? Were they to be treated like galley-slaves, to be forced to work at gun-point? He loved his pit, and felt quite sad at not having been down for two months. So he saw red at the thought of this insult, the threat to send down foreigners in his place. Then he remembered that he had been sent his booklet by the Company, and his heart broke.

'I don't know why I should get angry,' he muttered. 'I don't belong to their dump any more ... when they've driven me away from here I can just go out and die on the roadside.'

'Give over!' said Étienne. 'If you want, they'll take your booklet back again tomorrow. They don't want to lose good workmen.'

He broke off, astonished to hear Alzire laughing quietly in her feverish delirium. He hadn't yet noticed the stiff shadow of old Bonnemort, and the cheerfulness of the sick child shattered him. This time things had gone too far, if the children were starting to die. With his voice quivering he made his decision.

'Look, it can't go on like this, we haven't got a chance ... We must give in.'

La Maheude, who had been silent and motionless until then, suddenly burst out, and shouted in his face, forgetting propriety and swearing at him like a man:

'What d'you mean, mate? Bloody hell, what right have you got to say that?'

He wanted to explain his reasons, but she wouldn't let him speak.

'Don't keep on, for Christ's sake, or I'll punch you in the face, although I'm a woman . . . So we've been at death's door for two months, I've sold all my possessions, my children have fallen ill, and nothing's going to happen, the injustice goes on as before? . . . Oh, do you know what, when I think of that, I feel sick to the very heart. No, never! I'd rather burn it all down and kill the lot of them than give up now.'

She pointed at Maheu in the darkness, with a sweeping, threatening gesture.

'Listen to me. If my man goes back down the mine, I'll wait on the road for him and spit in his face and call him a coward!'

Étienne couldn't see her, but he felt her hot breath in his face as if she were a hound at the kill; and he drew back, overcome by this furious commitment that he had caused. He found her so changed that he hardly recognized her, from being such a good woman formerly, reproaching him with his violence, saying that one should never wish for another person's death, and now at this moment refusing to listen to reason, speaking of killing people all around her. It was no longer Étienne but La Maheude who was talking politics, demanding that the bourgeoisie be swept aside, calling for the revival of the Republic and the guillotine, to rid the earth of the thieving rich, who grow fat on the toil of the starving masses.

'Yes, I could flay them alive with my own two hands . . . Perhaps you're right, and we've had enough! Our turn has come, you said it yourself . . . When I think that our fathers and grandfathers and grandfathers' fathers, and all the family before them, have suffered what we're suffering, and that our sons and our sons' sons will still keep on suffering, it drives me mad, I could grab a knife and . . . The other day we didn't go far enough. We should have razed Montsou to the ground, to the last brick. And you know what? The only thing I regret is having stopped the old man strangling the girl from La Piolaine . . . They don't care if hunger strangles my kids, do they?'

She spat out her words as if she were wielding an axe, shattering the darkness. The blocked horizon had failed to clear, and the impossible ideal was turning to poison, in the depths of her mind crazed with suffering.

'You don't understand what I mean,' Étienne managed to say, beating a retreat. 'We could come to an understanding with the Company: I know that the mines have made heavy losses, I'm sure they'd want to make some arrangement.'

'No, not on your life!' she screamed.

And, at that same moment, Lénore and Henri came back empty-handed. A gentleman had given them two sous; but, because the sister had kept kicking her brother, they had dropped the two sous in the snow; and although Jeanlin had joined in the search with them, they hadn't been able to find the money again.

'Where is Jeanlin, then?'

'He ran off, Mum, he said he was busy.'

Étienne listened, his heart breaking. Previously she would have threatened to kill them if they tried to beg. Now she sent them out on the roads herself, and she said they ought all to go out, all 10,000 miners from Montsou, taking their sticks and their knapsacks like the olden-day poor, and roam round the countryside scaring the wits out of people.

Then the feeling of anguish in the dark room deepened. The kids had come back hungry, they wanted to eat, why wasn't anyone eating? And they grumbled, mooched around sulkily, and ended up treading on the toes of their dying sister, who gave out a feeble groan. Their mother was beside herself, and smacked them, as far as she could catch them in the darkness. Then, as they cried louder and louder for bread, she burst into tears, slumped down on the floor, and sat down to embrace all three of them in a single hug, the two kids and the little invalid; and her tears flowed for a long time, in a flood of nervous relief which left her weak and washed out, stammering the same phrases twenty times over, calling for death: 'My God, why don't you take us? God, take us, have pity on us, put an end to it!' The grandfather remained as motionless as a gnarled old tree, battered by the wind and the rain, while the father marched back and forth between the chimney and the dresser, without turning his head.

But the door opened, and this time it was Dr Vander-haghen.

'Heavens!' he said. 'You won't spoil your eyesight reading by candlelight . . . Quickly now, I'm in a hurry.'

As usual, he complained, because he was exhausted with work. Luckily he had some matches, and Maheu had to light six, one after the other, holding them up, while he examined the patient. They took off the blanket they had wrapped her in, and in the flickering light they saw her shivering, as thin as a little bird dying in the snow, so frail that only her hump stood out from her bones. Yet she was smiling, with the distant smile of the dying, her eyes staring wide open, while her poor hands clutched at her hollow chest. And while her mother asked in despair what was the sense in God taking the child before the mother, when she was the only one who helped her in the house, and so clever and gentle, the doctor raised his voice angrily.

'Look! There she goes . . . She's died of hunger, your damned child. And she's not alone, I saw another one just down the road . . . You all call me out, but I can't do a thing, what you need to cure you is meat.'

Maheu had dropped the match, which was burning his fingers; and the darkness closed in again on the little corpse, which was still warm. The doctor had run off again. Étienne could hear nothing in the dark room but the sobbing of La Maheude, who kept repeating her call for death in an endless and funereal lament:

'God, it's my turn, take me now! . . . God, take my man, take the others, for pity's sake, put an end to it!'

CHAPTER III

THAT Sunday evening, when it struck eight o'clock, Souvarine was already alone in the bar of the Avantage, at his usual place, leaning his head back against the wall. There wasn't a single miner who could find two sous to buy himself a pint, and the bars had never had so few customers. So Madame

Rasseneur, with nothing to do but wait at the bar, lapsed into an irritable silence; while Rasseneur, standing in front of the cast-iron fireplace, seemed to meditate studiously on the reddish smoke rising from the coals.

Suddenly the heavy peace of the overheated rooms was interrupted by three brief taps on one of the window panes, and Souvarine turned his head to look. He got up, having recognized the signal which Étienne had already used several times to call him, when he saw from the outside that he was sitting at an empty table, smoking his cigarette. But before the mechanic had reached the door, Rasseneur had opened it; and recognizing the man he saw in front of him by the light of the window, he said:

'Are you afraid that I'll sell you down the river? . . . You can talk better in here than out on the road.'

Étienne came in. Madame Rasseneur politely offered him a pint, but he brushed it aside. The publican added:

'It didn't take long for me to guess where you're hiding. If I was a spy like your friends say I am, I would have sent the gendarmes in a week ago.'

'You don't need to make excuses,' replied the young man. 'I know you never went in for that kind of game . . . You can have different ideas and still feel respect for someone, can't you?'

And silence fell again. Souvarine had gone back to his chair, and was leaning back against the wall, with his eyes gazing dreamily at the smoke from his cigarette; but his nervous fingers were twitching with anxiety, and he ran them over his knees, missing the warm fur of Poland, who was not there that evening; and he felt an unconscious malaise, there was something lacking, although he couldn't tell just what.

Étienne sat down at the other side of the table, and finally said:

'It's tomorrow they start work again at Le Voreux. The Belgians have arrived with young Négrel.'

'Yes, they waited till nightfall before they moved them in,' muttered Rasseneur, who was still standing. 'I hope we're not going to have another massacre!'

Then, raising his voice, he went on:

'Now, you know I don't want to start another argument with you, but it's going to turn nasty in the end, if you persist any longer . . . Look! Your own story is absolutely the same as the story of your International. I met Pluchart the day before yesterday in Lille, where I had some business. It seems his set-up is falling to bits.'

He gave the details. The Association, after winning over workers the world over in a surge of propaganda, which still made the bourgeoisie shiver to think about it, was now devoured and destroyed a little more each day by internal conflicts of vanity and ambition. Since the anarchists had taken control and expelled the gradualists* of the early days, everything was collapsing; the original goal, to reform the wage system, was getting lost through the bickering of sects, and the educated cadres were losing their power to organize because of their hatred of discipline. And already one could foresee the ultimate failure of this mass rising, which for a moment had threatened to blow away the old corrupt society with a single blast.

'It's making Pluchart ill,' Rasseneur went on. 'And he's lost his voice, into the bargain. Yet he will keep on speaking, he wants to go to Paris to speak . . . and he has told me three times that our strike has had it.'

Étienne kept his eyes fixed on the floor, and let him have his say, without interrupting him. The day before, he had spoken with some comrades, and he felt blowing over him a wind of suspicion and resentment, the first signs of unpopularity, and omens of defeat. And he sat looking gloomy, although he refused to admit his discouragement to a man who had predicted that the crowd would boo him in his turn, the day when it wanted to avenge itself of some mistake.

'No doubt the strike has had it, I know that as well as Pluchart,' he went on. 'But that's not surprising. We were reluctant to accept the strike, we didn't think we were going to beat the Company . . . But people get carried away, they start hoping for all sorts of things, and when things turn nasty, they forget that it was bound to happen, they bewail their fate and they argue over it as if it was a plague sent from heaven.'

'Well then,' said Rasseneur, 'if you think the game is over, why don't you get your comrades to see reason?'

The young man stared at him.

'Listen, that's enough of that ... You've got your ideas and I've got mine. I came in here to show you that I still respect you despite everything. But I still think that even if we kill ourselves trying, our starving bodies will serve the cause of the people more than all your sensible politics ... Oh, if one of those bloody soldiers could strike me down with a bullet to the heart, what a fine way to go that would be!'

His eyes had watered as he uttered this cry, which echoed with the secret desire of the vanquished for the last refuge, where he might have been released from his torments for ever.

'Well said!' declared Madame Rasseneur, who cast her husband a glance blazing with contempt, fuelled by her radical opinions.

Souvarine, whose eyes were swimming with tears, made nervous gestures with his hands, although he seemed not to have listened. His fair, feminine face, his fine nose, and small sharp teeth took on a primitive air of mystical reverie, full of bloodthirsty visions. But he had started dreaming out loud, and responded suddenly in the middle of the conversation to a comment made by Rasseneur about the International.

'They are all cowards, there was only one man who could have turned their set-up into a terrible machine of destruction. But they'd have had to really want to, nobody has the will, and that's why the revolution will abort once again.'

He continued in disgusted tones to lament the imbecility of men, while the two others felt disturbed by these sleepwalker's confidences, this voice arising from the depths of night. In Russia, nothing was going right, he was in despair at the news which he had received. His former comrades were all turning into politicians, these famous nihilists who had made all Europe tremble; these sons of priests, these petty bourgeois or merchants, couldn't see further ahead than national liberation, they seemed to believe that killing their own tyrant would lead to the salvation of the world; and, as soon as he spoke to them of razing the old human race to the ground like a ripe cornfield, as soon as he pronounced the childish word 'republic', he felt himself misunderstood, treated as a dangerous refugee from his class, henceforth enrolled among the number of the failed princes of revolutionary cosmopolitanism. Yet his patriotic heart continued to struggle, and he repeated his favourite slogan with painful bitterness:

'A load of rubbish! . . . They'll never get anywhere, with their load of rubbish!'

Then, lowering his voice again, he repeated in bitter phrases his old dream of fraternity. He had only renounced his rank and his fortune and joined the workers in the hope of at last seeing the foundation of this new society of communal work. All his money had long since found its way into the pockets of the lads in the mining village, and he had shown himself as kind as a brother to the colliers, smiling at their suspicions, and persuading them to appreciate him as a peaceful, quiet, and conscientious workman. But despite everything, he hadn't been able to get through to them, he remained an alien, with his contempt for all bonds, his desire to remain modest, with no thought for bravado or personal enjoyment. And that very morning he had been particularly exasperated by a news item which had been in all the papers.

His voice changed, his eyes cleared and lit upon Étienne, and he addressed himself directly to him.

'Can you understand this? Some millinery workers at Marseilles who won the first prize of a hundred thousand francs in the lottery, and who immediately bought investments, declaring that they were going to live a life of idleness! . . . Yes, that's what you all want, all you French workers, you want to find some buried treasure, and then hide yourselves away and live a life of selfish idleness. You may well complain about the rich, but you don't have the courage to give to the poor the money that fortune sends you. You will never be worthy of happiness, as long as you possess anything yourselves, and your hatred of the bourgeoisie stems solely from your furious urge to become bourgeois in their place.'

Rasseneur burst out laughing, for the notion that the two workers from Marseilles should have given up their first prize seemed stupid to him. But Souvarine turned pale, and his distressed face became frightening, as he was seized by one of those righteous angers that exterminate nations. He cried:

'You will all be mown down, cast aside, scattered to the

winds. There will come a man who will annihilate your race of clowns and hedonists. And then, mark my words, look at my hands, if I could, I would seize the whole earth between my hands and shake it until it crumbled into pieces and buried you beneath the rubble.'

'Well said,' repeated Madame Rasseneur, with polite enthusiasm.

There was another silence. Then Étienne talked again of the workers from Le Borinage. He asked Souvarine for information on the measures that had been taken at Le Voreux. But the mechanic had relapsed into his own preoccupations, and hardly bothered to answer, he only knew that they were going to supply the soldiers guarding the pit with cartridges; and the nervous twitching of his fingers on his knees increased to the point where he finally realized what was missing, the soft, soothing fur of his pet rabbit.

'Where has Poland got to?' he asked.

The landlord laughed again, and looked at his wife. After a brief, embarrassed silence, he made up his mind.

'Poland? She's nice and warm.'

Since her escapade with Jeanlin, when she must have been injured, the fat rabbit's litters had all been stillborn; and so as not to feed a useless mouth, they had resigned themselves, that very day, to serve her up with boiled potatoes.

'Yes, you've already had one of her legs for dinner . . . Eh? You were licking your lips all through the meal!'

At first Souvarine failed to understand. Then he turned very pale, and clenched his teeth to fight back a wave of nausea; while, despite his stoic intentions, two large tears swelled his eyelids.

But nobody had time to notice how upset he was, for the door suddenly burst open, and Chaval appeared, pushing Catherine before him. After getting tipsy on beer and boasting in all the bars of Montsou, he had hit on the idea of coming to the Avantage to show his former friends that he wasn't afraid. He entered, saying to his mistress:

'God almighty, I swear you're going to drink a pint in there, and I'll punch anyone in the face if they give me any dirty looks!'

When Catherine saw Étienne, she stopped short, and turned dead white. And when Chaval saw him too, he grinned unpleasantly.

'Madame Rasseneur, two pints! We're toasting the return to work.'

She poured the beer, silently, for she was a woman who never refused anyone a glass of beer. Silence had fallen, neither the landlord nor the other two men had moved from their places.

'I know some people who said that I'm a snout,' Chaval continued, with an arrogant air, 'and I'm waiting for those people to try to repeat it to my face, so we can see what they mean at last.'

Nobody replied, the men turned their heads and looked absent-mindedly at the walls.

'On the one hand you have your idle buggers, and then you have those as aren't idle buggers,' he continued, speaking louder. 'I have nothing to hide, I've left Deneulin's lousy dump and I'm going back under tomorrow at Le Voreux with a dozen Belgians, that they've asked me to look after, because they respect me. And if anyone sees anything wrong in that, he's only got to say so, and we'll have a chat about it.'

Then, since every provocative statement he made was met with the same disdainful silence, he flew at Catherine.

'Will you drink, for Christ's sake! . . . Drink to the death of all the bastards who refuse to work!'

She raised her glass, but her hand trembled, so that you could hear the slight clinking of the two glasses. Now Chaval had brought out of his pocket a handful of shiny coins, which he showed off with drunken ostentation, saying that he had earned it with his own sweat, and he challenged the buggers to show as much as ten sous. He was exasperated by the attitude of his colleagues, and launched into outright insults.

'So, when it's safe and dark the moles creep out of their holes, do they? Do we have to wait till the gendarmes are asleep before we can see the bandits?'

Étienne rose to his feet, very calm, but his mind made up.

'Listen, you're getting on my nerves . . . Yes, you are a snout, your money stinks of some fresh plot, and I feel

revolted at the idea of touching your mercenary skin. But
never mind that, you take it from me, it's been clear for a long
time that there's not room here for both of us.'

Chaval clenched his fists.

'Well then, it does take a lot to get you worked up, doesn't
it, you cowardly bastard! Just you on your own, that suits me
fine! And you'll pay me for the shit that I've had from you!'

Catherine made as if to get between them, pleading with
open arms; but they didn't need to push her out of the way,
she felt that the fight had to happen, and she slowly drew back
of her own accord. She stood back against the wall, remaining
unable to speak, and paralysed with anguish, staring wide-eyed
at these two men who were about to kill each other for her
sake.

Madame Rasseneur coolly removed the beer mugs from the
bar, so they wouldn't get broken. Then she sat down on the
bench, showing no unseemly curiosity. Yet you couldn't let
two old mates tear themselves to pieces like that, and Rasseneur
stubbornly tried to intervene, but Souvarine had to take hold
of his shoulder and lead him back to the table, saying:

'It's nothing to do with you ... One of them's got to give,
the weak must give way to the strong.'

Without waiting to be attacked Chaval lashed out into the
air with his fists. He was the taller man, and loose-limbed, he
aimed a series of savage, slashing blows at Étienne's face with
both fists, one after the other, as if he had been wielding a pair
of sabres. And he kept on talking, and striking theatrical poses,
working himself up with volleys of insults.

'Ah, you bleeding swine, I'll have your nose, I will, I'll have
your nose and stuff it! ... Let's have a look at your mug, let's
see that little slut-fucking face, I'm going to mash it into
pigswill, and then we'll see if the tarts still lift up their skirts
for you.'

Étienne said nothing, but clenched his teeth, and settled
down to defend his small frame, in the regulation pose, one fist
guarding his chest and the other his face; and every time he
got a chance, he unleashed a punch like an iron spring, jabbing
fiercely at his opponent.

At first neither did the other much harm. Chaval's flailing

arms and Étienne's cautious parries didn't make for a decisive encounter. They knocked a chair over, and their heavy shoes trampled the white sand all over the stone floor. But they eventually became out of breath, and you could hear them wheezing, while their red faces shone as if lit from inside by braziers, whose flames shone out of their eyes.

'Got you,' screamed Chaval, 'a hit, on your carcass!'

And in fact his fist, swinging sideways like a scythe, had pummelled his opponent's shoulder. Étienne held back a groan of pain, and all that could be heard was a dull thud that battered his muscles. And he countered with a blow to the centre of Chaval's chest which would have split his ribs if he hadn't sidestepped with one of his typical goat-like leaps. All the same, the punch landed on his left side still hard enough to make him stagger and gasp for breath. He was furious to feel his arms going weak with the pain, and he rushed forward like a wild beast, aiming a kick at Étienne's belly, hoping to tear it open with his heel.

'Hey, mind your guts!' he stammered in a choking voice. 'I'll rip them out and throw them to the dogs!'

Étienne sidestepped the kick, so indignant at this infringement of the rules of decent fighting that he broke his silence.

'Shut up, you brute! And no feet, for Christ's sake, or I'll get a chair and knock your head off.'

Then the battle grew fiercer. Rasseneur was shocked, and was ready to try to intervene again, if his wife hadn't stopped him with a stern look; didn't two customers have the right to settle their affairs in their establishment? So Rasseneur merely placed himself in front of the hearth, for he was afraid they might tumble into the fire. Souvarine still looked untroubled, and had rolled himself a cigarette, although he had forgotten to light it. Catherine stayed motionless against the wall; but her hands rose unconsciously to clutch her waist; and she twisted and tore at her dress, in rhythmical spasms. She put all her effort into not crying, into not getting one of them killed by shouting for her favourite, and she was so desperate that she couldn't even remember which one it was she preferred.

Soon Chaval grew weary and drenched in sweat, and started lashing out at random. Despite his fury, Étienne continued to maintain his guard, parrying almost all of the punches, although one or two struck him glancingly. He had an ear split, one of Chaval's nails had gouged a strip of flesh out of his neck, and he was so feverishly hot that he too started spitting out oaths, as he thrust out with a murderous right jab. Once again, Chaval jumped to move his chest out of the line of fire; but he had lowered his head, and Étienne's fist struck him in the face, smashing into his nose and battering his eye. Blood immediately started gushing from his nostrils, while his eye swelled up, and turned blue and puffy. And the poor fellow, blinded by this red flood, dazed by the battering his head had taken, his arms milling wildly around in mid-air, walked straight into another punch right in the centre of his chest, which finished him off. There was a crack, and he fell flat on his back, collapsing like a sack of plaster being dumped on the ground.

Étienne waited.

'Get up. If you want any more, we can carry on.'

Chaval did not answer, but after lying stunned for a few seconds, started moving on the ground, stretching his limbs. He struggled painfully to his knees, and stayed bent double for a moment, plunging his hand deep into his pocket, groping for something Étienne couldn't see. Then when he had managed to stand up he rushed forward again, his throat throbbing with a savage scream.

But Catherine had seen; and despite herself a great cry came from her throat, astonishing her as it revealed a preference she hadn't been aware of herself.

'Look out! He's got a knife!'

Étienne only just had time to ward off the first thrust with his arm. The wool of his jersey was cut by the wide blade, which was held in its boxwood handle by a copper hoop. Étienne immediately grabbed hold of Chaval's wrist, and a frightening struggle ensued, for he realized that he was lost if he let go, while his opponent shook his arm violently, trying to get free to strike him again. The blade gradually dropped downwards, their stiff limbs started to ache, and twice Étienne felt the cold touch of steel against his skin; and he forced himself to make a supreme effort, screwing Chaval's wrist into such a vice-like grip that the knife fell from his open hand. They both threw themselves to the floor, but it was Étienne who picked up the knife and now it was his turn to brandish it. Pressing Chaval backwards under his knee, he threatened to slit his throat.

'Now, you bloody bastard of a traitor, come and get it!'

A dreadful voice rising from deep inside him deafened him. It came from the pit of his stomach, and throbbed like a hammer inside his head, shrieking its frenzied lust for murder, its need to taste blood. He had never felt so shaken by an attack before. Yet he wasn't drunk. And he fought down this hereditary evil, shivering desperately like a crazed lover teetering on the brink of rape. He finally brought himself under control, and threw the knife behind him, stuttering in a husky voice:

'Get up, go away!'

This time Rasseneur had rushed over, but without quite daring to get between them, in case he fell victim to a stray cut. He didn't want any murders on his premises, and he became so angry that his wife, standing upright at the bar, told him that he was getting too nervous, as usual. Souvarine, who had nearly been knifed in the leg, decided it was time to light his cigarette. Did that mean that the fight was over? Catherine stood watching, dazed at the sight of the two men, both of whom were still alive.

'Go away!' Étienne repeated. 'Go away or I'll kill you!'

Chaval stood up, used the back of his hand to wipe away the blood that was still pouring from his nose; and, with blood-streaked jaws and blackened eye, he stumbled away, furious at his defeat. Catherine walked mechanically after him. Then he stopped short, turned to face her, and spat out his hatred in a stream of vile oaths.

'Oh, no, oh no you don't, it's him you want, so you can sleep with him now, you filthy cow! And don't come near my house again if you value your bloody hide!'

He slammed the door violently. A deep silence settled on the warm room, and nothing could be heard but the crackling and spitting of the coal in the fire. The only signs of the struggle were an upturned chair and a trail of blood, whose drops were soaked up by the sand on the stone floor.

CHAPTER IV

WHEN they had left Rasseneur's, Étienne and Catherine walked on silently. A slow, chilly thaw had started, dirtying the snow without melting it. The outline of a full moon could be seen in the livid sky behind the ragged clouds billowing high above as the raging wind whipped them furiously on; and on the earth below not a breath of wind stirred; all you could hear was the water dripping from the roof and the occasional soft fall of a white lump of snow.

Étienne was embarrassed by this woman that he had suddenly acquired, and was so ill at ease that he could think of nothing to say. The idea of taking her along with him and hiding her at Réquillart seemed ridiculous. He would have liked to take her back to her parents' home in the village; but she refused, looking terrified: no, not that, anything rather than be a burden to them again after leaving them so unfairly! And neither of them said another word, and they tramped on at random down the roads which were changing into rivers of mud. At first they went down towards Le Voreux; then they turned off to the right, and passed between the slag-heap and the canal.

'But you've got to sleep somewhere,' he said at last. 'If I had a room, I'd be pleased to take you in . . .'

But a strange attack of shyness interrupted him. He remembered their past, their urgent desires of former times, and the feelings of tact and shame which had prevented them from coming together. Might he still want her? For he felt disturbed, he felt a new warmth of desire rise in his heart. The memory of the slaps which she had given him, at Gaston-Marie, excited him now, instead of filling him with resentment. And he couldn't help being surprised, as he found the idea of taking her to Réquillart becoming perfectly natural, and easy to accomplish.

'Look, you decide, where do you want me to take you? . . . Do you really detest me so much that you refuse to come along with me?'

She followed him slowly, delayed by the awkward slipping

of her clogs in the ruts; and, without looking up, she murmured:

'I've got enough trouble, God knows, without you causing me more. What good would it do us, what you're asking, now that I've got a lover and you've got a woman yourself?'

It was La Mouquette she was referring to. She thought he had taken up with her, as the rumour had been going the rounds for the last fortnight, and when he swore that it wasn't true, she shook her head, she reminded him of the evening when she had seen them kissing on the mouth.

'It's a crying shame, all that nonsense, isn't it?' he went on, under his breath, and stopped still. 'We would have got on so well together!'

She trembled slightly, and replied:

'Come on, no regrets, you haven't lost much; if you only knew what a weed I am, I've got no more flesh on me than a pat of butter, and I'm so badly made that I'll never grow into a woman, that's for sure!'

And she continued talking quite openly, blaming herself for her long-delayed puberty as if it were her fault.

For, despite the man that she had had, this diminished her, and relegated her to the ranks of the children. At least you've got an excuse, when you can have a baby.

'My poor child!' said Étienne quietly, seized by a great feeling of pity.

They were at the foot of the slag-heap, hidden in the shadow of its enormous mass. An ink-black cloud passed in front of the moon at that moment, and they could no longer see each other's faces, but their breath mingled, and their lips were drawn together, towards the kiss that they had yearned for in agony for months. But suddenly the moon reappeared, and they saw the sentry at the top of Le Voreux standing high above them on the rocks, which shone in the white light, silhouetted against the moon. And still without ever having kissed, a feeling of modesty drew them apart, that old modesty which was mingled with anger, vague distaste, and a great deal of friendship. They set off again awkwardly, trudging through ankle-deep slush.

'So you've made up your mind, you don't want to?' asked Étienne.

'No,' she said. 'You after Chaval, eh? And after you, someone else . . . No, that's disgusting, I don't enjoy it at all, so
why should I bother?'

They fell silent and walked a hundred or so paces further
without exchanging a word.

Étienne broke the silence:

'Do you at least know where you're going? I can't leave you
out alone on a night like this.'

She replied openly:

'I'm going home. Chaval's my man, there's no reason to
sleep anywhere else.'

'But he'll beat you to a pulp!'

They fell silent again. She shrugged her shoulders, resigned
to her fate. He would beat her, and when he was tired of
beating her, he'd stop: but wasn't that better than tramping
the roads like a beggar? Besides, she was getting used to
getting knocked about by him, and said, to console herself,
that eight girls out of ten were no better off than she was. And
if her sweetheart were to marry her one day, it would be really
nice of him.

Étienne and Catherine had been walking unconsciously in
the direction of Montsou, and the nearer they came, the longer
their silences grew. It was already as if they had not been
together. He found no argument to convince her, despite the
heavy sadness he felt at seeing her return to Chaval. His heart
was breaking, but he hardly had anything better to offer her;
with his life of misery and hiding, any night might be their
last if a soldier's bullet were to blow his head off. Perhaps, in
fact, it was more sensible to carry on suffering just as they
were, without tempting fate to make them suffer more. So he
led her back to her sweetheart, not looking up at her, and he
made no protest when she stopped him on the main road at
the turning to the yards, twenty metres away from Piquette's,
saying:

'Don't come any further. If he saw you, that would cause
more trouble.'

The church bells chimed eleven, the bar was closed, but
light could be seen through chinks in the shutters.

'Farewell,' she murmured.

She had held out her hand to him. He kept hold of it, and she had to wrench it free, slowly and awkwardly, in order to leave him. Without turning back, she entered by the side-door, which was on the latch. But Étienne didn't withdraw, he stood motionless on the spot, staring at the house, worried by what was going to happen inside. He strained his ears, trembling at the thought that he would hear her being beaten. The house remained dark and silent, he only saw one window light up, on the first floor, and, as that window opened and he recognized the slim figure leaning out and looking down at the road, he went closer.

Then Catherine whispered very quietly:

'He hasn't come home, I'm going to bed . . . Please go away, I beg of you!'

Étienne went away. The thaw was increasing, the roofs were running with water, and a damp sweat broke out on all the walls, fences, and murky buildings of this industrial suburb, lost in the darkness. At first he headed towards Réquillart, sick with fatigue and sadness, having only one desire, to disappear below ground, to be swallowed up by the earth. Then the thought of Le Voreux came to him, he thought of the Belgian workers who were due to go down there, of his comrades in the village exasperated by the soldiers, and determined not to tolerate foreigners in their pit. And he went back along the canal bank again, amid the piles of slush.

Just as he was passing the slag-heap again, the moon came out very brightly. He raised his eyes to look at the sky, where the clouds were racing by, lashed on by the great wind blowing high up; but they started to grow whiter, break up, and become thinner, taking on the milky transparency of troubled water as they crossed the face of the moon; and they followed each other so rapidly that the moon only stayed veiled for a few moments at a time before constantly reappearing, clear and bright.

His eyes dazzled with this pure light, Étienne averted his gaze, but stopped suddenly as he noticed something happening at the top of the slag-heap. The sentry, stiff with cold, was walking up and down now, taking twenty-five paces towards Marchiennes, then returning towards Montsou. You could see the white flash of the bayonet, above his black silhouette, which showed up clearly against the pale sky. But what caught Étienne's attention was a shadowy figure moving behind the hut where old Bonnemort used to shelter on stormy nights; it was the shadow of an animal crouching low and stalking its prey, and he immediately recognized Jeanlin, by his back, which seemed long and boneless, like a weasel's. The sentry couldn't see him, and the piratical child must have been preparing some practical joke, for he was constantly fuming against the soldiers, asking when they would be rid of these murderers that they sent out with rifles to kill people.

For a moment Étienne hesitated, wondering whether he should call out to him, in case he was about to do something stupid. The moon was hidden again; he had seen Jeanlin crouch down ready to spring, but when the moon appeared again the child was still crouching. At each turn the sentry marched up to the hut, then turned his back to it and marched off again. Then suddenly, as a cloud cast its shadow, Jeanlin jumped on to the shoulders of the soldier, with an enormous leap like a wildcat, hung on with his nails, and plunged an open knife into his throat. The horse-hair collar resisted the blade, and he had to press on the handle with both hands and put all of the weight of his body behind it. He had often cut the throats of chickens that he had caught behind some farm outbuilding. It was over so quickly that there was just one muffled cry in the darkness, as the rifle fell to the ground with a metallic clatter. The moon had already reappeared and was shining with its bright white light as before.

Étienne was struck dumb with astonishment, unable to move or to stop watching. He strangled a cry that rose at the back of his throat. The slag-heap above him was bare, no shadow now stood out against the frantic racing of the clouds. And he ran up, to find Jeanlin on all fours by the corpse, which lay flat on its back with its arms outstretched. In the snow, beneath the limpid moonlight, the red trousers and the grey greatcoat showed up starkly. Not a drop of blood had flowed, the knife was still up to its hilt in the throat.

Without pausing to reflect he lashed out furiously with his fist and felled the boy, beside the body.

'Why did you do that?' he stammered, bewildered.

Jeanlin got to his knees, and stretched forward on his hands, with his narrow spine arching like a cat's; his big ears, green eyes, and prominent jaw quivered and burned, still trembling with the thrill of his exploit.

'For Christ's sake! Why did you do that?'

'I don't know. I just felt like it.'

And he stuck at that. For three days he had felt the urge. It had been torturing him, his head had been aching, there, behind the ears, from thinking so much about it. Why should they worry, with these bloody soldiers who had come to push the colliers around in their own backyard? From the violent speeches in the forest, and the cries of death and devastation that tore through the pits, he had retained five or six words, which he kept repeating, like a child playing at revolution. And that was all he could say, no one had pushed him into doing it, it had come to him just like that, like the urge to steal onions he saw in a field.

Étienne, who was horrified by the grisly birth of this crime in the depths of a child's mind, kicked him away again, as if he were a dumb animal. He trembled to think that the garrison at Le Voreux might have heard the stifled cry of the sentry, and he stole a glance at the pit each time the moon came out. But nothing had stirred, and he bent forward, touching the hands, which were turning to ice, listening to the heart, which had stopped beating beneath the greatcoat. All you could see of the knife was its bone handle, where the gallant motto 'Love' was carved in black letters.

His eyes went from the throat to the face. Suddenly, he recognized the young soldier: it was Jules, the new recruit, who had spoken to him that morning. And he was seized by a great feeling of pity, seeing this mild, fair face, covered in freckles. The blue eyes were wide open, looking at the sky, with the staring gaze that he had seen him turn towards the horizon, seeking out his homeland. Where was this Plogoff, which appeared to him bathed in sunshine? Over there, over there. Far away the sea was roaring in the stormy darkness. The wind which passed by so high overhead had perhaps blown over his native moors. Two women stood there, the mother and the sister, holding their windswept bonnets, and they too were watching, as if they could see what their boy was doing at this moment, beyond the leagues which separated them from him. Now they would wait forever. What an abominable thing it was for poor wretches to kill each other for the sake of the rich.

But he had to dispose of the corpse, and at first Étienne thought of throwing it into the canal. But he abandoned this idea because they would be certain to find it. Then his anxiety became critical, time was pressing, what should he decide? He had a sudden inspiration: if he could carry the body to Réquillart, he could bury it away for ever.

'Come here,' he said to Jeanlin.

The boy was suspicious.

'No, you'll only hit me. And anyway, I've got business. Good-night.'

And in fact he had arranged to meet Bébert and Lydie in a hide hollowed out underneath the stack of timber at Le Voreux. It was part of a major plan, to spend the night out, to be there in case people were going to stone the Belgians and break their bones when they went down next morning.

'Listen,' Étienne repeated, 'come here, or I'll call the soldiers, and they'll cut off your head.'

And as Jeanlin consented to obey, he rolled his handkerchief into a bandage to tie round the neck of the soldier, without taking the knife out, for it was preventing the blood from flowing. The snow was melting, and there were neither bloodstains nor footprints to betray the struggle.

'Take the legs.'

Jeanlin took the legs, Étienne grabbed hold of the shoulders, after fixing the rifle on his back; and the two of them walked slowly down the slag-heap, trying not to disturb any loose rocks. Luckily the moon had gone behind a cloud. But as they walked quickly along the canal bank it came out again and shone brightly: it would be a miracle if the garrison didn't notice them. They hurried along without exchanging a word, although they were handicapped by the swaying of the corpse, and had to put it down every hundred metres. At the corner of the road to Réquillart, a noise sent shivers down their spines, and they only just had time to hide behind a wall to avoid a patrol. Further on, a man bumped into them, but he was drunk, and went off, cursing them. And when they eventually arrived at the old pit, they were covered in sweat, and so upset that their teeth were chattering.

Étienne had guessed that it would not be easy to get the soldier down the ladder well. It was terribly exhausting. First of all, Jeanlin stayed up above and slid the body down, while Étienne, holding on to the undergrowth, accompanied it, to help it past the first two landings, where there were broken rungs. Then with every ladder he had to start the same procedure, going down ahead of it and taking it in his arms; and there were thirty of these ladders, 210 metres in all, and all the time he felt the body pushing down on top of him. The rifle was digging into his spine, and he didn't want the boy to go and find the candle end, which he was jealously keeping for himself. There was no point, anyway, for the light would only have got in their way, in this narrow channel. However, when they arrived at the loading bay, out of breath, he sent the boy to get the candle. He sat down beside the body, waiting in darkness for Jeanlin to return, his heart beating furiously.

As soon as Jeanlin reappeared with the light, Étienne asked his advice, for the child had searched through these old workings, including the chinks in the rock where grown men couldn't pass. They set off again, dragging the dead man nearly a kilometre, through a labyrinth of ruined tunnels. Finally the roof got lower and they found themselves on their knees beneath a crumbling rock face, held up by some half-broken props. It was like a long chest, which made a coffin for the young soldier to lie in; they deposited the rifle by his side; then, kicking hard with their heels, they broke right through the props, taking the risk of burying themselves into the bargain. The rock face immediately started to crack, and they only just had time to crawl out on their hands and knees. When Étienne turned round, unable to resist the urge to look, the roof was still collapsing, slowly crushing the body under its enormous mass. And then there was nothing left to see but the dense mass of earth.

Once they were back home, Jeanlin stretched out on the hay

in the corner of his bandit's lair, and murmured, broken with fatigue:

'Damn! The kids will just have to wait for me, I need an hour's sleep.'

Étienne had blown out the candle, of which there was only a small scrap left. He too was aching all over, but he couldn't sleep, he was assailed by painful, nightmarish thoughts hammering away at his brain. Soon only one of them subsisted, tormenting him, and confronting him with a question which he couldn't answer: why had he not struck Chaval down when he had him at knife-point? And why had this child just slit the throat of a soldier whose name he didn't even know? His revolutionary faith was deeply shaken by his disturbing feelings over the courage it took to kill a man and when it was right to do so. Was he a coward, then? In the hay, the boy had started to snore sonorously like a drunkard, as if he had a hangover from the intoxication of the murder. And Étienne was repulsed and irritated to know that he was there, and to have to listen to him. Suddenly he shuddered, a gust of panic had blown over his face. Something seemed to brush past him as a sob arose from the depths of the earth. The image of the young soldier, lying back there with his gun by his side, underneath the rocks, sent a shiver down his spine and made his hair stand on end. It was ridiculous, but the whole mine seemed to fill with voices, he had to light the candle again, and he didn't regain his composure until he could see by its weak light that the tunnels were empty.

For another quarter of an hour he reflected, still ravaged by the same struggle, his eyes staring at the burning wick. But it started spluttering, the wick was doused, and everything was plunged in darkness. He felt himself gripped by another fit of shivering, and he could have hit Jeanlin for snoring so loudly. The boy's company became so unbearable that he ran off, tortured by a need for fresh air, hurrying along the tunnels and up the well as if he had heard a ghost hot on his heels.

Once above ground, amid the ruins of Réquillart, Étienne was at last able to breathe freely. Since he hadn't dared kill, it was for him to die; and this thought of death, which he had already intuitively entertained, became lodged in his mind, as a last hope. To die pluckily for the revolution would solve everything, it would settle his account for better or for worse, it would save him from any more worries. If his comrades attacked the Belgians, he would be in the front line, and with a bit of luck he might get shot. So his step became firmer as he went back to prowl around Le Voreux. Two o'clock struck, and a loud buzz of voices emerged from the deputies' room, where the garrison which held the pit was billeted. The disappearance of the sentry had deeply upset the garrison; they had gone to wake the captain and, after carefully examining the ground, they concluded that the sentry had deserted. And watching from the shadows, Étienne remembered what the young soldier had told him about this republican captain. Who knew whether he might not be persuaded to go over to the side of the people? The troops would point their rifles down at the ground, and that could give the signal for a massacre of the bourgeoisie. A new dream swept him away, and he no longer thought of dying; for several hours he stood with his feet in the mud, and a drizzle of melting snow dripping on his shoulders, excited by the hope that victory might still be possible.

He watched out for the Belgians until five o'clock. Then he noticed that the Company had been clever enough to house them at Le Voreux overnight. The descent was already under way, and the handful of strikers from village Two Hundred and Forty who were posted as scouts were wondering whether to warn their comrades. It was Étienne who warned them that they had been tricked, and they ran off, while he waited behind the slag-heap on the tow-path. Six o'clock struck, and the muddy sky was growing paler, in the russet light of dawn, when Father Ranvier emerged from a path, with his cassock hitched up around his skinny legs. Each Monday he went to say mass at the chapel of a convent, the other side of the pit.

'Good-morning, my friend,' he cried loudly, after taking a good look at the young man, with his fiery eyes.

But Étienne didn't answer. Far off he had seen a woman passing under the trestles of Le Voreux, and he rushed over, full of anxiety, for he thought he had recognized Catherine.

Since midnight Catherine had been wandering along the

slushy roads. When Chaval had arrived home and found her in bed, he had hit her to make her get up. He shouted at her to leave straight away by the door unless she wanted to go out through the window; and weeping, hardly clothed, her legs kicked black and blue, she had had to go downstairs, to be thrown outside with a last punch. She felt so numb at this brutal separation that she had sat down on a milestone, looking at the house, waiting patiently for him to call her back; for it couldn't be true, he must be waiting for her, he would tell her to come back up when he saw her shivering away there with no one to invite her in.

Then, after two hours, dying of cold from sitting motionless like a dog thrown out into the street, she made up her mind and left Montsou. But then she walked back again, without daring to call up from the pavement or knock on the door. At last she went off again, straight down the cobbles of the main road, deciding to go to her parents' in the village. But when she arrived there, she felt such a wave of shame that she raced past the gardens, fearing that someone might recognize her, despite the fact that everyone was fast asleep, slumbering heavily behind drawn shutters. And then she started wandering about, terrified by the slightest noise, scared stiff of being picked up and taken as a tramp to the house of ill fame in Marchiennes, the threat of which had been haunting her like a nightmare for months. Twice she stumbled into Le Voreux, took fright at the loud voices coming from the garrison, ran away breathlessly, looking over her shoulder to see if she was being pursued. The narrow lane which led to Réquillart was still full of drunken men, but she returned there in the vague hope of meeting the man she had sent packing a few hours earlier.

Chaval was intending to go down that morning; and the thought of this drew Catherine back to the pit, although she realized that it was useless to talk to him: it was all over between them. There was no longer any work at Jean-Bart, and he had sworn he would strangle her if she went back to work at Le Voreux, where he was afraid she would compromise him. So what could she do? Go somewhere else, die of starvation, or yield to every passing man who wanted to beat her into submission? She dragged her feet along the road, stumbling over the ruts with aching legs, splashed with mud right up her back. The thaw was now making the roads run with rivers of mud, but she waded in deeper and deeper, walking ceaselessly, not daring to seek out a rock to sit on.

Day dawned. Catherine had just recognized Chaval's back as he cautiously walked round the slag-heap, when she espied Bébert and Lydie, peeping out of their hiding-place under the stack of timber. They had spent the night on the look-out, without daring to go home, because Jeanlin had ordered them to wait for him; and while he slept off the aftermath of his murder at Réquillart, the two children had huddled up in each other's arms to keep warm. The wind blew between the poles of oak and chestnut, and they cuddled up close together, as if they were in some abandoned woodman's hut. Lydie didn't dare declare openly how she suffered to be treated like an under-age battered wife, nor could Bébert pluck up the courage to complain of the blows that his leader bruised his cheeks with; but when all was said and done he had gone too far, risking their lives and limbs in his crazy escapades, then refusing to share any of the spoils; and their hearts rose in revolt, and they finally got round to kissing each other, although he had forbidden them, even if they ran the risk of their absent leader coming to beat them as he had threatened. But no blows materialized, so they continued to kiss gently, without thinking of doing anything more, putting into their kisses all their growing, pent-up passion, all their latent, martyred tenderness. They had kept each other warm in this way all night long, so happy hidden in the depths of their secluded hideaway that they couldn't remember when they had ever been happier, even at the Sainte-Barbe fair, when they had had fritters to eat and wine to drink.

A sudden loud trumpeting made Catherine tremble. She looked up, and saw the garrison at Le Voreux taking up their arms. Étienne came running up, and Bébert and Lydie tumbled suddenly out of their hide. And in the distance, against the growing light of dawn, they could see a mob of men and women coming down from the village, angrily waving their arms.

CHAPTER V

ALL the entrances to Le Voreux had just been closed; and the sixty soldiers, with their rifles at their sides, were blocking the way to the only door left open, the one that led to the entrance hall by way of a narrow staircase, which gave on to the deputies' room and the changing shed. The captain had drawn his men up in two lines, with their backs to the brick wall, so that no one could attack them from behind.

At first the mob of miners from the village kept their distance. There were no more than thirty of them, and they raised their voices in harsh confusion as they tried to agree what to do.

La Maheude was the first to arrive, having hastily tied up her dishevelled hair in a kerchief; she was carrying Estelle still asleep in her arms, and repeated feverishly:

'No one must enter and no one must leave! We must trap them all inside!'

Maheu agreed, when old Mouque just at that moment arrived from Réquillart. They tried to stop him getting through. But he struggled, he said that his horses still had to eat their oats and he didn't give a stuff for the revolution. And anyway, one horse was already dead and they needed him to get it out. Étienne helped the old stableman through, and the soldiers let him go up to the pit. And a quarter of an hour later, as the mob of strikers, which had been growing gradually larger, became threatening, a wide door on the ground floor was reopened, and some men appeared, dragging the dead horse, still wrapped in the rope net, a pitiful bag of bones, which they then abandoned amid the puddles of melting snow. The crowd was so shaken that no one prevented them from going back inside and barricading the door again. For everyone had recognized the horse from its head, which was bent back stiffly against its flanks. A whispered rumour ran round the crowd.

'It's Trompette, isn't it? It's Trompette.'

And it was indeed Trompette. Since he had gone underground, he had never been able to become acclimatized. He remained listless, taking no pleasure in his work, as if he were tortured by the thought of the missing daylight. In vain Bataille, the longest-serving horse in the mine, nuzzled up to his ribs in friendly fashion, and nibbled his neck, to pass on a little of his ten years' experience of underground resignation. These caresses only aggravated Trompette's melancholy, and his skin shivered as he felt the confidences of this comrade who had grown old in the darkness; and both of them, every time they nuzzled each other in passing, seemed to be lamenting, the old one for not being able to remember, the young one for not being able to forget. In the stables they were neighbours at the same stall, and they spent their time with heads hung low, breathing into each other's faces, endlessly exchanging their reminiscences of daylight, visions of green grass, white roads, yellow light, and so on. Then when Trompette was drenched in sweat, and lay dying in agony on his bed of straw, Bataille started to nuzzle him desperately, with short sobbing sniffs. He felt him growing cold, the mine was taking away his last pleasure, this friend who had fallen from above bringing fine fresh smells reminding him of his youth in the open air. And he had broken his tether, whinnying with fear, when he realized that the other horse had stopped moving.

Mouque, meanwhile, had alerted the deputy a week before. But why should they worry about a sick horse at such a moment! These gentlemen were not keen on moving horses. But now they'd have to remove it. The day before the stableman had spent an hour tying Trompette up, with the help of two other men. They harnessed Bataille to take him to the shaft. Slowly, the old horse pulled and dragged his dead comrade through a tunnel so narrow that he had to push his way through, running the risk of skinning him; and he shook his head from side to side, distressed by the sound of the heavy body rubbing along the face of the rock on its way to the knacker's yard. At the pit bottom, when they had unharnessed him, he followed with weary eyes the preparations for raising him up, as the body was pushed on rollers, over the sump, and the net fixed underneath a cage. Finally the loaders rang their dinner bells, and he raised his neck to watch him leave, gently at first, then suddenly plunging into darkness, flying away for ever up into the heights of this black hole. Thus he remained with his neck stretched out; perhaps his flickering animal memory recalled something of the world above. But it was all over, his comrade would never see anything again, and he too, one day, would follow him up there, tied up in a miserable bundle. His legs started to tremble, the draught of air from the distant countryside stifled him; and he seemed intoxicated when he lumbered back to the stables.

In the entrance hall the colliers were downcast, looking at the corpse of Trompette. A woman said:

'At least a man can decide whether he wants to go below or not!'

But a new flood of people arrived from the village, with Levaque marching at their head, followed by La Levaque and Bouteloup, and shouting:

'Death to the Belgians! No foreigners here! Kill them, kill!'

They all rushed forwards, and Étienne had to stop them. He approached the captain, a tall thin man, hardly more than twenty-eight years old, with a desperate but resolute face; and he explained things to him, trying to win him over, and studying the effect of his words. What was the point of taking the risk of starting a useless massacre? Wasn't justice on the side of the miners? All men were brothers, they should be able to reach an agreement. When he heard the word 'republic', the captain reacted nervously. But he maintained his military bearing, and said roughly:

'Keep back! Don't force me to do my duty.'

Three times Étienne tried again. But behind him his comrades were getting impatient. The rumour spread that Monsieur Hennebeau was at the pit, and they threatened to winch him down by the neck, to see if he wanted to hew his coal himself. But it was a false rumour, only Négrel and Dansaert were there; both of them showed their faces momentarily at a window of the entrance hall: the overman held back, embarrassed since his adventure with La Pierronne, while the engineer boldly raked the crowd with his small, gleaming eyes, smiling with the cheerful contempt that he cast over all men and all things. There was a round of booing, then the two men disappeared. And in their place, only Souvarine's fair features could be seen. It happened to be his turn on duty, he hadn't left his engine for a single day since the start of the strike, and he spoke to nobody, as he had become more and more absorbed in his obsession, which seemed to gleam like a dagger from the depths of his pale eyes.

'Keep back!' the captain repeated at the top of his voice. 'I don't have to agree anything with you, I have to guard the pit, and guard it I shall ... And if you don't stop trying to push my men back, I'll have to stop you by force.'

Despite his firm voice, he had grown paler, as he felt ever more anxious, faced with this rising tide of miners. He was due to be replaced at midday; but fearing that he would not be able to hold out that long, he had just sent one of the pit boys to Montsou to ask for reinforcements.

He was answered with vociferous shouting.

'Death to the foreigners! Death to the Belgians ... We want to be masters in our own house!'

Étienne fell back, discouraged. It was all over, the only thing left to do was fight and die. So he stopped holding his comrades back, and the crowd swept forward towards the small squad. They were nearly 400 strong, as the local villages emptied and more people came running up. They were all shouting the same cry, and Maheu and Levaque said furiously to the soldiers:

'Clear off! We've got nothing against you, clear off!'

'It's got nothing to do with you,' La Maheude went on. 'Mind your own business and let us mind ours.'

And behind her La Levaque added, more violently:

'Do you want us to have to eat you alive to get through? Please be so kind as to bugger off!'

And even Lydie, who had plunged into the thick of the action with Bébert, could be heard piping up in her shrill little voice:

'Useless bunch, all in a row!'

Catherine, standing a few steps further back, watched and listened, looking bewildered at this new outbreak of violence which her bad luck had led her into yet again. Hadn't she suffered enough already? What wrong could she have done to be so hounded by misfortune? Right up to the previous day she had understood nothing of the passions aroused by the strike, thinking that, when you already have more than your fair share of being knocked about, there's no point in going out looking for more trouble; but now her heart was bursting with a need to express its hatred, she remembered what Étienne used to tell them in the evening by the fireside, she tried to hear what he was saying to the soldiers now. He was calling them his comrades, reminding them that they came from the people too, so that they should side with the people, against those who exploited their suffering.

But then a long, rippling movement passed through the crowd and an old woman rushed forward. It was old Ma Brûlé, terrifyingly thin, her neck and her arms uncovered, and she had dashed up at such a speed that strands of her grey hair had blown into her eyes and were blinding her.

'Ah, God be praised, I made it!' she stammered, fighting for breath. 'That traitor Pierron shut me up in the cellar!'

And without further ado she flew at the troops, spewing forth insults from her black mouth.

'Load of scoundrels! Load of scum! You lick your masters' boots and you only dare to fight the poor!'

Then the others joined in and the insults flew thick and fast. Some of them still cried, 'Up with the soldiers! Down the shaft with the officer!' But soon there was only one clamour: 'Down with the bastards, blast their red trousers!' But these men, who had listened unmoved, with silent, fixed expressions, to appeals for fraternity and friendly attempts to persuade them to change sides, maintained the same passive stiffness under this hail of insults. Behind them, the captain had drawn his sword; and, as the crowd moved in closer and closer, threatening to crush them against the wall, he ordered them to present bayonets. They obeyed, and a twin line of steel spikes sprang forward, pointing at the chests of the strikers.

'Oh, the bastards!' screamed old Ma Brûlé, as she fell back.

But already everyone had started to move back towards them in an intoxicated contempt of death. Some of the women rushed forward. La Maheude and La Levaque cried:

'Kill us then, kill us! We want our rights.'

Levaque, ignoring the danger of cutting himself, had

grabbed a bunch of bayonets in his hands, and he shook the three blades, pulling them towards him, in an attempt to tear them off the rifles; and he twisted them, with his strength magnified tenfold by his anger, while Bouteloup stood aside, wishing he hadn't followed his comrade, and calmly let him get on with it.

'Come on, then, let's see what you're made of,' Maheu went on. 'Come on and have a go, if you've got any guts!'

And he opened his jacket and unbuttoned his shirt, showing off his naked chest, with his hairy flesh tattooed with coal. He pushed up against the tips of the bayonets, and his terrible insolence and bravado forced the soldiers back. One of the blades had pricked his chest; this goaded him furiously and he tried to push it further in, to crack his ribs.

'Cowards, you don't dare . . . There are another ten thousand behind us. Oh yes, you can kill us, but there will be ten thousand more to kill.'

The position of the soldiers became critical, for they had received strict orders not to use their arms except as a last resort. But how could they stop these madmen from skewering themselves if they wanted to? Besides which they had less and less room for manœuvre, for they had been forced up against the wall and could retreat no further. But their little squad, a mere handful of men against the rising tide of miners, held fast, and carried out their captain's crisp orders coolly and carefully. The latter stood there, with his eyes gleaming and his lips nervously sealed, possessed by a single fear, which was to see them lose their self-restraint under the volley of insults. Already one young sergeant, a tall thin man whose sparse moustache was bristling, had started blinking with alarming nervousness. Close by him, a hardened veteran of a dozen campaigns, whose skin was worn from exposure to all kinds of hardship, had turned pale when he saw his bayonet twisted like a straw. Another, who must have been a raw recruit, fresh from ploughing the fields, went bright red every time he heard himself called a bastard or a swine. And there was no let-up in the abuse, as the miners shook their fists at them and blasted their faces with vile words, and broadsides of accusations and threats. It needed all the force of their strict instructions to keep them there, their military discipline imposing on their expressionless faces a proud but sad silence.

A clash seemed inevitable, when they saw Richomme, the deputy, whose white hair made him look like a friendly old gendarme, emerge from behind the troops, shaking with emotion. He spoke up.

'For heaven's sake, isn't this stupid! We can't let this ridiculous state of affairs continue.'

And he thrust himself between the bayonets and the miners.

'Comrades, listen to me ... You know that I'm an old workman and I've never stopped being one of you. Well then, in God's name, I promise you that if you don't obtain justice I'll go to see the bosses myself and tell them what to do ... But this is going too far, you won't get anywhere by using foul language on these decent men and trying to get your own stomachs cut open.'

They listened to him, and hesitated. But just then, unfortunately, young Négrel's sharp profile appeared overhead. He must have been afraid that they would accuse him of sending a deputy, instead of taking the risk of going himself; and he tried to speak. But his voice was drowned in such an awful tumult that he was forced simply to shrug his shoulders and leave the window again. After that, however hard Richomme begged them repeatedly in his own name to settle the dispute among friends, they rejected his arguments, and treated him with suspicion. But he persisted, and stayed in their midst.

'For heaven's sake! They can break my head open along with yours, but I'm not going to leave you, while you're still acting so foolishly!'

Étienne, whom he begged to help him get them to see reason, shrugged his shoulders in despair. It was too late, they numbered more than 500 by now. And it wasn't only the extremists who had gathered to throw out the Belgians: there were the curious onlookers, and the jokers who had come to enjoy the fun of a fight. In the middle of one group, some distance away, Zacharie and Philomène were standing watching the show, so unperturbed that they had brought the two little children, Achille and Désirée. A new crowd came flooding in from Réquillart, including Mouquet and La Mouquette: he immediately went over to see his friend Zacharie, grinning and clapping him on the shoulder; while La Mouquette trotted along excitedly at the front of the wildest group.

Meanwhile, the captain kept turning round once a minute to look down the road towards Montsou. The reinforcements that he had requested hadn't arrived, and his sixty men could hold out no longer.

Finally he thought he would risk a dramatic gesture, and he ordered his men to load their rifles in front of the crowd. The soldiers obeyed the order, but the disturbance increased, with an outburst of bravado and mockery.

Old Ma Brûlé, La Levaque, and the other women sneered:

'Look, the idle buggers are going to the range for some target practice!'

La Maheude, with Estelle's small body clinging to her breast, because the child had woken up and started crying, came so close that the sergeant asked her what she meant by dragging the poor little kid along with her.

'What the hell has it got to do with you?' she replied. 'Take a shot, if you dare.'

The men shook their heads in contempt. Not one of them imagined that anyone would shoot at them.

'There aren't any bullets in their cartridges,' said Levaque.

'Are we Cossacks?' shouted Maheu. 'You can't shoot at Frenchmen, for God's sake!'

Others repeated that, when they had fought in the Crimean War,* they hadn't been afraid of bullets. And they all continued to throw themselves at the rifles. If the soldiers had started firing at that moment the crowd would have been mown down.

La Mouquette, who was in the front row, was choking with fury at the thought that the soldiers wanted to shoot holes in the women's bodies. She had spat out her foulest oaths at them, and couldn't find any more demeaning insults, when suddenly, attacking the troops with the last and most mortally wounding weapon in her repertory, she displayed her arse under their very noses. She lifted her skirts with both hands, and thrust out her buttocks, exaggerating their enormous size and roundness.

'There you are, that's what I think of you! And it's a shame it's so clean, you dirty bastards!'

She bowed and bobbed and turned so that everyone had his share of the vision, and with every thrust that she offered, she repeated:

'One for the officer! One for the sergeant! And one for the troops!'

A gale of laughter arose, Bébert and Lydie were doubled up with laughter, and even Étienne, despite his gloomy apprehensions, applauded this impertinent show of nudity. Everyone, from the jokers to the fanatics, started to boo the soldiers, as if they had seen them bespattered with a volley of filth; only Catherine stood to one side, standing on a pile of old timbers, and kept silent, her throat choked with a rush of blood, filled with a hatred whose heat she felt rising within her.

But there was another rush at the soldiers. The captain decided to take some prisoners, to calm his men's nerves. La Mouquette jumped quickly out of their grasp, dodging between the legs of her comrades. Three miners, Levaque and two others, were snatched out of the most violent group, and kept under arrest in the deputies' room.

From the window above, Négrel and Dansaert shouted to the captain to come inside and shut himself up with them. He refused, for he sensed that these buildings, whose doors had no locks, would be taken by storm, and that if he were inside he would suffer the shame of being disarmed. Already his small band of men was straining at the bit, and they couldn't retreat from a crowd of wretches in clogs. The sixty men, with their backs to the wall and their rifles loaded, faced the crowd again.

At first there was a movement of withdrawal, and a deep silence. The strikers remained astonished at this show of strength. Then a cry arose, demanding that the prisoners be released immediately. Voices could be heard claiming that they were being stabbed to death inside the building. And without being prompted, they were all swept along by the same urgent need for revenge; they all ran over to the nearby stacks of bricks, made of clay from the local marl, and baked on site. The children lugged them out one by one, the women filled their skirts with them. Soon everyone had his own munitions at his feet, and the stoning commenced.

It was old Ma Brûlé who was the first to take up position. She cracked the bricks over her bony knees, and, first with the right hand, then with the left, she threw both halves. La Levaque almost put her shoulders out of joint, and, being fat and flabby, had to go in very close in order to hit her target, despite the pleas of Bouteloup, who dragged her back, in the hope of leading her away now that her husband was safely out of the way. All the women got excited. La Mouquette, unwilling to cover herself in blood by trying to break the bricks on her far too fleshy thighs, preferred to throw them whole. Even the children went up to the front line, and Bébert showed Lydie how to dispatch them by bowling them underarm. There was a series of muffled thuds as they landed like a storm of giant hailstones. And suddenly, amid all these furies, Catherine could be seen, her fists in the air, brandishing half-bricks herself, throwing them with all the force her small arms could muster. She couldn't have said why, but she was suffocating, and was overcome with a desire to kill. Surely it would have to stop soon, this life of blasted misery. She had had enough of being beaten and thrown out by her man, of wading like a stray dog through the mud on the road, without even being able to ask her father for a bowl of soup, for he was as starving as she was. Things had never got any better, in fact they had only got worse, for as long as she could remember; and she broke her bricks, and threw them straight ahead of her, with the one idea of sweeping all before her, her eyes so flushed with blood that she couldn't even see whose jaw she might be breaking.

Étienne, who had been standing facing the soldiers, nearly had his skull split open. His ear swelled up, and as he turned round, he was shaken to realize that the brick had been flung by Catherine's frenzied hands; and he risked his life standing there looking at her instead of moving out of range. A lot of other people stayed there out of sheer fascination for a fight, without trying to lend a hand. Mouquet commented on the throws, as if it were a coconut shy: 'Oh, good shot, there!' and 'Bad luck, try again!' He laughed and nudged Zacharie, because he was arguing with Philomène now, after smacking Achille and Désirée, who had wanted to climb up on to his back to see better. There was a whole group of spectators lining the road far into the distance. And, at the top of the hill leading to the village, old Bonnemort had just appeared, limping along on a walking stick, and then stopping motionless, silhouetted against the rust-coloured sky.

As soon as the first bricks had started flying, Richomme, the deputy, had taken up his stance again between the soldiers and the miners. He pleaded and urged alternately, heedless of the danger, so desperate that great tears were running down his cheeks. His words were lost in the din, but his large grey moustache could be seen quivering.

But the hail of bricks became harder, for the men had now followed the women's example and started throwing.

Then La Maheude noticed that Maheu was hanging back, looking unhappy. His hands were empty.

'What's up with you, then?' she cried. 'Are you going to let your comrades down and send them to prison? . . . Oh, if I didn't have this child with me, you'd see something!'

Estelle was clutching her neck and screaming, preventing her from joining old Ma Brûlé and the others. And as her man didn't seem to be paying attention to what she was saying, she used her feet to shove a pile of bricks between his legs.

'For God's sake! Will you take hold of those! Do you want me to spit in your eye in front of everyone to give you the courage to act?'

He went very red, broke the bricks, and threw them. She lashed him with her tongue, dazing and numbing him with the murderous words that she spat out behind him, crushing her daughter in her arms against her breast; and he kept moving forwards, until he found himself facing the rifles.

The small squad of soldiers almost disappeared beneath the hail of stones. Luckily they were aimed too high, and merely pitted the wall. But what could they do? The idea of turning round and going home struck the captain momentarily and turned his face purple; but by now it wasn't even possible, for they would be skinned alive if they made the slightest move. A brick had just broken the peak of his cap, and blood was dripping from his forehead. Several of his men were wounded; he realized then that they had lost patience, and that an unbridled instinct for self-preservation would soon take precedence over any orders from their superiors. The sergeant suddenly shouted, 'God almighty!' as his left shoulder was nearly dislocated, his flesh bruised by a dull blow, thwacking into him like a paddle into a pile of washing. Twice the recruit had been hit glancing blows; one of his thumbs was broken, and his right knee was smarting fiercely: would they have to put up with it much longer? A piece of brick bounced up and hit the veteran in the groin; his face went green, and he raised his rifle with his thin arms trembling. Three times the captain almost gave the order to fire. He was tortured with anguish, and for a few seconds, which seemed to last an age, he felt struggling within him all the conflicting ideas, duties, and beliefs he held as a man and a soldier. The hail of bricks increased, and he was just opening his mouth, ready to shout, 'Fire!' when the rifles went off all by themselves, first three shots, then five, then a broadside from the whole squad, and finally a single shot after a long pause, amid a deep silence.

Everyone was stupefied. They had fired.* The crowd was staggered, and remained motionless, unable to believe it as yet. But some heart-rending cries arose, while the bugle sounded the order to cease fire. And there was a frenzied panic, as they ran desperately through the mud to escape the hail of bullets like a herd of stampeding cattle.

Bébert and Lydie had collapsed on top of each other, hit by the first few shots, the little girl struck in the face, and the boy with a bullet hole beneath his left shoulder. She had been knocked flat off her feet, and lay lifeless on the ground. But with the last convulsive movements of his death agony he seized her in his arms as if he had wanted to take her again, as he had taken her in the depths of the dark hideaway where they had just spent their last night together. Then Jeanlin, who had arrived from Réquillart at that very moment, still drowsy with sleep, came hopping through the smoke, and saw him embrace his little wife, and die.

The next five shots had felled old Ma Brûlé and Richomme, the deputy. Struck in the back just as he was pleading with his comrades, he had fallen to his knees, and, slumping on to one hip, he lay on the ground gasping, his eyes full of the tears that he had wept. The old woman, with her breast blasted open, had fallen flat on her back as stiff and brittle as a bunch of firewood, spluttering a last oath as she choked in her own blood.

But then the squad's main broadside had swept over the terrain, mowing down the bystanders a hundred paces away who had come to enjoy watching the fight. Mouquet received a bullet in his mouth, which smashed him open and knocked him down at the feet of Zacharie and Philomène, whose two kids were splashed with red. At the same moment La Mouquette was hit in the stomach by two bullets. She had seen the soldiers take aim and, with an instinctive movement of generosity, had thrown herself in front of Catherine, shouting to her to watch out; she screamed out loud, and fell down backwards, knocked over by the force of the shots. Étienne ran up intending to pick her up and take her away, but she gave a sign which said that it was all over. Then she choked, without ceasing to smile at both of them, as if she was happy to see them together, now that she was going away.

It seemed to be all over; the storm of bullets had even swept as far as the fronts of the houses in the village, when the last, single shot was fired, some time after the others.

Maheu was struck right in the heart; he bent double and fell face downwards in a black, sooty puddle.

La Maheude bent down, uncomprehending.

'Hey, old man, get up. It's nothing serious, is it?'

Her hands were still encumbered with Estelle, so she had to tuck her under her arm, in order to turn her man's head towards her.

'Come on, speak up! Where does it hurt?'

His eyes were empty, and his mouth dribbled bloody foam. She understood: he was dead. Then, with her daughter stuck like a bundle under her arm, she stayed sitting in the mire, looking at her man with a bemused air.

The pit was clear. The captain had nervously removed his cap, which had been torn by a stone, and then nervously put it back on again; yet he maintained his stiff, pale demeanour, even in the face of the greatest disaster of his career, while his men reloaded their rifles with expressionless faces. The terrified faces of Négrel and Dansaert could be seen at the window of the landing-stage. Souvarine was standing behind them, his brow marked with a great frown, as if his obsession had been printed threateningly across it. On the other side of the horizon, at the edge of the plateau, Bonnemort had not moved, propped up on his walking stick with one hand, the other hand shading his eyes to help give him a better view of his family and friends being slaughtered down below. The wounded were screaming, and the dead were freezing in their broken postures, spattered with the liquid slush from the thaw, and sinking into the mud here and there between the inky patches of coal which had reappeared through the dirty shreds of melting snow. And amid these tiny little human corpses, looking so poor and wretchedly thin, lay the carcass of Trompette, a great pile of dead flesh, monstrous but tragic.

Étienne had not been killed. He was standing watching over Catherine, who had collapsed with fatigue and distress, when a vibrant voice made him start. It was Father Ranvier, who had returned from saying mass; he raised both his arms into the air and, in a prophetic fury, called down the wrath of God on the assassins. He announced the arrival of the age of justice, and the imminent extermination of the bourgeoisie by fire sent from heaven, since they had brought their crimes to a climax by having the workers and the poor of the earth massacred.

PART VII

PART VII

CHAPTER I

THE shots fired in Montsou had rung out with a formidable echo that was heard as far away as Paris. For four days all the opposition newspapers had been indignant, spreading the story of the atrocities all over their front pages: twenty-five wounded, fourteen killed including two children and three women; and there were prisoners as well: Levaque had become a sort of hero, he was reputed to have answered the examining magistrate with classical wisdom. The Emperor's government, struck to the heart by these few bullets, showed the superficial calm of a great power, without being properly aware how seriously it had been wounded. It was simply a regrettable clash, an isolated incident out there in the black country, far away from the Parisian street corners where public opinion was moulded. People would soon forget, the Company had been ordered unofficially to hush up the affair and to get the strike over with, for its persistence was irritating and threatened to disturb the social peace.

Thus on the Wednesday morning Montsou witnessed the arrival of three members of the Board. The little town, sick at heart, and hardly daring till then to rejoice in its massacre, now breathed freely and at last tasted the joys of salvation. That very day the weather had turned fine, and the sun shone bright; it was one of those sunny early February days whose warmth turns the tips of the lilac trees green. They opened up all the shutters of the offices of the Board, and the vast building seemed to spring to life again; the most encouraging rumours circulated; it appeared that the gentlemen were very affected by the catastrophe, and had rushed to open their paternal arms to the lost sheep of the mining villages. Now that the blow had been struck, doubtless more cruelly than they would have wished, they were lavish in their task as saviours, and decreed a series of excellent albeit tardy measures. First, they banished the Belgians, surrounding this extreme concession to the miners with a great deal of publicity. Then they put an end to the military occupation of the pits, which

were no longer threatened by the crushed miners. They also
ensured that nothing should be said about the sentry who had
disappeared from Le Voreux: they had searched high and low
without finding either the rifle or the corpse, and they decided
to record the soldier as a deserter, although they suspected
foul play. In everything they attempted to soften the blow of
the events, trembling with fear for the morrow and judging it
unwise to do anything that might encourage the implacable
savagery of the people, who were capable of trampling the
whole rickety framework of their ageing world into the dust.
And besides, this work of reconciliation did not prevent them
from carrying out purely administrative tasks; for Deneulin
had been seen calling on the Board, where he met Monsieur
Hennebeau. The negotiations for the purchase of Vandame
continued, and people were certain that he would accept what
these gentlemen offered him.

But what particularly stirred up the countryside were the
large yellow posters* that the members of the Board had had
pasted up all over the walls. They stated in a few lines of very
large print: 'Workers of Montsou, we do not want the errors
whose sad consequences you have witnessed over the past few
days to deprive decent and well-disposed workmen of their
livelihood. We shall therefore open all pits on Monday morning, and as soon as work has resumed we shall examine
carefully and conscientiously any problems that we may be
able to resolve. In short we will do everything in our power to
ensure that justice is done.' In one morning all 10,000 colliers
filed past these notices. No one spoke, many shook their heads,
and others walked away wearily, showing no trace of reaction
in their expressionless faces.

Until then village Two Hundred and Forty had persisted in
its fierce resistance. It was as if the blood of the comrades that
had reddened the mud at the pit blocked the way for the
others. Fewer than ten had gone back down. The men watched
balefully as Pierron and other like-minded creeps came and
went, but without offering any threatening words or actions.
They greeted the poster pasted on to the church wall with
sullen suspicion. There was no mention in it of the booklets
that had been returned: was the Company refusing to accept

them back again? The fear of reprisals, and the fraternal spirit of protest against the dismissal of the people most compromised, made them even more obstinate. It was suspicious, they'd have to wait and see, they'd go back to the pit when those gentlemen were prepared to speak out plainly. The low houses were slumped in silence, even their hunger made no impression on them now, they all felt they might as well die, now that violent death had swooped down over their rooftops.

But one house, the Maheus', remained even more dark and silent than the others, crushed under the weight of its mourning. Since she had accompanied her man to the cemetery, La Maheude hadn't relaxed for a moment. After the battle, she had let Étienne bring Catherine back home, covered in mud and half-dead; and, as she was undressing her for bed in front of the young man, she thought for a second that her daughter too had come home with a bullet in her stomach, for her shirt was covered in large bloodstains. But she soon understood, it was her menstrual flow that had broken out at last under the shock of this dreadful day. Oh yes, what good fortune that wound would bring, what a rich reward it was, to be able to spawn children that the gendarmes would immediately gun down! And she wasn't on speaking terms with Catherine any more than with Étienne. He was sleeping alongside Jeanlin now, at the risk of being arrested, for he was gripped with such repulsion at the idea of returning to the darkness of Réquillart that he preferred prison: he was shaken by a shudder, a fear of the dark, after all those deaths, a suppressed fear of the young soldier who lay sleeping under the rock back there. Besides, he dreamed of prison as a refuge amid the torment of his defeat; in fact no one even tried to find him, and he felt the hours drag by wretchedly, not knowing what to do to tire his body out. Only occasionally did La Maheude look at the two of them, Étienne and her daughter, with a resentful air, as if to ask them what they were doing in her house.

Once again they snored away *en masse*, old Bonnemort using the former bed of the two kids, who slept with Catherine now that poor little Alzire no longer dug her hump into her big sister's ribs. It was when she went to bed that the mother felt

how empty the house was, for her bed was cold and had
become too big for her. In vain she took Estelle to bed with
her to fill the gap, but that couldn't make up for her man; and
she wept soundlessly for hours on end. Then the days started
to flow by as before: still bringing no bread, and not even the
good fortune to let them die once and for all; the poor
wretches were sufficiently unlucky to pick up enough scraps
here and there to keep body and soul together. Nothing had
changed in their lives, except that her man had gone.

On the afternoon of the fifth day, Étienne, who was in
despair at the sight of this silent woman, left the room and
walked slowly down the cobbled street of the village. The
enforced idleness which weighed heavily on him spurred him
to take endless walks, swinging his arms, looking at the ground,
tortured by the same thought. He had been tramping around
like this for half an hour when he sensed from his increasing
unease that his comrades were standing in their doorways
watching him. The scant popularity that he had left had gone
up in the smoke of the shooting, he couldn't walk by a house
without feeling hostile stares following him as he passed.
When he raised his head, he saw the men standing there
threateningly, and the women holding their net curtains open
to look out of their windows at him; and, under this as yet
silent accusation, under the restrained anger of these staring
eyes, gaping with hunger and tears, he became ill at ease, and
almost forgot how to walk. And all the time, behind his back,
these sullen reproaches were growing. He became seized with
such a fear of hearing the whole village coming out screaming
their poverty at him that he went back home, trembling.

But at the Maheus' house the scene which awaited him
made him even more distressed. Old Bonnemort had remained
near the fireless chimney, stuck to his chair, since the day of
the slaughter, when two neighbours had found him alongside
his broken walking stick, lying on the ground like an old tree
struck by lightning. And while Lénore and Henri tried to
cheat their hunger by scraping away deafeningly at an old
saucepan which had had some boiled cabbage in it the day
before, La Maheude had placed Estelle on the table, stood
stiffly upright, and was threatening Catherine with her fist.

'Just let me hear you say that again, so help me God, just you dare!'

Catherine had announced her intention of returning to Le Voreux. The thought of not earning her living, of being barely tolerated by her mother, like a useless animal that did nothing but get under her feet, became daily more unbearable to her; and if she hadn't feared being badly beaten by Chaval, she would have returned on the Tuesday morning. She repeated, stammeringly:

'What do you expect us to do? We can't stay alive if we don't do anything. At least that way we'd have some bread.'

La Maheude interrupted her.

'You listen to me . . . the first one of you lot that goes back to work I shall strangle in person . . . Oh, no, that would be too much, killing the father and then going on to exploit the children! We've had enough, I'd rather see you all six feet under, like the one they've already taken.'

And her long silence exploded in a flood of words. A fine help it would be to have the bare thirty sous that Catherine would bring home, even added to the twenty sous that scoundrel Jeanlin could earn if the bosses wanted to find him something to do. Fifty sous to feed seven mouths! All the kids were able to do was sit around knocking back soup.

As for the grandfather, something must have given out in his brain when he fell, for he appeared to have become an imbecile, unless he had had his stomach turned over at seeing his comrades shot at by the soldiers.

'Isn't that so, old man, they've finished you off? It's true you've still got some strength in your arms, but you've had it, haven't you?'

Bonnemort looked at her uncomprehendingly with his dead eyes. He spent hours staring into space, he only had wit enough left to spit into the basin filled with ashes that they put down by his side for the sake of cleanliness.

'And they haven't agreed to his pension,' she went on, 'and I'm sure they'll refuse to, because of our ideas . . . No, I tell you, we've had enough of these cursed people!'

'Yes, but', Catherine said hopefully, 'on the poster they promise . . .'

'Will you shut up with your poster! ... It's written on flypaper to trap us and kill us. It's easy enough for them to act friendly now they've cut us to ribbons.'

'But Mum, in that case, where can we go? They won't let us stay in the village, surely.'

La Maheude made a vague but terrible gesture. Where could they go to? How should she know, she preferred not to think about it, it drove her crazy. They would go somewhere, somewhere else. And as the noise of the saucepan was becoming unbearable she flew at Lénore and Henri and smacked them. And Estelle, who had been crawling around on all fours, fell over and added to the chaos. Her mother shut her up with a good hiding: what a bit of luck it would have been if she had killed herself while she was about it! Then she started talking about Alzire, wishing that the others might have the same good luck. Then suddenly she burst out into a fit of sobbing, leaning her head against the wall.

Étienne simply stood there without daring to intervene. He no longer had any influence in the house, even the children shrank away from him suspiciously. But the tears of this unhappy woman broke his heart, and he murmured:

'Come on, bear up, you'll see, we'll try and get by.'

She didn't seem to hear what he said, and she carried on complaining in one endless, monotonous lament.

'Oh, misery, how can it be true? Even with all these horrors we kept going. We only had dry bread to eat but at least we were all together ... And now what's happened, God only knows! Whatever have we done to be in such sorrow, some in their graves and the rest of us only wanting to follow them? ... It's true enough that they hitched us like horses to the plough, and there was no justice in it, we just got beaten for our trouble while we made the rich get richer and we never had a hope of tasting any of the good things in life. There's no pleasure in life when you've lost your hope. Yes, it couldn't go on any longer, we needed to breathe ... And yet if we'd known! How can it be true, how can we have made ourselves so unhappy when we were only looking for justice!'

Her breast heaved with sighs and her voice choked with immense sadness.

'Then there's always some bright spark promising you things will improve if you only try harder . . . You get all excited, you suffer so much from what you've got that you ask for what you can't have. I was already daydreaming like a beast in a field, I saw a life where everyone lived in friendship, and believe me, I was floating on air, my head in the clouds. Then you fall down in the mud and you break your neck . . . It wasn't true. There weren't any of those things we dreamed of out there at all. All that there was was more suffering, oh yes, all the suffering you could ever wish for, and gunfire into the bargain!'

As Étienne listened to this lament each tear stung him with remorse. He couldn't think of anything to say that would soothe La Maheude, who was shattered by her terrible fall from the heights of her ideal. She had come back into the middle of the room; she looked into his eyes and, abandoning all pretence of politeness, directed one last cry of rage at him:

'And you, Étienne, my friend, are you so keen on going back to the pit, too, now you've thrown us all into the shit? . . . I've got no quarrel with you. But if I was you, I'd have died of sorrow already from doing so much harm to my comrades.'

He wanted to answer her, then he shrugged his shoulders in despair: what was the point of giving her reasons that she wouldn't understand because of her suffering? And his heart ached too much, he walked away, and went outside to wander helplessly around again.

There again he found himself plunged in a village which seemed to be on the look-out for him, the men at the doors, the women at the windows. As soon as he appeared, a crowd gathered, and started muttering, A storm of gossip had been brewing for four days, and now it burst in a hail of curses. Fists were raised at him, mothers pointed him out to their children with spiteful fingers, and old men spat when they saw him pass. It was the backlash following their bitter defeat, an inevitable reaction to his previous popularity, a contempt exacerbated by all the fruitless suffering they had endured. He was paying for their hunger and their deaths.

Zacharie, who had just arrived with Philomène, bumped into Étienne as he came out of the house. And he sneered unpleasantly.

'Look who's putting on weight, and getting fat on other people's carcasses!'

La Levaque had already come out on to her doorstep accompanied by Bouteloup. Referring to her own kid, Bébert, who had been gunned down by the troops, she shouted:

'Yes, there are cowards who have children killed in their place. Why don't they go and dig mine up out of the ground for me if they want to give him back to me?'

She had forgotten that her man was a prisoner, for there was no gap in the family since Bouteloup was still there. However, the memory suddenly returned, and she continued in a shrill tone:

'Get away with you! There are thugs walking around free as the air while the honest men are locked up in the dark!'

Étienne avoided her but in so doing came across La Pierronne, who had run across the gardens to catch him. She had welcomed her mother's death as a liberation, since her violence had threatened to get them hanged; and she was no more upset by the death of Pierron's little girl, that stupid goose Lydie, she was well rid of her. But she took her neighbours' side in the hope of being reconciled with them.

'And how about my mother, then? And my little girl? We saw you hiding behind them when they were mopping up bullets in your place!'

What could he do? Strangle La Pierronne and the rest of the women? Fight the whole village? Étienne was tempted for a moment. His blood boiled in his head, he felt now that his comrades were brutes, he was exasperated to find them so unintelligent and barbarous that they blamed him for the blind course of events. How stupid! But he felt disgusted at his own inability to bring them back under his sway; and all he could do was quicken his stride as if he were deaf to their insults. Soon he was in full flight, as every household booed him on his way, snapping at his heels, the whole population cursing him with voices that gradually grew thunderously loud, as their hatred overflowed. He was the exploiter, the assassin, the single cause of all their misfortunes. He left the village, pale and distraught, racing off with the mob screaming behind him. When he finally got out on to the open road, a lot of them gave up the chase; but one or two persisted, until, at the bottom of the slope, in front of the Avantage, he met another group, leaving Le Voreux.

Old Mouque and Chaval were there. Since the death of his daughter La Mouquette and his son Mouquet, the old man had carried on his duties as stableman without a word of regret or complaint. But suddenly, when he caught sight of Étienne, he shook with fury, tears streamed from his eyes, and a jumble of foul words spilled out of his mouth, blackened and bleeding from constantly chewing tobacco.

'You bastard! You sod! You rotten bugger! ... Just you wait, you'll pay for my bloody children, you will, you won't get away with it!'

He picked up a brick, broke it in half, and threw both pieces at Étienne.

'Yes, you're right, let's get rid of him!' cried Chaval, sneering delightedly, working himself into a frenzy at the idea of getting his revenge. 'It's about your turn ... Now you've got your back to the wall, you filthy slob!'

And he too rushed at Étienne, throwing stones at him. A wild clamour arose, everyone took up bricks, broke them, and threw the pieces, trying to tear him apart as they would have liked to tear the soldiers apart. He was so dazed that he gave up trying to escape, and turned to face them, trying to calm them down by reasoning with them. His former speeches, which had been welcomed so warmly in the past, sprang to his lips. He repeated the words that he had used to intoxicate them in earlier days, when he held them in the palm of his hand like an obedient flock; but the spell failed to work, and the only response he elicited was a hail of stones; he instantly received a bruising blow to the left arm, and was retreating, in mortal danger, when he found that he was hemmed in against the wall of the Avantage.

Rasseneur had been standing in his doorway for the last few moments.

'Come in,' he said simply.

Étienne hesitated, for he felt depressed at the idea of having to take refuge there.

'Come on in, and I'll go and talk to them.'

He resigned himself, and went to take shelter at the back of the room, while the landlord filled the doorway with his broad shoulders.

'Now look, my friends, let's be reasonable ... You know perfectly well that I've never led you up the garden path, don't you? I've always been for taking things calmly, and if you'd listened to me you certainly wouldn't be in the mess you're in now.'

Expressing himself with animated movements of his shoulders and his stomach, he let his natural eloquence carry all before it, flowing over his audience as soothingly as warm water. And he achieved the same success that he had in former times, regaining his old popularity effortlessly, spontaneously, as if his comrades had never booed him and called him a coward a month earlier. Voices were raised in approval: right! They agreed! That was how to talk! A thunder of applause broke out.

At the back of the room Étienne felt quite faint, his heart steeped in bitterness. He remembered Rasseneur's prediction in the forest, when he had warned him of the ingratitude of the crowd. What stupid brutality! What disgraceful contempt for the services he had rendered! It was a blind force which constantly bit the hand that fed it. And in his anger at seeing these brutes spoil their own cause, there was also despair at his own collapse, the tragic end of his own ambitions. Well, then! Was it all over already? He remembered how under the beech trees he had heard 3,000 hearts beating in time to his own. That day he had felt the power of his popularity, the people belonged to him, he had felt that he was their master. At that time he had been intoxicated with the wildest dreams: Montsou at his feet, Paris just over the horizon, Member of Parliament perhaps, crushing the bourgeoisie with his eloquence, the first speech made to Parliament by a working man. And it was all over! He awoke to find himself wretched and hated, his own people had just banished him under a hail of bricks.

Rasseneur raised his voice.

'Violence has never prospered, you can't remake the world in a day. Anyone who promises to change everything for you all at once is either a fool or a rogue!'

'Bravo! Bravo!' cried the crowd.

So who was the guilty party, then? And as Étienne asked himself this question he felt completely overwhelmed. Was he truly to blame for this misfortune, which made his heart bleed too, some dying of hunger, others slaughtered by the troops, all these women and children, reduced to skin and bone, with not a scrap to eat? He had had this dreadful vision one night earlier on, before disaster had struck. But at that time he had felt buoyed up by some superior power, which carried both him and his comrades away. Besides, he had never dictated to them, it was they who had taken him along with them, who forced him to do things he wouldn't have done without the drive of that powerful mob behind him. With each outbreak of violence, he remained dazed by the turn events had taken, for he hadn't foreseen or wanted it at all. For instance, how could he have imagined that his faithful disciples from his own village would one day want to stone him? These fanatics were lying when they accused him of having promised them a life of banqueting and idleness. And behind this justification, in the very terms that he used to try to overcome his own remorse, there flickered the vague anxiety of having lacked the qualities necessary to carry out his task, a doubt that constantly assailed him as a self-taught student. But he felt that he was running out of courage, that he no longer even had any fellow feeling for his comrades, he was afraid of them, of their enormous numbers, of the blind, irresistible force of the people, sweeping onwards like some natural disaster, ignoring all rules and theories. He had started feeling repelled by them, and had grown away from them; his refined tastes made him feel uncomfortable, as he gradually moved into a higher class with every fibre of his being.

At that moment Rasseneur's voice was drowned out by enthusiastic cheers.

'Long live Rasseneur! He's the greatest, bravo, bravo!'

The publican closed the door behind him while the crowd dispersed, and the two men looked at each other silently. Both shrugged their shoulders. In the end, they drank a pint together.

That same day there was a grand dinner at La Piolaine to

celebrate the engagement of Négrel and Cécile. The Grégoires had started polishing the dining-room and dusting the sitting-room the day before. Mélanie reigned in the kitchen, supervising the roasts and stirring the sauces whose scent wafted right up to the attic. They had decided that Francis, the coachman, would help Honorine to serve at table. The gardener's wife was going to wash up while her husband would also act as doorkeeper. This patriarchal household, usually so staid and comfortable, had never had such exciting festivities.

Everything went off perfectly. Madame Hennebeau was charming to Cécile, and she smiled at Négrel, when the Montsou notary gallantly proposed to drink to the future happiness of the young couple. Monsieur Hennebeau too was absolutely charming. The guests were struck by his cheerful manner; the rumour had got around that he was back in favour with the Board, and that he would soon be appointed an officer of the Légion d'honneur on account of his vigorous suppression of the strike. They avoided mentioning the recent events, but there was a triumphal note in their universal joy, with the dinner turning into an unofficial victory ceremony. At last they had been delivered, they could start to live and eat in peace again! Someone made a discreet allusion to the dead, whose blood had hardly dried in the mud of Le Voreux: it was a necessary lesson, and everyone felt sad about it, when the Grégoires added that now it was the duty of everyone to go out and heal the wounds in the villages. Having resumed their placid benevolence, they had now excused their good miners, already seeing them back down the mine giving a good example of age-old resignation. The Montsou establishment, now that they no longer trembled for their lives, agreed that the question of the men's wages should be prudently investigated. By the time they reached the roast, the victory was complete, when Monsieur Hennebeau read out a letter from the Archbishop, who announced that Father Ranvier was to be transferred to another parish. All the bourgeoisie of the province commented furiously on the affair of this priest who was calling the soldiers murderers. And the notary, as the dessert was served, firmly declared his free-thinking opinions.

Deneulin was there with his two daughters. Amid all this

light-heartedness he tried to hide the melancholy caused by his ruin. That very morning he had signed the sale of his Vandame concession to the Montsou Company. With his back to the wall and his throat slit, he had accepted all the demands of the Board, at last leaving them the prize that they had coveted for so long, and receiving in exchange hardly enough money to pay his creditors. And at the last moment he had even accepted as a stroke of good luck their wish to keep him on as divisional engineer, thus resigning himself to earning his living supervising the pit that had engulfed his fortune. This sounded the death knell of small family businesses, soon to be followed by the disappearance of the individual entrepreneur, gobbled up one by one by the increasingly hungry ogre of capitalism, and drowned by the rising tide of large companies. He alone was paying for the strike, and he realized well enough that they were toasting his downfall in toasting Monsieur Hennebeau's decoration; and he only felt slightly consoled at the brave front put up by Lucie and Jeanne, looking charming in their mended clothes, laughing in the face of disaster, as if their feminine charms and boyish courage made them indifferent to money.

When they went into the lounge to take coffee, Monsieur Grégoire took his cousin to one side and congratulated him on his courageous decision.

'What can you do about it? Your great mistake was to gamble away the million you got from your share of Montsou by spending it on Vandame. You had to work yourself to the bone, and then it all disappeared in this rotten business, while my share just slept in a drawer and still keeps me fed and clothed in idleness, and will continue to do so for my children and grandchildren.'

CHAPTER II

ON Sunday Étienne escaped from the village as soon as night had fallen. A very bright, star-spangled sky lit the earth with a dusky blue glow. He went down towards the canal and walked slowly, following the bank up towards Marchiennes. It was his favourite walk, a grassy tow-path two leagues long in a straight line along this geometrically neat waterway which unfurled like an endless strip of molten silver.

He never met anyone there. But that day he was annoyed to see a man coming towards him. And beneath the pale light of the stars the two lone walkers didn't recognize each other until they came face to face.

'Oh, it's you,' murmured Étienne.

Souvarine nodded his head without answering. For a moment they stopped still; then side by side they set off for Marchiennes again. Each of them seemed to continue with his own train of thought as if they were a long way apart.

'Did you see in the paper the success Pluchart had in Paris?' Étienne asked at last. 'They came out on the pavements to wait for him and they gave him a standing ovation at the end of that meeting in Belleville ... Oh, his career is made now, despite his cold. He can do what he likes from now on.'

The mechanic shrugged his shoulders. He despised smooth talkers who were really just layabouts who took up politics as people take up the law, to make a good living out of making speeches.

Étienne had now got up to Darwin.* He had read some fragments summarized and popularized in a five-sou volume; and from this half-digested reading, he formed a revolutionary idea of the fight for existence, the lean swallowing the fat, the strong people devouring the sickly bourgeoisie. But Souvarine got angry and held forth about the stupidity of the socialists who accepted Darwin, that apostle of scientific inequality, whose famous natural selection was only fit for aristocratic philosophers. However, his comrade persisted, and wanted to argue about it, so he expressed his doubts as hypotheses: say the old society no longer existed, and every last crumb had been swept away; well then, wouldn't there be a danger that the new world might grow up gradually spoiled by the same injustices, some people sick and others healthy, some more skilful and intelligent, succeeding in every venture, others stupid and lazy, becoming slaves again? And then, faced with this vision of eternal misery, the mechanic cried out in a ferocious voice that if justice was impossible in a world of men, then mankind would have to disappear. For every corrupt society there should be another massacre, until the last human being had been exterminated. And they fell silent again.

For a long time, Souvarine walked over the soft grass, with his head lowered, and so lost in his thoughts that he followed the very edge of the water with the tranquil certitude of a sleepwalker wandering along the gutter. Then he shuddered for no apparent reason, as if he had met a ghost. He raised his eyes, and his face showed up very pale; then he said quietly to his companion:

'Did I tell you how she died?'

'Who do you mean?'

'My wife, back there in Russia.'

Étienne looked puzzled, astonished to hear this usually impassive fellow speaking with a quaver in his voice and feeling a sudden need to confide, for he was usually so stoically detached from others and himself. He only knew that the wife was a mistress, and that she had been hanged in Moscow.

'Our plans hadn't worked out,' Souvarine recounted, his eyes gazing out at the long white canal, stretching out endlessly between the bluish colonnades of the tall trees. 'We had spent fourteen days at the bottom of a hole, mining the railway line; and instead of the Imperial train it was a passenger train that we blew up . . . Then they arrested Anoushka. She used to bring us our bread every evening, disguised as a peasant girl. And she was the one who lit the fuse, too, because a man might have got himself noticed . . . I followed the trial, hidden in the crowd, for six long days . . .'

His voice faltered, and he was seized with a fit of coughing as if he were going to choke.

'Twice I wanted to cry out and leap over the heads of the crowd to get to her. But what was the point? Each man we lost was one soldier less; and I could tell that she was telling me not to with her great staring eyes when she looked into mine.'

He coughed again.

'The last day, I was there, in the square . . . It was raining, and the clumsy oafs lost their nerve, they were upset by the pouring rain. It took them twenty minutes to hang the other four: the rope broke, they couldn't finish off the fourth man

... Anoushka was standing there waiting. She couldn't see me, though she was looking for me in the crowd. I got up on to a milestone and she saw me, and we kept our eyes locked on each other. Even when she was dead she kept looking at me ... I took off my hat, and waved goodbye, then I went away.'

There was another silence. The white route of the canal stretched away to infinity, they both walked on with the same soft tread, as if each had fallen back into his private world again. Over on the horizon the pale water seemed to pierce the sky with a thin sliver of light.

'It's our punishment,' Souvarine continued harshly. 'We were guilty of loving each other ... Yes, it's a good thing she's dead, a new race of heroes will spring up from her spilled blood, while I've lost all trace of cowardice in my heart ... Oh, nothing, no family, no wife, no friends! None of the things that make your hand waver the day you have to take someone else's life or lay down your own!'

Étienne had stopped still, shivering in the cool night air. He didn't argue, he simply said:

'We're a long way out, shall we go back now?'

They slowly returned towards Le Voreux, and he added, after a few more paces:

'Have you seen the new posters?'

The Company had had another lot of large yellow placards pasted up during the morning. They looked clearer and more conciliatory, seeming to promise to take back the booklets of any miners who went down the next morning. Everything would be forgotten, and even those who had most compromised themselves would be offered a pardon.

'Yes, I've seen them,' the mechanic replied.

'Well then, what do you think?'

'I think that it's all over ... They'll all go flocking back down there. You're all too cowardly.'

Étienne argued urgently to excuse his comrades: a man can be brave but a crowd that is dying of hunger has no strength. Gradually they had got back to Le Voreux; and as they reached the dark mass of the pit, he continued, he swore he would never go below again; but he forgave those who did decide to. Then, as there was a rumour that the carpenters hadn't had time to repair the lining, he wanted to find out. Was it true? Had the timber framework which formed the lining of the shaft become so swollen by the sheer weight of the earth pushing in on it that in one place the cage was scraping against the side of the shaft for at least five metres? Souvarine had fallen silent again, but he replied briefly. He had just been working there the night before, and the cage was indeed scraping against the side of the shaft; the mechanics had even had to double its speed to get it past that spot. But all the bosses greeted such observations with the same irritated phrase: it was the coal they wanted, they would reinforce the lining of the shaft later.

'Imagine if it burst!' Étienne murmured. 'Then we'd really be in it up to our necks!'

With his eyes staring at the pit, which was dimly visible in the shadows, Souvarine concluded calmly:

'If it bursts our comrades will know all about it, since you're advising them to go below.'

The Montsou clock tower was just striking nine o'clock; and as his companion said he was going home to bed, Souvarine added, without even shaking hands:

'Well then, farewell. I'm leaving.'

'What do you mean, you're leaving?'

'Yes, I've asked for my booklet, I'm going somewhere else.'

Étienne looked at him, stupefied and shocked. They had been out walking for two hours and now suddenly Souvarine told him this, and in such calm tones, whereas the mere statement of this sudden separation made his own heart sink. They had got to know each other, they had worked together and shared their problems; it always makes you feel sad when you think that you'll never see someone again.

'So, if you're going, where are you going to?'

'Out there somewhere, I don't know where.'

'But shan't I ever see you again?'

'No, I don't think so.'

They fell silent, and remained face to face for a moment without finding anything else to say to each other.

'So, farewell.'

'Farewell.'

While Étienne walked back up to the village, Souvarine turned round in the other direction and went back along the canal bank; and there, alone at last, he started walking on endlessly again, looking down at the ground, so plunged in darkness that he seemed to be no more than one of the moving shadows of the night himself. From time to time he stopped, counting the chimes of a distant clock. When midnight struck, he left the canal bank and went off towards Le Voreux.

At that hour the pit was deserted, and the only person he met was a deputy, rubbing his eyes with sleep. They weren't going to start stoking up until two o'clock, to prepare the start of work. First of all Souvarine went up to get a jacket that he said he had left in the back of a cupboard. Rolled up in this jacket were some tools, a brace fitted with a bit, a small, strong saw, a hammer and chisel. Then he left. But instead of going out through the entrance shed, he went down the narrow corridor which led to the ladder well. And with his jacket tucked under his arm, he went slowly down without a lamp, measuring the depth by counting the ladders. He knew that the cage was scraping against the fifth section of the lower part of the lining of the shaft at a depth of three hundred and seventy-four metres. When he had counted fifty-four ladders, he reached out and felt with his hand. He felt the swollen pieces of timber. That was the spot.

Then, with the skill and resolve of a good workman who has carefully prepared his plan of campaign, he set to work. He started immediately by sawing a panel out of the partition wall, so that he could reach through from the ladder well to the winding shaft. And using a series of matches, which died out almost as quickly as they flared up, he was able to assess the state of the timber lining and the recent repairs that had been carried out.

Between Valenciennes and Calais it was exceptionally difficult to sink a mine-shaft, because of the need to cross great masses of underground water lying in vast tables at the level of the lowest valleys. It was only by constructing these shaft linings, and dovetailing the panels into each other like the staves of a cask, that they managed to contain the gushing springs, and insulate the shafts from the surrounding lakes, whose dark unseen waters lapped up against their walls. When they had sunk Le Voreux, they had had to build two linings: one for the upper level, in the shifting sand and white clay which lay next to the cretaceous rock, fissured on all sides, swollen with water like a sponge; then another for the lower level, directly above the coal measures, in a yellow sand as fine as flour, flowing like a liquid. That was where they had encountered the Torrent, an underground sea, the terror of the coalfields in the Nord Department, a sea with its storms and shipwrecks, an unknown, unfathomable sea, whose black waves broke more than 300 metres underground. Normally the linings held up under the enormous pressure. The only real threat to them was from the subsidence of the neighbouring rock if it was undermined by the continuing movement of the disused tunnels as they collapsed and filled up. During this process of slippage, sometimes the rock would develop a fault, which would spread gradually to the framework, so that it eventually became warped and bulged out into the shaft; and there lay the great danger, the threat of a rock fall, followed by flooding, which would fill the pit with an avalanche of earth and a deluge of water.

Souvarine, sitting astride the opening he had made, noted that the fifth section of the lining was very badly warped. The planks had started to belly out beyond their frames; some had even come away from their grooves. There were a great many leaks, which the miners called 'pichoux', spurting from the joints, having broken through the tow and pitch lagging which sealed them. And the carpenters, who were pushed for time, had merely fixed iron brackets across the corners, so negligently that they hadn't even fitted all the screws. There was obviously a lot of movement in the sands of the Torrent behind.

Then with his brace he undid the screws in the brackets, so that a last blow would tear them all off. It was a task of appalling rashness, and a dozen times he nearly toppled over and fell 180 metres down to the bottom of the pit. He had to hang on to the oak beams, which served as guides for the cages; and hanging out over the void, he moved along the cross-pieces which joined them at regular intervals, he slid along, sat down, leant over backwards, propped himself up on a single elbow or knee, coolly defying death. A breath of wind would have knocked him over; three times he only just stopped himself from falling, but didn't bat an eyelash. First he felt around with his hands, then he got to work, only lighting a match when he lost his way amid the greasy beams. When he had undone the screws, he started on the panels themselves; and the danger increased. He had been looking for the linchpin, the panel that held the others; he attacked it fiercely, pierced it, sawed it, whittling it down to weaken its resistance; while through the holes and the cracks the water which spurted through in fine jets blinded him, and drenched him in icy spray. Two matches went out. The whole boxful had got soaked, and he was plunged into the bottomless darkness of the subterranean night.

From then on he was carried away in a frenzy. He was intoxicated by the breath of the invisible; the stark horror he felt in this hole lashed with streams of water threw him into a fury of destruction. He tore haphazardly at the lining, striking where he could, hitting out indiscriminately with his saw or his brace and bit, seized with an urge to tear it to shreds and pull it down on top of him without delay. And he put as much ferocity into it as if he had been slashing away with a knife at the skin of some hated living being. He would kill it at last, this evil beast of Le Voreux, with its ever-open jaws which had swallowed up so much human flesh! The sound of his tools rang out as he hacked away; he arched his back, he crawled, he climbed up and down, keeping his grip by some miracle amid this perpetual flurry of movement, like some night bird flitting among the beams of a belfry.

But then he calmed down, annoyed with himself. Couldn't he do things carefully? Slowly he regained his breath, then climbed back into the ladder well and blocked up the hole he had made, replacing the panel that he had cut away. That was enough, he didn't want to alert people by causing too much damage, which they would have immediately tried to repair. The beast had been cut to the heart, time would tell if it would still be alive that evening; and he had carved his initials in its flesh, the world would learn to its horror that it had not died a natural death. He took the time to wrap up his tools methodically in his jacket, and he climbed slowly back up the ladders. Then, when he had emerged unseen from the pit, he didn't even think of changing his clothes. Three o'clock struck. He stood in the road, rooted to the spot, waiting.

At the same time, Étienne, who was lying in bed awake, was disturbed by something stirring in the deep darkness of the room. He made out the soft breathing of the children, the snores of Bonnemort and La Maheude; while next to him Jeanlin was whistling one long note like a flute. He must have been dreaming, and he curled up to try to go back to sleep, when he heard the noise again. It was a mattress creaking, the surreptitious sounds of someone getting out of bed. He thought Catherine must be unwell.

'Hey, is that you? What's the matter?' he asked under his breath.

No one replied, the others just kept on snoring. For five minutes nothing moved. Then there was another creak. And this time he was certain that he wasn't mistaken, and he crossed the room, stretching out his arms in the darkness to feel for the bed opposite him. He was greatly surprised to find the girl sitting on the bed holding her breath, wide awake and on the look-out.

'Well then, why didn't you answer? Whatever are you doing?'

At last she answered:

'I'm getting up.'

'You're getting up, at this time of night!'

'Yes, I'm going back to work at the pit.'

Étienne was quite shaken, and he had to sit on the edge of the mattress, while Catherine explained her reasons to him. She suffered too much living in idleness like this, feeling reproachful gazes weighing on her all the time; she preferred to run the risk of going back there and being pushed around by Chaval; and, if her mother refused her money when she brought it home to her, well, she was old enough to sit it out and make her own soup!

'Go away, I'm going to get dressed. And don't say anything, will you, if you want to help.'

But he stayed close to her, he had taken her by the waist in a caress of sorrow mingled with pity. They were sitting pressed close up against each other on the edge of the bed, which was still warm with the night's sleep, and they could feel the heat of each other's bare skin through their nightshirts. Her first reaction had been to try to struggle free, then she had started crying very quietly, and putting her own arms round his neck now, to keep him close to her, in a desperate embrace. And they remained like that, without desiring to go further, haunted by all the unhappiness of their past, unconsummated love. Was it over for ever? Would they never dare to love each other one day, now that they were free? It would only have taken a little happiness to dispel their shame, the embarrassment that prevented them from getting together, because of all the thoughts they had that they couldn't even interpret themselves.

'Go back to bed,' she murmured. 'I don't want to put the light on, it would only wake Mum up . . . Leave me alone, it's time I went.'

He wouldn't listen to her, and he clasped her desperately, his heart drowning in an immense sadness. A need for peace and an uncontrollable need for happiness invaded him; and he pictured himself married, in a nice clean little house, with no other ambition than for the two of them to live and die together inside it. They would only need a little bread to eat; and even if there was only enough for one of them, he would give her the whole piece. What was the point of wanting anything else? Was there anything in life worth more than that?

But she disentangled her bare arms.

'Leave me alone, please.'

Then, with a spontaneous surge of affection, he whispered in her ear:

'Wait, I'm coming with you.'

And he himself was astonished at what he had said. He had sworn not to go below again, how had he come to this sudden decision, which he had blurted out without arguing about it or even dreaming about it for a second? Now he felt such a deep calm within him, such a complete healing of his doubts, that he persisted, like a man saved by chance when he has stumbled into the only door leading out of the labyrinth. And so he refused to listen to her, but she took fright, realizing that he was sacrificing himself for her, fearing the insults that would greet his arrival at the pit. He took no notice of all that, the posters promised a pardon, and that was good enough for him.

'I want to work, it's my own decision . . . Let's get dressed, and don't make any noise.'

They dressed in the darkness, taking every possible precaution. She had secretly prepared her mining clothes the night before; he took a jacket and a pair of breeches out of the cupboard; and they didn't wash, for fear of making a noise with the basin. Everyone else was still asleep, but they had to cross the narrow corridor where her mother slept. Unfortunately, as they were leaving they bumped into a chair. La Maheude awoke, and asked, still dazed with sleep:

'Hey, what's up?'

Catherine had stopped still, trembling, and squeezed Étienne's hand violently.

'It's me, don't worry,' he said. 'I can't breathe, I'm going outside for a bit of air.'

'Oh, all right.'

And La Maheude went back to sleep. Catherine hardly dared to move. But at last she went down into the living-room, divided up a slice of bread that she had set aside for herself from a loaf that a lady from Montsou had given them. Then quietly they went out and closed the door.

Souvarine had been standing waiting near the Avantage at the corner of the road. For the last half-hour he had been watching the miners going back to work, vague shapes in the shadows, moving past him with the heavy tramping of a herd of cattle. He stood there like a butcher counting them in through the slaughterhouse door; and he was surprised to see how many of them there were, for even in his most pessimistic moments he hadn't guessed that there would be so many cowards. The queue grew longer, and he grew stiff with cold, but he clenched his teeth and kept on watching, his eyes gleaming.

Then he shivered. Among this file of men, whose faces he couldn't make out, he had none the less recognized one of them from his gait. He walked up to him and stopped him.

'Where are you going?'

Étienne was taken by surprise and, instead of answering him, stammered:

'Hey! Why haven't you left yet?'

Then he admitted that he was going back to the pit. Well, yes, he had sworn he wouldn't, but that was no life for a man, to wait with his arms folded for something which might not happen for another hundred years; and besides, he had other reasons, too.

Souvarine had listened to him, trembling. He seized him by the shoulder, and pushed him back towards the village.

'Go back home, I want you to, do you hear?'

But Catherine had arrived and he recognized her too. Étienne protested, declaring that he wouldn't let anyone judge his actions. And the mechanic's eyes went from the girl to his comrade and back again; while he took a step backwards and suddenly threw up his hands in despair. When a man had a woman in his heart, the man was finished, he might as well die. Perhaps in a fleeting vision he saw himself miles away in Moscow, his mistress hanged, severing his last fleshly bond, and freeing him from all responsibility for his own life or anyone else's. He merely said:

'Go.'

Étienne waited awkwardly, trying to find the words to express his friendship, so that they would not be lost to each other for ever.

'So you're going for good, then?'

'Yes.'

'Well then, let's shake hands, my friend. *Bon voyage*, and no hard feelings.'

Souvarine held out an icy hand. Never would a friend, nor a woman . . .

'Farewell for good, this time.'

'Yes, farewell.'

And Souvarine stood motionless in the dark, following Étienne and Catherine with his eyes as they entered Le Voreux.

CHAPTER III

AT four o'clock they started to go down. Dansaert, who was presiding in person at the controller's desk in the lamp depot, registered the name of each workman who presented himself and had him given a lamp. He accepted everyone, making no comment, keeping the promise announced on the posters. None the less, when he saw Étienne and Catherine at the window, he started, and turned very red, opening his mouth ready to refuse to register them, but then contented himself with expressing his triumph sarcastically: Aha, so the mighty were fallen? So the Company had its good points after all, if the great giant-killer from Montsou was coming back asking for bread? Étienne remained silent and took his lamp up to the pit-head, followed by his tram girl.

But it was there at the landing-stage that Catherine feared the worst insults from their workmates. And sure enough as they walked in she recognized Chaval in the midst of a score of miners, waiting for an empty cage. He came up to her in a fury, when the sight of Étienne brought him to a halt. Then he decided to laugh it off, shrugging his shoulders ostentatiously. Very well, he didn't give a damn, as long as the other bloke had taken his place in bed, it was a bargain! It was up to the other man to decide if he was happy with left-overs; yet, as he made this display of disdain, he was trembling with a jealousy that made his eyes burn. Meanwhile his comrades stayed where they were, and lowered their eyes in silence. They merely looked askance at the newcomers; then, feeling depressed but without anger, they went back to staring at the mouth of the shaft, holding their lamps, shivering beneath the thin cotton fabric of their jackets, in the perpetual draughts of the great hall.

At last the cage was anchored into its keeps and the call to embark was given. Catherine and Étienne squeezed into a tub where Pierron and two hewers had already settled. Beside them, in another tub, Chaval was telling old Mouque at the top of his voice that the management had been wrong not to take advantage of the situation to get rid of the worms that were gnawing away at the foundations of the pits; but the old stableman, who had already assumed his usual dogged resignation and was no longer angry about the death of his children, merely replied with a conciliatory gesture.

The cage was unhitched and they sped down into the night. Nobody spoke. Suddenly, when they were two-thirds of the way down, there was a terrible scraping. The iron creaked and groaned, and the men were thrown against each other.

'My God!' Étienne muttered. 'Are they trying to flatten us? We'll all end up down below at this rate, with their damn lining. And they said they had mended it!'

However, the cage got past the obstacle. But now it was going down through a stormy deluge so violent that the workmen couldn't help listening anxiously to the sound of the water crashing down. There must be an awful lot of new leaks in the caulking?

They asked Pierron about it, because he had been working for some days now, but he refused to show his fear, in case it might be interpreted as an attack on the management; and he replied:

'Oh, there's no danger, it's always like that. I suppose they haven't had time to plug all the leaks.'

With the torrent still roaring down over their heads they arrived at the pit bottom, at the last loading bay, to find themselves greeted by a veritable whirlpool. None of the deputies had thought of going up by the ladders to check what was happening. The pump would do the trick, and the caulkers would see to the joints the following night. The reorganization of work in the tunnels was difficult enough already. Before letting the hewers return to their coal-faces the engineer had decided that for the first five days all the men would carry out some extremely urgent repair work. They were threatened with rock falls on all sides; the floors of the tunnels had been so affected that there were whole stretches, hundreds of metres long, where they had had to reinforce the props. So as soon as they arrived at the bottom of the shaft they formed teams of ten men, each led by a deputy; then they were sent to work at the places where there was the most damage. When everyone had disembarked they calculated that 322 miners had come below, about half the number that would be at work if the mine was functioning at full capacity.

It transpired that Chaval was a member of the team that Catherine and Étienne had joined; and it was no coincidence, for he had first hidden behind a group of comrades, then forced the deputy's hand. Their team went off to the end of the northern sector nearly three kilometres away to clear a rock fall which was blocking one of the routes along this 'Eighteen-Inch' seam. They hacked away at the fallen rocks with picks and shovels. Étienne, Chaval, and five others cleared the rubble, while Catherine and two pit boys pushed the tubs full of rock up to the incline. They hardly exchanged a word, for the deputy stayed close by. However, the two rivals for the tram girl's favours reached the point where they were ready to exchange blows. Although he grumbled all the while that he didn't want to have anything more to do with the slut, her former lover kept after her, jostling her on the sly, until her new pretender threatened to make him see stars if he didn't leave her alone. They were eyeball to eyeball, and had to be separated.

Towards eight o'clock Dansaert came round to see how the work was getting on. He seemed to be in a foul mood, and he lost his temper with the deputy: nothing was going right, each prop should have been replaced as they came to it, what a bloody awful job they were doing, as far as he could see! And off he went, announcing that he would return with the engineer. He had been waiting all morning for Négrel, and couldn't think why he was so late.

Another hour went by. The deputy had stopped them clearing the rocks to get his whole team to work at propping up the roof. Even the tram girl and the two pit boys had stopped pushing, so as to prepare the pieces of timber and bring them up to the men. At the far end of their gallery the team was in the front line, so to speak, manning a border post at the last frontier of the mine, without being able to communicate with the other coal-faces any longer. Three or four times strange noises like people stampeding in the distance made the workmen turn their heads: what was up, then? It sounded as if the tunnels were emptying, as if their comrades were going back up already and wasting no time about it. But the noise died away into a deep silence; they went back to wedging in the props, their heads ringing with the sound of the great hammer blows. At last they were able to begin clearing the rocks again, and the tubs started rolling.

As soon as she had made her first trip Catherine returned in a fright saying that there was nobody at the incline.

'I called but nobody answered. They've all buggered off.'

They were so struck with fear that all ten men threw their tools away and bolted. The idea that they could have been abandoned at the bottom of the pit so far from the loading bay made them panic. They ran off in single file, the men, pit boys, and then the tram girl, taking nothing but their lamps; and even the deputy lost his head, crying out for help, as he became more and more terrified by the silence of the deserted tunnels which stretched endlessly before them. What could have happened, for them not to meet a living soul? What accident could have carried off all their comrades like that? Their terror was increased by their ignorance of the nature of the danger, feeling themselves in the presence of a close but unknown peril.

Finally, as they reached the pit bottom their route was blocked by a torrent. They immediately had water up to their knees; and they could no longer run, they waded laboriously through the flood, thinking that every minute's delay could cost them their lives.

'God almighty! The lining's burst,' cried Étienne. 'I told you we'd never make it!'

Since the shift had gone down Pierron had been very worried to see how the deluge pouring down the shaft had increased. While he was loading tubs with two other men, he looked up; his face was drenched with great drops of water, and his ears drummed with the roaring of the tempest above him. But he trembled even more when he looked downwards and noticed that the 'bog', the ten-metre-deep sump, was filling up: the water was already spurting up from underneath and spilling over the iron plates on the floor, proving that the pump wasn't powerful enough to soak up the leaks. He heard it straining, coughing, and spluttering with the effort. So he alerted Dansaert, who swore furiously, replying that they must wait for the engineer. Twice Pierron went back to Dansaert, without getting any reaction from him other than an exasperated shrug of the shoulders. All right, so the water was rising, what could he do about it?

Mouque arrived with Bataille, leading him to work, but he had to hold him steady with both hands, for the sleepy old horse had suddenly reared up, straining his head towards the shaft, neighing for his life.

'What's up then, my fine philosophical fellow? What's upset you? . . . Oh, it's raining, is it? Come on then, it's nothing to do with you.'

But the animal was shivering from head to tail, and had to be dragged away to pull the tubs.

Almost at the same instant that Mouque and Bataille disappeared down the end of a tunnel, they heard a cracking sound up above them, followed by a prolonged clattering as something came crashing downwards. It was a piece of the lining which had come away, falling a hundred and eighty metres, bouncing off the sides of the shaft as it came down. Pierron and the other loaders managed to move out of the way as the oak plank ploughed into an empty tub. At the same time a wall of water flooded down, surging like the tide released by a burst dyke. Dansaert wanted to go up and take a look; but while he was still debating, a second piece came hurtling down. Faced with the threat of catastrophe he stopped wavering, gave the order to go back up, and sent the deputies running off to warn the men at their workings.

Then there was a terrible stampede. From every tunnel queues of workmen rushed up and besieged the cages. They crushed each other underfoot, prepared to kill in order to get up first. One or two who had thought of going up the ladder well came back down again crying that the way was already blocked. There was a wave of general panic as each cage left: that one had made it, but who could tell if the next would get through the wreckage that was starting to block the shaft? Up above, the destruction must be continuing, for they could hear a series of muffled detonations, as the timber split and burst amid the ever-increasing roar of the deluge. One of the cages was soon out of action, shattered and no longer held by the guides, which must have broken. The other was scraping so badly that the cable was surely bound to break. And there were still a hundred or so men to get out; they were all groaning, bleeding, and drowning, as they strained to hang on. Two men were killed by falling planks. A third, who had leapt on to the outside of the cage, fell from fifty metres up and disappeared into the sump.

However, Dansaert tried to keep things under control. Armed with a pick, he threatened to split the skull of the first man to disobey; and he tried to order them into a queue, shouting out that the loaders should be the last to leave, when they had sent up their comrades. But they wouldn't listen to him and he had to stop Pierron, who had turned deathly pale, from rushing off in cowardly fashion to be one of the first to escape. He had to hit him away from each cage that left. But he found that his own teeth were chattering, too; in another minute he would be engulfed: everything was falling apart up above, and pieces of timber rained murderously down, as if a river had burst its banks. There were still a few more workmen arriving when he jumped into a tub, crazed with fear, letting Pierron jump in behind him. The cage ascended.

At that moment Étienne's and Chaval's team arrived at the loading bay. They saw the cage disappear, and rushed forward; but they had to draw back as the lining finally collapsed: the shaft was blocked, the lift would not descend again. Catherine was sobbing, and Chaval was choking with the oaths he was shouting. There were nearly twenty of them, would the bloody bosses just leave them to die? Old Mouque had walked slowly up bringing Bataille with him, still holding him by the bridle, and now both the old man and the animal stood looking in stupefaction at the rapid rise of the flood. The water was already up to thigh level. Étienne said nothing, but clenched his teeth, and picked Catherine up in his arms. And all twenty of them stood dumbfounded, screaming desperately and staring up at the shaft, a gaping hole that was spewing forth a torrent of water, and which could deliver them no succour.

Once he had disembarked and regained terra firma, Dansaert noticed Négrel running to meet him. As ill luck would have it,

Madame Hennebeau had kept him at home that morning after breakfast looking through catalogues to help him choose his wedding presents for Cécile. It was ten o'clock.

'Why, whatever's happening?' he cried out from afar.

'The pit's been destroyed,' replied the overman.

And he explained the catastrophe, stammering, while the engineer shrugged his shoulders incredulously: come now, could a lining just disintegrate like that? They must be exaggerating, they'd have to go and see.

'There's nobody left below, is there?'

Dansaert lost his composure. No, nobody. At least he hoped so. Although there might be some workmen who were still on their way.

'But for Christ's sake!' said Négrel. 'Why did you leave then? You can't leave your men like that!'

He immediately gave orders to count the lamps. That morning they had issued 322; and only 255 had been returned; however, several workmen admitted that they had left theirs behind in the chaos and panic. They tried to call a roll, but it was impossible to arrive at an accurate estimate: some miners had run off, others didn't hear their names. Nobody could agree how many comrades were missing. Perhaps there were twenty of them, perhaps forty. And there was only one thing that seemed certain to the engineer: there were men left below; if you leant over the mouth of the shaft, you could hear them screaming amid the sound of the water rushing through the shattered woodwork.

Négrel's first concern was to send for Monsieur Hennebeau and try to get the pit-head shut off. But it was too late now, the colliers who had stampeded over to village Two Hundred and Forty, as if the collapsing lining were still raining down at their heels, had already spread terror through every household, and bands of women, old men, and children came running down screaming and sobbing. They had to be repulsed, and a team of supervisors was detailed to hold them back, for they would have interfered with the rescue operation. A lot of the workmen who had just come up from the pit remained there, dazed, without thinking of changing their clothes, held by a kind of fearful fascination for this terrifying hole that had nearly cost them their lives. The women milled desperately round them, pleading with them, grilling them, asking them for names. Was so and so with them? And this man? And that? They didn't know, they stammered, they shivered violently and made incoherent signs, gesticulating madly as if to ward off an abominable vision that was still haunting them. The crowd grew rapidly, and a sound of lamentation came up from all the roads nearby. And high above them, on the floor of Bonnemort's hut on top of the slag-heap, was Souvarine, who had never left the scene, and still sat looking on.

'Names, tell us their names!' cried the women, their voices choking with tears.

Négrel appeared for a moment, and said a few quick words:

'As soon as we know the names we'll tell you. But don't give up hope, we'll save them all . . . I'm going down.'

Then mute with anguish the crowd waited. And indeed with calm bravery the engineer prepared to go down. He had had the cage disconnected and ordered a bucket seat to be hooked on to the end of the cable instead; and, as he guessed that the water would affect his lamp, he got them to fix another under the seat to keep it dry.

Some white-faced deputies, openly trembling and disturbed, helped get things ready.

'You'll come down with me, Dansaert,' said Négrel curtly.

Then when he saw that nobody dared, and noticed the overman tottering, drunk with terror, he pushed him aside with a contemptuous gesture.

'No, you'd only get in my way . . . I'd rather go alone.'

He immediately climbed into the narrow seat which was swinging at the end of the cable; then, holding his lamp in one hand and clutching the signal rope in the other, he himself called out to the mechanic:

'Easy does it!'

The engine started the drums turning, and Négrel disappeared into the abyss from which the screaming of the lost wretches still rose.

At the top of the shaft, nothing was out of place. He noted that the upper lining was in good condition. As he hung in the

middle of the shaft, he swivelled round, shining his light on
the walls: the leaks between the joints were few enough not to
endanger his lamp. But 300 metres further down, when he
reached the lower section, it went out as he had foreseen, and
his seat was inundated by a surge of water. From then on he
had to rely on the lamp hooked underneath which preceded
him, lighting the darkness. And despite his temerity he paled
and shivered as he discovered the horror of the disaster. There
were odd pieces of wood still in place, while others had
collapsed along with their frames; enormous caves could be
glimpsed through the broken lining; considerable masses of
yellow sand, which was as fine as flour, flowed through the
gaps; while the waters of the Torrent, that underground sea
with its uncharted tempests and shipwrecks, spilled forth as if
a sluice had been opened. He went further down, lost in the
midst of greater and greater gulfs, battered and spun by a
maelstrom of springs, so weakly lit by the little red star that
flew downwards beneath him that he thought he saw the
streets and the crossroads of a ruined city far off in the
patterns made by the great moving shadows. It was no longer
humanly possible to do anything about it. He had one last
hope, to try to save the men whose lives were in danger. As he
got further down, he heard the screams increase; but he had to
stop, for the shaft was blocked by a mass of frames, the broken
beams of the guides, the split partitions of the ladder wells, all
tangled up with the levers that had been ripped away from the
pump, which created an impassable obstacle. As he slowly
contemplated the scene, with heavy heart, the screaming suddenly stopped. The wretches must have just fled into the
tunnels to avoid the rapidly rising waters, unless the water had
already reached their mouths.

Négrel had to resign himself and pull on the signal rope to
have himself hauled back up. Then he had himself stopped
again. He remained stupefied by the suddenness of the accident, and couldn't comprehend its cause. He wanted to find
out, and examined the few pieces of the lining which were still
in place. From a distance he had been surprised by the scores
and notches in the wood. His lamp was thoroughly soaked,
and the flame was dying out, so he reached out with his fingers

to touch, and felt quite clearly the cuts made by the saw and
the holes gouged out by the brace and bit, the whole abominable work of destruction. It was obvious that the catastrophe
had been deliberately engineered. As he looked on transfixed,
the planks cracked and crashed down complete with their
frames in a last collapse which nearly swept him away with
them. His bravery vanished, and the thought of the man who
had done the deed made his hair stand on end and filled him
with the sort of religious awe that the presence of pure evil
inspires, as if, mingled with the shadows, the man had loomed
up again like some giant to commit his gargantuan crime once
more. He cried out, and shook the signal with a feverish hand;
and it was in any case high time, for he noticed that 100
metres higher up the upper lining in its turn had started to
move: the joints were opening, losing their tow caulking, and
letting the water stream through. Now it would only be a
matter of hours before the shaft lost all its lining and collapsed.

Back in daylight, Monsieur Hennebeau was anxiously waiting for Négrel.

'Well, how is it?' he asked.

But the engineer couldn't utter a word, he was choking and
feeling faint.

'I can't believe it, it's never happened before . . . did you
examine it?'

Négrel nodded, but looked around cautiously. He refused to
explain in the presence of the handful of deputies who were
listening, and took his uncle ten metres away, but decided it
wasn't far enough and went further still, then whispering very
quietly in his ear he told him of the sabotage, how the planks
had been sawn through and perforated, cutting the throat of
the pit and condemning it to death. The manager turned white
and lowered his voice too in an instinctive need to keep silent
about the monstrous nature of any great crime or obscenity.
There was no point in being seen to tremble by the ten
thousand miners of Montsou: later they would see. And both
of them continued to whisper, shattered by the thought that a
man had had the courage to go down and hang in the middle
of the abyss, risking his life ten times over, to commit this

dastardly act. They couldn't begin to comprehend this mixture of bravado and destructive frenzy, they refused to believe the evidence as one is led to doubt the truth of some famous escapes made by prisoners who have flown from their prison cells thirty metres up.

When Monsieur Hennebeau approached the deputies his face was affected by a nervous twitch. He made a despairing gesture, and gave the order to evacuate the mine immediately. The exodus was as lugubrious as a funeral procession; the men glanced behind them in silence as they abandoned the great brick structures, which were still standing, but deserted and doomed.

And as the manager and the engineer came down last from the landing-stage the crowd met them with an obstinately repeated clamour.

'Names! Names! We want names!'

Now La Maheude was there with the other women. She remembered the sound she had heard in the night, her daughter and the lodger must have gone off together, they must surely have been left below; and after crying that it served them right, that they deserved to die down there, the heartless cowards, she had run to the mine, shivering with anguish. Moreover she dared doubt no longer, as she was soon informed by her neighbours' discussion of the names. Yes, it was true, Catherine was there, Étienne too, a comrade had seen them. But as for the others there was no agreement. No not him, but perhaps the other man was, maybe Chaval, yet a pit boy swore he had come up with him. Although La Levaque and La Pierronne had no one missing from their families, they agitated as fiercely as the others, and lamented as loudly. Zacharie had been one of the first to emerge, and despite his air of unconcern he had wept as he embraced his wife and his mother; and keeping close to the latter's side he shivered as much as she did, displaying an unexpected upsurge of tender feelings for his sister, refusing to believe she was down there until it was officially confirmed by the bosses.

'Names! Names! The names, for God's sake!'

Négrel said loudly and nervously to the supervisors:

'For heaven's sake get them to shut up! It's tragic enough as it is. We don't know any names.'

Two hours had already gone by. In the first wave of panic nobody had thought of the other shaft, the old shaft at Réquillart. Monsieur Hennebeau announced that they would make a rescue attempt over there, when a rumour went round: five workmen had in fact just escaped from the flooded mine by climbing up the rickety ladders of the old, disused ladder well; they said old Mouque was one of them, which caused a surprise because nobody thought he had gone below. But what the five escapees had to tell increased everyone's sorrow: fifteen comrades had been unable to follow them, having lost their way and been walled up by a rock fall, and it was impossible to save them for Réquillart was already under ten metres of water. They knew all the names, and the air was thick with the wailing of a slaughtered people.

'Do shut them up!' Négrel repeated. 'And get them to move away! Yes, I mean it, a hundred metres away! It's dangerous, push them back, push them back.'

They had to struggle to get the poor wretches to move. They thought that they were being sent away to hide the number of deaths or that there were other dark secrets; and the deputies had to explain that the shaft would swallow up the whole mine as it collapsed. They were transfixed and fell silent at this news and they finally allowed the deputies to push them back step by step; but the number of guards keeping them at bay had to be doubled; for people were fascinated in spite of themselves and kept trying to come back. A thousand people were milling around on the road, and more were running up from every village, even from Montsou itself. And up there on top of the slag-heap the fair-haired man with the girlish face kept smoking cigarettes to calm his nerves, but never once turned his pale eyes away from the pit.

Then the long wait started. It was midday and nobody had eaten but nobody would leave. Rust-coloured clouds drifted slowly over the misty, dirty grey sky. Behind Rasseneur's hedge a big dog was barking furiously and incessantly, upset by the almost animal agitation of the crowd. And this crowd had gradually spread on to the neighbouring land and created a circle around the pit a hundred metres away. Le Voreux seemed to rise up from the centre of this great hole, uninhabited, soundless, barren; the windows and doors still hung open, revealing the abandoned interior; a ginger cat which had been left behind, scenting disaster in the solitude, jumped off a staircase and disappeared. The generator furnaces must still be hot, for some small puffs of smoke still drifted out of the tall brick chimney up towards the sombre clouds; while the weather-cock on the headgear, squeaking in the wind with a piercing little shriek, was the only melancholy voice to emerge from these great buildings which had just been sentenced to death.

By two o'clock still nothing had moved; Monsieur Henne-beau, Négrel, and other engineers who had rushed to the site formed a group of frock coats and black hats in front of the crowd, and they weren't going to leave either, though their legs were shaking with fatigue, and they were sick and feverish at the thought of standing helplessly by in the face of such a disaster, whispering only the occasional word, as if they were at the bedside of a dying man. The last pieces of the upper lining must be collapsing now, for they could hear the echo of a series of violent crashes, and the erratic sound of objects tumbling endlessly downwards, followed by long periods of silence. The wound was gaping wider and wider: the avalanche had started down below and was rising up ever nearer to the surface. Négrel was seized with a fit of nervous impatience, he wanted to see what was happening, and he was moving in alone towards the terrifying void when someone grabbed him by the shoulders. What was the use? He couldn't do anything useful. And yet someone else, an old miner, got past the guards, and rushed over to the pit-head; but then he reappeared quite calmly, he had gone to fetch his clogs.

Three o'clock struck. Still nothing. The crowd had been soaked by a shower but didn't budge an inch. Rasseneur's dog had started barking again. And it was not until twenty minutes past three that the earth was shaken by a first tremor. Le Voreux shook, but stood its ground solidly, and nothing fell. But a second tremor followed, and a long cry burst from every mouth: the pitch-roofed screening shed tottered twice, then came tumbling down with a mighty crash. Under the enormous pressure the iron struts split and splintered so violently that they sent out showers of sparks. From then on the earth shook continuously, and the shock waves followed each other in quick succession, as the mine started subsiding below them with a roaring noise like a volcano erupting. In the distance the dog had stopped barking, and had started whining plaintively, as if announcing the tremors to come, and not only the women and children, but the whole community of onlookers, were unable to repress a clamour of distress as each wave rocked them on their feet. In less than ten minutes the slate roof of the headgear collapsed, and the entrance hall and the engine-room were split asunder, opening up a great, yawning chasm. Then the noise died down, the collapse was halted, and there was another long silence.

For an hour Le Voreux stayed like this, as if it had been sacked by an army of barbarians. Nobody cried; the spectators had widened their circle, but remained looking on. Under the pile of beams from the screening shed could be seen the shattered tipplers and the crushed and mangled hoppers. But it was above all at the landing-stage that the most debris had accumulated amid the shower of bricks and surrounded by whole stretches of wall that had disintegrated into rubble. The iron framework that had carried the pulleys had fallen half-way down the shaft; one cage was still hanging from it, with a length of torn cable dangling, then there was a whole scrap-heap of tubs, iron plates, and ladders. By chance the lamp depot had remained intact and its bright rows of little lamps could be seen over to the left. And at the back of its gutted chamber the engine could be made out, still set squarely on its massive block of masonry: its copper surface gleamed, its great steel limbs looked like invincible muscles, and the enormous crank rod, bent upwards in the air, looked like the knee of some powerful giant, lying back tranquilly enjoying his display of strength.

After this hour's respite Monsieur Hennebeau felt his hopes rise again. The ground must have finished moving, so there was a chance of saving the machine and the rest of the buildings. But he still forbade anyone to approach, for he wanted to wait another half-hour. The waiting became unbearable, the hope made the anguish more acute, everyone's hearts were racing. A dark cloud growing on the horizon hastened the end of the day, and a gloomy twilight started to cover the wreckage left by this terrestrial hurricane. They had been there for seven hours without moving and without eating.

And suddenly, just as the engineers were cautiously advancing, a final convulsion racked the ground and put them to flight. Underground detonations rang out, like a monstrous artillery barrage raking the abyss. On the surface the last buildings toppled over and collapsed. First a sort of whirlwind swept away the remains of the screening shed and the landing-stage. Next the boiler-house burst and disappeared. Then it was the turn of the square tower, where the drainage pump gave a death-rattle and fell flat on its face, like a man mown down by a bullet. And then there was a terrifying scene; they watched as the engine was wrenched from its base, fighting for its life as its limbs were splayed: it straightened out its crank rod like a giant knee, as if attempting to rise to its feet; but then it was crushed and smothered to death. Only the great thirty-metre-high chimney remained standing, battered like a ship's mast in a hurricane. It looked as if it was about to crumble to pieces and disappear in a cloud of dust, when it suddenly plunged straight downwards, swallowed up by the earth, melting like a giant candle; and nothing was left showing above ground level, not even the tip of the lightning conductor. It was finished. The evil beast crouching in its underground cave was sated with human flesh and its harsh wheezing had at last died away. The whole of Le Voreux had now fallen down into the abyss.*

The crowd ran for their lives, screaming as they went. Women covered their eyes as they ran. Men were swept onwards by a gust of panic like a pile of dead leaves. They didn't want to scream, but scream they did, their throats swollen and their arms waving at the sight of the vast hole that had opened up in front of them. It was like the crater of an extinct volcano, gaping fifteen metres deep and at least forty metres wide, and reaching from the road to the canal. The whole surface of the pit-head followed the buildings, the gigantic trestles, the overhead tracks, a complete train of tubs, and three railway wagons: not to mention the whole supply of timber, a forest of freshly cut poles, all swallowed up like pieces of straw. Down in the depths all that could be seen was a tangled mess of beams and bricks, iron and plaster, horribly crushed remains, mangled and defiled by the fury of the catastrophe. The hole grew still rounder and wider, and cracks started forming around the edges, then spread right across the fields. One fissure reached Rasseneur's bar, and cracked its front wall. Would the village itself be the next victim? How far did they have to flee to be safe, on this tragic night, piled high with leaden clouds, which looked as if they too were about to come crashing down on top of the crowd?

But Négrel gave a cry of despair. And Monsieur Hennebeau, who had stepped back to survey the scene, broke into tears. For there was worse to come. One of the banks burst and the canal suddenly poured in a foaming tide along one of the cracks. It disappeared down inside, falling like a waterfall into a deep valley. The mine drank up its waters; the flood would now drown the galleries for many years. The crater soon filled, and a lake of muddy water took the place where Le Voreux used to be, like a lake beneath which slept some haunted city. A terrifying silence had settled, and nothing could be heard but the falling water, thundering down into the bowels of the earth.

Then Souvarine stood up, on top of the shaken slag-heap. He had recognized La Maheude and Zacharie sobbing at the débâcle, with this enormous mass weighing so heavily on the heads of the wretches who were dying down below. And he threw away his last cigarette, and walked off into the deepening darkness without a backward glance. His shadowy figure diminished in the distance and disappeared into the shades of night. He was heading for the unknown, however far. He went away calmly like an exterminating angel, headed for anywhere that he could find dynamite to blow up cities and the men who live in them. He will doubtless be to blame when the bourgeoisie in its death throes finds the cobbles starting to split open under its feet with every step that it takes.

CHAPTER IV

THE night after the collapse of Le Voreux Monsieur Henne-beau had left for Paris, wanting to inform the Board in person before the newspapers had had time to report the events. And when he arrived back the next day, he appeared to be very calm, the very model of managerial decorum. He had apparently disowned any personal responsibility, and he seemed not to have fallen from favour; on the contrary, the decree which appointed him an officer of the Légion d'honneur was signed twenty-four hours later.

But although its manager had saved his skin, the Company itself was left reeling from the terrible blow. It wasn't so much the few millions it had lost as the body blow of the secret but unceasing fear for the morrow, now that one of its pits had been slaughtered. The Company was so afflicted that once again it felt bound to keep silent. What was the point of digging any deeper into this abominable affair? And why should it make a martyr of the criminal, if it did discover his identity? For his terrifying heroism could turn other heads, and breed a whole line of arsonists and assassins.

Besides, the Company had no idea who the real guilty party was; it came to suppose that there was a whole army of accomplices, since it seemed unbelievable that one lone man could have had the audacity and the strength to execute such a deed; and that in fact was the thought which obsessed the Company, this notion of a gradually growing threat to all of its pits. The manager had received instructions to organize a vast system of espionage, then to sack the dangerous men discreetly one by one as soon as any one of them was suspected of having had something to do with the crime. The Company's policy was to limit itself to a highly cautious purge.

There was only one immediate sacking, that of Dansaert, the overman. Since the scandal at La Pierronne's he had become a liability. And they used as a pretext his behaviour when confronted with danger, the cowardice of a captain who abandons ship before his men. And besides, it was a covert concession to the other miners, who detested him.

Meanwhile rumours had started to surface in public, and the management was obliged to send a disclaimer to one newspaper, to deny its version of events, according to which the strikers had lit a barrel of gunpowder. Already after a rapid inquiry the report by the government engineer concluded that the lining had burst from natural causes, under the pressure of local subsidence; and the Company had preferred to keep silent and take the blame for inadequate supervision. In the Parisian press only three days after the event the catastrophe had become one of the most topical news items: no conversation was complete without mention of the workmen dying at the bottom of the mine, and the public was avid to read each morning's new dispatches. In Montsou itself the bourgeoisie turned pale and speechless at the very sound of the name of Le Voreux, and a legend grew up which even the boldest trembled to repeat under their breath. The whole region showed its great sympathy for the victims, organizing excursions to the stricken pit, whole families rushing to take in the awesome sight of the wreckage that hung over the heads of the buried wretches.

Deneulin, who had been appointed divisional engineer, had taken up his new functions at the height of the disaster; his first concern was to redirect the course of the canal into its bed, for this torrent of water was aggravating the damage by the hour. Major works were necessary, and he immediately sent a hundred workmen to construct a dyke. The force of the torrent carried away the first two dams that they built, but then they installed pumps and struggled feverishly to win back the lost land step by step.

But the rescue of the buried miners roused even more passion. Négrel was asked to mount a last attempt, and there was no lack of willing hands; all the miners rushed to offer their services in a surge of fraternal feeling. They forgot the strike, they stopped worrying about their wages; they didn't mind if they weren't paid, they asked nothing better than to risk their lives now that their comrades were in mortal danger. They all arrived with their tools, trembling in anticipation, waiting urgently to be told where to start digging into the rock. Many of them who had fallen ill with shock after the accident, and had been afflicted with nervous tics, drenched in cold sweat, or haunted by obsessional nightmares, left their sick-beds despite their suffering, and these men proved to be the most desperate to fight their way through the earth, as if they wanted to take their revenge. Unfortunately, as soon as they tried to decide what was the best course of action, confusion ensued: what could they do? How should they get below? Which way into the rock should they choose?

Négrel's opinion was that none of the unfortunate wretches could have survived, all fifteen must surely have perished, drowned or suffocated; but in mining catastrophes it is the rule always to assume that men who are walled in down below are still alive; and he acted on this presumption. The first problem to tackle was calculating in which direction they would have fled. The deputies and the old miners whom he consulted were all agreed on one point: faced with the rising flood their comrades would certainly have climbed up from gallery to gallery into the highest coal-faces, so that they must be trapped at the end of one of the higher tunnels. Moreover, that tallied with the information given by old Mouque, whose confused story even made it sound as if the panic-stricken flight had separated the team into small groups, leaving escapers behind at every level along the way. But then the opinions of the deputies were divided as soon as they came to discuss practical solutions. Since even the tunnels that were nearest to the surface were 150 metres underground, there was no question of sinking a shaft. There remained Réquillart as the only point of access, the only way they might reach them. The worst thing was that this old pit, which was also flooded, no longer communicated with Le Voreux, and the only parts of it that remained above water were some stretches of gallery leading to the first loading bay. It would take years to drain the pit, so their best hope was to check these galleries to see if any of them might lie close to the submerged tunnels where they suspected that the distressed miners might be lying. But before they arrived at this logical conclusion they had had long arguments in order to eliminate a host of impractical suggestions.

When they had made up their minds, Négrel burrowed into all the dusty archives, and when he had found the old plans of both pits, he identified the points where they should direct their search. Gradually this pursuit excited him, and in his turn he was seized with a self-sacrificing urge, despite his usual ironic lack of concern for people and things. There were some immediate obstacles to going down Réquillart: they had to clear out the mouth of the shaft, cut down the mountain ash, hack away the hawthorn and the sloe bushes, and then they still had to repair the ladders. After that they mounted an exploratory search. The engineer, who had taken ten workmen down with him, had them tap with the metal of their tools against certain parts of the seam that he indicated; and then in complete silence each pressed his ear to the coal-seam, listening out in case some distant tap might come in reply. But they went the whole length of every accessible tunnel, and not a single echo came in reply. Their confusion increased: where should they cut into the rock? Whose call for help could they answer, since there seemed to be nobody there? Yet they persisted, they kept looking, becoming increasingly nervous and anxious.

From the very first day La Maheude came to Réquillart every morning. She sat down on a beam facing the shaft, and didn't move again till the evening. When one of the men emerged, she jumped up and questioned him with her eyes: nothing? no, nothing! and she sat down again and kept waiting, without saying a word, her face hard and closed. Jeanlin, too, seeing that his lair was being invaded, had come to prowl around with the fearful air of a beast of prey whose den will reveal his pillage: he also thought of the young soldier lying under the rocks and was afraid that his peaceful slumber would be disrupted; but this side of the mine was flooded, and, besides, the search party was working further over to the left, in the western sector. At first Philomène had come regularly, to accompany Zacharie, who was a member of one of the search parties; then she had enough of needlessly exposing herself to the cold, with nothing to show for it: she stayed in the village, mooching around lethargically all day, losing interest in everything, and spending her time coughing from morning to evening. Zacharie on the other hand had suspended all normal living, and would have eaten his way through the earth if it could help him get through to his sister. He cried at night, he saw her wasting away with hunger, and he heard her voice, hoarse from her efforts to call for help. Twice he had wanted to start digging without authorization, saying that he knew the spot, that he could feel she was there.

The engineer wouldn't let him go down any more, but he refused to leave the pit that he was banished from; he wouldn't even sit down and wait with his mother, he paced restlessly up and down, tormented by the need to act.

It was the third day. Négrel was in depair and had resolved to give up entirely that evening. At noon, after lunch, when he returned with his men to make one last attempt, he was surprised to see Zacharie emerge from the pit, his face bright red, gesticulating and shouting:

'She's there! She answered me! Come on, hurry up!'

He had slipped past the guard on the ladders and he swore that he had heard tapping down there in the first tunnel of the Guillaume seam.

'But we've already gone past the place you're talking about twice,' Négrel pointed out incredulously. 'All right, we'll go and take a look.'

La Maheude had got to her feet; and they had to stop her going down. She stood waiting at the edge of the shaft, staring down into the darkness of the hole.

Down below, Négrel himself gave three well-spaced knocks; then he pressed his ear up against the coal, urging the workmen to keep absolutely quiet. Not a sound came in reply, and he shook his head: obviously the poor boy had been dreaming. Zacharie took it upon himself to start knocking again, in a frenzy; he heard it again, and his eyes gleamed, his limbs trembled with joy. Then the other workmen tried the same experiment, one after the other; and they all became excited as they detected the distant response quite clearly. The engineer was astonished, he pressed his ear to the rock again, and at last he perceived a faint, ethereal sound, a hardly perceptible rhythmical drumming, the familiar cadence of the miners' signal to retreat which they hammer out against the coal-seam when in danger. Coal transmits sound over great distances with the clarity of crystal.

A deputy who was there estimated that the block separating them from their comrades was at least fifty metres thick. But they felt as if they could already reach out and touch them, and they exploded with joy. Négrel had to undertake the preliminary cutting immediately.

When Zacharie saw La Maheude again back above ground they embraced each other.

'Don't let it go to your heads,' La Pierronne was cruel enough to say. She had come out to look that day out of sheer curiosity. 'If Catherine wasn't there, you'd be too upset afterwards.'

It was true, Catherine might be somewhere else.

'Bugger off, why don't you!' Zacharie cried furiously. 'She is there, I know she is!'

La Maheude had returned to her place, mute and expressionless. And she settled down to wait again.

As soon as the news had reached Montsou, a new crowd of people arrived. There was nothing to see, yet they stayed there just the same, and the curious onlookers had to be kept at bay. Down below they were working day and night. In case they met some obstacle, the engineer had got the men to cut out three tunnels sloping down through the coal, converging towards the point where they presumed that the miners were trapped. Only one hewer at a time could cut the coal at the cramped face of each narrow tunnel; he was relieved every two hours; and the coal was loaded into baskets and passed from hand to hand back along a human chain which became ever longer as the tunnel progressed. At first the job progressed very rapidly; they covered six metres in one day.

Zacharie had been allowed to take his place among the élite workers who were sent to do the cutting. It was a place of honour which was jealously fought for. And he got angry when they tried to relieve him after his two hours of regulation hard labour. He pinched his comrades' turns, he refused to drop his pick. His tunnel soon moved ahead of the others, and he tore into the coal with such furious energy that you could hear him puffing and panting deep down in the tunnel, sounding like the roaring of some subterranean forge. When he emerged, black and muddy, drunk with fatigue, he fell down and had to be wrapped in a blanket. When he went down again he was still tottering, and the struggle recommenced, with great muffled blows and muttered curses, as he fought for success in a frenzy of destruction. The worst thing of it was that the coal was getting harder, and he broke his pick twice, in his impatience at not progressing fast enough. He also suffered from the heat, a heat which increased with every metre gained, and became unbearable in the depths of this narrow gully where there was no fresh air. They set up a hand-operated ventilator, but the ventilation was sluggish, and on three occasions they had to drag out a hewer who had fainted, choking with asphyxia.

Négrel took up residence underground with the workmen. He had his meals sent down to him, and sometimes he caught a couple of hours' sleep on a bale of straw, rolled up in a coat. What kept their courage up was the call from the abandoned wretches in the distance, the tattoo that they drummed out to hasten the rescue. It became more and more distinct, ringing out quite clearly now with a musical sonority as if it were being struck on the keys of a xylophone. It was guiding them in the right direction; they burrowed towards its crystalline sound as soldiers walk towards the sound of gunfire in battle. Each time that one of the hewers was relieved, Négrel went down, tapped, then pressed his ear to the rock; and each time, so far, the answer had come, swiftly and urgently. He had no doubt now, they were progressing in the right direction, but with what fatal slowness! They would never arrive in time. At first they had managed to get through thirteen metres in two days; but the third day they had fallen to five; then to three on the fourth. The coal was getting harder, so solid that they had great difficulty in getting through two metres a day. By the ninth day after a superhuman effort they had covered thirty-two metres, and they calculated that they had another score to go. For the prisoners the twelfth day commenced, twelve periods of twenty-four hours without food or heat in the icy darkness! This appalling thought brought tears to their eyes and strengthened their arms as they fought on. It seemed impossible for one of God's creatures to live any longer; the distant tapping had already become feebler the day before, and they feared at every moment that they would hear it stop.

La Maheude still came regularly to sit at the mouth of the shaft. She brought Estelle in her arms, as she couldn't leave her alone all day long. She followed their progress hour by hour, sharing their hopes and disappointments. There was a

feverish sense of expectation, accompanied by endless speculation, among the groups who stood waiting at the pit, and even
back in Montsou. Throughout the region, every man's heart
beat with those down below.

On the ninth day, at lunch-time, Zacharie didn't answer
when they called him to be replaced. He seemed half-crazed,
and continued in a frenzy, swearing all the while. Négrel, who
had left for a moment, couldn't get him to obey; and in fact
there were only a deputy and three miners down there. Zacharie, who couldn't see what he was doing, and was furious with
the failing light that held up his progress, must have been rash
enough to light his lamp. Yet they had been given the strictest
orders, for they had detected escapes of firedamp, and the gas
had collected in vast pockets in the narrow, badly ventilated
corridors. Suddenly there was a thunderclap, and a jet of flame
burst out of the gully, like grapeshot exploding from the
muzzle of a gun. Everything was on fire, the air was burning
like gunpowder down the whole length of the galleries. This
torrent of fire swept the deputy and the three workmen aside,
flew up the shaft, and erupted explosively into the open air,
spewing forth rocks and fragments of timber framework. The
onlookers fled, and La Maheude leapt to her feet, clutching
the terrified Estelle to her breast.

When Négrel and the workmen returned, they were shaken
by a terrible anger. They kicked the earth brutally with their
heels, as though it were a wicked stepmother who had killed
her children at random in a state of crazed and wanton cruelty.
They were sacrificing so much already in the effort to go to
their comrades' assistance, and now there was an even higher
price to pay! After three long hours of effort and danger, when
they finally got through to the galleries, they had the lugubrious
task of bringing up the victims. Neither the deputy nor the
workmen were dead, but they were covered with terrible
wounds, and gave off a scent of charred flesh; they had
breathed in the flames, and had burns deep down inside their
throats; they screamed continuously, begging to be put out of
their misery. One of the three miners was the man who during
the strike had burst the pump at Gaston-Marie with a last
blow of his pick; the two others had their hands covered in

scars and their fingers skinned and cut from throwing bricks at the soldiers. The crowd, all pale and trembling, uncovered their heads as they passed.

La Maheude stood and waited. At last Zacharie's body appeared. The clothes were burnt off, the body was no more than a black mass of coal, charred and unrecognizable. There was no head, it had been blown to smithereens by the explosion. And when they had placed these ghastly remains on a stretcher, La Maheude followed them with mechanical steps, her eyes burning, but shedding no tears. She held Estelle, who had fallen asleep, in her arms, and she walked off like a tragic heroine, her hair dishevelled by the wind. At the village Philomène was stupefied, cried buckets of tears, and immediately felt relieved. But Zacharie's mother had already returned with the same tread to Réquillart: she had accompanied her son on his last journey, now she was returning to wait for her daughter.

Three more days went by in like fashion. The rescue attempt had started again amid unexpected difficulties. Luckily the approach tunnels had not collapsed after the firedamp explosion; but the air was still burning, and it was so heavy and polluted that they had to have more ventilators installed. The hewers were now relieved every twenty minutes. They kept going, and they were hardly more than two metres away from their comrades. But now they were working with heavy hearts, hacking away fiercely in a simple spirit of revenge; for the sounds had died away, the tattoo no longer sounded with its bright little rhythm. They had been working for twelve days, and it was fifteen days since the disaster; and, since that morning, the place had been as silent as the grave.

The new accident had renewed the curiosity of the inhabitants of Montsou, and the local bourgeois organized excursions so enthusiastically that the Grégoires decided to follow the fashion. They arranged a party, and it was agreed that they would travel to Le Voreux in their carriage while Madame Hennebeau would bring Lucie and Jeanne in hers. Deneulin would show them round his site, then they would return via Réquillart, where Négrel would give them the latest news on how the tunnels were progressing, and whether there was any hope left. And then in the evening they would all have dinner together.

When the Grégoires and their daughter Cécile went down towards the flooded pit, they found that Madame Hennebeau had arrived there first, dressed in navy blue, and using a parasol to protect her complexion from the pale February sunshine. The sky was beautifully clear, and there was a springlike warmth in the air. Monsieur Hennebeau happened to be there with Deneulin; and she listened absent-mindedly to the explanations given by the latter about the work they had had to undertake to dam the canal. Jeanne, who always took a sketch-book with her, had started drawing, excited by the horror of the subject; while Lucie, sitting beside her on the remains of a wagon, also heaved sighs of satisfaction, finding it 'fantastic'. The dyke, which wasn't finished yet, was riven with leaks, whose tumbling, foaming streams cascaded fiercely downwards into the vast abyss of the buried pit. And yet this crater was emptying, as the waters that had soaked into the earth receded, revealing the dreadful chaos that lay on its bed. Beneath the soft azure sky of the spring morning there lay a veritable cesspool, the ruins of a city lying smashed and melting in the mud.

'Is that what we've come all this way to see!' cried Monsieur Grégoire, very disappointed.

Cécile, who was pink with health and happy to breathe such fresh air, became lively and playful, while Madame Hennebeau pulled a face to show her revulsion, murmuring:

'The truth is that it's not at all a pretty sight.'

The two engineers started to laugh. They tried to capture the interest of their visitors, taking them everywhere, explaining how the pumps worked and how the pile-driver drove in the stakes. But the ladies were starting to fret. They shivered when they learned that the pumps would have to work for years, perhaps six or seven, before the pit was rebuilt and all the water drained. No, they preferred to think of something else, all this turmoil would only give them bad dreams.

'Let's go,' said Madame Hennebeau, walking away to her carriage.

Jeanne and Lucie protested. What, so soon! And her drawing

wasn't finished! They wanted to stay, for their father could bring them round to dinner later that evening.

Monsieur Hennebeau took his place alone beside his wife in the carriage, for he too wanted to question Négrel.

'Well then, you go on ahead,' said Monsieur Grégoire. 'We'll follow on, we've got to pay a quick visit in the village ... Go on then, it'll only take five minutes, we'll be at Réquillart at the same time as you.'

He got back up behind Madame Grégoire and Cécile; and, while the other carriage sped along the canal side, theirs slowly climbed the hill.

Their excursion was to finish with a charitable gesture. Zacharie's death had filled them with pity for the tragedy which had struck the Maheu family, which everyone was talking about. They weren't worried about the father, a bandit who killed soldiers and who had had to be put down like a mad dog. But they were touched by the mother, that poor woman who had just lost her son after losing her husband, and whose daughter was perhaps already lying dead underground; not to mention what people said about the invalid grandfather, the child who walked with a limp after a rock fall, and a little girl who had died of starvation during the strike. So although this family deserved its share of misfortune because of its reprehensible attitude, they had resolved to display the generosity of their charitable spirit, their desire to forgive and forget, by taking them alms in person. Two carefully wrapped parcels lay under one of the seats of the carriage.

An old woman told the coachman where the Maheus' house was, number sixteen in the second block. But when the Grégoires had alighted, holding their parcels, they knocked in vain, and even when they banged on the door with their fists they still got no answer: the house remained lugubriously quiet, lying frozen and bleak, like a house emptied by death and abandoned for years.

'There's nobody here,' said Cécile, disappointed. 'What a nuisance! What are we going to do with all this?'

Suddenly the door of the next house opened, and La Levaque appeared.

'Oh Sir, oh Ma'am, I beg your pardon, I'm sure! Excuse me

Miss! . . . It's the neighbour you want. She's not there, she's at Réquillart . . .'

She told them the story in a flood of words, emphasizing how everyone had to help each other, and how she was looking after Lénore and Henri so that their mother could go over there and wait. Her eyes, gleaming eagerly, had lit on the parcels, and she brought the conversation to bear on her daughter, who had just become a widow, in order to point out her own deprivation. Then, with a hesitant air, she murmured: 'I've got the key. If Sir and Ma'am really insist . . . The grandfather is there.'

The Grégoires watched her, stupefied. How could the grandfather be there? Nobody had answered! Was he asleep, then? But when La Levaque had made up her mind to open the door, what they saw brought them to a halt on the threshold.

Bonnemort was there, all on his own, rooted to his chair, staring with wide eyes at the cold hearth. Around him the room appeared bigger, without the cuckoo clock, and without the varnished pine furniture which had previously livened it up; and all that was left on the crude greenish walls were the portraits of the Emperor and the Empress, whose pink lips smiled with ceremonial goodwill. The old man didn't move, nor did he bat an eyelid when the door let the light in; he looked like an imbecile, as if he hadn't even seen the crowd of visitors come in. At his feet was his ash-filled dish, like a litter tray for a cat.

'Don't take any notice of him if he isn't very polite,' said La Levaque, obligingly. 'People say he's got a screw loose. That's all he's had to say for himself for the last fortnight.'

But just then Bonnemort was shaken by a deep croaking which seemed to rise up from his stomach; and he spat a thick gobbet of black phlegm into his dish. The ash was soaked, and it looked like muddy coal, as if he were now dredging back up all the coal from the mine that had gone down his throat. Then he immediately fell motionless again. He only ever moved when he needed to spit, every now and again.

The Grégoires were upset, and their stomachs queasy with disgust, but they tried to utter a few friendly, encouraging words.

'Well, my good fellow,' said the father, 'have you caught a cold?'

The old man kept looking at the wall without turning his head. And a heavy silence fell once again.

'We should make you some tea,' said the mother.

He remained rigid and mute.

'Oh dear, Daddy,' said Cécile, 'they did tell us he was poorly; but we forgot all about it . . .'

She broke off, in great embarrassment. After she had placed on the table some stew and two bottles of wine, she undid the second parcel, and took out a huge pair of shoes. This was the present for the grandfather, and she held one shoe in each hand, inhibited by the sight of the swollen feet of the poor man, who would never walk again.

'Hey, they've come a bit late in the day, haven't they, old fellow?' Monsieur Grégoire went on, to cheer him up. 'Never mind, who knows when they might come in useful.'

Bonnemort neither heard them nor replied, and his face remained terrifying, cold and hard as stone.

Then Cécile put the shoes down furtively beside the wall. But although she took every possible precaution, the nails rang out on the floor; and the huge shoes stood out ostentatiously in the room.

'Go on, he's not going to say thank you, is he!' cried La Levaque, who had cast deeply envious eyes on the shoes. 'You might as well give a duck a pair of glasses, begging your pardon.'

She kept up her patter in order to entice the Grégoires into her house, counting on moving them to pity her. Finally she found the pretext, praising Henri and Lénore, who were so nice and sweet; and so intelligent, answering any questions you asked them like angels! They would tell Sir and Ma'am everything they wanted to know.

'Will you come along with us for a moment, my dear daughter?' asked Monsieur Grégoire, pleased to be able to leave.

'Yes, I'll be round in a minute,' replied Cécile.

Cécile remained alone with Bonnemort. What kept her there, trembling and fascinated, was that she seemed to recognize this old man: where had she come across that square, livid face, tattooed with coal? And suddenly she remembered; she saw a tide of screaming people surrounding her, and felt the cold hands squeezing her neck. It was him, she had found the man who did it; she looked at his hands, which lay in his lap, the hands of a workman who had spent his life on his knees and whose whole strength was now concentrated in his wrists, still powerful despite his age. Gradually Bonnemort seemed to have woken up, and he noticed her, and he scrutinized her now, with his vacant air. A fire rose in his cheeks, and a nervous twitch twisted his mouth, from which a thin sliver of black saliva trickled. Each felt drawn to look at the other, the girl blooming, plump and fresh from her life of leisure and generations of comfortable luxury, the man swollen with water, showing the deplorable ugliness of a race of worn-out beasts, destroyed from father to son by a hundred years of toil and starvation.

Ten minutes later, when the Grégoires, who were surprised not to see Cécile, went back into the Maheus' house, they let out a dreadful scream. Their daughter lay strangled on the floor, and her face was blue. Bonnemort's fingers had marked her neck with the red imprint of his giant's hand. His dead legs had given way, and sent him crashing down beside her, and he couldn't get up again. His hands were still clenched, and he lay there looking up at them with his imbecile features and wide, staring eyes. As he fell he had broken his dish, spilling the ash and splashing the room with his muddy black spittle; but the large pair of shoes stood neatly side by side, safe out of harm's way against the wall.

Nobody ever managed to ascertain exactly what had happened. Why had Cécile gone so close to him? How had Bonnemort, despite being stuck to his chair, managed to seize her by the throat? It was clear that once he had her in his grip he must have been possessed, squeezing tighter and tighter, stifling her cries, tumbling and tossing in time to her dying spasms. Not a murmur, not a whimper had traversed the thin party wall dividing them from the neighbouring house. Presumably he had succumbed to a sudden fit of madness, an inexplicable temptation to murder, when faced with the sight of the girl's white neck. Such savagery was incomprehensible in a sick old man who had always lived an honest life, showing blind obedience, and resisting new ideas. What resentment had slowly poisoned him, without his knowing, creeping up from his bowels to his brain? The horror of it made people conclude that it was unconscious, a crime committed by an idiot.

Meanwhile the Grégoires had fallen on their knees, weeping, and choking with grief. The daughter that they had worshipped, that they had waited so long for, and then showered with all their wealth, that they had tiptoed to watch as she slept in her bedroom, that they had always found undernourished and never plump enough! And their whole life collapsed in front of their eyes; what was there left to live for, now that they would have to live without her?

La Levaque cried out wildly:

'Oh, the old devil, whatever has he done? How could anyone have guessed such a thing! . . . And La Maheude won't be back till this evening! How about it, shall I run and fetch her?'

The father and the mother were both too shattered to answer.

'Hey, don't you think I'd better . . . I'll go, then.'

But before she left La Levaque considered the shoes again. The whole village was in a turmoil, a crowd was jostling for position already. Someone might even steal them. And besides, there wasn't a man left at the Maheus' to wear them. She walked off with them, discreetly. They ought to be just the right size for Bouteloup.

At Réquillart the Hennebeaus had been waiting for the Grégoires for ages, in Négrel's company. He had come up from the pit and gave them the latest information: they hoped to be able to get through to the captives that very evening; but they would certainly not bring them out alive, for there was still a deathly silence down there. Behind the engineer, La Maheude was sitting on her beam, and listening white-faced, when La Levaque arrived to tell her what the old man had been getting up to. She merely made a sweeping gesture of impatience and irritation. But she followed her home.

Madame Hennebeau felt faint. What an abomination! That

poor Cécile, who had been so cheerful that day, so lively an hour earlier! Hennebeau had to take his wife inside old Mouque's hovel for a moment. With his awkward hands he unbuttoned her corsage, disturbed by the scent of musk that this open garment revealed. And as she wept floods of tears she embraced Négrel, horrified by this death which put an end to his marriage, while, released from at least one of his worries, her husband watched them commiserate. This misfortune would settle everything, he preferred to keep the nephew, since he feared he might well have been succeeded by the coachman.

CHAPTER V

AT the bottom of the pit, the wretched men who had been left stranded were screaming with terror. Now the water was up to their stomachs. They were deafened by the noise of the torrent, and the final collapse of the lining sounded to them like the world exploding as it came to an end; and what made them even more panic-stricken was the neighing of the horses shut in the stables, the terrifying, unforgettable death-rattle of slaughtered beasts.

Mouque had unharnessed Bataille. The old horse was there, trembling, his eyes dilated and staring at the water which was still rising relentlessly. The loading bay was filling up rapidly, and the great green tide could be seen swelling beneath the reddish glow of the three lamps which were still burning beneath the vaulted roof. And suddenly, when he felt this icy mass soaking his coat, he stretched his legs and took off at a full and furious gallop, and disappeared into the depths of one of the haulage galleries.

Then there was a general free-for-all, as the men ran off, following the animal.

'Sod all here!' shouted Mouque. 'Off to Réquillart.'

The idea that they might be able to get out through the old pit nearby, if they could get there before the passage was blocked, swept them along now. All twenty of them bunched

up in a close line, holding their lamps up high, so that the
water didn't put them out. Luckily the gallery sloped imperceptibly upwards, and they went forward for 200 metres, struggling against the current, without the water rising higher.
Long-buried superstitions stirred anew in the depths of their
lost souls, and they called out to the earth, for it was the earth
that was taking its revenge, which was shedding the blood of
its veins because its artery had been cut. One old man stammered some half-forgotten prayers, pointing his thumbs
outwards to calm the evil spirits of the mine.

But at the first turning an argument broke out. The stableman wanted to go left, some of the others swore that it would
save time to take the right turn. They lost a minute deciding.

'Hey, why not sit down here and drop dead, I don't care!'
Chaval shouted crudely. 'I'm going this way.'

He took the right fork, followed by two comrades. The
others stuck to old Mouque and charged off behind him,
because he had grown up underground at Réquillart. Yet even
he hesitated, not knowing which way to turn. Their heads
were spinning, and even the old-timers couldn't recognize the
route any more, as if its plans had been rubbed out as they
looked at them. At each fork, they hung back and hesitated,
yet they had to decide. Étienne brought up the rear, running
slowly because Catherine, who was paralysed with fatigue and
fear, was holding him back. He would have taken the right
fork, like Chaval, for he believed he was heading in the right
direction; but he let him go, even if it meant he would be left
down below. In any case, the rout continued, for another
group of comrades had gone off on their own, and there were
only seven of them left following old Mouque.

'Hang on to my neck, and I'll carry you,' Étienne said to
her, as he saw that she was weakening.

'No, don't bother,' she murmured, 'I've had enough, I'd
rather die straight away.'

They were losing time, they were fifty metres behind the
others, and he was about to lift her up despite her reluctance,
when the gallery was suddenly blocked: an enormous slab of
rock collapsed and cut them off from the others. The flood
was already soaking into the rocks, which were crumbling and

collapsing on all sides. They had to beat a retreat. Then they didn't know which way they were heading. That was it, they had to abandon the idea of getting back up through Réquillart. Their only hope was to reach the upper seams, where they could perhaps be rescued if the waters subsided.

At last Étienne recognized the Guillaume seam.

'Right!' he said. 'Now I know where we are. For heaven's sake, we were going in the right direction; but what the hell difference does that make now ? . . . Listen, why don't we just go on straight ahead, and we'll climb up the chimney.'

The water was lapping up against their chests, and they could only walk very slowly. As long as there was some light left, there was hope; and they blew out one of the lamps, to save the oil, thinking that they would pour it into the other lamp. As they reached the chimney, a noise behind them made them turn round again. Was it their comrades? Had they too been cut off and decided to return? They heard a distant panting, an incomprehensible, tempestuous sound as something drew near them, thrashing and churning the water. And they screamed as they saw a giant whitish mass emerge from the shadows and struggle to squeeze a way between the pit-props, which were too close together, in order to join them.

It was Bataille. He had set out from the loading bay, and galloped frantically along the dark tunnels. He seemed to know his way around this subterranean city where he had lived for eleven years; and he saw quite clearly through the endless night that had always surrounded him. He galloped and galloped, lowering his head and lifting his feet, slipping through the narrow bowels of the earth, filling them with his great body. Road followed road, crossroads offered their options, but he never hesitated. Where was he heading for? Maybe for that far-off vision of his youth, at the mill where he was born, on the banks of the Scarpe, driven by vague memories of sunshine, burning in the sky like a great lamp. He wanted to live, his memories of animal life revived, the urge to breathe the air of the plains once more drove him onward, hoping to discover the hole, the way out into the warm air and the light. And his age-old resignation was swept aside by a wave of revolt, now that he was dying in this pit, after being merely blinded by it.

The water which rushed along after him whipped at his hind legs and bit icily into his rump. But as he plunged onward, the galleries became narrower, the roof sloped downwards, and the walls swelled inwards. He kept on galloping regardless, tearing the skin off his legs as he scraped past the pit-props. The mine seemed to close in on him from all sides, to seize hold of him and suffocate him.

Then as Étienne and Catherine were watching him approach he got stuck, and started choking. He had crashed into the rock face and broken his two front legs. He made a last effort and dragged himself forward a few metres; but his flanks were too wide to get through, and he remained buried and strangled by the earth. And he stretched out his bleeding head, still looking for a crack to slip through, with his great bleary eyes. The water was covering him rapidly, and he started to neigh with the same hideous long-drawn-out death-rattle that the other horses in the stable had uttered as they died. This old creature's agony was atrocious, as he struggled, shattered and pinioned, so far down below the light of day. His distressed screams went on and on, the waters swept through his mane and seemed to curdle the sound emerging from his desperately gaping mouth. He made one last snort, sounding like the last gurgle of a barrel filling with water. Then there was a deep silence.

'Oh, dear God, take me away!' sobbed Catherine. 'Oh, dear God, I'm afraid, I don't want to die . . . Take me away! Take me away!'

She had looked death in the face. Neither the collapse of the shaft nor the flooding of the pit had struck her with such terror as the clamour of the dying Bataille. And she could still hear it ringing in her ears, setting her whole body quivering.

'Take me away, take me away!'

Étienne took hold of her and carried her away. And only just in time, for they were soaked up to the shoulders as they pushed on higher up the chimney. He had to help her up because she no longer had the strength to hold on to the timbers. Three times, he thought that he was going to lose her and see her slip back into the dark sea whose tide was rolling threateningly beneath them. However, they managed to catch their breath for a few moments when they came out into the first level, which was still free. Then the water rose, and they had to haul themselves higher up again. And for hours they kept climbing, as the rising tide chased them from level to level, forcing them to keep climbing higher. At the sixth level, a momentary lull in the rising tide made them burn with sudden hope; it looked as if the water might settle at that height. But then it surged upwards even more strongly, and they had to climb up to the seventh level, and then the eighth. There was only one more left, and when they had reached it, they watched anxiously as the water continued to rise centimetre by centimetre. And if it didn't stop, would they die there, like the old horse, crushed against the roof, their throats choking with water?

At every moment another rock fall rang out. The whole mine was shaken, its frail entrails were bursting under the strain of the great flood that was pouring into it. The air trapped at the end of the tunnels became so compressed that it set off a series of formidable explosions, which echoed through the splitting rocks and buckling passages. There was a terrifying din from these deep catastrophes, echoing dimly with the age-old conflict when the waters had covered the earth and buried the mountains beneath the plains.

And Catherine, who was shaken and dazed by this endless avalanche, clasped her hands and kept ceaselessly stammering out the same phrase:

'I don't want to die . . . I don't want to die.'

In order to reassure her, Étienne swore that the water would rise no higher. They had been fleeing for six hours, someone would be down to rescue them soon. And he said six hours without knowing, for they had lost all sense of time. In fact a whole day had gone by while they had been climbing up through the Guillaume seam.

Soaking and shivering, they settled down. She stripped off to wring out her clothes with no sense of shame; then she put her breeches and jacket back on to let them dry on her. As she was barefoot, he handed her his clogs and forced her to put them on. Now they had time to sit back and wait; they had lowered the wick of the lamp, keeping just the faint glow of the pilot light. But their stomachs were racked with hunger pangs, and they both realized that they were dying of starvation. Until then they had hardly felt any living sensation. When disaster had struck they hadn't had lunch. Now they found their sandwiches were bloated with water and changed into gruel. She had to insist and force him to eat his share. As soon as she had eaten, she fell asleep on the cold ground from sheer fatigue. Although he was burnt out with lack of sleep, he watched over her, staring at her with his forehead propped up on his hands.

How many hours passed like this? He couldn't have said. What he did know was that in front of him at the mouth of the chimney he had seen the swirling black flood reappear, like a beast whose back was swelling and swelling until it could reach them. At first there was just a thin line, a sinuous serpent growing gradually longer, then it grew into the heaving spine of some rampant beast; and soon it had reached them, soaking the feet of the sleeping girl. He hesitated to wake her, wondering anxiously whether it wasn't too cruel to shake her out of her restful and oblivious ignorance, where perhaps she was cradled in dreams of life out in the fresh air and the sunshine. Besides, where could they flee to? And as he racked his brains, he remembered that the incline which had been built in this part of the seam ran end on into the incline that served the loading bay on the next level up. That was a way out. But he let her sleep on as long as possible, watching the tide rising, waiting until it drove them away. At last he lifted her gently, and she shuddered violently.

'Oh, dear God, it's true . . . It's starting again, dear God!'

She screamed as she remembered that death was staring her in the face.

'No, calm down,' he murmured. 'We can get through, I swear we can.'

To get to the incline, they had to walk bent double, and once again they were soaked right up to their shoulders. And the climb began again, but more dangerous this time, up the tunnel which was totally lined with wood along its whole hundred-metre length. At first they tried to pull on the cable, in order to secure one of the trucks down below; for if the other fell down while they were climbing up it would crush them. But nothing moved, some obstacle was blocking the mechanism. They took the risk of going ahead, but didn't dare use the cable, although it got in their way and they tore their nails on the slippery woodwork. Étienne brought up the rear, using his head to take her weight when she fell back with bleeding hands. Suddenly they butted into some broken beams which were blocking the incline. There had been a rock fall, and a mound of earth prevented them from going any higher. Luckily there was a door there which led out into a passage.

They were stunned to see a lamp glowing in front of them. A man shouted at them furiously:

'Another bunch of fools who had the same bright idea as me!'

They recognized Chaval, who had been cut off by the same rock fall that had covered the ramp in earth; and the two comrades who had been with him had succumbed, their skulls stove in. He had been wounded in the elbow but had summoned up the courage to crawl back on hands and knees to search them and steal their sandwiches. Just as he was getting away a last rock fall had cut off the gallery behind him.

He immediately swore that he wouldn't share his provisions with these jokers who had suddenly sprung up out of the ground. He felt more tempted to kill them. Then he too recognized them, and his anger died away, he started laughing, with malicious pleasure.

'Oh, it's you, Catherine! You came a cropper, so you've come running back to your man. Well, that's fine, now we're in this together, we might as well enjoy it.'

He pretended not to notice Étienne. The latter was shaken by the encounter, and had moved to protect the tram girl, who huddled up closer to him. But there was no way out of the situation. He merely asked his workmate, as if they had parted on good terms an hour earlier:

'Have you looked down the bottom? Can't we get through by the coal-face?'

Chaval sneered.

'Oh, right, the coal-face! That's all collapsed too, we're caught between two walls like rats in a trap . . . But you can always go back down the incline, if you're a good diver.'

And in fact the water was still rising, they could hear it lapping. Their retreat was already cut off. And he was right, it was a trap, a dead end because the gallery had been blocked fore and aft by heavy rock falls. There was no way out. They were all three walled in.

'So you've decided to stay?' asked Chaval sarcastically. 'Okay, that's the best thing to do, and if you leave me alone I won't even talk to you. There's still room for two men in here . . . We'll soon see who dies first, unless they manage to find us, and that's hardly likely.'

Étienne persisted:

'If we tapped on the wall perhaps they might hear us.'

'I'm sick of tapping . . . Go on, try it yourself, there's a stone.'

Étienne picked up the piece of sandstone, which had already become chipped from Chaval's efforts, and he struck out the miners' tattoo against the floor of the seam, the long drum roll used by workmen in peril to signal their presence. Then he pressed his ear to the rock to listen. Twenty times he tried, and tried again. Not a sound came in answer.

All the while Chaval made a show of proceeding methodically with his own affairs. First he tidied his three lamps away against the wall: only one was lit, the others would come in handy later. Then he placed his two remaining sandwiches on a loose piece of timber. That was his larder, and it would last him two days if he was careful. Then he turned round and said:

'You know that half of it's for you, Catherine, if you get hungry.'

The girl remained silent. Her suffering was complete, now that she found herself caught between these two men again.

And so the terrible existence began. Neither Chaval nor Étienne opened his mouth, although they were both sitting on the ground only a few steps apart. Chaval advised Étienne to extinguish his lamp, and he agreed, it was a pointless waste of light; then they relapsed into silence again. Catherine had lain down on the ground near Étienne, worried by the looks she was getting from her former lover. The hours passed, and they could hear the quiet splashing of the water as it kept on rising;

while from time to time deep shocks and distant reverberations announced the final collapse of the mine. When the lamp went out and they needed to light another, they hesitated briefly a moment, for fear of igniting the firedamp; but they preferred to be blown up in one go rather than survive in the darkness; however there was no explosion, there couldn't have been any firedamp. They lay back again, and the hours started to pass once more.

Étienne and Catherine were surprised by a noise, and raised their heads. Chaval had decided to eat, and had cut a sandwich in two. He was eating slowly, so as to avoid the temptation of swallowing the lot. The other two watched him, racked with hunger.

'So you really don't want any?' he asked the tram girl, provocatively. 'That's a mistake.'

She lowered her eyes, fearful of yielding, for her stomach was racked with such hunger pangs that her eyes were swollen with tears. But she understood what he wanted; already that morning he had breathed down her neck; he had been seized by one of his familiar attacks of frenzied desire on seeing her with the other man. The looks he darted at her burnt with a flame she knew well, the flame of his attacks of jealousy, when he fell upon her with fists flying, accusing her of vile doings with her mother's lodger. But she didn't want to, she trembled at the consequences of returning to Chaval and throwing these two men at each other's throats, in this tiny cell where they were already at their last gasp. Dear God! Could they not end their lives as good friends!

Étienne would rather have let himself die of hunger than beg the tiniest morsel of bread from Chaval. The silence deepened, and it seemed to last an eternity, as the minutes ticked by one by one, monotonously and hopelessly. They had been trapped together for a day. The second lamp burnt itself out, and they started on the third.

Chaval bit into his second sandwich, and he grunted:

'Come on, stupid!'

Catherine shivered. To leave her free, Étienne had turned his face away. Then, as she didn't move, he said to her under his breath:

'Go on, my child.'

Now the tears that she had been choking back overflowed. She wept for a long time, without even the strength to get to her feet, not even sure whether she was hungry any more, suffering from pains all over her body. Étienne stood up and walked back and forth, hopelessly tapping out the miners' tattoo, furious at having to spend the last few hours of his life stuck up against his hated rival. There wasn't even room to die apart! As soon as he had walked ten paces he had to retrace his steps and bump into the other man. And the girl, that poor girl, they were still fighting over her even now that they were almost dead and buried! She would belong to the last man to die, this man would steal her from him again if he died first. There was no end to it, hour after hour, their revolting promiscuity increased, aggravated by their foul breath and their need to relieve themselves in front of each other. Twice he stormed up against the rock face as if he intended to break it open with his fists.

Another day drew to a close, and Chaval had sat down next to Catherine, sharing his last half-sandwich with her. She had trouble chewing each mouthful, as he made her pay for every one with a caress, persisting in his jealous desire not to die before having had her once more in front of his rival. She was exhausted, and let herself go. But when he tried to take her, she complained.

'Oh, leave me alone, you're breaking my bones.'

Trembling, Étienne had pressed his forehead against the timber so as not to see. He came rushing back, beside himself.

'Leave her alone, for Christ's sake!'

'What's it got to do with you?' asked Chaval. 'She's my woman, she belongs to me, doesn't she!'

He grasped her again, squeezed her in his arms with bravado, crushing his red moustache up against her mouth, and continued:

'Leave us in peace, damn you! Do us a favour and look over there to see how things are getting on.'

But Étienne, whose lips had turned white, shouted:

'If you don't let go of her, I'll strangle you!'

Chaval stood up quickly, for he had understood from

Étienne's strained voice that he meant to force a show-down. Death seemed to be taking too long to arrive, they needed one of them to give way to the other straight away. Their old battle had recommenced, in the earth where they would soon be sleeping side by side; and they had so little room that they couldn't even shake their fists without grazing them.

'Look out,' thundered Chaval. 'This time I'll have your guts.'

At that moment Étienne went mad. His eyes swam in a reddish mist, and his throat swelled with a surge of blood. He was seized with an irresistible urge to kill, a physical need, as if his tonsils were swollen and choking his throat, forcing him to spew up or suffocate. It rose and burst within him beyond the control of his will, under the impulse of his hereditary flaw. He grabbed hold of a slab of shale projecting from the wall, shook it loose, and ripped it out in one great heavy lump. Then raising it in both hands with superhuman force, he brought it crashing down on Chaval's skull.

Chaval had no time to leap back. He fell, with his face smashed in and his skull split open. His brains spattered the tunnel roof, and a purple stream flowed from the wound like a fountain bubbling from a spring. In no time there was a pool of blood, reflecting the smoky starlight shed by the lamp. Darkness invaded their sealed tomb, and his body lay slumped on the ground like a black heap of slag.

And Étienne looked at him, his eyes staring. So it was done. He had killed him. In confusion all his struggles returned to his memory, his useless struggle against the poison that slumbered in his muscles, against the alcohol that his people had slowly accumulated. Yet he was drunk only with hunger, the drunkenness of his parents years before had been enough. His hair stood on end at the horror of this murder, and yet despite the revulsion he felt as a civilized man, his heart fluttered with a kind of animal joy from a physical appetite satisfied. And then there came pride, the pride of the victor. He recalled the little soldier, his throat slit by the knife of the child who had killed him. Now he too had killed.

But Catherine stood bolt upright and screamed out loud.

'My God! He's dead!'

'Do you wish he wasn't?'

She choked and stuttered. Then she swayed and threw herself into his arms.

'Oh, kill me too, oh, let's both of us die!'

She clung to his shoulders in a close embrace, and he embraced her too, and they wished they might die. But death was in no hurry, and they disengaged their arms. Then, while she covered her eyes, he dragged the wretched body over to the incline, where he dumped it, to remove it from the cramped space that they still had to live in. Life would have been impossible with a corpse under their feet. And they felt terrified when they heard it plunge down amid a great surge of spray. So the water had already filled that hole? They realized that it was now overflowing into the tunnel.

Then the struggle began again. They had lit the last lamp, but it guttered as it lit the swelling flood, whose regular, persistent rise never flagged. First the water reached their ankles, then it wet their knees. The passage sloped upwards, and they took refuge at the top, which gave them a few hours of respite. But the waters caught up with them again, and they were in it up to their waists. They stood upright with their spines flattened against the rock and watched it growing deeper and deeper. When it reached their mouths it would all be over. The lamp, which they had hung up on the wall, tinted the surging flood of little waves with its yellow light; but as it grew paler, they could see no more than an ever-diminishing semicircle, as if the light were being swallowed up by the darkness which seemed to grow with the flood; then suddenly they were covered in darkness; the lamp had just gone out, after spitting out its last drop of oil. Then absolute darkness fell, it was dead of night in the middle of the earth where they would soon fall asleep and never open their eyes again to see the sunlight.

'God almighty!' Étienne swore softly.

As if she could feel the darkness grab hold of her, Catherine clung to him for shelter. She repeated under her breath the miners' proverb:

'Death blows out the lamp.'

And yet, faced with this new threat, their instincts rebelled, and a rage for life revived them. He started to dig into the shale violently with the hook of the lamp, while she helped him with her nails. They gouged out a kind of shelf half-way up the wall, and when they had hauled themselves up on to it, they managed to get seated, with their backs bent, for the sloping roof forced them to lower their heads. Now only their heels were frozen by the icy water. But soon enough they felt the cold eating into their ankles, then their calves, then their knees, in an irresistible and unrelenting movement. Their seat was uneven, and so soaked and slippery that they had to hang on tight to avoid falling off. This was the end, for how long could they hold out, imprisoned in their niche, exhausted and famished, with no bread and no light, and terrified of making the slightest move? And they suffered above all from the darkness, which prevented them from seeing death when it came. A great silence reigned, the mine overflowing with water lay still at last. Now all they could sense was this sea beneath them, its silent tide swelling up from the tunnels below.

Hour followed hour, each as black as the next, without them being able to measure their exact duration, as they increasingly lost all sense of time. Their torment, which should have made the time seem longer, made the minutes pass more swiftly. They thought they had only been trapped for two days and a night, when in fact the third day was already drawing to an end. All hope of salvation had vanished, nobody knew they were there, nobody would be able to get down to them, and they would die of hunger if they were spared by the flood. They decided to tap out the tattoo one last time; but their stone had disappeared under water. And besides, who would hear them?

Catherine had given up hope, and was resting her throbbing head against the seam, when she suddenly sat upright, trembling.

'Listen!' she said.

At first Étienne thought she was referring to the gentle sound of the water as it kept rising. He lied, hoping to reassure her.

'It was me you heard. I moved my legs.'

'No, that's not what I meant . . . Over there, listen!'

And she pressed her ear up against the coal. He understood, and did the same. They waited in breathless agony for a few seconds. Then, far away, they heard three very faint blows, clearly spaced out. But they still wondered if it was true; perhaps their ears were ringing, or it might be merely the seam creaking. And they couldn't think what to use to tap back in reply.

Étienne suddenly thought of something.

'You've got my clogs. Lift your feet up and bang with your heels.'

She knocked, beating out the miners' tattoo; and they listened, and again they heard the three blows, far away. Twenty times they tried again, and twenty times the blows came in answer. They wept, and they embraced, despite the danger of losing their balance. At last their comrades had come, they were on their way. They burst with joy and love which swept away the anguish of waiting and the panic of their previous vain appeals, as if their saviours had only to point at the rock with their fingers in order to split it asunder and deliver them.

'Hey!' she cried gaily. 'Wasn't it lucky I leant my head on the wall!'

'Ah, you've got an ear for it!' he replied. 'I didn't hear a thing.'

From that moment on they took it in turns for one of them to be constantly listening, ready to respond to the slightest signal. Soon they could hear the sound of the picks: they were starting the approach works, opening up a gallery. They didn't miss a single sound. But their joy diminished. Although they kept laughing, in order to deceive each other, they were gradually seized with despair again. At first they thought of all sorts of explanations: they must be coming in from Réquillart, the tunnel had to go down through the coal-seam, and perhaps they were opening up more than one gallery simultaneously, for they heard three different men at work. But then they spoke less, and finally lapsed into silence, when they started to calculate the enormous mass of rock that separated them from their comrades. They continued their reflections in silence, counting the long number of days it would take a workman to cut through such a mass. They would never get there in time, they would have died ten times over. And as their anxiety increased they became sullen and unwilling to risk conversation, they answered every signal with a volley of blows with the clogs, but with no hope, merely reacting with an automatic instinct to tell the others that they were still alive.

A day passed, and another day. They had been underground for six days. The water had reached their knees. It rose no further, but neither did it go down; their legs seemed to dissolve in this icy bath. They could pull them out of the water for an hour, but the position was so uncomfortable that they got dreadful attacks of cramp, and they had to let their feet fall back down again. Every ten minutes they had to wriggle their backs up again, as they kept sliding down the wall. Fragments of coal dug into their spines, and their necks ached with a sharp and relentless pain from being constantly bent in order to avoid hitting their heads on the roof. And the atmosphere became more and more suffocating, as the air was compressed by the mass of water and packed into the kind of diving bell where they lay enclosed. Their muffled voices seemed to come from miles away. They had fits of buzzing in the ears, they heard sudden peals of bells tolling madly and herds of horses galloping endlessly through hailstorms.

At first Catherine suffered horribly from hunger. She clutched at her throat with her poor tense hands, she breathed in great hollow wheezing gasps, moaning continuously and piteously as if her stomach were being torn by pincers. Étienne, who was choked with the same torment, felt feverishly around him in the darkness until his fingers encountered a piece of half-rotten wood beside him. He broke it up with his nails and gave Catherine a portion, which she greedily swallowed. They survived for two days on this worm-eaten wood, and they ate the whole plank, until they found to their despair that they had finished it, and scraped their skin trying to break up other planks, which were still intact, and resisted their efforts to splinter them. Their torment then increased, and they were furious when they found that they were unable to chew the material of their clothes. Étienne's leather belt satisfied them briefly. He cut it into little pieces with his teeth, and she chewed at them and forced herself to swallow them. It kept their jaws busy, and gave them the impression that they were eating. Then, when the belt was finished, they started on the cotton fabric of their clothes, sucking it for hours on end.

But soon the violent attacks passed, their hunger became only a deep, muffled pain, as their strength gradually ebbed away. They would have died soon enough, without a doubt, if they hadn't had the water, as much water as they wanted. They only had to lean forward and drink out of their hands; and they did so time and time again, burning with such thirst that no water could quench it.

On the seventh day Catherine leant forward to drink, when her hand felt something floating alongside.

'Hey, look . . . What's that?'

Étienne felt around in the darkness.

'I don't understand, it feels like the cover of a ventilation door.'

She drank, but as she bent down to take a second draught, the thing floated back and bumped into her hand. And she released a terrible scream.

'God almighty! It's him!'

'Who's that?'

'You know who . . . I felt his moustache.'

It was Chaval's corpse, which had been floated up to the top of the ramp by the rising tide. Étienne stretched out his arm, and he too felt the moustache and the crushed nose; and he shuddered with fear and revulsion. Seized with a ghastly wave of nausea, Catherine had spat out the water that was left in her mouth. She thought that she had just drunk some blood, and that the whole mass of liquid lying before her was now that man's blood.

'Hang on,' Étienne stuttered, 'I'll push him back.'

He gave the corpse a kick, which sent it away. But soon they felt it butting up against their legs again.

'In the name of God, will you go away!'

But the third time Étienne had to leave it. Some current kept bringing him back. Chaval refused to leave, he wanted to stay with them, wanted to touch them. He was a dreadful companion, and made the air even more foul. For a whole day they fought their thirst and stopped drinking, preferring to die; and only the following morning did they yield to their suffering: they pushed the corpse away before each draught, but they did drink none the less. There had been no point in smashing his skull, it hadn't stopped him coming back to lie between them, driven by his unquenchable jealousy. Even dead, he would remain there till the bitter end, to prevent them coming together.

Another day, and another. With every ripple of the water, Étienne received a slight blow from the man he had killed, as if he were nudging him with his elbow to remind him of his neighbourly presence. And every time, he shuddered. He saw him continuously, swollen and greenish, with his red moustache and smashed face. Then he forgot that he had killed him; his rival was swimming towards him and trying to bite him. Now Catherine was shaken with long, interminable bouts of weeping, which left her drained and depressed. She finally slipped into a state of unshakeable somnolence. Étienne woke her, and she stammered a few words, but went straight back to sleep again without even raising her eyelids; so he slipped one of his arms round her waist, for fear that she might drown. Now it was up to him to reply to their comrades. The blows of the pick were getting nearer, he could hear them, behind his back. But at the same time his strength was ebbing, he had lost all desire to tap. They knew they were there, so what was the point in tiring themselves out? It was of no interest. Let them come. In his state of expectant stupor, he sometimes forgot for hours on end what he was waiting for.

One thing came to bring them some relief and comfort. The waters fell back, and Chaval's corpse floated away from them. They had been waiting for their rescuers for nine days, and just as they were able to take a few steps down the tunnel for the first time, they were thrown to the ground by a dreadful commotion. They felt for each other in the dark, and held each other in their arms, not understanding what had happened, but crazed with fear at the thought that disaster had struck once more. But nothing stirred. The sound of the picks had ceased.

In the corner where they were sitting side by side, Catherine laughed quietly.

'It must be fine outside . . . Come on, let's go out.'

At first Étienne resisted this madness. But although his mind was firmer, he found it contagious, losing his sense of reality. All their senses were distorted, especially Catherine's, as she was tossing with fever now, and tormented with a need for words and gestures. The drumming in her ears had become babbling brooks and singing birds; she smelled a vivid scent of trampled grass, and she clearly saw great yellow shapes swimming in front of her eyes, so large that she thought she was outside by the canal in a wheatfield, on a bright, sunny day.

'Hey, isn't it warm! . . . Take me, why don't you, let's stay together for ever and ever!'

He held her tight, and she rubbed up against him for a long time, chattering on in a happy, girlish way:

'Haven't we been silly to wait so long! I wanted to accept you straight away, but you didn't understand, and you sulked . . . Then, do you remember, at home at night, when we lay on our backs wide awake looking at the ceiling, listening to each other breathing, and wanting each other so badly?'

Étienne was won over by her good humour, and joked about the memories of their silent passion.

'You hit me once, you did! You slapped me on both cheeks!'

'That was because I was in love with you,' she murmured. 'You see, I refused to let myself think about you, I told myself it was all over; and deep down I knew that one day sooner or later we would be bound to get together . . . We only needed an opportunity, just one lucky break, didn't we?'

Étienne felt an icy shiver run down his back; he wanted to shake her out of this dream, but then he replied slowly:

'Nothing is ever final, you only need a bit of happiness to be able to start all over again.'

'So this time it's all right, isn't it, you'll keep me for good?'

And she swooned, and slipped. She was so weak that her tiny voice died away altogether. He clasped her to his heart in a state of panic.

'Does it hurt?'

She sat up in astonishment.

'No, not a bit . . . Why?'

But the question had shaken her out of her dream. She

peered desperately into the darkness, wrung her hands, and
was shaken by a renewed fit of sobbing.

'Oh God, oh dear God, how dark it is!'

There was neither wheat nor the scent of grass nor the song
of the skylarks nor the great yellow sun; just the flooded and
destroyed mine, the stinking darkness, and the macabre sound
of dripping inside this tomb where they had been living out
their death agony for so many days. Her warped senses now
increased her horror, she was seized by the superstitions of her
childhood, and she saw the Black Man, the old dead miner
who came back to the pit to strangle naughty girls.

'Listen, did you hear that?'

'No, I didn't hear anything.'

'But there was . . . that Man, you know the one? . . . Look!
There he is . . . The earth is soaking us in blood from all her
veins to punish us for cutting one of her arteries; and there he
is, you can see him, look! He's black as night . . . Oh I'm
afraid, so afraid!'

Shivering still, she fell silent. Then, in a very small voice,
she went on:

'No, it's just the other man.'

'What other man?'

'The one that's in here with us, the one who's passed on.'

She was haunted by the vision of Chaval, and she spoke
ramblingly of their rotten life together, of the one day when he
had been nice to her, at Jean-Bart, and the other days when he
was stupid and hit her, when he beat her black and blue and
then crushed her half to death in his embrace.

'I tell you he's come back to stop us being together! . . .
He's got one of his old fits of jealousy . . . Oh, send him away
again, oh, take me and keep me all for yourself!'

She threw herself energetically on to him, seeking out his
mouth and thrusting hers passionately against it. The darkness
cleared, she saw the sun again, and she laughed once more,
happily and tenderly. Étienne trembled to feel his body touch
her half-naked flesh through the tattered shreds of her jacket
and breeches, and in a sudden surge of revived virility he took
her. And they had their honeymoon at last, in the depths of
this tomb, on a bed of mud, caught by the urge not to die

before they had had their moment of happiness, by the obstinate urge to live, to make themselves come alive for one last time. They loved each other desperately, knowing that all was lost, knowing that they were dying.

Then there was nothing. Étienne was sitting on the ground in the same corner, with Catherine lying motionless in his lap. Hours went by, and more hours. For a long time he thought that she was sleeping; then he touched her; she was very cold. She was dead. And yet he refused to move in case he woke her. The idea that he was the first to enjoy her as a grown woman, and that she might be pregnant, moved him. Other thoughts, the urge to go away with her, the joy of imagining what they would do together later on, came to him at times, but they were so insubstantial that they hardly seemed to skim his brow, like the breath of sleep itself. He grew weaker, and had only the strength to make a slight movement with his hand to check that she was still lying there stiff and cold, sleeping like a child. Everything disappeared, the darkness itself dissolved, he was nowhere, out of space, out of time. Yet something was beating near his head, violent blows which were coming closer and closer; but first he had felt too lazy to go and answer, numbed with an enormous fatigue; and now he was no longer aware what was happening, he was dreaming that she was walking in front of him and that he could hear the gentle tapping of her clogs. Two days went by without her moving, but he touched her mechanically, and was reassured to feel how peacefully she lay there.

Étienne felt a shock. Voices rumbled, rocks rolled down towards his feet. He saw a lamp, and sobbed. His eyes blinked as he followed the light, he couldn't stop looking in ecstasy at the tiny reddish glow which hardly made any inroads into the darkness. But he was carried away by his comrades, and he let them push some spoonfuls of soup between his clenched teeth. It was only when they were in the Réquillart tunnel that he recognized somebody, Négrel, the engineer, standing in front of him; and these two men who despised each other, the rebellious workman and the sceptical boss, fell on each other's necks, heaving great sobs, as they felt a common humanity well up deep within them. They were filled with great sadness, with generations of misery, with that overflowing of suffering that life sometimes leads to.

Up in the open air, La Maheude had collapsed beside the body of her daughter. She screamed, and screamed again, and then again, in a long series of endless, long-drawn-out wails. Several bodies had already been brought to the surface and laid out on the ground; Chaval, whom they assumed had been crushed by a landslide, a pit boy and two hewers whose brains had also been dashed out and their bellies swollen with water. Some of the women in the crowd lost their heads, tearing their skirts, and scratching their faces.

When Étienne had been given time to grow gradually accustomed to the lamps and taken a little food, he was finally brought out. He looked all skin and bones, and his hair had turned white; the crowd drew apart and trembled at the sight of this old man. La Maheude stopped crying and looked at him in stupefaction, staring with gaping eyes.

CHAPTER VI

It was four o'clock in the morning. The cool April night warmed gradually as day drew nearer. The stars started fading in the limpid sky as the first light of dawn tinged the orient with purple. And the black countryside, still sunk in slumber, stirred ever so gently with the faint murmuring that precedes awakening.

Étienne strode out down the road to Vandame. He had just spent six weeks at Montsou, in a hospital bed. He was still very pale and thin, but he felt strong enough to leave, and so he left. The Company, which still feared for its pits, and had already laid off several waves of men, had warned him that they couldn't keep him on. However, they offered him a lump sum of a hundred francs, as well as their paternal advice to give up coal-mining, which was now too strenuous for him. But he had turned down the hundred francs, for he had already been called to Paris by Pluchart, who had enclosed the money for the fare in his letter. This meant that his old dream was about to come true. The previous night on leaving the hospital he had slept at the Bon-Joyeux, Widow Désir's inn. And when he had got up early that morning he had only one last wish, which was to say goodbye to his comrades before he went to Marchiennes to catch the eight o'clock train.

Étienne stopped for a moment on the road, which was tinged pink. It was so good to breathe in the pure air of this precocious springtime. It looked like being a magnificent morning. Gradually the light spread, and the sun started to draw life up from the earth. And he began to walk again, striking the ground firmly with his dogwood stick, and watching the distant plain emerge from the mists of night. He hadn't met any of his acquaintances; La Maheude had come once to the hospital, but had no doubt been unable to return. But he did know that all the inhabitants of village Two Hundred and Forty would be going down at Jean-Bart now, and that she herself had gone back to work.

Gradually the deserted roads filled with people, and Étienne kept passing colliers with pale, silent faces. The Company, so people said, was exploiting its victory. When the workmen had succumbed to hunger and returned to the pits after two and a half months out on strike, they had had to accept the timbering tariff, that disguised cut in wages, which was even more repugnant now for being stained with the blood of their comrades. They were being robbed of the fruits of an hour of their labour, they were being made to renege on their oath not to submit, and this perjury stuck in their throats, as bitter as gall. Work started up again everywhere, at Mirou, Madeleine, Crèvecœur, and La Victoire. Everywhere in the morning mist the human herd was trampling down the shadowy roads, lines of men plodding onward with their noses to the ground, like cattle being led to the slaughterhouse. They were shivering in their thin cotton clothes; they crossed their arms, arched their backs, and hunched up their shoulders, which, with their sandwiches stashed between their shirt and their jacket, made them look like hunchbacks. And, from this mass of dark, silent forms on the march back to work, looking neither left nor right and refusing to laugh, you could guess at the teeth clenched in anger, the hearts brimming with hatred, and the resignation due only to the needs of the stomach.

The closer he came to the pit, the more Étienne saw their numbers grow. They were nearly all walking alone, and those who came in groups were walking in single file, already exhausted and sick of themselves as well as their workmates. He saw one very old man, whose eyes glowed like cinders in his livid face. Another man, a young one, was breathing heavily in a state of controlled fury. Many held their clogs in their hands; and you could hardly hear the soft sound of their thick woollen stockings on the ground. They passed by in a constant stream, like a routed army forced to march in retreat, moving ceaselessly onwards with their heads hung low, filled with a quiet but furious rage at the thought of needing to start struggling all over again, and seek revenge.

As Étienne arrived, Jean-Bart was just emerging from the shadows, and the lanterns hanging on the trestles were still burning in the nascent light of dawn. Above the dark buildings, a plume of white vapour rose like the crest of an eagle, delicately tinted with carmine. He went past the stairs of the screening shed to go to the landing-stage.

The descent was starting, and workmen were coming up out of the shed. For an instant he remained motionless amid all the din and commotion. The tubs shook the iron plates on the floor as they rolled past, the drums span round as the cables unwound, while all around you could hear orders shouted down a loud hailer, bells ringing, rappers raining blows on the signal block; and he recognized the monster swallowing down its ration of human flesh, the cages emerging and then plunging back down out of sight, sinking with their load of men, without ever stopping, gulping them down effortlessly like a greedy giant. Since his accident he had felt a nervous horror at the thought of the mine. As the cages went down, they made his stomach heave. He had to turn and look away, the pit made him feel too upset.

But in the vast hall still cloaked in shadows, which the guttering lamps lit with an eerie glow, he didn't recognize a single friendly face. The miners who were waiting there, barefoot, holding their lamps in their hands, watched him wide-eyed and anxiously, then lowered their gaze and drew back with an air of shame. No doubt they recognized him, and felt no more bitterness towards him; on the contrary, they seemed to fear him, blushing at the idea that he might reproach them with cowardice. This attitude made his heart feel heavy, and he forgot that these wretches had stoned him, and he started to dream again of changing them into heroes, of leading the people, to save that force of nature from tearing itself apart.

One cage embarked its load of men, the batch disappeared, and as others arrived he at last saw one of his lieutenants from the strike, an honest man who had sworn he was ready to die.

'You too,' he murmured, heartbroken.

The man went pale, his lips quivered, then he made a sign of apology, and said:

'What do you expect me to do? I've got a wife to look after.'

Now as the new crowd came up from the shed he recognized all of them.

'You too! And you! And you as well!'

And they all trembled, and stammered in stifled voices:

'I've got a mother to look after ... I've got children ... We've got to eat.'

The cage hadn't come back up again yet, they waited for it sullenly, suffering so acutely from their defeat that they avoided looking him in the eyes, and stared obstinately at the pit.

'And what about La Maheude?' asked Étienne.

Nobody answered. One of them made a sign that she was about to come. Others raised their arms, trembling with pity: oh, the poor woman, what a wretched state she was in! The silence continued, and when their comrade held out his hand to say farewell, they all shook it firmly, putting into this silent embrace all their fury at having yielded and their feverish hopes for revenge. The cage had arrived, and they embarked and disappeared, swallowed up by the abyss.

Pierron had appeared, sporting the open lamp that the deputies used to fix on to their leather caps. It was now a week since he had been appointed deputy at the loading bay, and the workmen moved aside to let him pass, for he showed his pride in his new honour. He was embarrassed to see Étienne, but he went up to him, and was finally reassured to hear from the young man that he was leaving. They chatted. His wife was now landlady of the Progrès Inn, thanks to the support of a number of gentlemen who had been so kind to her. But he broke off, and shouted at old Mouque, accusing him of not having brought up his horse dung at the proper time. The old man listened, bowing his shoulders. Then before he went back down again, choking with surprise at this reprimand, he too took Étienne's hand to shake it, with the same slow movement as the others, hot with suppressed anger, trembling with future rebellion. And Étienne was so deeply moved to feel this old hand shaking in his, and to realize this old man was forgiving him for the death of his children, that he watched him leave without being able to say a word.

'Isn't La Maheude coming this morning, then?' he asked Pierron, after a moment.

At first the latter pretended not to understand, for sometimes you can attract bad luck just by opening your mouth. Then, as he moved off on the pretext of having an order to give, he finally said:

'Who? La Maheude . . . here she is.'

And there she was, in fact, emerging from the shed holding her lamp, dressed in her breeches and jacket, her cap pulled down over her head. And it had taken a charitable exception to the rules of the Company, who had taken pity on this cruelly stricken woman, to allow her to go back down underground at the age of forty; but as it seemed difficult to send her back to pushing tubs, they used her to work a little ventilator that they had just installed in the north gallery, in the infernal regions under Tartarus which suffered from lack of air. There she spent ten hours at a time turning the wheel, with her back breaking, and her flesh roasting in forty degrees of heat down at the end of a burning-hot gully. She earned thirty sous.

When Étienne saw her, looking pathetic in her man's clothes, her breasts and belly seeming still swollen from the dampness of the coal-face, he stammered in confusion, he couldn't find the words to explain that he was leaving and that he had come to bid her farewell.

She looked at him without listening, and finally said to him, calling him by his first name:

'So, you're surprised to see me here, Étienne . . . True

enough, I did threaten to strangle the first person in my family to go back down; and now here I am, and down I go, so I ought to strangle myself, didn't I? . . . Well, my friend, I would have done it already if I hadn't had the old man and the children at home!'

And on she went in her tired, low voice. She didn't make excuses, she told her story simply; they had nearly died of hunger, and she had decided to go back, so as not to be thrown out of the village.

'How is the old man?' asked Étienne.

'He's still gentle, and he's clean . . . But he's completely off his head . . . You know he didn't get sentenced for that business, don't you? They said they'd send him to the mad-house, but I didn't want them to, they would only have slipped something in his soup . . . But those goings on caused us no end of trouble, because he'll never get his pension, one of the gentlemen told me it would be immoral if they gave him one.'

'Is Jeanlin working?'

'Yes, the gentlemen found him a surface job. He earns twenty sous . . . Oh, I can't complain, the bosses have been very kind, as they explained to me themselves . . . Twenty sous for the kid, and my thirty sous, that makes fifty. If there weren't six of us, we'd have enough to eat. Estelle is really wolfing it down now, and the worst thing is that we're going to have to wait four or five years until Lénore and Henri are old enough to go down the pit.'

Étienne couldn't help remonstrating unhappily.

'Them too!'

A flush had come to the pale cheeks of La Maheude, while her eyes started to gleam. But her shoulders slumped as if they were unable to bear the weight of her fate.

'What do you expect? First the others went, now it's them . . . They've none of them come back, now it's their turn.'

She fell silent, as the labourers pushing the trucks were disturbing her. Through the tall sooty windows the thin light of dawn entered, drowning the lamps in a greyish glow; and the vibrations of the engine started up anew every three minutes, the cables unwound, and the cages continued to swallow up the men.

'Come on, you idle buggers, get a move on!' cried Pierron. 'All aboard, we'll never finish in time today.'

He looked at La Maheude, but she didn't move. She had already let three cages go by. Then, as if she had fallen asleep on her feet, and, reawakening, remembered only Étienne's opening words, she said:

'So you're leaving, are you?'

'Yes, this morning.'

'You're right, you're better off leaving, if you can . . . And I'm glad I've seen you, because at least you'll know I've got no axe to grind with you. There was a time I wanted to kill you, after all that butchery. But then you think it over, don't you? You realize that in the end it's not really anyone's fault . . . No, it's really not your fault, it's everyone's fault.'

Now she went on to talk tranquilly of her dead, her man, Zacharie, and Catherine; and the tears only came to her eyes when she mentioned the name of Alzire. She had resumed the calm demeanour of a reasonable woman, judging things with equanimity. It wouldn't help the bourgeoisie at all to have killed so many poor people. Of course they'd be punished one day, you have to pay for everything. The workers shouldn't even have got mixed up in it, the roof would cave in all by itself, the soldiers would open fire on the bosses just as they had gunned down the workers. And her age-old spirit of resignation, whose hereditary instinct was bending her once more to its discipline, was being gradually weakened, as her certainty grew that, even if there was no longer a Good Lord, another would spring up in his place, to avenge the needy.

She was speaking under her breath, looking suspiciously about her. Then, as Pierron had come up to them, she added out loud:

'Well then, if you're leaving, you'd better come back home to collect your belongings . . . There are still two shirts, three handkerchiefs and an old pair of breeches.'

Étienne raised his hand to brush aside her offer of these few old clothes that had escaped the pawnshop.

'No. it's not worth the trouble, they'll do for the children . . . I'll get some more in Paris.'

Another two cages had gone down, and Pierron decided to call La Maheude directly.

'Hey, you there, we're waiting for you! How much longer are you going to go nattering on?'

But she turned her back on him. Why should that damn mercenary try to be so zealous? He wasn't supposed to have anything to do with the descent. The men at his loading bay already hated him. So she stubbornly refused to move, holding her lamp between her fingers, and freezing in the draught, despite the mildness of the weather for the season. Neither she nor Étienne found anything further to add. They stood looking at each other, their hearts so heavy that they wished they could find something more to say.

In the end she spoke for the sake of speaking.

'La Levaque is pregnant, Levaque is still in prison, and Bouteloup's taking his place while he's away.'

'Oh yes, Bouteloup.'

'Oh yes, wait a minute, did I tell you? . . . Philomène has left.'

'What do you mean, left?'

'Yes, she walked out, she went off with a miner from the Pas-de-Calais. I was afraid she'd leave me the two brats. But not a bit of it, she took them with her . . . How about that, not bad for a woman who coughs up blood and who always looks as if she's about to choke to death!'

She dreamed for a moment, then went on, with her slow voice.

'You wouldn't believe what people have said about me! . . . You remember, they said I was sleeping with you. My God, after my man died it could easily have happened, if I'd been a bit younger, couldn't it? But now I'm glad it didn't, because I'm sure we'd regret it.'

'Yes, we'd regret it,' said Étienne.

And that was all, they spoke no more. A cage was waiting for her, and the deputy called out to her angrily, threatening her with a fine. Then she made up her mind, and she shook his hand. Étienne was deeply moved, and kept looking at her, so ravaged and worn out, with her livid face, her greying hair slipping out from under her blue cap, her body beneath the breeches and the cotton jacket sagging from repeated confinements. And in this last handshake he recognized the same long silent embrace that his comrades had offered, making a date for whenever they might be able to take up the struggle once again. He understood perfectly well, he saw her tranquil faith in the depths of her eyes. See you soon, and the next time it would be the real thing.

'What a godforsaken idle bitch!' shouted Pierron.

La Maheude was pushed and jostled as she crammed herself into a corner of a tub with four other people. They pulled on the rope to ring out that dinner was served, the cage swung free and plunged down into the darkness, until all that could be seen was the swift flight of the cable.

Then Étienne left the pit. Down below, beneath the screening shed, he noticed someone sitting on the ground, in the middle of a great sheet of coal, with his legs stretched out wide. It was Jeanlin, employed as 'rough sorter'. He was holding a block of coal between his thighs, and hitting it with a hammer to knock out the fragments of shale; and he was drowned by such a fine, powdery cloud of soot that Étienne would never have recognized him, if the child hadn't lifted his monkey-like snout, revealing his prominent ears and his tiny blue-green eyes. He gave a farcical laugh, broke the block with a last blow of the hammer, and disappeared behind the cloud of black dust he had created.

Once outside, Étienne followed the road for a while, lost in thought. All sorts of ideas were milling around in his head. But he felt that he was at last out in the fresh air, under the open skies, and he breathed in greedily. The sun appeared majestically on the horizon, the whole countryside was experiencing a joyous awakening. A wave of gold light flowed from east to west across the vast plain. This life-giving warmth spread wider and wider, vibrating with youthfulness, throbbing with all the sighs of the earth, with birdsong, and with all the murmurs of the rivers and forests. It was good to be alive, the old world wanted to live for another springtime.

And, filled with this hope, Étienne started walking more slowly, looking distractedly all about him, drinking in the cheerful signs of the new season. He thought about himself, and felt strong and mature after his experience down the bottom of the mine. His education was finished, he was leaving with a new suit of armour, as a philosophical soldier of the revolution having declared war on society as he saw it, and condemned it. His joy at joining Pluchart, at the thought of becoming a respected leader like Pluchart, moved him to write speeches in his mind, which he kept revising. He considered extending the scope of his policies, for the bourgeois refinement that had lifted him out of his class gave him an ever-greater hatred of the bourgeoisie. As for the workers, whose stench of poverty now offended him, he still felt the need to cover them in glory, and he pictured them as the only heroes, the only saints, the only nobility, and the only force which could redeem humanity. He already saw himself on the rostrum leading the people to triumph, if the people didn't eat him alive before he got there.

He looked upwards towards a skylark he heard singing in the highest heavens. Tiny red clouds, the last vapours of night, dissolved in the limpid azure; and the faces of Souvarine and Rasseneur seemed to be vaguely figured there. To be sure, everything always went downhill as soon as each individual tried to seize power for himself. Thus, this famous International which should have remade the world had aborted, proving itself powerless to prevent its formidable army splitting up and falling to pieces in interminable bickering. Was Darwin right, then, was the world nothing but a battlefield where the strong ate the weak, for the beauty and the survival of the species? He found this question disturbing, although he was sure enough of his scientific knowledge to have his own answer. But one idea in particular dissipated his doubts and enchanted him, that of using his old explanation of the theory, as soon as he could make his first speech. If one class had to go under, wouldn't the people, who were still fresh and vital, trample all over the bourgeoisie, who were debilitated by their endless pleasure-seeking? New blood would create a new society. And in his expectation of a barbarian invasion which would regenerate the decadent old nations, there reappeared his absolute faith in a forthcoming revolution, the real one, that of the workers, who would set fire to the dying century with the same purple blaze of the rising sun that he saw now bleeding across the heavens.

He kept walking onward, daydreaming all the while, striking the stones on the road with his dogwood stick; but as he cast his eyes around him, he recognized bits of the countryside. It was just at La Fourche-aux-Bœufs, he remembered, that he had taken charge of the mob, the morning that they had sacked the pits. And today the brutal, lethal, underpaid work was starting all over again. Under the ground, far away, 700 metres down below, it was as if he could hear the regular, relentless, muffled blows struck by the comrades he had just seen descending, who were hacking away in black and silent anger. Of course they had been beaten, they had lost money and lives; but Paris would not forget the shots fired at Le Voreux, and the blood of the Empire itself would drain out of this incurable wound; for even if this industrial slump was drawing to a close, and the factories were reopening one by one, a state of war had none the less been declared and peace was no longer possible. The colliers had stood up and been counted, they had flexed their muscles, and their call for justice had stirred the hearts of working men throughout France. Therefore their defeat brought no reassurance, and the bourgeois of Montsou, whose victory was tainted by the secret misgivings that always follow the end of a strike, were looking over their shoulders to see if the writing wasn't in fact already on the wall, despite the deep silence that reigned. They realized that the revolution would always be able to rise again at a day's notice, but now it would be accompanied by a general strike and agreements between all the workers with relief funds, enabling them to hold out for months without going short of food. Their crumbling society had received another body blow, they had heard the foundations cracking beneath their very feet, and had felt the first shock waves of tremors to come, which would grow in number until the whole rotten, tottering edifice would come crashing down and disappear into the abyss, like Le Voreux.

Étienne turned left, down the road to Joiselle. He remembered, that was where he had prevented the mob from rushing to take Gaston-Marie by storm. In the bright sunlight he could see the headgear of several distant pits, Mirou to the right, and Madeleine and Crèvecœur side by side. The sounds of labour rumbled all around him, and the picks that he thought he could hear tapping away in the depths of the earth were echoing now across the whole length and breadth of the plain. A single blow, then a second, and then more and more, hacking relentlessly away under the fields, roads, and villages which lay smiling in the sunshine: the whole dark labour of this underground penal colony was so successfully suppressed by the enormous mass of rock overhead that you had to know it was there underneath before you could detect its lingering, suffering sighs. And now he started to wonder whether violence really made things happen any faster. Cut cables, torn rails, broken lamps, what a waste of effort! What was the point of getting 3,000 men together just to stampede through the countryside causing death and destruction? He felt confusedly that legal measures might one day prove to be much more devastating. Now that he had sown his wild oats, and outgrown his immature resentment, his ideas were maturing. Yes, La Maheude was right when she said, with her usual good sense, next time it would be the real thing; they would form a peaceful army, make sure they knew and understood each other, form trade unions* as soon as the law allowed it; and the day would come when they would find themselves shoulder to shoulder, when they would be millions of workers, facing a mere handful of layabouts, able to seize power and become the masters. Ah, what a rebirth of justice and truth! Then the crouching, sated god, that monstrous idol who lay hidden in the depths of his tabernacle untold leagues away, bloated with the flesh of miserable wretches who never even saw him, would instantly give up the ghost.

But Étienne was leaving the road to Vandame and came on to the main paved highway. To the right he made out Montsou sloping away into the distance. Opposite him were the ruins of Le Voreux, the cursed abyss that three pumps worked tirelessly to empty. Then over on the horizon there were other pits, La Victoire, Saint-Thomas, Feutry-Cantel; while towards the north, smoke from the high chimneys of the blast-furnaces and the batteries of coke ovens curled up through the clear morning air. If he wanted to catch the eight o'clock train he'd have to hurry up, for there were still six kilometres to go.

And far below, beneath his feet, the stubborn tapping of the picks continued. His comrades were all down there, and he could hear them following his every step. Wasn't that La Maheude under the beetfield, her back broken, and her raucous breathing rising up to the accompanying rumble of the ventilator? Further away, to the left and to the right, he thought he could recognize others, beneath the wheat, the green hedges, and the young saplings. High in the sky the April sun now shone down in its full glory, warming the bountiful earth and breathing life into her fertile bosom, as the buds burst into verdant leaf, and the fields quivered under the pressure of the rising grass. All around him seeds were swelling and shoots were growing, cracking the surface of the plain, driven upwards by their need for warmth and light. The sap flowed upwards and spilled over in soft whispers; the sound of germinating seeds rose and swelled to form a kiss. Again, and again, and ever more clearly, as if they too were rising towards the sunlight, his comrades kept tapping away. Beneath the blazing rays of the sun, in that morning of new growth, the countryside rang with song, as its belly swelled with a black and avenging army of men, germinating slowly in its furrows, growing upwards in readiness for harvests to come, until one day soon their ripening would burst open the earth itself.

EXPLANATORY NOTES

1 *Germinal*: this was the name given to the seventh month of the Revolutionary calendar (21 March to 19 April). Germinal year III (1795) was the occasion of hunger riots by the Parisian people against the Convention government. It thus has overtones both of violent insurrection and revolutionary renewal.

5 *Marchiennes*: an industrial town situated half-way between Douai and Valenciennes in northern France.

Montsou: a fictitious town, whose name echoes that of the real Montceau-les-Mines, but also the themes of poverty and greed ('mon sou' = 'my cash').

6 *tippler*: a frame or cage into which a tub of coal would have been run, and which was then revolved so that the tub was turned upside-down and unloaded its contents.

Étienne Lantier: the son of Auguste Lantier and Gervaise Macquart (the heroine of *L'Assommoir*, 1877). Étienne inherits a tendency to alcoholism from Gervaise (who is also the mother of the promiscuous heroine of *Nana*, 1880).

7 *Le Voreux*: the name of the pit immediately suggests that it is 'voracious', 'devouring' the men who work in it. The whole novel is permeated with such Dickensian names.

headgear: the overground structure at the pit-head, whose framework supports the pulley wheels which winch the cages up and down.

Les Forges: the local foundry clearly belongs to the recently founded (1864) mine and factory employers' union Le Comité des Forges, the largest industrial combine in France. The fact that such a 'big name' is affected indicates the gravity of the slump.

8 *black phlegm*: this is 'black spit', or silicosis, a disease caused by the inhalation of stone dust. It was actually less common than miners' asthma, or pneumoconiosis, caused by the inhalation of coal-dust, which was so common that every miner seems to have been afflicted by it to some degree in the course of his working life. Bonnemort appears to have contracted a bit of both.

8 *people laid off, workshops closing down*: the policy of financial and industrial expansion followed throughout the Second Empire was translated in practice into years of boom interspersed with years of slump: the slump of 1866, where the novel appears to be situated, was one of the most severe.

the Emperor's: a nephew of Napoleon Bonaparte, Louis-Napoleon (1808–73) had led the Bonapartist opposition to Louis-Philippe's bourgeois monarchy (1830–48). He entertained liberal economic theories based on the ideas of the utopian thinker Saint-Simon. After the 1848 Revolution he was elected President of the Second Republic. He asserted his personal power, however, by his *coup d'état* of 2 December 1851, reinforced by a plebiscite on 2 December 1852, when he abolished the Republic and proclaimed himself Emperor. The Second Empire (1852–70) was the period chosen by Zola as the setting for his whole Rougon-Macquart cycle. It was marked throughout by Napoleon III's commitment to popular dictatorship and industrial growth.

America: Napoleon III's foreign policy brought him initial popularity, when he sent troops to support Italian freedom from Austria in 1859, and final disaster, when he challenged Prussia and was forced to capitulate at Sedan in 1870. The Mexican war referred to here (1861–7) was in its death throes in 1866. In 1861 Britain, Spain, and France had sent troops to Mexico to challenge the new President Juarez, who had founded a republic and refused to honour foreign debts. Britain and Spain, however, made peace in 1862, leaving Napoleon III to conduct the war on his own and impose an unpopular puppet emperor, Maximilian of Austria, in 1863. In 1867 the United States forced France to withdraw, leaving Maximilian to his fate. (His execution is ironically commemorated in a famous painting by Manet.)

cholera: there was an epidemic of cholera in the Lille and Valenciennes region in 1866. Roger Magraw, in *France 1815–1914: The Bourgeois Century*, states that there were 2,000 deaths in Lille alone. Sanitation in the industrial cities was minimal, and even apart from this epidemic other fatal diseases—typhoid, diphtheria, tuberculosis—were rampant. Average life expectancy in Lille was 24 years, and 40% of children died before the age of 5.

10 *Bonnemort*: Zola's French literally means 'Nice Death'. (An equivalent nickname might be 'Barebones'.)

11 *trammer*: the usual British terms for the person who pushed the coal-tub were 'putter' and 'trammer', depending on the region. But these terms do not differentiate between male and female workers. So I have used 'trammer' for male workers or mixed groups and 'tram girl' for females.

under my skin: in fact Bonnemort appears to have contracted rheumatism and inflammation, caused as much by the constant chafing of the joints against the walls of the narrow underground tunnels as by the damp. Here, as elsewhere, Zola deliberately makes Bonnemort naïvely underestimate the gravity and the causes of his afflictions.

13 *good long family history*: the history of the accidents which befell Bonnemort and his family is intended to be typical rather than extraordinary. John Benson, in *British Coalminers in the Nineteenth Century* (New York, 1980), notes that there were about 1,000 deaths a year in British mines at this period, and that there were about 100 non-fatal accidents for every death.

d'Anzin: Anzin is an industrial town on the outskirts of Valenciennes. The d'Anzin Mining Company was the real mining company whose pits (the Renard pit at Denain and the Thiers pit at Bruay, a small town near Anzin) Zola had visited between 23 February and 3 March 1884. Zola's notes on his visit are recorded in 'Mes notes sur Anzin'. Zola also took information from Louis L. Simonin's *La Vie souterraine* (1866), and Émile Dormoy's *Topographie souterraine du Bassin houillier de Valenciennes* (1867). Zola's readers might have been expected to appreciate the irony that, during the period in which *Germinal* is situated, it was Adolphe Thiers, later to head the Versailles government which crushed the Paris Commune in 1871, who was president of the Board of Directors of the d'Anzin Company.

15 *village number Two Hundred and Forty*: the numbering rather than naming of the purpose-built mining villages draws our attention to the fact that these were mass-produced workers' settlements, rather than communities that had evolved naturally, and that the employers who built them were motivated by utility as much as philanthropy.

19 *stoneman*: the stoneman's job is explained on p. 41

overman: the official in charge of day-to-day operations at the pit-head.

20 *fortnight's pay*: throughout most of the nineteenth century

miners in France as well as Britain were usually paid fortnightly. Since pay-day usually meant a day off work, employers resisted moves towards weekly payment, which would have made family budgeting easier.

21 *sous*: the familiar name for the five-centime piece.

the bourgeois: the term 'bourgeois' is often used nowadays in France to refer loosely to the rich, or simply the middle classes. Here the term has more of the force intended by Marx, who used the term to refer to an élite of *rentiers* living off unearned income, typically from rented property, land ownership, or investment in stocks and shares.

a hundred sous: what La Maheude hopes for is actually a five-franc piece. Zola's workers reveal their poverty by counting the sum as a formidable number of the small coins they usually handle.

22 *Empress*: Empress Eugénie (1826–1920), Napoleon III's wife, was a staunch Catholic, of Spanish origins. The twin portraits displayed in a workman's cottage underline the extent to which the Imperial regime projected a popular image encouraging traditional family values as well as hierarchical respect. One cannot help thinking of the popularity of images of their contemporaries Victoria and Albert.

23 *'slab'*: the French term for this makeshift sandwich, 'briquet', makes derisory reference to a brick or a slab ('brique').

25 *deputy*: the equivalent of a foreman, or team-leader.

32 *Davy lamps*: in 1815 Sir Humphrey Davy (1778–1829) designed the safety lamp which avoided the explosions which naked light had previously provoked. The Davy lamp's flame was encased in a fine metal gauze mesh which allowed it to burn while keeping out the inflammable methane gas given off by the coal.

35 *onsetters*: pit boys who load the cages at the pit bottom.

38 *boys are stealing the girls' bread*: female labour underground was not abolished until 1874, whereas it had been banned in British mines in 1842. Nor is there anything unusual in children under 12, like Lydie, Jeanlin, and Bébert, working underground. John Benson, in *British Coalminers in the Nineteenth Century* (New York, 1980), notes that 5,000 children between the ages of 5 and 10 were working underground in Britain towards the middle of the nineteenth century. Girls were traditionally used

to push the tubs, while young boys operated ventilation traps until they were old enough to become hewers. The miners themselves tended to resist attempts to control or suppress female and child labour, since allowing a grown man to perform their tasks would mean that a miner's family would lose the extra income his children might have brought home.

46 *long line of alcoholics*: Zola believed, on the best scientific evidence available at the time, that alcoholism was inherited. This fatal flaw in the Rougon-Macquart family is one of the covert motors of the whole novel-cycle. Étienne's mother Gervaise and father Lantier, who figure in *L'Assommoir* (1877), are the immediate transmitters.

Paris . . . she's a laundress, in the rue de la Goutte d'Or: Étienne's mother Gervaise lives in a dilapidated tenement building in a poor working-class street situated between Montmartre and the Gare du Nord. She tries to earn an honest living as a laundress, but readers of *L'Assommoir* (1877) would have already been aware of her fatal descent into prostitution and squalid death, although this has not yet 'happened' at the time of *Germinal* (published in 1885 but set in 1866).

49 *flame of his lamp had turned blue*: when the Davy lamp's flame turned blue, this signalled the presence of firedamp in the atmosphere.

50 *firedamp*: the popular term for the inflammable gas methane, given off by the coal-seams, which is one of the worst hazards facing the coal-miner.

59 *Bataille . . . Trompette*: 'Battle', 'Trumpet'—the triumphal military names given to these equine drudges echo the martial ambitions of the Second Empire (the struggle for Italian unity, the Crimean War, the Mexican adventure). But the effect for Zola's readers would have been bathetic, given their knowledge of the Mexican and Prussian fiascos (1867, 1870).

62 *Volcan*: 'the Volcano'—one of several local pubs which announces its true colours; in this case a potent mixture of sex and alcohol. Theodore Zeldin, in *France 1848–1945*, calculates that there were around 1,000 pubs in Lille alone in the middle of the nineteenth century.

65 *Avantage*: 'the Advantage'—a more socially responsible-sounding pub, as befits an establishment belonging to Rasseneur.

66 *Rasseneur*: the figure of the pragmatic, reformist socialist Rasse-

neur was probably inspired by the characters of Émile Basly, an ex-miner who became a pub-owner, then leader of the new miners' union in Denain in 1883 (his nascent union was in fact broken by the strike of 1884, but he became a Member of Parliament in 1885), and Dr Paul Brousse, leader of the 'possibilist' opposition (Federation of Socialist Workers, 1881) to Jules Guesde's overt Marxism.

70 *river Scarpe*: the Scarpe flows through Arras, Douai, and Marchiennes on its way towards Belgium. It is linked by a system of canals to the Channel ports of Calais and Dunkirk.

75 *brioche*: a sweetish tea-cake.

79 *sou ... gold standard ... deniers ... pounds ... crowns*: this flood of financial terms from the *ancien régime* (the official nineteenth-century currency being denominated in francs and centimes) serves to emphasize how the rich have grown richer, while the poor are left to scrape a few coins together in order to buy a crust of bread. The phenomenal increase in value of the Montsou shares is based on the real history of the d'Anzin Company.

revolutionary regime: the French Revolution of 1789 had confiscated the lands of the aristocracy, and sold them to those of the middle classes able to afford them.

overthrow of Napoleon: Napoleon Bonaparte (1769–1821) had consolidated many of the innovations of the Revolutionary State, as First Consul (1799) and Emperor (1804), but after fighting off most of Europe on behalf of the French nation he was forced out of office by the allies in 1814, and defeated again, at Waterloo, after his escape from exile in 1815.

82 *Salon*: the annual Paris art exhibition, which showed thousands of paintings chosen from a vast number submitted by amateur and professional painters. To have an exhibit selected would help a painter make a name and sell his or her works. In 1863 so many major artists and important works (including Manet's *Déjeuner sur l'herbe*) were rejected by the traditionally minded selection committee that Napoleon III himself inaugurated an alternative Salon, the Salon des Refusés. Zola's novel *L'Œuvre* (1886) shows the unsuccessful struggle of an archetypal Impressionist painter, Claude Lantier (Étienne's brother), to be accepted by the Salon.

89 *Nord*: this Department (roughly equivalent to a British county) includes the port of Dunkirk and the industrial cities of

Lille and Valenciennes. It lies along the northern frontier of France.

94   *farthing*: the French is 'liard', an *ancien régime* coin of little worth, no longer current during this period.

96   *bread … brioche*: in Cécile Grégoire's ineffectual and absent-minded generosity there may perhaps be an ironic reminder of Marie Antoinette's famous answer to the plight of the starving Parisian people when she heard that they had no bread to eat, 'Qu'ils mangent donc de la brioche'—'Then why don't they eat cake?'

128   *Piquette's*: 'piquette' means a weak and vinegary wine—not a good advertisement for a pub.

139   *Souvarine*: Souvarine's theories seem to be based on those of the Russian anarchist Bakunin, and his personal history on the lives of more than one Russian terrorist.

140   *Tsar*: On 17 February 1880 there was an explosion in the dining-room of the Winter Palace in St Petersburg, which failed to kill the Tsar. On 13 March 1881 he fell victim to a successful assassination attempt. These events refer Zola's contemporary readers to incidents in their own day rather than to the 1860s, the period at which the novel is situated.

141   *'Poland'*: this unhappy rabbit's name is perhaps deliberately chosen by the anarchist Souvarine because of the prolonged martyrdom of that country, whose people's struggle for freedom was repeatedly crushed by tsarist Russia throughout the nineteenth century. France was a favourite haven for Polish refugees.

      Pluchart: he seems to share some of the characteristics of the careerism of Basly, but with a more Marxist programme, inspired perhaps by Zola's conversations with Jules Guesde, the founder (in 1879) of the first French socialist party based on Marxism (Le Parti des Travailleurs Socialistes), whose aims included the revolutionary overthrow of bourgeois democracy. Marx helped Guesde draw up its programme.

142   *the Workers' International Association*: it was founded in London in September 1864 under the impetus of Karl Marx (1818–83), who solicited the seizure of power by the proletariat after the demise of the capitalist economy. The International aimed to found a world federation of socialist associations—French sections were formed in 1865—and this 'First International' lasted until 1876.

144 *tablets of bronze*: the British economist Ricardo, influenced also by Malthus' pessimistic views on demography, formulated this 'bronze law of wages', which was reported in E. de Lavelaye's *Le Socialisme contemporain* (1883), read by Zola. Zola may also have had in mind the reformulation by the German socialist Ferdinand Lassalle (1825–64) of the same 'iron law of economics', expressed in his Open Letter of 1863, that wages tend to sink towards the vital minimum necessary for the subsistence of the family.

Anarchy: the movement is actually called 'anarchism', as promulgated by Mikhail Bakunin and by Proudhon, that is, not a totally random and chaotic society, but a community based on autonomous, small-scale units, rejecting the hierarchical and universal structures of the traditional State. Souvarine himself is a rather extreme example of a Russian 'nihilist', who seems not to entertain Bakunin's vision of industrial democracy.

145 *co-operative societies*: these were part of the social project of Pierre Joseph Proudhon (1809–65), a socialist militant, journalist, and thinker. His social theory was a kind of anarchism, formulated before Bakunin's, but it was relatively mild and structured, involving trade unions, co-operatives, and friendly societies. Marx attacked his *Philosophie de la misère* (1846) in *Misère de la philosophie* (1847), accusing Proudhon of not being revolutionary enough.

147 *Ducasse*: this annual festival was specific to the Nord region. It may remind us of the kind of festival enjoyed by Flemish peasants in earlier centuries, as shown in paintings by Brueghel, for instance.

148 *the Imperial Prince*: Eugène Louis Napoleon (1856–79), about 10 years old at the time of the novel. The portrait pinned up in a worker's cottage gives us another example of the penetrative power of the regime's image of the ruling family as an idealized version of the popular family.

151 *provident fund*: this develops one of the key ideas of Proudhon's anarchism, the structuring of society around 'mutuality'—a federation of small, quasi-autonomous workers' mutual self-help associations.

152 *Lenfant ... Progrès ... Tison*: 'The Child', 'The Progress', and 'The Burning Coal'—pubs implying varying degrees of family morality, social evolution, and hard work.

154 *Walloon*: the Walloons are the Belgians who speak a dialectal

form of French, as opposed to the Flemish, who speak a Dutch dialect.

155 *Tête-Coupée*: the 'Severed Head'—a violent, either criminal- or revolutionary-sounding pub.

finch contest: the miners' interest in finches or linnets may go back to the days before the Davy lamp, when caged birds were taken down the mine, because they succumbed to any gas escape more quickly than humans, and a dead bird constituted a timely warning of danger. See Benson (note to p. 13), and also Theodore Zeldin on the nineteenth-century games and pastimes practised by miners' clubs in Lille at the period.

156 *Bon-Joyeux*: the 'Jolly Good Fellow'.

164 *Miners' Hygiene*: Zola himself consulted a tome by Dr Boens-Boisseau, *Traité pratique des maladies, des accidents et des difformités des houilleurs* (Brussels, 1862).

167 *hand you your booklet*: since 1803 workmen had had to possess a professional record booklet, stamped by each successive employer and certified by the municipality. This requirement was finally abolished by a law of 25 April 1869. When a workman was sacked his registration booklet was returned to him.

187 *'Chicot'*: Berloque's nickname means a 'squirt' or 'cud' of chewed tobacco.

199 *the strike had just broken out*: the strike at Anzin in 1884 (19 February–16 April) had been precipitated by a change in working rates. Jules Guesde, following Karl Marx, believed in the strike as a revolutionary weapon, whereas Proudhon rejected this illegal means. 'Combination' (including striking) was legalized by a law of 25 May 1864.

telegraph: before the invention of wireless telegraphy and the telephone towards the end of the nineteenth century, the telegraph was the only means of instant long-distance communication.

Prefect at Lille: the Prefect was the representative of the State in each Department, responsible to the Minister of the Interior and empowered to deploy armed police. The Prefect was also in control of the civil apparatus and at this period could appoint teachers and mayors.

211 *Louis-Philippe*: Louis-Philippe (1773–1850), the 'Bourgeois

Monarch', brought to power by the Revolution of 1830, had signed a Charter acknowledging that he governed according to a constitution agreed with the nation. However, he was deposed in 1848 because of his authoritarianism. After the seizure of power by Napoleon III (in whose Second Empire the 'Rougon-Macquart novels are set), Louis-Philippe came to seem liberal in retrospect.

211 *dangerous concessions*: Napoleon III ruled by a mixture of authoritarian decree and demagogic plebiscite. The press was severely censored, but in some ways the workers were (equally arbitrarily) favoured. He went against the employers' advice to legalize strikes. See Roger Magraw, *France 1815–1914: The Bourgeois Century*.

1789: the date of the first French Revolution.

216 *contador*: a kind of bureau, originally used by merchants for their accounts.

portières: curtains drawn across a door to keep out draughts.

229 *the 1848 Revolution*: the Revolution of February 1848 which overthrew Louis-Philippe was triggered by spontaneous working-class discontent as much as by bourgeois design (unlike the earlier Revolutions of 1789 and 1830). But the radical provisional government was unable to prevent the spread of unemployment, poverty, and famine. Its experimental socialism seemed to fail, and it was replaced by a more conservative assembly after the April elections, which finally confronted a second workers' insurrection in June and used the National Guard to crush it. Hence La Maheude's disillusion.

239 *the confused remnants of a number of theories*: Étienne has indeed conflated several scarcely compatible kinds of socialism. It was Proudhon who declared that 'property is theft', in a notorious pamphlet of 1840, *Qu'est-ce que la propriété?*, and who pleaded for a society based on 'equivalent exchange', where labour would be rewarded in kind. Lassalle's *Open Letter* of 1863 actually rejects the idea that friendly societies, insurance funds, and consumer co-operatives could reform society unaided. Karl Marx, in his *Misère de la philosophie* (1847), attacked Proudhon's naïve refusal of government machinery, and, in his 1848 *Communist Manifesto*, written in collaboration with Friedrich Engels, advocated collective ownership of the means of production. Marx argued that, although it was the workers through their

labour who created wealth, society still had to regulate the process of remuneration.

242 *Bakunin*: Mikhail Bakunin (1814–76) was an active revolutionary militant involved in uprisings all over Europe, and a leading theorist of anarchism (*Statehood and Anarchy*, 1873). He adopted a theory of 'co-operatism' inspired by Proudhon, but he also called for the immediate and revolutionary suppression of the State. His extremism led him and his followers to be excluded by Marx from the International in 1872.

243 *hanged one rainy morning in Moscow*: Sophie Perovskaia was hanged at St Petersburg with four companions on 15 April 1881 after the assassination of Tsar Alexander II. With the nihilist Leo Hartmann, she had also tried to blow up the Tsar's train near Moscow on 1 December 1879 (see pp. 451–2).

246 *Citizens*: Pluchart deliberately uses the form of address popularized by the 1789 Revolution, 'Citoyens' rather than the more usual greeting of 'camarades' ('workmates' or 'comrades'), in order to signal his revolutionary and egalitarian intentions.

265 *cross*: a primitive type of cross-country golf. The 'cross' is the stick, or club. It is believed that the Roman legions originally brought the game with them as they spread across northern Europe.

269 *ventilation system*: the existing system of ventilation at Le Voreux, whereby a roaring furnace draws air down the main shaft, through the tunnels of the mine, and back up a ventilation shaft, is shown as an inefficient anachronism. By this period most modern mines used steam pumps to drive air through their passages, as is shown to be the case at Jean-Bart.

279 *great clearing*: with public meetings banned, miners were obliged to hold secret meetings in the woods, as for example at Anzin in 1878 and at Montceau-les-Mines in 1882.

283 *destruction of the State*: Proudhon tended to argue that, if inheritance and property were abolished, a society of small-scale producers would exist in a condition of natural harmony, with no call for central government. But he was opposed to strikes and violent revolution. Marx's theory supposed rather that competition and exploitation would recur, unless the proletariat seized control of the State, and used it to regulate the economy. It was Bakunin who called for the immediate destruction of the State.

295   *'What is it?'* ... *'Sir, it's a rebellion'*: Deneulin's innocent
       question and its shock answer may well be intended to recall
       the famous words of Louis XVI in 1789—'Is it a rebellion?'—
       and the reply they elicited—'No, Sire, it's a revolution.'

298   *brothel*: the French is 'maison publique', a polite euphemism
       for a registered, legally tolerated, 'public' brothel. Prostitution
       was legally tolerated where prostitutes registered with the police,
       lived in brothels ('maisons de tolérance'), and submitted to
       regular medical inspection. If caught wandering destitute and
       arrested as an unregistered streetwalker, Catherine might well
       be locked up in a women's prison and reformatory. There is not
       much to choose between this likelihood and that of being
       picked up and taken to the brothel by a violent client, nor
       between that and being forced by the authorities to register and
       reside there. In *Nana*, another novel from the 'Rougon-Mac-
       quart' series, Zola focuses on prostitution and high society in
       Paris.

303   *Tartarus ... La Côte-Verte*: one of Zola's sources, Simonin,
       records instances of permanent underground fires from spon-
       taneous combustion at Le Brûlé, near Saint-Étienne, and at
       Burning Hill, in Staffordshire.

308   *bad air, or dead air*: carbon dioxide, usually called 'chokedamp'
       by British miners. Whereas firedamp (methane) is lighter than
       air, and inflammable, chokedamp extinguishes burning, and is
       heavier than air. Hence the failure of Catherine's lamp, and the
       greater danger of suffocation when she falls to the ground. This
       is why Chaval has to hold her up off the ground and run up to
       a higher level. (See also note to p. 50.)

312   *cutting the cables*: similar incidents had occurred at Montceau-
       les-Mines in 1882 and demonstrations at Denain in 1884.

328   *We want bread*: historically, a famous and emotive outcry,
       uttered by the Parisian market women who marched on Ver-
       sailles with La Fayette at their head in October 1789 to take the
       royal family back to Paris as hostages; and also by the Parisian
       crowds rioting in protest against the famine they suffered under
       the Convention government in 1795. (See also note to title, p. 1.)

348   *the 'Marseillaise'*: the 'Marseillaise', the battle hymn and na-
       tional anthem of the French Republic, composed by Rouget de
       l'Isle, was banned under the Second Empire.

373   *the army had come*: the army had picketed the pit-head at
       Anzin in 1884.

Le Borinage: the Borinage region, an area of the northern coalfield situated in Belgium.

383   *Cossacks*: originally a tribe of nomadic warriors, the Cossacks had settled in the Ukraine, and their soldiers formed a famous corps of the Russian army. They had held out fiercely against French and British troops for a whole year (September 1854 to September 1855) at the siege of Sebastopol during the Crimean War.

399   *set-up is falling to bits . . . anarchists . . . gradualists*: Zola benefits from a little retrospective foresight here, in his reference to the debilitating conflict between Marx's scientific socialists and Bakunin's anarchists, who joined the International in 1867. The anarchists were expelled in 1872, the year after the defeat of the Paris Commune. The International finally collapsed in 1876. See Leszek Kolakowski, *Main Currents of Marxism*, i: *The Founders* (Oxford 1981), for the history of the International and an analysis of the theories of Marx, Bakunin, Proudhon, Lassalle, etc.

427   *the Crimean War*: this complex religious and territorial dispute (1854–5) between Russia and Turkey involved France and Britain as signatories of a mutual defence pact with Turkey. The allies' military success gave the nascent Second Empire illusions of imperial grandeur.

431   *They had fired*: troops had fired on miners at La Ricamarie (near Saint-Étienne) on 16 June 1869, killing thirteen, including two women; and at Aubin (in the Aveyron) on 7 October 1869, killing fourteen.

438   *large yellow posters*: Zola takes this detail from what happened during a miners' strike at Fourchambault in 1870.

450   *Darwin*: Charles Darwin published *On the Origin of Species*, on natural selection and evolution, in 1859. A French translation was published in 1865. Souvarine's doubts as to whether the process of natural selection and the survival of the fittest, in making the survival of a species depend on the ability of its strongest members to mate and procreate, would lead naturally towards socialism, were shared by some socialists, since the theory seemed to devalue personal and social morality, and make the question of the eventual triumph of the proletariat over the bourgeoisie seem to depend on arbitrary violence rather than the objective of a just cause. These doubts were shared by Engels, who debated the question in *Ludwig Feuer-*

bach. Later in the novel Étienne too starts to lose confidence in the scientific inevitability of this theory.

475 *fallen down into the abyss*: Simonin's book described how a mine collapsed at Marles in the Pas-de-Calais on 28 and 29 April 1866.

523 *trade unions*: like strikes, these were illegal during the Second Empire. They were finally legalized by the Waldeck-Rousseau Act in March 1884.